CW00842346

Hope Springs

Books 4-6

Not Until Us

Not Until Christmas Morning

Not Until This Day

Valerie M. Bodden

Hope Springs Books 4–6 © 2020 by Valerie M. Bodden.

NOT UNTIL US

NOT UNTIL CHRISTMAS MORNING

NOT UNTIL THIS DAY

Not Until Us Copyright © 2019 by Valerie M. Bodden. All Rights Reserved.

Not Until Christmas Morning Copyright © 2019 by Valerie M. Bodden. All Rights Reserved.

Not Until This Day Copyright © 2020 by Valerie M. Bodden. All Rights Reserved.

Scriptures taken from the Holy Bible, New International Version®, NIV®. Copyright © 1973, 1978, 1984, 2011 by Biblica, Inc.™ Used by permission of Zondervan. All rights reserved worldwide. www.zondervan.com The "NIV" and "New International Version" are trademarks registered in the United States Patent and Trademark Office by Biblica, Inc.™

All rights reserved. No portion of this book may be reproduced in any form without permission from the publisher, except as permitted by U.S. copyright law.

This is a work of fiction. Names, characters, places, and incidents either are products of the author's imagination or used in a fictitious manner. Any resemblance to any person, living or dead, is coincidental.

Valerie M. Bodden

Visit me at www.valeriembodden.com

Hope Springs Series

Not Until Forever
Not Until This Moment
Not Until You
Not Until Us
Not Until Christmas Morning
Not Until This Day
Not Until Someday
Not Until Now
Not Until Then
Not Until The End

River Falls Series

Pieces of Forever
Songs of Home
Memories of the Heart
Whispers of Truth
Promises of Mercy

River Falls Christmas Romances

Christmas of Joy

A Hope Springs Gift for You

Members of my Reader's Club get a FREE book, available exclusively to my subscribers. When you sign up, you'll also be the first to know about new releases, book deals, and giveaways.

Visit www.valeriembodden.com/gift to join!

Need a refresher of who's who in the Hope Springs series?

If you love the whole gang in Hope Springs but need a refresher of who's who and how everyone is connected, check out the handy character map at https://www.valeriembodden.com/hscharacters

Not Until Us

A Hope Springs Novel

Valerie M. Bodden

Remember, Lord, your great mercy and love,
for they are from of old.
Do not remember the sins of my youth
and my rebellious ways;
according to your love remember me,
for you, Lord, are good.

Psalm 25:6-7

Chapter 1

How had she messed up again?

Jade swiped at her cheeks as she slid the key into the lock of her apartment door. If the God her roommate Keira kept telling her about had any decency, Keira would still be in bed. She wasn't in the mood to be reprimanded by her squeaky clean friend right now. She already knew last night had been a mistake.

One she'd made far too many times.

She inched the door open slowly but let out a frustrated breath as her eyes fell on her roommate, perky as ever, sitting on the couch with some kind of kale-soy-banana-protein drink in hand.

Apparently God didn't have any decency. Or he had one wicked sense of humor.

"Good morning." Keira eyed Jade's clothes—the same ones she'd been wearing when she'd left for work last night.

Jade held up a hand. "Don't say it."

"Say what?" Keira took a long sip of her drink, still watching Jade.

"Fine. I screwed up. Again." She tried to sound defiant, but even as the words came out, a bone-crushing weariness descended on her. She was trying to be a better person. She really was. But old habits were hard to break. Last night had been just one more name to add to her list of lifelong mistakes. Or it would be if she knew his name.

She buried her face in her hands. She was an awful person. "I don't know why I keep doing this."

When the guy had walked into the bar where she worked, she'd told herself to ignore him. But she'd been bored. And he'd had nice eyes and witty banter. Plus, he was only passing through town on business. There was no chance things would get messy or complicated. He'd go on his way, she'd go on hers, and neither of them would worry about it again.

Besides, he'd practically challenged her to go back to his hotel room with him. What was she supposed to do?

Walk away. The voice in her head sounded an awful lot like her big sister Violet. Not that Violet had any idea what Jade's life was like, aside from the sanitized version Jade fed her on their weekly phone calls.

Keira crossed the small space and pulled Jade's hands away from her face, holding the protein drink out to her. Jade wrinkled her nose and pushed it away. After eight years in Los Angeles, she still had no interest in the stuff that passed for breakfast around here. Give her a donut and a strong cup of coffee any day.

"Change is hard." Keira wrapped an arm over her shoulder and steered her to the couch. "You should pray about it."

Jade shook her head. If there was anything she was less interested in than protein shakes, it was prayer. "I need to pack. My plane leaves in a couple hours."

She still wasn't sure what had compelled her to give in to her sister's pleas that she spend the summer in Hope Springs. But maybe it would do her some good to get away from this town of broken dreams for a while.

Besides, the way Violet talked about Hope Springs made Jade almost homesick for it. Almost.

Mostly, though, she was going because she owed it to Vi. After six years of completely cutting her sister out of her life, Jade didn't deserve the second chance Vi had given her. The phone calls they'd been exchanging for the past couple years weren't enough. The least she could do was spend the summer helping her sister finalize plans for her wedding.

"Well, look at it this way." Keira sucked down the last of her shake. "Maybe you'll meet a nice, wholesome man in Hope Springs, and you'll get married and live happily ever after."

Jade snickered. "You read too many small town romances. Trust me, there's no one in Hope Springs I'd consider dating, let alone marrying. Besides—" She flopped onto the couch. "I'm not really the happily ever after kind of girl."

Keira tipped her head to the side, studying Jade. "Everyone's a happily ever after kind of girl. It just takes some of us longer to get there than others." She moved to the cramped kitchen to rinse out her glass.

Jade stared after her. Keira could dream about happily ever after all she wanted. But Jade knew the truth. There was no such thing. She'd learned that lesson early, and she wasn't going to forget it anytime soon.

Chapter 2

Dan hadn't known it was possible to sweat this much.

This had to be the hottest Hope Fest parade on record. Of course, that might have something to do with the heavy lion costume he was wearing. Grace had borrowed the local high school's mascot, insisting that if they were going to have a Noah's ark float, they needed the animals too. Lucky for him, he was exactly the right size for the costume.

Despite the sweltering heat, Dan had to admit that the float had turned out better than he could have imagined. And judging from the crowd's cheers as they walked past, he wasn't the only one who thought so.

Dan swiveled to catch a glimpse of the others marching with him. There had to be nearly one hundred people representing Hope Church in the parade—all of them in some sort of animal costume or another.

His heart filled. He knew many of them were there in tribute to his father, who had been their spiritual leader for nearly forty years. Dan had almost canceled the church's entry in the parade this year. His grief over Dad's death was still too raw for him to dedicate the time needed to plan it. But when he'd brought it up to the church board, they'd reminded him that the congregation was looking to him as their new head pastor for guidance in how to move on. He was glad now that he'd listened to them. The parade seemed to have brought his members together in a way nothing else had lately.

"Hey. This turned out really well." His sister Leah sidled up to him, decked out in a colorful parrot costume. "Dad would have loved it. I could totally see him hamming it up in that costume."

"I was just thinking that. Thank goodness Grace came through with all this stuff." It was almost a miracle, considering he'd asked her to be in charge of the parade only two weeks earlier. And she'd done it all with a smile.

"Speaking of which—" Leah poked him in the side, and Dan knew what was coming. "How was your dinner last night?"

"You mean the one you tricked us into?"

Dan, Leah, and Grace had worked on the float until late the night before, and afterward Leah had suggested they grab a bite at the Hidden Cafe, before conveniently remembering she had to take care of a friend's cat.

"How was the cat, by the way?"

"What cat?" Leah waved to the cheering crowds. "Oh, yeah. The cat was good."

Dan gave her a little shove. "There was no cat."

Leah laughed, completely unashamed. "Nope. But you didn't answer my question. How was dinner with Grace?"

Dan sighed into his costume, then wished he hadn't, as his breath only made the small space steamier. "It was fine."

"And?" Leah poked him, as if waiting for more.

He lifted his hands, the claws of his costume clacking. "And that's it."

There'd been no fireworks. No amazing revelation that this was the woman for him. Just some good food, a bit of conversation, and a wave goodnight.

Which was fine.

Just fine.

"You should ask her to the fireworks tonight."

This time Dan managed to contain his sigh—barely. "I just don't see this going any-where, Leah."

It wasn't like he was looking for a relationship anyway. Sure, he'd been performing marriage ceremonies for his friends more frequently lately, and every once in a while, he longed for what they had. But mostly, he was too busy with his ministry to consider marriage and a family.

"Famous last words." Leah flitted away to pass out candy to the parade goers.

Dan shook his head at her. His sister was a meddler, there were no two ways about it. Her heart was in the right place, but sometimes he sure wished that place was somewhere else.

By the time they reached the final stretch of the parade, Dan was tempted to pull his lion head off. But he forced himself to wait until they'd gone past every last spectator.

When he'd finally taken the costume off, he grabbed an abandoned water bottle from the float and poured it over his head. The few kids whose parents hadn't yet plucked them from the realistic-looking ark giggled, and he grabbed another half-empty water bottle and gently tossed a few drops their way. They shrieked but laughed harder.

"You're good with them." Grace came up next to him, looking cool and comfortable in her shorts and t-shirt. She'd ridden along in the truck to manage the speaker system. She started pulling decorations off the float.

"Ah, kids are fun." Dan lifted a little guy dressed as a turtle down from the ark and passed him a lollipop from the bag of extra candy. Soon, a group of kids had gathered around him. Dan couldn't help but smile. He knew the kids were surrounding him more for the candy than for his company, but that didn't make him feel any less like a rock star.

"Bribing them again?" Dan's friend Nate, who really was a rock star—or at least the lead singer for the church's worship band—clapped him on the back.

Dan grinned. "Whatever it takes. I'd better bring some of these along to camp next month." Dan was excited to resurrect the annual trip to Camp Oswego that the church had taken when he was a kid.

"Oh." Grace popped up from the other side of the float. "I almost forgot to tell you. Cassandra Murphy said she could chaperone, so we should be all set."

"Seriously?" Dan could have hugged her. He'd been trying for weeks to find one more female chaperone. He'd asked Cassandra himself at least twice, but she'd said it'd be impossible to get time off. Apparently Grace really was a miracle worker.

"I don't know how you did it, but thank you." He pulled a stuffed giraffe off the side of the ark. "And thank you for putting this float together. It looked amazing."

Grace ducked her head. "It was nothing."

Leah bounced over to them. "What was nothing?"

"The float." His voice was guarded. The last thing he needed was for his sister to overreact to his compliment to Grace. Next thing he knew, she'd have them walking down the aisle.

But to his relief, Leah turned away from him to Grace. "Oh my goodness, yes. Thank you so much for designing it. My attempts the last few years have been kind of . . ."

"Pathetic," Dan filled in for his sister.

"Ouch." Leah swatted at him. "But yes. Pathetic is a good word to describe it." She slid the parrot wings off. "Are you coming to the fireworks tonight, Grace?"

There it was. Dan shot his sister a look, but she only winked at him.

Grace shifted the handful of stuffed animals she'd picked up from the float. "There are fireworks?"

"Oh yeah, better than the fourth of July." Leah gestured toward the sky, as if she could see them already.

Even though he knew what was coming, Dan couldn't figure out a way to prevent it. He took a step away from the float, but that didn't stop his sister.

"Actually, I know Dan is going. I bet he could pick you up on the way. He has to drive right past your house anyway."

Dan froze but didn't turn around.

After last night, Grace would recognize his sister's blatant matchmaking and say no. Wouldn't she?

"If that wouldn't be too much trouble, I'd love to go."

"It's no trouble," Leah assured Grace, and Dan almost snorted out loud. Of course it was no trouble for her. She'd just set her little brother up on a date. He'd have to thank her later. Once he'd come up with a suitable revenge.

But for now he turned to Grace. It wasn't her fault he had a meddlesome sister. And he really did owe her after all she'd done to make the parade a success. "It's no problem at all. How about I pick you up around eight?"

Leah beamed at them both, then sashayed off, saying something about making sure everyone handed in their costumes.

"I'm sorry if you don't want—" Grace said. "I don't need to go."

"No, it's fine. I'm looking forward to it." He offered her the most genuine smile he could muster. "It'll be fun." Anyway, it wasn't like a trip to the fireworks was a marriage proposal.

He stood awkwardly, trying to figure out something else to say. Thankfully, Nate's fiancée, Violet, walked up at that moment, winding her arm through Nate's as he leaned down to kiss her forehead. Dan couldn't have been happier for his two friends, whose wedding was coming up at the end of summer.

"We'd better get going. We need to be at the airport by seven." Violet tugged Nate toward the parking lot.

Nate patted her arm. "It's only four now."

"I know, but there could be traffic, or . . ." She gave him a playful swat on the arm. "Stop laughing at me. I'm excited."

"Are you two skipping out of town? Without seeing the fireworks?" Dan's heart fell. He'd been hoping he and Grace could sit with them, so it'd seem less like a date.

"Nope." Violet's face lit up brighter than any firework. "We're going to the airport to pick up Jade."

Dan fought to keep his expression neutral, even as his heart surged at the name.

It had been eight years. He shouldn't still react that way to something as insignificant as her name.

"I didn't know Jade was coming home."

If possible, Violet's smile got even brighter. "I've been begging her for weeks to come home for the summer, and she must have gotten sick of it because she finally said yes. She's staying until after the wedding." Violet pulled on Nate's arm. "Come on. We have to go."

Nate shrugged at Dan, then followed his future wife toward the parking lot.

"Save us a seat for the fireworks," Violet called over her shoulder. "We may be late."

"Who's Jade?" Grace's question made Dan jump.

"Violet's sister." And his— His what?

His almost-girlfriend?

They hadn't dated. Not officially. But they'd spent so much time together in the last few months of high school that they'd forged a connection deeper than dating ever could.

At least that's what he'd thought.

Right up until she disappeared, leaving him only a note. He hadn't seen or heard from her once since then.

But apparently that was about to change. So he'd better get a grip on how he felt about it.

Fast.

Chapter 3

Thirty thousand feet in the air probably wasn't the best place to change her mind. As the captain announced over the intercom that they had started their descent, Jade's eyes went to the window, where the sun was low on the horizon, throwing a blinding light across Lake Michigan. She pressed a hand to her stomach.

She'd left eight years ago with the intention of never returning. So what was she doing here now?

She had let herself get caught up in her sister's excitement, had let herself believe that she'd left behind all the shame and regret that had driven her to flee Hope Springs in the first place. But now that she was almost home, it squeezed against her lungs, as if someone had over-pressurized the cabin.

It may have been eight years since she was in Hope Springs, but one thing she knew about small towns—they had long memories.

And Jade had given the people of Hope Springs plenty to remember—even if no one there knew the worst of it. None of them knew the real reason she'd fled.

Jade straightened in her seat. *And they never will.*

She caught her breath as the plane skimmed over the runway, then bounced lightly as the wheels touched down.

Her heart was suddenly thrumming faster than the jet's engine. She couldn't do this.

Maybe she could sneak off the plane and skip picking up her luggage. Then Vi wouldn't see her, and she could sneak onto another plane to somewhere else—anywhere else—and no one would ever have to know.

Jade let herself indulge in the fantasy for all of ten seconds. But the thought of what that would do to Vi put an end to it.

She was lucky her sister had forgiven her for running the first time. She couldn't do that to her again.

Anyway, she was stronger than this.

She steeled her shoulders and stood. She wouldn't worry about what any of them thought.

She was Jade Falter, and she was proud of it.

A nagging voice at the back of her head said she shouldn't be, but she shoved it away, along with all the other nagging voices she'd ignored over the years.

She clutched her carry-on and followed a white-haired woman off the plane, forcing herself to keep her chin up.

But the moment she stepped off the plane and into the airport, a wave of memories slammed against her. Of course she'd have to be in the same terminal she'd fled from that last day. Everything looked almost identical to how it had then. There was the bank of chairs in the corner she'd huddled in as she'd waited for her flight to be called. The terminal had been crowded, and at least a dozen people had approached the seats next to her. But they'd all walked away the moment they'd spotted her. Not that she blamed them. She'd been unable to stop sobbing, her arms wrapped around her middle, rocking back and forth.

Tears sprang to her eyes for the scared girl she'd been then, but she blinked them away.

She wasn't that girl anymore.

She pointed her head forward and made her way to the baggage claim without another look back.

The moment she neared the luggage carousel, she heard her name shrieked, and then arms were engulfing her.

"I'm so happy to see you. I can't believe you're here. You look so good." Violet squeezed so hard that Jade couldn't lift her arms to return the hug.

"It's not going to do much good to have your sister home if you crush her before she gets out of the airport." A man with a light layer of scruff and slightly shaggy hair gently pulled Violet's shoulder.

Vi laughed, wiping at her cheeks as she took a step back. "I'm sorry. It's just so— I can't believe this is real. That you're really here."

"I'm here." Jade swallowed down her own unexpected tears. When was the last time someone had been so happy to see her? "I just need to grab my bag."

She stepped around Violet toward the luggage carousel, giving herself a minute to collect her composure. It wasn't like her to lose it over a little thing like this. Probably just all the emotions of the day catching up with her.

Nate insisted on taking her bag for her as they made their way to Violet's car. At the vehicle, he opened the door for each of them. Jade climbed into the backseat with a weary sigh. All she wanted was her pajamas and a bed.

She settled back into the seat, training her gaze out the window. The familiar sights were more of a balm than she'd expected, and her eyes drooped with fatigue from the long day.

"I don't think we have time to stop at home. Hope Street will be closed by now anyway." Vi's voice broke into her half sleep, and when she opened her eyes, dusk had already fallen. As she peered into the graying night, she picked out the town's various landmarks. The Old Lighthouse. The giant sunfish. The church.

Her heart jumped as her gaze swept over the beach below the church. The beach where she'd thought maybe her life would change. Where she'd let herself hope that she'd found a man—he was really a boy then, she supposed—who could love her in spite of her reputation, in spite of her past. Who could believe that she'd changed. The man she'd fled the moment she'd had to confront the fact that there was no changing who she was.

She briefly considered asking Vi what had ever become of Dan but then thought better of it. There was no point in rehashing old dreams that could never be. Besides, Vi would probably find the question odd, since Jade had never told her—or anyone else, for that matter—that she and Dan had spent time together at the end of senior year. Had developed feelings for each other. Anyway, that was a long time ago. If Dan had followed his plans, he'd moved far away by now.

"Why don't you park here? It's probably as close as we're going to get." Nate gestured down a side street, which was almost parked full.

13

Vi nodded and pulled up to the curb. Throngs of people funneled down the sidewalk toward the lake.

"What's going on tonight? Why's everybody out?" Jade leaned forward to watch a mother trying to quiet a crying baby. The familiar pang jabbed her behind the belly button, and she looked away. She kept waiting for the guilt to end, but it was always there, hovering like her own personal cloud of regret.

The young mother moved down the street, and Jade sat back. If things had been different, if *she* had been different, would she be like that young mother?

"It's Hope Fest." Vi put the car in park and opened her door. "We're going to have to hurry or we'll miss the beginning of the fireworks."

Jade's stomach plummeted. Vi didn't really expect her to go to the town's annual celebration, did she?

"Come on." Vi opened her door.

"I'll wait for you guys here. I need a nap." Jade forced a yawn that even she could tell wasn't believable.

"It's going to be too loud to sleep." Vi planted a hand on her hip. "Come on, everyone is dying to see you."

Jade sincerely doubted that. If there was one person besides Vi in this town who wanted her to come back, she'd eat her left shoe.

Nate opened her door. "I didn't think I'd like it either when Violet made me come last year. But it was actually pretty fun. Come on. I'll buy the popcorn."

Jade threw her hands in the air. "If you two are going to gang up on me, I guess I don't have much choice, do I?" She slid to the door, and Nate stepped aside to let her out.

Vi and Nate closed the car doors, and she let them pass in front of her. The two linked hands, and Nate leaned over to drop a light kiss on Vi's cheek.

Jade's stomach clenched as she fell into step behind them.

She was happy for her sister. No one so young should have to experience the loss of a spouse like Vi had.

But Jade hadn't even gotten one happily ever after. So how was it that Violet had been given two?

As they approached the marina, Violet glanced over her shoulder, as if to make sure Jade was still there, and Jade offered her a tight smile. It was the best she could do.

"Dan texted that he's saving us a seat in front of the gazebo," Nate said.

Jade almost stumbled but caught herself at the last second. "Dan?" She forced the name out.

Violet's brow wrinkled. "Dan Zelner. You remember him, don't you? I'm pretty sure he was in your class."

Jade nodded but couldn't answer. Her mouth went completely dry. Dan was here? As in *here* here?

A huge crowd covered the hill of the public park above the marina, and Jade let a momentary relief wash over her. The gazebo was on the far side of the hill. There was no way they'd be able to get through the crowds to it—and even if they did, the chances they'd find Dan in this mess of people were small at best.

"There he is." Nate held up a hand to wave, then started weaving through the people toward the gazebo.

Jade's feet wanted to remain planted, but Violet reached back and grabbed her arm, tugging her forward.

She was about to be reintroduced to her past. Whether she wanted to be or not.

Chapter 4

"You were saying?" Grace's voice reached Dan's ears, but he had no idea what he'd been saying. He'd just spotted Violet and Nate—and being dragged behind them as if being taken to detention—Jade.

His stomach rolled uncomfortably, and his pulse rocketed past any heart rate he'd ever achieved on the treadmills at the gym. He had a sudden urge to give himself a quick sniff test, even though he'd gone home and taken a shower after the parade. How was it that one glimpse of Jade had sent him right back to feeling like a self-conscious teen?

He kept his hand raised in the air until he was sure Nate had seen it, then turned toward the lake as if he couldn't care less that the woman he'd once dreamed of spending the rest of his life with was coming his way at this very moment. Anyway, he reminded himself, she was also the woman who'd torn his heart out and left it to rot in the sand.

"About camp." Grace's prompt reminded Dan that she was still sitting next to him on the blanket Leah had called to tell him to pack. If his sister micromanaged this date any more, she might as well be the one on it. Then again, since she was sitting right behind them, she practically was.

"Look who I brought with me." Violet stood to the side and motioned Jade forward, but Jade barely moved. "Sophie, Dan, you remember Jade, right? Everyone else, this is my sister, Jade."

"Welcome home." Sophie stepped forward to hug Jade, her husband Spencer following with a handshake. The rest of the group—Jared and Peyton, Emma, Grace, and Tyler—stepped forward and introduced themselves.

Finally, Dan was the only one left who hadn't said hi. Jade lifted her eyes to meet his for a second, then let them dart away. A tiny worm of satisfaction crawled through Dan's gut. At least she had the grace to look embarrassed to see him. But a moment later he reprimanded himself. He'd forgiven her long ago, so he had no right to hold the past over her head.

He took a step closer, thinking he'd give her a hug, but then changed his mind at the last second and held out a hand instead. She stared at it, as if not sure what to do with it, then put her hand in his. He tried not to notice the warmth her grip sent up his arm.

She could have stepped right out of the pages of their high school yearbook. Same white-blonde hair, same smooth complexion. Same standoffish confidence she'd worn like a shield through most of high school, except in those rare moments when she'd dropped it with him.

"It's nice to see you again, Jade." Lame, but what else was he supposed to say?

Jade's nod was slow and deliberate, but her eyes drifted from him to Grace, and he groaned inwardly. She was going to think he was here with Grace.

You are here with Grace.

Dan shook himself. Of course he was here with Grace. And so what if Jade knew? She wasn't here to see him. And he most definitely wasn't here to see her.

"I think the fireworks are about to start." He laid a hand on Grace's elbow to steer her back to her seat on the blanket, then sat next to her. "Have a seat, you guys. There's plenty of room."

He kept his gaze directed toward the lake as he felt people shuffling next to him.

A second later, someone's leg brushed his as they sat. He risked a glance over.

His eyes landed on Jade just as the first firework exploded overhead, lighting her in a wash of blue.

She tilted her face up at the sound, but he noticed the lines of tension around her lips.

As if she felt him watching her, Jade turned toward him. Her eyes were the same shade he'd remembered—like a summer sky on a perfect day. But there was something new in them—something broken. Dan pressed down the urge to ask what it was.

She'd chosen to run. Whatever had happened to her since then was none of his concern.

Still, he had to say something, or this would get awkward. "How have you been?"

"Good." She bobbed her head vigorously. "Fabulous."

"Oh. Good." Dan fumbled for something else to say. What did you say when the girl of your dreams suddenly showed up in real life again?

Girl of your former dreams, he reminded himself.

His new dreams had nothing to do with her.

A sharp prod in his back made Dan jump. He cast a quick look over his shoulder at his sister, who jerked her head toward Grace on his other side.

Dan returned Leah's glare but turned his attention back to Grace. Her legs were stretched out in front of her as she leaned back on her elbows to watch the fireworks, her lips slightly parted like she was mesmerized. Her relaxed demeanor was a perfect contrast to the tension exuding from Jade on the other side of him.

As Dan lifted his eyes to the sky, Grace leaned a fraction closer. "Your sister wasn't exaggerating. These are the best fireworks I've ever seen."

Dan nodded, fighting every impulse to glance at Jade when she shifted next to him, causing her arm to brush his.

"I didn't think you'd still be in Hope Springs." Jade's voice was low but closer to his ear than he'd expected, and he leaned slightly away. It would be dangerous to let her get too close. He'd made that mistake once already.

"I thought you were going to go to seminary and then go off and do big things for God." Her words held a trace of a sneer, but under that he sensed something softer—curiosity, maybe?

He frowned at the white streaks flashing above them. "I guess I was meant to do smaller things for him." He let himself glance at her out of the corner of his eyes, but she was looking toward the sky. "I'm actually head pastor at Hope Church."

In his peripheral vision, he saw her head snap toward him. "You are?"

"Yeah. I am. I was serving with my dad, but he died a few months ago." He swallowed past the sharp jab the words brought.

"I'm sorry." Jade set a hand on his arm for the briefest second.

But the touch was enough to send him back to those few months in high school, when the touch of her hand meant everything to him.

Sometimes, he wondered if it had all been a dream after all—their relationship was just too unlikely. He was the pastor's son. She was the rebel.

All through grade school and middle school, she'd teased him mercilessly. In high school, she'd finally lost interest and ignored him.

Until they were paired as lab partners for chemistry senior year.

He'd nearly groaned out loud when Mr. Burns had read out their names. So much for a peaceful final year of high school.

To his surprise, though, she hadn't said an unkind word to him all year. Hadn't said more than a handful of words to him at all, actually.

She always showed up to class with one guy or another. Dan lost count of how many boyfriends she went through during first semester alone. One constantly called her crude names, another couldn't seem to keep himself from grabbing at her, and another was always giving her compliments on various parts of her anatomy.

Dan had kept his head down and his mouth shut.

But one day right before spring break, she'd walked into the room earlier than usual, with a hand pressed to her ribs.

Dan tried to focus on the homework he'd come in early to finish up. He told himself not to say anything, but when she winced as she sat, he couldn't help it. "Are you okay?"

He could have sworn he saw tears in her eyes. But if there was one thing he knew about Jade Falter, it was that she didn't cry. Ever. Not even in grade school when she'd taken a baseball to the nose.

He leaned closer, keeping his voice low. "What is it?"

She shook her head and blinked hard enough to clear the tears. "Let's just say Brett wasn't a big fan of being dumped." Her laugh was sardonic.

The lead of Dan's pencil snapped, leaving a jagged line across his paper. He threw it down.

"Did he hurt you?" He fought to get the words out past his gritted teeth.

Jade shrugged, but her hand tracked to her side again.

"Let me see." Dan reached toward her, but Jade slapped his hand away.

"I didn't expect you of all people to try to take my shirt off." Her smirk was calculated to irk him.

"Whatever," he muttered under his breath, picking up his pencil and crossing the room to sharpen it.

"What?" Jade watched him as he sat down again. "Now you're not talking to me?"

"You wouldn't listen anyway."

"You never know." She gave him an exaggerated wink. "I just might surprise you."

He almost let it go at that. But something about her tone told him she needed to hear what he'd been wanting to say to her for months.

"I don't understand why you keep dating all these jerks." He clamped his mouth shut. He shouldn't have said it. He knew it the moment the words were out.

But Jade fixed him with a look he'd never forget. One that told him whatever she was about to say was from her most vulnerable place.

"The good guys don't tend to ask me out." She shuffled through her bookbag and pulled out her textbook. It was the first time he'd seen her with the book all year. A curtain of hair shielded her face, but he could have sworn her cheeks were tinged with pink.

"I'm sure—" Dan stuttered, not knowing where he was going with the sentence. "I'm sure there are plenty of good guys who want to go out with you. They're probably just scared of you." Now he could feel his own neck warming. That wasn't supposed to come out as an insult.

Jade lifted her head and raised an eyebrow. "Like you?"

"I'm not scared of you." Which wasn't entirely true, but why make a bad situation worse?

But Jade shook her head, her eyes right on his. "I mean, like you. Are there guys like you who want to go out with me?"

Dan couldn't free his gaze from hers. "Yeah. Sure. I'm sure there are plenty of guys like me who want to go out with you."

He finally managed to break the stare she'd had him trapped in and paged through his book.

Jade sighed. "You don't get it."

His first instinct was to ignore her. But she was so different today. So clearly hurting.

He closed the book and gave her his full attention. "What don't I get?"

She bit her lip, almost as if she were nervous. He threw a glance over his shoulder to make sure Brett hadn't come back to harass her. But there were only a few other students in the room, and none of them were paying attention to his conversation with Jade.

"I mean like *you*. Do *you* want to date me?"

Dan had to grab at the table to keep from falling off his lab stool. When she'd said she might surprise him, he definitely hadn't expected *that*.

"Well, I mean, I—" Why wasn't the bell ringing?

She didn't really expect him to answer that, did she? It was a hypothetical question, right?

Jade's face slid back into its typical hostile expression. "See? That's what I mean." She turned away but not before Dan read the hurt in her eyes.

He drew in a breath, as if he could suck courage straight from the air. This whole thing was likely a trap to make him look like a fool.

"Yeah, I'd go out with you." He forced himself to keep his eyes on her, so he caught the moment the creases in her forehead eased.

"But I'm pretty sure a girl like you wouldn't want to go out with me." There was no way she was serious about this. The two of them couldn't be more opposite.

"Try me."

"Try you, what?"

She rolled her eyes. "Try asking me out."

Don't do it. It's a trap.

But the words had come out anyway. "Would you like to go to a movie with me Friday night?"

Jade's reply had been immediate. "No."

Told you.

"But I would like to hang out with you at the beach."

"At the beach?" Dan's mind had barely been able to comprehend what was happening. Had he just made a date with Jade Falter?

She'd given him what may have been the first genuine smile he'd ever seen from her. "The beach."

Another jab in his side brought Dan back to the present.

"Sorry about that." Leah leaned forward, extending her leg between Dan and Jade as she stood so that Dan had no choice but to scoot closer to Grace. "I'm going to grab some popcorn. Anyone else want some?"

Dan frowned at Leah as Jade shook her head. Leah offered him an innocent smile and dropped a hand onto his shoulder, subtly pushing him away from Jade and toward Grace.

As he turned back to the fireworks, he saw that Jade had widened the distance between them even more. On his other side, Grace slid closer and sent him a sweet smile. It didn't make his heart flip the way Jade's smile did. But maybe sweet smiles—ones that didn't raise fireworks in his heart—were safer.

He returned her smile and clasped his hands in his lap, telling himself he could be happy in a world without fireworks.

Chapter 5

Jade stretched, the half-filled air mattress Violet had set up on her bedroom floor creaking beneath her. But she couldn't convince herself to get up.

Last night had only been a bad dream, hadn't it? A nightmare that she'd come face-to-face with the one man she'd ever had feelings for, and he was with another woman. A woman who looked exactly like the kind of wholesome, virtuous woman he should be with.

She peeled her back off the mattress and swung her legs over the side.

You had your chance. What she needed was a stern talking to. *And you messed it up.*

The same way she always did.

It was just, did he have to look so good? Like *good* good. The once lanky and somewhat gangly teen had filled out into a broad-shouldered yet trim man. But his smile. That was the same as always. Still warm and easy—though maybe a bit guarded with her. Not that she blamed him for that.

And his smell. She'd had to stop herself from leaning closer to soak up the light, sporty scent she'd recognized from high school.

It had made her think of that first night they'd hung out at the beach. They'd spent hours together, first walking, then settling into a cozy spot in the sand between two dunes.

That night was the first time Jade had ever felt like the guy she was with was listening to her with his full attention, not nodding along while wondering how long it would be before she'd stop talking and he could feel her up.

In fact, Dan kept a healthy couple of feet between them all night. Even when she moved closer, complaining of the chill, he pulled off his sweater and passed it to her but didn't make a move toward her. At first, she found it strange. Maybe he wasn't attracted to her. But then she'd realized he was being respectful.

The realization had filled her in a way she'd never expected. It had made her feel precious and protected.

It was a feeling she hadn't experienced again in the eight years since she'd left Hope Springs. She shook herself out of the memories and stood. She didn't need to feel precious and protected. She needed to be strong and independent.

She *was* strong and independent.

The bedroom door opened a crack, and Vi poked her head through slowly. "Oh, good, you're up. I didn't want to wake you since you had a long day yesterday. But if you're up for it, I'll be leaving for church in about an hour."

Jade startled. Was today Sunday? Despite Keira's constant nagging, Jade hadn't set foot in a church in eight years.

But for some reason, the idea of going to Hope Church appealed to her today.

Maybe it was the nostalgia of being home.

Maybe it was guilt for all the things that had driven her from Hope Springs in the first place.

Or maybe it was the desire to see a certain dark-eyed preacher—even though she knew how much it would hurt.

At any rate, she could tell by Vi's hopeful expression that nothing would make her sister happier than Jade agreeing to go to church with her.

"Let me just grab a quick shower."

The light in Vi's eyes chased away any lingering doubts. Jade had a lot to make up to her sister.

Someone knocked on the apartment door, and Vi broke into a huge smile. "That's Nate. He always comes over for breakfast before church. He'll have to eat right away, so he can get to church to warm up the band, but we'll save you some pancakes if you want to shower first."

Jade eyed her sister. She and her fiancé had the oddest living arrangements Jade had ever heard of, living in apartments across the hall from each other, even though Vi had told her they'd closed on a house they planned to move into after the wedding.

"Wouldn't it be easier if you two moved in together right away? Your wedding is in a couple months, anyway."

Vi hit Jade with a penetrating gaze that made her squirm. "Easier isn't always right. We want to honor God with every part of our marriage. Living together now would open the possibility for too many temptations."

Jade rolled her eyes. That was so old-fashioned. Didn't her sister know that times changed? She shoved aside the twinge of conscience that said her own life hadn't exactly been God-honoring and padded down the hall to get ready for church.

The low buzz of voices didn't let up as Jade followed Vi through the lobby of Hope Church. But she felt as if every eye in the building had zeroed in on her. She could practically hear their thoughts:

Isn't that Jade Falter?

What's she doing here?

Jade Falter in a church? You've got to be kidding me.

She ducked her head and kept walking.

Anyone who wasn't trying to figure out what she was doing in church was probably wondering how she'd turned out so bad when she had such a perfect mother and sister.

Well, let them wonder.

Hadn't she wondered the same thing a thousand times herself?

Maybe someone here could figure it out. She sure never could.

Vi passed the pews at the back of the church, where Jade would have preferred to hide out, and stopped at a pew nearly at the front. Several of the people Vi had introduced her to last night were already seated. Jade fiddled with the edges of her cutoff shorts as she eyed Grace in a light floral print dress. Vi gestured for her to enter the pew first, so she slid in and settled next to Grace with a half smile.

But Grace leaned over and gave her a one-armed hug. "It's so nice to see you again. I take it you and Dan go back a long time."

Jade eyed her warily. "We went to high school together." Best to leave it at that. No one had known they were seeing each other in high school, so no reason to bring it up now.

"That's so neat." Grace patted her hand as if they were old friends. "I bet y'all have a lot of catching up to do."

Jade moved her head noncommittally. She was pretty sure she and Dan wouldn't be doing any catching up. In fact, he probably wished she'd never come back.

Not that knowing that kept her stomach from dipping as he stepped to the front of the church and offered his warm smile to everyone seated there. Nor did it keep her from remembering the days when that smile was reserved for her.

But at least she didn't long for those days again.

Much.

Chapter 6

"Hidden Cafe?" Dan flipped off the last bank of sanctuary lights and turned to the dozen or so friends waiting for him in the lobby. His eyes automatically went to Jade, standing with Violet and Nate, looking completely uncomfortable and as if she'd rather be far from here.

"Where else?" Spencer clapped a hand on his back. "Good sermon today, Pastor."

"Thanks." Dan still hadn't gotten used to being called by that title. For as long as he could remember, that's what people called his dad. Thankfully, his friends generally called him by his first name—although Spencer preferred to address him as pastor when they were talking church things.

He followed his friends to the parking lot, where they all got in their own cars for the short drive to the cafe.

While he waited for everyone else to leave, he loosened his tie and tugged it off, then slipped out of his suit coat.

Much better.

If he could get away with preaching in jeans, he'd be perfectly content. But that probably wouldn't go over very well with his congregation.

He reached into the backseat to dig for one of the water bottles he kept stocked there. By the time he turned around, only Grace's car was left, but she appeared to be talking on the phone.

He debated—should he pull out ahead of her or be a gentleman and wait?

Before he'd made a decision, she hung up, then looked over and smiled at him. He waved for her to go ahead. But when she tried to start the ignition, the engine only coughed. She tried twice more with no result.

Dan groaned. Fixing a car wasn't really on his agenda for today. But he couldn't leave her stranded here.

He started his own engine and eased his car into place across from hers. It probably needed a jump start. At least that would only take a couple minutes. He was starving.

Grace slid out of her car and approached with a sheepish look.

He closed his car door. "Car trouble?"

She nodded. "I meant to fill up with gas on my way to church this morning."

Dan stared at her. "It's out of gas?" He resisted the urge to rub his temples. The nearest gas station was across town. And he'd used up the last of the gas in his gas can when he'd mowed the lawn yesterday.

"Don't worry about it. Grandpa was doing pretty well this morning. I'll call him and ask if he can fill up a gas can and bring me some. Y'all go ahead and eat without me."

Dan sighed. He couldn't do that. "Tell you what, why don't you ride with me to lunch and then afterward we'll get you some gas and get your car going again."

Grace looked uncertain. "You're sure?"

A loud growl from his stomach sealed the deal. "I'm sure."

Grace's smile was sweet, and again Dan tried to feel something for her. But it didn't spark anything.

"I talked to your friend Jade this morning," Grace said as he drove out of the parking lot.

"Yeah?" He hated the way his heart gave that jolt every time he heard her name.

He thought about correcting Grace and telling her Jade wasn't his friend. Once upon a time, he'd thought she was more than that. But he'd been wrong.

He should have realized when she never wanted to be seen with him in public that she wasn't serious about him. He finally got the message when she left—what she'd claimed to feel for him had never been real. And it never would be.

"She seemed nice," Grace continued, and Dan had to bite his tongue to keep from asking if they could talk about something else.

Anything else.

"A little aloof, though." Grace looked at him, as if to confirm whether he agreed.

He raised a lip. Aloof was putting it mildly.

"I wonder what happened to make her that way?" Grace tapped a finger to her chin. "Some kind of hurt early in life, I'd bet."

When Dan didn't say anything, she laughed at herself. "Don't mind me. I've been watching way too many daytime talk shows with Grandpa."

He laughed too and shifted the conversation to the grandfather Grace had moved here to take care of.

Unlike Jade, who'd fled from everyone who loved her, Grace had upended her whole life to be there for those she loved.

If that wasn't something he should be looking for in a woman, he didn't know what was.

So why did his eyes track to Jade the moment they entered the Hidden Cafe?

You were just looking for the right table. It's not your fault she's the first one you saw there.

Dan wanted to believe his own excuses.

Violet was on one side of Jade, Leah on the other. The moment his sister noticed him, standing in the doorway with Grace, a ginormous smile tipped her lips.

Great. Now she was going to assume her matchmaking had worked.

Dan followed Grace to the table and sat next to her in the only two chairs that were empty. He took a quick survey of the restaurant. It was a popular after-church destination, and he recognized at least six or seven families from his congregation. He waved to them.

He loved to see the members of his flock out and about, but sometimes he felt like he was always on display. Were they just waiting for him to say or do something that would prove he wasn't ready to be head pastor?

He picked up his menu, but his gaze flicked to Jade as he opened it. She was staring intently at her own menu, even though she must have had ten minutes to read it already.

By the time they'd ordered, she hadn't glanced toward him once.

So that was how she wanted to play this? They'd ignore each other?

That was completely fine with him.

Better than fine. It was ideal. Now he wouldn't have to keep rehashing the past—all their moonlit walks on the beach, talking about everything and nothing in their special spot between the dunes, feeling like she knew him better than anyone besides God.

None of that would have to cloud his mind for even a second.

Dan gave his attention to a conversation with Grace and Tyler, who were both serving as chaperones on the trip to Camp Oswego in two weeks. By the time his omelet was almost gone, they'd worked out most of the details of who needed to bring which supplies.

"Who's going to watch the boys?" Grace turned to Tyler, whose twin five-year-old boys had gone home with their grandparents after church.

"Only their coolest aunt and uncle," Sophie called from the other end of the table.

Dan smiled. He loved the moments when they all felt like one big happy family. Well, one big happy family, plus Jade now. She hadn't lost any of the tension Dan had noticed in her face last night. It was as if she expected someone to jump out and ambush her at any moment.

A heavy hand fell on Dan's shoulder, and he nearly jumped. Talk about ambush.

He hadn't noticed Terrence Malone, president of Hope Church's board, walking over.

"Pretty good sermon this morning, Danny. I remember the last time your dad preached on those verses. He had a slightly different take." He coughed. "But you're still young. You'll get there."

"Thank you." Dan forced himself not to grit his teeth. Terrence was only making small talk, not trying to insult him. Since he'd taken over his dad's role as head pastor, he'd come to recognize that there were two types of people in his congregation, at least when it came to how they saw him: There were those who put him on a pedestal, and those who saw him as a little boy playing church. He wasn't sure which group he was more afraid of disappointing.

Terrence patted him on the back. "Your father left some pretty big shoes to fill. But you know that already." With one more shoulder clap, Terrence left. Across the table, Jade looked from Terrence to Dan. For some reason, it unnerved him that he couldn't read what she was thinking.

Next to him, Grace set her napkin on her plate. "I didn't know your daddy, but I do know you'll fill his shoes well."

Dan nodded, wishing he could be as sure.

Chapter 7

J ade clicked on her phone to check the date. It was Friday, which meant she'd been in Hope Springs one day short of a week. Why did it feel so much longer?

The familiar claustrophobia this town had always given her was creeping up on her already.

It didn't help that she'd spent all week holed up in Vi's apartment. But there wasn't anything she wanted to do or anyone she wanted to see.

And there was one person she very much *did not* want to see.

She raised her hands to her face and rubbed it. Why was it in the six days she'd been home she'd thought about Dan at least six million times? Over the past eight years, she'd managed to leave thoughts of him behind, but now that she was here, it was like he'd invaded her head.

The head is fine. Just don't let him get to your heart again.

Jade pulled her hands down, firming her resolve. Of course Dan wouldn't get to her heart again.

Anyway, he was with another woman now. When he'd walked into the Hidden Cafe with Grace after church on Sunday, she'd told herself she was fine with it. But the longer the meal had gone on, the more painful it had been to watch him with her, laughing and planning their trip. And when that guy from church had come over to tell Dan what big shoes he had to fill, it had hit her.

Even if he weren't with Grace, he would never consider a relationship with her. He had a role to fill here, a reputation to maintain. And being with her wasn't the kind of reputation he needed.

Not that she'd wanted to get back together with him. That wasn't the point. The point was, she'd burned any hope of a future here before she'd left in the first place.

She shook her head at herself. It wasn't like she wanted a future here anyway. All she had to do was make it through the summer, and then she could get back to her real life in LA.

The real life with the dead-end job, string of meaningless men, and, oh, don't forget the generous helping of self-loathing.

Jade shut off the voice and grabbed her phone again, swiping at her contact list. She needed someone to help her get her head on straight.

Keira answered before the phone had even rung.

"Wow. Were you waiting for me to call?"

"Yep." Keira's voice was reassuringly familiar. "I figured you were due to be going crazy right about now."

Jade snorted. "You could say that."

"So those wholesome Hope Springs guys aren't enticing you, huh?"

Jade closed her eyes. She'd had a wholesome Hope Springs guy once. "I already told you I wasn't coming here to date."

"Ah, well, the summer is young. Don't give up yet."

"Actually—" Jade fiddled with the small turquoise ring her mother had given her for her sixteenth birthday. It was the one piece of jewelry she never took off. "I'm not sure I can make it the whole summer. I might just come back to LA. I'll tell Vi I have an audition." No need for Vi to know she'd quit going on auditions two years ago when she'd realized that even if she ever got a decent part, she actually hated acting.

"What about the shower and the wedding?"

"I don't have to be here all summer for those. I can just fly here for those weekends." The more she talked about it, the better the plan sounded.

"Jade Lynn Falter."

Jade winced at her roommate's use of her middle name.

"Do you remember how many nights you spent crying to me about what an awful sister you've been?" Keira's voice was sharp and sympathetic at the same time.

"It wasn't that many nights," Jade muttered.

"It *was* that many. And if you come back now, it's going to be that many more. And I can't take that—my tissue budget is empty for the year."

Jade let herself laugh a little. She pushed out an exaggerated sigh. "Fine. I'll stay."

"Good girl." Keira's voice gentled. "It can't be that bad there, can it?"

This time Jade's sigh was too real, pulling with it all the mistakes from her past. She'd never told Keira about Dan, and she didn't feel like getting into it now. Next thing she knew, Keira would be telling her God had brought her back into Dan's path for a reason. And unless that reason was to torture her, Jade couldn't agree.

"There's just not much to do, I guess."

"What did you used to do?"

The question was innocent enough, but Jade flinched. "Nothing I'm proud of or want to repeat."

Keira paused. "Okay, what does your sister do?"

"Works in her antique store."

"There you go then."

Jade wrinkled her nose. She'd popped down to the store below Vi's apartment a couple times during the week to ask her sister where things were, but she hadn't hung around long. Too dull for her taste.

"I'm not sure that would be much more fun than sitting around staring at the walls," she told Keira.

"Jade." For a single woman with no children, Keira sure had a good mom voice. "You're supposed to be spending the summer there to catch up with your sister. Wouldn't it be easier to do that if you actually spent some time with her? I'm sure it'd mean a lot to her."

"Well—" But she had no counterarguments. "Ugh. I hate when you're right."

"But I always am. Gotta fly, but call me soon and let me know how antiquing goes."

Jade sighed again as she hung up the phone, but she dutifully got dressed and made her way downstairs to her sister's antique shop.

It may not be fun, but at least it should help get her mind off Dan.

Chapter 8

"Thanks, Pastor Dan."

"Anytime." Dan ushered the young newlyweds he'd been counseling to the door of his office. When he'd married Colton and Sierra two weeks ago, both had been radiating happiness. So he'd been more than a little surprised when they'd knocked on his office door this afternoon, both near tears, asking if he had time to talk.

Thankfully, the issue hadn't been anything serious. Just some difficulties in adjusting to married life and setting realistic expectations of each other.

"Why don't you two go out and get a nice dinner together and keep talking?"

"We will." Colton shook his hand, but Sierra gave Dan a hug.

"I know you told us before the wedding that marriage would be hard, but I didn't know you meant *this* hard," she said.

Dan laughed as he released her. He may not have any personal experience with marriage, but he'd done enough couple's counseling to know marriage took work.

"It's worth it though." Colton draped an arm over his wife's shoulders and dropped a kiss onto the top of her head.

"Stay in the Word together and pray together," Dan reminded them as they started down the hall. He watched them until they turned the corner into the church lobby, a deep sense of satisfaction filling his soul. The impromptu counseling session had been an interruption to his plans for the day, no doubt about that. But for him, one of the most rewarding parts of ministry was moments like this, when he could sit down with people one-on-one and help them work through their problems. Most importantly, he could point them to God's Word.

Help them to keep you at the center of their relationship always. He offered a silent prayer for the couple, then checked the time.

Four-thirty. Which meant he had just enough time for a short run before dinner at Violet's.

He switched off the lights in his office and pulled the door closed. But as he came to the end of the hallway, he heard the church's door open, followed by footsteps.

He paused, undecided.

He could backtrack and take the side exit, so he wouldn't run into whoever had just come in. But he dismissed the thought. What if it was Colton and Sierra with more questions?

He continued toward the lobby, promising himself he'd give whoever was there the time and attention they needed, even if it meant missing his run.

But the only one in the lobby was Leah.

"Oh, it's just you." He moved toward the door, gesturing for her to follow him.

She slapped his shoulder as he passed. "That's a nice way to greet the sister who brings you good news."

Dan held the door open for her, then stepped outside, locking it behind him. "What good news?" He took a deep breath of the lake-scented air. The day was warm, but the usual humidity of late June hadn't hit yet, and the light breeze off the water was refreshing. Perfect running weather.

"I was just talking to a certain someone, and I get the impression she'd be more than happy to go on another date with you."

Dan's thoughts jumped to Jade, before he realized his sister was talking about Grace.

He rolled his eyes. "It's tough to go on *another* date with her since we haven't gone on *one* date."

"Yes you have. Dinner last week. And the fireworks."

"Those were not dates. They were setups. By you."

Leah shrugged. "Same difference. Anyway, I'm not the one who made you bring her to the Hidden Cafe after church on Sunday. That was all you."

Dan threw his hands in the air and walked across the parking lot toward his house next door. "Her car was out of gas. What was I supposed to do, leave her?"

35

Leah fell into step next to him. "Still, it was pretty chivalrous, especially the way you insisted on filling her car up afterward, at least the way she tells it."

Dan scrubbed a hand down his face. "I told you, I just don't see it going anywhere, Leah."

"Why not?"

But he didn't have a good answer. Grace was a nice woman, and he appreciated all her help at church. But that was the extent of his feelings for her.

When he didn't answer, Leah's hand went to her hip. "Dan, if she's not perfect for you, I don't know who is. She's a pastor's daughter, she jumped right into volunteering at church, she has all kinds of ideas for ministry and the ability to carry them out. Oh, and she was helping me out in the kitchen the other day—she knows her way around in there."

All of that was true—Dan knew that. On paper, Grace would make a perfect pastor's wife.

"This is about her coming back, isn't it?" His sister's sharp stare made him look away.

"Her who?"

Leah whacked his arm. "You know who."

He shook his head. "It's not about Jade, if that's what you're implying."

"Good." Leah was still watching him too closely. "Because that is a high school dream that's over. You know that."

"Yeah." Dan kicked at a rock in front of him. "I do."

He wished, not for the first time, that he'd never told her about his short-lived relationship with Jade.

Leah stopped as they reached the front of his house. "I'm serious, Dan. Grace is a great woman. Promise me you won't get so blinded by what was that you don't notice what's in front of you. Give Grace a chance, at least."

"Yeah, fine. I promise." He jogged up the porch steps. "Now get out of here. I want to go for a run before we have to be at Violet's."

"Fine." Leah backed toward the church parking lot, where she'd left her car. "But just so you know, I invited Grace tonight. So you can start keeping your promise right away." With a wave and a laugh, she skipped off.

Dan closed the door harder than necessary behind her. His sister's meddling got worse every year. For some reason, she couldn't bear to see Dan single, even though she herself rarely dated and claimed she'd be perfectly content to end up alone.

As he was changing into his running clothes, Dan's thoughts wandered to Leah's accusation that his lack of interest in Grace had something to do with Jade's return.

That was ridiculous. What he'd had with Jade—if it had ever been anything—was long over.

He tied his running shoes and headed out the back door, jogging across his yard to the wooden staircase next to the church, which led down to the beach.

Telling himself it was the better workout, he turned to the south, images of Jade chasing him all the way. When he reached their special spot between the dunes, he stopped short, sucking in sharp breaths. He'd avoided this place for the past eight years, but in the last week, he'd found his runs ending up here every day.

He moved closer and squinted, as if that would make it possible to see into the past. To figure out what had gone wrong.

For two months, everything had been as close to perfect as possible. The beach had become their refuge, the spot where they sat close and talked about everything from school to his plans to enter seminary to her mom's cancer. He'd even worked up the courage to hold her hand.

He'd tried for weeks to find exactly the right moment to kiss her, but every time he thought he might go for it, he chickened out.

A couple weeks before graduation, Jade's mom died. He ached to be there for her, but the more he tried, the further she pulled away. She didn't want him to sit with her at the funeral. She shut down all his requests to meet at the beach. Eventually, she quit coming to chemistry class too, although he saw her in the halls at school, always with some guy or another. The same guys who'd treated her so badly at the beginning of the year.

Dan had tried to be understanding, tried to tell himself she was going through a lot. That she just needed time.

Finally, on graduation day, she slipped him a note as they rehearsed the recessional.

Meet me at our spot tonight after graduation?

He looked up to meet her eyes, not caring who saw his grin. Giving her time had worked. Now things could get back to normal.

Looking back later, Dan realized that her return smile had held a trace of sadness behind it, but at the time, he'd been too ecstatic to notice.

He barely paid attention to the graduation ceremony. He couldn't wait to get out of there and get to Jade. When he finally made it to the beach after his family had given him about a gazillion hugs, she was already there.

The night was dark, clouds completely obscuring the moon, but as his eyes fell on her silhouette, the clouds slid aside, letting a slice of moonlight illuminate her face.

Dan's breath caught as it hit him: He was in love with Jade Falter, and he would be for the rest of his life.

"Hi." Jade's voice was thick with emotion, and he wondered if she'd had the same realization as he had.

He stepped closer, all the fears that had held him back so many times falling away.

He knew it then.

This was it. Exactly the right moment.

As he'd leaned toward her, he'd never been so uncertain and so sure of something all at once.

The kiss had been . . . awkward. But also sort of magical.

Dan hadn't had much practice in the kissing department, and his lips had fumbled against hers. He didn't remember doing it, but somehow he'd lifted his hands to her shoulders, and he still remembered the simultaneous warmth of her skin with the chill of the night air.

Jade had sighed against his lips, and it was the most beautiful sound he'd ever heard.

When she'd pulled away, she'd given him a smile he'd never seen on her. Sort of happy and scared and overwhelmed all at once.

For some reason, it had made him self-conscious. "Sorry if that wasn't very good. I don't—"

But her hand had brushed against his cheek. "That was perfect."

"Hey, man, can you get that?" The guy's voice yanked Dan out of his memories, and he shook himself, eyes tracking to a Frisbee that lay a few feet from where he stood. He stooped to pick it up, then tossed it to the guy.

As the guy called out a "thank you," Dan lifted a hand to wave, then started toward home at a slower jog.

Apparently the kiss wasn't as good as Jade had let him believe.

The next day when he went to meet her again, all he'd found was a note.

And, until last weekend, that was the only word he'd heard from her in eight years.

Leah was right.

He should give Grace a chance.

Jade was a dream who had walked out of his life.

He'd be a fool to let her back in.

Chapter 9

Jade took a second to survey her handiwork.

"That's looking pretty good." Vi stepped over to examine the dining table Jade had been sanding down for her. "Tomorrow I'll teach you how to refinish it."

Jade groaned, but she couldn't help smiling. When she'd taken Keira's advice to come down here, she'd planned on talking with Vi for an hour or so and then making her escape. When Vi had asked if she wanted to help, she'd said yes only out of a sense of obligation.

But she had to admit that she'd enjoyed working with her hands. And seeing the fruits of her labor left her feeling more satisfied than she'd been in a long time.

Satisfied and exhausted.

She lifted her arms in front of her to stretch them. "How do you do this every day?"

As she'd watched her sister move from helping customers to repairing broken table legs to taking care of the accounts, Jade had been amazed.

Vi shrugged. "I love what I do. Just like you love acting."

Jade turned away. She'd wanted to love acting, so maybe that counted for something. Truth be told, she'd never found anything that she really loved. Or that she was good at.

"I flipped the sign out front to closed," Vi said, "so as soon as we get this all cleaned up, we can head upstairs for dinner."

"Already?"

"Yep." Vi held out what looked like a piece of netting.

"Fishnet stockings?"

Violet burst into laughter. "Cheesecloth."

Jade wrinkled her nose as the fabric hit her fingertips. Instead of the smooth silkiness she'd anticipated, it was gummy.

"You use it to wipe off the dust from sanding." Vi pantomimed wiping the cloth over the table.

Jade followed her sister's instructions as Vi put away her tools. Ten minutes later, the workshop looked just as it had this morning, with the exception of a couple items she and Vi had managed to maneuver onto the sales floor.

"This was nice." Vi flipped off the light and pulled the door closed.

"It was." To her surprise, Jade meant it.

One of the things she'd worried about most when she'd agreed to come to Hope Springs for the summer was that things would be awkward between her and her sister after not seeing each other for so long. But thankfully they'd been able to pick up right where they'd left off—better than they'd left off, actually, since they'd never been terribly close as kids.

She followed Vi up the stairs at the back of the building.

"We should have just enough time to get ready before everyone gets here," Vi said over her shoulder.

Jade glanced up. "Get ready for what?" She'd been looking forward to slipping into some pajamas and spending the night binging Netflix.

But before Vi could answer, the door at the bottom of the stairs opened. They both glanced over their shoulders.

"Hey! I didn't expect you to be home yet." Instantly, Vi turned and skipped down the steps to greet her fiancé. Jade smiled at the clear adoration on Nate's face as he looked up at his future bride.

But her smile wilted as Dan stepped through the doorway behind Nate. His eyes met hers for half a second before he looked away, his jaw tight.

"Sorry I'm early," he said to Vi, who had already pulled him into a quick hug.

"Don't be silly. Come on up. Jade helped me in the shop today, and we were just heading up ourselves."

"Yeah?" Nate smiled up at Jade. "How'd you like it?"

"It was good." If they wanted more intelligent conversation from her, she was going to need to know what was going on. Why Dan was here. "So what are you guys up to tonight?"

Vi slapped a palm to her forehead. "I can't believe I forgot to tell you. Everyone's coming over for dinner tonight. I hope that's okay?"

"Of course." It was Vi's place, after all. Jade only wished she'd known ahead of time so she could have made plans to escape.

Maybe it wasn't too late.

But no matter how much she wracked her brain, she couldn't come up with somewhere to go by herself on a Friday night around here.

She let Nate and Vi pass her on the stairs. Dan was still at the bottom, though, busy with his phone, so she turned to follow them up. After a second, Dan's footsteps sounded below her, but she refused to let herself look back. The same way she'd done when she'd left that note on the beach years ago.

In the apartment, Vi and Nate were already bustling around the kitchen, gathering the taco fixings Jade had smelled Vi making before she'd left for work this morning. The way they moved together, handing each other plates, sidestepping to move out of the way, occasionally pausing for a smile or a quick kiss, made them seem like a married couple already.

Jade had pretty much always been sure she didn't want anything like that, but watching them now almost made her change her mind.

She crossed through the apartment to take refuge in the bedroom. She didn't really need anything in there—aside from a minute to compose herself.

After spending all week fighting to get Dan out of her head, having him in the next room wasn't helping.

She pulled her hair into a ponytail, just so it would look like she'd come in here for a reason, then forced herself to rejoin the others. In the few minutes she'd been in the bedroom, the small apartment had filled up. Emma, Leah, Grace, and Sophie had joined Vi and Nate in the kitchen. Sophie's husband—Jade thought she remembered his name was Spencer—and his brother—Tyler, maybe—were talking to Dan in the living room.

And there was Jade, all by herself between the two, not belonging anywhere. Story of her life.

She took a tentative step toward the kitchen, but the apartment door swung open, and before she knew what was happening, everyone was oohing and swarming the couple who had just come in. It wasn't until the group shifted positions that she saw why. The woman was holding a small, squirming bundle.

Jade retreated to the kitchen to busy herself with something. Anything. She couldn't coo over the baby. Not with this terrible ache in her throat.

"She's getting so big already." Vi stroked the baby's cheek as she led the couple to the living room.

"She's a month old today," the woman said, never taking her eyes off the baby.

Vi moved toward the kitchen. "Jade, you haven't met Ethan and Ariana yet, have you? They weren't at the fireworks the other night because of the baby." Vi grabbed Jade's arm and dragged her to the living room, not stopping until they were right in front of the happy family. "Ethan. Ariana. This is my sister Jade."

They both smiled and said hello.

"And this is little Joy." Vi leaned down to touch the baby's hand, and instantly Joy grasped her finger. Vi looked like she was in heaven. "Isn't she just the most precious thing?"

Everyone was watching her expectantly. Waiting for her to—what? Play with the baby? She nodded mutely and turned toward the kitchen.

The apartment door opened again, and the woman Vi had introduced as Peyton at the fireworks held up a pink box. "Sorry we're late. But I brought cake, so you can't be mad."

Her husband followed her through the door. "It's my fault. I was on a call."

"Ask him what it was." Peyton laughed as she opened the box, revealing a beautifully decorated cake covered in swirls of flowers.

Jared groaned. "It was a first for me. Some kid got stuck in a laundry chute."

A mixture of laughs and gasps went up from the group.

"Did you get him out?" Grace asked.

"Her," Jared corrected. "And yes. But it took several hours, and I'm afraid the parents are going to be facing some pretty costly repairs."

"Great." Ariana sighed. "Add one more thing to worry about as a new mom."

Ethan kissed her forehead and took Joy from her, snuggling the baby against his shoulder. "We don't even have a laundry chute."

Ariana laughed along as the others giggled. When they stopped, she stood, grabbing a diaper bag from the floor. "I know, but seriously you guys, I had no idea how much there was to worry about as a parent. I pray for this little one constantly."

"And that's the best thing you can do for her," Dan said.

Jade glanced at him, then at the others, who were nodding in agreement. Did they really believe it was that easy? Just pray and everything would be fine?

"Dinner's ready," Vi called from the kitchen.

The noise swelled as there was a mass surge for the food. Jade watched everyone for a minute. They were all comfortable together. Relaxed. Like a family.

One she didn't belong to.

But as dinner wore on, Jade had to admit that the others were striving to include her—everyone except Dan, who'd chosen a spot as far from her as possible in the small quarters.

Sophie had asked about life in LA. Ariana had complimented her earrings. And Grace had been interested in knowing what it was like on a film set—which Jade could only answer with details she'd picked up from friends since the closest she'd come to an actual film set was the training video she'd starred in for an insurance company.

When the dishes were cleared and washed—by the men, since they apparently traded off turns between the sexes—they all settled on various pieces of furniture or the floor of the living room. Jade took a spot on the floor with her back against the wall. To her surprise, she had to admit she enjoyed listening to the flow of their conversation.

There was no talk of parties or clubs or who wore what when. But they all seemed to care about the mundane details of each other's lives, like Ariana and Ethan's sleepless nights with the baby and Peyton's plan to expand her bakery and Tyler's tales about the twins' latest mischief.

Jade let herself wonder briefly what it would be like to have a group of friends like this—people she was one hundred percent comfortable around and never worried would judge her. But she dismissed the thought. She'd never needed a close friend group like this before—and she didn't need one now. Besides, she wasn't hanging around long enough to form friendships.

"I know!" Grace chirped during a lull in the conversation.

Jade had tried not to notice that Grace had chosen a spot next to Dan on the couch, along with Vi and Nate. The four of them were crammed on there so tightly that Grace's shoulder was pressed up against Dan's.

"Let's play Bible Pictionary." Grace's enthusiasm was almost alarming.

Jade made a face. She had to be kidding, right?

But apparently Jade was in the minority with her opinion, as Vi was soon pulling out a large pad of paper and some markers.

Tyler did a quick count of the room. "It'll be uneven teams, unless baby Joy plays."

As if she'd heard her name, the baby cooed in her sleep, and everyone aahed over her again.

Jade stretched her cramped legs and pushed to her feet. "That's okay. You guys play without me. I'm going to get a little air."

She ducked her head so she wouldn't have to see Vi's disappointed look. But her sister followed her to the landing outside the door.

"Everything okay?" Vi asked in a low voice.

"Of course." Jade lifted her lips into a smile. "Your friends are great. I just need a little break."

Vi laughed. "That's understandable. They are pretty great, but they can be a bit much to get used to." She squeezed Jade's arm. "Be careful out there."

Jade resisted rolling her eyes. She'd lived in LA for eight years. There wasn't much about Hope Springs that could scare her. But she dutifully answered, "I will," before trundling down the steps.

She paused outside the exterior door. Where was she going to go?

The sound of the waves reached up the long hill behind the apartment building. She'd been working to avoid the beach all week. It held too many memories of what could have been.

So she absolutely shouldn't go there now.

But apparently her feet hadn't gotten the memo, as she was already halfway there.

Chapter 10

"Samson and Delilah," Grace shouted, and Dan pumped a fist in the air.

"See," he said to the rest of the group. "I can draw."

"I have no idea how she got that." Spencer tilted his head to the side. "It looks like a potato to me."

"You two must have some kind of connection," Leah piped up.

Dan shot his sister a look as Grace beamed at him.

"It was the scissors that did it." Grace pointed to an *X* on Dan's drawing.

"That was supposed to be a braid." Dan held his hand up to her for a high five. "But whatever works."

He deliberately ignored his sister, who was probably exploding with googly eyes right now.

"And on that triumphant note, I must bid you all adieu."

They all protested, telling him to stay, but he held up a hand. "Some of us have a sermon to finish preparing for Sunday." Not to mention, some of them wanted to escape before Jade came back inside.

She'd been gone at least half an hour already, and if he didn't get out of here soon, he was going to have to see her again. And if he saw her again, he was going to have to remind himself all over again of all the reasons he should avoid her, same as he'd been doing all night. It was getting exhausting.

He said goodnight, then jogged down the stairs and out the door, savoring the cool night air after Violet's warm apartment.

"Oh, hey." He stopped short as his feet hit the parking lot.

Great plan. Not only was Jade standing right here in front of him, but now they were alone together.

"Hey." Jade ran a hand through her hair, which she'd pulled out of its ponytail. It was now dancing in the lake breeze.

"Were you down by the beach?" He didn't intend to ask, but the words slipped out right past the wall he'd meant to erect around his heart.

She nodded wordlessly.

"Oh." Was that really all he had to say? *Oh?*

But what else was he going to do? Ask her if being down there made her think of him? Ask if she remembered the time they'd kissed down there?

If she could tell him why she'd left?

"I was just heading out." He pointed to his car behind her as if his words weren't clear enough to explain what he was doing.

She nodded again but looked away, biting her lip.

The gesture was so familiar that he had to remind himself that it was eight years since the last time he'd seen her do that.

But he still knew what it meant. "What is it?"

"Can we get something in the open?" Jade gave him a direct look, and he forced himself to return it.

"Of course," he said evenly. Maybe she was finally going to tell him why she'd left. Not that he was sure he actually wanted to know anymore. Some things were better left buried.

"I understand if you don't want me to hang out with you all anymore." She gestured toward the upper floor of the apartment building behind him just as a burst of laughter sounded through Violet's open apartment window. "You have every right to hate me."

Dan scrubbed a hand against his jaw, staring past her toward the lake. Moonlight reflected from the foamy tops of the waves. She didn't really think he hated her, did she?

"I don't hate you." He couldn't look at her as he said it. Otherwise, he might be tempted to tell her that far from hating her, he was beginning to fear that he was as taken by her as ever. Even though he very much shouldn't be.

"Of course not. You're a pastor. You don't hate anyone."

Dan laughed and brought his eyes to her face. But she was staring at her feet. "I'm human, Jade. I struggle with emotions just like everyone else. But I don't hate you. I never did."

She looked at him then, skepticism written all over her face. "Why not?"

He lifted his shoulders. How could he tell her that no matter what happened in this world, he was pretty sure he could never hate her?

"You did what you thought you had to do." His gaze swung back to the lake. Much as he hadn't wanted to see it then, it was probably for the best that she'd left. "Anyway, I'm here doing what I'm supposed to be doing. You're in LA doing what you're supposed to be doing. So it all worked out." He forced a tight smile, and she half returned it.

"So you weren't angry with me for leaving?"

Dan pondered the question. She deserved an honest answer. "I was maybe a little angry at first. But mostly I was confused."

He waited, hope and dread colliding over the possibility that she might take the hint and fill him in on what had driven her away.

When she remained silent, he stepped past her to his car. "But then, you always were the most confusing girl I knew."

Jade's soft laugh followed him.

"Anyway—" He paused with his hand on the car door. "I don't want you to stop hanging out with everyone. You should feel comfortable with your sister and her friends. And if me being around makes you uncomfortable, I'll step back for the summer." He had plenty to keep him busy at church, although the thought of not spending time with his friends left him empty.

Jade shook her head. "You don't make me uncomfortable."

"Good." He pulled the car door open. "Then you should join us all for dinner again next Friday. My place."

He dropped into his seat and closed the door. It'd been a dumb thing to say, and he didn't want to hear her answer, whether it was yes or no.

Chapter 11

"Here we are." Vi parked the car in the driveway of a cute little house after church on Sunday. "What do you think?" Vi was clearly enchanted with the place.

"It's sweet." Jade could easily picture her sister and Nate starting a family here. She unclicked her seatbelt and followed Vi onto the front porch, with its white railing, decorative pillars, and cozy swing.

Vi paused with her hand on the front door. "The house needs some work on the inside, but we'll get to that eventually. When we have time."

Jade gave her sister's arm a reassuring pat. Vi didn't have to worry about impressing her.

"I'm sure it's— Whoa." She stopped as she entered the house. She didn't know where to look first. Wallpaper in every pattern imaginable covered every wall—and even some doors. The entryway was a checkered red plaid, while the living room walls boasted a pink floral print. Jade made her way slowly through the first floor, taking in the jungle print on the dining room walls and the fruit basket border in the kitchen.

"There's more upstairs." Vi laughed at Jade, who struggled to ease her features into an expression somewhere short of horror.

"More?"

"It's no big deal. We'll take it one room at a time after we move in, and eventually it'll get done."

"And in the meantime, you'll be happy living here?"

"Of course." Vi rubbed a hand over the kitchen wall. "I don't care what our home looks like. Nate and I will be here together. That's what matters."

Jade nodded, even though she'd have no idea about any of that. She walked to the French doors that looked out onto the backyard.

"It's an amazing view, though." The house overlooked an empty section of beach below the town.

"Yep." Vi pulled the doors open and led the way onto the patio. "That's what drew us here."

Jade shielded her eyes against the morning sun as she watched the water. It was completely still today. Completely peaceful.

"So—" Vi poked her shoulder. "What's up with you and Dan?"

Jade wrinkled her nose at her sister. "What are you talking about?"

"I saw the way he looked at you the other night at the fireworks and the way you kept staring at him Friday night when everyone was over."

"He wasn't looking at me any way." Jade tried to keep her voice disinterested. "He was probably trying to remember who I was. We didn't exactly run in the same circles in high school." Which wasn't a complete lie. Aside from each other, they'd had no mutual friends—something she'd worked hard to maintain since the kind of people she called friends would have had a field day picking on the preacher's son if they'd known she was seeing him. Dan would have beat his own school record in the one hundred meter dash running away from her if he'd spent any time with them.

"What about you, then?" Vi tipped her head to the side, scrutinizing her. "You can't deny you were staring at him. A lot."

"I can deny it." Jade took a few steps toward the edge of the patio. "And anyway, if I *was* staring at him, it's because I was thinking about his sermon from last week." She didn't know why she was so determined to keep her feelings about Dan from her sister. Probably because she didn't have any feelings for him. Just silly memories that were better left in the past.

"Oh." Vi seemed to take her at her word. "I'm glad you came to church with us again today."

Jade offered a noncommittal nod.

Vi's brow creased. Not for the first time since she'd been home, Jade felt Vi studying her. She wasn't sure what her sister was looking for, but she clearly wasn't finding it. Big surprise there. Jade rarely had what people wanted.

"Did you not like the service?" Vi finally asked.

"The service was fine." In fact, a couple of the songs had reminded her of going to church with Mom and Vi as a kid, and she'd been surprised to find their familiarity comforting. And Dan's sermon about God's grace had actually pulled her in. Even if she remained skeptical about the message, she had to admit that Dan was an engaging speaker. His love for what he did came through so clearly as he preached, and she couldn't help but admire his passion.

"What is it, then?" Vi sat in one of the chipped Adirondack chairs and gestured for Jade to sit in the other.

Instead, Jade leaned against its back. "I guess I don't feel like I belong there. I can feel everyone wondering what I'm doing there."

Vi turned in her seat to stare up at her. "You know no one thinks that, right? Everyone at Hope Church is very warm and welcoming."

"Easy for you to say," Jade muttered.

"What do you mean by that?" Vi's eyes were wide, as if she had no idea what Jade was talking about.

"Oh, come on, Vi." Jade threw her hands in the air. "You know you were always the good one. Of course everyone at church loves you." She paced to the other side of the patio. "I know you were away at college my last couple years of high school, but even you must know that I didn't exactly have—" She cut off, suddenly not wanting to continue. If by some miracle her sister had lived in Hope Springs all these years without hearing rumors of Jade's less than savory past, she didn't want to be the one to shatter her sister's image of her.

"Have what?" Vi's voice was gentle, her eyes searching, although Jade had a feeling Vi knew exactly what she had been about to say.

"Never mind." Jade strode toward the door. "We should get going. You and Nate promised to be at Peyton's by two for the cake testing."

Vi pressed her lips together but got up and crossed toward the door. Jade didn't wait for her.

It wasn't until they were almost home that Vi turned to her. "Whatever happened in the past is in the past. You're forgiven for all of it. And no one here is thinking about it." She squeezed Jade's arm. "Got it?"

Jade kept her gaze directed out the window and made herself nod to placate her sister. It was a nice sentiment.

And Vi probably really did believe it was true.

But Jade had seen enough of the world to know it wasn't.

Not for girls like her.

Chapter 12

She shouldn't be here. It was all Jade could think as she followed Nate and Vi to the front door of Dan's house Friday night. Dan's invitation last week had been made out of pity—not a desire that she'd actually show up. But Vi had insisted that if she wanted dinner she'd have to come, since there was no food left in the apartment.

Plus, as Jade had joined Vi in the antique shop all week, a brilliant plan had occurred to her. But she was going to need the help of Vi's friends to pull it off. And this was the only way she could think of to talk to all of them without raising Vi's suspicions.

Now that she was here, though, she wished she had tried harder to come up with another way.

She paused at the bottom of the steps leading up to Dan's front door, waiting for Vi to ring the doorbell. At least she'd have a few more seconds to come to grips with being here before Dan answered the door. But Vi grabbed the knob and let herself in.

Jade shot Nate an alarmed look, and he shrugged. "That's how we do things around here."

Jade pushed down the swirl trying to flutter from her belly toward her heart and followed Nate into the house. There was nothing to be nervous about, now that she and Dan had cleared the air and she knew that at least he didn't hate her.

But instead of reassuring her, the conversation in the apartment parking lot last week had left her shaken. Probably because Dan had incomplete information about why she'd left. If he knew the real reason, he would hate her, pastor or not.

But he would never know the real reason, she reminded herself. She didn't understand why that didn't make her feel better.

Inside, the house was bigger than Jade had expected. Though the furniture was worn, it was tasteful and gave off a homey vibe. Not exactly what she'd expected in a bachelor pad. But then, she supposed Dan wasn't your typical bachelor. Aside from her, she didn't know of anyone else he'd dated in high school. Of course, that was a long time ago. He could have dated a whole slew of women since then. But somehow Jade knew he hadn't. Probably no one besides Grace.

Jade's gaze traveled to the kitchen, where Grace and Leah were chatting and cutting up vegetables while Dan rolled out dough.

He lifted his head as Jade closed the door behind her.

"Glad you could make it," he called in the general direction of the door, keeping his eyes off hers. He could as easily have been talking to Vi and Nate as to her. In fact, she was sure he was.

"Hope you guys don't mind pizza." He slid the crust onto a pizza stone, his movements deft and sure. "We have an early morning. The bus for Camp Oswego leaves when the sun comes up."

"Oh, I almost forgot." Grace laid a hand on Dan's arm. "I picked up some snacks for the ride."

Dan smiled at her, and Jade looked away. Listen to those two throwing around that word, "we."

That's what couples do.

Of course it was. That was why Jade had been so careful not to use that word with Dan in high school. It was always, "Meet me at the beach." Or "I'll grab some sandwiches." Never "We should go to the beach" or "we" anything.

We meant attachment. It meant opening yourself up to hurt when there was no longer a *we*.

Nate and Vi moved to talk to Dan, but Jade took a seat next to Sophie and Spencer, with her back to the kitchen.

"Hey, Jade." Sophie offered her a kind smile. "Vi said you were a lot of help in the store this week."

"I'm not sure help is the right word. I'm pretty sure I slowed her down more than anything. But I was there, anyway."

"I'm glad." Sophie patted her leg. "Vi works way too hard and never knows when to ask for help."

Jade couldn't have hoped for a more perfect opening. "I've noticed." She lowered her voice, not enough to draw suspicion, but low enough that no one would be able to hear from the kitchen, especially over the rest of the chatter. "I was thinking, maybe we could all get together and take down that hideous wallpaper in their new house and paint for them. You know, as part of their wedding gift or something."

Sophie's grin grew as Jade talked, and she reached one arm to give Jade a quick squeeze.

"That's a great idea." In her enthusiasm, Sophie practically shouted, and her eyes widened.

"Sorry," she whispered. "That's a great idea."

"What's a great idea?" Peyton asked from the chair across from them.

Jade peeked over her shoulder, but Vi and Nate were deep in conversation with Dan and Grace and didn't even glance toward the living room.

As stealthily as she could, Jade made her way around the room to the others as they ate, cleared the dishes, and talked.

Finally, the only ones she hadn't talked to were Dan, Grace, and Leah. She figured if she talked with any one of them, they could tell the other two. So now it was a matter of who she saw first. If she were a praying woman, she'd pray that it was Leah or Grace.

Chapter 13

The clamor of his friends eating and talking and laughing at his house always filled Dan's heart with a special kind of contentment. As the kid who was always picked on, he'd never imagined this would be his life.

In the short time he'd been back in Hope Springs, this small group of people had become a second family to him.

If she let them, they could be a second family to Jade too. Hard as he'd tried not to watch her, he had noticed how she spent time talking to everyone here tonight. Well, everyone except him. She hadn't so much as been in the same room as him all night. He'd told himself it was a coincidence at first, but as he moved into the living room now, she got up and headed for the kitchen.

He briefly considered doubling back to see what she would do but decided against it. He'd respect her wishes. If she didn't want to be near him, he wouldn't push it.

Grace offered him an open smile as he sat on the couch next to her. "That was the most delicious pizza I've ever had. And I'm Italian, so that's saying something." She leaned closer and nudged him with her shoulder.

"Thanks." Dan returned her smile. Much as he hated to admit his sister was right about anything, he had to agree that Grace was sweet and easy to be with. "Did everyone get enough?"

"Ugh. Too much." Sophie rubbed her stomach. "Not that I'm complaining. It was all delicious."

"That's good." Spencer wrapped an arm around his wife and snuggled her close. "Since you're eating for two now."

"Spencer!" Sophie slapped at his thigh. "We agreed to wait another month to tell everyone."

But the whole group had already gotten to their feet to take turns engulfing the couple in hugs. When it was Ariana's turn, she held Joy out toward Sophie's tummy.

"That's either your future best friend or future husband in there," she cooed to the baby, and everyone laughed.

Dan jumped to his feet and headed for the kitchen to grab some celebratory apple juice, since he had no wine in the house—and Sophie couldn't drink it even if he did. He counted out enough paper cups, since he had nowhere near enough wine glasses for everyone either, then passed the juice around.

But when he was done, he had an extra left. He scanned the room, trying to figure out who he'd missed. But everyone had a cup—even Ariana, who was struggling to keep hers out of Joy's grabbing fingers.

Maybe he'd miscounted. But then he realized one person was missing.

Jade.

A clunk from down the hallway caught his ear.

Oh no. Please tell him she hadn't found—

He strode down the hallway.

Sure enough, there she was, right in the middle of his Star Wars room, bending to pick up a storm trooper mask. As she straightened, her eyes fell on him, and she jumped as if she'd been caught toilet papering the principal's office again.

"Sorry." She set the mask on its stand and stepped away from it. "I don't think I broke it."

Dan shrugged. He was more worried about the fact that Jade Falter was standing here in the middle of his Star Wars collection. It was the one thing he'd kept hidden from her in high school—because if there was anything that proved they didn't belong together, it was this. She was the too-cool-to-care girl, and he was the nerdy guy who collected Star Wars toys.

"I'm sure it's fine," he finally said. "What are you doing in here?" He didn't mean for it to come out so harsh, so he passed her the juice to soften the words.

She raised an eyebrow and took a sip. "Apple juice?"

"Yeah." He toed the edge of the Millennium Falcon-shaped rug that had seemed like such a find when he'd picked it up at a garage sale. "Sophie and Spencer announced they're expecting."

"I heard." Jade's voice was quiet, and he almost thought he detected a wistful note in it.

"It's crazy, isn't it? Everyone getting married and having babies?" A pang he'd never felt before tugged at his gut. A pang that said maybe he'd like that too—someday.

"Yeah." This time he definitely heard a layer of sadness in her voice.

He took a step closer. "You okay?"

"Of course." She walked over to the set of shelves where his Star Wars action figures were lined up. "So, you like Star Wars, huh?"

Dan laughed. There was no point in denying it. "You could say that. I watched the movies with my dad all the time growing up." He cleared his throat. He hadn't been able to watch them since Dad died.

"You never told me." Her words were soft, but the look she gave him was searching.

He found that he had to look away. "It didn't exactly seem like the kind of thing that would impress you. I figured it'd ruin any chance I had with you." A half laugh slipped past his lips. "Not that I had much of a chance in the first place."

When she didn't answer, he made himself look at her. She'd picked up a Luke Skywalker action figure and was bending its arms and legs.

"Maybe I didn't want to be impressed. Maybe I just wanted to know the real you."

Dan nodded slowly. That's what he'd wanted—to know the real Jade. And he'd thought he was starting to—until she left.

"Jade." He didn't know what he was going to say, but she shook her head and cut him off.

"So, who is this guy?"

He studied her. He didn't believe for a second that she cared about any of the Star Wars characters. But this was probably the safest topic to stick to. He took a few steps closer—close enough to point out the figures but far enough to fit at least three people between them—and started telling her about the various items.

She did a good job of feigning interest. So good she almost had him convinced. Until he remembered that she'd spent the past eight years in Hollywood, pursuing an acting career. Feigning was what she did for a living.

He was in the middle of telling her about the difference between the first trilogy and the second trilogy when his phone rang. He pulled it out of his pocket, frowning at the number. He didn't recognize it, but he didn't have every one of his congregants' numbers in his phone. And if someone was calling after nine on a Friday night, it could be an emergency.

"Sorry, I have to take this."

Jade nodded and slipped out of the room.

As Dan answered, his mind was still on her. He couldn't help wondering, if she hadn't left, would they be planning their own wedding or preparing for the arrival of their baby?

He shook his head at himself. The idea was ridiculous.

He and Jade Falter had never been intended for each other.

And they never would be.

Chapter 14

Jade wandered toward Dan's living room, her thoughts still on the Star Wars collectibles he'd been showing her. Much as she could tell he was trying to downplay it, it was clear that he loved everything having to do with the movies. But before today she'd never heard him utter the words Star Wars. Had he really been afraid to let her know that side of him in high school? Had he really thought that would impact how she felt about him?

"There you are." Vi glanced up as Jade entered the room. "We were just figuring out a date for Sophie's baby shower. She and Spencer are expecting!"

"I heard." Jade took half an awkward step forward, wondering if she was supposed to hug Sophie. But she pulled back, settling for a feeble "congratulations" and a low wave to the expectant parents.

"So where'd you wander off to?" Vi slid over on the couch, gesturing for Jade to sit next to her.

Jade took the seat, wedging herself between Vi and Grace. "I was looking for the bathroom, but then I ended up in this room with all kinds of Star Wars memorabilia."

"Oh no." Vi patted Jade's leg. "I'm sorry. I completely forgot to warn you about the Star Wars room. At least Dan must not have known you were in there, or you'd be stuck listening to him talk about all that stuff for a few hours."

Everyone else joined in the laughter—all except for Grace, who looked confused.

"The what now?" Grace asked.

"Oh, the Star Wars room." Spencer leaned forward. "Dan has spent his whole life collecting Star Wars stuff, and once he gets someone in there, he doesn't let them go until he's told them every last detail of every last item."

"Oh, it's not that bad." Nate defended Dan from the other side of Vi.

"No, it's worse," Emma chimed in.

Jade laughed along with them. "Actually, I think it's kind of neat that he has something he's so interested in." To her surprise, she'd enjoyed listening to him, not so much because she cared about the movies but because he was fun to listen to.

"Yeah," Grace spoke up from beside her. "It sounds neat. I'd like to see it."

Jade cut a look at her. Dan hadn't shown her the Star Wars room? Surely he wasn't afraid this perfect woman would judge him for it. Or maybe they weren't as serious as she'd assumed. An unnamed hope spread through her at the possibility, but she pushed it away. It didn't matter how serious Dan and Grace were. They could be about to announce their engagement for all Jade knew—and for all it mattered to her.

Grace got to her feet, but before she made it out of the living room, Dan rushed in, his face drawn.

"That was Cassandra." He held up his phone. "She tripped on her kids' toys and fell down the steps. Her leg is broken pretty badly."

Everyone gasped.

"Is she okay?" Grace moved to Dan's side lickety-split and laid a hand on his arm.

Jade ignored the unpleasant flash of feelings in her stomach. The fact that this was the seventh time Grace had touched Dan tonight didn't affect Jade in the least.

"She's going to be fine." But Dan's face remained grim. "But she can't chaperone for camp tomorrow. Which means we have to cancel the trip."

Grace's hand flew to cover her mouth, and Jade almost rolled her eyes.

Talk about overreacting. It wasn't the end of the world. In fact, if she were scheduled to go on the trip, she'd be relieved. Who wanted to spend the weekend in the middle of nowhere, with a bunch of bratty kids?

"But it's all the kids have been talking about for weeks." Grace looked near tears. "They'll all be crushed."

"I know." Dan seemed pretty crushed himself. "I really wanted this to happen."

A twinge of regret went through Jade for his sake.

"I know you did." Grace patted his shoulder. Make that eight times she'd touched him tonight.

"Unless—" Dan scanned the room, a gleam in his eyes as if he'd had a brilliant idea. "One of you wonderful ladies wants to save my life by filling in." He folded his hands in front of him, as if praying. "Sis?"

Leah raised her shoulders. "You know I would have been the first to sign up, but I'm catering a wedding tomorrow and then I'm slammed all week."

"And I'm doing the cake for the wedding. Sorry." Peyton gave him a sympathetic look.

"I don't think you want Joy keeping your campers up all night with her crying," Ariana added.

"Violet?" Dan turned to Jade's sister, eyes pleading.

Vi chewed her lip. "You know I would, but between the store and the wedding plans and . . ."

"I know." Dan waved her off. "Forget I asked."

His gaze moved to the chair across the room. "Emma? Pretty please? You're my last hope."

Emma shook her head. "I'm sorry. Any other time, I would. But I have a new horse arriving tomorrow, and I've been told he's a handful."

Dan's shoulders fell, and he slumped into a chair. "I guess that's it then." He pulled out his phone, his voice sharp with defeat. "I hate to call everyone so late, but I don't want the kids to show up bright and early tomorrow only to find out we're not going."

"Wait!" Vi shouted, making everyone jump. "What about Jade?"

Jade felt all the eyes in the room shift to her.

She gave an uncomfortable laugh. "What about Jade?"

"You could do it." Vi said it as if it was the most obvious thing in the world.

Jade was pretty sure this time her laugh came out as more of a desperate gulp for air. "Do what?"

"Chaperone." Vi nudged her.

"Oh— I— Well—" Jade could feel the heat climbing up her neck to her cheeks, and she resisted the temptation to give her sister a quick elbow to the ribs.

"Oh, that's so perfect." Grace beamed at Jade as if she'd agreed to do it.

"No. I mean, wait. I mean—" Jade stopped to sort out her flustered thoughts. "Camp isn't really my thing. I don't know the first thing about the outdoors or survival or kids."

"We can help you with that." Dan spoke for the first time since Vi had volunteered her, and Jade let herself meet his eyes.

Which was a mistake. The look he gave her—head tilted to the side as if waiting for her to say yes—almost made her lose her resolve.

She contemplated the front door. Too bad it was too far across the room to make a quick, unobtrusive escape, especially with everyone watching her.

"I'm supposed to be here to spend time with Vi. I can't just up and leave for a weekend." There. That tactic had to work.

"Of course you can." Vi patted Jade's knee. "I have you all summer. I can spare you for five days for a good cause."

Five days?

Jade almost choked. She'd been unsure when she'd thought the camp was only for a weekend. But five days? She'd never survive.

"But—" More arguments spun through Jade's brain, but the way Dan was looking at her made her forget every single one.

His eyes pleaded with her. But more than that, his look said he believed she could do it. That he was counting on her.

She took a deep breath. For once it would be nice to live up to someone's belief in her.

"Okay," she finally said. "What time do we leave?"

The whole room erupted in cheers, and Jade had to admit to herself that it felt good to be the reason.

But it felt even better to be the recipient of Dan's quiet smile and mouthed "thank you."

Chapter 15

When Jade's alarm went off at four o'clock the next morning, she asked herself for the thousandth time what she'd gotten herself into.

It didn't help that she'd spent half the night dreaming about all the creepy crawly critters she might encounter at the camp. Twice, she'd woken up and had to turn on the flashlight on her phone to make sure there were no bugs in her bed. And that was here in Vi's apartment. How much worse would it be in a cabin tonight?

She picked up the small bag she'd packed last night and stepped silently into the bathroom to get ready without waking Vi.

If she was honest with herself, it wasn't the bugs that scared her most about camp. It was that this was a Jesus camp—not exactly somewhere she'd fit in. Even though she'd been going to church with Vi since she'd come back, that didn't exactly make her an expert in all things Jesus. What if one of the kids called her out on her lack of Bible knowledge? Or, worse, what if they asked if she believed in God? It'd be wrong to lie to them, wouldn't it? But in this case, she was pretty sure it'd be worse to tell them the truth: that she hadn't been sure there was a God for many years now. And even if there was, she wasn't sure she wanted anything to do with him.

She sighed as she applied a light layer of makeup. Faith seemed to come so easily to Vi and her friends—it was something they simply talked about in the course of regular conversation, as if it were as natural as talking about the weather.

Even when she was little, Jade had never been completely comfortable talking about God. But now, after everything she'd done, she was the last person who should be taking a group of kids to church camp.

You're just there to chaperone, she reminded herself. *It's not like you have to preach.*

Besides, she was an actor. How hard could it be to play the role of Miss Holy Camp Leader?

She fixed her hair in a loose ponytail. At least she looked the part, in a cutoff pair of khaki shorts and a short-sleeved white blouse.

She was as ready as she'd ever be. She grabbed her bag and padded out of the bathroom, stopping to pull Vi's blankets up over her shoulders. She kissed her fingertips and pressed them to the top of Vi's head. All those years in LA, she'd told herself she didn't need her sister, even if she was her last remaining family, but she'd been wrong. Being home with Vi had filled spots in her heart she hadn't realized were empty.

With one last glance at her sleeping sister, Jade tiptoed out of the apartment. The door across the hall opened at the same time as she stepped onto the landing, and Jade pressed a hand to her heart.

"Good morning." Nate grinned at her, his dog Tony straining at the leash to get a sniff of her legs.

"Ugh. Violet warned me you were a morning person." But she smiled at him. The truth was, she liked Vi's fiancé.

Nate laughed. "Guilty as charged. But you look pretty chipper yourself. All ready for camp?"

Jade shrugged. "Honestly? I have no idea what I'm doing."

Nate let the dog tug him down the steps, and Jade followed.

"Thanks for doing this," Nate said over his shoulder. "It means a lot. To all of us."

Jade nodded as he opened the door for her. She got the impression that their church was more important to Vi and her friends than pretty much anything else.

"Wish me luck." She passed through the door and headed to Vi's car, which her sister had said she should take and leave in the church parking lot.

"You won't need luck." Nate's voice followed her. "You've got God on your side."

Jade closed the car door without responding. She wasn't so sure of that.

A soft spray of light was just creeping over the lake as Jade turned onto Hope Street. She couldn't remember the last time she'd seen the sun rise because she'd gotten up so early instead of because she'd stayed up so late.

Something about the muted light and the quiet of the morning stirred a longing in her soul, but she couldn't place what it was she longed for.

Peace, maybe.

But as she drove into the church parking lot, she suppressed a groan. Peace was the last thing she was going to find today.

Dozens of kids surrounded an old school bus that had been repainted green and gold. Some of the kids looked sleepy, but others had already started a game of tag.

Jade sucked in a deep breath and let it out. She could do this.

She opened the car door and grabbed her bag out of the backseat, the early morning humidity clinging to her skin. She made her way toward the bus, thankful that other than a few curious glances, most of the kids ignored her.

As she came around the side of the bus, her eyes fell on Dan, who was squatting next to a boy with red hair and two missing front teeth.

"All right, bud, you're all set. Why don't you go grab a seat?" Dan rumpled the kid's hair and straightened as the boy scampered toward the bus door.

"Thanks for coming." His smile was warm but guarded.

"Did you think I wouldn't show?"

He looked away, and she could almost hear the unspoken words. *It wouldn't be the first time.*

"So how does this work?" She jumped to fill the silence.

"Well, we get on the bus and we sit down, and the driver drives us there." Dan gave her a lazy grin.

"You know what I mean." She resisted the playful push she was tempted to give him. Grace may feel free to touch him whenever she wanted, but Jade most definitely did not.

"For now, we'll just be one big group. But when we get there, I'll give out cabin assignments. Each chaperone will lead a cabin of about a dozen kids. You'll take your cabin to their activities, oversee meals, make sure they go to bed on time, that sort of thing."

Jade gaped at him. That sort of thing?

She'd figured she was along as an extra pair of hands and eyes. Not as a leader.

"Is that all you brought?" Dan gestured to the gym bag slung over her shoulder.

"Yeah. Why? Is it not enough?" Leave it to her to forget all the important things.

"No, it's good." Dan rubbed a hand over his hair. "I'm just surprised."

"Why?" She slid the bag off her shoulder and looked at it. It was just an ordinary bag.

"To be honest, I had these visions of you showing up with three suitcases." He cringed. "Sorry."

She let herself laugh. "I guess I'm full of surprises."

He studied her, as if trying to solve a riddle. "Yes. I guess you are." After a second, he seemed to shake himself. "If you want to get on the bus, we'll be leaving soon. We're just waiting for a couple more kids."

Jade nodded, but as she turned toward the bus door, a woman about her age approached, pulling a crying little girl behind her.

"Sorry we're late, Pastor Dan." The woman stopped in front of them, the little girl cowering behind her. "Penelope got cold feet right as we were leaving, but I told her—" She broke off as she noticed Jade. "What are you doing here?" The woman's voice was filled with resentment.

"I'm sorry?" Jade's back stiffened, and every muscle in her shoulders tightened. Did she know this woman?

"Oh, I'm sorry." Dan stepped in smoothly. "Brianna, this is Jade Falter. She grew up in Hope Springs and is visiting for the summer. Jade, this is Brianna Miller. She was a few years ahead of us in high school."

Jade tried to smile, but her face had gone numb.

"I believe you knew my ex-husband Derrick." Brianna's stony look could have rivaled the boulders that littered much of the shoreline.

Jade could feel the color slip right off her cheeks. Of course it was Brianna. President of the senior class the year Jade was a freshman. Head cheerleader. All-around popular girl.

"I'd heard you were home. You're helping with this?"

Jade heard the implication, the subtle suggestion that she, of all people, wasn't fit to be chaperoning a church camp.

More to escape the look Dan was directing between her and Brianna than for any other reason, Jade crouched at the still-crying girl's side.

"Do you want to know a secret?" Jade cupped a hand around her mouth, then mock whispered, "I'm nervous about camp too."

The girl's eyes widened, but she let out a small giggle.

Jade held out her hand. "Maybe if we stick together, we'll both be braver."

After a second, the girl reached out a tentative hand and set it in Jade's.

The warmth of her fingers sent a jolt right to Jade's heart.

She swallowed down the sudden lump of emotion and stood up, leading the girl to the bus door.

"What's your name?"

"Penelope." The girl had a slight speech impediment, which only endeared her to Jade more.

"Nice to meet you, Penelope." Jade stopped with one foot posed on the bus step. "Better say goodbye to your mommy."

Penelope waved toward Brianna and called out a goodbye, then bounded up the bus steps.

As Jade followed, she pretended not to notice the sharp glare Brianna hit her with. Someday, she owed Brianna a proper apology. But for now, she'd have to settle for taking good care of her daughter. She only hoped she didn't mess that up.

Dan stared after Jade, completely dumbfounded. He was eternally grateful she'd agreed to chaperone, of course, but he had to admit he'd had his doubts about the whole plan. First, that she'd show up at all, and second, that she'd be prepared for what camp involved. But she'd shown up—on time and without a heap of luggage—and now she'd helped calm poor Penelope, who'd been going through such a rough time since her dad had split a few months ago.

"Can I talk to you for a minute?" Brianna shuffled next to him, and Dan turned to her. She was frowning at the spot where her daughter had disappeared onto the bus.

"Of course." From the few times Brianna had come to him for counseling, he knew the divorce had been messy, so it was understandable that she was apprehensive about Penelope.

She led him a few steps away from the bus, looking around as if she didn't want to be overheard.

"Don't worry about anything." Dan gave her a confident smile. "Take some time for yourself this week to relax. Penelope is in good hands."

Instead of seeming reassured, Brianna crossed her arms in front of her. "Jade Falter's hands?"

Dan tensed. "Yes. Jade and Grace and Tyler and I."

"Pastor, maybe you don't remember Jade's reputation, but I do. She was the first one Derrick cheated on me with. Under the bleachers. At homecoming."

Dan fought the urge to cover his ears. He'd known of Jade's reputation, of course, but he'd always tried to avoid learning any specifics.

"That was a long time ago, Brianna." He worked to keep his tone gentle. "I'm sure you don't still hold that against her."

Brianna grimaced. "Girls like her don't change."

Dan clamped his jaw against his instinct to jump to Jade's defense. Brianna's father was Terrence, the church president, and Dan couldn't afford to get into an argument with his daughter.

"The fact of the matter is, we have no one else who can chaperone, since Cassandra broke her leg. If Jade hadn't stepped up at the last minute and volunteered, we'd have had to cancel the whole trip." Not exactly the glowing defense he owed Jade for saving the trip, but maybe it was a neutral enough middle ground to diffuse Brianna's anger.

"Canceling might have been the smarter option." Brianna smoothed her hair. "Trust me, *she* is not the kind of woman you want influencing young people."

Dan kneaded at a kink in his neck. "Penelope seems to like her."

Brianna's cheeks reddened. "She likes chocolate cake too. But that doesn't mean it's the best thing for her."

The bus driver honked, and Dan peered at the vehicle. It was loaded with rambunctious kids eager to be on their way to camp.

"We need to get going." Dan sought his most mollifying tone. "Thanks for sharing your concerns. If you'd prefer for Penelope to stay home, we can get her off the bus. Otherwise—" He gestured toward the bus, indicating that he needed to go.

Brianna threw her hands in the air. "I'm cleaning out the rest of Derrick's stuff this week, and I don't want her there for that. Take her. But—" She flailed a wild arm toward the bus. "I don't want her anywhere near Jade. Put her in someone else's cabin." She strode toward her car without a backward glance.

The tension in Dan's jaw shot up through his forehead, but he jogged to the bus. He couldn't worry about what Brianna thought right now. He had fifty excited kids to keep happy.

And one chaperone he was going to have to avoid.

Chapter 16

"We're here." Penelope's squeal nearly burst Jade's eardrums. The little girl pointed to a wooden sign with the name Camp Oswego carved into it.

Jade picked up on the girl's contagious grin. In the two hours they'd been on the bus, Penelope had talked nonstop, and her childish enthusiasm had captured Jade's heart.

She had learned that Penelope was seven, that she loved unicorns, and that she absolutely did not like the dark. Jade tried not to think about what that last one meant for tonight.

The bus bumped down the long gravel driveway, and Jade watched as the trees on either side of them closed in, shutting out the rest of the world.

"Look." She pointed to a stand of trees, where a buck stood staring at the bus, his tail quivering.

Penelope turned her head toward the spot. "That's a daddy deer." Her know-it-all voice made Jade smile. A second later, the deer sprang into the forest and was gone.

Penelope turned away from the window. "Do you think that deer has any babies?"

"I don't know. Maybe."

"But it's not with them. Maybe it left them like my daddy left me."

Jade's smile shriveled. "Oh, I'm—" But she had no idea what to say to that.

Penelope's lip quivered, but she shook her head. "Mommy said not to think about it this week."

"That's a good idea." Not that Jade had ever succeeded in trying not to think about something. Just look at the way her eyes had been glued to Dan during the entire bus ride.

The bus stopped in front of a dilapidated building of weathered gray boards.

"Is that where we sleep?" Penelope's eyes were wide.

"I sure hope not," Jade muttered.

"I can be with you, though, right, wherever we sleep?" Penelope grabbed Jade's hand in her sweaty palm, and Jade squeezed.

"I don't see why not."

Dan stood in the aisle at the front of the bus, holding up a hand until the kids quieted. "Grab your things and let's gather right over there in front of the lodge—" He pointed to the tumbledown building, and Jade almost fell off the bus seat. If that was a lodge, she was a princess. But she dutifully helped shepherd the children to the spot he'd indicated.

Once everyone was there, Dan pointed down a narrow footpath. "The cabins we'll be staying in are a little hike down this trail. Once I've called out your assigned cabin, you can follow your leader to it and get settled in."

He first called off the campers in Tyler's cabin, then in his own, putting one of the older boys in charge of getting the others settled while he gave out the girls' cabin assignments.

Jade watched with interest. Maybe she could have an older girl in her group take on some of the responsibility.

"For those of you who don't know, this is Miss Jade. She'll have Melody, Dakota, Sarah, Libby, Lily, Andrea, Abby, Brooklyn, and Madison."

A group of girls moved to surround her. A couple looked about Penelope's age, but most looked to be about nine or ten and two of the girls were probably closer to their early teens.

"Miss Jade." Someone shook her arm, and Jade looked down as Dan read off Grace's campers. "He didn't say me."

"Oh." Jade listened as Dan called Penelope's name for Grace's cabin. "I'm sure we can get that switched."

She surveyed the other girls in her group. "Hang tight a second. We just need to talk to Pastor Dan."

Dan was making a few scribbles on his list, but he looked up with a smile as they approached. "You got the best cabin. It's the shortest walk too."

"Oh, thanks. Just real quick, is there any way to put Penelope in my cabin instead of Miss Grace's? We kind of became BFFs on the bus." She held up their linked hands as proof, and Penelope giggled.

Dan's smile dimmed, and he avoided her eyes. "Actually, we can't change up the cabin assignments." He held up his list as if that were all the evidence he needed, and she grabbed it out of his hand. How difficult was it to swap Penelope's name from one list to another?

"Why not?" Her finger slid down the list of names until it landed on her own. "Oh."

Penelope's name had been printed under hers, but it had been crossed out and added in pencil under Grace's. Her memory cut to watching Dan talking with Brianna outside the bus this morning. She'd wondered what that was about. Guess she didn't have to wonder anymore.

Dan scrubbed a hand down his face. "I'm sorry. I—"

Jade thrust the clipboard back at him. "It's no problem."

She crouched to be at eye level with Penelope, whose cheeks were streaked with tears. "Here's the deal. We'll still see each other lots, but you'll sleep in Miss Grace's cabin. If you want to know the truth, Miss Grace is much better at camping than I am, so you'll be in good hands."

But Penelope threw her arms around Jade. "You said we'd make each other brave. I can't be brave without you."

Jade's heart cracked, but she kept her voice soothing. "You've already been so brave. And you've made me brave. If you can do this, you'll be the bravest person I've ever met."

Penelope let out a hiccupping cry. "I want to go home." Her hiccups soon escalated to deep sobs, and Jade clutched her close. She had no idea what else to do.

"Oh, sweetie, you're going to have so much fun with Miss Grace. She—"

"Take her to your cabin." Dan's voice cut through her own.

Jade looked up at him. "But—"

Dan shook his head. "Don't worry about it."

"You're sure?"

Dan reached a hand to help her up and nodded. "I'm sure."

She eyed his hand but stood without taking it—which was a challenge with Penelope wrapped around her. Still, she'd take the risk of falling flat on her back over the risk of one simple touch of his hand. "Thank you."

Dan's eyes searched hers, and she forced herself to look away.

"Come on." She pulled Penelope away from Dan toward the rest of their group. "Let's go check out our cabin."

He'd done the right thing. Hadn't he? Letting Penelope switch to Jade's cabin.

He wasn't sure if it was Penelope's tears or the look of hurt on Jade's face when she realized why he had assigned Penelope to Grace's cabin that had made him change his mind.

There would likely be consequences when they got home. There was no way Penelope wouldn't tell Brianna about all the fun she'd had with Jade. But hopefully by then Brianna would realize that Jade hadn't been a bad influence and would rethink her judgment.

He plopped his small bag onto the bottom of one of the bunks and broke up a fight between two boys who each wanted the top bunk.

"Why don't we—"

But his words were cut off as a sharp scream ripped through the open door of their cabin. Dan's head jerked up. That was a woman's scream. Jade?

He was already tearing out of his cabin, his feet pounding over the packed dirt trail that led to the girls' cabins on the other side of the small clearing.

As he ran, he realized he should have grabbed the first aid kit. Or maybe a weapon. Who knew what was going on over there?

He burst in the door of Jade's cabin without knocking. "What's wrong?"

He pulled up short, a dozen girls gaping at him as he stood in the doorway gasping for air. "I thought I heard a scream."

Everyone appeared to be in one piece, and there were no apparent signs of danger.

Until he spotted Jade standing on a rickety old chair in the far corner of the room.

"There are ladybugs." She pointed to the opposite corner.

"Ladybugs?" Dan repeated dully. What did ladybugs have to do with anything?

"Miss Jade doesn't like ladybugs." Penelope let out a giggle, and the other girls joined in.

"Oh." Dan raised an eyebrow at Jade, and she gave him a chagrined look.

"I got bit by one once."

"By a ladybug? I don't think they bite."

Jade gave him an indignant look. "They do when you accidentally lay on one that has crawled into your bed."

The girls laughed harder, and Dan pressed his lips together to keep from joining in.

"Who wants to help me save Miss Jade from the ladybugs?" He strode to the corner she had indicated. Sure enough, a dozen or so ladybugs were scattered across the wall and floor there. With the girls' help, he scooped them up and transplanted them outdoors.

"There." He crossed to the chair Jade was still perched on and held out a hand. "Now will you get down? I think that chair is more dangerous than all the ladybugs in the woods combined. It looks like it's about to fall apart."

She stared at his hand, as if afraid it was leprous. But he grabbed her arm as she wobbled. She might not want his help, but he didn't need a camp leader with a broken neck.

He ignored the zing that shot from his hand, up his arm, and right to his heart at the feel of her skin under his fingers. It had been a long time since he'd held her hand.

She pulled away the moment she was on the ground, and he backed toward the door. "We're going to do a devotion in ten minutes. Then how about a swim before lunch?"

The girls all cheered, but Jade looked panicked.

"Don't worry." He couldn't resist teasing her. "There shouldn't be any ladybugs in the water." He waited for the look of relief on her face, then added, "Just snakes."

The ladybug thing was embarrassing, Jade could admit that. But there was no way she was going in that lake if there was even a remote chance there were snakes in it. Dan, Tyler, and Grace had all reassured her repeatedly that Dan had only been teasing, but she wasn't taking any chances.

Besides, she and Penelope and a few of the other girls were making the most incredible sandcastle known to man. So far, they had three levels, plus a tower and a moat. And she was in the middle of constructing a drawbridge right now.

She'd probably have it done already if her eyes didn't keep drifting to the water, where Dan and Grace and Tyler had started a game of water volleyball with the kids. She worked hard not to notice the nicely defined muscles of Dan's chest and torso. Or the way he and Grace exchanged high fives every time their team scored a point—which seemed to be every five seconds.

"How about this for the bridge, Miss Jade?" Penelope held a piece of bark out to her, and Jade took it.

"Perfect, Penelope." She placed it in the opening of the castle wall. "There. I think it's done."

"Now what?" Penelope's eyes traveled to the water.

"You can swim, Penelope. I'll be right here watching you."

"No." Penelope's sigh held a trace of annoyance. "I want to stay by you."

Jade watched the little girl. Was she really going to let her own hang-ups keep Penelope from having fun?

"Tell you what, what if I come in a little way? Then will you swim?"

"Yes!" Penelope was already dragging her toward the water.

Jade cringed the moment she stepped into the shallows, but the water wasn't as cold as she'd anticipated. She always forgot how much warmer inland lakes got than Lake Michigan. And with no waves to speak of, at least she wouldn't get splashed.

She walked in until the water skimmed her knees, and Penelope seemed content to swim right in front of her.

She resisted as long as she could, but eventually her eyes were drawn back to the water volleyball game—just in time to see Dan laughing at something Grace was saying. Jade dropped her gaze to Penelope. There was no point in giving Dan another thought.

It wasn't like she could ever compete with a woman like Grace. And it wasn't like she wanted to anyway.

She'd known when she left Hope Springs that she'd never have a shot with Dan again. And she'd been fine with that.

"Watch this, Miss Jade."

Jade turned to watch Penelope as she porpoised up and down in the water.

"Wow, Penelope, that's very— Yikes!" A wave of water hit her square in the back.

She spun around, her mouth still open with shock. Which was how she ended up with a mouthful of water as another wave hit her.

"Sorry." But Dan was laughing too hard to be sincere. "*Now* you're in the water."

She stared at him, water still dripping from her face and hair.

"Why would you do that?" She infused her voice with as much anger as she could.

Dan's mouth fell open. "Oh, wow, Jade, I'm sorry." He stopped laughing and stepped closer. "I didn't mean—"

She waited, hands on her hips, keeping her lips in a straight line.

"I mean, I shouldn't have—" Two more steps closer. "I thought—" Another step.

Jade bent at the waist, slicing both hands into the water, then lifting them to send a huge splash cascading over him.

He froze as the wave hit him, eyes closing instinctively.

But when he opened them again, they were wide. All around them, the kids were laughing and clapping.

"I can't believe you did that." But he was grinning too.

"You totally deserved that," Grace called from behind him, and he laughed, sloughing the water off his face.

"I guess I did. Truce?" He held out a hand, and Jade eyed it. When he'd touched her arm in the cabin, the electricity had almost sent her sailing into the air.

But everyone was watching. Waiting.

Slowly, she placed her hand in his.

The moment his fingers wrapped around hers, she was yanked forward and off her feet. Water closed over her head, and she flailed to regain her footing.

When she came up spluttering, Dan smirked at her. "I can do this all day. Want to try again?"

But she shook her head and wrung out her hair. The offer to touch his hand again was too tempting.

"Smart decision. Truce for real this time?" Dan held out his hand, looking one hundred percent sincere. But Jade wasn't falling for that again. Just because the guy was a pastor didn't mean he was above tricking her a second time.

She dropped her hands into the water and sent a small splash toward him. "*Now* we can have a truce." She dashed out of the water and up the beach before he could retaliate.

When she reached the spot where their sandcastle stood, she chanced a glance at the water. Dan was still watching her, an expression she didn't recognize on his face. He took a couple steps toward the beach, and Jade's stomach tumbled. He was going to come up by her.

Out of the corner of her eye, she spotted something sailing through the air toward him. "Watch—"

But her warning was too late. The volleyball smacked into the back of his head. He lifted one hand to his head and with the other scooped the ball out of the water.

"Sorry, Pastor Dan," an older boy with dark hair called.

"That's okay." Dan threw the ball back, then with one last look at Jade, rejoined the volleyball game.

Jade plopped into the sand to add a few decorative details to the castle, telling herself she was relieved.

It was like he'd said—he was where he belonged, and she was where she belonged.

And that was just the way she liked it.

Chapter 17

The campfire crackled in the growing dark, and Dan had to smile from his perch on the top of the picnic table. The first day of camp had gone even better than he'd hoped. The kids all seemed suitably worn out and happy. And other than one minor scrape and Jade's ladybug emergency, the day had been incident free.

As soon as the kids finished making their s'mores, they'd have a devotion, sing a few songs, and turn in for the night. His gaze drifted over the group. The older kids sat together on camp chairs, while Tyler had taken some of the younger kids to the other side of the clearing for a game of tag. Grace helped some kids make s'mores, while Jade led a group of chocolate and marshmallow covered kids to the bathroom to wash up.

He allowed himself a contented sigh. This was exactly what he'd wanted camp to be—a chance for the kids to get together and enjoy God's creation and time with each other. Maybe some of these kids would remain lifelong friends and encourage each other in their faith as they confronted all the things out there that were waiting to steal them from the truth. Dan had lost count of how many times he'd prayed for them, but if he had one hope as a pastor, that would be it.

"Pastor Dan, Pastor Dan." A little girl named Melody pulled Jade toward him, one hand clasped in front of her as if she were holding a precious treasure. His eyes traveled to Jade's face, and he almost laughed out loud at her repulsed expression. He wondered if Melody's treasure was a ladybug. But when she opened her hand, a big juicy nightcrawler wriggled there.

"It's a worm! Isn't it cute?" Melody sounded as if she'd found a puppy instead of a worm. "Do you want to hold it?"

She held the worm out toward Dan, and he opened his hand so she could drop it in. Jade took a large step backward.

"It *is* cute." He let the worm squirm in his hand a few seconds, then passed it back to Melody.

"Do you want to hold it, Miss Jade?" Melody asked.

Dan coughed to cover his laugh as Jade's face contorted. "That's okay, sweetie. I'm good just looking at it."

"Do you want to pet it at least?" Melody thrust her hand at Jade.

Dan was going to have to jump in and come to Jade's rescue.

But Jade poked out a tentative finger and inched it toward the worm, eyes squinted as if she couldn't bear to watch what she was about to do.

With a half gasp, she gave the worm the slightest brush of her finger, then snatched her hand back.

"Oh, it's slimy," she choked out.

Dan couldn't hold back his laugh any longer, and Jade shot him a look.

"What?" He held up his hands. "I'm actually impressed." Which was the truth. This had to be so far from Jade's normal life, but here she was, putting on a brave face and touching worms to make a little girl happy.

"What y'all got there?" Grace came up alongside them and peered into Melody's palm. "Oh, that's a good one." She held out her hand, and Melody dropped the worm into it.

"Miss Jade didn't want to hold it," Melody said. "I think she's scared of it." Her stage whisper made them all laugh.

"That's the great thing about God. He made us all unique. So not everyone likes the same things." Grace returned the worm to Melody. "But I happen to love worms. They remind me of fishing with my daddy. Come on, let's go find it a nice home before it dries out."

Grace and Melody moved toward the cover of the trees, leaving Dan alone with Jade. He cleared his throat. Now what?

"She's made for this, isn't she?" Jade's gaze had followed Grace and Melody.

"Her dad was the resident pastor at a church camp for a few years, so it's in her blood."

᾿

"Ah." Jade sat on the very edge of the picnic table, leaving plenty of space between them.

"You're doing a great job too." He kept his eyes on his hands but looked up when she snorted.

"This isn't exactly my thing, if you hadn't noticed."

"I know." He looked her in the eye. "But you're doing it anyway. And the kids really like you. You have a gift for working with them."

Jade's lips parted, but she didn't say anything. The voices of the kids around them faded, and the quiet stretched between them, softer than the night.

"Okay. Worm is in a good home." Grace was all business as she returned to the picnic table. "Should we start the devotion?"

Dan jumped. Why did he feel as if he'd been caught doing something wrong? He pulled out his phone, scrolling to his Bible app.

Nothing like a good devotion to clear his head of the unwanted thoughts that had crept in. Thoughts about how Jade's lips shone in the firelight. Thoughts about what it might be like to feel those lips on his again. Thoughts that maybe, just maybe, God had brought her back to Hope Springs to give them a second chance.

He pushed every last one of those thoughts aside.

They were all ridiculous and unrealistic.

But when he let himself chance another glance at her, he couldn't help it: They all came rushing back in.

"Sleep well, girls." Jade clicked off the cabin light. She had never been more exhausted in her life, but somehow she knew she wouldn't be able to sleep yet, so she slid out the cabin door, zipping up the sweatshirt she'd put on over her blouse—which was now covered in dirt stains and chocolate from little fingers.

"Miss Jade?" Penelope's voice followed her out the door, and Jade turned to find the nightgowned girl standing in the doorway behind her.

"What is it, Penelope? You're supposed to be going to sleep."

"I'm scared." The girl's lower lip trembled, and Jade moved closer. How could she have forgotten that Penelope was afraid of the dark?

She held out a hand to the little girl and led her to the rickety-looking porch swing. She sat tentatively, and when it held, she pulled Penelope onto her lap. They sat like that for a couple minutes, listening to the squeak of the swing, as Jade tried to figure out what she could possibly say to help Penelope sleep.

"See all those stars?" Jade pointed to the night sky, which was filled with more stars than she had probably ever seen in her life. They made her feel small and yet important all at once.

Penelope nodded. "They're so far away."

"Yes, but—" Jade swallowed, hoping she wasn't about to accidentally say anything blasphemous. She wasn't exactly fluent in God talk. "Do you know who made them?"

"God made everything." Penelope said it with such conviction that Jade almost envied her. Had she ever been that sure about anything in her life?

"Right. And remember what Pastor Dan said in his devotion tonight?"

Penelope didn't say anything, so Jade answered for her. "He said that God is your Father, and he'll never leave you. So, if God made the stars and—"

But she broke off as Penelope sniffled and a drop of water fell on her shoulder.

"Pen?" She held the little girl back to examine her. Silent tears slipped down Penelope's face. "Oh, Penelope, what's wrong?"

Penelope nuzzled into Jade's neck, leaving her skin wet, and Jade tightened her arms. Just when she'd thought she was getting the hang of this camp leader thing, she went and made a little girl cry.

"My daddy left," Penelope finally said.

"I know." Jade rubbed a hand up and down Penelope's back. It'd been insensitive of her to mention fathers when she knew Penelope didn't have a father at home anymore.

"Does that mean God is going to leave me too?"

"What?" Jade stopped rubbing Penelope's back so she could adjust their positions and look the little girl in the eyes. "Of course not. Pastor Dan said God will never leave you." Jade only hoped she was getting that right—and that Penelope didn't ask for too many more details.

"That's what my daddy used to say too. But then he left." Penelope swiped a finger under her runny nose.

"Well—" Jade tipped her head back, thinking. "The thing is, God is even better than our daddies. And when he promises something, he always has to keep his promise."

"He has to?" Penelope's eyes widened.

Jade nodded. She was pretty sure that was how it went.

"Did your daddy keep his promises?"

The question hit Jade right in the gut. She hadn't thought about her dad in years.

"No, he didn't. He left when I was a little girl. Littler than you, actually. But I had a great mommy just like you do."

Penelope looked thoughtful. "But God never left you?"

Jade had to think about that one. Had God ever left her? He'd sure felt far from her for many years.

But maybe it wasn't that he'd left her so much as she'd left him. She'd wanted to live her life the way she wanted to live it, so she'd pushed him away. But lately, since she'd been home, she'd started to wonder if he was still there, waiting for her to come back.

Penelope was still watching her, so Jade finally gave her as honest an answer as she could. "No, I guess maybe he never did." She slid Penelope to her feet. "Come on, let's get you to bed. Do you think you can be brave and sleep now?"

Penelope nodded and let Jade lead her into the cabin. They tiptoed past the other sleeping girls, and as Jade tucked the blankets around her, Penelope reached up to hug her again. "Goodnight, Miss Jade. I love you."

Moisture gathered behind Jade's eyelids. When was the last time anyone besides Vi had said those words to her?

"I love you too," she whispered into Penelope's hair.

The little girl gave her a sleepy smile and rolled over, leaving Jade to watch her fall asleep.

Chapter 18

Jade was pretty sure this wasn't how scrambled eggs were supposed to look. Liquid seeped from the grainy, almost white lumps in her pan.

Oh well. There wasn't much she could do about it with hungry campers lined up for breakfast. They'd just have to fill up on Grace's perfectly golden pancakes.

Jade had no idea how the other woman did it. Grace had been in about a million places at once as the two of them managed breakfast duty while Dan and Tyler led the morning devotion.

It had been all Jade could do to man her egg station. And look how that had turned out.

"Good morning." Dan reached them, offering a warm smile. "Everything go all right last night?"

"Perfect." Grace slid three delicious looking pancakes onto his plate with a bright-eyed smile.

"We had one little issue in my cabin." Jade fought to suppress a yawn but failed. "Penelope was scared of the dark, but we talked for a bit, and she went to sleep."

She cringed inwardly as she scooped a large pile of eggs onto Dan's plate.

To his credit, he didn't blink. "Thanks." Despite the mess on his plate, his smile was genuine.

"You might want to take some more pancakes and ditch the eggs." Jade wrinkled her nose at the egg juice that was spreading to fill his plate.

"The eggs look great. Thank you for making them."

Jade waved him off. "Pastors aren't supposed to lie, you know."

"No lie." He grabbed a fork and stabbed a big bite. Jade winced as he shoved it in his mouth. She hadn't been able to bring herself to taste them.

"They're better than they look." He grinned at her and stabbed another forkful. "See?"

Jade rolled her eyes, but her cheeks grew warm.

She brushed off the compliment. "So what's on the agenda for today?"

"Not much. Some swimming, hiking, high ropes, crafts—"

Jade's head jerked up. "What did you say?"

Dan wrinkled his brow. "Crafts?"

"No." She brandished her spatula at him. "Before that."

"Oh. High ropes. It's this course where you—"

But Jade held up a hand to stop him. "I know what it is. But I did *not* know I was signing up for that when I agreed to come. You probably don't remember the time freshman year when I totally froze on that high ropes course we went to for phys ed, but I swore then that there was no way I would ever do something like that again." It had been the single most embarrassing moment of her high school career. Everyone had seen her weakness and her need for help.

"I remember." Dan's voice was quiet. "It wasn't that bad."

Jade groaned. "It was worse."

"Yeah, it was."

She hid her face in her hands. Even Dan couldn't deny that she'd made a fool of herself. Mr. Henning, the phys ed teacher, had been forced to climb up and lead her down one step at a time. It'd taken her two days to stop shaking afterward.

"But look at it this way." Dan's voice brimmed with optimism. "It's a chance to redeem yourself. Prove to yourself you can do it."

"But I can't." Jade wanted to stomp her foot.

Nothing he said was going to get her up there.

"I believe in you." Dan gave her a look and moved off to find a seat.

Jade sighed. That line came close to making her want to try. But not close enough.

She managed to make it through hiking and swimming—and even found she was halfway decent at helping the kids with their crafts—but when they got to the high ropes course, the shaking started.

She tried not to let the kids notice as she directed them into a line.

"You don't have to do this if you don't want to." Dan's voice was low in her ear, and she didn't turn around. She simply pressed her lips together and nodded.

She was relieved. Of course she was. But that didn't explain the small dip in her stomach. Was it because she didn't want to disappoint Dan? Or maybe for once she didn't want to disappoint herself. Still, it was probably better if she didn't try. Because if she did try, she would likely only fail again.

"Miss Jade?" Penelope grabbed her arm. "It's too high. I'm scared."

"Oh, it's not that high." Jade crossed her fingers, hoping the little white lie was innocent enough. Besides, too high was relative. "I promise you'll be fine. You're so brave, remember?"

"I'm not brave about this." Penelope stuck out her lower lip. "I'm scared about this."

"Well—" Jade took both of Penelope's shoulders in her hands. "That's good."

"It is?" Penelope seemed unconvinced, and Jade thought fast.

"Yep. Because the only way to be brave is to do something you're scared of."

Before Dan could say anything, she raised her head to meet his appraising look. "Yeah, I heard myself."

He grinned at her, and she turned to Penelope with a resigned sigh. "That's why I'm going to go up first to show you how to be brave. Because I'm scared too."

Dan was pretty sure he'd been holding his breath for at least five minutes. His eyes were locked on Jade's form as she grabbed the rope above her head. With each step she'd taken up the rope ladder, he'd been sure she was going to give up and turn around. But she'd made it to the top. Now all she had to do was step out onto that thin rope.

Dan double-checked the belay line in his hands. He was sure she wouldn't fall, but if she did, he'd be there to catch her.

As Jade placed a foot onto the rope, the kids let out an encouraging cheer. Dan yelled along but didn't take his concentration off Jade as she took first one step and then another.

She was doing it! If he had a hand free, he'd pump it in the air. But he had to settle for the biggest grin that had ever stretched his face. He hadn't been this proud the first time he'd accomplished this course himself.

Climbing, camping, all this outdoorsy stuff was square in the middle of his comfort zone. But for Jade—wow—her comfort zone had to be so far from this that it looked like a dot from here.

Dan fed out more line as Jade approached the middle of the rope, where it started to slope uphill, increasing the difficulty. Jade hesitated a second, then lifted her left foot. But as she did, her other foot slipped. She screamed as she started to fall to the side. Around Dan, several of the kids screamed as well.

Before he could register what he was doing, Dan had pulled on the rope with his brake hand. The belay device reacted just as it was supposed to, locking the rope in place. Jade's feet hung only a few inches below the lower rope, her hands still gripping the upper rope. She scrambled to replant her feet.

Even from here, he could see the trembling in her legs. His own heart was thundering at supersonic speeds, but he forced his voice to come out calm and controlled. "You okay, Miss Jade?"

He saw her helmet bob once, but her shaking didn't ease, and she didn't say anything.

Dan waited, giving her time to shake it off—and giving himself a second to get his heart rate under control.

After a few minutes, the kids around him started to murmur.

"Is she stuck, Pastor Dan? I could go get her." Penelope had sidled up next to him and shielded her eyes against the sun as she peered up at Jade.

"That's very brave of you, Penelope." Dan kept his eyes fixed on Jade. "But I think Miss Jade is braver than she realizes. Just like you. I bet she can do it."

"You can do it, Miss Jade," Penelope yelled.

On the rope, Jade's helmet shook back and forth.

"She can't," Penelope whispered.

"Jade!" Dan moved so that he was standing where she could see him. "Look at me."

She gave her head a minute shake. "I can't look down." Her voice was so quiet he could barely hear her.

Dan tightened his grip on the belay rope. "Look at me. I'm right here."

He waited, holding his breath again. She stared straight ahead for another thirty seconds, but finally she tilted her head slightly downward.

He started talking the moment she made eye contact. He didn't know how long she'd give him. "I've got you." He held up the belay line. "I'm not going to let you go. I'm not going to let anything happen to you. I promise."

He waited, trying to ignore the doubts that she'd trust him. He wasn't sure she'd ever trusted anyone, really.

After several seconds, she lifted her head. When she didn't move, he called Tyler over. He'd have to hand off the belay and go up there to help her down.

But before he could pass the equipment off, Jade took a tiny step. Then another. And another.

The kids broke into wild cheers and chanted, "Go, Miss Jade. Go, Miss Jade."

Though he was too far away to see her face clearly, Dan was almost sure it had relaxed into a smile. And when she finally climbed down ten minutes later, he was certain of it.

The kids all swarmed her with hugs and high fives, but Dan resisted the temptation to do the same, instead concentrating on cleaning up the equipment.

When she passed him her safety harness, she said a quick, low "thank you."

But that radiant look on her face right now—that was all the thanks he needed.

Every muscle in Jade's body protested as she lowered herself onto the tree stump in front of the dying campfire.

She'd gotten all the kids tucked into bed without incident tonight, but she'd felt like she needed a little time to decompress before she went to sleep.

"Hey." Dan stepped into the clearing, and she jumped.

"Sorry." He gestured to the pail of water in his hand. "I was going to put the fire out."

"Oh. Sorry." Jade moved to stand, but Dan motioned for her to sit.

"It can wait." He set the pail down and pulled a stump over next to hers. When he sat, their knees were only a few inches apart, and Jade readjusted to put more space between them.

"Quite a day, huh?" Dan picked up a thin stick off the ground and twirled it between his fingers.

Jade gave a sharp laugh. "You could say that. I'm sorry I'm not very good at all of this." To her surprise, the back of her throat burned, and she had to swipe a quick hand under her eyes.

"Jade, what is it?" Dan swiveled on his stump so that he was facing her head-on, his brow creased in concern.

The look was too much, the connection too strong. She looked away, blinking hard. Why was she being so stupid and emotional about this? It was just a silly church camp. It wasn't like it meant anything.

"It's nothing." But she couldn't lie to him this time. Not when he was looking at her like that. Like he really wanted to know what was troubling her.

"Let's face it. I'm not cut out for this." The admission stung more than it should. Why did she suddenly want to be the kind of person who could handle camping and working with kids and making a difference?

"Is that all?" Dan nudged her shoulder. "I was afraid it was something serious, like you wanted to bail on me."

Jade opened her mouth, then closed it. It *was* serious. She shouldn't be here. She was probably the worst camp leader the kids had ever had. For all she knew, she was harming their faith instead of helping it.

"I know you don't see it yet, but I do." Dan turned to the fire, which had lowered to a few flickering embers.

Jade waited for him to make sense of that cryptic line, but when he didn't say anything else, she sighed. He was going to make her ask.

"See what?" She tried not to sound too curious. She didn't want to give him the satisfaction.

"Your gifts," Dan said simply, as if that were any clearer.

"What gifts?" Had he gotten her something? That would be awkward.

"Well, for starters, you're great with the kids. They all love you. And as much as you try to hide it, you have a big heart for them."

Oh. *Those* kinds of gifts.

Dan turned his head to give her a smile that made her pulse speed up nearly as much as it had when she'd slipped on the ropes course.

She reminded herself that he was just being nice.

"And—" Dan continued. "You're willing to try new things and push out of your comfort zone and—"

"And I screamed at ladybugs, massacred the eggs, and froze on the ropes course," Jade filled in, hitting him with a scowl. He needed to stop looking at her through rose-tinted glasses. If he wanted to talk about the perfect camp leader, he should go find Grace, who'd set a new record on the high ropes course after Jade had finally gotten down.

But he shrugged. "Those things aren't what matter. You're being a Christian role model for these kids."

She almost snorted. Christian role model was the last thing she would describe herself as.

"I'm serious, Jade." Dan's gaze landed directly on her, and she found she couldn't break it. "You have no idea the impact you're having on these kids just by being there for them."

Jade studied her chipped fingernails. Whether she was a good influence on the kids or not, she owed Dan a thank you. "Thanks for talking me down up there. I was half afraid we'd have to call Mr. Henning to come get me down again."

"Thanks for trusting me." Dan's voice went soft, and Jade turned to look at him.

He was watching her with a hint of that look he used to give her. The one that said he wanted to know her—really know her, not assume he knew her based on what he'd already seen or heard from others.

"You're the only one I would have trusted." She probably shouldn't have said it out loud, but for some reason it was suddenly important to her that he know. She wasn't sure why she'd trusted him. Other than the fact that he was the one person in the world, aside from Vi, she knew would never do anything to hurt her.

But now that the words were hanging between them, she wished she could draw them back in.

"Anyway, I guess I have trust issues." She attempted a lighthearted laugh but failed miserably.

The truth was, she didn't want to be like this. She didn't want to be afraid that the moment she let down her guard with someone, they'd take off on her. Didn't want to always be the first one to bail so the other person couldn't.

"Why?" Dan asked.

"Why what?"

"Why do you think you have trust issues?"

She scratched at a mosquito bite on her leg. "It's just who I am, I guess."

"Jade." Dan's voice held that tone he'd always used to call her out when she put on what he called her "tough guy" act.

"I don't know." She dragged her fingers through her hair. How many sleepless nights had she spent trying to figure out why she was so broken? "Blame it on my dad, I guess."

"He left when you were little, right?"

"Yeah." Jade didn't know what was going on. She almost never talked about her dad, and now this was twice in two days that she'd mentioned him.

"He didn't say goodbye. We came home from school one day, and he was gone." Jade bit her lip. That sounded a little too familiar.

But Dan was too good of a guy to point out that she'd done the same thing to him.

"That must have been awful." He looked like he was going to reach for her hands, so she tucked them under her legs.

"It was no big deal. I don't know why I brought it up." It was time to shut this conversation down before she let herself get drawn into wanting something she couldn't have.

"Jade—"

But she jumped to her feet. "I should get to bed. That awful wake-up bugle of yours comes painfully early."

He stood too, still eying her, and she shifted on her feet.

"I know you don't think you're good at this." He gestured at the woods and cabins surrounding them. "But you are. And—" He scuffed his shoe on the ground. "I'm glad you came."

"Yeah. I'm kind of glad too." She tapped his foot with hers, then turned to walk to her cabin.

The night had grown chilly, but she barely noticed, with Dan's words warming her from the inside.

Chapter 19

*W*ow.

It was the only word that came to Dan's mind as he watched Jade cross the clearing in the early morning light. Her face was animated as she chatted with the group of girls surrounding her. In the four days they'd been at camp, he'd seen a more dramatic change in her than he'd perhaps ever seen in anyone in his life.

She'd lost the sullen look that had been her nearly perpetual expression as long as he'd known her. Now it was only in rare moments that he caught her without a smile. And when she was with the kids, she seemed to almost glow. Working with them definitely brought out the best in her.

"Good morning, Pastor Dan." Jade directed her smile toward him but didn't look him in the eyes.

Which didn't keep his insides from lighting up—something that had been happening more and more lately.

Jade shepherded the girls to sit behind the boys, who were already seated on the ground. Since Tyler and Grace were on breakfast duty today, he and Jade would oversee the morning devotion.

Once the girls were all seated, Jade lowered herself to the ground in the back row, but Dan shook his head. She may have assumed she was only here as an observer, but she was wrong.

"Uh, Miss Jade?"

"Yes, Pastor Dan?" Still that beautiful smile. Still not looking him in the eyes.

"Usually the devotion leaders sit up here." He patted the top of the picnic table, right next to where he was sitting.

If it weren't for the fact that the kids were watching him and the fact that he didn't want to embarrass her, he'd have burst into laughter at the way her eyes widened and her chin dropped.

"Oh, I thought I'd—"

"Make me do all the work?" Dan grinned at her as the kids giggled. "Not a chance. Come on."

Jade's mouth closed into a tight, unhappy smile. She wasn't comfortable with this. He knew that.

But he also knew she could do it, even if she didn't realize it yet.

Keeping her back to the kids and her teeth clenched, she leaned toward him. "I have no idea how to lead a devotion." If he read her expression right, she was ready to punch him.

"You'll be great." Dan passed her the Bible, which he'd already opened to the day's reading. "Start right there." He pointed. "Psalm twenty-five, verses four through seven."

Jade hit him with one more disapproving look, then yanked the Bible out of his hands and spun to face the kids. He had to give her credit—the kids would never know by looking at her that she'd wanted to poke his eyes out a second ago.

Probably still did.

But this would be good for her. He knew it would.

Please let it be. He sent up the quick prayer as Jade began to read.

"Show me your ways, Lord, teach me your paths." Jade's voice shook slightly, and her finger traced a line under the words. "Guide me in your truth and teach me, for you are God my Savior, and my hope is in you all day long."

Her voice had grown stronger as she read. She picked her head up to survey the kids, who had all quieted and were listening attentively.

"Remember, Lord, your great mercy and love, for they are from of old. Do not remember—" Jade paused, and he could tell she was letting her eyes scan ahead. She swallowed, but when she spoke, her voice was clear. "Do not remember the sins of my youth and my rebellious ways; according to your love remember me, for you, Lord, are good."

As Jade finished the verse, she closed her eyes. It may have been a trick of the rising light, but when she opened them again, he was almost sure they sparked with unshed tears. He blinked away the sudden emotion that overcame him as well.

He never failed to be moved when he saw God's Word taking hold in someone's heart. And the fact that someone was Jade right now was the answer to about a million prayers he'd offered for her over the years.

He cleared his throat and turned his attention to the kids. "Does anyone have any questions or anything they want to talk about from those verses?"

A few of the kids raised their hands, and Dan allowed himself an internal fist pump. It was early, these kids hadn't had breakfast yet, and here they were, eager to discuss God's Word.

He called on Oliver, a precocious eight-year-old he'd had to get out of more than one sticky situation this week.

"That sounded like a prayer, not the Bible," Oliver said.

Dan nodded. "Good observation, Oliver. That's what the psalms are—prayers and songs to God."

Henry, Oliver's cohort in crime, raised his hand. "Whose prayer is it?"

"King David." Jade answered before he could, and his head swiveled to her in surprise. She looked as shocked as he felt. "Right?"

"Yeah. It's King David's prayer."

"But why would a king need to pray that?" Henry called out without raising his hand. "He's the *king*."

Jade kept her eyes on Dan, clearly waiting for him to take this one, but he gestured for her to go ahead.

She licked her lips. "Well—" She stopped, her eyes pleading for him to step in and help. But he knew she knew this.

"Well—" She dragged the word out. "Everyone needs to pray—even kings."

Henry nodded, apparently satisfied, and Dan got ready to call on another student, but Jade tapped the Bible she still held.

"I mean, even kings sinned, right? And if I remember correctly from my Sunday school days, David sinned a lot. So I guess he needed God's forgiveness a lot." She looked at Dan meekly. "Or am I totally off base here?"

"You're right on base."

Her face relaxed, and she pointed to Samantha for the next question. Dan sat up, on alert. He'd counseled Sam after the young teen had been picked up for shoplifting. She could be tough to get through to.

"But God can't really forget, can he?" Sam's voice was defiant, as if challenging Jade to answer the question.

"What do you mean forget?" Jade's tone was gentle and non-defensive, and Dan could have hugged her. Any other tone likely would have made Sam shut down.

"I mean, David's praying that God won't remember the sins of his youth. But good luck with that. I mean, he's *God*. He's perfect. So he can't forget, right?"

Jade pointed at Sam. "*That* is an excellent question. In fact, I was wondering the very same thing. Pastor Dan, could you help us out here?"

Dan leaned forward with his elbows on his knees. "You're right." He sought out Sam's eyes. "God is perfect. So I guess that means he never forgets anything. Which would be a great skill to have when it comes to a science test, right? How many bones does a giraffe have? God knows because he created them, and he never forgets a single detail."

Sam's face fell, and Jade slid closer to Dan on the picnic table, pointing to a verse in the Bible. But Dan kept going, giving each of them a gentle smile. "But God would totally bomb a test where he had to name each one of our sins. Because when he looks at us, he sees Jesus. He sees the perfect life Jesus lived for us and the innocent death he died to pay for our sins. Jesus took them all away. They are gone. God can't remember them because they don't exist anymore."

Sam nodded, looking relieved, but Jade frowned at him. "Why would he do that?"

Dan leaned close enough to read the Bible over her shoulder, his finger landing at the end of verse seven. "According to your love."

Jade lifted her eyes to his. There was still doubt there, but behind it, there was something more.

Something that looked a lot like hope.

The big dinner bell outside the mess hall clanged, making both of them jump.

"Okay, campers, off to breakfast and then we've got all kinds of stuff planned for today, since it's our last full day here."

As the kids scampered toward the food, Jade passed him his Bible. "Sorry I didn't have all the answers."

He almost reached to tuck a stray hair into her ponytail but stopped himself at the last second. "It's okay not to have all the answers. It was actually good for the kids to see that faith doesn't depend on knowing everything."

"And you really believe God forgets about all our past sins?"

Her gaze was intense, but he returned it without flinching. "I really believe that."

"Well." Jade started toward the mess hall. "Even if God forgets, people don't."

Dan thought about arguing. About saying that he'd forgotten.

But no matter how much he wanted that to be true, it wasn't.

Chapter 20

S weat rolled down Jade's neck, and she took a swig from the water bottle on her hip. They must have hiked at least four miles already, and the girls in front of her were starting to lag. Their chatter had long since quieted, and now they simply plodded, one foot in front of the other.

But the long walk was exactly what Jade had needed. She tipped her face skyward, taking in the tops of the trees that arched over the trail, spots of flawless blue sky showing through the foliage. It didn't take much effort to believe in God when she was surrounded by all this majesty.

On the first day of camp, she'd watched her feet as she walked, simply hoping to survive the week. But now that camp was almost over, she found herself wishing it could last longer. Church camp was nowhere near where she'd imagined her life taking her, but after spending most of her life feeling directionless, it was nice to wake up each day with a purpose. She wouldn't miss the bugs, but these kids had grown on her, and she didn't know how she would fill her days without them. Plus, she'd finally mastered cooking scrambled eggs and putting together woodsy crafts—and she'd even managed to complete the high ropes course yesterday with a respectable time. But her most shocking accomplishment of all had to be this morning's devotion. She'd never imagined she could enjoy reading the Bible, let alone talking about it. But now that she'd done it, she found she kind of craved a chance to do it again. But once she returned to her real life, all of this would be only a memory. There was no way to make it last.

"Miss Jade, Penelope's off the path." Melody's voice cut into her thoughts.

She dropped her eyes to the girls. Sure enough, Penelope had wandered a few steps off the trail to a patch of purple coneflowers.

"Aren't they pretty?" Penelope asked, reaching to touch the petals.

"Let's keep going, Pen." Jade stopped to wait for the little girl, letting her gaze drift to the lake below. They'd kayaked across it yesterday—something else she'd never thought she'd enjoy.

"Ouch!" Penelope's scream made Jade's head snap to her.

"What happened?"

Penelope stood in front of the flowers, her right hand clutching her upper left arm. Her face was scrunched in pain, and tears ran down her cheeks as she continued to scream.

Jade ran to her side and crouched next to her, reaching to lift Penelope's hand off her arm so she could take a look. But Penelope tightened her grip and refused to let go.

"Pen, you have to let me see it so I can help." Jade pried the little girl's hand off, but Penelope clapped it right back onto her arm.

"Madison," Jade called to her oldest camper. "Run ahead and get Pastor Dan. The rest of you stay put for a minute."

Dan's group was in the lead, so they were probably at least a quarter mile ahead. Madison sprinted off, and Jade lowered herself to sit on the ground next to Penelope. The little girl was crying so hard she was shaking, and Jade wrapped her arms around her, pulling her in close. If only she could do more to make the small girl feel safe.

After a few minutes, footsteps pounded toward them.

Thank goodness. Dan would know what to do.

"What happened?" Dan crouched at her side, worry filling his eyes.

"I don't know. She was smelling some flowers, and I looked away for a second, and then she started screaming."

Why had she looked away? Penelope was her responsibility, and she hadn't protected her. Dan never should have trusted her with the kids.

Dan turned to Penelope. "Do you think I could peek at your arm?"

Penelope shook her head.

"What if Miss Jade looks at it? She'd never do anything to hurt you, right?"

At Penelope's slow nod, Jade let out a breath.

"Good girl." Jade smoothed Penelope's hair off her cheek. "You're so brave."

98

Penelope lifted her hand to reveal a small red dot with a white center. Jade breathed a sigh of relief. "Okay, sweetie. You have a bee sting. Pastor Dan is going to remove the stinger, and then it will feel a lot better."

But Penelope squirmed away as Dan reached to touch her arm.

She buried her face in Jade's neck. "I want you to do it."

Jade grimaced. She'd had an allergic reaction to a bee sting once as a kid. It hadn't been too serious, but it was enough for the doctor to prescribe her an EpiPen. Which she should probably have with her now, come to think of it. Instead of in her purse back in the cabin.

She pushed the thought aside. What were the odds that she would get stung by a bee too?

But no one had ever told her if it was dangerous to simply remove a stinger from someone else.

Penelope's fresh wails made the decision for her. "Okay, sweetie. I'll get it out. But you have to be super brave and hold very still."

At Penelope's nod, Jade shifted her so that she could reach her arm, then placed her fingernail at the edge of the stinger and scraped.

Penelope screamed, and Jade almost pulled her hand away, but she made herself keep going. Stopping now would only make it worse.

Finally, the stinger was out, and Jade flicked it to the side of the trail, wrapping Penelope in a big hug. "You did it. Does it feel a little better?"

Penelope nodded, and Jade stood up.

Dan met her eyes, looking at her with . . . what? Admiration, maybe.

She looked away.

His admiration was the last thing she deserved.

"Let's head back to camp and get some medicine on that to make it all better." He smiled at Penelope, who offered him a wobbly return smile, even as tears continued to drip down her cheeks. "How about if I walk with you and Miss Jade?"

In spite of herself, Jade was relieved. If Dan was with them, at least nothing else bad would happen to Penelope. Brianna had been right not to want her daughter in Jade's care.

They set out again, Dan and Jade falling in with Penelope behind the rest of the group.

Penelope clutched Jade's hand as they walked.

The silence stretched between them until Jade couldn't stand it anymore. "I'm sorry I didn't watch her more closely."

Dan reached a quick hand to rest on her shoulder before pulling it back. "Kids get bee stings, Jade. There's nothing you could have done to prevent it."

Jade nodded but looked away. Why was this man always so kind to her? Why did he always see the best in her? Even when there was so little good to see.

Penelope tripped, and Jade tugged her hand to keep her from falling. "You okay, sweetie?"

"I feel kind of funny."

Jade stopped and squatted at the girl's side. Penelope's face was red and splotchy, and Jade tried to remember if she'd gotten sunburned earlier.

"Funny how?"

"Like I'm spinning. And my tummy hurts." Tears welled in her eyes again, and Jade leaned in to hug her.

"It's going to be okay." She sized the girl up. Penelope was small, but not *that* small. She wasn't sure she could carry her all the way to camp. But she could at least get her partway there. "How about I give you a piggyback ride?"

But Dan reached a hand to stop Jade from picking Penelope up. "Is it okay if I give you the piggyback ride, Penelope? I'm a little stronger than Miss Jade."

Penelope coughed but nodded, and Jade helped her onto Dan's back.

The little girl's cough seemed to get worse as they walked.

"Does she have a cold?" The words came out in puffs as Dan kept going with Penelope on his back.

"I don't think so." Jade bit her lip, anxiety coursing through her. Something wasn't right, but she didn't know what it was.

"How you doing, Pen?" She couldn't help asking every few minutes.

"I'm . . . okay," Penelope answered for the third time. But something about the way she hesitated between words drew Jade up short. She set a hand on Dan's arm to stop him.

"Let's give her a break."

Dan stopped and eased the girl to the ground.

Jade helped her lie back and lifted her water bottle to Penelope's lips as Dan jogged ahead to check on the other hikers, who'd kept up a faster pace.

As Jade capped the water bottle, Penelope pulled at her t-shirt, as if it were too tight. "I want to breathe."

Something cold washed down Jade's back as she watched the little girl.

"Dan!" Jade had never screamed louder in her life. She scrambled to her feet, sucking in air to scream again, but Dan was already sprinting back to her.

Jade pulled out her phone and dialed 911.

If she was right, Penelope didn't have much time.

But there was no sound from the phone. Jade yanked it away from her ear.

No service.

"Aargh."

Now what? They had to be at least a mile from camp yet. By the time they got Penelope back, it might be too late.

"What's going on?" Dan's usually calm expression was twisted into a look of fear. It was the first time Jade had ever seen him anything less than collected, and it shook her. But it also spurred her into action.

"Is Penelope allergic to bee stings?"

"I don't know. I don't think so. Her mom didn't say anything—" Dan's head swiveled, as if he was looking for the answer in the bushes that surrounded them.

"Dan." Jade's voice was sharp. He had to get it together. "I think she's in anaphylactic shock."

He blanched, but his eyes locked on hers, and he nodded. "What do we do?"

"I have an EpiPen in my purse. It's on my bunk. You need to run and get it."

Dan was sprinting down the trail before she could finish.

"And have someone call 911 as soon as they have a signal," she hollered behind him.

She dropped to her knees next to Penelope. There had to be something she could do to help her.

She tried to remember what the doctor had told her when he'd diagnosed her allergy, but her own reaction had been so mild, and her mind was stuck on the image of Penelope struggling for air.

Think, Jade.

Raise her feet. She should raise Penelope's feet to help her circulation.

She peered around wildly, her eyes landing on a fallen log off to the side of the trail.

She lunged for it and lugged it toward Penelope. It was heavier than she'd expected, but she used every ounce of energy she had left to maneuver it into position. She piled her pack on top of it, then gently lifted Penelope's feet onto it.

She moved to Penelope's side and brushed the hair off her face, grabbing the little girl's hand in hers. "It's okay, kiddo. You're going to be fine. You just hold on for a few minutes, and Pastor Dan will be right back with some medicine for you." Somehow, her voice was steady, even though she was certain her whole body was shaking.

Penelope nodded, her lips slightly swollen.

Jade bowed her head and brought Penelope's hand to her cheek. "Hurry, Dan," she murmured. "Please let him hurry." She only hoped he'd kept up with his running since his days as a track star.

"Oh no."

"Is she okay?"

"Why are her feet on that log?"

Jade looked up at the chorus of voices. The rest of the campers surrounded them, and some of the younger girls started crying.

Grace knelt and rested a hand on Jade's back. "Dan told us what happened as he ran past, so we came back. What can we do for her?"

"Pray." The word was out before Jade could think. But she knew, somewhere deep in her heart, that prayer was what Penelope needed more than anything right now.

Grace told the other children to fold their hands. Then, with her hand still on Jade's back, she started to pray. "Dear Heavenly Father, please hold Penelope in your loving arms. Protect her and keep her safe. We pray that you would give Pastor Dan swift feet to bring the medicine Penelope needs and that you would help Mr. Tyler's phone get a signal so he can call for help."

Jade squeezed her eyes shut and let Grace's prayer wash over her. Did she even believe it could make a difference?

She wasn't sure, but right now, it was all she had.

Grace's hand was firm on Jade's back as she continued with her prayer. "Most of all, we ask that you would help us all to trust in you. To trust that just as you are the all-powerful God who created this world, you are the loving Father who created each one of us and watches over us daily. To trust that you love us without condition and that in you we have the promise of eternal life, whenever you choose to call us home to you."

The tears were coursing down Jade's cheeks now, but somehow she was more at ease than she had been in months. There was nothing she could do in this moment.

So she had to do the only thing there was left to do.

She had to trust.

The group fell silent, most of the campers standing with their hands folded, a few hugging each other and whispering, all of them watching Penelope. With every movement of the little girl's chest, Jade gave a prayer of thanks.

Just let her keep breathing. The words circled through her mind in a continuous loop.

"Here he comes."

Jade's head popped up at the shout. The campers all cheered Dan on as he closed the remaining yards, holding the EpiPen out to Jade like a relay baton, a look of sheer determination on his face. Jade didn't know how much time had passed, but she'd be willing to bet that his run had broken the records he'd set in high school.

The moment the EpiPen hit her hand, she pulled off the protective cap and jabbed it into Penelope's leg. The little girl flinched but didn't have the energy to cry out.

Jade held completely still, vaguely aware of Grace's hand on her back, of Dan standing above them, breathing heavily. But mostly watching Penelope's chest.

After a few seconds, the little girl's breathing eased, her chest rising and falling more deeply. The swelling in her lips went down.

"Thank you, Lord." Jade wasn't sure if she'd spoken the words aloud as she bent in half and kissed Penelope's cheek.

She jumped to her feet. "She needs to get to a hospital. She could relapse and need another dose."

"Tyler got a signal when we were halfway to the cabins. He said they were sending flight for life since we're too remote for an ambulance. They're going to land in the clearing by the lake."

Jade nodded. "We should get her there. Can you carry her?"

But Dan was already scooping Penelope into his arms. "Let's go."

Chapter 21

The flight nurse circled his hands and pointed down, and Dan nodded, glancing out the window to see the hospital below at last.

He let out the breath he'd been holding the entire chopper ride.

Thank you, Jesus.

They'd had to give Penelope two more shots of epinephrine on the way here, and each time, Dan had been sure his own heart was going to stop. He was responsible for this little girl, and if anything happened to her . . .

But nothing had happened to her.

No thanks to him. He'd had no idea what was wrong with Penelope or what to do to help her. He'd promised the parents of these children that he'd keep them safe, and the first emergency that had come up had left him helpless.

But not Jade.

Thank you, Lord, that she knew what to do. It was at least the tenth time he'd uttered that prayer since the moment she'd said the words anaphylactic shock. He didn't know how she'd known what to do or why she happened to carry an EpiPen, but he trusted that God had brought all that together at just the right time for a reason.

Jade had accepted his decision to be the one to ride with Penelope with a resignation that had almost broken him. He knew how much she cared about this little girl. And after the bond she'd formed with Penelope, she should be the one here with her. But he'd also known how it would look to Brianna if Jade was the one to greet her at the hospital with her daughter, when she'd specifically asked him to keep Penelope away from Jade.

The moment the chopper landed, a team unloaded Penelope's stretcher, and Dan followed them into the building. He was here often enough to visit sick congregation members, but he never quite got used to the unnatural smell of the place.

"I'm going to go check if your mom is here yet. I'll bring her to you." He squeezed Penelope's hand, grateful that her return squeeze was strong.

The moment he stepped into the waiting room, a blonde blur rushed him. Brianna stopped inches from him, her normally pristine makeup smeared in streaks under her eyes and across her cheeks. "Where's Penelope? Is she okay?"

Dan set a comforting hand on her shoulder. "She's doing much better now. They want to observe her, but they think she's past the worst of it. I'll take you to her."

As he led her through the hallways, he filled her in on what had happened.

"I didn't know she was allergic to bees." Brianna's face paled when Dan told her about the bee sting and Penelope's reaction.

"The flight nurse said that's pretty common. You can't know until someone has a reaction, unfortunately. I had no idea what was wrong, either. It was Jade who figured it out."

Brianna froze, the click of her heels coming to a sudden halt. "She was with Jade?" She threw her hands in the air. "I thought I made my feelings about that clear. If she hadn't been with Jade, she probably—"

"She'd probably be dead."

Brianna gaped at him, grabbing the wall for support. "Dead?" She said the word as if she'd never heard it before.

"Yeah." Dan ran a hand through his hair. He had to get his personal feelings under control before he said something he'd regret. "She was in anaphylactic shock. If Jade hadn't realized that's what it was, if she hadn't had an EpiPen along, if she hadn't done first aid . . ."

"I didn't realize." Brianna hugged her arms around her middle and bent over at the waist. "I could have lost my baby."

Compassion rose in Dan's chest, and he moved closer, placing a light hand on Brianna's back. "But you didn't. God protected her. And he used Jade to do that. That's something to be thankful for."

Brianna didn't look at him. "Can I see Penelope now? I really need to see her."

"Of course." Dan steered her to Penelope's room. "I'll be in the waiting area if you need anything."

Brianna stepped into the room, then seemed to think twice. She stopped, turned around, and gave him a quick hug. "Thank you for keeping my little girl safe."

He returned her hug. "Thank God for that." He let her go and started down the hall. "And Jade."

Fire burned behind Jade's eyelids, but even though the bus was unusually silent—the kids much more subdued than they'd been on the way to camp—she couldn't close them.

Every time she'd started to fall asleep last night, she'd seen Penelope strapped to that stretcher, being loaded onto the helicopter. Eventually, she'd given up on sleeping and spent the night watching the stars until they'd faded in the gray dawn light. She'd tried to find the majesty of God she'd seen in the forest, but it was all tainted now.

Dan could say God loved them all he wanted, but if that was true, why had he allowed this to happen to Penelope?

This morning, Tyler had led the kids in a short devotion, then he, Grace, and Jade had agreed it was best to skip the few activities that had been planned and head home. The kids were all too worried about Penelope to have any fun, and they wouldn't be able to get an update on her until they got within decent cell range. Apparently, it had been a fluke that Tyler had gotten a signal to call for emergency services yesterday, since none of them had been able to get any reception since.

Jade leaned her head against the window, the trees outside a blur of brown and green. How had she thought yesterday that she'd found purpose in working with these kids? It turned out that getting close to them could be just as painful as getting close to anyone else.

"I've got a signal." Grace's shout from the front of the bus drew everyone's attention. All around Jade, the kids shifted in their seats, everyone leaning forward as if their proximity to the phone would help Grace's call go through.

Jade's heart sped up, but she resisted the urge to pray. If God wanted to try to convince her he loved her, he could go ahead. But she was done begging him.

"It's ringing," Grace called. A second later, she held up a finger for silence, even though no one was talking.

"Hi, Pastor Dan, it's Grace." Her voice carried to the back of the bus. "We're almost back to Hope Springs, but I have a bus full of kids here wondering how Penelope is doing."

She kept her finger poised as she listened. But Jade doubted anyone on the bus was so much as breathing. She knew she wasn't.

After a few seconds, Grace's face relaxed. "She's doing great," she called out.

The kids erupted in cheers, and several of the girls exchanged hugs.

Jade leaned her head on the window and closed her eyes, ignoring the tears that slid out from under her lids.

It couldn't have been more than a few seconds later that one of the kids was shaking her shoulder. "Miss Jade, wake up. We're home."

Jade peeled her eyes open and waited for them to focus. The bus had stopped, and kids were waiting in the aisle to get off.

She glanced out the window. Dan must have contacted the kids' parents to let them know they'd be back early, as parents milled in the church parking lot, waiting for their kids and hugging them extra tight when they found them.

Once all the kids had disembarked, Jade made her way up the aisle, checking each seat to make sure no one had forgotten anything. By the time she got off the bus, the parking lot was empty, aside from Grace and Tyler.

Grace wrapped her in a hug the moment she stepped onto the pavement. "I'm so glad you came along. If you hadn't . . ." Grace squeezed tighter. "But you did, and thank the Lord for that."

When Grace released her, Tyler gave her a quick hug too. "Get some sleep."

She nodded numbly.

"Where's Violet?" Grace looked around the empty lot. "Do you need a ride home?"

"No thanks." She hadn't called Vi to let her know they'd be back early. She didn't want to make her sister leave the store in the middle of the day. "I think I need the walk." What was a couple miles compared to the distances they'd hiked at camp?

Grace gave her another hug, then headed for her car, while Tyler made his way to his truck.

Jade lifted a hand to wave to each of them as they pulled away. Then she started walking.

But instead of heading for the road, her feet took her toward the beach. The events of the past few days swirled through her mind, and she needed some time to sort them out.

The waves pulled at Dan's feet, beckoning him farther into the water. He'd love nothing more than to dive in and forget the past twenty-four hours had ever happened.

He should be up in the parking lot, making sure all the kids got picked up, but he trusted the rest of his leaders to take care of that. He couldn't handle the thought of facing the parents right now. Calling to tell them what had happened and request that they pick their kids up early had been humiliating enough. No one had come out and said it, but he knew they were thinking it—if his dad had been in charge, this never would have happened.

He kicked at the water, sending a spray into the air in front of him.

"Good to know it's not just me you splash."

He spun, a smile almost lifting his lips at the sound of her voice. "How'd you know I'd be down here?"

She walked toward him, balancing on the thin border where the water barely kissed the sand. "I didn't. Just felt like I needed a walk."

"Me too."

As she reached him, they fell into step, the same way they had dozens of times before.

"So she's really all right?" Jade grabbed his arm, and he stopped walking so he could look her in the eyes.

"She's great. They released her this morning. She—"

But the hug she launched at him was so powerful, it knocked the air out of him.

"Oh, thank goodness." Her words were a half sob.

Before he could decide whether to return the hug, she'd let go.

"Sorry, I was just so worried—" Jade ran a hand over her wrinkled shirt and started walking again.

"I'm sorry we couldn't both go to the hospital with her. I would have had you go, but—"

Jade waved him off. "You did what you needed to do."

They walked in silence for a few minutes.

"You believe in God, right?" Jade finally asked.

"Of course." He debated with himself a second before asking, "Do you?"

Jade's feet slowed. "I thought I was starting to. But then this happened. I mean, what kind of God lets a little girl get sick like that?"

Dan considered her question. A flippant answer wouldn't do any good here. "This world isn't a perfect place. It's tainted by sin. Which is why bad things happen." Before she could take his comment as meaning that it was her sin that had caused it, he continued. "Even things that are no one's fault."

Jade looked thoughtful, as if she were considering his words. "But he could have made it not happen, right?"

"He could have." Dan leaned down to pick up a shell and passed it to her, delighting in the look of surprise in her eyes. "But he has a bigger plan at work than we can see. He tells us that in all things he works for the good of those who love him. He can bring good even out of this." He didn't add that he could see some of the good right here, in her, in the softening of her heart even as she asked the hard questions about God.

Now that she'd asked her question, he supposed he could be brave enough to ask his. "How did the parents seem when they picked up the kids? Were they angry?"

Jade gave him a curious look. "Why would they be angry?"

Dan's feet dragged through the sand. "Obviously, the trip didn't go quite to plan. I'm guessing that's the last time anyone will send their kids to camp with me."

Jade's hand on his arm was so light, he probably wouldn't have noticed it if he hadn't seen it, but it pulled him to a stop.

"Dan, you brought everyone home safely. You said yourself that Penelope is fine, and—"

"That's no thanks to me. I had no idea what to do. If you hadn't been there—"

"But I *was* there. And that was because of you."

His head snapped up. Had she meant that the way it sounded? The slight blush of pink in her cheeks said maybe she had.

"Anyway." She started down the beach again. "Why are you so concerned about what they think?"

Dan gave a dry laugh. She had to be kidding, right?

"There are a lot of people counting on me. You knew my dad. He was a giant of the church. Everyone loved him. It's a lot to live up to."

Jade didn't say anything for a while, and Dan let his gaze slide to her.

"I guess I can understand that," she said at last. "But maybe people don't want you to be your dad. Maybe they want you to be you."

"Yeah, maybe. But half of them still remember me as the five-year-old who threw up in front of the whole church when we were singing on Easter Sunday."

"No." Jade laughed but quickly slapped a hand over her mouth. "You didn't."

"You don't remember that?"

Jade shook her head, still laughing, and he groaned. "I really wish I hadn't brought it up then."

When Jade's giggles had subsided, she turned to him, her expression earnest. "But you love it, don't you? Being a pastor."

He ran a hand over his chin. "With all the stress of the past few months, I'd started to forget that, but, yeah, I do. Being at camp with the kids"—and with her, but he couldn't exactly say that—"reminded me why I entered the ministry in the first place. It's probably how you feel about acting."

But she looked away. "I gave up on acting a long time ago."

He stared at her, trying to process. "But Violet is always talking about your auditions and—"

"I lied."

He tried to keep the question from coming out but failed. "Why?"

She sighed and stared out at the lake. "Because I knew otherwise Vi would ask me to come home."

"And you didn't want to?"

Any hopes he'd been beginning to build collapsed like a sandcastle under the waves.

Her laugh was laced with sarcasm. "I never belonged in Hope Springs, Dan. We both know that. I've burned too many bridges. No one wants me here."

"Violet wants you here."

I want you here.

But he wasn't entirely sure that was true. Having her here made things complicated. Messy. Uncertain.

Jade watched him for a minute, as if waiting to see if he had the courage to say more.

When he didn't, she smiled softly and looked over her shoulder, toward the dunes.

He saw the moment she recognized where they were.

"This is it." Her words were almost a whisper, and she took a few steps up the beach toward the dunes.

But then she stopped. "That was a long time ago."

Dan stood at her side. "It was."

But somehow his hand had found hers, and now they were facing each other, holding hands. His eyes went to hers, then slid to her lips.

This was nearly the exact spot he'd kissed her once before. The desire to do it again almost overwhelmed him. If he kissed her right now, would they get a second chance?

Jade's eyes closed a fraction, and Dan leaned toward her. His heart took up the pounding rhythm of the waves.

But maybe instead of a second chance at love, all he'd get was a second helping of heartbreak. She'd said herself that she wasn't made for Hope Springs.

He cleared his throat and stepped back, letting her hand fall. "We should probably get going."

"Yeah." Her eyes opened slowly, and she gave the dunes a wistful glance as they walked away. He almost thought she'd stop and say they should stay.

But she didn't.

And neither did he.

Chapter 22

Jade stretched a kink in her back, then bent to slide her roller through the paint tray again.

She had to hand it to Nate and Vi's friends. They'd joined her here every moment they could spare in the week since camp. She and Sophie had pulled down the last of the hideous wallpaper last night. And this morning she'd started painting the living room the subtle blue she'd picked out.

She surveyed the enormous room. This was going to be a big job. She hadn't even completed one wall yet. Dan had said he might come by to help, but with any luck at least one or two others would be here before then. She and Dan hadn't been alone since that afternoon last week when she'd mistaken his kindness for a desire to kiss her. Now there was this weird tension between them. They should probably talk about it, but she much preferred pretending it had never happened.

"Good morning."

The voice behind her made Jade jerk upright and spin around. Too late, she remembered the fully loaded roller in her hand. She watched, mouth slack, as flecks of blue paint scattered through the air, landing everywhere—including the hardwood floor and Dan's t-shirt.

Dan stood there for a minute, staring down at his shirt as if he wasn't sure what had just happened.

"I'm so sorry." But she couldn't hold back the giggle that sneaked out. The look on his face was too comical.

"It's fine." Dan took a step closer and picked up another roller, loading it with paint. "Now I look like I've been working for hours."

Did this guy never get upset about anything? She lifted her roller to the wall, picking up where she'd left off, but something wet and sticky sloshed onto her forearm. Jade gasped and spun on Dan, who was grinning maniacally.

She held up her now-blue elbow. "You did not just do that."

But Dan concentrated on the up and down motion of his roller on the wall. "Now we're even."

Jade could be mature about this and start painting again. Or—

She lunged forward and painted a stripe down his back.

Before she could retreat, Dan had grabbed both her wrists and snatched the roller out of her hand.

"No," Jade shrieked around a laugh. "I'm sorry. Truce. I give up."

But Dan held her hands above her head. "I've seen how you keep truces." He painted a line down each of her sides.

"Hey, that was two for one." Jade made a futile effort to free herself, but she was laughing too hard to put any strength behind it.

"You're right. That probably wasn't fair." Dan loosened his grip on her wrists, and she lunged for the roller. But in one deft movement, Dan had wrapped an arm around her shoulders and pulled her in close enough to slap paint onto her back.

"Hey." Jade gave a halfhearted wriggle but leaned her head into his chest to catch her breath. She hadn't laughed this much since— She had no idea when she'd last laughed like this.

But as her laughter slowed, she became alarmingly aware of Dan's arms still around her, of his heart beating under her ear.

As if realizing it at the same moment, Dan loosened his grip and gave her a gentle nudge away from him.

But he didn't take his eyes off her. "Now that we both look like robin's eggs, I guess—"

"Oh my goodness! What happened?"

Both of them spun toward the door, where Grace was standing with her mouth open, staring from one of them to the other. Out of the corner of her eye, Jade saw Dan open the space between them. She told herself she didn't care.

"It was my fault." Of course Dan was going to take the blame. He always did the right thing, no matter what it cost him.

"Actually—" Two could play this game. "I started it."

"Oh." Grace's mouth was as round as her eyes, but after a second she seemed to decide it was best to ignore whatever had just been happening between Jade and Dan. A pinch of conscience stirred in Jade's tummy, but she reminded herself she hadn't done anything wrong.

"Well." Grace stepped into the room, holding up a bag. "Leah sent lunch."

The smell of fried chicken drifted through the room. For some reason, it set Jade's stomach churning. Or maybe that was still the effect of being too close to Dan.

"Is it lunchtime already?" She checked the time. "I'm supposed to meet Vi for a dress fitting in ten minutes. And thanks to *someone*, I have to find a way to sneak home and change first so Vi doesn't ask what I've been up to."

"She really has no idea?" Dan wiped the paint flecks off the floor as he talked.

Jade felt her face pull into a frown. "I feel bad, though. I think she's starting to worry that I'm avoiding her."

She'd seen the flash of disappointment in Vi's eyes every time she'd declined to help in the store this week.

"Tell her you're meeting a mystery man," Grace said with a wink and a laugh.

Reflexively, Jade's eyes went to Dan, who seemed to be scrubbing at the paint spots on the floor with more vigor than necessary.

She forced a laugh. "I'm not sure she'd believe that."

Chapter 23

The ball swished through the hoop, and Jared lifted his hands in triumph. "That's three in a row, man. What's up with you today?"

Dan grabbed the rebound. "Nothing's up with me."

Jared checked the ball but didn't move in for the block as Dan made his way down the half-court that had been painted off to the side of the church parking lot for youth group events. For the past year or so, he and Jared had been playing a quick game of one-on-one every Friday morning.

"You know, for a guy who's always encouraging others to talk about their problems, you aren't so quick to share your own."

Dan shrugged. He was here to play basketball, not talk about his problems.

Not that he had any.

"You remember what you told me when I needed someone to talk to about Peyton?"

Dan drove to the basket for a layup. The ball went in easily, only because Jared didn't take so much as half a step to block him.

"Are we playing basketball or talking?" Dan tried to keep the annoyance out of his voice.

But Jared was standing with the ball clasped in his hands. "Talking."

Dan stared at his friend a second, then jogged to the sideline to grab his water bottle.

"You said—" Jared walked over, setting the ball in the grass and grabbing his own water. After a long swig, he continued. "You said you were human."

Dan looked up. Of course he was human. "I don't think I've ever said I wasn't."

"No." Jared scooped the ball up and tossed it from hand to hand. "But you act like you're superhuman. You don't share your problems because you don't want people to know you have any."

"I *don't* have any." But he'd known Jared long enough to realize his friend wouldn't let him get away with that.

He dragged a hand through his hair. "Fine. It's Jade. And Grace."

Jared nodded but didn't say anything, just kept tossing the ball from hand to hand. He was using Dan's own technique of waiting silently to draw him out. Dan would think it was nicely played, if it weren't so frustrating.

Jared was right. Dan didn't want anyone to think he had problems. After all, he was the pastor. He was supposed to solve everyone else's problems, not come to them with his own.

But Jared was a good friend. And Dan did need some advice.

He reached to steal the ball from Jared and started dribbling. "Not many people know that Jade and I went on a few—I don't know if you'd call them dates—but we spent some time together at the end of high school, right before she left Hope Springs. We were actually getting pretty serious. At least that's what I thought. But then—" Dan gave an extra-strong dribble that made the ball bounce up to his head. "Then she left. And it seemed pretty clear the path God had laid out for me. And then Grace moved here, and everyone kept telling me how perfect she is for me. But now Jade is back and—" He caught the ball and shrugged helplessly. Why was this all so confusing?

"And you still like her."

Dan nodded. "Quite a lot, actually. But Grace is the smarter choice."

Jared snorted. "Spoken like a true romantic. I believe the exact words you asked me were, 'Do you love her?' So I'll ask you that too."

Dan shook his head. He liked Grace well enough as a friend, and he certainly appreciated all her work at church. But what he felt for her was nowhere near love. As he'd eaten lunch with her at Nate and Violet's house yesterday after Jade had left, he couldn't help mentally comparing the two women. In his mind, Grace came out ahead every time. It was as if God had created her to be a perfect pastor's wife. She was warm, open, hospitable, a natural when it came to serving at church—and she even played the piano and sang in the choir. In short, she was everything Jade wasn't. But no matter how much he told himself all of that, he couldn't get his heart on board.

"Maybe I could grow to love Grace. If I try hard enough, you know? I mean, her dad was a pastor, she grew up in the church, she's right at home jumping into ministry. She's the perfect match for a pastor." So what if he didn't see fireworks when her arm brushed up against his? There was more to a relationship than that. She was the sensible choice. The choice everyone would approve of.

"And Jade? Do you love her?"

Dan wanted to say it was way too early to call what he felt for Jade love. And yet he knew it wasn't too early. He'd never fallen out of love with her in the first place. He never would.

But love wasn't everything. He had his responsibilities to think about. And his first responsibility was the welfare of his church.

"I'm trying to keep everything going here, trying to show everyone that I can handle things on my own, trying to live up to what my dad started."

"Okay—" Jared attempted to steal the ball, but Dan pivoted too quickly for him. "Nice. But what would dating Jade have to do with any of that?"

A hollow opened in Dan's stomach. He didn't like to think it, let alone say it out loud. But he had to get it out there. "I care about Jade. A lot. But you know what her reputation was in high school. And I've heard whispers even now. I try not to pay attention to them. But I don't think the congregation would ever accept me dating her."

This time Jared was successful in stealing the ball. He placed it deliberately on the ground and braced his foot on it. Then he gave Dan a piercing stare. "I hate to throw your own words back at you, but a few weeks ago, you preached a sermon about the kind of people Jesus hung out with. They weren't the people with the best reputations."

Dan looked away, toward the lake where he'd been so tempted to kiss Jade the other day.

"I know." He couldn't deny that Jared was absolutely right. "But Jesus didn't have a whole church just waiting for him to mess up so they could point out he wasn't as good as his father."

"Sounds to me like it's not Jade's reputation you're worried about. It's yours." Jared picked up the ball and passed it to him, hard.

Dan caught it with a grunt.

"Maybe God brought Jade back so you could have a second chance. Maybe not. But you owe it to yourself—and to her—to find out."

"Yeah, maybe."

Dan lobbed the ball absently toward the hoop. It clanged against the rim, then bounced off in the other direction. Which was probably exactly what would happen with Jade if he told her how he felt.

"You don't think so, do you?" Grace's voice cut into Dan's thoughts and he realized that he'd lost track of their conversation for the fifth time since they'd arrived at the Hidden Cafe.

He scooped up a forkful of French toast to give himself a moment to return his focus to her. "I'm sorry. What was that?"

"You seem sort of distracted this morning. Is everything all right?"

"Sorry. Just have lots of things on my mind." After a sleepless weekend, he'd gotten up this morning certain of his choice. He had to do what was best for the church. So he'd called Grace and invited her to breakfast. Too bad he'd proceeded to spend the entire meal thinking about Jade.

He had to snap out of it. "What were you saying?"

Grace waved a hand in the air. "Nothing much. I was just talking to hear my own voice, as my mama would say. Is there anything I can do to help? With whatever's on your mind, I mean."

He sincerely doubted that. "It's nothing." He grasped at the thread of conversation he remembered. "You were saying you think we need some more people to help with VBS?"

"Oh yeah." She nodded. "I have all kinds of new things I want to try. I thought maybe Jade could help with the crafts and . . ."

She was still talking, but his mind was gone again, drifting to Jade. He hadn't seen her for a couple of days now—Violet had said she wasn't feeling well yesterday, so she hadn't been in church—and he missed her.

"So you're on board with that?"

Dan blinked at Grace. "Yeah. Sounds great. Just let me know if you need anything else."

He finished the last bite of his French toast and signaled for the check.

"Now what?" Grace asked.

Dan's mind drew a blank. Now what *what*? And then he realized she meant now what should they do.

"Oh. I— Um—" He hadn't thought beyond the meal. He'd planned to go to the office afterward. But apparently Grace had taken his invitation to breakfast as an offer to spend the whole day together.

Both of their phones dinged with a text, and Dan breathed a silent thanks.

The message was from Jade, to their group chat about Violet and Nate's house. *The house is open if anyone wants to paint today. I'm still not feeling the best, so I won't be able to make it.*

"Oh, poor thing." Grace clicked off her phone. "Hope she feels better soon."

Dan nodded, but the worry that hummed through him, the desire to be with Jade and make her feel better, told him what he hadn't wanted to admit.

He was with the wrong woman.

"I'm sorry." He didn't have any desire to hurt Grace, but it wasn't fair to let her believe there was something here that wasn't. "I think you're a wonderful woman, and I am so grateful for everything you've done for our ministry. But—"

Her bright blue eyes fell on him, and he had to look at the floor. He'd had a lot of unpleasant conversations with people in his day, but this was one of the worst.

"The thing is, I just don't feel that way about you. I'm sorry." He kept his hands folded in his lap.

Grace gave a soft laugh. He'd been prepared for a lot of reactions from her. But not that one.

He ducked his head. "Sorry. Was I totally off base in thinking you liked me?" He groaned. "I was, wasn't I? That's embarrassing. I don't have a lot of experience with this sort of thing. Can we just pretend none of this ever happened?" Or better yet, they could both hit their heads against the table and get amnesia.

"No, no." Grace shook her head. "Sorry. You weren't wrong. I did like you. Do like you." Her face grew fiery, but she didn't look away. "But I told your sister it was never going to happen. It's pretty clear your heart already belongs to someone else. I'm just surprised it took you this long to realize it."

He could pretend he had no idea what she was talking about, but he wasn't going to insult her intelligence like that.

"Thanks for understanding." A twinge of regret pinched at him. His life would be so much easier if Grace were the one he had feelings for. "I hope this won't make things awkward between us. I want to still be friends if that's okay with you."

She slugged his arm lightly. "Try to stop me. Now go get the girl you're really after."

Dan swallowed. The problem was, he wasn't sure she wanted to be gotten.

Chapter 24

Jade stared around the room, trying to place the sound that had made her open her eyes. She pushed slowly to an upright position, waiting for the wave of nausea that had rolled over her every time she sat up this morning. She hadn't been feeling the best the last few days, and yesterday she'd finally given in and stayed in bed instead of going to church.

She'd thought she was doing better last night, but when she'd woken this morning, the prospect of standing had made her nearly vomit, so she'd regretfully bailed on working at Vi and Nate's house. They had plenty of time to get the painting done, but she had been looking forward to seeing everyone.

To seeing Dan.

She silenced the thought.

She hadn't been looking forward to seeing Dan any more than anyone else. In the short time she'd been back in Hope Springs, Vi's friends had started to feel like an extended family.

If she wasn't careful, she was going to start thinking of this town as home.

A soft knock on the apartment door drew her attention. That must have been what woke her in the first place.

She pushed herself off the air mattress. Thankfully, the room didn't spin. "Coming."

She combed her fingers through her hair, but they got stuck halfway. Whoever was at the door was going to have to deal with seeing her like this.

But the moment she opened the door, she regretted that decision. Her eyes landed on the hyacinths Dan held, then swept down to her baggy plaid pajama pants and stained Minnie Mouse t-shirt.

"What are you doing here?" The words came out almost as an accusation, and she berated herself. It was pretty clear he was bringing her flowers, and she was thanking him by yelling at him. "I mean, I figured you'd be at church, doing official business."

"This is official business." He passed her the flowers. "One of my flock is sick, and I came to see how she's doing."

Jade didn't point out that she wasn't technically part of his flock. Or any flock, for that matter.

She lifted the flowers to her nose, taking in their soft perfume. How had he remembered they were her favorite? She'd only mentioned it once in passing years ago, when they'd found a patch of them sprouting on a dune.

"So, can I come in for a minute?"

"Oh." Jade jumped back. "Sorry. Of course. Have a seat." She gestured to the living room. "I'm just going to put these in some water."

In the kitchen, she dug around the cupboards until she found a suitable vase. While it was filling, she yanked her fingers through her hair a few times, trying not to cry out as they snagged on snarls. She almost always kept a rubber band on her wrist for emergency ponytails, but of course today was the one day she hadn't.

When the vase was full, she added the flowers and carried it to the living room. Dan was seated on the couch. She set the flowers on the table next to it, then shuffled across the room to sit on the chair farthest from him.

"Sorry, I wasn't expecting visitors. I'm still in my pajamas, and my hair—" She touched a self-conscious hand to her head.

"You look . . . fine."

Jade laughed and eyed him. "Careful. Your high praise will go to my head."

Dan grinned. "Actually, you look beautiful, but I wasn't sure how to say that."

"Oh." A smart remark would be helpful right about now. Or, barring that, some way to change the subject. "You do too."

Dan chuckled. "Thanks. That's the look I was going for today."

Jade joined in his laughter. "I mean— Oh, never mind." She threw her hands in the air. She was making a complete fool of herself. And the odd part was, she didn't care. She felt comfortable here with him, pajamas and messy hair and all.

"But seriously, how are you feeling? Any better?" Dan's mouth turned down, and Jade had to force herself to take her eyes off his lips.

"Much better, actually. Must have been something I ate. The weird thing is, I'm starving now." She got up and moved toward the kitchen again. "Want anything?"

"No thanks." Dan's voice was relaxed and easy. "I had breakfast with Grace a little while ago."

Jade's back stiffened, and she stopped rummaging through the cupboards for a second. Why was she surprised? Everyone could see that Dan and Grace were perfect for each other.

She dug through the food for another second, then slammed the cupboard shut. Why was there nothing that looked good?

She returned to the living room emptyhanded and flopped onto the chair with a dejected sigh.

Dan raised an eyebrow. "I thought you were starving. Where's your food?"

Jade lifted a shoulder. "Nothing here looks good."

"What are you in the mood for?"

Jade didn't even have to think about it. "Ice cream."

"The Chocolate Chicken it is. Let's go." He stood and held out a hand to help her up.

She only hesitated a second before setting her hand in his. His fingers closing around hers felt like the most natural thing in the world. She pulled her hand away the moment she was on her feet. No point in getting used to that sensation.

"Give me a second to change and do something with this hair." It was bad enough Dan had seen her looking like this. No way was she going in public.

"I like the jammie look on you. But if you want to change, go for it."

She shot him a mocking grin and disappeared into Vi's room.

Ten minutes later, she emerged wearing a pair of cutoff shorts and her favorite yellow tank top. She'd thrown her hair into a messy bun. It wasn't stellar, but it would have to do.

Dan surveyed her. "I think I liked the jammies better, but this is good too."

She swatted at him. She'd seen the appreciation in his eyes as he looked at her. Not the lustful kind of appreciation other men had always directed her way, like they were wondering what she looked like under her clothes. Dan's look was more tender—a look that made her feel sheltered and safe.

Downstairs, she popped into the antique shop to let Vi know she was going out, then followed Dan to the parking lot.

He started for his car, but she grabbed his arm. "Do you mind if we walk? It's so nice out, and I've been cooped up inside all day."

"Of course." Dan matched her pace, and they fell into an easy silence. The day was warm, but a gentle breeze played with the hairs that had fallen out of her bun. Jade tilted her face to the sky and sighed.

"Something wrong?" Dan looked at her with concern.

"Nope. I just feel—" She didn't know how to describe it. "Like I wouldn't change anything right now."

Dan's footsteps stuttered, but he quickly resumed walking, picking up his pace slightly. Great. Now she'd scared him off. Again.

She had to stop implying that she wanted to be with him. It was pretty clear he already had a future. And it wasn't with her.

"I'm glad," Dan said finally, and it took her a minute to figure out what he was glad about.

She should undo what she'd done. But she didn't know what else to say. She couldn't take it back because it was true.

Fortunately, they arrived at the Chocolate Chicken, and the crowds made further conversation impossible. Apparently, ice cream sounded good to everyone on a hot day like today. Vacationing families, local teens, and a few senior citizens filled every last table, and the line to order stretched outside the door.

As they waited for their turn, Dan talked easily with a few people in front of them in line. Jade recognized them from church. She watched as Dan laughed at their jokes, listened to their concerns, offered to pray for them. This all came so naturally to him. Jade hovered awkwardly by his side, saying hi when he introduced her but not saying much else.

More than one person cast a curious eye at her. She knew what they were thinking because she was thinking it too. She wasn't the kind of woman he should be taking out for ice cream. He needed a woman who could support him in the ministry. They all knew who that woman was. And—spoiler alert—it wasn't her.

When they got close enough to see the counter, Jade busied herself examining the ice cream flavors.

"I'll take a scoop of cotton candy ice cream in a waffle cone with chocolate syrup and . . ." She tapped her lip, thinking. "Maybe some crushed candy cane."

Dan gave her a revolted look. "Is that even a thing?"

She shrugged. "It sounds good."

"If you say so." He turned to the high school kid taking their order. "I'll have a double scoop of triple chocolate in a dish."

"A dish?" Jade scoffed. "Does that qualify as real ice cream?"

"Hey, no comments from the woman who ordered the world's weirdest ice cream combination." He took out his wallet and passed the kid his credit card.

"Oh, wait. Let me get—"

But it was too late. The kid was already passing the card back.

Dan winked at her. "You can get it next time."

She told herself that the temporary bump in her heartbeat was not because of those two little words, *next time.*

Three minutes later, when she grabbed her ice cream cone, Jade had to admit that it looked rather disgusting.

"Want to go down to the marina to eat these?"

Jade glanced around the crowded restaurant. "Yeah. It doesn't look like there's a single table open."

"Oh, I'm not worried about that. I just don't want anyone else to have to watch you eat that." Dan gestured at her ice cream cone.

"Haha." Jade gave him her most dramatic eye roll. "It's going to be good. You'll see."

The moment they stepped out the door, the ice cream dripped down her hand, and she had no choice but to take a lick.

She gagged and yanked it away from her tongue. Too late, she realized Dan was watching. She tried to make herself take another lick. But she couldn't do it. How could she have thought cotton candy, chocolate, and mint would taste good together?

To his credit, Dan managed to avoid laughing for all of five seconds. Then a huge chuckle burst out of him. "So not the most delicious thing in the world?"

Jade pouted. She'd really wanted ice cream. But there was no way she could eat this. "I may have been a little off in my calculations. Apparently, watching Top Chef doesn't actually qualify you to choose flavor combinations."

"To be fair, it was unique." Dan chortled again. "I'm sure no one else has ever tried it before."

"Want to trade?" Jade held it out to him as a joke.

"Sure." His answer was instant, and she had to stop to look at him.

"I was joking."

"I wasn't."

Before she realized what he was doing, he'd grabbed the cone from her and placed his dish of decadent looking triple chocolate into her hands.

"Dan, no. We aren't going to switch. There's no way you're going to eat that."

"Nope." Dan tossed the cone into the trashcan they were passing. "I'm not."

Jade's mouth fell open. "I'm not going to eat your ice cream."

"Of course you are. We traded fair and square."

"Not fair *or* square." She would have placed a hand on her hip, but she was afraid of dropping the dish. In which case neither of them would have the ice cream Dan had paid for.

"Come on." Dan laid a hand lightly on the small of her back to lead her forward. The jolt of his touch kicked her legs into gear, but his hand lingered there a second longer than was necessary. When he pulled it away, Jade concentrated on keeping her expression neutral. She didn't need him—and the whole town—knowing how much that simple, protective gesture meant to her.

And anyway, it hadn't meant anything to him. He'd simply wanted to get her moving again. He probably wanted her to finish up the ice cream so he could get back to his office. He had more important things to do than eat ice cream with her.

"Why don't we sit over there?" Dan pointed to the worn wooden bench at the end of the breakwater that protected the marina.

Jade swiveled to survey the area. It was rather exposed. Did Dan really want everyone to see him with her?

Then again, if it didn't bother him, it didn't bother her.

She followed him and settled on the bench, pressing herself all the way to the far side. Was this a standard-sized bench? It seemed way too small.

"Eat up." Dan angled his body toward her and slung an arm over the back of the bench.

Jade inched the last centimeter closer to the other end of the bench and held the ice cream out to him. "I told you, I'm not going to eat your ice cream."

Dan's eyes crinkled in a smile as he leaned closer to her face. All the breath got caught in her lungs. What was he doing? He wasn't going to—

"That would be a lot more convincing if you weren't drooling."

His comment caught her completely off guard, and a laugh burst out of her. But she reined it in and put on a mock hurt expression. "That wasn't very nice."

"I'm sorry." Dan's lips folded into a fake frown and he fluttered his eyelids at her. "Here, I'll make it up to you." Before she could react, he'd reached over, grabbed the spoon from the ice cream, and popped it into her mouth.

"Hey," she protested around the spoon. But a microsecond later, she closed her eyes in bliss as the creamy chocolate coated her tongue.

"Good, right?" Dan pulled the spoon slowly from her mouth.

She nodded, letting the cool cream slide down her throat. When she opened her eyes, Dan was studying her like watching her eat ice cream was the most fascinating thing he had ever done.

"Fine. You win." Jade grabbed the spoon and dipped out a heaping scoop. She lifted it toward her lips but at the last second diverted it into Dan's mouth. "We'll share it."

His eyes widened, but his mouth curved into a grin around the spoon. "Fair enough," he mumbled through the ice cream.

For the next ten minutes, they were busy passing the spoon back and forth, though Jade noticed Dan always took tiny spoonfuls for himself.

When all that remained was a melted soup covering the bottom of the bowl, Dan passed it to her. "The rest is all yours."

Jade eyed him but took it. "You really would have given me the whole thing, wouldn't you?"

Dan shrugged. "Of course."

Jade leaned against the back of the bench and scooped the soupy mess into her mouth. The last time she'd splurged on good ice cream, the guy she'd brought home with her had found it in her freezer and eaten it while she slept.

"Thank you." She licked the spoon clean and set it and the bowl to the side.

Somehow, as they ate, the distance between them had closed, so that Dan's shoulder was almost pressed against hers now.

She should move.

But she was too comfortable like this.

She closed her eyes. The sun baked pleasantly on her hair, and the refreshing breeze slid against her skin. She gave a contented sigh, letting the sound of the waves lapping against the rocks lull her.

Just for a moment, she'd pretend this was her life.

Chapter 25

An itch in the middle of his back was driving Dan crazy, but if he moved to scratch it, he'd disturb Jade. He hadn't realized she'd fallen asleep next to him until her head had slid onto his shoulder.

He couldn't stop looking at her. In sleep, all the guardedness she normally wore like a hockey mask faded away. With the wind blowing tendrils of hair across her cheeks, she looked sweet and almost . . . fragile. Dan resisted the temptation to brush her hair off her cheek and tuck it behind her ear.

He cast his eye on the lowering sun, trying to calculate the time, but he'd never exactly been a Boy Scout. It had to be nearly dinnertime by now. Much as he didn't want to move, he did have to get home and get ready for a meeting tonight. He still had a couple of reports to write up for it.

A gust of wind carried a tendril of hair across Jade's nose, and she shifted on his shoulder. Forgetting his earlier resolve, Dan hooked his finger under the hair and slid it gently off Jade's cheek.

She stirred again, this time blinking up at him, and he pulled his hand back quickly.

Jade blinked again, her eyes clouded with confusion, then bolted upright, wiping at the line of saliva that had trickled down her cheek.

"I'm so sorry. I didn't mean to— Oh my goodness, I drooled on your shirt." She lifted a hand to swipe at a small wet spot on his shoulder.

Dan caught her wrist gently and lowered it to the bench between them. "Don't worry about it. You should see the puddle Nate's dog leaves on me all the time."

Jade laugh-groaned. "Thanks for comparing me to a dog." She swiped self-consciously at her cheek again. "I'm sorry about falling asleep. I don't know what's wrong with me."

"You've been working too hard. And you're sick. You're allowed to fall asleep." Dan stood and held out a hand to help her up, not letting go until he was sure she was steady on her feet. Then he reached behind him to scratch desperately at the spot that had been itching for the past twenty minutes.

But his arm didn't bend like that.

"Here." Her fingers found the exact spot and scratched back and forth.

"Ahh." Dan could have crumpled in relief. "Thank you."

Much as he wanted to stay there with her the rest of the night, he couldn't. "Should we head back? I was going to ask if you wanted to grab some dinner, but I actually have to get to a meeting. Plus, I don't know about you, but I'm still full from that ice cream."

"Dan." Something in Jade's voice made him stop, but he was afraid to look at her. She sounded too gentle, too un-Jadelike.

"What's up?"

She took a step closer, so they were standing side by side.

"This was nice." She studied the bench, as if there was still a shadow of them sitting there. "And I appreciate it. But don't you think Grace is the one you should be taking out to dinner?" She didn't meet his eyes.

He tried to tamp down the hope sprouting in his heart. Was it possible she was jealous?

"Jade." He waited for her to look up at him. When she did, her expression was unreadable. But he was used to that. Typical Jade.

"Grace and I aren't a couple."

Jade broke their eye contact and started walking. He fell into step beside her.

"Maybe not yet." Jade's stride was rapid. "But you will be eventually. Everyone sees it. She's perfect for you."

He grabbed her arm and pulled her to a stop. "*I* don't see it, Jade. I know Leah already has Grace and I walking down the aisle. And I couldn't tell you the number of older women from church who have given me their blessing to court her. They've pointed out all her good qualities—she loves ministry, she sings, she plays the piano, she cooks, she—"

"Yeah, it really sounds like you don't see a future with her." Jade's sarcasm cut through his list, and he broke off.

"But those aren't the things I'm looking for." He licked his lips. He had to stop now. Before he went too far.

"What are you looking for then? Because if Grace doesn't meet your standards, I don't know who will." Was that a note of bitterness he detected?

Dan raised his hands helplessly. "I don't have a list. I just want someone who makes me laugh. Someone I can spend time with for hours and never get tired of their company. Someone I look at and think, 'Wow, God really knew what he was doing when he put this person in my life.'"

Someone like you.

But if he said those words, there'd be no taking them back.

"Oh, is that all?" The sarcasm was back, but under it, Dan thought he caught a note of hope.

"Anyway, I told Grace this morning that I thought it was best if we didn't pursue a relationship."

"Oof." Jade let out a breath. "Poor girl. How'd she take it?"

Dan considered. How much did he want to reveal? "Surprisingly well, actually. She seemed to be expecting it. She seemed to think—" But no, that would definitely be revealing too much.

"To think?" Jade prompted.

Dan scrambled for an explanation that was the truth—but not enough of the truth to scare Jade away. "She seemed to think it was for the best too. Anyway, she didn't seem to have any hard feelings, so . . ." What was the end of that sentence? So he was free to marry Jade? Or at least to confess his love for her? Maybe start with dating her?

Jade raised an eyebrow, waiting. Was that a challenge? Did she think he was too chicken to say the rest of it?

He opened his mouth, then snapped it closed. She was right—he was too chicken.

They started walking again, and with every step, Dan's cowardice mocked him.

Tell her. Tell her.

You didn't tell her.

When they arrived at Violet's apartment building, Dan opened the door and stood aside for Jade to enter.

She gave him a long look, then stepped up.

Before he could rethink it, he darted out a hand to stop her. "Actually, there was something I wanted to ask you."

"So ask." Jade's voice was all business, but her eyes brightened.

For some reason, that scared him more than anything else.

"Would you be willing to help out with VBS in a couple weeks?" He shuffled his feet as her face fell. That was so *not* the question he'd wanted to ask, but now that he'd started, he couldn't undo it. "You were so good with the kids, and they really loved you, so I was hoping . . ."

"Yeah, of course. I'd be happy to." Jade reached for the door.

It was halfway closed when he stuck his arm out to brace it open. "Also, one more thing."

She tilted her head, lips in a straight line.

Dan heaved in a quick breath. He wasn't likely to get another chance if he blew it again. "Would you like to go to dinner with me tomorrow night?"

Watching the slow smile spread across her face was like watching the sun rise over the lake on a perfect morning.

"Yeah." Her smile stunned him more than any sunrise ever had. "I would."

Chapter 26

Jade did a slow spin in front of the bathroom mirror. She'd taken a few minutes off of working on Vi and Nate's house this afternoon to buy the dress, but now she was having second thoughts.

Maybe it was too much.

She needed another opinion.

"Vi?" She checked the time as she wandered to the kitchen. Fortunately, she'd started getting ready for dinner plenty early, so she could change if Vi gave the dress a thumbs down.

"Whoa." Vi set down the knife she'd been using to chop garlic. "I guess you're feeling better."

"Yep." She'd felt a little off again this morning, but it had passed rather quickly. "Is it too much?"

She spun to give her sister the full effect of the pink off-the-shoulder dress.

"It's not something I would have pictured you wearing," Vi said. "But you look amazing. What's the occasion?"

Jade bit her lip, suddenly feeling shy about telling her big sister she had a date.

"I'm meeting a friend for dinner."

Vi gave her a knowing look. "Is this the same *friend* who brought you those heavenly smelling flowers?"

Jade's face heated way beyond any fever she'd ever had. But she couldn't stop the silly smile that kept threatening to lift the corners of her mouth as she nodded.

"So?" Vi prompted. "Who is he?"

"Uh—" Jade busied her hands straightening a pile of mail on the counter. "It's Dan." She chanced a glance at her sister.

Vi's mouth widened into an almost perfect *O*, and she dropped her knife. "You like *Dan*?"

Instantly, Jade's hackles rose. "What's wrong with Dan? He's a great guy, and—"

Vi waved her hand. "Nothing's wrong with Dan." She picked up her knife and resumed chopping. "I know he's a great guy. I just didn't think he was your type."

"I'll have you know that we actually dated—well, not really dated, but spent a lot of time together—at the end of senior year."

"You and Dan dated?" Vi shrieked.

Jade pressed her hands down in midair, as if that could calm her sister. "It wasn't that big of a deal. We were just friends."

But the word mocked her.

She hadn't been willing to see it at the time, but she'd realized it after she'd left. She was in love with him.

And it wasn't some high school infatuation. It was that soul-deep love you only read about in novels.

"Did he know you were going to leave?" Vi concentrated on scooping the chopped garlic into a sauté pan, but Jade could hear the hurt.

She touched her sister's arm. "No one knew, Vi. Not even me, really, until I did it."

Vi nodded with a quick sniffle. "Well, be careful. You're leaving again eventually, and you don't want to hurt him." She set the pan on the stove. "Unless you're not leaving?"

Jade shook her head, trying to ignore the hope that had replaced the sadness in Vi's eyes. Of course she was leaving. This wasn't her real life. It was just a break, a diversion.

But something sank in her stomach at the prospect of going back to her so-called life in LA. It was so empty compared to what she had here—her sister and Nate, their friends, who were starting to feel like her friends, Dan, and even church. What did LA have that compared to any of that?

Still, it wasn't like she could just pretend the past hadn't happened, move back here, and live happily ever after.

Could she?

This was really happening. Dan had to keep reminding himself of that as he watched Jade, sitting across the table from him, smiling a real smile at him, laughing that full laugh that made her whole demeanor soften. The setting sun lit her hair and reflected in her eyes as they sat on the patio outside the Hidden Cafe. He'd wanted to take her somewhere nicer for their first real date, but she'd insisted that this was where she wanted to go.

He was glad now that he'd let her talk him into it. She seemed so at ease here, so comfortable. He could sit and watch her all night. He caught his breath as her eyes landed on his.

"What?" She gave him a self-conscious smile.

"What, what?"

"You're staring at me. Do I have spinach in my teeth?" She covered her mouth with her hand, and he impulsively reached across the table, entwining his fingers in hers and bringing their hands to rest between them.

"No spinach. I was just thinking about how much I enjoy being with you."

"Dan." She tried to pull her hand away, looking at the other tables around them, but he wasn't going to let go. She struggled for another second but finally let her hand relax in his.

Her lips slid into a gentle smile. "I like being with you too." She said it so begrudgingly, he had to laugh.

"You don't have to sound so happy about it."

She stuck her tongue out at him. "I tried not to, you know. Nothing good can possibly come of this." She gestured between them. "I'm only here for a couple more months, and you're a pastor and—"

He raised his hand to stop her, then closed it over her other free hand. "We'll let God worry about all of that. For now, let's just focus on being together."

"But—"

"Please?" He stood, pulling her to her feet too. He had all the same fears she did about this—maybe more, since his heart was already fully invested. But he also trusted that if

Jade was the woman God had created for him, his Heavenly Father was powerful enough to make things work out.

"Come on. Let's go for a walk."

"I'd like that." She grabbed her purse. "Let me just use the restroom first."

As Dan watched her walk away, he offered a short prayer. *If this is your will, Lord, help me not to screw it up.*

Jade could not erase the stupid grin from her face even as she used the restroom. She'd tried to keep the date from getting too serious by insisting on dinner at the Hidden Cafe, but somehow even the little restaurant had become magical tonight.

The way Dan had looked at her. The way he'd held her hands. How did that simple gesture feel more intimate than anything she'd ever done with any other man?

With everyone else, the sensations had been purely physical. Her mind and emotions had never been part of the picture. And forget her soul.

But with Dan—

With Dan, simply holding hands felt like forging a deep connection. Like something bigger than themselves was bringing them together. Could it be that it was God?

But that was crazy, wasn't it?

God would never intend for someone like her to end up with a pastor.

Jade stood and fixed her dress. She heard the bathroom door open, a woman's voice echoing in the tiled space.

"Did you see who he's with tonight?" The woman's voice was high-pitched and gossipy, and Jade rolled her eyes. How many times had she said that same sentence to her friends in LA? Did she sound as ridiculous as this woman?

She pivoted to flush the toilet but stopped mid-motion as a second woman chimed in.

"Jade Falter?" Her voice oozed disdain. "I guess he doesn't know about her reputation."

"Or he does." Yet another woman, whose voice sounded vaguely familiar, added. "And he's tired of being a good boy."

A chorus of giggles and "Stop" and "That was bad" filled the room.

Jade pressed a hand over her mouth. She was plenty used to being talked about like that. But it wasn't fair to Dan to let them slander his name because of her.

She steeled her shoulders, then flushed and pulled the stall door open.

The three women were still smiling as they reapplied their makeup in the mirror. She only knew one woman's name—Heidi—but she recognized all three from church.

Heidi noticed her first, and her smile disappeared, her eyes widening. The other two women took a moment to realize what was going on, but within ten seconds, they wore matching expressions.

Jade let the silence unreel as she deliberately washed and dried her hands. Tension consumed the space behind her as she pushed out the bathroom door.

Only after it had closed did she let her shoulders fall and allow herself a few quick blinks to clear her eyes.

She'd been delusional to let herself believe anything real could develop between her and Dan. She'd set the course for her life as a kid. And it didn't include a relationship with a preacher.

The smile Dan greeted her with as she met him at the front door almost brought the tears she'd buried to the surface.

"Ready to go?" He reached for her hand, but she pulled it away, gripping her purse instead.

He frowned, studying her. "Everything okay?"

"Yep." She strode ahead of him toward the door. "Let's go."

Chapter 27

The evening still felt warm, but apparently a cold front had gone through Jade. They'd been walking down the beach together for twenty minutes, but every time Dan came within two feet of her, she moved away.

Pretty soon, she'd be walking knee-deep in the water to avoid him. Already her feet had to be soaking from the waves that pounded the sand.

He'd asked a few times if everything was okay, and every time she'd answered with a short "Yep" and kept walking in silence. He was trying to give her the space she needed to deal with whatever it was that had changed between the time she'd left their table at dinner and the time they'd walked out the door of the Hidden Cafe, but that would be a lot easier to do if she showed some small sign that she was still remotely interested in being here with him.

He slowed, then stopped walking, watching the flecks of light spark off her hair as she kept going.

She made it another fifty yards before she seemed to realize he was no longer next to her.

She whirled around and raised her arms out to her sides. "What's wrong?" He could tell she was yelling, but he could barely hear the words over the constant refrain of the waves.

"You tell me," he called back.

She watched him, her hands still raised, and he wondered if she'd heard him. Then she dropped her arms and spun back around, walking farther away from him.

He huffed out a breath. Why was she making this so difficult?

He bent over and dropped his hands to his knees, considering. Maybe he should give up on this whole thing.

But half a minute later, he sprang up and sprinted down the beach after her. He knew how he felt about her, and that wasn't going to change because she spent one evening pushing him away.

In less than a minute, he'd closed the space between them. Although his instinct was to grab her and demand to know what was wrong, he was careful to give her the two feet of space she seemed to need.

"So in case you didn't realize, I'm not terribly experienced at this dating thing." He stuck his hands in his pockets. She had to know that already, but it was still embarrassing to admit.

Jade appeared to be fighting a smile, as the edges of her lips curved the slightest fraction. He chose to take it as a positive sign.

"So if I did something wrong at dinner—if I used the wrong fork or sneezed too loudly or didn't tell you enough times how beautiful you are—you have to tell me so I can fix it."

Jade completely lost the battle with her smile now, but it wasn't the open, easy smile she'd worn at dinner. This smile was laced with sadness.

"There was only one fork," she said, her voice subdued.

"And I don't think I sneezed at all, so that leaves not telling you how beautiful you look enough times. Which is a huge mistake, and I'm so sorry for it. Because you do. Look beautiful."

He risked taking a step closer to her. Miraculously, she didn't move away.

"Dan." The way she said his name like that, like it was goodbye, made his stomach drop.

"What is it, Jade? Why aren't you willing to give us a chance?"

Jade's mouth twisted. "There is no *us*."

But he wasn't going to give up that easily. Not this time. "I'd like there to be."

He took another step closer and reached for her hand. He knew she'd felt the connection between them at dinner. They needed to get back to that.

But she yanked her hand out of his. "Don't you understand?" Her eyes were wild and filled with a pain he couldn't comprehend but wanted desperately to erase.

"No, I don't," he said honestly. "I thought things were going well. I thought, when we held hands—" He looked away. How big of a fool had he been? "I thought there was something between us. I thought you felt it too."

"You know who else felt it?" Jade's words were caustic, and he couldn't help but look at her.

What on earth was she talking about? As far as he knew, it had only been the two of them.

"All of Hope Springs, that's who." Jade spun away from him and walked toward the water.

He watched her back for a moment. Her bare shoulders heaved, as if she were trying to catch her breath.

"What do you mean?" He finally let himself walk to her side. An icy wave washed over his feet, soaking the cuffs of his pants.

"Everyone up there saw us holding hands." Jade sounded completely defeated.

"And that's a problem?" He'd understood her desire to keep their relationship secret in high school. After all, she was the cool girl and he was the nerdy preacher's son. But he'd figured they were old enough to be beyond that now.

"Of course that's a problem." Jade fired the words at him.

"Because you're embarrassed to be seen with me?"

"What?" Jade turned sharply toward him. "Why would I be embarrassed to be seen with you?"

He shrugged. "You never wanted to be together in public in high school, so—"

"Because I didn't want my so-called friends to make problems for you. I was afraid they'd scare you off."

Dan opened his mouth to speak, but all that came out was a long breath. All these years he'd been under the impression that she'd been ashamed of liking him and somehow that had been the reason she'd left. But she'd wanted to protect him?

A new tenderness for her filled him. "What is it then? Why don't you want people to see us holding hands?"

"Because of me, Dan." She met his eyes, letting him see everything she was thinking for the first time maybe ever.

She looked tormented. "I'm not the kind of woman you should be holding hands with."

He almost laughed, the statement was so ridiculous. But the look on her face stopped him.

"Why not? It just so happens that you have the perfect hands for holding." He moved closer and slowly reached for her hand, giving her time to pull away if she wanted to.

This time, she let him wrap his hand around hers, and he smiled as the warmth of his skin transferred to her cold fingers. "See?"

She didn't smile back. "You know my reputation, Dan. You pretend not to, but you do."

He squeezed her hand tighter. "I don't see what that has to do with holding hands."

She shook her head. "Don't play dumb. If people see us holding hands, they'll start talking."

Dan laughed. Was that what she was worried about? "I think people have more interesting things to talk about than who I hold hands with."

"Tell that to the women in the restroom." Jade withdrew her hand from his, crossing her arms in front of her.

"The women?" In the restroom? Is that what had transformed her from open, lighthearted Jade into sullen, closed-off Jade? "Who?"

Jade shrugged. "I don't know their names. They're from church, I think. It doesn't matter."

"And they said something to you?" It was probably just a misunderstanding she'd blown out of proportion.

"They didn't know I was in there. They were talking about you and me. Holding hands." She gave him a grim look.

"So what? It doesn't matter if they were talking about us holding hands. I don't care who knows. In fact, I think it's great people know. I'll tell everyone myself." He cupped his hands around his mouth and yelled to the waves. "I held hands with Jade Falter. And I want to do it again."

He grinned at her. "There. Now everyone knows."

"Stop, Dan." Jade's eyes flashed. "They weren't just talking about us holding hands. They implied that you were with me because of my reputation. Because you wanted to do more than hold hands. A lot more." Even in the quickly fading light, he could see the red rise to her cheeks.

His chest tightened. What right did anyone have to make assumptions like that about Jade?

"I'm so sorry." He stepped in front of her so that she had no choice but to look at him. "They never should have— The thing about the church is that it's made up of sinners. Me included. But—"

Jade stopped him with a glare. "I don't care what they said about me, Dan. I'm used to it. But don't you get that if people see us together, my reputation is going to rub off on you? That's why we can't hold hands. Why we can't be together." Her delicate throat rippled as she swallowed, and he wanted nothing more than to wrap her in his arms and make all the pain of the encounter go away.

"You've changed, Jade. You're not the girl you were in high school. We'll just have to make sure everyone sees that. They already know you volunteered at camp, and soon they'll see you volunteering at VBS. They'll realize you're the perfect girl for a pastor in no time."

Jade lifted her head, her eyes wide enough to reflect the full moon that was rising. "And if they don't?"

"If they don't, I don't care. I don't care what they think."

Jade gave a disbelieving laugh. "Yes, you do. It's why you were so worried about how camp went and why you couldn't talk to the parents afterward."

Dan almost flat out denied it, but he stopped himself. She was right.

"I don't care what they think about this, Jade. About us."

"I don't know." She chewed her lip, and suddenly her lips were the only thing he could focus on. He lifted his hands to her face.

"Do you remember the first time we kissed?" he murmured.

She nodded, her eyes softening. "It was perfect."

Dan's thumb slid back and forth on her cheek. "Not true. I had no idea what I was doing, and I'm sure you could tell."

Jade's laugh was low and throaty. "Maybe it wasn't the most technically perfect, but it was still perfect."

Her eyes fell closed, and Dan leaned forward. It had been eight years since that kiss. But in this moment, it felt as if no time had gone by at all.

"Dan." Jade whispered his name.

The last thing Dan saw before he closed his own eyes was the smile playing on her lips.

And he could feel that smile when his lips at last met hers.

All the magic of that first kiss eight years ago was still there—with none of the awkwardness. Jade's hands slid from his shoulders to wrap around his neck, and she pulled him closer. He let his hands travel to her hair, deepening the kiss.

Jade sighed softly against his lips, then pulled back. He pulled her into a tight hug.

"I hope that was better than last time," he said into her hair.

She tightened her arms around him. "Your technical performance has definitely improved. But it was still perfect."

They stood like that for a few minutes, until Jade tried to disentangle herself. But Dan wasn't ready to let her go.

She shook her head but leaned into him again. "Maybe it'd be best if people didn't see us doing that," she whispered.

He turned to look up and down the beach. "I don't see anyone here."

He dropped his head for another kiss.

Chapter 28

J ade twirled her way across the tiny living room of Vi's apartment as she waited for Keira to answer her phone. She must look like an absolute lunatic right now, but she didn't care. She had to do something with all this extra joy building inside her.

"About time you called." Keira's cheerful voice belied her gruff words. "I was starting to worry Hope Springs had finally done you in."

"Nope." Jade lifted a mini replica of the Old Lighthouse off Vi's shelf. Maybe she and Dan could go there sometime soon. "Everything's good here."

"What do you mean everything's good there?" Keira's disbelief sounded through the phone. "Last time we talked, you were ready to hop a plane back to LA."

"Let's just say things are better now." Jade set the lighthouse down and moved to look out the window at the lake. And the beach. The beach where she and Dan had walked every night for the past week and a half. Where they'd kissed every night for the past week and a half.

"What do you mean things are better? Did you fall in love with working in your sister's antique shop or— Oooh." Keira gasped. "Or did you fall in *love*? You met a wholesome Hope Springs guy, didn't you?" She squealed, making a sound Jade had only ever heard from three-year-olds.

"Nope." Jade dragged out her answer. The suspense would kill her roommate, but she couldn't resist. "I didn't meet him. I already knew him. We sort of, almost, dated, I guess, a long time ago."

"You *almost* dated? What does that mean?"

"It's a long story. But the point is, he's still in Hope Springs and so am I for the moment and—"

"Oh my goodness, it's a second chance romance." Keira's shriek was so loud that Jade pulled the phone away from her ear. "I love those."

Jade chuckled. "Slow down, Keira. I—"

But once Keira got going, nothing could stop her. "I'll come for your wedding. Wouldn't miss it. Wait— Does that mean you're not coming back to LA?"

"That was the exact opposite of slowing down. No one's getting married." But she had to admit that the same questions had been going through her head. And she wasn't sure she had the answers yet.

"You're going to stay there, aren't you?" The excitement had partially faded from Keira's voice. "I'm going to miss you."

"I haven't decided anything yet, Keira. At this point, I'm still planning to come back to LA."

"But you're considering staying? For this guy?"

"Yes. No. I mean—" Jade forced herself to slow down and explain. "I am considering staying. But not for the guy."

Keira snorted.

"Well, not *just* for the guy," Jade amended. "My sister's here too, and she has this great group of friends who have welcomed me, and I don't know. . . . It's kind of starting to feel like home here."

"I'm happy for you, Jade." Keira sounded sincere. "I've never heard you call anywhere home. So this is pretty huge."

"Not huge." Jade didn't want to overplay it. "And nothing's decided yet."

But in her heart, she knew—it was huge.

"Ready for this?" Dan's smile as he met her at Vi's car the next morning sent the same pool of warmth surging through her stomach as always. Even after a week of spending every spare moment together, she still hadn't gotten used to that feeling.

He picked up the oversize beach bag she'd packed and leaned down to drop a kiss on the top of her head. Jade squirmed even as she acknowledged the flip in her heart. She still felt slightly uncomfortable about letting others see them together. But Dan's naturalness about the whole thing eased her worry a little.

She caught Vi's grin as she and Nate also emerged from the car.

"Good morning, Dan," Vi called.

"Hmm?" Dan lifted his head. "Oh, morning."

"So are you?" Dan took Jade's hand and drew her toward the ferry landing. "Ready for this?"

This time it was Jade's stomach that flipped. "Have I mentioned I'm not the biggest fan of boats?" Just the thought of getting on the ferry that was supposed to take them to Strawberry Island had left her feeling queasy all morning.

"I know." He leaned over to kiss her head again as they walked. "But I promise not to leave your side."

The tenderness in his eyes unwound something that had been coiled tight in Jade's gut. "Then let's do it."

Dan wrapped an arm around her and held her against his side as they came to the pier where the rest of their friends had already gathered. Most of them already knew about Dan and Jade's developing relationship—a word she had to admit she liked the sound of—and they greeted them with smiles.

"You two are so adorable together," Sophie called when they were close enough.

"We know." Dan squeezed her close, and she swatted at him, but she couldn't deny that the fact that he wanted everyone to know about them meant everything to her.

The only one who didn't seem to approve was Leah, who was busy rummaging in her bag, though Jade doubted she was searching for anything in particular. She couldn't blame Dan's sister for being less than thrilled with her baby brother's choice of women, especially since she'd been trying so hard to set Dan up with Grace.

Thankfully, Dan had been right when he'd said Grace had taken things well. She'd taken it so well that if it weren't for the fact that Jade knew Grace was the most sincere person alive, she'd think it was all an act.

But when Grace's eyes fell on them now, she immediately grabbed her phone. "Y'all need a picture of this." She snapped the photo, then swiped at her phone for a few seconds. "There."

Both Dan's and Jade's phones dinged with a notification, and they pulled them out at the same time.

"That's a great picture. Thanks," Dan said to Grace.

Jade could only stare at the image on her screen. She was looking at the camera, smiling a smile she didn't recognize—one that made her appear completely comfortable and at home.

But Dan wasn't looking at the camera. His eyes were on her, and the look in them made Jade's breath hitch.

She'd seen that look before. That was the way Nate looked at Vi, the way Spencer looked at Sophie, Ethan looked at Ariana, and Jared at Peyton. It was a look that said the words neither of them had spoken yet.

It was a look that said he loved her.

"Don't you like it?" Dan asked quietly enough that only she could hear.

"I love it." She blinked and turned her phone off, tucking it into her pocket.

"Me too." Dan tugged her forward. "Come on, we don't want to miss the boat."

They followed the others, who were already crossing the narrow walkway onto the ferry.

"I really don't like boats." A fresh wave of nausea hit her as she stepped onto the deck of the ferry, and the whole thing heaved under her feet.

"It's going to be great. I promise."

Tucked against the warmth of Dan's side, she could almost let herself believe it.

He led her past the rest of the group to a spot at the front of the ship. Taking his arm off her, he leaned over the railing, stretching his fingers toward the water, as if he could reach the waves, which were at least ten feet below.

"Are you kidding me?" Jade clutched at the railing as the boat dipped in the waves.

"Sorry." Dan pulled himself upright. "My dad used to dare us to touch the water every time we rode the ferry."

Jade softened. "You really miss him, don't you?"

Dan's smile shifted from playful to wistful. "Yeah, I do. But I'll see him again someday."

"In heaven." Jade ran a hand over Dan's smooth cheek. They'd had several conversations about God and life and death and heaven over the past couple weeks, and Jade had felt a joy she'd never known before as Dan told her that getting to heaven didn't depend on what she'd done or not done. It was all about what Jesus had done for her. Part of her

147

knew that was too good to be true. But the other part of her—the part she was coming to recognize more and more—held onto the hope that it was.

"In heaven," Dan repeated, bending down to brush a light kiss onto her lips. "But for now, I think I'm going to enjoy my day on earth. With you."

"Me too." She popped onto her tiptoes to give him another kiss, but just then the ferry's engine gave a loud roar, and the boat surged forward.

Knocked off balance, Jade toppled into Dan, whose arms went around her.

"Wow. I knocked you off your feet, huh?" Dan quipped.

But Jade could only nod, pressing her lips tight together. The boat's movement had set her stomach churning.

"You okay?" Concern filled his voice.

She closed her eyes and leaned into him, trying to fight off the nausea.

But it was a losing battle.

"I need a bathroom," she gasped.

Chapter 29

Dan stood with his forearm pressed to the outside of the bathroom door, waiting for the sound of Jade's retching to pass. This was her third rush trip to the restroom since they'd gotten on the ferry, and he couldn't have felt more awful if he were the one throwing up.

When she'd told him she didn't like boats, he should have listened, instead of convincing her to come anyway. But he'd been so excited about the prospect of spending an entire day with her that he hadn't been able to resist.

Inside the bathroom, he heard a toilet flush and then the sound of running water. He stepped back from the door to give Jade room to exit.

The moment she did, he gathered her into his arms. "Feel any better?"

Her head bobbed against his chest. "A little." But her face was pale and drawn, and a cold sweat dampened the hair he brushed off her neck.

"Just hold on a little longer. We're almost there." He led her slowly toward the exterior deck again, bracing her against his side to minimize the impact of the ferry's rolling motion.

At least the fresh air seemed to help. A little color returned to Jade's cheeks as he steered her to a row of low benches. He passed her the water bottle Violet had brought her.

"I wish there was something I could do to make you feel better." He hated being useless like this.

"Sitting with you makes me feel better."

Dan looked over at her. Her head was tilted back, her eyes closed, but the slightest smile edged her lips.

Just then, the engine sounds changed as the ferry slowed. Dan watched the approaching island with relief. He had no idea how Jade was going to survive the trip back to the mainland this evening. But they had a whole day to enjoy together before they had to worry about that.

"We can get off this bucket in a few seconds," he told her.

"That's good." She leaned into him, and he rested his chin on top of her head, taking a second to soak in the tropical scent of her hair. On second thought, maybe they should sit here like this all day.

At last, the engines cut off, and the ferry's forward movement stilled.

"Ready to put your feet on dry land?" He held out a hand to help her up, anticipating the moment her fingers intertwined with his.

"Yes, please." She offered him a weak smile and let him lead her onto the pier.

When they'd gathered everyone, the whole group wandered as one down the wide cobblestone street.

"Where to?" Violet asked. "Stores, beach, or food?"

"Beach and food." Sophie veered to the right, where a short boardwalk led down to perfect white sands. "I have such a craving for some of those soft pretzels. Oh, and maybe a chili dog."

Everyone laughed. Sophie had been eating nonstop since announcing her pregnancy, and the latest joke was that maybe she was carrying both a best friend *and* a husband for Ariana's baby, since twins ran in Spencer's family.

The others followed, but Jade stopped with one foot on the boardwalk.

Dan stopped next to her. "Not in the mood for the beach?"

She shook her head. "Not really. Would you mind terribly if we did something else?"

"Jade, the only thing I need to make me happy today is to be with you," he said honestly.

When she grabbed his hand, it was all he could do to keep from cheering out loud. It was the first time she'd been the one to take his hand instead of the other way around.

"How about a walk?" she asked.

He lifted her fingers to his lips and pressed a kiss onto her knuckles. "Lead the way."

Jade had no idea where they were. They'd taken a left turn here and a right turn there, until she was hopelessly lost.

"Do you know the way back to the ferry landing?" she asked Dan.

"Nope." He looked completely relaxed. "Does that worry you?"

"Not in the least." As long as she was with Dan, she could be lost in Siberia and she wouldn't mind.

"I figure we're on an island, so if we keep walking long enough, we should come to the water, and we can always follow the shoreline to where we started."

"You have it all figured out, don't you?" she joked.

But he appraised her with a searching look. "I think I'm starting to figure it out."

The intensity of his gaze made her glance away. He'd looked at her like that so often, and yet it caught her off guard every time.

"Look." She pointed to a sign half covered by the dense trees at the side of the road. "Mercy's Bluff. I wonder what that is."

"Only one way to find out." Dan pointed to the faint remnant of a trail that had long since grown over. Six weeks ago, Jade would have wrinkled her nose and said he was crazy if he thought she was going in there.

"Let's check it out," she said.

They cut through the underbrush that had almost obscured the trail, a few times nearly losing it entirely. After a while, Jade picked up a low rumble.

She paused, holding up a hand like a stop sign. "What's that? It's not going to storm, is it?" She lifted her face, but the trees were so thick here that she couldn't make out more than a speckle of sky.

Dan tilted his head to the side, as if straining to hear. "That sounds like . . ." He trailed off and strode forward again, grabbing her hand and pulling her along.

"Was there supposed to be an end to that sentence?" She fought to catch her breath as he pulled her faster.

Instead of answering, he came to a stop so quickly she nearly ran into him. The low rumbling had intensified and seemed to come from below them.

"Dan. What's going on?"

He stepped aside, giving her a full view. She caught her breath.

They were at the edge of a horseshoe-shaped cliff that dropped straight down to the lake. Below them, huge waves smashed against the rock face, sending spray high into the air.

"Wow." The juxtaposition of the power of the waves and the immensity of the water that stretched until she couldn't see it anymore touched on something deep in the middle of her chest.

"Welcome to Mercy's Bluff." Dan spread his arms wide, inviting her to take it in.

But she didn't need an invitation. She strode a few feet closer to the edge of the bluff so she could look straight into the water below.

"I thought you were afraid of heights." Dan's voice was light, but he moved closer and wrapped an arm around her waist, as if to keep her from falling.

But she wasn't scared. Not of this.

She was . . . in awe.

"I bet that rock at the bottom used to look like this." Dan pointed to the jagged rock that jutted out closer to the top of the cliff. "But it's been worn smooth over time." He gestured to the lower part of the cliff, where the water had worn away all the bumps and rough patches.

Jade nodded. She knew how that rock felt. The same thing had been happening to her since she'd come back to Hope Springs.

Jade couldn't stop smiling at herself in the bathroom mirror as she washed her hands. She and Dan had made their way back to the ferry landing—apparently, he'd known the way all along—just in time to eat dinner with the others. Now she only had to survive the ferry ride to the mainland. But somehow knowing Dan wouldn't leave her side even if she was sick made the prospect of getting back on the boat easier to bear.

She ran her fingers through her hair, trying to bring some sense of order to it. But it was way too messy to go for anything but the windblown look.

Oh well.

She had a feeling she could stick a paper bag over her head, and Dan would still find her attractive.

152

That was one of the things that drew her to him most. Whenever he looked at her, it was as if he was seeing right past her outer appearance to her heart.

Once, that had scared her. It was why she hadn't said goodbye to him in person all those years ago.

She'd been afraid he'd take one look at her and discover the ugly secret swelling inside her.

But now she didn't have any secrets to keep from him. She wanted him to see her, faults and all.

Giving her hair one last tousle, she reached for the door just as it opened and Leah bowled into the room.

"Sorry. I didn't see you." Jade grabbed the door handle. The sooner she escaped Dan's sister, the better. Leah was nice enough, but her feelings about Jade had been plenty clear in the way she'd kept watch over Jade and Dan at dinner.

"Actually." Leah stood in her way. "I was hoping to find you in here. I wanted to talk for a minute."

Jade swallowed. Why did she feel like she was sitting in Principal Jessup's office all over again? "Sure. What did you want to talk about?"

Leah studied her. "First, I want to say I'm sorry."

"Uh—" Jade reached for the door again. "Okay." She had no idea what Leah had to be sorry for, but this conversation had been much easier than she'd anticipated.

She opened the door a crack, but Leah was still talking. "I should have been more welcoming. It's just, I know how devastated Dan was when you left the first time, and I don't want him to go through that again."

Jade let go of the door and stepped farther into the room. "Neither do I."

"But—" Leah stepped forward and grabbed Jade's forearm. "Even I can see how good you two are together. So I wanted to tell you how happy I am for you."

"Thank you?" Jade didn't mean for it to come out as a question, so she tried again. "That means a lot."

"You're welcome." Leah met her eyes. "But that's not all I wanted to say."

She inhaled audibly, clearly uncomfortable. "If you leave again, it's going to break his heart. So unless you're planning to move back to Hope Springs, it might be best to end things now, before this goes any further." She said it without a trace of malice, and Jade could tell she truly only wanted what was best for her brother.

She swallowed past the dryness in her throat. "The last thing I want to do is hurt Dan."

"I'm glad." Leah squeezed her arm, then moved to the sink.

Jade pushed the door open slowly, savoring a deep breath of the damp night air. She didn't want to hurt Dan. Ever.

Which meant she knew what she had to do.

Chapter 30

"For you." Dan held out the small paper bag he'd gotten from one of the shops, fighting to keep from grinning at Jade.

Her eyes met his for a second, then dropped to the bag. "You shouldn't have gotten—" She opened the bag, looked inside, and laughed. "It's Dramamine. Thanks." She took out the box and dropped a tablet into her hand.

He held out the bottle of water he'd also grabbed for her.

"You thought of everything." She swallowed the medicine, then fell into step with him as they boarded the ferry. This time she was the one to lead the way to the front railing.

"So," she said as the ferry's engine churned. "I ran into your sister in the restroom."

Dan braced himself. What had Leah done now? "Whatever she said, don't listen to her. She can't help meddling in my life, but she's harmless. Mostly."

Jade studied him, and he wondered what she was searching for. "She said you were devastated when I left last time."

Dan gazed far out over the water, where he could just pick out the pinpricks of light on the mainland. Simply remembering when she'd left made his chest ache. "I was."

"Dan, I'm sorry. I owe you an explanation."

But he lifted a finger to her lips. "You don't owe me anything, Jade. I forgave you a long time ago, remember?"

She opened her mouth to say something, but he leaned down to give her a long kiss. That should quell any lingering doubts she had.

When he pulled away, Jade kept her eyes closed for a second.

"She also said," she continued once she had opened them.

Dan dropped his head. "Are we still talking about my sister?" That was not exactly his idea of a romantic topic of conversation.

"Yes." Jade shoved him lightly. "We are. She also said that if I'm leaving again, maybe we should end this now, before it goes any further, so I don't hurt you again."

Dan's shoulders tensed. He was going to throttle Leah the next time he saw her. Forget next time. He was going to find her right now.

Just because she didn't like his choice of girlfriend didn't give her the right to ruin things for him. It was his life.

"Look, Jade, Leah's an idiot. I'm crazy about you. I know the stakes. I know it's going to be like tearing my heart out when you leave again. But I don't care." He grabbed her hands and brought them to his chest. "I don't care. This is too good to give up on. *We* are too good to give up on."

He let his eyes rest on hers, praying she wouldn't say there was no "we."

"I agree." Jade's voice was barely above a whisper, and he leaned closer to make sure he'd heard right. "That's why I was wondering how you'd feel if I moved back to Hope Springs. Permanently."

It took him a moment to process the words, but the instant he did, he wrapped his arms around her and lifted her off her feet. "You're serious?"

His heart was beating a tap dance all around his chest, and he was smiling so big that the muscles in his cheeks hurt.

"Put me down." But even as she said it, she tightened her arms around his shoulders. "And, yes, I'm serious."

Dan set her back on the boat deck. "Remind me to thank my sister later."

But first, news this good called for a kiss.

Chapter 31

How had she been so happy only yesterday?

Jade pulled the cap low over her forehead as she reached for the package on the drugstore shelf. She watched her hand land on the box and pick it up. But it was as if it was someone else's hand. Someone else's life.

This couldn't be happening to her.

Not again.

She fought the tears that had threatened all morning. She was wrong. She was sure of it. She was only buying the test to confirm it.

She ventured a quick glance around the store before making her way to the counter. Fortunately, everyone else was at church right now.

When she'd woken feeling nauseous, she'd begged off church again, assuring Vi it was just residual effects of yesterday's ferry ride.

But as she'd lain in bed, her mind had flashed over the past couple weeks. She'd been feeling nauseous most mornings. She'd ordered that bizarre ice cream at the Chocolate Chicken. And her emotions were all over the place. Any one of those things by itself, she could have explained away. But the combination of all three had her worried.

Really worried.

So she'd done some quick calculations.

She'd always kept track of her period rather religiously. But she hadn't thought about it once since she'd come to Hope Springs. Six weeks ago. If she remembered correctly, she'd last had her period a couple weeks before that.

"Just this?" The cashier was a cheerful girl who looked to be about a high school senior. The same age Jade had been the last time she'd bought one of these.

She kept her head down and passed the girl some money, her eyes too blurred to tell if it was the right amount. Then she snatched the bag off the counter and ran to the front door, ignoring the girl's cries that she'd forgotten her change.

By the time she got to Vi's, her breath was coming in ragged gasps, even though it was only a few blocks.

Inside the apartment, she made a beeline for the bathroom but drew up short outside it.

She couldn't go in there. Couldn't do this. That little plus sign had exploded her world last time, just as she'd thought she'd finally found happiness.

She couldn't let that happen again.

You have to know. Then you can deal with it if need be. The thought sent a fresh wave of nausea rolling over her. She'd fought for the past eight years to forget what she'd done last time. But she still thought of it every single day. How could she possibly go through it again?

She forced herself to inhale through her nose and let it out through her mouth. She had to get this over with before Vi got home from church.

Her hands were remarkably steady as she pulled the test out of the box. It was as if she'd separated from her body. This was all an act, part of a movie. She was just an actor following a script. This wasn't really her life.

It couldn't be.

She sat on the toilet, stuck the test in her urine stream, capped it, washed her hands, set the timer on her phone for three minutes, and then stood staring in the mirror. In her bloodshot eyes, she saw the reflection of the scared teenager she'd been eight years ago. She'd thought she'd left that girl behind, but apparently there was no escaping who you really were.

The alarm on her phone rang, but she ignored it, letting its constant trill wear on her nerves. Last time, the moment she'd seen the results, she'd known what she needed to do.

She'd packed a small bag, scrawled two notes—one for Vi and one for Dan—then jumped on the first bus headed for the airport.

This time, if the test had the same result, she didn't know what she'd do. She couldn't disappear again, at least not right away. That wouldn't be fair to Vi. She had to at least stay for her sister's shower and wedding.

But after that?

After that, she'd have to go. She only hoped she could keep anyone from finding out before then.

Maybe it's negative. The little whisper of hope was even more maddening than the still-chirping timer.

She tapped the button to turn it off, then made herself look down.

The stick was still there.

The results window glared up at her, the plus sign that had materialized seeming to grow bigger and bigger until it took over the whole bathroom.

She folded in half, bracing her hands against the sink.

"Noooo." The word hurt coming out—hurt her throat, but more than that, hurt her heart.

How could she have let this happen? How could she be in the exact same spot today as she was eight years ago?

Her stomach rolled, and she lunged for the toilet.

She knelt there dry heaving for several minutes. But nothing came up. Her stomach was empty. Her mind was empty. Her heart was empty.

When she finally managed to get herself under control, she wiped her eyes, washed her hands, and wrapped the spent test and packaging in the drugstore bag. Her movements were deliberate and methodical, and she wondered with an odd sense of detachment if this was what it was like to be a robot. To not feel, just do.

Evidence in hand, she made her way down the stairs to the dumpster at the far end of the building's parking lot. Once she'd disposed of the test, her feet turned as if pro-grammed by some outside force, taking her down the hill to the beach below.

How could this same beach be the place where her dreams for the future had formed and died—twice?

She dropped into the wet sand.

She'd always known she wasn't good enough for Dan.

The plus sign on the pregnancy test had only confirmed it.

Chapter 32

"How are you feeling?" Dan had been waiting for Jade since the moment he'd opened the church doors for vacation Bible school this morning. He'd been worried when she hadn't been at church yesterday, but when he'd called after the service, she'd flat out refused his offer to come over.

He'd told himself he'd feel better once he saw her, but the way she brushed past him now had him more anxious than ever.

"Let me help you with that." He moved to take the box of crafting supplies she was carrying, but she hugged it tighter to herself.

"I've got it." She picked up her pace.

"So, I was thinking." He cleared his throat. He'd been so sure about asking her the other night, but that seemed to have been a different Jade. "My family has this tradition where we go to my aunt's house every year for a reunion. This will be the first year without Dad, which is going to be really hard on my mom. But I thought it might cheer her up if I brought you. To, you know—" He cleared his throat again. Maybe this had been a bad idea. "Meet her."

Jade kept walking.

"It's this weekend," he added. "So VBS will be done by then."

She finally stopped and looked at him, but her eyes lacked the warmth they'd taken on over the past few weeks. "Sure. Sounds fun." She moved toward the door to the Sunday school classroom they were standing outside of. "I have to get these crafts set up."

"Yeah. Of course." He stepped aside, hovering in the doorway to watch her for a few minutes. She bustled around the room, grabbing supplies and setting them on the front table.

He told himself it was only because she was busy that she didn't glance up at him even once.

But after two more days of VBS, Dan had to admit it to himself—she was avoiding him. He ran through every possible reason but came up empty again and again.

Last he knew, she was planning to move back to Hope Springs to be with him. And now she could barely look at him, let alone talk to him.

The only plausible explanation he'd come up with was that she was afraid. Of what, he wasn't sure. Maybe that he'd change his mind. Or that people would talk. Or maybe she was scared because she'd never felt this way about anyone before.

He knew he hadn't. But if anything, it made him feel less afraid than he had in months.

He waited until the kids had all left on Wednesday afternoon, then ducked into Jade's classroom, where she was cleaning up the day's painting project.

Dan collected paint brushes from the tables and rinsed them in the sink. "These turned out well." He nodded toward the mini terracotta pots the kids had painted today.

"We're going to plant mustard seeds in them tomorrow." Her voice was flat.

"That's a good idea." He watched the water flow over the brushes, washing blues and purples and reds down the drain. "I have a meeting later tonight, but I thought maybe we could go grab some dinner before that."

"I have an appointment," Jade mumbled.

"Oh." He fought to keep the disappointment out of his voice, then had an idea. "Is it something for Violet's shower? I could come with you. Especially if it's cake testing."

Jade rewarded his effort at levity with a tight smile. "It's not for the shower. But thanks." She put the last of the paints away. "I'll see you tomorrow." She crossed to the door.

"Jade, wait." He shut off the water and set the brushes down. Drying his hands on his shorts, he stepped toward her, trying not to notice the stiffness in her shoulders.

He stopped a few feet from her, scared that if he moved any closer, she'd bolt. "I've missed you."

Her lips lifted into an imitation of a smile. "We've been together every day this week."

He watched her, but she wouldn't meet his eyes. "Yeah. You're right." He dropped a soft kiss onto her lips, but she barely returned it.

When she pulled away, the sadness in her eyes nearly did him in. Something between them had broken. And he had no idea how to fix it.

She was right here in front of him, but he was losing her as surely as he had the first time.

Jade sat in the car she'd borrowed from Vi, staring through the rain that lashed the windshield in pounding sheets. She could barely make out the squat gray building at the other end of the parking lot.

But she didn't need to see it to know what it looked like inside. She'd been in a clinic like this once before. She'd seen the stark waiting room, the plain white walls, the lonely table surrounded by instruments she wished she could erase from her memory.

The rain kept up its relentless thrashing on the car roof.

I can't do this again.

The thought struck her square in the middle of her stomach—right where she imagined her uterus must be. Right where her baby was.

Her baby.

Even in her head, the words sounded surreal.

Just go in there and get it taken care of, and you'll never have to think those words again.

Her hand went to the door handle.

But she couldn't open it.

She couldn't go in there.

She couldn't do it all again.

The weight of the guilt from last time pushed on her every single day. If she added to it, it might sink her for good.

I can't do it. The prayer sounded in her head before she realized that was what it was. *I can't have another abortion. But I can't have this baby, either. You know that. You know I'm not fit to be a mother. Please spare this baby and take it from me right now.*

A dry sob escaped her. It was the worst prayer she'd ever prayed—probably the worst prayer anyone had ever prayed—and she was likely going straight to hell for it.

But please answer it, Lord. I can't do what I did last time. I can't. I need you to do it for me.

She started the car and drove slowly out of the parking lot, squinting through the rain.

If God didn't answer her prayer, she didn't know what she was going to do. There was always adoption.

Or she could keep the baby.

Her lip curled into a sneer. The idea of her as a mother was ludicrous. Look at the mess she'd made of her own life. She didn't even want to imagine how badly she could screw up a baby's life.

Her grip on the steering wheel tightened. It wasn't like it mattered what happened now, anyway.

Things with Dan were over no matter what. She only hoped he would get frustrated enough with the way she'd been treating him that he'd give up on her.

Because she wasn't sure she was strong enough to be the one to walk away this time.

Chapter 33

Jade didn't know how she'd made it through the entire week of VBS. When she was working with the kids, she could at least compartmentalize and allow herself to forget the secret growing inside her womb for a little while. But whenever Dan looked at her with that expression of mixed hope and sadness, it all came back to her.

As she waited now for the last of the kids' parents to pick them up, she pressed a hand to the fabric of her loose-fitting shirt. It was much too early to worry about showing, but she wasn't taking any chances.

When the kids had all finally left, she stood there, staring out the church doors. If anyone had told her a month ago that this place would feel like her second home, she would have accused them of indulging in too much communion wine.

But everything about the church had grown on her—the big, comfortable lobby that invited people to stand around talking after services, the bright sanctuary with the large cross on the front wall, the music, the people, and especially the richness of God's Word. She'd never heard another preacher who made it come alive so vividly—in a way that she could understand how it related to her life.

Dan had a real gift—and she wasn't going to get in the way of his ability to use it.

She took a shaky breath, then made herself walk into the sanctuary, where Dan was cleaning up the props he'd used for his final message to the children.

"Hey there." His face brightened the moment she walked through the door, and she knew it was because this was the first time she'd sought him out all week.

Her heart strained with a wish that things were different. That she'd come in here to tell him she was sorry and things were all better.

But none of her wishes had come true lately, so why should this one be any different?

"Hey." She let herself walk halfway down the aisle but no farther. This would be impossible if they were within touching distance. The slightest brush of his hand against hers, and she'd lose her resolve.

"I just wanted to tell you that I won't be able to make it to your family thing tomorrow." She watched her shoe poke at the crushed cracker crumbs scattered among the flecks of brown and gold in the carpeting.

"Oh."

She could tell Dan was trying not to let her see how disappointed he was—which only made this that much harder.

"Maybe we could do something on Sunday then." Dan's voice was measured, as if he already knew what her answer would be.

She stuffed her own longing into a deep part of her soul. She had to do this for his sake.

"I don't think so," she made herself say. "I don't think we should see each other anymore."

"You don't?" Dan's voice had gone dull, and this time he didn't even attempt to cover the hurt.

She couldn't look at him.

"I don't," she choked out.

Then she turned and ran out the church doors, praying he wouldn't follow.

Chapter 34

"Hey, Jade. It's Dan. Again." He closed his eyes, picturing her as he left the message a week after she'd broken things off. Her face had been so twisted with anguish when she'd told him they shouldn't see each other anymore that he hadn't known what to do. His instinct was to follow her, tell her whatever it was that had her spooked, they could work through it. But he'd known he wouldn't be able to reach her. That pushing her would only drive her further away.

His resolve to give her space had lasted all of three days, before he'd decided maybe he was wrong. Maybe what she needed was to know he wasn't going anywhere, no matter what. So he'd spent the past four days calling every few hours. So far, she hadn't answered once. And the one time he'd shown up at Violet's apartment, Jade had opened the door only long enough to tell him she was too busy preparing for Violet's bridal shower to talk.

"I know you're scared," he said to her voice mail now. "But I'm not going to give up on you. So if you want me to stop leaving these annoying messages, you're going to have to answer one of these times." He swallowed the *I love you* he wanted to add and hung up the phone. She was already skittish enough. If he said those three words right now, he might send her flying right back to LA.

He hit the phone absently against his hand as he thought through his next move. It had to be something that wouldn't scare Jade away—but that would give him a chance to show her what she meant to him. To show her that she was his world.

"I know you feel something for me, Jade," he muttered to the silent phone.

There had to be something he could do to get through to her. Or if he couldn't do it, maybe someone else could help him.

He swiped his phone on and scrolled to Violet's number.

"Dan." Violet's sympathetic tone was enough to tell him she knew what had happened between him and Jade. "How are you?"

"I'm—" He ran a hand through his hair. "I'm kind of going crazy without her, to be honest."

Violet's sigh crackled over the phone. "I know. I can tell Jade is hurting too, but she won't talk about it."

"Yeah, I'm pretty sure you got all the talkative genes in your family."

Violet offered a strained laugh. "Don't give up on her, okay? I don't know what happened, but she needs you."

Dan swallowed. "I'm not giving up on her." Until she came out and told him to leave her alone, he wouldn't give up. And maybe not even then. "I actually called because I need a favor."

"Anything." Vi's answer was immediate.

"Tomorrow, after your bridal shower, could you convince Jade to take a walk on the beach with you?"

"Sure." Violet sounded confused. "I can probably do that. And then what?"

"Well—" How did he say this without sounding rude? "After you get her to the beach, you leave."

Violet's laugh rang through the phone. "Ah, I see. And I assume you'll be there waiting for her?"

"Of course." Not just waiting for her. Waiting for her with a romantic dinner and flowers and music and . . . anything else he could think of to show her his love.

"I'm in." Violet sounded almost as excited about the plan as he was.

"Thanks, Violet. I appreciate it."

"You know I'd do anything for Jade."

"Me too." As soon as Dan got off the phone with Violet, he dialed the florist.

Tomorrow was going to be perfect. The first day of the rest of his life with Jade.

He could feel it.

Jade pretended not to notice the number that flashed on her screen as she applied her mascara Saturday morning.

She'd muted the ringer so she wouldn't have to feel guilty every time he called, but that didn't keep her from noticing when the screen lit up with his number.

Each time, she told herself she wasn't going to listen to the voice mails. But each time she only managed to obey herself for three minutes max before lunging for her phone and listening to his recorded voice as if it were a lifeline.

By now, he should have given up. Or he should at least be sounding annoyed or defeated. But if anything, his messages got brighter and more optimistic with each call.

She finished putting on her makeup, then grabbed the phone, tapping to listen to her newest voice mail even as she chided herself not to.

"Hey, Jade. Dan again. But you probably recognize my voice by now, huh?"

She closed her eyes as the warm tones washed over her. She would recognize his voice anywhere.

"Just wanted to say I'm thinking of you today. And I hope to see you soon. That's all for now. Have fun at Violet's shower."

Jade lowered the phone slowly, resisting the urge to replay the message. She wanted to see him more than anything, but she couldn't let that happen. It would only make everything harder.

She was already exhausted from dodging him all week. How was it that not being with him sapped all her energy?

Over the last couple days, she'd started to have a crazy idea. What if she told him? He would understand, wouldn't he? He was the one who was always preaching about how Jesus forgave all sins.

She picked up her phone and ran her hand over it. Should she call and ask him to meet her later? Was she brave enough to do that?

A knock on the bathroom door made her jump and almost drop the phone.

"You ready, Jade?" Violet called.

"Yep." Jade stuffed her phone in her purse. She'd get through this shower first, then she'd decide whether or not to talk to Dan.

She opened the door to find Vi waiting for her in the hallway, her long, dark curls swept into a neat twist, her skin almost glowing under the white sundress she'd chosen.

"Wow, Vi, you look beautiful." Without thinking, Jade leaned over to hug her sister. The affection that had seemed so foreign to her when she'd first returned to Hope Springs came more naturally every day.

"You look pretty spectacular yourself." Vi gestured to the empire-cut blue dress Jade had chosen mainly because its loose fit hid the ever-so-slight bulge that had started to form in her waistline this week.

She wouldn't be able to hide her secret from Violet much longer. But every time she thought about telling her sister, she broke into a cold sweat.

There wouldn't be any celebration or cooing over her tummy when she announced it. No jokes about how her baby might one day marry Ethan and Ariana's baby.

There would only be shame and regret and disappointment.

Jade forced her thoughts off the baby. That was another day's problem. For today, her focus needed to be on making Vi's shower perfect.

Fortunately, Violet kept up her usual chatter on the drive to the church, where she'd insisted she wanted to hold her shower. Seeing Vi so happy helped Jade forget about her own mountain of problems at least a little bit. Even if she'd lost her brief chance at a happily ever after, she couldn't begrudge her sister this second chance.

Vi pulled into the church parking lot, but instead of getting out of the car, she turned to Jade and grabbed her hand. "Thank you, Jade." Tears sparkled in her eyes. "You have no idea how much it means to me that you came home and that you've done so much to make sure my wedding is special. Honestly, just having you here would be enough—"

"In that case, maybe I'll have Peyton take the cake back." But tears pricked at her eyes too, and she leaned over to pull Violet into another hug. "I love you, big sister."

One of Violet's tears dropped onto her shoulder. "I love you too, little sister."

Jade closed her eyes, but it was too late. A tear had sneaked out and trailed down her cheek.

Thank goodness she hadn't told Vi about her wild idea to stay in Hope Springs. That had only been a temporary delusion. One that was over already. She'd called Keira yesterday to let her know to expect her back in a month after all.

She just had to figure out how to survive in Hope Springs until then.

Chapter 35

"You did a lovely job planning the shower." Sophie squeezed Jade's arm as she walked past.

"Thanks again for taking care of the decorations. Everything looks amazing."

Sophie had transformed the church hall so thoroughly that Jade barely recognized it. Elegant tablecloths were topped by beautiful bouquets of wildflowers, and fairy lights were strung across the ceiling, with ivy trailing down the walls. It looked like they'd been transported to an enchanted forest.

"Did you get some cake?" Sophie held out a plate to Jade, but Jade gestured it away.

"I'm fine for now thanks. I'd better check if Leah needs any more help in the kitchen." But halfway there, she had to stop as a wave of pain tightened her belly. It had been happening for the past couple hours, but so far she'd been able to ignore it.

Now she couldn't deny that the pain was getting worse.

It was probably because she'd been on her feet all day. Once she had a chance to sit down, she'd feel better.

She shoved away the niggling fear that something was wrong with the baby. If God had been planning to answer her prayer to take the baby, he'd have done it by now.

As the pain passed, she stepped into the kitchen. Leah was bustling around, refilling bowls and handing them off to Brianna, who was bringing them to the serving line.

Jade froze.

She'd been disappointed—but not surprised—that Brianna hadn't enrolled Penelope in vacation Bible school. Though she missed the little girl terribly, even when she saw them in church she went out of her way to avoid them. The last thing she needed was a run-in with Brianna.

"Oh, sorry, I was just— Looks like you have everything under control." Jade stepped backward out the kitchen door.

"Jade. Wait." Brianna followed her, and Jade stopped like an obedient schoolgirl.

She deserved whatever horrible things Brianna wanted to say to her. A mother had a right to decide who took care of her children, and Jade had disregarded her request to stay away from Penelope at camp.

She ignored the fresh onslaught of pain in her belly as she waited for Brianna to tear into her.

"I wanted to say—" Brianna fidgeted, eyes on the floor.

"Brianna, I'm sorry. I should have respected your request that I stay away from Penelope. She's your daughter, and—"

Before she could finish her apology, Brianna's arms were around her, nearly smothering her with the strength of her hug. "Thank you." Her voice was muted. "Penelope is the only thing in this world that matters to me, and if I had lost her . . ." She shuddered.

Jade had no idea what to do. She'd been prepared for yelling, even a slap to the face, but a hug was so unexpected that she could only respond by hugging Brianna back.

After a full minute, Brianna pulled away, straightened her shirt, and strode back to the kitchen, leaving Jade standing there, completely dumbfounded.

She made her way over to Vi to ask if she was ready to open her gifts or if she preferred to play the goofy games Jade had looked up online first.

But as she was waiting for Vi to finish up a conversation with an older lady, her insides cramped so tightly that she had to wrap her arms around her middle.

"Excuse me," she managed to gasp to no one in particular, before she rushed for the bathroom.

When she got there, she locked the door and leaned her forehead against it, letting the metal surface cool the sweat beaded there.

The cramp eased slightly, and Jade made her way to the toilet. Her hands shook as she lifted her dress to pull down her underwear.

She blinked at the three perfect red circles that had stained the fabric.

"Oh." All the breath left her lungs as she sat. Her thoughts spun, trying to get a fix on what this meant.

She was pregnant. So she shouldn't be bleeding. But she was.

She didn't want the baby. So she should be relieved. But she wasn't.

At the sight of more blood on the toilet paper, she closed her eyes.

Legs shaking, she pulled her underwear up and washed her hands. Then she stood staring at herself in the mirror. Her face was pale, her eyes too big.

How could she go out there and pretend nothing had happened?

But she had to, didn't she? All those people were here for Vi's special day. And she wasn't going to ruin it. As far as any of them knew, she wasn't pregnant and never had been. She might as well keep it that way. If the blood meant anything, pretty soon she wouldn't be pregnant anymore, anyway.

A knock on the door made her jump. "Coming." She splashed a little cold water on her face to put some color back in her cheeks.

"Everything all right in there, Jade?" Vi's voice was muffled through the door.

Jade dried her face and opened the door, fully intending to tell her sister that everything was fine. But one look at the concern on Vi's face, and Jade crumpled. She could feel the tears working their way up, but she was helpless to stop them.

"What is it, Jade?" Vi's expression morphed to confusion, and she stepped into the bathroom, closing and locking the door behind her. "Is this about Dan?"

But that only made Jade cry harder.

She could barely get the words out past the panic that had lodged in her throat. "I'm bleeding."

"Where?" Vi looked her up and down, as if expecting to find a giant, gushing wound.

Jade raised her hands helplessly, then gestured to her midsection. "I'm bleeding, Vi."

Vi's forehead wrinkled. "Like you have your period? I think I have some meds in my purse if you have cramps. I forgot that you used to get them so bad."

"No, Vi." Jade reached a hand to stop her sister, who had turned to the door, apparently ready to fetch her purse and make everything all better. "I'm bleeding. And I'm—" She swallowed so hard it hurt. Could she really say the word? "I'm pregnant."

Time stopped as Violet just looked at her. It was several seconds before she even blinked.

Jade wanted to beg her to say something, but she had to give her time to process.

She bent double as a fierce cramp ripped through her belly, setting it on fire.

"Let's get you to the hospital." Violet placed one hand on Jade's back and the other on her elbow, steering her to the door.

"No, Vi." Jade planted her feet, but she didn't have the strength to fight Violet and breathe through the cramp at the same time. "You are not going to leave your shower. And neither am I. I'll be fine."

But Vi had already steered her down the hallway to a side door. "Stay here a second while I go tell Sophie. She'll take care of everything."

Jade wanted to protest. But she was in too much pain to do more than lean up against the wall and wait.

Within two minutes, Violet was back at her side, steering her out the door. "It's going to be okay."

"What did you tell them?" Not that it mattered. It wasn't like her secret was going to be a secret much longer.

"I told them to pray."

Jade closed her eyes as she settled into the passenger seat.

Maybe it wouldn't be a bad idea to pray herself. But now that God was in the middle of answering her last prayer, of giving her what she'd thought she wanted, all she could think was, *I take it back, Lord*.

Chapter 36

Everything was perfect. Dan had spent the past hour carrying the bistro table and chairs from his patio down to the beach and laying out the meal of seared salmon and scallops. It wasn't super fancy, but he'd prepared it himself, and that had to count for something. He double-checked that he had a lighter for the candles and rearranged the flowers in the center of the table for the fifth time. Maybe he should take them off the table altogether. He wanted to be able to see her while they ate. He gave everything one last glance to make sure he hadn't forgotten anything.

The blanket! He'd planned to lay it out so they could sit on the beach after they ate. But he must have set it down when he was gathering the dishes. He could picture it balanced on the back of the dining room chair closest to the patio door.

He glanced at the time on his phone. The shower should be getting done any moment. He didn't want Jade to walk down here and find him missing. But he wanted everything to be perfect. If he sprinted, he'd only be gone a few seconds.

Mind made up, he dashed down the beach, up the stairs alongside the church, and toward his house. He grabbed the blanket and was back out the door in less than two minutes.

As he sprinted back toward the steps, he peered at the church to check if any shower guests were on their way out yet.

But the parking lot was empty.

Odd.

He glanced at the time again. Maybe the shower had ended early. But if it was done, where was Jade?

His heart dropped. Had she refused to take Violet up on her request to walk on the beach? Had he lost his chance?

He pulled out his phone to call Violet, but before he could dial, it rang.

He had it to his ear before the first tone had finished. "Hey, Violet. She caught on, didn't she? What if I just come over and sweep her away?"

Muffled voices sounded from the other end of the phone, but Violet didn't say anything.

"Violet?"

"I'm sorry, Dan. I should have called sooner, but in all the commotion, it didn't occur to me."

"Commotion?" Dan drew up short, watching the dark church. "What commotion?"

"I had to take Jade to the hospital during the shower."

The words nailed Dan right in the chest, and he was already backtracking to his house. He needed his keys. "What happened? Is she all right?" His chest constricted. Of course she wasn't all right, or she wouldn't be at the hospital.

"She's okay. But Dan—" Something in the way Violet hesitated as she said his name made the hairs on his neck stand on end.

"What's wrong then? Tell me." He needed to know right now.

Violet's sigh was heavy. "She's pregnant. She had some pain and bleeding. The baby has a heartbeat, but it's too soon to say if she's miscarrying."

Dan grabbed blindly for a chair. Jade was pregnant? As in carrying a child? Another man's child?

He tried to swallow, but his throat had gone completely dry. "What? I don't—" He closed his mouth. He didn't know what he wanted to say.

"I'm sorry, Dan. They're sending her home pretty soon, if you want to see her. Otherwise . . ."

Dan stared at the car keys in his hand. Otherwise, what?

"Okay," he said dully. But nothing was okay about this. Nothing at all. Tonight was supposed to be the night he won Jade over forever. And now he was learning that he'd never had a chance. That she was pregnant with another man's child.

"Dan?" Violet's voice was tentative. "Could you pray? For her and the baby?"

Dan scrubbed a hand over his mouth and chin. "Yeah." The word came out all scratchy, but it was the best he could do. "I'll pray."

He hung up and glared at the phone in his hand. Dropping it on the kitchen table, he made his way to the beach and packed up the meal and the candles. He grabbed the flowers out of their vase and chucked them onto the dune.

Why, Lord? he cried out in his heart. *Why did you let me think she was the one when you've known this would happen all along?*

The constant rhythm of the waves was his only answer. He moved closer to the water and plopped into the sand, dropping his head between his knees. He had never felt so defeated in his life.

He didn't know how long he sat like that, resisting the urge to pray, but finally his instincts took over, and he found himself pouring out his heart to his Heavenly Father. *I don't know why this is happening, Lord, but you do. You have promised that you work all things for the good of those who love you. Help me to trust that even in this you can work good—even if I can't see how right now. Please be with Jade and keep her safe. Help her to know that your love surrounds her no matter what happens.* He bowed his head deeper. He didn't know how he could say this next part, but he had promised Violet he would pray for Jade—and her baby. *Please protect the little one inside of Jade. Keep him or her safe until they reach full term, and help Jade to deliver a healthy baby when it is time. Help her to raise that baby to know you.*

He lifted his head and tilted it toward the sky. *And help me to surrender to your will. This is not what I want, Lord. Not what I planned. But I leave it all in your hands.*

Chapter 37

The baby's heartbeat was good. Jade clung to that. When she'd heard it, her own heart had filled her chest until she'd been sure she'd burst. Seeing the tiny form on the ultrasound had undone something inside Jade. This was her *child*. Flesh of her flesh. There was something awe-inspiring and almost miraculous in that.

And now that she'd seen it, she wanted this baby to live more than she'd ever wanted anything in her life.

But even after hearing the heartbeat, the doctor hadn't been able to guarantee that the baby would survive. Jade had wanted to argue with him, to talk him into giving her some kind of promise, but she'd known he didn't have that kind of power. So she'd meekly followed Vi to the car. There was nothing more they could do for her at the hospital.

All she could do was wait.

You can pray too, a little voice at the back of her head whispered as Violet drove her home.

But every time she tried to pray, she drew a blank. How was she supposed to ask God to save this baby when she'd despised the last one he'd given her? When she'd been so concerned with how a baby would affect her life that she'd decided to end its life?

Tears gathered behind her lids, and she closed her eyes. Her sorrow over that one decision would never leave her.

And now if she lost this baby too—how would she ever recover from that?

"We're here." Violet's voice was gentle—too gentle. She'd done nothing but take care of Jade's every need since the moment Jade had told her she was pregnant. She hadn't scolded Jade once or reminded her of what an awful person she was.

Jade almost wished she would.

The second Violet shut off the engine, she jumped out of the car and rushed around to Jade's door. She helped Jade out of the car and up the stairs to the apartment, as if she were an invalid.

Jade should tell her not to, but she didn't have the energy.

Nate stood at the top of the stairs waiting for them, his face lined with worry. He moved to open the door for them and squeezed her shoulder as she passed.

Jade closed her eyes. Why were they being so nice to her? She didn't deserve it. Here they were, doing everything possible to honor God with their relationship, and now Vi was stuck with a knocked-up sister.

Violet shepherded her to the bedroom. "Let's get you settled in so you can rest."

Jade should argue that she didn't need to rest. The doctor had said there was nothing she could do to affect things one way or the other. But that didn't mean she wasn't going to try. If she had to lay in bed for the next seven months straight to keep this little one safe, that's what she would do.

Instead of settling her onto the air mattress, Vi pushed her gently onto her own bed, then bent to take off her shoes.

"I can take off my own shoes, Vi." Jade bent toward her feet, but another pang seized her stomach and she stopped with a grunt.

"Lie back, Jade."

This time she obeyed Vi's command. She couldn't deny that it felt good to be taken care of.

Once Vi had her shoes off, she tucked the blankets around Jade's legs, then scurried around the room, closing the curtains. "Do you want anything? Some water or tea or something?"

Jade shook her head, watching her sister. A question burned on the tip of her tongue, but she was afraid to ask it.

But not knowing the answer was worse. "Vi?" Her voice was barely a whisper, but Vi was instantly at her side.

"Do you think—" Jade licked her chalky lips. "Do you think God is punishing me?"

"Of course not." Vi dropped onto the bed next to her. "Why would you ask that?"

Jade gulped back the tears. If she didn't tell Vi now, she never would. And she had to tell her. Had to confess to someone.

"Do you know why I left?" Even as she said it, her brain screamed at her to stop. Once she told Vi, there was no going back. Her sister's opinion of her would forever be tainted.

"You wanted to pursue acting. And there was nothing wrong with that. I should have been more supportive and—"

Jade dropped her hand onto Vi's lap. "I didn't want to act. I mean, I guess I did a little. But the reason I left the way I did, without telling anyone I was going, is because I was pregnant."

Violet couldn't suppress her gasp this time, but to Jade's surprise she didn't get up and walk away.

"Whose baby—" Vi waved a hand in the air. "You know what, it doesn't matter. What happened? Did you miscarry? Did you give the baby up for adoption?"

Jade grabbed her sister's hand and looked at her, really looked at her, until a mixture of horror and pity swirled in Violet's eyes. "Oh, Jade."

The sobs she'd been suppressing for the past eight years tore loose. "I got rid of it, Vi. I got rid of it, and I can't bring it back."

She buried her head in the pillow, but Vi's arms were around her, pulling her closer. She tried to slide away. She didn't deserve Vi's comfort.

But Vi refused to let go. Instead she clutched Jade, letting their tears mingle.

When they'd both quieted, Violet smoothed a hand over Jade's hair.

"I'm sorry," Jade whispered. "I was so scared, and I didn't know what else to do. I thought if I could just take care of it, I could forget about it and go on with my life as if nothing ever happened." Her lip quivered involuntarily, and she waited until she had it under control again. "But I couldn't. I think about that baby every day. And I regret what I did every single day. And that's why God is punishing me."

Vi wiped at the tears on her own cheeks, then on Jade's. She gave a gentle smile. "He's not punishing you, Jade. What you did was wrong, yes."

Jade closed her eyes. Violet was only telling her what she already knew, but it still hurt.

"But—" Violet wrapped her hands around Jade's. "He's forgiven you, Jade. For everything."

"Not—"

Violet shook her head. "Even for this, Jade. You know how much you love that little one inside you, how you would do anything to protect that baby?"

Jade nodded. It made no sense. This baby was the result of one of the biggest mistakes of her life, and she'd thought she didn't want it. But already she knew she loved it more than she loved her own life.

"That's how God feels about *you*, Jade. He loves you more than you could ever imagine. And he wants to protect you—not just physically but spiritually. Maybe all of this is his way of doing that."

Jade bit her lip, letting the words sink in. "I don't understand why he would do it like this," she finally said.

Vi laughed. "Yeah, we usually don't understand it. But we have to trust that he knows what we need, even when we don't."

"If you say so." But a hint of peace settled in Jade's heart. Somehow, she believed Violet was right about this. More than that, she trusted that God held her and her baby in his hands.

It was a new feeling. One she wanted to get used to.

Dan was stalling, and he knew it. Church had been over for twenty minutes already. He'd spent as little time mingling with his parishioners as possible today, seeking refuge in the small room behind the altar instead.

Most people had already filtered out, but he could still hear Violet's voice. He debated hiding here until she left.

He was sure she was waiting to talk to him about Jade. And that was one topic he had no interest in discussing.

Yesterday's shock of finding out she was carrying another man's baby had worn off sometime in the middle of the night as he stared at the wall in the dark. It had been replaced by anger, hurt, shame—you name it, he'd probably felt it. Most of all, though, he'd felt foolish. He'd ignored every single person who'd told him not to get involved with Jade, who'd reminded him of who she'd once been. He'd thought he knew better, thought she'd changed.

Joke was on him.

181

And some joke it was.

One that left his heart shredded into a pulpy mess.

It was his own fault. He couldn't blame Jade. Not really. She'd tried to keep him away, tried to warn him that she wasn't the right kind of girl for him.

He should have realized she knew herself better than he knew her. After all, she'd never let him get close enough to think differently.

He slammed down the water bottle he'd just drained and drew in a breath.

He couldn't stay in here forever. He squared his shoulders and stepped into the sanctuary, where Violet was talking in a low voice with Nate.

"You guys getting excited for the big day?" His lame attempt at small talk fell short.

"Hey, Dan." Violet gave him a sad half smile. "I know this is awkward. And I wouldn't ask if I didn't think it was important, but could you come by to visit Jade? I think she's really struggling right now, and she could use someone to talk to."

Dan tried to keep his expression neutral but had to assume he'd failed based on the pity in her eyes. "I'm guessing she doesn't want to talk to me."

"No, probably not." Violet lifted her eyebrows. "But you've never let that stop you before."

He looked away. He couldn't deny that. But this time was different.

"How is she doing?" Much as he wished he could shut off his feelings for her and be indifferent, he couldn't. He needed to know she was okay at least, that she wasn't in danger.

"She's doing a little better. The pain seems to have stopped, but she still has a little bleeding."

Dan had to force himself to ask the next question. "What does that mean for the baby?"

Tears clouded Violet's eyes, and Nate wrapped an arm over her shoulder. "I don't know. The doctors said we'd have to wait and see." She swiped at her cheek. "I know Jade is really worried. The only way I can get her to eat is by telling her it's good for the baby."

Dan nodded. "I have a couple visits to make at the hospital today. But I'll try to come by later this week."

Violet's face fell, but it was the best Dan could offer right now. He wasn't ready to see Jade yet.

"Thanks, Dan." Violet gave him a quick hug. "And for the record, I'm sorry. I had no idea . . ."

"Yeah." Dan returned her hug and ushered them to the door. "That makes two of us."

Chapter 38

"The baby is looking good." The doctor switched off the ultrasound machine. "Heartbeat is strong, all measurements are normal, and since you're no longer bleeding and cramping, I think it's safe to say that this little one is out of the woods."

Jade could have hugged him she was so happy, but she settled for a heartfelt "thank you" as Vi squeezed her hand.

This had been the longest six days of her life. She'd barely ventured from Vi's bed the entire week, and every time she'd gone to the bathroom, she'd held her breath, dreading the possibility that she'd see blood.

"That's good news." Vi pulled her into a hug as soon as she was on her feet. "Let's get you home."

Jade nodded and followed her. Violet hadn't asked once who the father of the baby was or how Jade could have been stupid enough to make the same mistake twice. She'd simply loved Jade and taken care of her. Violet's friends, too, had been nothing but wonderful. Sophie and Spencer had stopped by earlier in the week, and Grace had sat with her nearly all day Wednesday. Peyton had brought her a cake. Even Leah had called to check on her.

The only person she hadn't heard from was Dan.

Not that she'd expected to.

She'd known it was over from the moment Vi had told her Dan knew.

She reminded herself yet again that it was for the best.

But that didn't make it hurt any less.

"Have you heard from Dan lately?" She hated how meek she sounded as she asked Violet the question on the way home from her appointment.

Vi shot her a quick glance, and Jade looked away. "Never mind. It doesn't matter."

"Maybe you should call him."

Jade snorted. "And say what? Sorry I'm pregnant?" She watched the shops roll past as Vi turned onto Hope Street.

"You could tell him how you feel about him. He's hurt right now, but maybe if you talked—"

"It's better this way." She kept her voice abrupt. This conversation was pointless, and she was done with it.

Fortunately, Vi took the hint and remained silent the rest of the way to the apartment.

She finally spoke as she parked the car. "I'm not sure how this fits into your plans, but that's Dan's car." She pointed to the beat-up Camry at the other end of the lot, near the dumpster where Jade had thrown away her pregnancy test.

Jade's heart gave an unwanted leap, but she scolded herself. She had no business being happy to see Dan.

She got out of the car and looked around, half expecting him to ambush her from behind one of the vehicles. But there was no one in the parking lot. He must have gone inside already.

"I can't—" Her heart rate surged. "Can you tell him I'm not here? Tell him—"

"Tell him what?"

She spun toward his voice, her blood pounding so loudly in her ears she could barely hear herself as she said his name.

He walked toward her from the hill behind the parking lot, hands in his pockets.

Jade swiveled in desperation. She couldn't see him right now. Couldn't talk to him. Couldn't bear to feel his disappointment in who she'd turned out to be.

He took a few more steps toward her but stopped a good fifteen feet away, just looking at her.

She dropped her eyes. She'd never be able to meet his gaze again.

"Will you walk with me?" he finally asked.

Every instinct told her to say no. To turn and go in the house and lock the door and not come out until her baby was grown. But she found herself nodding instead.

"I'll be inside." Vi's voice from behind her was quiet, and Jade could hear the worry in it. But she wasn't sure which of them it was directed toward.

Dan waited, his face stony, as Jade closed the distance between them. When she reached his side, he pivoted and started walking down the hill toward the beach. He kept his hands in his pockets, his crooked elbow ensuring she couldn't walk too close. Not that she'd try.

Neither of them said a word as they stepped onto the beach and turned north, away from the beachgoers sprawled in the sand to the south.

Finally, she couldn't stand it any longer. "Do you hate me now?"

"No." His answer was swift but emotionless, and he didn't look at her.

She bit her lip, parsing through all the things she could say. But nothing would be adequate.

"I didn't know," she whispered. "Not at first. Not when we started spending time together. When I found out, I didn't know what to do. I didn't want to ruin everything with you. But I also didn't want to deceive you. I was planning to tell you the night of Vi's shower."

He let out an ironic laugh. "The night I was going to tell you I loved you, you were going to tell me you're pregnant with another man's baby."

Her sharp inhale cut at her lungs. Loved. Past tense.

He had loved her. But he didn't anymore.

Not that she'd expect him to. She only wished she could turn off her feelings for him as easily. She swallowed down the ache at the back of her throat and kept walking.

But Dan pulled up short and turned to her. "I thought you'd changed. You told me you'd changed."

Jade reared back. He may as well have struck her. "I have—"

But he was still going. "I vouched for you. Stood up for you."

"I didn't ask you to do that." Her hands balled into fists. "You did it because you were afraid of what people would think of you. Even when you claimed you weren't."

"Yeah, well—" Dan pulled his hands through his hair. "Guess I was right to be. Do you know how many people have asked me if it's my baby? I had an elder stop by yesterday, talking about disciplinary action. About asking me to leave."

Jade's hands covered her mouth. How did she always manage to hurt the people she loved most?

"I'm so sorry. I'll tell them. I'll stand before the whole church and tell them it's not yours." It didn't matter how much that would humiliate her. All that mattered was making things right for Dan.

"That won't be necessary. I told them it wasn't mine, and they took my word." He stopped short, as if suddenly struck by something.

"Whose is it?" The question came out slow and deliberate. "Someone you're in a relationship with?"

Jade hesitated, then nodded. Better he think that than find out the truth—that she didn't even know the name of her child's father.

Dan's stricken look made her want to take it back.

"Then why did— I thought we—" Dan raked his hands through his hair again. Watching the pain on his face tortured her. How could she have done this to him?

She laid a hand on his arm, but he pulled away. She completely deserved that, but it didn't ease the sting.

Dan stared out over the water. "So now what? Are you going back to California? To be with this guy? With the father?"

Now what? Hadn't she been pondering those two words every minute since she'd found out she was pregnant?

"Yeah." The single syllable sliced her heart open. "I'll go back to California."

Dan gave a sharp nod and started walking again. She gave him a few seconds on his own, then followed more slowly. There was nothing for her in California. Everything she wanted in the world was right here. But she'd blown what she had here.

After a few more minutes, Dan stopped and just stood there.

Finally, he said, "I think we should go back."

His voice was so quiet, so defeated, it was all Jade could do to keep from throwing her arms around him and begging him for forgiveness.

She wouldn't do that to him.

She didn't deserve his forgiveness.

And she wasn't going to ask for it.

Chapter 39

Dan escorted Sierra and Colton to the door of his office. The young couple gave him a last wave, then walked down the hallway hand in hand. They'd dropped by simply to thank him for being there for them.

Sighing, Dan wandered back into his office and picked up the Bible on his desk, flipping aimlessly through it. He didn't even know what he was looking for.

Answers.

Yes, answers would be nice. How was it that he had the answers for everyone else, but he didn't have any answers for himself?

He needed someone to tell him how to patch this gaping wound in his heart. Because if it wasn't fixed soon, he might lose all ability to feel permanently.

Actually, what he needed to do was get Jade out of his head. It shouldn't be too difficult, since in the three weeks since they'd last talked on the beach—when she'd told him she was going back to California to have another man's baby—he'd seen her only at church. Even then, she'd taken to slipping in right as the service began and ducking out during the final prayer.

But somehow seeing her less only made him think about her more.

Dan slammed his Bible shut. He was starting to drive himself crazy.

Air. That was what he needed. Maybe a good run too.

He strode through the hall to the lobby but drew up short the moment he reached it.

Jade was on the other side of the room, bent over the reception table. She didn't notice him at first, and he let himself take a moment to soak her in.

Her hair was pulled back into a messy bun, and she had no makeup on, but she'd never looked more beautiful.

He had to leave.

Right now.

He took a step back and started to turn away, but before he could, her head snapped up, as if she'd sensed he was there.

Their eyes met and held. She didn't smile, and neither did he. From this distance, he couldn't read what she was thinking.

When she straightened, her shirt stretched over her midsection, and he looked away. In case he'd forgotten why he couldn't be with her, that bump should be reminder enough.

"Hi," he finally croaked.

She held up a piece of paper. "Vi asked me to stop by to proof the wedding programs." She sounded defensive, as if he might kick her out otherwise.

"Oh." He couldn't get his feet to move. "How are you feeling?"

He grimaced at his own question but found that he wanted to know.

"Okay. The morning sickness is starting to pass."

"That's good." His feet shuffled forward. "I'm sure you're excited to get back to California after the wedding next week. To see the baby's father again." He hated himself even as he said it. And yet, he had to admit that it was satisfying to get one last dagger in.

Until he saw the hurt look on Jade's face and the tears that overflowed her lids.

"I'm sorry." He moved closer. What was done was done. There was no need for him to be a jerk about it. "That was uncalled for."

She shook her head and wiped at her eyes. "There is no father."

"What do you mean there is no father?" Dan could feel his brow wrinkle. There obviously had to be a father.

Jade had gotten her tears in check, but she looked more lost than he'd ever seen her.

"I mean, I don't know who the father is. He was some random guy who picked me up at the bar one night. I don't even know his name."

Dan's head reeled. Why had she said she was in a relationship with the baby's father? For the past three weeks, he'd believed she'd been stringing him along this whole time—a diversion to bide her time until she went home to her real relationship.

"But you're still going back to California?"

Her laugh was mocking. "What else am I going to do, Dan? Hang out here with a baby everyone thinks is yours? It will be better if I go—for both of us."

Dan pinched his chin. She wasn't wrong. But that didn't eliminate the sharp pain in his chest at the thought of her leaving.

"So you're going to raise the baby on your own? Or are you going to give it up for adoption?"

"I'm going to keep it." Her voice was filled with a conviction he'd never heard from her before. For some unexplainable reason, he was proud of her.

"For the record, I think that's really brave."

She shook her head. "Not brave. I'm totally terrified."

He tried a smile. "I heard someone say once that that's what makes it brave."

He thought she was brave?

Jade scoffed.

Nearly everything she'd done in her life was motivated by fear. And she didn't deserve to have him think otherwise.

"I thought about getting rid of it." She didn't know why she said it. Maybe to shock him—to make him stop being so nice to her when she deserved only his wrath.

"Getting an abortion," she added, in case he didn't understand what she was implying. He needed to know the full extent of her vileness.

Dan's face twitched, but he didn't say anything at first.

She could see him running through the possible responses in his head.

Finally, he settled on, "What made you decide not to?"

The question caught her off guard.

She clutched the already crumpled wedding program tighter but made herself look him in the eyes. "Because I couldn't go through with that again."

The way his mouth twisted told her she'd done it—she'd finally killed every last feeling he had for her.

Good, she told herself even as she felt a fissure larger than this room opening right through the middle of her heart.

"Again?" His voice was hoarse.

She followed a crack in the floor with her toe. "It's why I left. The first time. I was pregnant."

The air between them went completely still. Jade heard the air conditioner kick in, but there was no other sound. She couldn't even hear Dan breathing.

She made herself look up at him.

He was staring toward the wall, his face blank. But a muscle jumped in his clenched jaw.

"I'm sorry." The words were so small, but they were the only words she had.

When Dan still didn't move, she walked to the door.

Before opening it, she glanced back, half hoping Dan would tell her to stop. But she already knew he wouldn't.

Chapter 40

Follow her.

Dan ignored the voice in his head. Following her was the last thing he wanted to do.

When he'd first found out she was pregnant, he hadn't thought things could get any worse.

But now? Finding out she'd left Hope Springs to have an abortion?

That meant she'd slept with some other guy—it didn't matter who—while they'd been together last time.

That fact kept circling through his head. He'd loved her, and she'd never seen him as anything more than a—what? He didn't even pretend to know.

He wasn't sure how long he stood in the church lobby before he dragged a resigned hand through his hair and shuffled out the door and across the parking lot to his house.

But he didn't know what to do there. He tried watching TV, but everything he turned on annoyed him. He picked up a book, but after he'd reread the same page half a dozen times, he set it down. He was getting up to change into running clothes when the doorbell rang.

His stupid heart jumped, but he thrust his hope aside.

There was nothing to hope for now, even if it did happen to be Jade at the door.

"Hey, bro." Leah opened the door before he'd reached it. "Just stopped by to— What's wrong with you?"

"Nothing's wrong with me." Leave it to Leah to sour his mood even more.

"Yeah. That's why you look like you did when Patches ran away."

Dan rolled his eyes. He'd give anything to have his biggest problem right now be a runaway cat.

"What do you want, Leah?" He dropped into the worn chair he'd picked up from Goodwill when he'd first moved in, suddenly sapped of all energy.

"I brought some leftovers from a birthday party I catered, in case you're hungry."

"I'm not." The thought of food made bile rise in his throat.

"It can be your dinner then."

He heard her walk into the kitchen and open the refrigerator, but he didn't follow. Instead, he leaned his head back and closed his eyes. He didn't open them when the couch across from him creaked with the sound of her settling into it.

"So how long are you planning to mope around before you come to your senses?" Leah's voice was lighthearted, but he heard the rebuke in it.

"I'm not moping."

"Look, I know you're hurting." Leah's voice was uncharacteristically gentle, the voice she used with her friends, not her brother. "But did you ever think that maybe she's hurting too?"

Dan ignored the gut punch of her words. He knew Jade was hurting. And not only because of the unplanned pregnancy. She was hurting because of him. But he didn't know what he was supposed to do about it.

He cracked an eye open. "I thought you didn't like Jade."

Leah sighed. "It's not that I don't like her. I just didn't want to see you get hurt."

"Well, I did get hurt. So I guess you were right."

"And, what? You want to hurt her back?"

"No." He opened his eyes and stood to pace the room. He didn't want to hurt her. But he also didn't know if he could get over the way she'd hurt him.

"Then stop acting like a spoiled little boy and forgive her. Work things out."

He stared at his sister. Did she really think it worked like that? "It's not that easy."

"Why not? Do you love her?"

He threw his hands in the air. "She's having another man's baby." He practically shouted the words at his sister. How was she not getting this?

"And?" Leah blinked at him way too calmly.

"And she doesn't know whose it is. Probably some jerk who only wanted to use her." His hands tightened into fists. "Why does she always choose guys like that?"

"She also chose you, Dan." Leah folded her feet under her on the couch. "Twice."

But Dan gave his head a vigorous shake. "No, she didn't. I was just a distraction until another jerk came along."

"Or maybe—" Leah speared him with an intense look. "You were her lifeline and she lost her grip. Don't push her farther away, Dan. Swim out and save her."

Dan shook his head at his sister. Hadn't Jade proven more than once that she didn't want to be saved?

"She told me she was pregnant when she left, Leah. When we were together. She was pregnant with some other guy's baby then too." He could barely say the rest—barely believe it. "She had an abortion."

His sister's expression didn't change. "So, two strikes and she's out? How many times has God pursued you when you've messed up? Or me?"

Dan looked away, his jaw working. He'd seen the remorse in Jade's eyes. The shame. The fear. But instead of reassuring her of God's forgiveness, he'd beaten her down further, heaped more shame and guilt on her instead of loving her.

He groaned long and low. He hated when his sister was right.

"Anyway—" Leah uncurled from the couch and stood. "What are you going to do? Pretend you never knew her?"

He shrugged. "She'll live her life, and I'll live mine. Just like we did before. Everything will be fine."

Except it wouldn't be. He knew already that his life would never be fine without Jade in it.

Leah opened the front door. "You know I'm perfectly content being single. But if someone were to come along who was as perfect for me as Jade obviously is for you, I'd like to think I'd be smart enough not to throw it away."

She stepped outside and closed the door behind her, leaving Dan staring at the wood grain.

She couldn't be serious when she said Jade was perfect for him. Jade was nothing like what he'd envisioned in a wife and ministry partner.

She was still young in her faith, she was impulsive, she didn't know the first thing about church procedures.

But she was also eager to learn and quick to jump in and help, and she was great with the kids. She'd be great with her kid too—Dan knew that.

He let out a ragged breath and strode to his Star Wars room. There, he opened the bottom drawer of a filing cabinet and grabbed a tattered shoe box. Dropping to the floor, he lifted the lid off.

There was the hyacinth they'd picked on the dunes. And an almost perfectly intact shell. There were wrinkled papers too—notes Jade had passed him during chemistry class.

He lifted them out and sorted through them. Someday maybe he'd be brave enough to reread everything. But for now, he needed to be reminded of how she'd left last time—of why he was doing the right thing in not being with her now.

Finally, he came to the short note.

The last one he'd ever gotten from her.

He closed his eyes for a second, then made himself read it.

I'm sorry, Dan. If I loved you less, I'd stay. But I can't do that to you. Forget about me and live the life you were made for. I'd only get in your way. Love, Jade

Dan looked up from the note, his eyes falling on the Luke Skywalker figure Jade had been standing here holding just a couple months ago.

This note was the only time she'd ever said she loved him, but he'd completely disregarded it. If she'd loved him, she would have stayed.

But rereading the note now, Dan saw it. She'd left to protect him. She'd known being associated with a pregnant girlfriend would keep him from doing the things he wanted to do, even if the baby wasn't his. She hadn't wanted him to know how she'd failed—hadn't wanted him to have any part of her decision regarding the baby.

An overwhelming sadness rolled over Dan that he hadn't been there for her. Then or now.

She'd distanced herself from him the moment she'd learned she was pregnant this time. And he'd let her.

He hadn't done anything to support her or love her through this.

She'd been trying to protect him. But it turned out that she was the one who needed protection—from him and his judgment.

But that was going to change.

Right now.

He jumped to his feet and jogged out of the house and back toward his office.

He had a sermon to rewrite before Sunday.

Chapter 41

"Come on, it's starting." Vi hurried Jade toward the steps that led down to the beach.

Today was the annual outdoor church service. It was the one service Jade had always loved, even as a kid.

But she preferred to get to church late these days. That way, there was no danger she'd run into Dan. It was the same reason she made her escape before the final prayer each week.

At first, she'd considered giving up going to church completely. But her tender faith was the only thing getting her through right now, and she wasn't willing to give up the opportunity to have it nourished. Whatever had happened between them, she still appreciated the way Dan shared God's Word. Lately, it seemed that each of his messages contained some truth she desperately needed to hear—which she chose to believe was a coincidence.

She kept her head down as she followed Vi onto the beach to the spot where rows of white folding chairs had been set up. Nate and his worship band were finishing the final verse of the first song as Jade and Violet slid into two empty seats at the back.

As Dan stood to deliver the day's readings, Jade couldn't look away. His eyes looked tired, as if he hadn't been getting enough sleep, but he had the same energy about him that he had every time he was in front of the congregation.

For a second, she let herself wonder what it would be like to serve with him in his ministry. Never in her wildest dreams would she have thought that would be something she'd enjoy. But helping with camp and VBS had given her a different perspective. And much as she'd been afraid to recognize it, Dan might have been right about her gift in working with children. She'd loved every moment of it.

She pressed a hand to the bump in her belly. Hopefully her gift in working with other people's children would extend to raising her own child. The prospect terrified her. She had no idea how she was going to do this alone.

Some nights, when she was so tired she could barely move, she let herself imagine a world in which she and Dan were married, and the child inside her was his and they raised it together.

She shook off the thought and tried to concentrate on the service as Dan stood to deliver his sermon.

"Today's message is from the book of John. Here we read about a woman caught in adultery." As Dan read the verses that described how the law declared the woman should be stoned for her sin, a high-pitched humming started in Jade's ears. She knew he was angry with her, knew he would never forgive her, but did he have to preach a sermon directed specifically at her? In front of all these people?

With her baby bump starting to show, it wouldn't take anyone much guesswork to figure out who he was talking about–if there was even anyone left in this town who didn't already know how she had messed up. Again.

She eyed the chairs between her and the end of the row. She could probably get over there without stepping on too many people's feet.

She shifted and started to stand, but Vi's hand landed on her leg and pressed gently. "Just listen," she mouthed.

Jade stared at her. She wanted Jade to listen to Dan reminding her of what a vile sinner she was? She already knew that. But she lowered herself back to her seat just as Dan was closing his Bible.

His eyes scanned the entire congregation. When they met hers, she felt the sear of the connection, but she didn't look away.

If he had something he wanted to say to her in front of all these people, he could go ahead and say it. It wasn't like the weight of guilt pressing her down could get any heavier than it already was.

"Do you ever read that story and wish the people had thrown their stones?" Dan bent and inspected the beach, then stood, holding up a fist-sized stone. "After all, she deserved it, didn't she?"

He tossed the stone from hand to hand and took a step toward the chairs. "You know that woman caught in adultery? She's here."

Jade flinched. He wouldn't really call her out in front of the whole church, would he? He was too kind, too decent for that. Then again, she'd hurt him pretty badly. That could change a person.

"So what should we do? Should we grab our stones?" He held the stone up again but then lifted a finger. "Before you decide, let me tell you about this woman. She's lied, she's cheated, she's lusted after things that weren't hers, she's hated, she's put anything and everything else before God." He paused, giving them time to absorb the list of her sins. "And do you want to know her name?"

Every instinct told Jade to run before he said her name. But she couldn't move.

"Her name is *you*." But Dan wasn't looking at Jade. His eyes were roaming over the entire congregation again. "Her name is *me*." He pressed a hand to his chest. "We are all that woman caught in adultery. We've all been caught cheating on the One who loves us more than we can comprehend. Every time we sin, every time we choose our way over God's way, every time we put something before him, we're committing adultery against our God. We deserve to be stoned. Worse, we deserve hell." He only hesitated for a second before continuing. "But—"

Jade's pulse quickened, and she leaned forward in her seat. She needed to hear that *but*.

"But listen to what Jesus says to the woman: 'Neither do I condemn you.' Do you hear that? He's saying that to you. To me. He does not condemn us. He frees us. He saves us." He held the rock up, then opened his hand and let it fall to the sand. "Those stones that were poised to be thrown at us? They're on the ground now. And that's where they'll stay. No one can throw them at us. Ever again. Our guilt is gone. We are washed clean in Christ's blood."

Jade let out a breath she hadn't realized she'd been holding. Those words sounded too good to be true. And yet, she knew in her heart that they were true. And that they were for her.

But Dan was still talking, and she didn't want to miss a word of this beautiful message. "When Jesus died for us, he freed us from our sin. He told the woman, 'Go and sin no more.' He didn't mean she had to go show him how good she could be. She didn't have to change to earn his love. It was never about change. It was never about her at all. It was about what Christ had done for her." His eyes landed on Jade, and he held her gaze. "He loved her no matter what. Loved her enough to die for her sins." He paused, his eyes still locked on hers, as she soaked in what he was saying. What it meant for her.

Finally, he pulled his eyes away and let them scan the congregation. "He meant that she wasn't a slave to her sin anymore. She was free to live for him, out of love for him. And so are we. Every one of us. It doesn't matter what you've done. You are forgiven, and you are given the power to live for God. Every last sin is erased. You are a new creation."

Jade's heart had climbed up past her chest, past her throat, and was beating so wildly to get out that she had to leave before she erupted in full-out sobs. It was too much, knowing that she was forgiven. Knowing that she was a new creation in Christ. That her past was erased.

This time when she stood, Vi didn't stop her.

She made it to the car before she collapsed into a sobbing heap.

She was free. She was finally free.

"Thank you, Jesus," she whispered into the empty vehicle.

Dan forced himself to loosen his grip on the hyacinths before he crushed them. He'd seen the look on Jade's face when she'd run out of church this morning, and he'd wanted to follow her so badly he'd almost lost his place in the service.

He could tell the sermon had touched her, but he'd written it for himself. He'd learned in seminary that he should preach to himself first of all, and he'd definitely needed to remind himself of God's forgiveness, of the Savior's refusal to condemn those who believe in him.

All this time, he'd been condemning Jade, but he was just as guilty a sinner as she was.

He'd been so busy worrying about what people would think of him if he was with her that he'd never considered what she was going through. Never paused to tell her she was forgiven, not only by him but by God.

But that was going to change. From now on, he was going to do everything he could to show her how much he loved her. Starting with these flowers and the scavenger hunt he'd spent all afternoon setting up. If everything went well, they'd end up at his house, where Leah would be waiting with a gourmet meal—and where dessert would be served with the infinity necklace he'd bought her.

He parked his car and ran up the steps to Violet's apartment.

Violet's smile as she opened the door and saw him standing with the flowers bolstered his confidence. Surely, this would be enough to show Jade how he felt. And if it wasn't, he'd come up with an even bigger gesture. And a bigger one after that if need be.

"I'm so glad you haven't given up," Violet whispered, stepping aside so he could come in.

Jade was sitting on the couch, reading a book, but the moment her eyes fell on him, she snapped it shut and pushed to her feet.

"I'll give you two a minute." Violet slipped out the door as Dan entered the room.

"That's all right, we don't need—" Jade started, but Violet had already disappeared into Nate's apartment across the hall.

Dan held the bouquet out to Jade, but she didn't take it.

"What's this for, Dan?"

"For you." He shook the flowers a little, but she crossed her arms in front of her, so that they rested on her baby bump.

This was going to be harder than he thought. But she was worth any effort.

"I was hoping you'd give me another chance. I have a whole scavenger hunt set up—" He passed her the first clue, which she didn't bother to read.

"You made your feelings about me clear when you found out I was pregnant." Jade's brow lowered.

Dan set the flowers on the table and took a step closer to her, but when he reached for her, she flinched.

He stuck his hands in his pockets. "I know. And I'm so sorry for that. I was wrong. That's what the flowers and the scavenger hunt are for. To show you . . ." He trailed off. He could hear how lame he sounded. He'd completely written her off, abandoned her, and he thought a little scavenger hunt was going to make up for that?

"I should have been there for you." His voice was quiet, and he couldn't look at her. "And I wasn't. And I'm so sorry for that. I hope you can forgive me someday."

He turned to the door, leaving the flowers on the table without water.

Chapter 42

"No peeking." Jade felt like Santa, the Easter bunny, and the tooth fairy all rolled into one as she led Vi and Nate up the walk to the front door of their house.

She and Grace had finished the painting yesterday, just in time for Vi and Nate to come home to it tomorrow night after their wedding.

"You can look!" She nearly jumped up and down at the shocked expressions on their faces.

"What—" Vi wandered from the living room to the kitchen, her mouth hanging open. "Where'd all the wallpaper go?"

"Do you like it?" Jade fought back the sudden fear that maybe she'd miscalculated. Maybe Vi had wanted to do this on her own.

"Are you kidding? It's perfect." Vi spun slowly, as if taking everything in.

"You did this?" Her sister was staring at her as if she didn't recognize her.

"No. I mean, yes. I mean, we all did it. Ethan and Ariana and Peyton and Jared and Tyler and Sophie and Spencer and Emma and Grace and Leah and—Dan." She tried not to hesitate before the last name but didn't quite succeed.

She pushed on, so she wouldn't dwell on it. "I hope the colors are okay. They were inspired by that pillow." She pointed to a gray-blue pillow she'd found in Vi's store right after she'd come home.

Or, rather, right after she'd come back to Hope Springs. She had to stop thinking of it as home. LA was home. And she'd be going back in two days.

"This is amazing, Jade. Thank you." Nate's voice was full of emotion as he pulled her into a hug. "I'm not sure what I did to deserve another awesome sister, but I'm glad I did it."

"You take care of my big sister, and we'll call it even." She hugged him back.

"That's the plan." Nate let go of her and smiled at his bride. "Forever."

Jade blinked and looked away. What would it be like to have someone who was willing to love her—faults and all—forever?

Vi crossed the room to hug her too. When she pulled away, she and Nate exchanged a significant look.

"What?" Jade swiveled from one to the other. Were they going to tell her they hated the paint colors after all?

"We were talking, and we'd like you to move in here with us." Vi's smile was wide but tentative. "After the wedding."

Jade stared at her sister. She couldn't be serious.

"You guys are newlyweds as of tomorrow. You don't want me around. Especially not with a baby that's going to disturb you at all hours of the day and night."

"We do want you here. Along with our little niece or nephew." Vi touched Jade's belly.

Jade sighed. They might think they wanted her here, but they'd forgotten about one little detail. "I'm an unwed mother. Wouldn't you be embarrassed to have me here?" She kept her eyes on her belly as she said it.

Vi rested a hand on her shoulder. "That's the amazing thing about God's grace. He can take even our weaknesses and our sins and use them for his purposes. The baby inside you is a blessing. And he or she is a blessing we want to know and spoil."

Jade laughed and swiped at her teary eyes. How had she taken her sister's love for granted for so long?

"Please," Vi pleaded. "It would be the best wedding present in the world."

"Better than house painting?" Jade raised an eyebrow.

"Better than anything." Vi grabbed her hand. "Please at least think about it. I feel like I'm getting a second chance at a family. And I want you to be part of it."

Jade opened her mouth to promise she'd call weekly, but Vi beat her to it. "I want you *here*, Jade. With us. A real family."

Jade turned to Nate. "And you're on board with this? Living with your sister-in-law?"

Nate grinned at her. "I'm afraid so. Can't use me as your excuse."

Jade wavered. She'd been trying to mentally prepare herself for returning to LA for weeks now. But she couldn't deny the hope that filled her at the thought of staying.

Sure, it'd be awkward seeing Dan on a regular basis. But so far, she'd been mostly able to avoid him, and eventually, she'd get over him completely.

Wouldn't she?

She looked from Nate to Vi one more time. Both were watching her expectantly.

"I'll think about it," she promised. Before she could warn them not to get their hopes up, they'd both engulfed her in a group hug.

Chapter 43

"You are the most beautiful bride there has ever been." Jade couldn't get over how amazing Vi looked in her wedding dress, with its delicate beadwork and slight flair.

"You could light up the room with your smile." Nate's sister Kayla maneuvered her wheelchair next to Vi to give her a hug. Jade couldn't have agreed with her more. She and Vi had spent some time at the cemetery this morning, talking about Vi's first husband, Cade, and Jade knew this day was one of mixed emotions for her sister. But now that they were here and she was about to walk down the aisle, Vi was positively radiant.

"What can I say?" Vi's smile grew even larger. "God is good."

Jade nodded. She hadn't thought so a few months ago, but now she saw it in every part of her life. She slid a hand over the seafoam green bridesmaid dress that had been let out to make room for her belly.

"I think we're ready." Sophie passed them their bouquets. Vi had asked each of her bridesmaids to choose their favorite flowers months ago. Which meant Jade was now holding a bouquet of hyacinths that looked a little too much like the bouquet Dan had brought her last week—the one she'd tossed in the trash.

She'd been so tempted to accept them and fall into his arms. But they'd tried too many times already. Clearly, they weren't meant to be together.

There was a knock on the door of the church conference room they'd been using as a makeshift dressing room, and all four women turned toward it expectantly. Jade was closest, so she opened the door.

Then she froze, her limbs going numb.

On the other side of the door, Dan seemed to be frozen in place as well.

He recovered first. Looking past her, he sought out Vi. "We'll be ready for the processional in five minutes. Nate is waiting upstairs."

Violet gave her dress one last check, then squeezed past Jade out the door. Nate had been teaching her to play piano, and the two of them were going to play a duet of Canon in D as the bridesmaids walked down the aisle, before taking their own positions at the front of the church.

"We'd better get lined up then." Sophie passed through the door too, followed by Kayla.

Still, Jade's legs wouldn't move.

"Can we talk for a second?" Dan stepped into the room, and Jade's legs finally came unstuck as she moved to open up more space between them.

"I just wanted to tell you—" Dan's Adam's apple bobbed. "It doesn't matter to me what you did in the past. In high school. That you cheated on me—"

"I didn't cheat on you." She hadn't been planning to tell him what really happened, but it suddenly seemed important that he know.

He tugged on his tie. "Yeah. I guess you can't cheat on someone you're not really with."

"No, Dan." She moved close enough to touch his arm, ignoring the sizzle that went through her fingertips. "I mean, I didn't cheat on you. At least not the way you think I did. I considered you my boyfriend. We were together, and it was the best thing that had ever happened to me. But after my mom died, I got kind of messed up. I didn't want you to see me like that, so I started hanging out with my other so-called friends. One night, I went to a party with them. I was only going to stay a few minutes." She closed her eyes. That one decision had changed the entire trajectory of her life. "But they offered me a beer. I didn't want it, but I figured they'd get off my back if I drank it. So I did. And then they convinced me to do a few shots. Before I knew it, I was drunk."

The look in Dan's eyes—she couldn't place it. Was it worry, anger, fear?

She had to tell him the rest before she lost her courage. "Brett was there. You remember him?"

Dan's nod was short, and his jaw twitched.

"He started talking about how we should get back together. I told him I was with someone else now, but I wouldn't tell him who because I was afraid of what he'd do to you."

"Jade, you didn't—"

She lifted her hand. She had to get through this next part. The part she had never told anyone. "He kissed me and pulled me into a closet. I tried to tell him no, but I was too drunk to put up much resistance." She shuddered. "I stopped fighting, telling myself it was no big deal." She dropped her head. "I never wanted you to know. But now you do."

She watched his feet. They remained planted for two seconds, then closed the space between them. Before she could look up, he'd pulled her tight against him. His palms pressed into her back, and her arms went up to wrap around him.

"I'm so sorry," he murmured into her hair. "If I'd known—" She heard him swallow.

"I should have told you," she whispered. "I shouldn't have left without telling you."

Dan drew in a breath, as if preparing to speak, but the door to the conference room banged open.

"Oh. Sorry." Sophie grinned at the two of them. "But it's kind of tough to have a wedding without the maid of honor and the pastor."

"Coming." Dan gave Jade one last long look. "Talk later?"

She nodded and followed him out the door. Her feelings were completely jumbled right now. But one thing she knew. No matter what happened next, she was glad she'd told him.

Chapter 44

"Could I have this dance?" Dan held out a hand to Jade, nerves winging through his stomach as if he were a gangly teenager again.

Jade shook her head but offered him a smile filled with regret. "What would people think?"

But he was done letting the fear of what people would think keep him from being with her. "That I'm with the most beautiful woman in the room." It wasn't just a line, either. Jade looked stunning in her bridesmaid's dress, which set off the glow of her skin. Her hair was swept up, revealing her perfectly curved shoulders.

He thrust his hand closer to her, but she didn't move.

"Fine. Have it your way. But just remember you brought this on yourself." He trotted up to the stage, where members of Nate's band were providing the evening's music. Fortunately, he knew them all well.

"Hey, Aaron. Can I borrow the mic for a second?" he called as the group finished their song.

"Sure thing, Pastor." Aaron passed him the mic.

"Excuse me." Dan spoke to the crowd without hesitation. One of the perks of being a pastor—standing in front of all those people didn't make him nervous. There was only one person whose reaction he cared about—and he wasn't at all sure what it would be.

As he waited for the room to quiet, he caught Violet's eye, hoping she'd understand why he was crashing her wedding dance, but she gave him a thumbs up.

"First, congratulations to Nate and Violet. I know we are all so happy for them and pray for God's blessings on their marriage." He waited for the applause to slow. "And second, I need your help. There's a young woman here I'd very much like to dance with, but she's a little shy. Could you all help me encourage Miss Jade Falter to give me this dance?" He held his hands up and started clapping, grinning as the wedding guests began to clap along.

At her table, Jade covered her mouth with her hands but not before he saw the smile starting there. He crossed the room, holding his hand out to her as the band played a slow, sweet melody. The crowd continued to applaud, and someone yelled, "Dance with him already."

Dan laughed, but his eyes met Jade's. "I don't think they're going to give up. And neither am I."

Not taking her eyes off him, Jade stood slowly and put her hand in his. He finally breathed out, as the crowd broke into cheers.

"Thank you," he leaned over to whisper in her ear.

"Well, you didn't leave me much choice." But she smiled as he wrapped his arms around her waist and her hands came up to his shoulders. He pulled her in closer, suddenly unable to say all the things he'd been planning to say. Right now, all he could think of was holding her. He prayed this wouldn't be the last time he'd ever have his arms around her, but if it was, he didn't want to forget a moment of it.

Too soon, the song ended, and Jade gently untangled herself from his grasp.

"Thank you." Her voice was full, and he wondered if she was overcome with as much emotion as he was.

He grabbed her hand. "Talk outside?"

She nodded and let him lead her.

But before they reached the doors, Terrence Malone stepped in front of them. Dan tried not to groan at the sight of the church president.

"I won't keep you." Terrence nodded a greeting to Jade, who offered a gracious smile that Dan could have kissed her for. "I just wanted to say that I enjoyed your wedding message today. Your father spoke on that First Corinthians text often, but you brought out some things that I'd never picked up on before." Terrence winked. "Your father would have been proud."

Dan cleared his throat at the unexpected compliment. "Thank you."

Terrence clapped him on the back, then gestured for them to continue out the doors.

The night was cool and damp, and Jade shivered as they stepped into the garden behind the ballroom. Dan slipped off his suit coat and draped it over her shoulders, then wrapped an arm around her. They made their way through the gardens, the fragrant scent of the flowers enveloping them, and he was afraid to break the silence.

When they came to a small stone bench, he gestured to it, and Jade sat. He lowered himself next to her.

"I screwed up." No point in denying it. He'd messed up big time. "I thought I could make it up to you with flowers and grand gestures." He turned his body toward her and took her hands in his. "But what you needed was my constancy. My promise not to give up on you or turn away from you no matter what. If you let me, I'm ready to give you that. To give you me. If you can forgive me."

Jade's smile was edged with both joy and sorrow. "I forgive you, Dan."

A thousand fireworks burst in Dan's heart. Asking for her forgiveness had been a long shot, but she'd given it so willingly. Hope infused him with new courage. He didn't want to spend another moment without her.

"So, what are you doing tomorrow?"

She looked at him in surprise. "I'm moving, actually."

All the hope that had filled him burst, leaving him as flat as a balloon that had been filled too full and then popped.

He slid as close to her as he could, his knees pressed against hers, and tightened his grip on her hands. She couldn't go. Not when they finally had their second chance. "Please don't go back to LA. I know I messed things up, big time. I let my own petty concerns get in the way, and I shunned you when I should have been holding you close and protecting you, and I'm so sorry."

"Dan, I—"

But he pressed a finger to her lips. "I have to say this, Jade. I should have said it sooner, I know I should have. But I'm saying it now. I love you."

Tears sprang to her eyes, and she opened her mouth, but he had to keep talking. If he let her get a word in, he was afraid it would be to tell him it didn't matter. To tell him she was leaving and would never be back.

"I've loved you since that first day when you told me to ask you out. And I admit that sometimes you confuse me and sometimes I don't know what you're thinking. But I want to figure it out. I want to understand everything about you. And even when I don't understand you, I still love you."

"Dan—"

He cradled her hands against his heart. "The thought of you disappearing and going back to California and living a life that's completely separate from mine—that scares me more than anything. The thought of losing you keeps me up at night. I want you to stay, Jade. I want you to stay and be with me."

He drew in a breath. What else could he say to show her the depth of his feelings for her?

Jade pressed her fingers to his lips. "Dan."

The way she said his name made him stop.

She slid her hand to his cheek. "I'm not leaving. I'm moving in with Vi and Nate. Into their house. They asked me to stay, and I said yes."

Dan stared at her, trying to comprehend what she was saying. "You're not going back to California?"

Her head shake was the most wonderful thing he'd ever seen.

"I belong here," she said. "Hope Springs is home. It's where I want to raise my baby."

"That's—" He wrapped his arms around her shoulders, pulling her close enough that he could feel her breath on his face. "That's good news."

He swallowed down the emotion that had blocked his throat.

But Jade pulled back a fraction, her eyes darkening. "We can't, Dan. It doesn't make sense, you and me."

"Us." He laid a palm against her cheek.

"There is no us," she murmured.

"There's always been an us, Jade. It just took us a long time to realize it. But now that we've found it, I'm not letting it go." He was determined. Nothing was going to change his mind.

"But people will think—"

"I don't care what people think."

Before she could come up with another argument, he slid his arms around her. When she lifted her face, he lowered his lips to hers.

This was right. He could feel it with every fiber of his being. Everything they'd been through had been leading them to this moment.

211

The kiss ended much too soon for his taste, leaving both of them breathless.

"Now—" Dan wrapped a strand of hair that had fallen from her updo around his finger. "Do you have anything else to say?"

"Yes."

Dan shifted his eyes to hers, half afraid she'd come up with another argument for why they couldn't be together.

But she smiled and brushed a kiss over his lips. "I love you too."

Epilogue

"Dan, say something."

Dan shook himself. He'd been staring at Jade, but he couldn't help it. She'd completely taken his breath away the moment he'd opened his front door. She was due in two weeks, and her belly protruded adorably from her small frame. But it was her eyes that had captivated him. Every day they got brighter, more joyous.

"Sorry." He leaned down to give her a deep kiss, savoring the warmth of her lips against his. "Come in."

"Have you been outside today? It's beautiful." Jade took off the light sweater she'd been wearing over her flowery maternity shirt. "I don't think there's a single flake of snow left on the ground. And it's only March first. That has to be a new record. Which is a relief because I don't want to deliver this baby in a snowstorm." She pressed her hands to her swollen belly.

Dan covered her hands with his. "And how's our little one today?"

"Busy." Jade rubbed at her tummy. "I feel like an inside out drum. Which made it extremely difficult to concentrate at school today. I'm pretty sure I bombed my philosophy of education test."

Dan dropped a kiss on her nose. "I'm sure you didn't." He'd helped her study for the test yesterday, and she'd known every single question he'd asked. Ever since she'd started working toward her teaching degree, he'd sensed a new purpose in her.

"What's that delicious smell?" Jade raised her nose to the air and sniffed.

Dan had to laugh. If this were a cartoon, she'd be following those little squiggly scent lines to the kitchen.

He took her elbow and led her toward the dining room table.

"Dan!" Jade's gasp made him smile. It was exactly what he'd been hoping for. "I thought we were ordering pizza."

He shrugged as if it had been no big deal. "You deserve something a bit more special than pizza." He dropped a kiss on the top of her head and pulled out a chair for her.

Jade eyed the spaghetti carbonara and garlic bread, then narrowed her eyes at him. "Did Leah bring this over?"

He pressed his hands to his heart. "I'm hurt." But he couldn't carry it off. "Fine, she brought over the pasta. But I made the bread. From scratch."

Jade whistled. "Wow. I'm impressed."

"Maybe you should wait until after you've tasted it to decide that." But inside he was glowing. He wanted everything about this night to be absolutely perfect.

He sat across the table from Jade, and they both folded their hands.

But before Dan could start the prayer, Jade cut in. "Would you mind if I pray tonight?"

He lifted his head in surprise. She'd grown so much in her faith over the past months that he was astounded. It'd been almost like watching a seed sprout and flower into a full-fledged plant. She'd even started attending a women's Bible study, and the two of them had been reading the Bible together whenever they had a chance. But she'd never volunteered to pray out loud with him before.

He had to clear his throat to swallow the emotion. If that wasn't a sign that tonight was the night, he didn't know what was. "Of course."

Jade gave him a hesitant smile, then closed her eyes and bowed her head. He followed suit.

"Heavenly Father," Jade began. "Thank you that we can call you that. Thank you that we can come to you with all our hurts, all our joys, all our needs. Tonight, Lord, I want to praise you for what you have done in my life. I was broken, Lord, you know that. I thought I was beyond repair. But you didn't. You put people in my life to show me your love. It wasn't always easy, and they probably should have given up on me long ago, but they didn't. Thank you for Dan, who has made me happier than I have any right to be. And thank you that you have taken even my worst sins and you have worked them for good. Thank you for the new life growing inside me. Please help me to be the mother this child needs and to dedicate my life to raising him or her in you. Amen."

Dan lifted his head and met her eyes. The joy in them was brighter than ever.

"That was—" He had to stop to swallow. "That was perfect."

She smiled as he passed her the bread. He would do anything to keep that joy on her face forever.

As they ate, he grew more and more certain.

He'd considered waiting until after the baby was born, to give her time to settle in and get used to being a mother before he asked her to become a wife too.

But he couldn't wait even a day longer. He had to tell her how he felt.

Now.

Tonight.

As soon as the dishes were cleared, he ducked into his bedroom and grabbed the tiny box he'd bought weeks ago. He tucked it into his pocket as he stepped into the living room, where Jade was sprawled in his chair, her feet up on the oversize ottoman.

He paused, soaking up her presence in his house. This is where he wanted her to be always.

But maybe it wasn't the right place for a proposal. "You want to go for a walk on the beach?"

"Sure." She held out her hands, and he tugged her up off the chair. "I'll be glad when it doesn't take a team to get me off the furniture anymore."

"Yeah."

She gave him an odd look. "Are you okay? You look kind of pale and sweaty all of a sudden."

"Yeah," he croaked again. The enormity of what he was about to do had just hit him. He wasn't afraid of the commitment he was about to make—he'd already made that in his heart long ago. But what if she said no? What if she couldn't bring herself to marry him and share in his life in the ministry? Although most people at church seemed to accept that he was with her, he knew there were still plenty who didn't. And while that truly didn't matter to him anymore, what if she thought she'd be protecting him by pushing him away again?

Forcing the worries aside, he led her across the lawn that separated his yard from the church and down the stairs toward the beach.

He had to trust this was in God's hands.

"You're sure you're okay?" Jade was a step in front of him, and she turned to look him up and down, concern pulling at her forehead. "You're so quiet."

"Sorry." He leaned forward to press a kiss onto her hair. "Just thinking."

"About what?" She smoothed a hand against his cheek, and he smiled and gestured for her to continue down the steps.

Much as he was bursting to drop to one knee right here and now, he wanted to wait until they'd reached their special spot. "I'll tell you in a minute."

She gave him a curious glance but continued down the steps.

As they walked, he ran through the options in his head. *Will you marry me?* Traditional but straightforward. *Will you be my wife? Will you make me the happiest man in the world? Will you let me love you forever?*

"Oh." Jade drew up short on the bottom step, and he had to stop quickly to keep from running into her. She inhaled sharply and pressed her hands to her stomach.

"What is it?" Every other thought fled as he stepped down next to her and wrapped an arm around her back. "Is it too far? Do you need to sit down?"

She shook her head. "I'm good." She gestured toward her feet. "But I think my water just broke."

Jade was exhausted, sweaty—and happier than she'd ever been in her life.

Her daughter, Hope Elizabeth Falter, was cradled in her arms, sleeping after an amazingly fast delivery. Dan stood next to her bed, leaning over to stroke the soft auburn fuzz on the baby's head. He hadn't left her side once since he'd sped her to the hospital, probably breaking more traffic laws than he'd ever broken in his life in his rush to get her here on time.

In the moments before her water had broken, Jade had sensed something shift in Dan. His sudden quiet, his almost nervous demeanor, had made her start to wonder if he was going to propose on the beach.

Just the thought had sent tingles all the way to her toes.

But now that he saw her here, with another man's baby—a baby who would never look anything like him, who would always be a reminder that she had fallen short—would he change his mind?

Was he secretly glad that her water had broken when it did? Had it saved him from making a terrible mistake?

"Jade." Dan reached for her hand, and she met his eyes.

What she saw there made her breath catch. He hadn't changed his mind about her—if anything his look held more love than ever.

He took something out of his pocket and lowered himself to one knee at the side of the bed.

With a half sob, Jade adjusted Hope in her arms so that she could lean closer to him. She didn't want to miss a single detail of this.

"I am so happy for you. And for little Hope. And I love you both. And I want to be there for both of you. Forever." He cleared his throat, and his eyes reddened. Jade's eyes welled at the emotion in his voice.

"I want to be your husband, and I want to be Hope's father." He opened the box, but Jade couldn't see the ring through the tears coursing down her cheeks. "Will you marry me?"

If she weren't holding the baby, Jade would have jumped out of the bed and flung herself at him. Instead, she let out the sob she'd been holding back, managing to squeeze out a yes around the cries.

In an instant, Dan was on his feet, leaning over to press his lips to hers. His kiss conveyed all the love words couldn't express.

When he finally pulled back, he took the ring out of the box and gently took her left hand, which was still cradled around Hope. Careful not to wake the baby, he slipped the ring onto her finger. Then he kissed his hand and pressed it lightly to Hope's head.

The baby opened her eyes and looked from one to the other of them, as if trying to figure out what all the commotion was about.

"Hope." Jade whispered her baby's name in awe. As unexpected as she'd been, this little blessing had helped her find her true Hope again. "I'd like you to meet your father. We're a family, you and me and him."

Dan leaned closer and kissed first her cheek and then the baby's. "We're an us."

"Yes." Jade snuggled closer to him and hugged Hope tight. "We're an us."

Not Until Christmas Morning

A Hope Springs Novel

Valerie M. Bodden

"Though the mountains be shaken and the hills be removed, yet my unfailing love for you will not be shaken nor my covenant of peace be removed," says the Lord, who has compassion on you.

Isaiah 54:10

Chapter 1

Please ring.

Austin stared down his computer, perched on the scuffed card table in his cramped eat-in kitchen. These moments before his brother was supposed to call were the hardest. The moments when his mind went to all the things that could have happened to keep Chad from calling.

He folded himself into the rickety chair next to the table, sliding his crutches to the floor and pulling up the leg of his sweatpants. It'd been almost a year, but the jolt still went through him every time his eyes met the rounded end of his left leg. Even though he knew intellectually that his foot wasn't there anymore—even though he accepted it to some degree—it was still surreal every time he saw the empty space where it should be. He rolled the silicone liner over his residual limb, which ended about eight inches below his knee, then grabbed his prosthetic and slid his stump into it, standing to walk in place until the pin on the end of the liner locked with a series of clicks.

He lowered himself to the chair with a groan, tucking his legs under the table as his computer blasted the sharp alarm he'd set to indicate an incoming video call. As always, the sound set his nerves firing, ramping his heart rate to levels it hadn't achieved since the first days of Ranger training. But he wasn't about to lower the volume, in case he was ever asleep when his brother called. If he ever actually slept, that is.

The moment his brother's face filled the screen, wearing the same goofy grin as always, his heart rate slowed, and he could breathe normally again.

"Hey, man, it's good to see your ugly face." There was a delay between Chad's words and the movement of his mouth, but Austin didn't care. Seeing that his brother was still safe—still whole—was what mattered.

"Likewise." He kept his voice gruff, so his big brother wouldn't know how much he lived for these too infrequent calls. It was the only thing he lived for anymore, really. That and getting in shape to redeploy. No matter what the doctors said.

Only two percent of soldiers with injuries like yours return to the battlefield.

Well, Austin was going to be part of the two percent. There was no other option. No way was he going to leave his brother over there alone.

"How are things?" Austin asked the same question every time they talked.

And every time, Chad repeated the same bogus answer: "It's raining peaches." It had been one of their mother's favorite sayings when they were growing up, and after she'd died, Chad had taken it over as if he'd inherited it the same way he'd inherited her curly hair.

Usually, Austin let him get away with it. When he'd been stationed over there, he hadn't wanted to talk about what was happening with anyone back home either. There was just no way to make them understand.

But this was different. He did understand. He'd been there. He'd lost buddies there. Tanner and—

No. He couldn't go there right now.

Austin squinted at his brother, trying to see what he wasn't saying. "Stop churching it up and give me a straight answer. How many missions are you running? You look tired."

Chad's grin slipped, and he ran a hand over his unshaven cheeks. "You know I can't, Austin. I'm fine. We're all fine. God's got our back."

Austin shoved his chair out and pushed to his feet. Supposedly God had their back last year too. Right up until the moment everything blew to pieces. He'd feel a lot better when he got back over there. Then he could be the one who had everyone's back.

"Austin, don't be like that." Chad's voice followed Austin as he took three steps to cross his kitchen.

"I'm not being like anything," he called over his shoulder, loudly so the computer would pick it up. "I'm hungry."

He yanked the refrigerator door open. But aside from a bottle of mustard and a gallon of milk he was pretty sure was at least three weeks old, it was empty.

"Did you go grocery shopping? Got something in there for a change?" Chad's voice carried across the small room, a rough mix of reprimand and concern.

Austin slammed the fridge door shut with a growl, then stood with his head braced against it, the stainless steel cooling his overheated skin.

"Austin—" Chad's voice was gentler now, laced with big-brother authority. "You can't keep living like this, man. Something has to change."

"Yeah." Austin nodded with his head still against the fridge. "I have to get back there."

"No." Chad's voice was firm, and Austin jerked toward the computer screen. His brother's face was grim.

"What do you mean, no?" The snap of his words carried across the room, bouncing off the walls.

Chad had never been anything but supportive of Austin recovering and redeploying. So what was he saying now?

"Maybe you'll get back here, Austin, maybe you won't. But either way, you have to learn to live with it."

"I *am* living with it."

"Yeah? When's the last time you left your apartment or ate anything besides takeout or went on a date or even talked to another human being?"

Austin opened his mouth to respond, but Chad jumped in. "And I don't count."

"I leave my apartment three times a week for physical therapy. I have no interest in dating. I talked to my mailman this morning." He couldn't argue about the takeout, though. Still, three out of four wasn't bad.

"That's not a life, Austin."

He almost argued again. But the little voice in his head that said Chad was right got the better of him. "I know. But what else am I supposed to do?"

"Get out of town for a while. Go somewhere warm. Florida or Hawaii or something. You've got the money from selling Mom's house."

Austin lifted his lip. Go to Hawaii? That was his brother's answer? He had no desire to go to Hawaii.

"Chad, I'm not going—" But he cut off as his eyes fell on the single picture he kept on his refrigerator. A family of four: Mom, Dad, Chad at maybe four years old, and little baby Austin.

He snatched it out from under the magnet and strode to the table, his gait sure despite the uneven floor that often tripped him up. He held the picture in front of the computer's camera.

"Do you remember this?"

Chad squinted, and Austin waited for his delayed answer.

"Yeah. That was right before Dad was called up. I think it's the last picture we have of all four of us together."

Austin pushed aside the familiar stab of jealousy that Chad had four years with their father before Dad was killed in action. Austin had been too young then to remember the man at all.

"What was the name of the town again?"

"Hope Springs? Why?"

Hope Springs. That was right. His parents had grown up there, but after his father's death, Mom had found a job opportunity in Iowa. Every once in a while, she'd tell them a story about the town, though, and to Austin, it had always sounded like the perfect place.

"I'm going to go there." He said it with certainty, as if it were the most logical thing in the world. Even though some part of him knew it was the exact opposite.

"Go where?" Even with the poor video quality, Austin could see Chad's brow wrinkle.

"To Hope Springs." He dropped into the chair next to the card table. "To see where we were born. Where Mom and Dad grew up."

"Okay." Chad dragged the word out, and Austin could tell he was trying to avoid saying a whole lot of other things. "If that's what you want to do. But November in Wisconsin sounds even less pleasant than November in Iowa. I still think somewhere warm and—"

"No." Austin peered at the picture again. This was where he wanted to go. Where he needed to go, even if he didn't know why.

And if he left right now, he could be there before dark.

Chapter 2

L eah had no idea why she'd agreed to this.

Scratch that. She did know. Her sister-in-law could be persuasive, that was why.

She arranged her face into what she hoped was a polite smile as the waiter set a salad in front of her. Across the table, her date—ugh, she hated that word, date, but there was no other word for a man you didn't know sitting across the table from you and trying to make small talk—stabbed a forkful of spinach and brought it to his mouth.

Leah followed suit. At least the food would give her an excuse to stop searching for topics of conversation. So far, they'd tried to talk about his job as an accountant, her catering business, and the Packers. When even the subject of the team's winning streak hadn't been able to sustain a conversation of more than five minutes, Leah had known the date was doomed.

Well, that wasn't true exactly.

She'd known it was doomed from before she got here. Not because there was anything wrong with this guy in particular. She was sure Robert was a perfectly nice man. But she wasn't interested in dating him—or anyone else.

But it seemed that every time she told that to Jade, her sister-in-law simply took it as a challenge. One she seemed determined to win.

No more. After tonight, Leah was putting her foot down. No more setups.

Still, that didn't mean she wanted to be rude to this guy. He was probably just as uncomfortable as she was. As she understood it, he was in one of Jade's classes at the university, where she was studying for her education degree. He'd probably rather be anywhere than here as well.

"So, Jade said you have a daughter?" Leah set down her fork to take a long sip of water. If she'd had her way, she'd be at home in a bubble bath right now, after a long week of catering a corporate retreat. *Later*, she promised herself. Maybe she'd stop at the candle shop on her way home and get something fall-scented—apple cinnamon or pumpkin spice—to add an extra touch of relaxation to her soak.

"I do." Robert set down his fork too. "Savannah."

"That's a pretty name." Leah waited for him to elaborate about his daughter, but when he didn't, she poked at another forkful of salad.

"Thanks." Robert resumed eating as well.

"How old is she?"

"Six."

"Oh." Leah's mind tripped over other possible topics of conversation as she scooped up another bite. Had they talked about the weather yet?

"Did you hear if it was supposed to snow? It feels like it could." If she wasn't afraid he'd think she was rolling her eyes at him, she'd roll them at herself. But it was true. When she'd walked out of the conference center earlier, the air had nipped at her uncovered ears, and low clouds had formed a flat ceiling overhead. It was only early November, but that didn't mean it couldn't happen.

"I hope it doesn't." Robert slid his empty salad plate to the edge of the table. "I hate winter."

Leah almost dropped her fork. The guy hated winter? Her favorite season? Had Jade gotten no info on him before she'd set them up?

"A dusting of snow is just what we need." She kept her voice light. "It will put everyone in the Christmas mood."

Robert drew in a breath to speak, and Leah marveled that she'd finally stumbled on a topic of conversation that lasted more than two sentences. But her phone trilled from her purse on the chair next to her. She reached to grab it as people at the nearby tables swiveled to give her dirty looks. "Sorry, I thought I silenced this."

She slid her finger to dismiss the call, but when she noticed the number, she couldn't help the gasp. She'd assumed it would be months yet before she got this call.

"I'm sorry. I have to take this. I'll be right back." She swiped to answer as she hurried toward the restaurant's doors so she wouldn't disrupt the other diners.

"Hello?" Her greeting came out at the same moment the sharp November air hit her skin, sending prickles up and down her bare arms. She probably should have grabbed her coat, but she didn't care.

"Is this Leah Zelner?" The woman on the other end of the line sounded matter-of-fact and clinical, with no hint of the excitement Leah could feel building in her own belly.

"This is Leah." Her teeth chattered, but she couldn't tell whether it was from the cold or from the possibility that this was really happening.

"Ms. Zelner. This is Jen Peters, a caseworker with Child Welfare Services. I see you have completed your home study and that you received your foster and adoption licensing certificates a couple months ago."

"Yes." She said it louder than she intended, and she imagined the woman on the other end pulling the phone away from her ear.

"And are you still willing to take a placement of an older child?"

Willing? She was more than willing. This was what she was supposed to be doing right now. She just knew it.

But she forced herself to keep her voice calm. "I'm willing."

"I'm glad to hear that. We have a child we'd like to place with you. However—"

"Yes. I'll take him. Or her."

"Slow down." The caseworker cut in. "I appreciate your enthusiasm, but there are some things we need to go over before you agree."

Leah made herself take a breath. She could be professional about this, even if her heart had taken up a giddy two-step. "Of course. I'm sorry."

"First, you should know that Jackson has had some disciplinary issues and has been removed from his last three foster homes because of them."

"Okay." But Leah's heart had latched onto the name—her child's name. Jackson.

"The issues include truancy, fighting at school, fighting with foster siblings, and running away, among others. Do you understand that should you accept this placement, these issues are likely to still be present?"

Leah swallowed. She'd known when she started this process what she was signing up for. Older foster children often came with special challenges. But that was exactly why she wanted to take in an older child. Babies would always find a home, but older children were often forgotten.

But Leah could change that. She could make a difference for them. Change their life.

"I understand," she answered.

"I hope you do." Jen sighed into the phone. "But I'd like to fill you in a little more on his case history. Can you come to the office right now? We have about an hour before Jackson arrives."

An hour?

That was fast. Really fast.

Leah was good at waiting. She'd been prepared for the woman to say they had a child who would need a home in a month or even a week. But right now?

That was nowhere near enough time to get everything ready. Sure, the guest bed was all made up, the dresser was just waiting for a young person to stash their clothes in it, and she'd stocked a bookshelf with some of her childhood favorites. But she'd been picturing how she'd make the child's transition to her home a celebration. She'd prepare a special meal, get a cake from her friend Peyton, and gather all her friends and family to welcome the child. To let the child know that they were going to have more love than they knew what to do with.

"Ms. Zelner? I'm sorry to rush you, but if you can't take Jackson, I'll need to make other arrangements for him."

Leah wrapped her arms around herself. What was she thinking? Was she really going to give up her chance to make a difference in a kid's life because she didn't have time to get a cake?

"Yes, of course, I'm available right now." A thrill zipped up her spine. After months of going through the licensing process and then waiting for a child, she was suddenly going to be a mother. Or, a foster mother, more precisely. But that didn't matter. She'd love the child as her own.

She knew she would.

As she hung up, Leah pulled in a long breath of the sharp air, sending up a quick prayer for wisdom.

"I can do all things through Christ who strengthens me," she reminded herself.

Then she hurried back into the restaurant to grab her purse and jacket and offer a hasty explanation to Robert. She was pretty sure she left him with the impression that she was crazy, but she couldn't worry about that right now.

She sped out of the restaurant and jumped into her car, following the winding streets through downtown Hope Springs toward the Child Welfare office, tucked along a residential street near her church. She hadn't known the office was there until she'd started researching foster care after watching her brother go through the process of adopting his wife's baby. Something in Leah had shifted as she'd seen her younger brother become a dad. She may be content without a husband, but that didn't mean she didn't want a family. And if she could improve the life of a child who might otherwise be without hope in the process, all the better.

As she pulled up to a stop sign, she reached for her phone and dialed Jade. Her sister-in-law answered immediately.

"Why are you calling me while you're on a date?" Jade demanded.

"I'm not on a date, I'm—"

"Leah." Jade's exasperated voice interrupted. "Tell me you did not cancel on poor Robert."

"I didn't cancel. I went, but—"

"You ditched him? That's even worse. Hope, not so loud." In the background, Leah could hear her eight-month-old niece pounding on something—probably one of the toy pots and pans Leah had gotten her.

"I didn't ditch him. I mean, I did, but—"

"Seriously, Leah. Why do you—"

"Jade." Leah raised her voice, and Jade must have sensed the urgency in her tone because she stopped scolding.

"What?"

"Child Welfare called. They need me to come pick up a kid tonight. Right now."

"Oh my goodness. Wow." Jade took a breath. "That's great. Do you want us to come along? Dan is over at church, but I can go get him, and I can rally the others too if you want."

Leah took a second to consider how she wanted this to go. She'd been so sure that a big party was the way to welcome a kid home. But if things had been as rough for Jackson as the caseworker had implied, maybe it'd be better to keep it low-key. "You know what, I think I'll go alone. And then maybe I can introduce him—Jackson—to all of you tomorrow night at dinner."

"Jackson. That sounds exactly like the name I'd picture your kid having." Jade's voice held the smile Leah was sure she was wearing. "Do you want to move dinner here? It's no trouble. I can throw together some pizzas or something."

Leah had to swallow the lump of emotion at Jade's enthusiasm.

"That's okay. I think maybe it will be good to have everyone over to my house. Let Jackson get settled in before I drag him around to everyone else's places."

Jade squealed, then laughed as Hope joined in from the background. "Sorry. I'm just so excited for you. I know how much you've wanted this."

"I have." Leah squealed too as she hung up. *Thank you, Lord, for answered prayers. Please help me be the mother this child needs right now.*

She finished the prayer as she drove into the parking lot of the Child Welfare office. She should be nervous. She should be freaked out. She was about to take responsibility for a child, for goodness' sake.

But she wasn't.

She was absolutely confident this was what she was supposed to be doing. And she was ready for it.

Chapter 3

Two hours later, with Jackson hunched into the passenger seat next to her, Leah was less confident.

If she'd thought making conversation with Robert at dinner was difficult, talking to Jackson was impossible. Every time she asked a question—What do you like to do? What's your favorite food? Do you have any homework tonight?—she was answered with a nearly inaudible grunt.

After what she'd learned from the caseworker, she probably shouldn't be surprised. When he was only six, Jackson's mother had died of an opioid overdose—and he'd been the one to find her. The thought of it twisted Leah's insides into such tight knots that she wasn't sure they'd ever loosen. According to the caseworker, Jackson had been placed with nine different foster families in the past six years, and his last placement had lasted only three weeks. If he weren't in the car with her right now, she'd probably break down into tears over what the poor child had already faced, being passed around as if he were nothing more than a piece of clothing that didn't fit anymore.

But that ended now.

She was going to make things better for him, give him a forever home and a forever family.

"So—" She tried a new conversation. "You'll be able to keep going to Hope Springs Middle School, so that's good." Although she wasn't one hundred percent sure that was true. According to the caseworker, in the three weeks he'd been enrolled at the middle school, Jackson had received four detentions and one in-school suspension.

Another grunt from next to her.

"Anyway—" She kept talking as if he'd answered. "I was thinking, we'll have to figure out what you should call me. I feel like Ms. Zelner is too formal." It's what the caseworker had suggested so that she could establish authority, but Leah hated it.

Jackson turned toward her and opened his mouth. Leah held her breath. Was he actually going to say something?

"How about—" His lips twisted into a smirk as he suggested a curse word that nearly made her gasp out loud.

She blinked and worked to keep her face neutral, telling herself he was only trying to shock her. And he'd done a pretty good job of it.

His satisfied sneer told her she'd utterly failed at hiding her reaction.

She made herself count to ten, then, keeping her voice flat, said, "How about Leah for now? Maybe someday, you'll call me Mom. If you're comfortable."

Jackson stared out the windshield, his face a complete blank.

"Hey." Leah slowed to turn onto her street. "I don't know if the caseworker told you, but my hope is that this will work out and that I'll be able to adopt you eventually." She glanced toward Jackson.

The boy was still staring out the window, but his hands were fisted in his lap, and his jaw was clenched.

"If you want me to," she added.

Jackson's jaw twitched. "You'll get rid of me long before that."

Leah shook her head. It was going to take a long time to get through to this kid. "Of course I won't—"

But she broke off as she pulled into her driveway and her eyes fell on her neighbor's house. Miranda had left for a year-long mission trip a few weeks ago. So why were the lights on in her house? And why was a strange truck parked in the driveway?

She threw her own car into park and opened her door. "Stay here a minute," she ordered Jackson. "I'll be right back."

It didn't occur to her to be scared until she was standing on the porch, hand poised to knock. Then she realized that it could be an intruder in there. Or a squatter.

But she'd promised Miranda she would keep an eye on things.

She gave the door a sharp triple rap, then stood back, glancing over her shoulder to check on Jackson. But he was still sitting in the car's passenger seat, still staring straight ahead.

She turned back to the house. It wasn't a huge place. Surely whoever was in there should have opened the door by now.

She lifted her hand to knock again, but before she could, the clatter of a lock turning had her scrambling backward. She drew in a sharp breath as the door opened, praying she hadn't just made the dumbest mistake of her life.

Beads of sweat prickled Austin's forehead, and he cleared them with a hasty swipe.

It's just someone at the door.

Nothing to get all bent out of shape about. Certainly nothing to send his heart rate ratcheting to pre-mission levels.

Night had fallen since he'd arrived, and he searched the bank of light switches near the door, flipping one after another until he found one that turned on the porch light.

It illuminated a petite blonde woman, arms crossed in front of her, mouth pulled into a frown.

"What are you doing here?" she demanded.

And here Austin had worried the people of Hope Springs would be too friendly for his taste.

"Excuse me?" His voice was hard and unyielding, and the woman took half a step back, her expression a cross between fear and indignation.

Her frown deepened, and she uncrossed her arms to gesture to the doorway he stood in. "This isn't your house. So what are you doing in it?" Her eyes flashed, blue-green swirls snapping at him.

"I'm renting it." Austin chopped each word short. He had no desire to continue this conversation. "I made arrangements with the owner this morning."

"You talked to the owner?" The woman's hands tightened into fists, and Austin smirked. Did she plan to physically remove him from the place?

"Yes." Austin kept his answers as clipped as hers.

"You talked to the owner?" The woman repeated. "In Croatia."

Austin shrugged. This morning he'd been talking to his brother in Afghanistan, so was it really so hard to believe he'd talked to someone in Croatia too? "I don't know where she was. I just know I talked to her."

The woman shook her head. "If Miranda had rented the house out, she would have told me."

Austin grabbed the door, closing it halfway. "I don't know what to tell you. I rented this house, and this is where I'm staying."

The woman's mouth opened wide, and Austin braced himself for whatever she was going to say next, but the sound of a car door closing drew her attention.

"Jackson!" Her shout was loud but uncertain, and Austin peered over her shoulder into the dark.

A car was parked in the driveway next door, and a smallish form trundled away from it. It was tough to tell in the dark, but Austin guessed the kid was about eleven or twelve.

The same age as Isaad.

He shoved the thought aside. Another person he couldn't think about. Isaad. Tanner. The list was too long, his capacity for forgetting too short.

"Jackson, come here." The woman's call was even less certain this time. Again, the kid ignored her, quickening his steps toward the sidewalk.

The woman threw one last look at Austin, then sprinted off his porch.

"Well, if that was all," Austin said wryly as he closed the door, but the woman was already halfway across his yard.

Chapter 4

Where on earth did Jackson think he was going?

Wherever it was, fortunately he didn't seem to be in a hurry, and Leah was able to catch up with him before he'd gotten halfway down the block.

She slowed her sprint to fall into step next to him. Her instinct was to grab his arm and pull him toward her house, but something told her if she did that, the boy would take off. Instead, she walked silently next to him for a few steps.

When he didn't acknowledge her presence, she took a deep breath and tried for a light tone. "Our house is actually the one we parked in the driveway of. So unless you're taking the long way to get inside . . ."

Jackson kept walking, giving no indication he'd heard her.

Apparently she'd have to try a different tactic. She worked to sound stern. "Mind telling me where you're going?"

Jackson didn't look toward her. "Got bored waiting for you to stop talking to your boyfriend. So I decided to go find something to eat."

Leah's back stiffened. "I don't even know that man. I was trying to figure out—" She broke off. This wasn't about her or the man who claimed to be renting her neighbor's house. Which she still had her doubts about. But that would have to wait.

One problem at a time.

"Let's go home, and I'll make us some dinner."

She set a tentative hand on Jackson's arm, wincing at his cold skin. The kid only had on a t-shirt, but when she'd asked at the Child Welfare office if he wanted to put on his coat, he'd shrugged and picked up a duffel bag that looked too light to contain a winter jacket. She made a note to herself to buy one tomorrow.

Jackson pulled out of her grasp but turned around and walked next to her as they retraced their steps to her driveway. She led him up the narrow cobblestone path to the house's small porch.

When she'd unlocked the door, she pushed it open and reached to flip on the lights, then stood aside and gestured for Jackson to enter.

She followed him inside, trying to gauge his reaction from his posture, since she couldn't see his face.

"I can see why you're fostering." Jackson strode through the living room and toward the back of the house. "Where's my room? Or am I sleeping on the floor?"

"I'll show you your room in a second. Why don't you come take your shoes off first?" Leah slid her feet out of her own shoes and tucked them into the front closet. "We keep shoes in here."

Jackson rolled his eyes as he turned back to her and dragged his feet toward the front door.

"What do you mean you can see why I'm fostering?" She kept her gaze on him, though he hadn't looked at her once since they'd met.

Jackson scraped his shoes off without untying them and kicked them into the closet, where they bounced off the wall before landing on top of Leah's favorite work shoes. She resisted the urge to straighten them.

"Obviously you need the money." Jackson gestured at her house, wrinkling his nose as if it were decrepit and falling apart. Which couldn't have been farther from the truth. Her house may not scream luxury, but it was cozy and welcoming.

"Actually, I have a successful catering company." She shrugged off her jacket and hung it in the front closet. "The money I get for fostering is to buy things for you. Like a winter jacket, for starters. Is there anything else you need?"

Jackson turned away from her. "Where's my room?"

Leah swallowed the sigh that almost escaped. Maybe she should have taken Jade up on her offer to get everyone together. This alone time with Jackson wasn't going so well.

But she stepped past him with a smile. "It's this way. I didn't know if I'd be fostering a boy or a girl, so I tried to make it kind of neutral." She stopped at the end of the hallway. "I hope you like it." She stepped aside to reveal the cream colored walls and navy quilt she'd chosen. "There are some books and some art supplies over there. And you can unpack your stuff in the dresser and—"

But Jackson launched his duffel bag across the room, and it hit the far wall with a thud. Before she could react, he'd closed the door in her face. She scrunched her eyes shut, willing the emotion back. So this wasn't going how she'd imagined. That didn't mean she couldn't salvage the night.

"I'll go make us some dinner," she called through the closed door. "I hope you like chicken."

She waited a few seconds, half hoping there would be an answer from the other side of the door but knowing there wouldn't be.

As she shuffled to the kitchen, she pulled out her phone to check the time. It was almost seven o'clock, which meant she'd have to make one of her quicker chicken dishes so she could get Jackson to bed at a reasonable time.

What even was a reasonable time for a twelve-year-old to go to bed?

She was about to Google the question, but an email notification from her neighbor popped onto the screen. She should warn Miranda about the guy next door while she was thinking about it. Find out what her neighbor wanted her to do about it.

But the moment she opened the email, her mouth fell open. Apparently the guy had been telling the truth. Miranda was emailing to let her know she'd rented the house out and not to be alarmed if there was someone staying there.

A little late for that.

She scanned the rest of the email, grimacing at Miranda's PS: *He sounds cute. And he'll be right next door. Just saying.*

Leah clicked the phone off, setting it on the counter harder than she meant to in her exasperation. Would no one ever get it through their heads that she didn't need—or want—to be set up with anyone?

And anyway, the guy next door may have sounded cute from 3,000 miles away. But in person he was rude and stubborn and condescending and . . .

Leah forced herself to stop. It wasn't like she'd exactly been the picture of a warm welcome, yelling at him like that. She rubbed at her temples. At some point, she'd have to apologize.

But for now, she had bigger problems.

Like the preteen boy sulking in his bedroom waiting for some food. She pulled the chicken out of the refrigerator and got to work.

Half an hour later, she knocked on the door of Jackson's room to call him to dinner.

She'd thrown together a quick stir fry, and it smelled so enticing—if she did say so herself—that she was surprised he hadn't come wandering out on his own already.

"What?" Even through the door, the hostility was almost enough to knock Leah back, but she stood her ground.

"Dinner is ready." She infused an extra helping of enthusiasm into the statement as if that could make up for the boy's attitude.

"I'm not hungry."

Leah blew out a quick breath. Heaven help her, she was going to need an extra measure of patience tonight. "You were so hungry you were going in search of something to eat half an hour ago."

"I changed my mind." Jackson's tone crawled with defiance.

"If you're not hungry, you can watch me eat. We sit together at the table for meals in this family." She bit her lip. The truth was, she usually sat wherever she felt like sitting for meals—sometimes at the table but more often on the couch or, on nice summer nights, the deck. Still, it sounded like something a parent would say. And from now on, it's what they would do.

Five seconds went by. Then ten.

Finally, the shuffle of footsteps, faint but definitely there, reached her through the door. A moment later, Jackson emerged, looking as sullen as ever.

"It's a stupid rule," he muttered as he passed her.

She chose not to respond, instead following him to the kitchen and taking out two plates. "Wash your hands please."

Jackson gave her a look but went to the sink and ran his hands under the water. "There." Leah held a towel out to him, but he wiped his hands on his shirt.

She debated with herself for half a second, then put the towel down. Maybe some things weren't worth arguing over.

"Do you like stir fry? It's my favorite." She scooped a generous portion onto her plate, then held the pan toward Jackson.

"I told you I'm not hungry." His eyes darted toward the living room window.

Leah's eyes followed, just in time to see a pizza delivery car backing out of Miranda's driveway—or for now, she supposed, that guy's driveway. She hadn't even gotten his name, she realized with a flash of shame. She usually prided herself on her hospitality.

She set the pan of stir fry down and folded her hands in her lap. "We say grace before we eat."

Jackson looked at her as if she'd grown a pair of horns on top of her head. "What's that?"

"We thank God for our food." Leah faltered. Had Jackson never lived in a home where people prayed? "Fold your hands and close your eyes please."

Jackson folded his hands, but he stared at her—more defiance. She decided it was good enough.

Closing her own eyes, she offered a prayer. "Lord, we come to you with hearts overflowing with thankfulness for bringing Jackson and I together tonight. We may have just met, but we know that you have a plan in all things, including making us a family, and we ask that you would bless us as we get to know one another. Thank you for the food you have given us and the home. Most of all, thank you for your love. Amen."

As she finished the prayer, she looked at Jackson. But he was staring ahead, stony faced.

"Are you sure you don't want some stir fry?" She held the pan out to him again, but he knocked it away.

The pan tumbled out of her hand and hit the floor with a loud clang that reverberated through the house. Chicken and vegetables splattered across the kitchen floor.

Jackson sprang from his chair before Leah could fully register what had happened. "I told you I didn't want any."

Before Leah could answer, he'd taken off down the hallway. A second later, the slam of his bedroom door shook the house.

Leah closed her eyes, gripping the edge of the table. One extra measure of patience wasn't going to be enough tonight. She was going to need a whole truckload of it.

After cleaning the floor, she sat to finish her now-cold stir fry. Not that the temperature of the food mattered since she barely tasted it. She'd known bringing an older child into her home wouldn't be easy. She'd known all the potential difficulties. She'd thought she was prepared for them.

But it turned out that knowing something and experiencing it were two different things.

But that didn't matter. She'd promised to give Jackson a home and a family, and that was what she was going to do. Plate empty, she pushed back from the table with a new resolve. She wasn't going to give up on this kid after a few hours.

Scratch that. She wasn't going to give up on him, period.

After she'd washed her dishes, she pulled out a loaf of the homemade bread she purchased from Peyton's bakery every week, a jar of the strawberry jam she'd made this summer, and some peanut butter. Jackson may not be willing to eat her stir fry, but she hadn't seen a kid yet who could resist a PBJ. Especially when they were as hungry as she was sure Jackson was.

When the sandwich was made, she brought it to his room and knocked on the door. When there was no answer after a few seconds, she pushed it open.

Jackson was sprawled on the bed, staring at the ceiling. He didn't look over when the door opened, though she noticed his shoulders tense.

"Hey." She crossed the threshold with one foot, holding out the sandwich. "I know not everyone likes chicken stir fry. So I made you a PBJ. You can eat it in here if you want. Just for tonight."

Jackson didn't so much as twitch. She bit back her desire to stand here until he said something—anything—reminding herself that this was all new to him too.

"I'll put it on your dresser, in case you want it." She crossed the room and set the plate down, then stepped to within a few feet of his bed. "I know this is going to be an adjustment. But you should know that I'm on your side here."

Jackson blinked slowly up at the ceiling, not a single emotion registering on his face.

"I'll always be on your side," she added as she retreated from the room. "I'm sure you're tired. Why don't you eat your sandwich if you want it and then go to bed."

Ever since she'd begun the process of applying to be a foster parent, she'd envisioned the bedtime hug she'd give her child. But it would clearly be a bad idea to attempt that tonight. Jackson would probably sprint out of the house so fast she'd never see him again. Ignoring her disappointment, she pulled the door closed.

In the living room, she settled into the chair at the desk in the corner, shoving aside the latest payroll sheets and pulling out a blank piece of paper.

So today hadn't gone as well as it could have. Tomorrow was another day, right? As was the day after that. And the day after that. She had a lifetime of days with Jackson to show him he could trust her, that she wanted to be his family.

All she had to do was brainstorm some ideas how.

First up was introducing him to her friends tomorrow night.

She could take him to the petting zoo too. And maybe ice skating. They could tour the Old Lighthouse, though she'd have to check if it had closed for the season.

Her pen stilled. What else?

She spent the next two hours searching the internet for every event in Hope Springs and the surrounding area, until her list sprawled from the front of the page across half of the back. But it felt like something was missing. She rubbed her eyes, grainy from the long day and hours on the computer. Maybe she should just go to bed. Surely this had to be enough opportunities to bond with Jackson. But as she moved to put the list away, her hand brushed the day's mail—and a postcard announcing the annual Christmas decorating contest.

That was it. They'd decorate the house together and win the contest. She'd make this the best Christmas he'd ever had—the best Christmas any kid had ever had.

She made a note on her paper, then put it in the desk drawer.

Every muscle in her neck and shoulders protested as she stood and stretched. The day had taken its toll on her, and she needed some sleep.

On the way past Jackson's room, she nudged the door open softly. The boy was asleep—still clothed, still lying on top of the blankets. Leah padded to the linen closet and pulled out a spare blanket, then returned to Jackson's room and draped it over him. For a few minutes, she stood watching him. In sleep, there were no traces of the rebellion he'd shown earlier. He was just a sweet little boy who needed someone to love him.

And Leah would be that someone.

She blew him a silent kiss as she tiptoed out the door, continuing down the hall to her own bedroom.

She'd just nuzzled her way under the blankets, snug in her comfiest sweats, when a loud thud jarred her upright. She sat still, listening again. She had no idea what the sound had been or where it had come from, but her first instinct was to run and check on Jackson.

Before she could swing her legs out of bed, though, the thud sounded again. This time it was louder—and clearly coming from outside.

She waited a few seconds, hoping whatever it was would go away, but the sound came again. And then again a few seconds later, taking up an oddly familiar rhythm.

She'd heard that sound plenty of times as a kid when her father had gone outside to chop wood. But it had always been during the day. Not at—she peered at her phone—nearly midnight.

It had to be the guy staying in Miranda's house. The elderly couple who lived on the other side of her had their lights out by eight o'clock every night.

Leah clenched her blankets in her hands as the thudding continued, seeming to grow louder with each thwack. She had to put a stop to this now—before the idiot woke Jackson.

What kind of person chopped wood at midnight?

Leah pounced out of bed and seized her robe, sliding her feet into her slippers.

Apparently, she was taking a midnight trip into the cold.

Chapter 5

The vibration of the ax making contact with the solid hunk of wood ran up Austin's arms. He savored the ache in his shoulders, the repetition of lifting the ax, swinging it in a downward arc, yanking it free, and starting again.

Another hour or so of this, and maybe he'd be exhausted enough to fall into a dreamless sleep. Though he doubted it.

It was why he rarely slept anymore. If he didn't sleep, he couldn't dream. And if he couldn't dream, he couldn't see that day again. Couldn't be dragged back into the horrifying images that he usually managed to keep at the edges of his consciousness when he was awake.

The doctor had prescribed sleeping pills for him and urged him to take them. But he had seen too many guys go that route. Become dependent on the pills. Turn to other pills to numb not only the physical pain but the emotional. That wasn't him.

A drop of sweat trickled into his eye, and he paused to blink it away, then lifted the ax again, bringing it down for one last whack. The log split with a satisfying crack.

He bent over the woodpile the owner had left unstacked and hefted another log onto the stump he was using as a chopping block.

He had the ax poised over his shoulder when a light sprang on in the backyard next door. His gaze jerked that direction in time to see a woman rushing outside. The same woman who had yelled at him earlier for being in the house he had rented and paid for.

With a barely suppressed groan, he dropped the ax. Why did he get the feeling she was going to yell again?

As she hurried toward him, her hair now pulled into a ponytail and a robe flapping around her sweats, his eyes caught on her feet. Hmm. He wouldn't have guessed she was a bunny slippers kind of woman.

Seemed more like a porcupine to him.

He leaned against the ax handle as he waited for her to reach him. Judging by her narrowed eyes and pinched mouth, she hadn't decided to make this a welcome visit either.

"What do you think you're doing?" she hiss-whispered the moment she was within five feet of him.

He gestured to the pile of split wood on the ground. That should be self-explanatory enough.

"It's nearly midnight." Her breath hung in the air between them. "I have a—" She caught herself, as if unsure how to continue, but when she spoke again, her whisper had sharpened. "I have a kid in there I'd like to get a good night's sleep. And this—" She gestured at the same pile of wood he'd pointed to, her lips twisting. "It's not exactly helping."

"Oh." Austin blinked at her. He hadn't considered the fact that normal people went to bed at normal times. That they slept through the night without worrying about being woken by nightmares. Or by a crazy neighbor chopping wood at midnight. "I'm sorry. I wasn't thinking."

The woman contemplated him, her face softening. "So you'll stop?"

He nodded. When had he become so inconsiderate? The guys had always razzed him about being Mr. Polite, but here he was, only thinking about himself. Then again, that was all he'd been thinking about for the past eleven months, wasn't it?

"Yeah." He leaned the ax against the stump. "I'll try to keep the midnight wood chopping to a minimum."

"Good."

He waited for her to turn back to her house, but she stood there studying him, her eyes raking over his face. In the dark, she probably couldn't see the jagged scar along his jawline, but still he shifted. He'd gotten plenty used to close scrutiny by doctors and nurses and therapists—but that didn't mean he liked it.

"Well, if that was all." He repeated the phrase from earlier, taking a step toward his own house.

The woman stepped closer, so that he could smell the tantalizing scent of apples and cinnamon that drifted from her. "Actually, I owe you an apology."

Now it was his turn to study her. Her cheeks were tinted pink, but he couldn't tell if it was from the cold of the night air or from embarrassment over admitting she needed to apologize.

"For what?" He couldn't resist asking. "Yelling at me now or yelling at me earlier?" The lightness in his tone sounded foreign, like he was speaking a language he'd once known but long since forgotten.

Her laugh sparkled on the crisp air. "Both. It's been a long day." She glanced over her shoulder toward her house. "It was my first day as a foster mom, and let's just say it could have gone better."

When she dragged her gaze away from the house, he caught the worry in her eyes. She looked as exhausted as he felt.

"But that's no excuse," she hurried to add. "I was rude, and I'm sorry."

"Apology accepted." Austin wasn't sure why it was important to him to see the tension in her face ease, but it was. "And you no longer believe I'm a squatter here?"

Her long ponytail flipped over her shoulder as she shook her head. "I got an email from my neighbor. Looks like you're on the up and up."

"That's a relief." He pretended to swipe a hand over his brow. "I was afraid you were going to call the FBI earlier."

"Honestly, I thought about it." There was that sparkly laugh again. "I'm Leah, by the way." She held out a hand, and Austin pulled off his glove to shake it. Her fingers were icy, and he felt an odd need to hold on longer to warm them.

"Austin."

He let go of her hand, and she slid it into the pocket of her robe. "So what brings you to Hope Springs?"

Austin stared over her shoulder. Beyond her house, everything was dark and quiet. Still. Peaceful.

"I was born here, but my mom moved us to Iowa when I was too little to remember. I guess I just wanted to see this piece of my history." He left out the part about how he was broken and had no idea where to go to be fixed. How for some reason, he thought this place might be it.

"That's so cool. What's your last name?"

"Hart."

She tipped her head toward the sky, apparently deep in thought. Austin followed her gaze until his eyes met the spread of stars far above. Hard to believe this was the same sky he'd slept under so many nights.

"I don't think I know any Harts," Leah finally said. "But I'll ask around to see if anyone remembers your family."

"You don't have to—"

"Nonsense." Leah's eyes twinkled almost as bright as the stars. "Figuring out how everyone in town is connected is sort of my hobby."

He was pretty sure the sound that came out of him was a laugh—but he couldn't be positive after so many months of not hearing it. "Strange hobby, but whatever you're into."

Leah's laugh was followed by a violent shiver.

"You'd better get inside before you freeze to death. Don't you know it's crazy to be outside at this time of night?"

Leah shook her head at him but turned toward her house. "Sleep well."

Austin sincerely doubted that would happen, but he appreciated the sentiment all the same. "You too."

He bent to stack the wood he'd chopped.

After a few seconds, her voice carried to him from the edge of her yard. "And Austin?"

He looked up in time to see her flash a grin. "Welcome to Hope Springs."

He gave a quick nod before returning to stacking the wood. It didn't make sense that his heart felt lighter after being here for only a few hours. But it did. Only a sliver, maybe. But a sliver was a start.

When he'd finished stacking the wood, he glanced toward Leah's house. The lights were now all off, and Leah was probably already asleep.

Austin tried to remember what it had felt like, once upon a time, to fall asleep instantly, to sleep through the entire night, to wake up feeling rested.

Maybe tonight he'd be able to do that.

He crossed the yard and returned to the house, letting its warmth thaw his raw face.

He puttered around for a while, but finally he couldn't put it off any longer. Between the drive, the cold, and the physical exertion, he had to admit he was exhausted.

He dropped to the side of the bed to pull off his prosthetic, then climbed under the blankets, sure he'd spend the next hour staring at the ceiling.

At least tonight he'd have something new to think about. This house. This town. The neighbor with the blue-green eyes.

But before he could decide what he thought of her, he was out.

Chapter 6

Today was a new day, Leah reminded herself as she set the plate of bacon and eggs in front of a glowering Jackson. He shoved it aside.

"Eat up." Leah infused her voice with all the enthusiasm she possessed in this world. "Big day at school today, and then afterward some of my friends and family are coming over for dinner so they can meet you."

If possible, Jackson's expression soured even more, but Leah pressed on. "I noticed you didn't have a backpack, so I dug one out of my closet. It's not in the greatest shape, but it should do for today. We'll get you a new one this weekend."

Jackson pushed away from the breakfast bar. But she wasn't sending him to school on an empty stomach.

"Eat at least half of that before we go."

"Or what?" Jackson shot a half-smirk, half-taunt at her. "What are you going to do to me?"

Leah's mouth opened and closed, and the breakfast she'd eaten before waking him rolled in her stomach. What would she *do* to him? Was he daring her to threaten him? Had he been threatened in the past?

"Or you're going to be hungry," she said simply, then turned to load the dishwasher. "What about lunch? Do you want me to make you something, or do you want to get lunch at school?"

Jackson didn't answer, so she responded as if he had. "How about a PBJ? I saw you ate the one I left in your room last night. Pretty good, right?" There hadn't been so much as a crumb left on his plate when she'd picked it up this morning.

"Whatever." But when she'd made the sandwich and passed it to him in a paper lunch sack, he took it.

Leah resisted cheering out loud at the minuscule sign of progress and led him to the car.

As she looked over her shoulder to back out of the driveway, she noticed a figure standing on the sidewalk. Although the hood of his sweatshirt hung low over his forehead, she immediately recognized Austin.

He waved to indicate he'd wait for her to back down the driveway, and as they passed, he flashed her a quick look. Not a smile, exactly—more an acknowledgment that he recognized her.

When she'd gone back inside last night, she'd lain in bed a while, her earlier exhaustion chased away by the cold night air. She'd tried to list in her head more things she and Jackson could do together. But she hadn't been able to focus as her thoughts kept drifting to the strange neighbor who felt the need to chop wood at midnight. She couldn't help wondering what his whole story was. The scar she'd noticed on his jaw earlier suggested there was a lot more to it than what he'd told her.

Not that it mattered. It wasn't like the guy owed her his whole life story. As long as he didn't chop wood at midnight anymore, that was all that mattered to her.

Not who he was. Or why he'd come. Or what had caused that haunted look in his charcoal gray eyes.

Leah pulled onto the street, watching Austin in the car's mirror. He took a few walking steps, bouncing a little as if warming up, then set out at a slow jog toward the outskirts of town. She made a mental note to tell him later that her brother was a runner too.

Jackson ignored all her attempts to start a conversation on the way to school, so she finally turned up the volume of the Christian radio station she always listened to.

When she reached the school, she pulled up to the curb where other parents were dropping off their children. "Have a good day."

Jackson didn't respond as he edged out of the car.

Groups of kids bubbled up the steps into the school, giggling and jostling each other. But none of them acknowledged Jackson. And he didn't acknowledge them.

An ache filled Leah's chest at the thought of how lonely the boy must be. According to the caseworker, this was the fourth school he'd attended in six years. No wonder he didn't talk to anyone.

The car behind her honked, and Leah forced her eyes off Jackson as she eased her vehicle toward the exit. After ten years of following the same routine every day, it felt strange to be starting her day by dropping a kid off at school. Strange but good.

The start of a new routine. One that would last for many years to come.

She didn't know what it would take to get it through to Jackson that he was here to stay, but she was going to figure it out. Even if it left her emotionally bruised and battered in the process.

The moment she reached the storefront that housed her commercial kitchen, she called the school to give them her contact information. The "oh" the secretary uttered when she said she was calling about Jackson was loaded with more meaning than any two-letter word should be able to carry. She chose to ignore it and simply relay the necessary information.

"Is there anything else you need from me?" she asked before hanging up.

"No, I'm sure we'll be seeing you soon." The secretary's voice hung with that same meaning she'd pushed into the word "oh."

Leah took a breath, commanding herself to ignore it. It wasn't going to help Jackson if she got into an argument with the school secretary. Besides, the caseworker had already warned her last night that Jackson was on thin ice with the school.

She only hoped his teachers would see his new circumstances as a chance for him to begin again.

She thanked the secretary and hung up the phone, throwing herself into preparations for the wedding she was catering tomorrow.

Wait, tomorrow. How could she cater a wedding tomorrow when she had Jackson to take care of?

Technically, at twelve, he was old enough to stay home alone, but was that wise? She supposed she could bring him with her—if nothing else, she could put him to work folding napkins.

By lunchtime, Leah was elbow-deep in prepping the pinot noir sauce she'd need for the filet mignon the bride had insisted on, when her phone rang. Normally, she'd let it go to voice mail if she got a call when she was in the middle of something like this, but she had a child to worry about now.

Please don't let it be about Jackson. She mouthed the prayer as she grabbed her phone off the counter. She didn't recognize the number, but it was local. Which she assumed was a bad sign.

"Hello?"

"Ms. Zelner? This is Hillary, the secretary from Hope Springs Middle School. We spoke this morning?"

Leah closed her eyes, still praying. "Yes? Did you need more information from me?"

"We're going to need you to come in and pick Jackson up. He's been suspended for the rest of the day."

Leah's chin dropped to her chest, but she forced herself to ask. "Why?"

"He was involved in a fight." Disdain dripped from the woman's voice. "Again."

Leah was already shoving ingredients back into the refrigerator. "I'll be right there."

When she pulled into the school parking lot fifteen minutes later, Leah slid into the closest spot. The sound of shrieking and laughter carried to her from the fenced yard behind the school. Most of the kids were apparently enjoying their lunch period.

But not Jackson.

Leah grimaced. This was not the first impression she wanted to make with the school.

She hurried toward the building and ran up the steps but stopped outside the doors to smooth her shirt, rubbing at the grease stain she'd gotten on the sleeve this morning.

Perfect.

Now they were going to think she was an incompetent mother *and* a slob.

She squared her shoulders and pushed through the front doors. It didn't matter what they thought of her. What mattered was that they give Jackson another chance.

The moment she said her name, the secretary pointed toward a door beyond the reception desk marked with the ominous word "Principal."

Mouth dry, Leah offered a grim thanks, then pushed the door open.

Jackson sat slumped in a straight-backed chair in front of the principal's desk, a bag of ice pressed to his cheek. Leah rushed to his side and dropped to her knee.

She hadn't been prepared to find him hurt. She silently lifted the ice bag off, wincing at the purple bruise that was starting to form on his cheekbone.

"Ms. Zelner. Thank you for coming so quickly."

Leah dutifully stood and shook the hand the older woman held out.

"I'm Mrs. Rice, the new principal here this year."

Leah simply nodded. She knew that Mr. Jessup—who had been principal when she was a student here—had retired last year, but she hadn't had an occasion to meet the new principal.

Until now.

"What happened?" Leah turned to Jackson, still slouched in the chair with the ice on his face. He stared at the floor. "Are you hurt?"

Mrs. Rice made a sound somewhere between a tsk and a snort. "It's the other boy you should be concerned about."

Leah's stomach lurched. "What happened?" she repeated.

"Jackson decided to—"

Leah raised her hand to stop the principal. "I'd like to hear it from Jackson, if you don't mind."

Mrs. Rice spluttered but gestured for Jackson to answer the question.

His mouth remained closed, his eyes focused on the floor.

From behind the desk, Mrs. Rice cleared her throat. "Nothing happened. Nothing ever does. He just decides he doesn't like the way a kid is looking at him that particular day and decides to beat the pulp out of them."

"Beat the pulp out of?" Leah reached for the back of the empty chair next to Jackson to steady herself. Was he that violent?

"Bryce now has a bloody nose and possibly a dislocated finger." Mrs. Rice gestured at Leah. "I understand you're his new foster mother."

Leah nodded, still clutching the chair back.

The principal rifled through a stack of papers on her desk, finally pulling out a puce sheet. "These are some resources we suggest for troubled students. I don't know how many of them his former foster parents have tried. But something has to be done. I'm afraid Mr. Young doesn't have many chances left."

Leah's shoulders tightened. What would happen then? Would Child Welfare take him away from her? Find her an unfit foster mother?

"Could I speak with you alone for a moment?" she managed to croak to Mrs. Rice.

The principal's lips flattened into a crooked line. "Jackson, go wait in the outer office."

Jackson didn't look at Leah as he slunk out of the chair and skulked to the door.

As soon as he'd closed it behind him, Leah drew in a deep breath. It felt like whatever she said now was going to set the course for the rest of Jackson's life.

No pressure.

She blew the breath out. "Mrs. Rice, I am so sorry that this happened, and I will talk with Jackson about it. It's not acceptable behavior, and I know that. I'm sure he does too."

Mrs. Rice raised an eyebrow. "Unfortunately, this is pretty regular behavior for him."

"Please try to understand." Leah stepped out from behind the chair to stand at the side of Mrs. Rice's desk so she could look the older woman in the eye. "Jackson has been through a lot in his life, and his circumstances—"

Mrs. Rice held both her hands up in front of her, as if erecting a barrier to the rest of Leah's explanation. "I know all about Jackson's circumstances. But I have a school to run."

"I know, and I can appreciate that," Leah jumped in. "But I hope you can also appreciate that Jackson is going through a period of transition, and he's struggling. I don't think we can even imagine what it's like to be moved from home to home like he has been." She touched a hand to her chest. "It breaks my heart."

Mrs. Rice's face softened. "Look, I appreciate what you're trying to do here. I really do. I hope you'll be able to make a difference for Jackson. And I'll do what I can to help. I'm just warning you that it might be a tough road. I hope you're prepared for that. Because if you're not, you might both be better off if you say so sooner rather than later."

Leah gripped Mrs. Rice's desk, every muscle in her body tensing. Did the principal really think Leah was just going to walk away from this boy? "Jackson is the way he is because he has been failed by every adult who has ever been part of his life." She spun on her heel and stalked to the door, her breaths coming in sharp gasps. "I refuse to be one of them."

Chapter 7

Three more reps, Austin pushed himself.

But the screaming pain from his knee stopped him after two more modified squats.

He cursed to himself. He could do this. He wanted to do it.

So why wouldn't his body cooperate?

He dropped to the couch, massaging what was supposed to be his "good" knee. The doctor had said it had some arthritis, but he'd assured Austin it shouldn't get much worse if Austin didn't work it too hard.

But not working it too hard wasn't an option. If he wanted to get off the temporary disability retired list and be fit for duty by the time of his next exam, he had to push himself as hard as he could.

The throbbing in his leg didn't abate, but Austin ignored it, reaching instead for his other leg to unfasten his prosthetic and pull off his liner. He massaged the end of his residual limb, feeling the spot where his tibia had been cut, refusing to wince as his fingers kneaded into the skin. The muscles of his lower leg had atrophied over the past eleven months, so that this leg was decidedly smaller than the other.

But just as strong, he told himself, bending to pick up the crutches he'd discarded on the floor this morning. He needed a shower. But as he settled them under his arms, a movement in his peripheral vision caught his attention. A flash of light against something metallic. He jerked his head toward the front window, breath catching in his chest. But it was only a car pulling into the driveway next door.

He meant to move away from the window then, but for some reason, he couldn't take his eyes off the car. Leah had gotten out and stood with her hand on her door, bending down to talk to someone inside. Must be her kid. The boy who'd taken off down the street last night.

Austin leaned his crutches against the couch and lowered himself onto the cushions. He didn't know why, but he felt compelled to watch them.

After a minute, the kid climbed out of the car, closing it with a force that made Leah jump. Her eyes followed him up the walkway to the front door. From here, Austin couldn't read her expression. But he was pretty sure it wasn't a happy one.

She closed her own car door so lightly that Austin doubted it had latched properly. Then she stepped toward the back door on the driver's side. But instead of opening it, she braced her elbows on it and dropped her head to her arms.

Austin recognized the move. How often had he done that over the past eleven months? Against his refrigerator, his apartment door, his bedroom wall?

It was a move of despair, of hopelessness.

Apparently, her second day as a foster mom wasn't going so well either.

As Austin watched her, he debated with himself. Something inside told him he should go out there, offer a kind word, maybe a listening ear. But another part of him—the smarter part—said that was absurd. Whatever was going on with his neighbor was none of his business—and he didn't want to make it his business. He had no desire to get close to her. And even less desire to get close to the kid. He wouldn't make that mistake again.

He rubbed at the scar on his jaw as he watched her slouched there, clearly in anguish. He tried to tell himself to look away, but he couldn't make himself obey.

After a few minutes, Leah lifted her head, swiped a quick hand over her cheeks and straightened her back. As she walked to the house, he could see the sheer force of will driving her there, and he was overcome by an irrational urge to cheer her on.

His phone dinged from beside him on the couch, and Austin glanced down at it, then looked away. It was an email notification. From the only person who emailed him anymore. The one person whose emails he couldn't bring himself to open.

Tanner's wife.

She'd been writing to him once a week every week since Tanner died. Which meant he had more than forty unread emails from her.

He had no idea what her messages said, and he couldn't risk looking. He was too much of a coward to answer the question she'd asked him the one time she'd visited him in the hospital.

How are you?

How was he? He was alive, that's how he was. When her husband was dead. And it was his fault. If he hadn't insisted on picking Isaad up. If he had been the one driving as he was supposed to be. If he had been watching the road instead of joking around with the kid.

But *ifs* didn't matter.

Austin had no idea how long he sat like that, staring at the phone screen even after it had gone blank. Finally, he put the phone away and lifted his head. The sun had dropped behind the trees across the street, leaving trails of deep pink and purple in the clouds. He glanced toward Leah's house, but she must have long since gone inside.

A set of headlights swept down the street, slowing as it approached, then turning into Leah's driveway. Before anyone had emerged from that car, another turned into her driveway. People spilled out of the cars, and their voices, indistinct but clearly joyful, carried across the yard and through Austin's closed windows. He counted four adults—and it looked like one of them was carrying a young child. As they made their way to the door, two more cars drove up, parking on the street in front of Leah's house. More people walked toward her door, more cheerful voices carried toward his house.

A grating kind of pain pressed at Austin's gut. He'd known camaraderie like that once. With Chad and Tanner and all the rest of the guys in his unit. If he were over there right now, if the past year had never happened, they'd probably all be sitting around, playing a game of poker and ribbing each other about whatever came to mind.

More *ifs* that didn't matter.

Austin grabbed his phone and hit the number for the pizza place—the only number he'd called since he got here. Then he pushed himself up from the couch, pretending not to notice as one more car pulled up to Leah's house.

He preferred to be alone, anyway.

Leah watched the timer on the oven tick off the seconds until the pan of meatballs was done.

Her friends were all in the living room, but she needed a few moments to herself. The day hadn't gotten any better after she'd picked Jackson up from school. She'd had no choice but to bring him to work with her, since she had to finish getting things ready for tomorrow's wedding. She'd tried to give him a job peeling carrots, but the moment she'd turned her back, he'd snuck off to a corner of the room, where he sat brooding the rest of the afternoon. She hadn't had time—or energy, frankly—to get him to do what she'd told him to do.

She'd hoped things might be better once he was surrounded by her friends and family tonight. But with each introduction, he'd grown more withdrawn, refusing to do anything but offer a limp handshake. He hadn't so much as said hello to anyone.

Last she saw, he was huddled in a chair, staring at the floor and refusing to answer even the simplest questions her friends asked.

She rolled her shoulders now, trying to ease the tension that had been building there all day. She was exhausted, frustrated, and much as she hated to admit it, embarrassed. When she'd told her friends she wanted to be a foster mother, they'd all been so supportive. They'd assured her she'd be a wonderful mother, that she'd make such a difference in a kid's life.

And now here she was, not even two days into fostering, and she was floundering big time.

Scratch that. She wasn't floundering. She was sinking. Fast.

"You need any help in here?" Her sister-in-law's voice nearly made Leah jump onto the countertop.

"Sorry. I didn't mean to startle you." Jade offered a sympathetic look. "Everything okay?"

Leah nodded. "Just thinking."

"About Jackson?"

Leah blew out a long breath. "Yeah. How'd you guess?"

"Give it time." Jade lifted a stack of plates out of the cupboard and set them on the counter.

"I don't know how to get through to him." Leah turned off the oven timer as it flipped to zero. "I know there has to be something I can do. I just haven't figured out what yet."

"You can pray about it," Jade prompted, and Leah marveled once again at the transformation in her sister-in-law. A year and a half ago, she would have scoffed if anyone suggested she pray—now she was the one offering that advice.

Still, it wasn't as if Leah hadn't thought of that. And she had prayed. Probably more than she ever had in her life. But it seemed like this was going to be one more prayer God answered with no.

She moved to the living room to let the others know dinner was ready. Her eyes went to Jackson, still slouched in his chair, not acknowledging the people who surrounded him. Beyond him, she caught the flash of lights out the window as a pizza delivery car pulled into the neighbor's driveway.

"Dinner time." She directed a pointed look at Jackson. "Why don't you lead the way, since you're our guest of honor tonight?"

But Jackson shook his head. "I'm not hungry."

That had to be a lie. He'd resisted eating the peanut butter and jelly she'd packed him for lunch until he thought she wasn't watching, then devoured it in about three bites. Was it just another act of defiance, his refusing to eat when she told him to? Or was there more to it than that?

Either way, he obviously needed food.

She tried to keep the frustration from creeping into her voice. "Jackson, you have to—"

But someone laid a gentle hand on her arm, and she glanced over to find Jade stepping past her into the living room, Hope on her hip. "Jackson, if you're not hungry, could you do me a favor and watch Hope while I get some food? I am absolutely starving, and she's at the age where she tries to knock everything off my plate."

"I'm not sure—" Leah jumped in. She appreciated what her sister-in-law was doing, but maybe putting the boy who'd been suspended for punching a kid in charge of a baby wasn't the best idea.

Jade shot her a look and set Hope on the floor by Jackson's feet, scattering a few toys around her. "She shouldn't be any trouble, but let me know if you need anything, okay?"

Jackson blinked at Jade, his expression shifting from opposition to something Leah hadn't seen on him before—a flicker of interest.

With a pat of Hope's head, Jade straightened and strode through the living room toward the kitchen, pulling Leah behind her.

"Do you think that's a good idea?" Leah kept her voice low so Jackson wouldn't hear her. "I told you about what happened at school."

"Trust me. Jackson's the one who better watch out. That little girl can soften even the hardest heart."

"What little girl?" Leah's brother Dan asked, dropping a kiss on his wife's cheek.

"Your daughter." Jade nudged him, and Leah was sure no father had ever lit up with a prouder grin.

The heaviness that had been dragging at Leah's heart since the car ride home with Jackson eased a little. Hope couldn't be more Dan's daughter if she had been his biological child. The same would be true of her and Jackson one day. It was like Jade had said, she had to give it time.

She joined the others in prayer, then dug into her own plate of meatballs, letting the sound of her friends' conversations soothe her frayed nerves. This was exactly what she needed—to be surrounded by all the people she loved best in the world.

"Leah, you have to come here." Jade's low, urgent tone carried to Leah from the opening to the living room as she was about to bite into one of the cupcakes Peyton had brought.

Appetite vanishing, Leah shoved her chair back and rushed to Jade's side. "What's wrong?"

But Jade didn't look horrified, she looked . . . awed.

Leah peered around Jade, and her breath caught. Was she seeing this right?

Jackson had slid out of the chair onto the floor, and Hope had crawled over to his side. Jackson was holding a rattle in one hand, shaking it gently as he held it out to her. But more amazing than all of that was his face—it was the first time Leah had seen him smile.

It made him seem both younger and older, vulnerable and responsible all at once.

"Wow," she breathed.

"I told you Hope could soften any heart," Jade whispered.

Chapter 8

The night air cut at Austin's lungs, but he drew in a deep breath, leaning his head against the back of the Adirondack chair he'd pulled off the deck and into the middle of the yard.

It was surreal, how like the Afghan night this was and yet how different. It had gotten this cold in the Afghan mountains, but the smells here were different. Less acrid smoke from the villagers' sawdust stoves, more pine trees and lake breeze.

It was nowhere near as dark here either. Although he'd turned off most of the lights in his house, warm patches of yellow light spilled from Leah's house next door onto his lawn.

The strangest part was that there was no danger here. He was sitting in the middle of a backyard, completely safe. While his brother faced who knew what on the other side of the world.

He flexed his left leg, wincing as needles stabbed through his nonexistent foot. The phantom pains weren't as bad as they'd been in the beginning, but they were still there, even when he wore his prosthetic. Still hampering his recovery.

He gritted his teeth and forced his mind off the pain. He was getting stronger. He knew he was.

He only hoped it was strong enough to prove he was fit to return to combat. He didn't have any desire to be stuck behind a desk somewhere. Or worse, retired from service entirely.

For the past fourteen years, the army had been his life.

Without it, he wasn't sure he knew who he was.

A clatter from next door pulled his eyes toward Leah's yard as she stepped out her back door, feet clad in boots this time instead of bunny slippers.

He meant to pretend he didn't see her, but instead his hand rose into a wave.

Leah did a double-take, then marched across her yard until she was standing in front of him. "What are you doing out here?"

Austin peered up at her. "Sitting."

Leah rolled her eyes. "I see that. I guess I should ask *why* you're sitting in the middle of your yard in hardly any clothes when it's like twenty degrees out here."

Austin snorted. Hardly any clothes? He was wearing his warmest fleece sweatshirt. The same one he'd worn so many nights in the mountains. And he'd never once gotten cold in it. "I'm good. What are you doing out here *in* clothes?"

Even in the dark, Austin could have sworn that Leah's cheeks flushed, and he chalked up a point for himself.

"I only wear my pajamas outside when I have to stop some lunatic neighbor from waking my kid. When I come out to get wood for my fireplace, I tend to dress more appropriately for the weather."

"How are things going?" Austin didn't know why he asked. He certainly hadn't planned to. And he didn't want to know the answer, not really. But when he pictured how defeated she'd looked earlier, he couldn't help it.

"A tiny bit better actually." Leah lifted her arms and drew her long hair into a ponytail, then let it fall. "I think we may have just had a breakthrough. He's in there playing with my baby niece. She has him wrapped around her finger already." The lightness in Leah's tone completely transformed her.

"So are you going to sit out here all night, or do you want to come meet some people?" Leah gestured toward her house.

If those were the two choices, he'd take sit out here all night. "No thanks, I—"

"You might as well say yes because I'm going to stand here and bug you until you do." Leah crossed her arms in front of her. "Plus, we have some food left. Meatballs. And cupcakes. I know all you've had for the past two days is takeout pizza."

So she was bossy *and* nosy. Good to know.

"I really should—"

"Come get some food? Yep." Leah held out a hand as if to help him up.

He contemplated it. He wanted to argue. Wanted to tell her to leave him alone, he was just fine on his own, thank you very much. But then he remembered the happy people he'd seen walking into her house earlier. The way they'd talked and laughed and joked together. The tightness in his chest that hadn't eased since then.

"Come on," Leah wheedled again. "I need some help carrying in firewood."

"Fine." He gave a resigned sigh. "But only to help with the firewood."

"Yay." She bounced on the balls of her feet.

He eyed her hand still stretched toward him but braced his hands against the arms of the chair to push himself upright.

An involuntary groan escaped him as he took a step.

Leah threw a concerned look over her shoulder. "You okay?"

"Yep." He tried to walk normally, ignoring the protest of his stiff leg muscles. "Just a little sore from my run this morning."

"Do you run a lot?"

It was an innocent enough question. She couldn't possibly know how fraught answering it would be for him.

"I used to," he answered finally. "I'm trying to get back into it."

She didn't seem to find anything strange about his answer. "My brother's a runner too. I bet he'd love to run with you."

Austin stared at her. Did she always go making plans for complete strangers?

They each loaded their arms with logs, then he followed Leah toward her back door.

"I guess we didn't think this through." Leah looked from her own full arms to his. With her elbow, she pounded on the door. "Hopefully someone will hear that. They're kind of loud in there."

But it was only a few seconds before someone opened the door.

"Thanks, Peyton." Leah smiled at the woman who held the door, then slid in past her. Austin followed Leah, trying to ignore the curious look the other woman gave him.

He kept his head down as he trailed Leah through the kitchen and dining room to the living room. People covered nearly every conceivable seating area, and Austin's eyes darted to the door. He forced himself to take a deep breath. As soon as he dropped this load of wood, he could get out of here. A couple of guys had sprung to their feet and were unloading the wood from Leah's arms. One started to grab logs off Austin's pile too.

"You should have told us you needed wood, Leah. We would have gotten it," one of the guys scolded.

"It's fine. I had a helper." As she passed the last piece of wood off, Leah gestured to Austin. "Everyone, this is Austin." She turned to him. "Ready for this?"

Before he could figure out what he was supposed to be ready for, she launched into rapid-fire introductions. "That's Sophie and Spencer over there, with their twins Rylan and Aubrey." She pointed to a couple seated on the floor, their legs extended to keep two crawling babies on the far side of the room. Both adults waved at him.

"And that's Peyton and Jared on the couch and Nate and Violet snuggled on that chair together. Ethan and Ariana on the love seat, and that's their little girl Joy eating a book." Everyone laughed as Ariana tugged the paper out of her daughter's mouth.

But Leah was still going. "Next to you is Tyler, and those are his twins running around. He's Spencer's brother." She leaned closer. "Twins run in their family."

"Someone could have told me that *before* I married into the family," Sophie called as she picked up one of her little ones to deliver a raspberry to her tummy.

"On the hearth here are Emma and Grace," Leah continued. "And over by the window is my brother Dan and his wife Jade."

Dan stepped around the others and held out a hand. Austin wiped his own hand subtly on his sweatpants before returning the gesture.

"And that's their daughter Hope on the floor next to Jackson. My—" She faltered, and Austin's eyes went to her. She took a quick breath, then said, "My foster son."

It was the first time Austin had seen the boy up close, and his heart jumped.

Dark hair. Bumpy nose.

Isaad?

But then he blinked, and the kid looked up, his expression surly.

Not Isaad.

His heart plummeted.

"So where'd you two meet?" The question came from the woman Leah had introduced as her sister-in-law.

Austin heard the undertone in her voice and nearly groaned. He never should have agreed to come inside. Not only was this place way too crowded for comfort. Not only was there a kid who looked disconcertingly like Isaad. But now he'd given Leah's friends—and probably Leah herself—the impression he was interested in her.

"We didn't meet," Leah jumped in defensively, a hand lifting to her hip as she shot her sister-in-law a look.

Okay, so maybe Leah, at least, hadn't gotten the wrong impression. That was a relief.

"So you brought a stranger over?" Dan sounded like he was only partially teasing.

"Wouldn't be the first time," the blonde woman on the couch chimed in. If he remembered correctly—which was unlikely—that one was Peyton. "Remember that time she brought home that hitchhiker and insisted on making him a warm meal before—"

"All right. All right." Leah held up her hands. "I promise Austin isn't a hitchhiker. He's renting Miranda's house for a while." She turned to him. "How long did you say?"

He shrugged. He had no idea. But if his physical went well, not long.

"His family was originally from Hope Springs. Hart. Sound familiar to anyone?"

They all shook their heads, but Dan stepped forward. "I can check through old church records. Chances are, if they lived in Hope Springs, they went to Hope Church."

Austin gave a noncommittal nod. Dan was probably right, since his mother had been a committed Christian and had raised him and his brother in the church. But whereas Chad remained a believer, Austin had long since come to his senses. Anyone who could still believe in God after the things they'd seen in battle was crazier than him.

"Come on." Leah tilted her head toward the dining room. "I promised you food. And food you'll get."

She smiled at him, and he tried to convince himself it didn't warm him. That was just the fire that one of the guys now had roaring in the fireplace.

Nothing else.

Chapter 9

"We still need those tartlets," Leah called across the wedding hall's kitchen to her assistant Sam.

"On it." Sam wiped her hands on the front of her already streaked apron and held up her mixing bowl.

Leah studied the schedule she'd laid out for the day. So far, there had been no major delays, and things were running smoothly. Which was something of a miracle, considering that her brain wasn't all here.

She was too busy worrying about her decision to leave Jackson home alone while she catered this wedding. She'd debated bringing him with her, but after the way he'd flourished with Hope last night, she hoped that perhaps giving him a little more responsibility and showing him some trust would improve things between them.

But that didn't mean she was certain about it. At all.

If only she could call to check on him, she'd feel better. But he didn't have a phone. She'd have to add that to the list of things she needed to get him, so they could stay in touch in situations like this.

Maybe she should call one of her friends and ask them to swing by the house. Or would that be too much like spying on him? Would he take that as a sign she didn't trust him?

She let out an exasperated breath and returned to her list. Why had no one warned her this parenting thing would be so hard? She was so used to feeling certain about everything, used to making snap decisions and not thinking twice about them. But now, she was questioning everything, second guessing herself at every turn. Was this what parenting was going to be like? For the rest of her life?

Okay, mushrooms. She needed to prepare the mushrooms. She pulled the carton out of the refrigerator.

Austin. The name popped into her head. She could call Austin and ask him to check on Jackson. It wouldn't be suspicious if the neighbor happened to stop by—maybe he needed to borrow some sugar or something.

She took out her phone and scrolled to his name. Good thing she'd made him give her his number last night, just as she'd done with all the rest of her neighbors when she'd moved into the neighborhood. Just as a way for everyone to watch out for one another.

Her finger hovered over the call button. Was this too weird?

Austin hadn't seemed entirely comfortable at her house last night. Of course, Jade's implication that the two of them had met and then intentionally sought each other out again hadn't helped.

But it seemed like there was more to it than that. He tried to hide it, but she hadn't missed the way his eyes had flitted to the door every few seconds, no matter what room he was in. And other than a quick glance, he'd entirely ignored Jackson.

Still, he didn't have to be Mr. Rogers to check on Jackson now.

She hit the button, cradling the phone against her shoulder and cleaning the mushrooms as she waited for him to answer.

When he did, he sounded winded.

"Did you just get back from a run?" She set the mushrooms down and leaned against the counter.

"No. Working out. What's up?"

Unbidden, an image of his broad shoulders sprang to mind. She banished it. "Could you do me a favor?"

"Maybe." Austin sounded hesitant. "Depends what it is."

Leah laughed. "That's fair. Can you look out your window and check something for me?"

"Sure. Check what?"

"Is my house still standing?"

The laugh that sped through the phone took Leah by surprise. She didn't know Austin well, but so far she hadn't gotten the impression he was the laughing type.

"It's still standing. Why? Are you expecting it to fall today?"

"I hope not." Leah had never been more fervent about anything. "Now for the favor."

"I thought that was the favor." Austin's bemusement crept through the phone.

"No. That was a question." Leah tucked her hair behind her ear and switched the phone to her other shoulder. "The favor is, can you go over to my house and check on Jackson?"

"Check on—"

"But don't let him know you're checking on him," Leah rushed on. "Tell him you need to borrow some sugar or something."

"I don't think—"

But now that Leah had hatched the plan, she was desperate to carry it through. It was the only way she'd have any peace of mind. "Then call me afterward and let me know how he's doing. Please."

"Leah, I think—"

"I'm sorry. I know this is weird. And I wouldn't ask if I wasn't desperate. But I need to know that he's okay there, or I won't be able to do my work here. And I don't want to ruin some poor couple's wedding dinner because I'm a basket case."

The moment Austin's sigh crackled through the speaker, she knew she had won. "Thank you so much, Austin. You're the best." She clicked the phone off before he could try to get out of it again.

"He's the best, huh?"

Leah jumped at Peyton's voice. She'd been so focused on her conversation with Austin, she hadn't seen her best friend come in and set her box of cake decorating supplies on the counter.

"He's going to check on Jackson. I've been so worried about leaving him home alone." Leah busied herself chopping the mushrooms. There was no reason she should feel embarrassed that she'd been on the phone with Austin.

But she knew the conclusion Peyton would jump to before her friend said it. "He seemed like a nice guy. Maybe you should—"

"No." Leah stilled her knife and lifted her head. "I'm not going to ask him on a date. I'm not going to ask anyone on a date. And for the record, none of you are going to ask anyone on a date for me either. Never mind the fact that I've told you not to a thousand times before."

Peyton's mouth opened, but Leah wasn't done. "Jackson is my priority right now. And he will be for a long time to come. So no more comments about asking Austin out. He's a nice guy, and I look forward to becoming friends with him. But that's as far as it goes."

Peyton raised her hands in front of her in a gesture of surrender. She started pulling supplies out of her box in silence, and Leah returned to her chopping.

But after a few minutes, Peyton slid her empty box off the counter and turned to Leah, watching her silently.

Leah blew a stray piece of hair out of her face. "What?" She'd rather pretend Peyton wasn't standing there just waiting to tell her something—something she probably didn't want to hear—but she knew Peyton would just bring it up another time—probably a time when it was even less convenient.

"It's just . . ." Peyton waved her piping bag at Leah. "You've put this guy into the friend zone before you've even gotten to know him. You're not giving him a chance."

Leah rolled her eyes. "Who says he wants a chance?" Austin had shown as little interest in her as she had in him.

"I'm not saying he necessarily does." Peyton opened a bag of powdered sugar and measured it into a bowl. "I'm just saying you're shutting him down before he can decide whether he does or not. It's the same thing you've done with every guy since Gavin."

Leah sucked in a breath. No one had mentioned Gavin in years, so why Peyton thought he had anything to do with anything now was beyond her.

"I got over Gavin years ago." Her voice was low, but there was a note of warning in it that she knew Peyton would recognize. And probably ignore.

"Maybe so." Peyton raised an eyebrow as if she didn't entirely believe Leah. "But that doesn't mean what happened hasn't affected you on some level. Affected the way you see men."

Leah pressed her lips together and pulled out a baking pan. Peyton knew the signal. The conversation was over.

"Come on, Leah." Apparently her friend didn't care about the signal today. "The guy dated you for two years. You thought you were going to get married. And then he decided he wanted to be friends."

Leah pushed past Peyton to grab a stick of butter out of the refrigerator.

"And then—" Peyton wasn't done yet. "He married someone else three months later. You can't tell me that didn't have an impact on you."

Leah dropped the cold butter into the pan harder than necessary. "Of course it had an impact on me. Then. Not now."

"So you're telling me that the reason you friend-zone every guy you meet has nothing to do with Gavin?"

"That's what I'm telling you." Why was it so difficult for Peyton to believe that the reason she was just friends with guys was because she was perfectly content as a single woman?

"Hey, Leah." Sam's call from the other side of the kitchen held a note of panic. "I don't think these Brie tartlets turned out."

Leah allowed herself a sigh of relief. She'd never thought she'd be grateful to hear that her star appetizer hadn't turned out. But anything was better than this conversation.

Chapter 10

Austin stared at the front door of Leah's house. How had she gotten him to agree to do this? And how stupid was he going to sound asking a twelve-year-old kid if he could borrow a cup of sugar?

Not that it mattered.

He was only here to do his good deed. He'd check on the kid. Ensure that both he and the house were in one piece. And then he'd get out of there, as fast as he could.

As he lifted his hand to knock, he steeled himself for the sight of the kid. *It's not Isaad.* He repeated it to himself as he waited for Jackson to come to the door. Maybe this way he wouldn't experience that painful jolt he'd felt every time he'd chanced a glance at the kid last night. The jolt that made him think just for a second that he'd gone back in time and Isaad was still alive.

He knocked again, but no one came to the door. He checked the time on his phone. Almost two o'clock. Even teenagers didn't sleep this late, did they?

He pounded on the door again, harder this time, the refrain *It's not Isaad* still playing in a loop in his head.

Another minute went by. Then another.

He debated. Technically, he'd kept his promise. He'd come over with the intention of asking for a cup of sugar. It wasn't his fault the kid had refused to answer the door.

But he'd also promised to let Leah know how it had gone. He could only imagine what would happen if he called and told her he hadn't seen or heard a sign of her foster son. He'd get yelled at again, for sure.

He tried the doorknob, but it was locked.

Great.

Was he going to have to break in?

Maybe before taking such drastic measures, he should try the back door. Pulling up his hood against the biting wind, he started around the house.

The moment he reached the backyard, he spotted Jackson, crouched under the large oak tree at the back of the lot, peering at something in the grass.

Despite his *It's not Isaad* mantra, the initial gut punch of the boy's dark hair drew Austin up short.

But as Jackson shifted, Austin got a glimpse of his face.

Not Isaad.

The boy glared at him, and Austin considered turning around. He could honestly report to Leah that Jackson was fine. But from the little he knew of her, that wouldn't be enough. He forced his feet forward.

Jackson reached into the grass, cupping his hands around something.

"What you got there?" Austin called out as he drew closer. The minute the words slipped from his mouth, he stopped. That was the first thing he'd ever said to Isaad too. The boy had been holding a rock, and Austin's first assumption had been that he was about to throw it at the American soldiers. But then the boy had pointed out the flecks of chlorite and serpentine in the stone, and Austin had realized he was a budding geologist. After that, Austin had made it a habit to search for interesting rocks to give the boy, who always knew exactly what they were.

He shook off the memory. This wasn't Isaad. It was Jackson. And whatever he was holding definitely wasn't a rock—it was moving.

Austin inched closer as Jackson regarded him, suspicion and mistrust fogging the boy's eyes. He turned his back to Austin, as if trying to protect his secret.

Austin shuffled closer, catching a glimpse of something squirming in Jackson's hands. "Is that a baby squirrel?"

Jackson eyed him again, then looked at his hands, giving a barely perceptible nod.

Stepping next to the boy, Austin bent to peer more closely. The squirrel fit entirely in Jackson's palm, a fine layer of fur covering most of its body. Its eyes were closed, as if it had curled up for a nap, and it's tail—nearly as long as its body—wrapped around its side.

Austin squinted upward, shielding his eyes as he searched the branches. Finally, he spotted a leafy nest near the top of the tree. "It must have fallen."

Too bad there was no way they could get it back up there. Strong as he was getting, there was no way Austin could climb this tree, and he was pretty sure Leah would skin him alive if he sent Jackson that high into the tree, especially considering the way the branches were whipping in today's wind.

"I'm going to keep it." It was the first time Austin had ever heard Jackson speak, and his voice was lower than Austin had expected.

"You should probably leave it. Its mom will come for it." Austin turned to leave. He'd done his job. Now he could go home, report to Leah that Jackson was alive and well, and maybe get in another workout before—

Before what?

Before he ordered another pizza and sat around all night with nothing to do?

It wasn't like his calendar was exactly full.

"The squirrel's mom isn't coming back." Jackson's voice jabbed at him, steelier than any twelve-year-old should ever sound.

Austin turned to the kid. "How do you know?"

Jackson studied the squirrel. "His body was cold when I picked him up. That means he's been there a while. If she hasn't come for him yet, she's not coming."

Austin scrubbed a hand across his short hair, letting it prickle against his fingers. *Go home*, he told himself. But he couldn't, not with that half-pleading, half-frightened look Jackson was giving him. Austin sighed. The kid was in foster care. Which meant he probably hadn't had the best experience with his own parents, right?

He was going to regret this. He knew he was. But he pulled out his phone and did a quick search for "how to take care of a baby squirrel." After a few minutes of reading, he looked up. Jackson was still cradling the squirrel, his left hand cupped over his right.

"It says to put a zipper bag filled with warm water in a box and cover it with a t-shirt and then put it at the base of the tree. That way the baby squirrel will stay warm, and the mom can come and get it."

Jackson shot him a challenging look.

Austin jumped in before he could argue. "You at least have to give her a chance to get her baby."

"What if she doesn't?" There was that hardness again.

"If she doesn't, then—" But Austin had no idea what they would do then. He couldn't go making promises to the neighbor's kid. But he wasn't about to be the one to tell him he couldn't keep the squirrel either. "Then we'll figure that out when we get to it. Deal?"

Jackson's nod was slow but emphatic. "Deal."

Satisfied, Austin held out his hand for a quick handshake. "I'll go get a box."

He sent Leah a text on his way back to his house to retrieve the shoe box he'd seen in the hall closet. *Everything fine here. Jackson playing outside.* No need to freak her out with the news that her foster son was hoping to adopt a squirrel. With any luck, the critter would be back in its nest with its mother within the hour, and he could get back to his own life—or lack thereof.

But three hours later, he was less optimistic. He and Jackson had been observing the box from inside all afternoon, and so far there hadn't been any sign of an adult squirrel. The temperature was dropping quickly—they'd already changed the bag of warm water half a dozen times to make sure the little squirrel didn't freeze—and now snow flurries were starting to fall. And it was getting dark. Austin didn't dare voice his fear that if the squirrel's mother didn't get it soon, it would become a meal for a hawk or a stray dog.

Jackson had been asking for half an hour already if they could bring the squirrel inside. Finally, Austin had to relent. He had no idea how it would traumatize the kid if the squirrel died—and he didn't have any interest in finding out.

As Jackson ran outside to collect the squirrel, Austin tried to figure out how he was going to explain this to Leah.

He couldn't quite decide if he dreaded the snap of fire in her eyes when she yelled at him—or if he looked forward to it.

"You're sure you don't mind finishing the cleanup without me?" Leah eyed Sam. Her assistant had only gotten married a few months ago and was probably eager to get home to her husband.

"For the twentieth time, I'm sure." Sam shoved Leah toward the door. "We're almost done. Go home to your son."

Leah couldn't help the grin. *Her son.* She hadn't gotten used to those words quite yet, but already she loved the ring of them. And Sam was right, she did feel a strong need to get home and check on Jackson. Austin's text earlier that Jackson was playing outside had given Leah enough peace of mind to get through the meal. But now that it was over, she wanted to get home and see for herself. Plus, if Jackson had ventured outside, maybe it meant he was over at least some of the sullenness that had followed him around like a chained puppy for the past two days.

As she drove home, careful not to press her foot to the accelerator too hard in her eagerness, her thoughts flitted to what Peyton had said earlier. About her friend-zoning guys because of what had happened with Gavin. It was absolute nonsense. Sure, she'd prayed Gavin would be her husband. And after things fell apart with him, she'd prayed that God would give her someone else to love.

But she'd stopped praying that prayer a long time ago.

It was clear that God's plans for her didn't include marriage. But just because she wasn't searching for a husband didn't mean she was deliberately sabotaging any relationship before it started.

And just because Austin was good looking and seemed fairly kind and even a little funny when he let himself be didn't mean she had to be interested in him as more than a friend.

Leah nodded to herself as she pulled into her driveway, vowing to put thoughts of Peyton and Austin and everything else that wasn't Jackson-related aside for the rest of the night.

But when she stepped through the door to her house, she realized that was going to be difficult, considering that Austin was sitting on the couch with Jackson. Her heart skipped at the picture of the two of them bent close together, peering into a small shoe box on the cushion between them. Anyone who didn't know them might assume they were father and son, despite Austin's light hair and Jackson's darker locks. They looked up as she closed the door behind her.

Both wore expressions of mixed guilt and hope.

"What's going on?" She concentrated on catching her breath after the surprise of seeing Austin in her house and seeing Jackson anywhere other than his room.

Austin gestured her over. "Jackson found this little guy on the ground, and he's taken care of him all afternoon."

"Little guy?" Leah took a cautious step closer. She wasn't sure she wanted to see anything that was described as little guy and fit into a shoe box. What if they had a spider in there?

Her eyes fell on a nearly naked creature, and she shrieked and jumped back. "Is that a rat?"

Two snickering laughs greeted her. "It's a baby squirrel." Jackson's voice held a note of *duh*.

"Oh." As long as it wasn't a rat, she could probably be brave enough to get a little closer. "What's a baby squirrel doing in my house?"

"It fell out of its nest, and we tried to find its mom, but she never came back for it."

Leah felt her mouth open. That was the longest string of words she'd ever heard Jackson utter.

"That was very kind of you." She kept her voice guarded. "We should call the humane society. If they don't take in squirrels, they'll know who does."

"Actually—" The rumble of Austin's voice cut her off as she was about to look up the phone number. "Jackson would like to keep it."

Leah froze. They wanted her to keep a squirrel? In her house? She glanced at Austin, who held her gaze, eyes pleading. Was it that Jackson wanted her to keep the squirrel, or that Austin did? But when she turned to Jackson the same pleading was reflected in his eyes.

She sighed. How was she supposed to say no to that? But her mind seized on something. A squirrel was a wild animal. "I'm sorry, Jackson. It's illegal to keep wild animals. Maybe we can get some fish or something." Fish were easy to take care of, weren't they?

But Austin and Jackson were both smirking at her. It was uncanny how much they looked alike when they did that.

"Actually, there are exceptions in Wisconsin, including . . ." Austin looked at her, and she could almost swear he was going to wink, but then he gestured to Jackson.

"Squirrels," the boy filled in. Austin grinned and held out a hand for a high-five, which Jackson returned with a matching grin.

Something twinged at Leah's middle, and she pushed it aside. She should be happy that Austin and Jackson had bonded today. Maybe it meant Jackson would open up to her too.

She reached behind her head and gathered her hair into a ponytail, thinking. Just because it was legal to keep a squirrel didn't mean she wanted one in her house.

"But we don't know the first thing about taking care of a squirrel. I'm sure they need special food and a cage and— What?"

They were both giving her that dorky grin again.

"I went to the pet store." Austin ran a hand over his cropped hair, as if self-conscious. "I got some food and a cage and some toys."

Jackson looked at Austin as if the man were his hero.

Leah stiffened. This had gone far enough. "You shouldn't have done that."

"It was no big deal. It was just a few things." Austin ducked his head as if she had thanked him.

"I mean, you shouldn't have done that without asking me first. I hope you can return it all. Because we're not keeping that squirrel. We'll call the humane society in the morning."

Both Austin and Jackson jerked their gazes to her. But this time, where Austin's was apologetic, Jackson's was insolent. He jumped to his feet, snatching up the box and stomping toward the hallway.

"I hate you." The ugly words were completely devoid of emotion, but Leah winced, turning away and blinking rapidly to clear the moisture that filled her eyes. She didn't need Jackson to know he'd hurt her.

She stared out the front window, where the flurries that had started falling earlier were now collecting in a thin layer on the grass.

"I'm sorry." Austin's voice was low. "I shouldn't have interfered."

She heard him push to his feet and cross the room but didn't turn her head.

A gust of cold air swept over her as he opened the front door.

"The way he took care of that squirrel, though. It was pretty amazing."

The door closed with a click, and Leah rubbed at her forehead.

Just when she thought parenting might be getting easier, her kid brought home a squirrel.

Chapter 11

Austin rubbed at his gritty eyes as he stared out his front window. When had the sun come up?

A nightmare had woken him well before dawn, and he'd been sitting here on the couch since then, but apparently he hadn't been paying attention to his surroundings.

He'd been too stuck in his own head, thinking about Chad and Tanner and Isaad. And Leah and Jackson.

Much as he tried, he couldn't get his mind off his new neighbors. Off the way spending time with Jackson had started to feel natural yesterday. Off the way he'd stopped thinking the boy was Isaad every time he saw him. Off the glint of tears in Leah's eyes when Jackson had said he hated her.

He never should have overstepped the way he had. He'd put Leah in an awkward position.

He should go over there and apologize. But she'd probably prefer if he left them alone. Pretended he'd never met them. Austin rubbed at his leg, but it didn't do anything to ease the tightness that constricted his chest.

He tried to shake himself out of it. He'd been on his own for months now. There was no reason to be disappointed that his budding friendship with his neighbors had ended. Hadn't he promised himself not to get close to anyone here anyway? He'd be leaving soon, and the fewer people he had to say goodbye to, the better.

Movement next door caught his eye, and he angled his head toward Leah's yard in time to see her stomping toward his house through the thin layer of snow that had settled on the grass. Apparently he'd been wrong about her preferring to leave it alone. She obviously hadn't yelled at him enough last night.

He got to his feet and pulled on his stocking cap, emerging onto the porch as Leah reached the bottom of the steps. The morning was sharp and clear, and the snow created a dazzling backdrop in the winter sun. For a second, Leah's hair seemed to glow, and he was almost tempted to reach out to see if it was real.

Fortunately, he had more sense than that.

"Good morning," he said cautiously.

"Good morning." She sounded equally uncertain as she climbed the porch steps to stand level with him.

"I'm sorry—" he said, at the same time she said, "I shouldn't have—"

They both broke off, then both started again. Austin forced himself to be quiet. Let her talk first, then he could apologize.

"I just wanted to say I was sorry about last night." She wrapped her arms around her down jacket, ducking her chin into the white fluffy scarf wound around her neck. "I was kind of blindsided by the whole squirrel thing. But I think you were right. I think I should let Jackson keep it."

Austin gaped at her. She wasn't yelling at him? She thought he was right?

"I just wanted you to know. And to apologize for yelling at you." She lifted her head so that her mouth was no longer covered by the scarf and offered him a slight smile. "Again."

Austin finally found his voice. "I'm sorry too. I shouldn't have overstepped like that. I was having fun with Jackson, but I didn't think long term." He tugged his hat lower over his ears against the sting of the morning chill. "What made you change your mind?"

She peered over her shoulder, toward her house. "Jackson's mother died when he was six. Drug overdose. He had no father, and he's been in foster care ever since. Nine families in six years."

Austin's stomach rolled. He'd seen kids in a lot of terrible situations in Afghanistan, but somehow he never thought of horrible things happening to kids in his own country.

Leah shrugged. "I started thinking about what it must be like for him, to find this baby squirrel that was abandoned. And the compassion he showed in wanting to take care of it. Maybe it's a sign that somewhere in there is a little boy who wants to be taken care of too." Leah tucked a stray piece of hair under her hat. "Anyway, it was pretty obvious he was happy with that creature." She hit him with a direct look. "And with you."

He lifted a hand, almost reaching for her arm, but then lowered it. "I shouldn't have shoved myself into a relationship with him like that." He'd seen the flash of envy in her eyes yesterday as she'd watched them together, and he couldn't blame her.

But Leah shook her head. "I'm glad you did. Right now, anyone who can get through to him is my hero. Speaking of which, maybe you should be the one to tell him he can keep the squirrel. You're the one who helped him take care of it, and he'd probably rather talk to you than to me anyway."

It would be fun to tell the boy, Austin had to admit that. But he wasn't going to take that joy from Leah too. "Nah. He should hear it from you. You're his mom."

Leah's brow creased. "I don't know if he'll ever consider me his mom." Her voice cracked, and this time he did touch her arm, only for a fraction of a second.

"Give it time. You care a lot. Anyone can see that. He'll figure it out eventually too."

"Yeah." She stuffed her hands in her coat pocket. "Aren't you freezing?" She gestured to his sweatshirt. "Why don't you ever wear a coat?"

"I'm good. You look cold, though. Do you want to warm up with some coffee? I've got a pot made." He didn't know where the invitation came from. For some reason, he had an urge to keep talking right now. Or maybe it was that he had an urge to keep talking to her.

"No thanks." Leah took a backward step down the porch stairs. "I need to wake Jackson up for church." She turned and bounced down the last two steps. At the bottom, she turned back, looking tentative. "You're welcome to come with us if you like. To church."

With the sun backlighting her like that, it wouldn't take much of a stretch to imagine she was an angel. But he'd long ago figured out angels weren't real. And neither was God.

He shook his head once, said, "No thanks," then turned to the house and stepped inside. On his way through the living room, he allowed himself a glance out the front window. Leah was almost back to her house already, and as he watched her walk through the snow, he let himself wonder, just for a second, what would have happened if he'd said yes to her offer.

Something tugged at his heart, but he ignored it.

"What do you want to do now?" Leah glanced at Jackson, who had sat stock still through the entire service, although at her prompting he'd at least stood at the appropriate times. With his blank expression, it was impossible to tell if he'd gotten anything from the service.

But her heart felt a million times lighter after worshipping her Savior. Dan's sermon about trust had been exactly what she'd needed to hear. A perfect reminder that God had never failed her—and he wasn't about to now.

Jackson shrugged. "I have to feed Ned."

Leah still didn't understand how the squirrel had gotten that name, but she wasn't going to fight it. At least Jackson was talking to her now. He'd offered a simple "thank you" when she'd told him he could keep the squirrel, but she'd seen the way his eyes brightened.

"What about after that? Is there anything fun you want to do? I'm not sure there's enough snow to sled yet, but we could go somewhere. I heard Rothman's Farm has opened their Christmas Wonderland. We could go feed some goats and stuff."

Jackson was silent so long Leah was sure he wasn't going to answer. Finally, though, he said, "Can Austin come?"

Leah forced herself to keep her expression neutral. Jackson wasn't trying to hurt her feelings, she was sure. "Don't you want to do something, just the two of us? Get to know each other better?"

But Jackson shook his head. "I want Austin to come."

Okay, maybe he *was* trying to hurt her. But she wasn't going to let him see how it affected her. "I guess we can ask him."

They rode the rest of the way home in silence, and the moment they entered the house, Jackson went to his room, presumably to feed Ned, whose cage they'd perched on Jackson's dresser. Leah set to work making him a peanut butter and jelly. She'd decided not to push him to eat with her—or to try other foods—for now. One step at a time.

She dropped the sandwich off in Jackson's room, then made one for herself and started to text Austin.

We're going to Rothman's Farm. Jackson wanted to know if you'd like to come.

She studied the words. She wanted to make sure it was abundantly clear that the invitation was from Jackson, not her. Finally satisfied that there was no way he could read more into it than was there, she sent it off. She tried to force herself to eat, but she couldn't help checking her phone every few seconds to see if he'd replied. She couldn't decide if she wanted him to say yes to make Jackson happy or to say no so that she and Jackson could spend the day alone together.

As she finished her sandwich, her phone dinged with his response.

Do you want me to come?

Ugh. Leah almost threw her phone across the room. How was she supposed to answer that question? And how did he even mean it?

If you want to. She eyed her response, then sent it off before she could change her mind.

This time she only had to wait a few seconds for his response. *Sure. Be over in a minute.*

Leah exhaled, relief and tension colliding in her belly. Much as she wanted to spend the day alone with Jackson, she had to admit that having Austin there as a buffer would almost certainly be helpful. Which was probably why her pulse quickened ever so slightly when she glanced out the window and saw him approaching.

"Jackson," she called down the hallway. "Austin's here. Time to go."

She opened the front door before Austin could knock, and he stepped inside, bringing with him the smell of the cold outdoors, but also something underneath that—something warmer and more masculine. She took a step back to widen the space between them.

"You're sure you don't mind if I come?" Austin spoke quietly, his face almost boyish with uncertainty.

"I told you—" Leah waved a hand as if it didn't matter to her one way or the other. "If you want to come, you should come. If you don't want to—"

"I don't want to get in your way."

She lifted a shoulder. "You—"

But before she could finish that sentence—which she had no idea how to end—Jackson traipsed into the room.

He went straight to Austin, who held out his hand for a fist-bump.

"I get to keep the squirrel." Jackson's voice was filled with more enthusiasm than Leah would have imagined he possessed.

"So I heard." Austin reached over to ruffle the boy's hair, and Leah pressed down a fresh pinch of jealousy. It was good for Jackson to have someone he could relate to, she reminded herself. Even if it wasn't her.

"Are we ready to go?" She took in Jackson's t-shirt and shorts. Clearly not.

She pointed toward his room. "There's snow on the ground. You need to wear something warm. Pants and a jacket."

Jackson nodded toward Austin. "How come *he* doesn't have to wear a jacket?"

Leah eyed Austin's sweatshirt in exasperation. Did no one around here know how to dress for the Wisconsin weather?

"I'm not his mom," she finally said. "Now go put on some warmer clothes."

"You're not my mom either," Jackson muttered, so low that Leah could almost convince herself she'd only imagined it—except for the searing pain cutting across her stomach. "And I don't have a jacket."

Leah dropped her head. That was true. Between his suspension on Friday and the wedding yesterday, she hadn't had time to get him one yet. Maybe this had been a bad idea. Maybe they should stay home after all.

"Go put on some pants like your mom told you to." Austin's voice was even. "I've got something you can wear for a jacket."

Leah braced for Jackson's outburst. But after watching Austin for a minute—who watched him in return, not blinking—Jackson spun and stomped down the hallway. Leah was pretty sure he muttered, "She's not my mom" once more before he ducked into his room.

She stared at the floor, trying to decide if she should thank Austin or ream him out for stepping in. Before she could make up her mind, he murmured, "I'll be right back" and disappeared out the front door.

She leaned against the wall and closed her eyes as she waited for both of them. *Please help us have a good day together, Lord. Help me have the patience to be a mother to Jackson.* She'd never had to pray for patience before—it generally came naturally to her—but she felt as if she'd used up her lifetime reserve of it, and now she was left without any right when she needed it most.

As she opened her eyes, they caught on Austin crossing the yard toward her house. He had a different kind of a walk—not swaggering exactly, but sort of stiff. She tried to decide if he had a limp or if it was her imagination.

Just as she'd decided it was her imagination, he looked up, and even through the window, his eyes seemed to snag on hers. She inhaled but found she suddenly couldn't exhale. After a second, he disappeared from the window as he reached the front steps, and she could at last breathe out again.

She sucked in a couple of quick extra breaths, working to get herself under control. That had been strange—and it wasn't something she wanted to repeat when he was standing right next to her, so she moved toward Jackson's room as she heard the front door open.

But Jackson had apparently been waiting for Austin, because he emerged from his room the moment the front door opened. At least he was wearing pants now.

"Here you go, dude." Austin held out a sweatshirt that matched his own, and Jackson shoved past Leah to grab it, immediately pulling it over his head. Great. In their matching shirts, the two looked even more like father and son.

"Now are we ready?" Leah grabbed her car keys and slipped past them to lead the way out the door. She and Austin reached for the door handle at the same time, their fingers brushing for an instant. She jerked hers back and let him hold the door open as she practically flew outside and down the steps, barely resisting the urge to stick her hand in the snow to cool the shock of warmth she'd felt at his touch.

Chapter 12

They'd been at the petting zoo for an hour already, and still Austin had no idea what had possessed him to accept Leah's invitation. Maybe it was the way she'd apologized earlier this morning. Or the earnest look she'd directed his way when she'd invited him to church.

Most likely, it was just that he'd enjoyed spending time with Jackson yesterday. One thing he knew: It had nothing to do with the warmth he felt every time he got anywhere near Leah. Sure, she was pretty, with that light hair and those enchanting green-blue eyes, and sure she was easy to talk to—when she wasn't yelling at him—and sure her smile was the most captivating he'd ever seen. But none of that meant he was interested in her as anything more than a neighbor. Or if he was, he shouldn't be.

Wouldn't be.

"Oh look." That captivating smile was back as she pointed past him. He followed the trajectory of her finger to a large sign that read "Christmas Wonderland."

His effort to suppress a groan failed, and Leah's eyes slid to his, the shock on her face almost comical.

"You don't like Christmas?"

Austin swallowed. That was a loaded question. He'd liked Christmas once upon a time. Looked forward to running downstairs with Chad to tear open the presents their mom had so lovingly picked out. There usually weren't a ton, but they were always just what Austin and his brother had wanted.

He'd had some good Christmases in the service too. Time spent with his brother and the other men in their unit. Usually, they managed to fashion some sort of Christmas tree or another. And they often received care packages with thoughtful gifts from people they didn't even know, which was always touching.

But last year had ruined Christmas for him. Losing your leg, your best friend, and the young Afghan boy you'd come to look at almost as a son would do that.

"I'll wait for you guys over here." He scraped the words out as he took a step toward a seating area made up of straw bales.

Leah tipped her head to the side, studying him. She opened her mouth as if to say something, then closed it and turned to Jackson, gesturing him toward the Christmas Wonderland.

But the boy shook his head. "I don't like Christmas either." He trailed Austin.

"What?" Desperation filled Leah's voice. "But I wanted to show you the Enchanted Forest and the First Christmas and—"

"I said I don't want to." Jackson folded his arms in front of him.

Leah's eyes met Austin's, pleading. The war in his chest was more heated than any battle he'd ever taken part in. Everything in him told him to avoid any reminders of Christmas. But then he looked at Jackson, defiant and clearly waiting for his lead. And Leah, broken and clearly needing his help.

He reached up with two hands to pull his knit cap lower over his ears. "Why don't we all go?"

Leah's relieved smile almost made the knot of anxiety crawling its way up his esophagus worthwhile.

But Jackson stood unmoving.

"I don't like Christmas," the boy repeated.

"This is going to be the best Christmas ever, you'll see." Leah took a tentative step toward her foster son. But Jackson shuffled away from her.

The renewed anguish in Leah's eyes was too much for Austin. "Come on." He clapped Jackson on the shoulder and led him toward the Christmas Wonderland. He wasn't sure if Leah's sigh as she fell into step behind them was one of relief or frustration, but he didn't turn around to find out.

As he steered them toward the sign, Austin scanned the area. It wasn't enclosed, so if he got in there and found he couldn't handle it, there were literally hundreds of escape

285

routes. Some of them went through what looked to be employee-only areas, but that was no big deal. As long as he could always find a way out, he'd be fine.

He hoped.

As they passed under the sign, Austin dragged in a long breath. So far, so good.

They made their way through a trail that led past dozens of trees, each decorated in a different style, some formal, some more festive. One was even decorated in red, white, and blue and had soldier ornaments hanging from its branches.

Austin kept walking, until they reached a life-size stable with actors dressed in nativity garb. He veered in the other direction—he had no need to sit here and watch people swallow this neat and tidy little story about a cute baby who was supposed to be the Savior of the world. If he couldn't save Isaad and Tanner, how could he save Austin—or anyone else, for that matter?

But Leah's hand on his arm stopped him. "I'd like to watch this for a minute, if you don't mind." Her words were soft, as if she knew he wanted to protest.

He pressed his mouth closed but led the way to a section of bleachers that had been erected to the side of the stable.

"Do you know the Christmas story?" he heard Leah ask Jackson.

"Like about Santa? Yeah, everyone does." The boy's tone implied what he thought of Leah's question. If he kept this up, Austin was going to have to have a talk with him about speaking respectfully.

But Leah smiled at the kid and said gently, "I mean the true Christmas story. About Jesus."

When Jackson didn't answer, Leah gestured for Austin to find them a seat in the bleachers.

He scanned the mostly full benches. He could probably get to the top if he had to. But he'd rather not attempt it right now. Instead, he led the way to a section of the front row that had just enough room for the three of them. He sat, and Leah followed, leaving room between them for Jackson to squeeze in.

But the boy stepped to Austin's other side, gesturing that Austin should slide over so he could sit there. Austin glanced at Leah, the hurt in her eyes lancing his gut, but at her subtle nod, he slid closer to her.

The space was so tight that he had to angle his shoulder behind her to make enough room for Jackson, and their arms pressed against each other.

Leah's back stiffened, but she gave him a strained smile. Her warm cinnamony smell played with his senses, and he tried to take his focus off of her.

"This is stupid," Jackson muttered from his other side.

Austin felt the same way, but he owed it to Leah not to show it.

"Give it a chance," he whispered to the boy as music started to play over the speakers.

Jackson gave him a disagreeable look, but Austin's gaze went to Leah. She was watching as a man and a pregnant woman—presumably Mary and Joseph—walked toward the stable. The look on Leah's face—it was a look Austin would love to see there all the time. She looked at peace, filled with hope and joy. The look stirred something familiar.

He'd felt that way once, hadn't he?

He shoved the question aside.

Even if he had, he'd never feel that way again. And there was no point dwelling on it.

"I'm sorry about the Ferris wheel." Austin's apology sent a renewed stab to Leah's belly, but she shook her head as they stood together in her driveway after returning from Rothman's. It wasn't Austin's fault that after the nativity play, she'd suggested they go on the farm's small Ferris wheel—the first suggestion she'd had all day that excited Jackson. It also wasn't Austin's fault that it was a two-person ride. Or that Jackson had insisted on riding with Austin or not going on it at all.

Austin had tried his best to convince the boy to go with her, even resorting to bribery—he'd ride with the boy *after* Jackson took a turn with Leah—but nothing had worked.

She swallowed past the hurt that had been building for the past four days into a constant ache at the back of her throat and fought off the questions that had been swirling through her mind all afternoon. Why was Jackson resisting her affection? Why did he seem to adore Austin and loathe her? And worst of all, had becoming a foster mother been a terrible mistake?

"Thanks for coming," she finally managed to say. "It was good for Jackson."

Austin touched a hand to her elbow. "It will get better."

She let out a breath. "Yeah."

In church this morning, sitting next to Jackson, surrounded by her church family, she'd been sure that was true. But now she was less certain than ever.

The front door burst open, and Jackson stepped outside. He'd peeled off his socks and shoes, but he still wore the sweatshirt Austin had given him.

"Don't come out here barefoot," Leah called, though she was pretty sure her reprimand lacked conviction. She was too exhausted to summon any up right now.

To her surprise, Jackson pulled his feet back into the house, though he leaned his torso farther out the door. "You want to see Ned?"

Though she and Austin were standing right next to each other, Leah knew the question was directed to her neighbor.

"Oh, uh—" Austin hesitated, and Leah could feel his gaze slide to her.

She shrugged. "Might as well come in and see the squirrel you roped me into keeping."

"I'm not sure you could be roped into anything," Austin muttered. He gave her shoulder a gentle nudge, then stepped past her toward the house.

Leah followed, her feet dragging through what was left of the snow. When was the last time she'd been this exhausted?

Inside, she busied herself heating up leftovers from yesterday's wedding. She'd make a plate for herself and one to send home with Austin. And a PBJ for Jackson.

She was pulling the last of the food from the microwave when Austin emerged from Jackson's room.

"You have to admit Ned is cute." Austin stepped into the kitchen, flashing her a smile that she couldn't help but return. If she didn't know better, she'd say today hadn't been good for only Jackson. It'd been good for Austin too. He still wore that haunted look, but at least he'd started smiling more.

"Don't even start." But she couldn't keep a straight face. Aside from looking like a rat, the baby squirrel was fairly adorable. And the little sounds it made were precious.

"I guess I'm going to head out. Let you guys get some dinner."

But Leah wasn't going to have any of that. "You aren't leaving until I give you your plate, young man. No takeout pizza for you tonight."

Austin opened his mouth, and she was sure he was going to argue, but then he said, "I was hoping you'd say that. That food smells delicious."

She couldn't resist laughing. She passed him the plate that held Jackson's sandwich. "Would you take this to Jackson? You don't have to make sure he eats it or anything. He'll eat it later when no one is watching."

Austin's brow wrinkled. "Why?"

"That I haven't figured out. But for now I'm happy he's actually eating something."

Austin's gaze lingered on her another moment, then he took the sandwich and brought it to Jackson's room. He was back within a few seconds.

Leah examined the plate she'd made him. "I should cover this, so it doesn't get cold as you're carrying it home. Or—" She didn't know why she stopped. She had friends eat here all the time. It was no big deal if she invited him to do the same. He was becoming a friend, wasn't he?

Still, what if he took the invitation the wrong way?

Better to play it safe.

"Or I could put it in a container." She ducked into one of her lower cabinets, sticking her head farther into it than strictly necessary to fetch her favorite large container, mainly to hide the flush rising to her cheeks.

There's nothing to be embarrassed about, she scolded herself. *It's not like you wanted to invite him as anything more than a friend.*

By the time she'd nabbed the container and its matching cover, her face had cooled. She stood and fit the food into it, then snapped the cover on and passed it to him.

"Thank you." His dark eyes held hers. "I'll enjoy this."

She offered a silent nod, and he turned toward the door.

"Austin, wait." She bit her lip as he turned toward her, eyes searching.

"Why don't you—" But his mesmerizing gaze made her change her mind again. "Why don't you take one of these too?"

She opened the box of leftover cupcakes Peyton had left and passed one to him.

"Thanks." He turned toward the door again, hesitating a second this time.

But she held her tongue, and after a moment, he was gone.

Chapter 13

The resistance band pulled taut as Austin finished his last set of leg lifts. He swiped at his forehead, then picked up his dumbbells, glancing at the clock on the wall. Four thirty. That gave him just enough time to finish his workout and shower before Leah stopped by with dinner.

At least if she continued the pattern they'd fallen into over the last few days.

Austin tried to feel guilty for taking advantage of her kindness. But she truly seemed to enjoy giving him food—which probably explained her career as a caterer. And, maybe he shouldn't admit it, but he'd come to look forward to the few minutes they spent together each day as they exchanged dishes, his empty ones for her freshly filled ones.

Those were the few moments each day when he could let himself focus on something other than his rehabilitation and getting back to Afghanistan. When his thoughts didn't track to what had happened over there—what could still be happening to his brother.

When Leah was here, he could think about other things. Like her sparkling laugh. And her swirly eyes. And her easy kindness.

Austin shook his head at the dumbbells, resting motionless in his hands.

He was acting like a kid with a crush.

Which was the furthest thing from what he was.

He was simply a man who appreciated a friendly neighbor—and good food.

One of these days, he'd have to start cooking for himself again. But how could he? After what Tanner had said the last time he cooked?

If this is the last meal I ever eat, I'll die happy.

What was he supposed to do with the fact that it *had* been the last meal Tanner ever ate?

The blare of a video call nearly made him drop the still uncurled dumbbell on his toes. He set the weights down and dove toward his computer. Thursdays were Chad's day to call. If someone was calling on a Wednesday—Austin's throat closed.

No, not Chad. Please don't let anything have happened to Chad.

The moment he clicked to answer and Chad's face appeared on the screen, Austin crumpled onto the couch.

Chad was alive. He was in one piece.

"Why are you calling?"

"It's good to see you too, brother." Chad wagged his eyebrows.

But the scare of the call hadn't worn off, and Austin wasn't ready to joke.

"Seriously, Chad. What's wrong? Why are you calling early?"

"I'm hurt." Chad pressed a mock hand to his heart. "Can't a guy just want to talk to his little brother?"

Under the joking, Austin heard what his brother wasn't saying. He was going on an assignment and wanted to call in case—

Austin couldn't let himself go there. He worked hard to match his brother's joking tone. "A guy can. *You* can't."

A flash of relief crossed Chad's face. He knew Austin had caught on.

"So, how's Hope Springs?"

"Pretty quiet. Kind of peaceful, actually."

"Good. And have you met some actual people? Other than the mailman this time?"

"Yes." He didn't know why, but he wanted to leave it at that.

Chad's eyes narrowed. "Name two people."

"Leah, Jackson, Sophie, Spencer, Peyton, Jade, Dan." He paused, trying to remember the names of the others he had met at Leah's house.

"Whoa. Whoa. Whoa." Chad's eyes went wide. "Are you making up names now?"

Austin snorted. "No. But thanks for the vote of confidence."

"Where did you possibly meet that many people in under a week?"

Austin shrugged. "Just my natural charisma."

Now it was Chad's turn to snort. "No, seriously."

"My neighbor dragged me over to her house when she had some friends over."

"She?" Chad's eyebrows lifted toward his slightly receding hairline.

"Knock it off." But Austin couldn't deny the heat radiating from his face. Hopefully Chad's connection wasn't good enough to detect it from the other side of the world.

"Aw, does little Austin like a girl?"

"Seriously, Chad. Knock it off. It's not like that."

"Like what?" Chad blinked at him innocently. "Seriously, though, Austin. I hope you do like her."

"Why? For all you know, she's hideous."

Chad gave him a knowing look. "Is she?"

Austin groaned. He'd walked right into that one.

"No." The word came out begrudgingly. But Leah was the farthest thing from hideous. "She's actually kind of gorgeous."

"I knew it." Chad's chortle shot through the computer.

"Don't get too full of yourself." Austin had to find a way to change the subject. "Just because she's pretty doesn't mean I'm interested."

A knock at the door made him lift his head. On the other side of the front window, Leah was waving at him, wearing a bright smile.

"Ah, look at your face." Chad's amused voice yanked Austin's attention back to the computer screen. "It's her, isn't it? You are such a goner."

Austin rolled his eyes. "I'm not a goner. She has food, and I'm hungry."

"Wait, you two are having dinner together? And you say there's nothing going on?"

"We're not having dinner together." They kept their relationship strictly neighborly. "She noticed that I was getting takeout all the time and apparently made it her mission to give me good food. She's a caterer, so—"

"Are you going to keep the poor girl out in the cold all night, or are you going to answer the door?"

"I'll answer the door if you ever shut up for a minute."

"Actually, I'd love to stick around to see how this goes, but I have to fly."

"Oh." Much as Austin didn't want Chad hovering in the background of his conversation with Leah, he wasn't ready to say goodbye to his brother yet. Not if it might be the last time—

Stop thinking like that.

"Take care of yourself, bro." He swallowed down all the other things he should say but couldn't.

"You too. I'll call when I can. But don't be worried if it's not for a while. And in the meantime, I wouldn't mind a prayer or two."

Fat chance he wouldn't worry. Or that he'd pray. But Austin worked his face into a stoic expression and nodded.

"And Austin?" Chad leaned closer to the camera. "I'm happy for you. And your girlfriend. Now go let her in." The screen went blank, and Austin shook his head as a chuckle escaped. Chad always had to have the last word.

He must have still been chuckling when he opened the door because Leah took one look at him, then peered over his shoulder. "What's so funny?"

"Nothing." Austin tried to straighten his lips, but seeing her didn't do anything to erase the smile. "I was just talking to my brother."

"Oh, I'm sorry. I didn't realize you had company. I can go get more food. Give me five minutes." She turned toward the porch steps, and without thinking, Austin reached for her arm.

"It's just me. I was chatting with him online." He kept his hand on her arm as she spun back toward him—maybe for a second or two longer than was necessary.

Fine.

Maybe Chad was right.

Maybe he did like her.

But so what? It wasn't like he was going to do anything about it.

"Where does he live?" Leah passed him the container, and he had no choice but to lift his hand from her arm to take the food.

"Afghanistan right now." As he did every night, he lifted the cover just enough to smell the contents. "Oh, pork." He allowed himself another sniff. "My favorite." He snapped the lid closed so the food wouldn't cool while he talked to Leah. Because now that she was here, he didn't want her to go.

"That must be hard." Leah stepped closer and jabbed her hands into her coat pockets. "Having a brother over there. Do you talk often?"

"Once a week or so when we can."

Until last year, they'd been together every day. But he didn't want to talk about that right now. "How's Jackson?"

293

Leah's sigh sounded like it carried the weight of the world. Or of a mother.

"I've already been to the principal's office three times this week, and Jackson still won't talk to me, so . . . not great."

"I was sure letting him keep that squirrel was going to score you points."

Leah lifted her hands to her mouth and blew on them. "I'm not sure anything I do could score points with him. Unless I could become you."

There was no bitterness behind her words, but still regret swamped Austin. For whatever reason, Jackson had taken a liking to him. Maybe the boy sensed that Austin was as broken as he was.

"Anyway—" Leah took a step backward. "Enjoy the pork. There are some mashed potatoes and corn in there too." She took another backward step, then turned toward the stairs.

"Leah."

She stopped, but he had no idea what to say. He only knew he wasn't ready for her to leave yet.

But that was ridiculous. What was he going to do, ask her to stay and watch him eat the food she'd brought?

"This smells delicious. Thanks."

She nodded and skipped down the steps, leaving him to eat alone.

Again.

Chapter 14

This was getting ridiculous.

Thursday night, Leah eyed the food she was about to bring to Austin.

It wasn't that she minded bringing him dinner. In fact, she quite enjoyed it. Sharing food with others was one of her greatest joys, and since Jackson refused to eat anything beyond peanut butter and jelly, it was nice to have someone else appreciate her cooking.

And, fine, she enjoyed her conversations with Austin too.

But it would make a lot more sense to enjoy those conversations over dinner, rather than standing at his door dropping off food. Plus, if he happened to come to her house to eat, maybe Jackson would emerge from his room longer than the three seconds it took him to refill Ned's water.

So why didn't she just invite Austin over for dinner already? It wasn't like he would misconstrue her invitation, especially since he'd shown zero interest in her.

What was she afraid of? That her friends would find out and jump to conclusions?

So what if they did?

She was an adult. She didn't have to be ruled by what her friends thought.

Mind made up, she grabbed her coat and charged for the front door before she could chicken out.

The smile Austin met her with knocked a little of the confidence out of her. This *was* the right thing to do, wasn't it?

Not that she could turn back now.

"Hey, I didn't bring dinner tonight," she blurted, then gave herself an internal kick. That wasn't exactly an invitation.

"I see that." Austin's grin didn't dim. "You know you don't have to have food to knock on my door though, right?"

Her laugh sounded nervous even to her own ears. "What I meant was, instead of bringing food to you, I thought it might make more sense to bring you to the food. If you want to come over. I mean, Jackson has been asking about you, and I figured that way you could kill two birds with one stone—eat and see Jackson and—"

"Leah."

"Yeah?" She forced herself to stop and take a breath. Had she been babbling?

"I'd love to come over and say hi to Jackson."

"Oh." A flutter rippled through her belly, but Leah ignored it. "Okay. Good."

She took a step away from the door and waited for Austin to pull on his stocking cap and follow her out.

"You look a little bit like a cat burglar in that." She gestured to his black track pants, black sweatshirt, and black cap.

Austin's rich, full laugh warmed her. "I prefer ninja. Sounds tougher."

Leah eased into step beside him as they crossed the yard.

See, this wasn't weird at all.

When they got to her front door, Austin opened it and gestured her inside.

He followed, pulling his cap off and running a hand over his hair. "Smells delicious, as always."

"Ravioli tonight. And garlic bread."

Austin groaned and patted his flat torso. "I'm going to have to start running twice as far if you keep feeding me like this."

Leah highly doubted that. There was no way a guy built like Austin didn't have a six pack.

She strode toward the kitchen to banish the thought. "Everything will be ready in a minute. Do you want to say hi to Jackson first?"

She directed a cooling breath toward her face as he moved down the hall toward Jackson's room. What was her problem tonight?

It wasn't like she'd never had a friend who happened to be male over for dinner before.

As she got out plates and silverware, she gave herself a strict talking to.

It's no big deal. You're two friends having a meal. It's no different than having Peyton over for dinner.

Except Peyton didn't have broad shoulders and mysterious, slightly haunted eyes.

Leah huffed at herself.

Clearly, this talking to wasn't working.

"Everything okay?"

She jumped, nearly dropping the pan of noodles covered in her homemade marinara sauce.

"Yep." She only hoped she sounded less flustered than she felt. "Could you grab the water?" She nodded toward the pitcher on the counter.

Austin slid past her, his warm scent washing over her. She scooted to the table and set the pan down harder than she meant to.

"Nice oven mitts." Austin pointed at her hands, protected by a ratty set of red and white checked mitts.

"They were my dad's. He always wore them when he grilled out. I should probably toss them, but I can't make myself do it."

Austin nodded, and though he didn't say anything, she could read the understanding in his eyes.

They both took a seat, and she folded her hands to offer a silent prayer for her food.

Normally, she invited her guests to join in. But after the way Austin had shut down her invitation to church last Sunday and the way he'd watched the nativity play with barely disguised contempt, she decided it best to let it go.

Silently, they each dug into their food, and for a few minutes neither of them said anything.

Great. This was going to be just like her date with Robert.

Not that this was a date.

"Do you mind if I ask you something?" The question came out before she could think better of it.

Austin's eyes met hers, his smile slightly guarded. "Can't promise I'll answer. But you can always ask."

Leah nodded. At least he was honest. "Why didn't you want to watch the nativity play or go to church?" If nothing else, the question should solidify that this wasn't a date. Wasn't that the number one rule of dating: Don't talk about religion?

Austin wiped his mouth with his napkin and took a long drink of water.

She lowered her gaze to her plate, scooping another bite. He had said he might not answer. So she shouldn't be surprised. Or disappointed.

"I used to go to church." His voice was flat, but when Leah looked up, she saw the conflict brewing in his eyes.

"But you don't anymore?"

He shook his head and took another bite.

"Do you mind if I ask why? Did something happen at your church or—"

Another head shake. "Nothing like that. I just don't believe any of it anymore."

"Any of it?" Leah swallowed against the sick feeling that swirled in her stomach. It broke her heart every time she learned of someone who had once believed but had fallen away.

"Any of it." Austin sat completely rigid, and Leah could tell the conversation was over. Fine. She'd let it go for now.

But if he thought that was the last he was going to hear from her on that topic, he was wrong. What kind of friend would she be if she sat back and watched him throw away his faith?

Their conversation turned to lighter topics, including Ned the squirrel, who had nearly doubled in size already. In spite of herself, Leah had to admit that the little critter was cute. And the way Jackson cared for the squirrel gave her hope that under the boy who got into fights at school, there was a sweet, caring young man.

They lapsed back into silence as they finished the meal, but Leah found she didn't mind.

After he'd scooped the last bite off his plate, Austin studied her. "My turn to ask you a question."

"And do I have to answer as thoroughly as you did?" She couldn't help the teasing note.

Austin returned her smile. "You can be as cryptic or as open as you want." At her nod, Austin continued, "What made you decide to become a foster mom?"

Leah pressed her hands to the table, thinking. There were so many reasons she'd wanted to be a foster mom—how did she begin to answer that question?

Austin apparently took her hesitation as a desire to be cryptic because he picked up his plate and moved to the sink. "You don't have to answer."

"No, it's not that. I'm just trying to figure out how to give you an answer that doesn't take all night."

Austin shrugged. "I don't have anything else to do."

"Okay." Leah lifted an eyebrow and led him to the living room. They settled on opposite ends of the couch but angled toward each other.

Leah lost track of time as she told Austin about how Dan had adopted Jade's baby after they were married. How right around that time she'd seen a news special about the great need for foster families. How there were twenty-five thousand kids over the age of eleven waiting to be adopted from foster care, and thousands of them would likely never find a permanent home. How her heart had broken for them and she'd known this was something she could fix. That she could make a better life for at least one kid. How it wasn't just something she *wanted* to do, it was something she felt *called* to do.

He didn't even roll his eyes when she told him how she'd prayed about it. How God had helped everything fall in place at just the right time so that she got this house right before she was due for the required home study.

"Plus, I've always wanted kids," she said now. "And time is kind of running out for me to have any biological children, so . . ."

Austin leaned forward, holding out a hand to stop her. "Hold on. You can't be more than thirty or so."

She laughed, not sure if she should be flattered or insulted that he'd gotten so close to her actual age. At least he'd been a couple years under instead of a couple years over with his guess.

"Thirty-two," she corrected.

"That's hardly running out of time to have kids. My friend Tanner—" But he broke off, clearing his throat. "People have kids into their forties these days."

"I know. But I have no plans to get married in the near—or distant—future. Which makes it a little harder." She smoothed her hands over her jeans. She had no idea why she'd told him all of this.

Or why he'd listened.

"Well, for the record, I think what you're doing is really great." With the haunted look buried farther in the background, Austin's eyes were warm, and she appreciated him saying it.

She only wished she could still be so sure it was true. "I hope so."

The couch shifted as Austin stood. "I should get home. You probably need to get Jackson to bed."

Leah lurched upright. "What time is it?" A quick look at her phone confirmed it was almost nine o'clock. Had they really been talking for two hours? She pushed to her feet and walked Austin to the door.

"Thanks for dinner." He reached for the door handle but didn't open it. His eyes searched her face, and he took half a step closer.

Panic flooded Leah's system, ringing in her ears and making spots pop in front of her eyes. Was he going to kiss her? Is that why he was looking at her like that?

She took two steps back, then spun and fled to the kitchen. "You should take some ravioli home," she called over her shoulder, barely able to get the words out between gasped breaths.

In the kitchen, she forced herself to count to ten and inhale through her nose as she found a container and scooped leftover pasta into it. She was overreacting. Austin hadn't wanted to kiss her. He'd simply been moving so he could get through the door.

But she made sure to stay just out of arm's reach from him as she passed him the food. His eyes lingered on hers a moment, his expression unreadable, then he said goodnight and was out the door.

As she locked it behind him, Leah drew in another deep breath, telling herself she didn't enjoy the subtle hint of him that still hung in the air.

Chapter 15

Keep going.

This was the farthest he'd run yet, and Austin could feel his muscles starting to give out. But he was only three blocks from home. He wasn't going to let himself quit before then. Even if his knees *were* screaming at him.

He lifted an arm to mop the sweat from his brow, trying to concentrate on his breaths. His stride was different with the prosthetic than it had been before—uneven now—and it always threw his breathing off.

He'd considered getting a running prosthetic, but he felt wrong doing that. Like it would be cheating. And he'd already cheated death. The least he could do was avoid making things easier on himself than they should be.

Inhale, two, three, four . . .

He lost count as his mind drifted to last night again. For the life of him, he couldn't figure out what had possessed him. Leah had invited him over for a nice, friendly dinner—emphasis on *friend*—and he'd ended up almost kissing her.

Good thing she had more sense than he did.

He couldn't remember the last time he'd kissed any woman, let alone one he'd known for only a week. Though it felt like he'd known her longer—like his days in Hope Springs were part of another life, one so far removed from his old life that he could escape it for a little while.

Maybe that was it. That was why he wasn't acting like himself.

In which case, he'd better get back to being himself if he wanted to be in shape for his physical.

No more distractions, he promised himself as he pulled up in front of his house. Even as he made the promise, though, he couldn't keep his eyes from traveling to Leah's house. Although it was still early afternoon, her car was in the driveway. Hopefully that didn't mean Jackson had been suspended again.

Maybe he should check in. Make sure everything was okay.

That was what neighbors did, right?

Or, it was the very definition of distraction.

Austin forced himself to walk up his driveway. Whatever it was, she could handle it on her own. And if she needed anything, she'd ask.

Unless he'd scared her away with that near kiss.

As he reached his porch, Leah's door opened, and she rushed outside. Seeing her did nothing to slow his heart rate.

But either she didn't notice him, or she'd chosen to ignore him. As she charged toward her car, disappointment hit Austin. She was leaving. He wouldn't be able to talk to her even if he wanted to.

But instead of getting into the car, she circled to the trunk and popped it open, loading bag after bag into her arms.

Don't get distracted.

But he couldn't just stand here and let her struggle with that heavy load alone.

Ignoring the voice of common sense blaring in his head, he crossed the yard, reaching her car as she turned to go inside.

"Oh, Austin." She jumped, looking ready to run.

Was it because he'd startled her? Or because he'd freaked her out last night?

"Sorry. It looked like you could use some help." He reached to take a few bags from her, then leaned into the trunk to lift out a red cake box tied with string. "This too?"

She nodded and closed the trunk. "Thanks. I had no idea this was going to take so long."

Austin followed her toward the house. "And what is this?"

Leah's sigh was exasperated. "I had the brilliant idea to throw Jackson a birthday party. So I had to go shopping to get stuff for it. But I had no idea what to get him for a gift, so it took forever. I ended up with this." She set her bags on the kitchen counter, then rummaged in one, pulling out a small box and passing it to him. "Do you think he'll like it?"

Austin opened the box, which held a sports watch. "I'm sure he'll love it."

Leah bustled around the kitchen to put groceries away. "I don't think he'll ever love anything I do, but as long as he doesn't hate it, that will be a start."

He held the watch out to her, and she scurried to take it, then began piling streamers and balloons on the counter before zipping across the kitchen to grab a punch bowl.

"Hey. Leah?"

"Yep?" She kept moving.

"Maybe you should slow down. You're moving faster than Ned the squirrel right now."

Leah threw him a frazzled smile. "Can't. I have way too much to do before I have to pick up Jackson and his friends. And—" Now she stopped and stared at him, her expression pure panic. "I have no idea what thirteen-year-old boys like to do."

Austin clapped his hands together and headed for the door. "I can help you with that."

"Wait. Where are you going?" Leah's voice trailed him.

Austin rushed to his own house, where he unhooked his video game console and gathered up his games and controllers.

He may not know how to act around Leah right now.

But boys and video games? *That* he did know.

Plus, maybe helping with Jackson's party would get things back to normal with Leah.

And neither of them would have to think about that almost-kiss anymore.

Leah could not stop thinking about how she'd been so sure Austin was going to kiss her last night.

All afternoon, as he'd set up the video game console and then helped her decorate, her eyes had tracked to him again and again. But not once had he shown anything other than friendly interest. Which could mean only one thing: She'd completely imagined his desire to kiss her.

What a relief.

So why did her eyes insist on going to him again now, as she stepped into the living room, balancing a tray of food?

"Oh! Smoked you!" Austin tossed his remote onto the couch and fist-bumped one of the boys she'd invited over.

She'd wanted Jackson to choose a few friends for the party, but when he'd refused, she'd asked one of his teachers who he got along with. After some hesitation, Mrs. Johnson had suggested Logan, Kayden, Tommy, and Braxton. Fortunately, all four had agreed to come.

And they all seemed to be having fun—even Jackson, whom Leah had heard cheering moments before. He'd even shown a smidge of interest in the watch she'd given him, though he'd set it aside without putting it on.

"You guys ready for some food?" She started toward the coffee table, but before she could take two steps, Austin was on his feet and lifting the tray of pigs in a blanket from her hands.

Jackson's friends lunged for the food the moment it hit the table.

"Aw, man." The boy who'd been playing the video game spoke around a mouthful of food. "Jackson, your dad is way too good at this game. It's not fair."

Austin froze, looking from her to Jackson. When Jackson shrugged, Austin turned back to her, the question clear in his eyes. Should he correct the boy and tell them he wasn't Jackson's father?

Leah gave a subtle head shake. So what if Jackson's friends thought Austin was his dad. It wouldn't hurt anything.

"Better come get some food, Jackson, before your friends eat it all." Leah tried not to sound too motherly so she wouldn't embarrass Jackson.

He didn't acknowledge that he'd heard her.

"This looks great." Austin leaned forward to grab one of the pigs-in-a-blanket.

"Jackson's mom, you make good food," Kayden said, helping himself to more.

Leah beamed at him. These boys were so polite. "Thank—"

But before she could finish the sentence, Jackson jumped in. "She's not my mom."

The rest of the boys fell silent, and aside from the sound of their chewing, the room went still. Leah worked to keep her smile in place even though it felt like her face had hardened into plastic. Her pulse roared in her ears, but fighting past it, she turned to Kayden. "You can call me Miss Zelner. Or Leah. Leah would be fine too." Her voice was too quiet, and she gave a single nod, then turned and walked out of the room.

But the kitchen wasn't far enough. She pushed through the door to the backyard, letting the Arctic blast of the cold front the forecasters had been predicting for days buffet her. Her face froze instantly, except in the spots where hot tears tracked down her cheeks.

I'm trying here, Lord, I really am. Please help me. If ever she could use a *yes* in answer to a prayer, this was it.

But she was starting to doubt she would get it.

Austin passed his controller off to one of the other boys, throwing Jackson a dark look as he stood and followed Leah. If the boy noticed the look, he didn't acknowledge it.

He tried the kitchen first, but it was empty, although another batch of hot dogs boiled on the stove. Austin checked on them, then walked toward the hallway. But as he passed the back door, he caught sight of movement on the dark patio.

He opened the door slowly, so he wouldn't bump her. She shuffled out of the way but didn't look at him.

"He's never going to accept me, is he?" Her voice was broken, her face wet. "Every time I think things are getting better, he goes and reminds me that they're not. Not really."

"Sure they are." He nudged her shoulder with his. "He didn't say he hates you. Just that you're not his mom. Which, biologically, is true."

"He didn't correct them that you're not his dad," she muttered. "Maybe he'd be better off with you."

He held up a hand. Befriending the kid was one thing. But he most certainly wasn't looking to become a father. "I'm not in the market for a kid."

Leah turned to him, her normally light eyes shadowed in darkness. "Why not? You'd make a great dad."

Austin shrugged. "I don't think I could go it alone like you're doing. If I ever had a kid, I'd need a wife first. And there aren't exactly a lot of candidates seeking after that position."

Why had he said *that*? It wasn't like he was looking for candidates.

Leah gave him a sideways glance but didn't say anything further. After a few minutes, she wiped her tears and turned toward the house. "We'd better get back in there."

As Austin followed her inside, the shoe on his prosthetic snagged on the threshold. He pitched forward, shuffling his feet quickly to catch his balance.

But it was too late.

He careened into Leah, shoving her forward before landing on his knees behind her.

She spun toward him, eyes widening. "Are you all right?"

"I'm sorry. Did I hurt you?" He was still on his hands and knees, but he was pretty sure he hadn't injured anything.

"I'm fine." Leah reached to help him up. "What happened?"

He ignored her hand. "Just tripped," he muttered. Bracing his hands against the floor, he pulled his good leg out from under him. Leah moved her hand closer, as if he hadn't seen it the first time.

"I've got it." The words came out with more force than he intended. "Go check on the boys. I'll be right there."

He didn't look at her, but he could feel her eyes drilling into him. Finally, she left the room.

When she was gone, he slowly pushed up onto his right leg, pulling his left leg behind him and readjusting his track pants over the prosthetic. He didn't know why it was so important to him to keep his prosthetic hidden. He'd worn shorts all summer without giving it a second thought. Sure, he got looks sometimes, but it didn't matter. He hadn't cared who had known how broken he was.

But here things were different. No one here knew what had happened to him. They didn't see him as someone broken. As far as they knew, he was whole and intact. And knowing there were people who thought that gave him hope that maybe he could be again.

Someday.

The shadows on the ceiling shifted as the trees outside bent in the whistling wind. It was the only movement in the room, other than the rise and fall of Leah's chest as she tried to take relaxing breaths.

Austin had sent her to bed at midnight, promising to hang out with the boys until they dropped off to sleep and then go home. That had been three hours ago, and the sounds from the living room had long since died down, but still she couldn't sleep.

Every time she closed her eyes, all she heard was Jackson's sneered words, "She's not my mother." How many times would he say that? Would he insist on it for the rest of his life?

She'd meant it when she'd told Austin the boy would be better off with him. Or at least with both of them.

Her eyes opened wider in the dark. What had brought on that thought? She didn't want to raise a child with Austin.

She'd just been thinking about how much easier it was to deal with Jackson when Austin was around. How he always seemed to know what to say to get Jackson to do what he was supposed to do. How on occasion he could even make Jackson smile. And her—he could definitely make her smile too.

Stop it.

This wasn't about her or her feelings for Austin.

Not that she had any.

She punched her pillow into a new position and settled her head into it. Finally, her eyes drooped closed, and she let the heaviness of sleep start to carry her away.

But only moments later, her eyes sprang open as a yell of some sort echoed from the front of the house. She bolted upright and sprang out of bed. That wasn't the fun kind of yelling the boys had been doing as they'd played.

This was more like a terrified yell. A genuine cry of pain or fear.

Maybe one of the boys had gotten up to go to the bathroom and been startled. Or maybe they were having a nightmare. Hopefully no one was fighting.

She clicked on the screen of her phone as she approached the living room, so she'd have enough light to find her way without waking the boys—assuming they were still asleep after that commotion.

Boys were spread across every inch of the living room floor, and all of them appeared to be out cold.

Another yell sounded, this time making Leah jump. She swung her phone to the other side of the room. Austin was sprawled on her couch, eyes clenched tight, arm flailing, as if he were trying to reach someone. His yell was quieter this time but filled with more anguish than she'd ever heard from a person before.

She hurried through the maze of sleeping boys, careful not to step on anyone. Miraculously, not a single one of them stirred. There was a small opening between where one of the boys slept on the floor and the edge of the couch, and Leah wedged her feet into the space, then bent over and laid a gentle hand on Austin's arm. Under her hand, his biceps were rigid, and his shirt was damp with sweat.

"Austin." She shook him lightly as she whispered. "Austin, wake up." She'd barely been able to hear herself, and yet Austin woke with a start, eyes wild as he searched her face, hands coming to her shoulders.

"Shh. It's okay. You were having a dream." Instinctively, she stroked his hair.

"Sorry." He sat up so quickly she had to clutch at his shoulder to keep from falling over the boy on the floor.

"I should go." His whisper was hoarse.

"Yeah, of course." She let go of him and made her way through the sleeping boys. She didn't hear any footsteps behind her, but the moment she'd crossed into the dining room, he was there.

"I'll go out the back door, so I don't wake them." Austin was still whispering.

She wanted to ask him what the dream had been about. If it had anything to do with whatever gave him that haunted look.

But she simply passed him his coat and opened the door for him. "I'll bring your games back tomorrow."

He waved her off. "Let Jackson keep them." And then he was gone.

Leah stood outside the door, letting the night air poke needles into her skin as she watched him cross their yards and enter his own house.

He'd been through something traumatic at some point in his life. Of that much she was becoming more and more certain.

Maybe it was why he was able to make a connection with Jackson so easily. Maybe if she could help fix whatever it was that had hurt Austin, she could figure out how to fix Jackson too.

At any rate, it was worth a shot.

Because she wasn't sure how much longer she could survive with things as they were.

Chapter 16

He never should have gotten close to them.

Austin's feet dragged to a walk, though he couldn't have run more than a mile. But his limbs hung heavy with the need for sleep.

He hadn't even tried to go to bed when he'd gotten home from Leah's. After that nightmare, sleep would have been worse than the exhaustion that weighed on him now.

Because this time when the IED went off, it wasn't only Tanner and Isaad he couldn't save. Leah and Jackson were there too. He couldn't shake the image of their broken bodies lying on the sand. It had been enough to drive him from the house at first light. But even now, as the wind cut at his skin and the sky hung gray and bleak above him, he couldn't escape it.

He scrubbed his hands over his face, as if that could banish the image seared into his mind.

He knew it couldn't happen to them. There were no explosives alongside the roads here. They weren't in a war zone. They were in the middle of sleepy Hope Springs.

But that didn't do anything to loosen the vise that choked the air out of his lungs every time he thought of it.

Was this what it was going to be like for the rest of his life? Every time he got close to someone, he'd see them being blown to pieces? How was he supposed to live like that?

A sudden need to talk to Chad gripped him. But he couldn't. Chad was on a mission, facing who knew what kind of danger.

And there was nothing Austin could do to keep him safe.

His brother's request from the other day kept popping into his head: "I wouldn't mind a prayer or two."

Chad had never asked Austin to pray for him before. Had he done it now because he knew something he wasn't telling Austin? Was he worried he might not make it back this time?

Austin shoved the thought aside.

More likely, it had been one more of Chad's lame attempts to get him to turn back to God.

Well, his brother could forget that. Believing in God had never done anything good for him. And it wasn't going to now either.

But the words came almost automatically. *Please keep—*

No.

He wasn't going to fall for that again. Chad was a good soldier. And good soldiers had his back. He'd be fine.

Austin hadn't been paying attention to where he was walking, but now he pulled up short at a scenic overlook he'd never come across before. The ground dropped away at the side of the road to the lake below, where waves frothed against the beach.

He drew in a ragged breath and eyed the drop-off. It was steep but not so steep he couldn't get down it.

He lowered his right leg tentatively into the thin covering of snow. When it held, he brought his left leg down. The movement was familiar, comforting. If it weren't for the pounding of the waves below, he could almost close his eyes and be back in the Afghan mountains.

At the bottom of the hill, he stepped cautiously onto the sand, packed hard by the cold. The sharp scent of the water sliced into the tension he'd carried all morning.

"What am I supposed to do now, Chad?" He called out, as if the waves could carry the message to his brother. "And don't say pray."

The lake foamed at his feet, and the sky loosed a sheet of thick, wet snowflakes.

Austin shook his head. He refused to believe the timing was anything more than a coincidence.

Anyway, he didn't need an answer. He already knew what his brother would say. "Talk to someone."

And Austin would scoff, just like he did now. Because he was tired of talking about it. The shrink he'd been required to see while he was in the hospital had been big about talking.

You lost your leg. Do you want to talk about it? Your best friend died. Do you want to talk about it? You saw a kid die and blame yourself. Do you want to talk about it?

No, he did not want to talk about it. Not with his shrink. Not with anyone.

Austin tilted his head at the water, Leah's face refusing to leave his mind. She'd listen, he knew she would. But he couldn't possibly tell her the things he'd seen, what he'd lived through. She was too innocent for that. She shouldn't have to know about the horrors the world held.

She'd understand.

Austin sighed. He supposed she might. After all, she was raising a kid who'd discovered his mother dead. But that didn't mean he should bother her with this too. She had enough to shoulder already.

No. This was his burden to carry.

And he'd keep carrying it. Alone.

Leah blew on her hands and shook out her stiff fingers, then gripped the frigid metal of the ladder. She'd hoped the snow might let up, but if anything, it fell faster as the morning went on.

She knew some people thought it was crazy to decorate for Christmas before Thanksgiving. But she wasn't one of them.

If things hadn't been so busy lately, she'd already have the decorations up, and she was determined to get it done today. She'd tried to coax Jackson to help her after his friends left, but he'd only shot her a look of contempt and holed up in his room again. Even the lure of the Hawaiian grand prize hadn't been enough to prompt any interest.

But when they won, he'd see. He'd be glad she'd entered. Glad they got to spend the week in Hawaii together. Making mother-son memories.

She ignored the voice that said if he didn't enjoy spending time with her here, he wouldn't enjoy it in Hawaii either. It was Hawaii—how could anyone not be happy there?

Stepping carefully onto the second step from the top of the ladder, Leah reached to grip the gutter above her head. With her other hand, she attempted to fasten one of the clips she'd bought for hanging lights. But it slipped out of her numb fingers, clicking against the ladder before disappearing into the snow. She sighed and dug in her pocket for another.

This might be more than a one-day job.

"What are you doing?" The gruff voice startled her, and she dropped another clip. If she kept this up, she was going to have to make another trip to the hardware store before she got a single string of lights hung.

"You should really give some warning when you sneak up behind a person on a ladder." She turned toward Austin, reminding herself that the extra kick to her heart was only because he'd surprised her.

"It wouldn't be very sneaky then, would it?" He peered into the snow, then bent at the waist and dipped his fingers into it, fishing out the clips she'd dropped.

"How did you . . ." She shook her head as he passed it to her. "You must have eagle eyes. Did you get any sleep after you went home?"

Austin shrugged, hands in the pockets of his sweatshirt. "So what *are* you doing out here? Don't you know it's a snowstorm?"

"What does it look like I'm doing?"

Austin scrutinized her. "Trying to catch your death."

She blew on her fingers again. "Every year, Hope Springs has a house decorating contest for Christmas. The grand prize is a trip to Hawaii."

Austin watched her, face blank. Did he not see where she was going with this?

"And I thought if we won, it would be a good chance for Jackson and me to spend time together. Away from everything else."

"Have you won before?" Austin looked skeptical.

"Of course not. I've never entered before."

Austin spluttered, but she pushed on. "But I have a plan." She climbed down from the ladder and pulled out her phone, scrolling to the inspiration board she'd created. She wanted to transform her home into a gingerbread house.

Austin's eyebrows lifted toward his stocking cap. "That looks like a lot of work."

"I know." But she could do it. She hadn't created a successful business by shying away from hard work.

"At least put on some gloves." Austin pulled his hands out of his pockets, and before she realized where they were headed, he had them wrapped around hers. "You're going to get frostbite." He rubbed his warm hands back and forth over hers.

Leah scrambled for something to say. But the only thing she could focus on was his hands on hers. Why did they feel so good? So right.

Because they're warm and you're cold, she told herself. *That's the only reason.*

She tugged her hands back and tucked them into her own pockets. "Much better, thanks. I can't hold onto stuff with my gloves on."

Austin's hands went back into his pockets too, but he was still watching her.

More to escape his gaze than from any burning desire to climb the cold ladder, she reached for a rung.

But Austin held an open hand in front of her. "Pass me the clips."

She blinked at him. "I thought you didn't like Christmas." But she reached into her pocket and started depositing clips into his hand.

"I don't." Austin shoved the clips into his own pocket and took a step up the ladder, moving cautiously. "But I like—" He turned away from her, falling silent.

"But I like to help," he finally mumbled.

Leah watched his deft movements as he snapped the clips onto the gutter.

For a second, she'd been sure he was going to say, "But I like you."

But he hadn't.

Thank goodness.

Just because he'd helped hang the lights didn't mean he liked Christmas any more now than he had before today.

Though Austin had to admit that he *did* like spending the day with Leah—and if hanging Christmas lights was the price he had to pay to do it, he'd gladly pay again.

Nice job following through with that whole not getting distracted thing.

Austin ignored the snarky reprimand in his head as he hung the last string of lights around the last window. He tossed Leah the end of the cord, and she plugged it in with the other ones.

"We need Jackson out here for this." She ducked into the house to call for the boy. That kid had no idea how good he had it. Leah had spent the entire day out here—in the middle of a blizzard—to make this perfect for him.

"Austin's here," he heard Leah call.

Much as Austin had come to enjoy spending time with Jackson, it irked him that the only time the boy showed any interest in anything Leah said or did was when it involved him. He hadn't done anything to deserve the kid's respect or devotion. Not the way Leah had.

Austin heard Leah negotiating with Jackson to wear a jacket and boots. Fortunately, when the boy emerged a few minutes later, it looked like Leah had won.

"Ready for this?" Austin fist-bumped the boy. "I'll turn it on. You two go stand on the sidewalk, so you get the full effect."

When they were in position, he couldn't resist doing a countdown. "One hundred. Ninety-nine. Ninety-eight."

"Austin." Leah's laugh from across the yard warmed through him.

"Fine. If you can't be patient. Three. Two. One." He rushed through the countdown and flipped the switch.

"Wow." Leah's awed gasp drew his attention more than the lights. He walked down the driveway to join them, his eyes fixed on her face—the way her lips curved into a smile, the way her cheeks were pink and bright with cold, the way the lights from the house reflected in her eyes.

"It's perfect," she breathed as he came to stand next to her and take in the house.

Even as someone who didn't enjoy Christmas, he had to admit they'd done a good job bringing Leah's vision of a gingerbread house to life. The eaves were all outlined in white lights, while colored lights rimmed every window on the front of the house. Leah had wrapped some old wreaths in lights to make them look like candies. She'd made Austin try them in about a thousand different places before she'd decided to put them back in the first spot. Not that he'd minded. A line of lighted candy canes traced the footpath to the front porch, completing the effect.

Closer to the sidewalk, a spotlight shone on a hand-carved wooden nativity set. When Austin had pointed out that it didn't really fit with the theme of the rest of the decorations, Leah had simply given him a look and said that without Jesus, there was no point to Christmas. Unwilling to get into a debate about religion, Austin had simply nodded and dutifully placed the heavy figures where she pointed.

"What do you think, Jackson?" Leah's voice was tentative.

Jackson shrugged. "It's okay." But under the nonchalance, Austin could read it in his eyes—he was impressed.

Apparently Leah saw it too, because she clapped her hands. "How about some cocoa?"

Jackson gave a slight nod, and Leah turned to Austin, eyes questioning. "Join us?"

He should say no. He hadn't gotten in a workout at all today, aside from climbing back up the overlook, which had been more challenging than he'd anticipated.

Plus, what had happened to not getting close?

But the idea of spending the night by himself with his weights and his resistance band didn't hold much appeal.

"Sure."

Weak, soldier. Weak.

He moved closer to her. "But first, there's something I've been waiting to do all day."

Leah's eyes widened, and she took a step backward. Was she afraid he was going to try to kiss her again? Surely, she didn't think he was that foolish?

He bent to the snow and scooped a handful into a ball.

Leah's shriek said she'd figured out what he was about to do.

She took two running steps into a snowdrift, but she was too slow. His lob easily hit her shoulder, and she shrieked again as snow cascaded down her coat.

Before she could retaliate, he reloaded, this time firing the snowball at Jackson. The boy didn't quite shriek like Leah. But he did grunt and bend to make his own snowball. Both his and Leah's hit Austin at the same time, and snow trickled down his back. But he didn't care.

Seeing both of them smiling at the same time made it so worth it.

Chapter 17

"Ready?" The nervous buzz that had been percolating in her belly all day was ridiculous.

Austin had come over for dinner every day in the week since they'd decorated her house. And none of his actions had been anything more than friendly.

Just because they were eating at Peyton's tonight didn't make things any different.

She knew that.

She was sure Austin knew it.

She only hoped—prayed—that her friends knew it too.

"Let's go." Austin looked as nervous as she felt.

Was it too much, bringing him to her friends' house? But it was either that or let the poor guy starve tonight.

Besides, plenty of her friends had brought new people to their get-togethers.

She tried to ignore the fact that most of them were now married to the people they'd brought. That had absolutely nothing to do with her and Austin.

Austin led the way to his truck and moved to open the passenger door. Leah forced down a fresh surge of panic. A guy could open a car door as a friend—it didn't have to mean anything. Besides, Jackson had to get in this way too, so technically Austin had opened the door as much for the boy as for her.

Austin must have started the car earlier because it was already toasty inside.

That was thoughtful.

Leah pushed the thought aside. She had to stop reading into everything.

"How's your brother?" Leah had avoided asking much about his brother, but she'd added him to her daily prayers.

"Haven't heard from him." There was an undertone of worry to Austin's voice, though Leah could tell he was working hard to sound unconcerned.

"That's probably pretty normal, though, right? I mean, I'm sure communication there is spotty and—" She cut herself off. And what? She didn't know the first thing about what it was like over there. But she felt an overpowering need to offer him some reassurance. "I've been praying for him."

Austin grunted. Apparently that conversation was over.

"Jackson, do you have homework this weekend?"

A grunt from the backseat. If only these two weren't so talkative.

Still, things had been going so much better this past week that she couldn't complain. That snowball fight with Austin last weekend seemed to have loosened Jackson up a bit. And with Austin coming over every night for dinner, Jackson had started eating at the table with them. He still only ate PBJ, but at this point, she'd take the small win. Plus, she'd only been called to Mrs. Rice's office once this week, and that was because he'd skipped science. But at least he hadn't punched anyone else.

As for Austin, he seemed to laugh more readily every day. And the look that had haunted his eyes—the one that made it seem like he wasn't entirely present—had receded farther and farther into the background, so that sometimes she didn't see it at all.

Now if they could just get through this dinner without her friends making things awkward between them.

Two hours later, Leah had to wonder what she'd been so worried about. Her friends had been on their best behavior—though Jade and Peyton did keep shooting her significant looks.

But Austin had gotten involved in a game of darts with the guys the minute they'd stepped through the door and had barely talked to her once since then. As they ate now, he sat in the living room, joining in an animated conversation with Jared and Ethan about their work as volunteer firefighters, while she sat in the kitchen with Sophie and Spencer and Ethan and Ariana and their little ones. A pang went through her middle every time Sophie wiped at her twins' faces or Ariana made a silly face at Joy.

Adopting an older child had been the right decision. She still believed that. But she couldn't deny that every once in a while she wondered what it would be like to have a baby too. Maybe next time she could adopt a little one.

If she survived this time.

She turned toward the living room to check on Jackson. She'd packed him a PBJ, but she knew he wouldn't eat it with everyone around. Maybe later, when everyone was involved in a game of charades or something, he'd find a quiet spot in the kitchen to eat it. She was learning not to push it. And for now, he seemed content playing on the floor with Hope.

One more sign that a little sibling would be good for him. Someday.

Her gaze left Jackson and traveled to the spot where Austin sat on the couch, right at home with her friends. His eyes caught hers, and he grinned. Her eyes jumped to the other side of the room, but it was too late.

She could already feel her face warming. Hopefully no one else noticed.

She stood, gathering her plate, along with those of her friends, and carried them into the kitchen, where Peyton was stacking a tray with Christmas cookies.

Her friend smiled. "It's a little early, but—"

"You know I don't mind." Leah chose a bell-shaped one and took a bite, closing her eyes as memories of Christmases with her family washed over her. "Perfect."

Peyton checked over her shoulder, as if to make sure they were alone. "Speaking of perfect, I'm glad you brought Austin."

Leah snorted. "Subtle, Pey."

But Peyton poked her shoulder. "I'm serious. He seems much more comfortable than the first time we met him. His eyes don't keep going to the door. Though they *do* keep going to a certain someone."

"Whatever." Thankfully, there was no way Peyton could see the warmth pooling in her middle.

"Don't be like that, Leah. It's obvious you two are good together."

"We haven't been together all night."

"My point exactly." Peyton shot her a triumphant smile. "You guys are working so hard not to be together that it's obvious you *are* together. Or you want to be."

"You're delusional. Go serve those cookies before you say something even more non-sensical." She shoved Peyton toward the living room. "Austin and I are friends. But that's all we're ever going to be. Capisce?"

"I think you're wrong—"

Leah held up a warning finger. "Capisce?"

Peyton gave a half nod, then shook her head vigorously and escaped the room.

"You are the most exasperating friend ever, did you know that?" Leah called after her. The only answer she got was Peyton's gleeful laugh.

That had been more fun than Austin had anticipated. He'd already known Leah's friends were nice from the first time he'd met them, but he hadn't been sure how he'd do with being in such a large crowd again. But now that he knew them, it turned out they didn't feel so much like a crowd—more like a good-sized family.

He'd also been more than a little concerned that Leah's friends would detect his interest in her. But he'd done a pretty good job of keeping that hidden, if he did say so himself.

Actually, he'd done such a good job that it felt a little ridiculous now as he pulled into Leah's driveway to drop her and Jackson off.

He hopped out of the car to walk them to the door. Jackson disappeared inside after giving him a fist-bump, but Leah turned to him.

"I hope you had fun." She could barely suppress her yawn.

"I did." *Do not tuck her hair behind her ear.* "Sorry if I was ignoring you. I didn't want your friends to . . ." He toed at the step with his prosthetic. How did he say this?

Leah looked at her own shoes. "It's fine. It's not like we're a couple."

"Right." He yanked his hat tighter over his ears and turned toward the steps.

"Wait. Austin."

His pulse slid upward. Was this the part where she said she wanted to be more than friends?

"There's this thing tomorrow at Jackson's school. Some kind of father-son event. I offered to take him, but you can imagine how well that went over." She met his eyes, and he could read the uncertainty there. "And he could really use a male role model. So I wondered if maybe you might be willing to go with him."

Austin swallowed against a sudden scratchiness at the back of his throat. She had so many male friends. And a brother. But she considered him a role model for Jackson?

"You know what, never mind. I shouldn't have asked. It was silly." Leah reached for the door, but Austin threw out a hand to stop her. Her fingers were warm under his, and he had to make himself pull his hand away.

"It's not silly." He cleared his throat and met her eyes. "I'd love to go."

"Thanks." Leah's whisper slipped right through to his heart. He couldn't take his eyes off hers. It would be so easy to bend down and kiss her right now.

But this was about more than the two of them. It was about Jackson. And he wasn't going to exploit her gratitude over this to get a kiss.

Assuming she'd even kiss him—and not run away again.

Which was highly unlikely.

He forced himself to reach past her and open the door. "Goodnight."

She stepped inside, and he pulled the door closed behind her, staring at it a few seconds longer.

Taking Jackson to a father-son event was a no-brainer. Figuring out what to do with these feelings for Leah?

That was a whole new level of complicated.

Chapter 18

Austin pulled into the driveway of the sports complex Leah had given him the address to, glancing over at Jackson. The boy hadn't said much on the way over, but Austin understood. He hadn't had a father either. He couldn't count how many times he'd watched his friends hanging out with their fathers, wishing that just once he could be like them. But his mom had never thought to ask another male role model to take him to these kinds of events.

It felt surreal to be going as a father figure now. But in a good way.

He tried not to worry about the fact that the event must be some kind of sporting activity. He'd always been athletic, and as long as they stuck to the basics, like basketball, he'd be fine.

He let Jackson lead the way to the front doors, then made him pause for a photo. "Your mom made me promise to take lots of pictures. Say 'fun.'"

Defiance sparked across Jackson's face. "She's not my mom."

"She is." Austin injected authority into his voice, the same way he had on the rare occasions he'd had to deal with insubordination among his men. "And she cares about you very much. I don't know if you realize this, but that's not the easiest thing to find in this world. You should be thankful for her."

He snapped the picture and texted it to Leah, hoping it was dark enough that she wouldn't notice Jackson's petulant expression.

"I don't need anyone to care about me."

Austin stopped in front of the boy, laying a hand on his shoulder. "That might be what you tell yourself. But we all need someone to care about us."

"Whatever." Jackson shrugged out of his grip. "You're not my dad."

The words shouldn't have cut at Austin the way they did. He knew he wasn't Jackson's dad and that he never would be. But that didn't lessen the sting.

"No, I'm not." He kept his voice even. "But I am your friend. And as your friend, I'm telling you—"

Jackson pushed through one of the building's glass doors, letting it swing shut behind him. Austin grabbed it just in time and followed him, trying to summon up some of that incredible patience Leah always showed.

Inside, a wall of noise hit Austin as boys and dads grouped in the lobby, dads laughing together, boys shouting and chasing.

Jackson had already tucked himself away at the far end of the bank of doors, and Austin followed him. He should probably encourage Jackson to greet the other boys, but the truth was, this spot as far from the crowd as possible suited him perfectly as well.

"Hey." A guy with reddish hair and a green sweater approached. "Is this your dad, Jackson?"

Jackson gave the man a disgusted look. "No."

"Oh." The guy looked taken aback.

"I'm a friend of the family." Austin shook the hand the man offered. "And you are?"

"Mr. Wickel. Jackson's science teacher."

Austin resisted the urge to increase the pressure on the guy's hand. If he was Jackson's science teacher, shouldn't he know the boy didn't have a father?

"We're going to get started in a few minutes. Looks like you don't have any gear, so you can head down the corridor to the right to rent some. We'll see you in there." Mr. Wickel held out a fist to Jackson for a fist-bump, but Jackson sneered at it.

Austin didn't blame him. "That guy is an imbecile," he muttered as Mr. Wickel moved off.

The comment earned him Jackson's first smile of the night. But Leah probably wouldn't approve.

"Don't tell your mom I said that."

This time he was almost sure he heard a laugh.

"Come on." Austin clapped a hand on Jackson's shoulder. "What kind of equipment do we need to rent?"

They followed the line of kids and dads down the hall. A couple of boys said hi to Jackson, but most ignored him.

"I wonder what we're . . ." Austin lost his words as the crowd ahead of them thinned enough for him to see what they were waiting to rent.

Hockey gear.

His heart dropped. He knew the military had a hockey team for amputees. Those guys were whizzes on the ice—the single-leg amputees on skates and the double-limb amputees on sleds—but Austin had never been a hockey player, and he'd had no inclination to learn during his recovery. He didn't figure there'd be much call for hockey players once he got back to Afghanistan.

He pulled at the collar of his t-shirt. Now what did he do? Should he try, for Jackson's sake? But maybe here, in front of a hundred kids and their dads, wasn't the place to reveal his prosthetic to Jackson. At the thought of all those eyes on him—all the questions he'd be asked—he almost bolted.

But he made himself stand his ground to talk to Jackson. Leaning close to the boy, he spoke in an undertone. "I can't play hockey."

Jackson rolled his eyes. "You stand on skates and hit a puck with a stick. It's not that tough."

The line shuffled forward, and a guy behind Austin cleared his throat, gesturing for Austin to move up. Instead, Austin reached for Jackson's arm and tugged him out of line, motioning for the next group to go ahead of them.

"We can stay if you want. I'll watch you. But I can't skate."

Disappointment flashed in Jackson's eyes, but he blinked, and it was gone. "Whatever. I didn't want to come anyway."

Austin nudged him toward the line. "Go on. I'll rent you some equipment. I bet you've got killer skills. I want to watch you."

But Jackson twisted out of his grip and marched toward the lobby.

Austin followed, the weight of the prosthetic he usually didn't notice dragging at him.

"Hey." He pulled up next to Jackson. "How about we do something else? Just the two of us." He racked his memory for what he'd liked to do at Jackson's age. "How about bowling?"

Jackson directed a withering look at him.

"Or we could hang out here. Shoot some hoops. I'm sure they have an open court."

But Jackson angled for the door. "I want to go home."

Austin followed him outside, his exasperated sigh fogging the air in front of him. He hit the key fob to unlock the truck and watched Jackson climb in. As he followed, Austin tried to figure out if there was a way to salvage the night.

But he came up empty.

Queasiness rolled through him at the knowledge that he was failing Jackson.

And what was Leah going to think?

She'd asked him for this one simple favor, and he couldn't even do that. The worst part was, he couldn't begin to explain why.

The ride home was silent, but when they pulled into Leah's driveway, Jackson spoke, not looking at Austin. "Don't worry. I'll tell Leah I had a good time. We all know that's the only reason you went anyway."

Austin's head whipped toward the boy. "Do you really believe that?"

Jackson shrugged.

"I like your mom. She's nice. And we get along well. But I went tonight because I like *you*. I wanted to spend time with *you*."

"Whatever." Jackson's eyes rolled back farther than Austin would have thought possible.

Before Austin could say anything else, Jackson jumped out of the truck and slammed the door. Austin watched him shuffle toward the house, debating whether he should follow or take the coward's way out and go home.

He really wished he didn't already know the right answer to that one.

Steeling himself, he followed Jackson's tracks to the front door. But Leah beat him there, stepping outside as he reached the bottom of the porch steps.

"What happened? Why are you back already? Did Jackson refuse to participate?" Little puffs of steam clouded in front of her as she spoke, and she wrapped her arms around her elbows.

Austin swallowed. Apparently, Jackson hadn't said anything. It'd be so easy to let Leah believe her assumption was correct. But he couldn't do that to her. Or to Jackson.

"It was me." He dug his hands into his pockets.

Leah's lips tipped into a frown. "What was you?"

324

"I'm the one who wouldn't participate. It was hockey, and I don't skate."

Leah's mouth worked, no words coming out, but her eyes snapped. Finally, she seemed to find her voice. "And you couldn't try? For him?"

"I'm sorry." In his pockets, his hands clenched. "I couldn't."

"Why?" There was fire in her voice. "Why couldn't you try? He wouldn't have cared if you were bad at it. All he cared about was being there with you. And you blew that."

"I blew that?" Austin puffed out a hot breath. "I blew that?"

This woman was incredible. He'd taken her son to a father-son event, as a favor to her, and now she was telling him he'd blown it when he hadn't been able to skate because he didn't have a leg?

"So what if you weren't the best? You could have tried anyway. There's no reason—"

But he'd had enough. He reached down and gripped the left leg of his track pants. "You want to know *why* I couldn't skate?"

His breaths were ragged and sharp, and he almost did it.

He almost pulled up his pants leg and revealed his prosthetic.

But he stopped himself.

This wasn't the way to tell her. Not in anger.

Her hand went to her hip, and she raised an eyebrow, her expression saying "I'm waiting" as clearly as words would have.

Austin breathed in and out. His grip on his pants leg loosened.

"I just couldn't. I'm sorry." He turned and stalked to his truck. He could feel her eyes on him as he backed out and parked next door.

But he didn't look over at her.

Leah leaned into the porch railing as Austin disappeared into the house next door.

A long sigh scraped against her trachea in the cold.

At least that was over. The feelings she'd had for Austin lately had been growing dangerously close to attraction, and she'd started to think it might be mutual. But if the guy couldn't spend one evening with her son, that had to end right now.

She and Jackson were a package deal.

Anyway, this made things easier. Austin had been occupying way too many of her thoughts lately. Thoughts that would better be spent on figuring out what to get Jackson for Christmas or finalizing plans for the annual community Thanksgiving meal she always managed.

She moved toward the door, its colorful lights winking at her. Lights she'd held as Austin hung them. They'd felt so much like a team that day.

Just went to show that feelings couldn't always be trusted.

What mattered now was providing Jackson with stability and with adults he could trust. She'd thought that might be Austin. But apparently she'd been wrong.

As she returned inside, she pulled in a breath. She'd close the door on whatever feelings she'd been starting to develop for him.

Now.

With a hard shove, she latched the front door.

She only hoped the door of her heart was closed as tightly.

Chapter 19

He'd wanted fewer distractions.

And now he had fewer distractions.

Austin curled the weight, an involuntary grunt exploding from his lips. He'd already punished his muscles harder than he should this morning. And it was only nine o'clock.

But his physical was just over a week away. And he had nothing else to do anyway.

He dropped the weight and reached for his water bottle, his eyes going to the window, the same way they had a million times in the past two days. And just like it did every time, that same ache rose in his middle.

Maybe he shouldn't, but he missed them. Two days of not seeing them, not talking to them, was too long.

He'd considered going over to apologize for everything that had happened the other night—he'd even gotten as far as opening his front door yesterday. But what was he going to say? Sorry I couldn't skate, but I don't have a leg?

That's a start.

But he pushed the thought away. It was better this way. It wasn't like he was going to be here forever. Next week, he'd have his physical, and then he'd be on his way back to Afghanistan.

That didn't exactly leave time for a relationship—with Leah or her kid.

He forced his eyes off their house and moved toward the bathroom. He should shower and get on with his busy day of doing nothing.

His eyes flicked to his laptop, open on the coffee table. Still no word from Chad.

He tried to ignore the dread that nearly strangled him every time he thought about his brother.

It had only been two weeks since they'd last talked—and Chad had warned that it might be a while before he could call again.

There was nothing to worry about.

Austin sat on the small stool he'd placed next to the shower and hiked up the leg of his track pants. He'd learned it was easier to take his prosthetic off first, then the pants.

He was about to push the button to release the pin that held the prosthetic in place when there was a loud bang on the front door.

He considered ignoring it. It was probably a solicitor.

Or it could be Leah.

He pulled the leg of his pants back down and stood, telling his heart to knock off its silly thumping as he strode to the front door.

Eagerness shot through him as he opened it.

But it wasn't Leah.

It was Jackson, shivering in only a t-shirt.

"Hey, dude." Austin reached for the boy's arm, dragging him into the house. "Get inside before you freeze to death."

Jackson's eyes darted around the room.

"I'm glad you came over." Austin gestured for Jackson to sit, but the boy didn't move. "I wanted to apologize—"

"Leah's not getting up." Jackson's voice was scratchy, and he blinked as if holding back tears.

"What?" Austin tried to switch gears, even as his heart heaved. "What do you mean, she's not getting up?"

"She's always up by now, but I pounded on her bedroom door, and she didn't answer." Jackson shook harder.

"Okay. It's okay." Austin locked a reassuring hand on the boy's shoulder. "Maybe she decided to sleep in, and she's wearing ear plugs or something." Though he had to admit that didn't sound like Leah.

"What if she's dead?"

Austin's mouth opened. Leah was a young, healthy woman. Why would Jackson jump to that conclusion?

And then he remembered—Leah had told him that Jackson had found his mother dead of a drug overdose. She'd probably been young and healthy as well.

"She's not dead." He grabbed his coat and threw it around Jackson's shoulders, then pulled his stocking cap onto his head and steered the boy to the door. "Come on. I'll check on her."

At first, Jackson's feet didn't budge, but after a few nudges, Austin got him moving.

They sped across the yard as fast as they could through the six inches of fresh snow.

"She's in her room." Inside, Jackson pointed down the hallway but seemed unwilling to step beyond the front door. He stood there, Austin's coat still draped over him, face pale, shaking.

Austin patted his shoulder, then strode down the hallway to Leah's closed bedroom door at the end.

He gave a gentle knock. "Leah?"

When there was no answer after a few seconds, he knocked and called again, a little louder this time. He glanced over his shoulder, but he couldn't see Jackson from here. He stuffed down his own mounting concern and raised his hand to knock again, but the door opened.

He allowed himself a tiny sigh of relief.

Until his eyes fell on her.

Her cheeks were flushed, sweat beaded on her forehead, and dark circles bruised her eyes, which she seemed barely able to open, although they widened when they fell on him, and a hand went self-consciously to her hair.

"What are you doing here?" She wrapped her arms around her middle as a shiver wracked her frame, despite the fleece pajamas she wore.

"Jackson came over. He said you weren't getting up." Austin reached for her elbow to lead her back toward the bed.

"I'm fine." Leah tried to escape his grasp but stumbled. His arm went around her to steady her, and he tried to ignore the warmth in his chest as she leaned into him.

"Yeah, you seem fine." He touched his free hand to her forehead, wincing at the heat that radiated from it. "You're burning up. Let's get you back to bed."

329

But Leah tried to pull away again. "I can't. I have to get everything ready for the community dinner tomorrow. I have twenty turkeys to cook and mashed potatoes and stuffing and—"

"There must be someone else who can do that." They'd reached her bed, and he lowered her gently onto the white comforter.

"I cook the meal every year. I like to do it. I want to help people."

Austin bent to lift her legs and swing them into the bed. "I know you like to help people." He made his voice gentle. "But this year, you're going to have to let people help you. Who should I call to make the meal?"

She closed her eyes and lifted a hand to cover them. "My assistant is the only one I'd trust. But she's out of town for Thanksgiving. Maybe if I rest for a little bit, I can go over later. It'll be tight but . . ." Her words had gotten slower, and she looked half asleep.

"That's right. You rest." Austin tucked the blankets around her, then strode to the bathroom and wet a rag with cool water. After ringing it out, he folded it into a neat rectangle, then placed it on her forehead. She half-sighed, half-moaned but didn't open her eyes.

Austin let himself watch her for a few seconds, until he was sure she was sleeping. Then he headed for the living room to recruit Jackson. They had a lot of work to do.

It looked like they were making Thanksgiving dinner.

For the entire town.

❧

"I knew there'd be a list." Jade waved the piece of paper triumphantly in front of Austin as she emerged from the office at the back of Leah's commercial kitchen downtown. "I'm always teasing Leah about all the lists she makes, but this time I have to admit that it's helpful."

Austin did too. He wasn't sure they'd be able to pull this off otherwise. Even with the list, it was going to be a challenge.

"I still can't believe Leah asked us all to help make the community Thanksgiving dinner. The last time we offered, she practically laughed in our faces." Jade's husband Dan came up behind her and read the list over her shoulder. "She must be really sick."

Austin nodded. No need to mention that technically it hadn't been Leah who had texted to ask her friends to help with the meal. It had been Jackson's idea to "borrow" Leah's phone and contact her friends to see if anyone would be able to help with the cooking. Austin had agreed, making it clear to the boy that the only reason it was acceptable was because they were doing it to help Leah.

He'd been apprehensive at first, but he had to admit now that it had been a good idea. In addition to Dan and Jade, Peyton and Jared, Ethan and Ariana, Grace, and Emma had made it.

Austin glanced toward the building's small lobby, where Jackson was keeping Hope and Ethan and Ariana's little girl, Joy, entertained.

"So, where do we start, chef?" Dan teased.

Austin scanned the list Jade passed him. He'd thought Leah had been exaggerating when she'd said she had to make twenty turkeys, but judging from this, she hadn't been.

He swallowed. "How many people does this need to serve?"

"A couple hundred. Mostly homeless people or people who have nowhere else to go for Thanksgiving." Jade was studying the list. "I can handle the mashed potatoes. Pretty hard to mess that up, right?"

Austin made a mark on the paper. "And I can take care of the turkeys." He divvied up the rest of the tasks among the others.

As they broke off to do their jobs, Austin rummaged in the industrial-size refrigerator for the herbs he'd need for the turkeys. He snapped off a piece of sage, the smell a punch straight to the gut.

He'd promised himself he'd never cook again, and everything in him rebelled at the idea, from his trembling hands to his churning stomach. But what else could he do?

You could turn around and leave. You don't owe these people anything.

But that wasn't true. Leah could have written him off that first night they'd met, when she'd found him chopping wood at midnight. Instead, she'd gone out of her way to make him feel at home here. And her friends had all been more than welcoming too.

Austin threw the sage back in the bag. Today was not the day to get caught up in those old memories. Today was a day to make new ones. If not for his own sake, then for Leah's.

With a quick breath, he grabbed the rest of the ingredients from the fridge.

For the rest of the day, the kitchen bustled with activity as everyone worked on their tasks. As Austin understood it, they'd make all the food today, then transport it to the church, where they'd let it warm tomorrow during the Thanksgiving service so that no one had to miss worship to prepare the meal.

"It smells good in here." Jackson stopped in front of Austin, carrying baby Hope. "Way better than she smells."

From next to Austin, Jade laughed and took her daughter. "Unless you want to change her?" She wiggled her eyebrows at Jackson, who gave her the kind of revolted look only a thirteen-year-old boy could pull off. "I'll take that as a no." Jade carried the still smiling baby off.

"So it smells good, huh? You want a bite?" Austin leaned closer and whispered. "I won't tell anyone."

But Jackson's mouth dropped into his more typical scowl. "I don't want it. It just smells good."

Austin studied the boy. There was a reason he wouldn't eat more than peanut butter and jelly, he was sure of it. But if Leah wasn't going to push it, neither was he.

"All better." Jade passed a fresh-smelling Hope back to Jackson. The baby immediately gripped his ear, and Jackson's scowl transformed into a smile as he tickled the little girl into letting go. Too bad Leah wasn't here to see that smile. On both kids.

Actually, it was too bad Leah couldn't be here, period. Surrounded by her friends, the dull longing he'd felt after not seeing her for two days had grown into a need to be near her. And it didn't help that they kept mentioning her name.

As Jackson took Hope back, Jade leaned her hip on the counter and regarded Austin. Peyton came and stood next to her. Austin eyed the two women. They were ganging up on him about something, he could feel it.

"It was nice that you did this for Leah." Peyton gave him a wry look that said he'd been busted.

He tried to play it off. "Oh, I didn't do— She was the one who—"

But both women were shaking their heads and laughing at him.

"Nice try," Jade said. "But Leah could be dead, and she still wouldn't give this up. You must really care about her."

"I didn't— I don't—" He turned his full attention to the turkey he'd been carving. "I was just trying to help," he finally mumbled.

Jade's grin gentled. "I know. And we all appreciate it." She gestured around the room, where everyone was now cleaning up. "And so will Leah."

He lifted the turkey pieces into the large roaster they'd use to warm it tomorrow. He tried to ignore the fact that the women's eyes were still on him.

"Can I tell you something about Leah?" Peyton asked.

Austin shrugged, as if he couldn't care less what she had to say about Leah. He doubted they bought it.

"If you like her, you're going to have to make it painfully obvious."

His eyes swung to Peyton, then to Jade. Both looked completely serious.

"And be persistent," Jade added. She grabbed a rag and wiped up the juices that had dripped from the turkey.

Austin opened his mouth to argue, but clearly there was no point. These two had already made up their minds.

And it wasn't like they were wrong.

Not that it mattered after the way he'd left things with Leah the other night.

Peyton set a hand on his arm. "I can tell she likes you too. Or, she would if she let herself. But you're going to have to fight if you want to get out of the friend zone. She's been hurt in the past. So she tends not to give men much of a chance, beyond friendship."

Austin's shoulders tensed. He hated the idea of anything hurting Leah. "Oh, I—"

But he had no idea how to finish the thought. Did she even consider him a friend anymore? And if she did, did he want her to think of him as something more?

No.

But the weak voice wasn't enough to convince even himself.

Chapter 20

With a gasp, Leah sprang upright, her eyes flashing open.

What was she doing in bed? How long had she been sleeping?

A faint trace of light leaked in through the curtains above her bed, and she reached to open them. The sun was low in the sky, faint lines of pink and orange oozing from its center into the clouds.

Could it really be sunset already?

But no, that couldn't be right. The sun set on the other side of the house.

It *rose* on this side.

She jumped to her feet but had to pause as a remnant of yesterday's headache pounded at her temples. She waited for the dizziness to pass, then sprinted for the bedroom door. Somehow, she'd slept through an entire day and night.

The day and night she was supposed to spend preparing the community Thanksgiving dinner.

She had to call Dan. Maybe he could get the word out that the event was canceled before people started showing up.

A sick feeling not at all related to her illness swirled in her stomach. She shouldn't have insisted that she had to be the one to prepare the meal. She should have listened to Austin yesterday when he'd suggested that she call someone else to make it. It would have been better than letting an entire community down.

Austin.

She stopped as her thoughts caught up with the spinning in her head.

Austin had been here yesterday. He'd tucked her into bed. She could still feel the soothing coolness of his hand on her forehead. The rag he'd placed there.

She'd woken once in the middle of the day yesterday to find a glass of water that she'd gulped down. She could only assume he'd left it. And the note.

He'd left a note.

Saying that he would take care of everything.

She rushed back to the nightstand, grabbed the note, then burst into the hallway. She'd run over to his house, find out what still needed to be done, and then get to work. Maybe the meal could be salvaged.

Jackson's bedroom door was open, but he wasn't in there.

She padded to the kitchen, already calling for him. "Jackson, do you know if . . ."

But she lost track of what she was going to say as her eyes fell on Austin standing at her kitchen island.

"Good morning." Austin raised a coffee cup toward her, his eyes finding hers and sending a tingle from her toes up her spine. "How are you feeling?"

"Much better." But her voice was scratchy and dry, and the words came out sounding more frog than human. She probably looked more like a frog right now too.

Austin grabbed a glass from the cupboard as if he'd lived here his whole life, filled it from the refrigerator, and passed it to her.

She took a long drink, letting the water soothe her throat, still struggling to recover from the shock of finding Austin in her house first thing in the morning. "Where's Jackson?" At least she sounded more like herself now.

"In the living room. I hope you don't mind, but I said he could watch TV."

"I got your note." She lifted it. "I'm going to go change and then I'll run over there and finish things up. What needs to be done yet?"

She braced for his answer. Hopefully she'd be able to accomplish at least some of it in the few hours before hungry people started to arrive.

"Nothing."

"What do you mean, nothing?" Even she usually left a few last things for the morning. "What about the turkeys?"

"Roasted, carved, and ready to warm."

"And the stuffing?"

"Stuffed."

"Potatoes?"

"Mashed. I think you can see where I'm going with this. Your friends all pitched in. Jackson too. He kept the little ones occupied all day. You would have been proud." He stepped around the counter and passed her a cup of coffee, his eyes seeking out hers. "I'm sorry about the other night."

But Leah couldn't worry about the other night right now. Or about how it felt to have his eyes on her. Or about how much she'd missed seeing him for the past few days. Those kinds of thoughts would only confuse her.

"Do you want some breakfast?" Austin cleared his throat and escaped to the other side of the counter. "You must be starving after not eating at all yesterday." He picked up her cast iron pan and started wiping it out with a paper towel. Somehow the guy who didn't cook knew not to submerge a cast iron pan. And had cooked a turkey dinner for the whole community.

"No thanks." Leah watched him a moment longer. She had so many questions. But now wasn't the time. "I should go check on Jackson."

"He didn't sleep very well last night. He got up every hour to go to the bathroom, but I think it was just so he could check if you were still—" Austin looked toward the living room and lowered his voice. "Still alive. He seemed pretty freaked out."

Leah pressed a hand to her chest. She highly doubted that Jackson cared what happened to her. But if her illness had triggered memories of what had happened with his mom, she was terribly sorry for that.

Something else Austin had said snagged at her. How did he know Jackson had been up? "Did you stay all night?"

A trace of pink rose in Austin's cheeks. "I didn't want to leave Jackson. And I didn't know if you might need anything . . ." He swallowed and directed his eyes to the now gleaming pan in his hands.

"Oh." Hopefully he'd figure the flush of her cheeks was still from her fever. "I'll go check on Jackson."

She gulped in a clearing breath as she made her way to the living room. Just because the man had taken care of her, taken care of her son, taken care of the meal she was supposed to prepare, didn't mean anything. Aside from the fact that he was a good friend. A *really* good friend.

336

Jackson looked up as she entered the living room. He looked smaller than usual, curled into a tight ball in his chair, and his eyes were heavy. He didn't say anything when she greeted him, but she could almost believe a flash of relief sparked in his eyes. Was it possible that Austin had been right? Had Jackson actually been worried about her?

"Happy Thanksgiving." She dared to slide a few steps closer, and Jackson went so far as to nod. "I'm going to go shower and get ready, and we'll leave for church right after that. Then we'll go serve the meal everyone made yesterday. Austin said you were a big help."

This time the corner of Jackson's lip lifted into what Leah could almost convince herself was a smile.

"Thank you for that." She wanted to say more. To tell him how much it meant to her. But maybe this was where she should leave it for now. Baby steps.

She padded back toward the kitchen to let Austin know it was okay if he went home now. She had things under control.

But at the sight of him wiping her counter, she paused, taking a moment to watch him. He looked up, and she snapped her head toward the refrigerator as if it were the most interesting thing in the world.

But she could feel her face heating again. There was no way he hadn't noticed her staring.

"I'm going to get ready for church," she mumbled, taking a step down the hallway. But halfway to her room, she turned back. "Would you like to come with us?"

She held her breath as she brought her eyes to his. He stopped wiping the counter and stared at her.

She should have known better than to ask. He'd already declined multiple invitations to church.

But he offered a slow nod. "I think I might."

She could feel the grin lifting her lips, and she didn't try to restrain it. Chalk one up to God for an answered prayer.

Chapter 21

Austin's shoulders tightened as he drove into the church parking lot. He'd insisted they take his truck, since a fairly heavy snow had started to fall about half an hour before they'd left. Already, a slick half-inch of snow covered the roads.

"Should I drop you off at the door and then find a place to park?" Austin glanced at Leah out of the corner of his eye. In her black leggings and an oversize pink knit sweater that hung almost to her knees, she looked cozy enough to snuggle.

He knew he should chase the thought from his mind, but he couldn't. He'd spent all night considering what Jade and Peyton had said. About how he must really care about her. About how he'd have to fight if he wanted to get out of the friend zone.

And somewhere around two in the morning, as he'd laid a hand on her forehead and been swamped by relief to find it at last cool and fever-free, he'd realized—he did want to get out of that zone. He wanted to tell her how much he cared for her. But he hadn't figured out exactly how to do that yet.

"That's okay." Leah's smile strengthened his pulse. "Let's all walk in together."

Austin nodded, pulling into one of the few remaining parking spots. He jumped out of the truck, then sped around to the other side to help Leah down from her seat. The feel of her warm hand in his made something in his throat jump. It didn't make any sense, how he felt about her. He'd only known her for three weeks. And yet, in that time she'd become a constant in his life.

She hit him with another smile as she walked around the truck with him. "I'm glad you came."

He nodded, but his muscles tensed as they joined the river of people flowing toward the building. He hadn't considered how many people might be here this morning. Sweat pricked the back of his neck even as snow landed on his face.

He never should have said yes to this. But he hadn't wanted to see the disappointment that flitted on Leah's face every time he declined her invitations to church. Plus, his mom had always taken them to church on Thanksgiving, and he'd felt a sudden, unexpected nostalgia for that family feeling this morning as he'd stood in Leah's kitchen.

As they stepped through the doors, Dan greeted him with a handshake and a pat on the shoulder. Austin's eyes darted around the large lobby, crowded with groups of people talking and greeting one another. Beyond them, the sanctuary was even more packed. His jaw tensed as he checked over his shoulder for the door. As long as he could see it—as long as he knew there was a way out—he'd be fine.

He was pretty sure.

"Where do you—" Leah cut off as her eyes searched his face. "What's wrong?"

He shook his head, clearing his throat and trying to put on a halfway normal expression. "Nothing. What were you going to say?"

Concern hovered in Leah's eyes, and she moved closer to his side. "I was going to ask where you want to sit."

He did a quick survey of the sanctuary. "How about there?" He pointed to a small section of open seats near the back. It might be a tight squeeze, but it was better than being in the middle of the crowd.

Leah gave him an odd look but led the way. He silently thanked her for not pointing out that there were at least two nearly empty rows near the front of the church.

After squeezing past three people's legs, they settled into the empty spots, Jackson on one side of him and Leah on the other. As Leah folded her hands and closed her eyes and Jackson picked at a hangnail, Austin concentrated on taking a few calming breaths.

He wasn't in danger here. There was no reason for him to count the number of steps from here to the exit.

Fourteen.

Solely to distract himself, he picked up a Bible from the rack hanging on the back of the seat in front of him. He paged through it, not paying attention to the words. It wasn't like they meant anything.

Next to him, Leah shifted, her arm brushing against his, and he couldn't resist turning toward her. Her smile was as ready as ever.

He almost leaned over and told her how beautiful she looked, but at that moment, her brother's voice came over the church's sound system.

Leah turned toward the front of the church, and Austin followed suit.

As he went through the familiar motions of the service, he worked to steel his heart against what he was hearing. Just because he was here didn't mean he was going to fall for all this mumbo jumbo again.

Every once in a while, he allowed himself a glance at Leah, who appeared to be loving every moment of the service.

Austin almost envied her. His life would certainly be simpler if he hadn't had to learn the hard way that God was no more than a fairy tale or a nice idea.

At the front of the church, Dan stood at a small podium.

He took a moment to look around the crowded sanctuary. "So, how's your Thanksgiving going so far? Do you have a lot to be thankful for? Food? A home? Family?" Dan bobbed his head up and down a few times, as did many of his listeners.

Austin stopped himself from rolling his eyes. Could this be any more cliché?

"Yeah, me too." Dan braced his hands on the podium and leaned forward. "Now, I know it's Thanksgiving and all, but let's be real here for a second. Are there some things you're *un*thankful for? Things you're maybe angry with God for?"

Austin stilled. Were preachers allowed to say things like that in church?

"Maybe you lost your job this year," Dan continued. "Or maybe you've had some health issues. Maybe someone close to you died."

Tension zapped through Austin's body, and he winced as a phantom pain sliced his missing foot.

"So what are we supposed to do with those things? Say, 'Thanks God, but no thanks? I'll thank you for everything else, but I can't really be grateful for *that*?'"

Dan paused, as if thinking, then picked up his Bible. "Actually, listen to what God calls us to do. In First Thessalonians, Paul says we are to 'Rejoice always, pray continually, give thanks in all circumstances, for this is God's will for you in Christ Jesus.'"

Dan closed his Bible and shook his head. "Unbelievable, isn't it? You're telling me God expects me to give thanks in *everything*—even the bad things? Not only that, but he wants me to *rejoice* while I'm going through them? What is he, crazy?" Dan held up a hand. "I know, I know. You're thinking I shouldn't be standing up here calling God crazy. But you know you're thinking it too. You're thinking, if God wants me to thank him for those things, he can think again."

Dan stepped out from behind the podium to pace in front of the church. "But that's exactly what God is saying we need to do. He says, 'Give thanks in *everything*.' Even the bad things."

Dan ran a hand through his hair. "But why? Why would God want us to thank him for the bad things that happen to us?" He stopped pacing and scanned the congregation.

Austin wanted to make himself look away, but he couldn't. He had to know—why would anyone give thanks for all the bad that had been heaped on them? Why should he give thanks after he'd lost his leg and his friends?

"It's because—" Dan spread his arms wide. "It's because God uses those things for our good too."

Austin let out a harsh breath and shook his head. Unbelievable. It was one thing to say he should be thankful that he'd lost so much. But to say it was for his good? That was taking things too far.

Leah glanced over at him, but he couldn't face the concern in her eyes. He needed to pull it together, think about something else until Dan was done talking.

But he couldn't shut out Dan's voice. "I'm not saying we're always going to see these things as good for us. We might never see how blessings could come out of them while we're on this side of heaven. But God sees. God knows. He knows how even these hard things, these things that make us so angry, are working for our good. In Romans 8:28, Paul writes, 'And we know that in all things God works for the good of those who love him, who have been called according to his purpose.'" Dan looked up, and Austin could have sworn that his eyes traveled straight to the back of the church. "It's pretty easy to see that, to believe it, when things are going well for us, isn't it? When we have the dream job and money in the bank and a healthy family. When we're coasting."

Austin tried to remember the last time he'd felt like he was coasting. Maybe before Mom died? Maybe longer ago than that?

Dan started pacing again. "But what about when things go wrong? What about when we hurt? What about when the people we love hurt? Is that all for our good? Because if it is, maybe I don't want all things to work for my good, right? I'll take okay, I'll take medium instead of good, if it means I don't have to have all these heartaches, right?"

Austin's jaw clenched until his teeth ached, and he was suddenly too aware of the press of bodies around him.

Only fourteen steps to the exit. It was no big deal. He wasn't trapped. He wasn't in danger.

And yet.

He couldn't sit here another second.

He half rose, and Leah leaned closer, whispering, "Are you all right?"

But he could only shake his head and try to remain inconspicuous as he climbed over first Jackson and then the three people at the end of the row.

Eight more steps.

He pushed through the doors into the lobby, sucking in a deep breath as they closed behind him. Away from the press of bodies, Austin's pulse slowed, and the squeezing in his chest loosened. But the lobby must have had speakers because Dan's voice had followed him out of the sanctuary.

"But God doesn't want okay for you," Dan was saying. "He doesn't want medium. He wants *good* for you. Eternal good. And sometimes the way he brings about that good is through hard things."

Austin eyed the exterior doors. Maybe he should wait outside. He took a few steps toward them, but something in Dan's voice made him slow and then stop. He dragged himself to the far side of the room, where a comfortable looking couch sat in front of a large stone fireplace.

"I'm going to ask you to do something now. Something that it's going to feel really weird to do on Thanksgiving. But humor me." Even from out here, Austin could hear the congregation's gentle chuckle before Dan's voice picked up again. "I want you to close your eyes." He waited a second. "Go ahead. If everyone does it, no one will look foolish." Another twitter from the crowd.

"Good. Now—" Dan continued. "I want you to make a list in your mind of all the things you're *not* thankful for this year. The things you're mad at God about. And I want you to confess those things to God. Tell him, 'God, I'm mad about this.' Don't worry, he's a big God. He can take it. I'll give you a minute for that."

Austin stared at the rough stone of the fireplace. He wasn't going to close his eyes, but that didn't stop him from making a list. He was angry about his leg. And Tanner. And Isaad. He was angry that Jackson had found his mother dead and had grown up without a family. He was angry that he'd grown up without a father. He was angry that he was too broken to ever be fixed.

"Got your list?" Dan's voice came over the speaker again, and Austin let out a shaky breath.

It wasn't rational. He knew that. How could he be mad at God when he didn't believe in God anymore?

But that didn't change the fact that he was.

"Now—" Dan lowered his voice, but Austin could still hear him too well. "Here's the tough part. I want you to surrender all of those things to God. Ask him to change your heart and to give you peace with each one of those things. Ask him to help you trust that he's using them for your good and his glory."

No.

Thankfully, there was no one else in the lobby to see how hard he was shaking his head, to see him get up and pace in front of the fireplace.

No.

This was where he drew the line.

He could maybe admit that he was mad at a God he claimed not to believe in. But he wasn't about to ask that same God to give him peace with those things. He didn't want peace with them.

He wanted to be angry.

He had a *right* to be angry

He worked on tuning out the rest of the service.

It didn't matter what Dan said.

It wasn't like Austin believed any of this anyway.

Chapter 22

L eah's eyes tracked to Austin.

Again.

Instead of working on the serving line with her, he'd chosen to stay in the kitchen, filling glasses of milk and juice. She'd tried to talk to him after church, to make sure he was okay, but all he'd say was that he'd needed some air.

But there was more to it than that, she could tell. That haunted look, the one that had started to fade over the past couple weeks, had overtaken his expression again.

She forced herself to dollop mashed potatoes onto the next plate. With one hand, she gripped the edge of the table to hold herself upright. She'd never tell anyone, but her head had started to pound again, and the whole room seemed to be swaying.

As she scooped another batch of potatoes, a warm hand covered hers. "Why don't you take a break?" Austin's voice was low and close to her ear, and a warm shiver went down her back. "I'll take over for you."

She shook her head. She hadn't been able to help prepare the meal. The least she could do was serve it.

But Austin had already stripped the spoon out of her hand.

He dropped a serving of mashed potatoes onto a plate. "I promise we'll come find you if we need anything. Why don't you go lay on that comfy couch in the lobby?" He rested the potato spoon in the bowl and stepped back from the serving line. In one deft movement, he pulled his blue sweater over his head, revealing a plaid button-down underneath. He held the sweater out to her. "Use this for a pillow. Or a blanket."

Leah took it, trying not to notice that it was still warm from the heat of his body. Or that it carried his pleasant scent.

She should argue, but the prospect of lying on a couch right now was too tempting. Reluctantly, she took off her apron and slipped out of the kitchen and through the quiet hallways to the lobby. Being sick for Thanksgiving hadn't been part of the plan. But at least she had people she could rely on to take care of things.

People like Austin.

It was her last thought before she nestled her head into Austin's sweater, closed her eyes, and was out.

She was pretty sure it was only ten minutes later that someone was shaking her.

"Leah."

The voice whispering her name was familiar, comforting, and her lips slid into a smile.

"Leah." The voice was more insistent this time, and she cracked her eyes open to find Austin's face inches from hers.

"Hey." His mouth curved into a teasing smile. "Going to sleep all day?"

She blinked, trying to focus. "Sorry. What do you need?"

"Nothing. Just you."

Her eyes snapped open all the way, and he seemed to realize what he'd said. "I mean— To take home— To come with me so I can drive you home."

Leah was pretty sure her face must be as red as his, but she pushed herself into a sitting position. The moment she did, the headache that had eased while she slept returned with renewed vigor. She closed her eyes and rubbed at her temples.

"Here. Let me." Even without opening her eyes, she could feel Austin step closer. His hands gently nudged hers out of the way, then his fingers were pressing gently into her temples, moving in slow circles.

Leah's shoulders tensed, but the motion eased her headache, and after a second, she relaxed into it. Austin's hands slid further back on her scalp, into her hair, still moving in those slow circles.

"That's much better," Leah murmured.

"Good." Austin's voice was low, but he kept massaging.

Leah should tell him to stop. Her headache was almost gone now. But having his hands in her hair felt too good.

"Dan sent me up to see what was taking so . . ." That was Peyton's voice. Leah would recognize it anywhere. Along with the laughing, I-told-you-so note to it as she trailed off.

Austin's fingers jerked out of her hair, and he took three quick steps backward before bumping into a chair.

Leah could only pray Peyton wouldn't say anything stupid that would make her friendship with Austin awkward.

As Peyton reached them, her eyes flicked from one to the other, and she could barely suppress her smile. But apparently God had heard Leah's prayer because Peyton simply said, "Dan wanted you to know your mom can't make it to dinner because of the storm. And he said to tell you not to feel obligated to come if you're not feeling up to it."

Leah had never missed Thanksgiving dinner with her family. But right now the idea of doing anything but going home and snuggling into bed was more than she could handle.

"I do have a headache." Leah rubbed at her head again to show Peyton that was why Austin's hands had been in her hair. And for no other reason. "Is it really that snowy out?"

"There's a good eight inches out there already." Austin glanced toward the church doors, where the afternoon was quickly darkening into dusk.

"Maybe I better skip it this year." She turned to Austin. "Unless you wanted to go? I'm sure I'll be fine."

Austin shook his head. "I think we should get you home."

Leah pretended not to notice the pointed look Peyton directed her way.

"I'll send Jackson up." And with that, Peyton was gone again, though Leah was almost sure she saw her friend shoot Austin a wink as she sauntered down the hallway.

An awkward silence descended on them. Leah started to rub at her temples again, then dropped her hands into her lap. The last thing she needed was for him to think she wanted another scalp massage.

"I'll go pull the truck up," Austin finally said. "That way you won't have to walk through the snow."

"That's all right. I'll be—" But Austin was already on his way out the door.

A minute later, his truck pulled up outside, just as Jackson entered the lobby.

"Hey, dude." Leah tried to gauge Jackson's mood. "How did you like helping with the meal?"

Jackson shrugged, but his eyes looked brighter than usual.

The moment they stepped through the front doors, Leah gasped. She knew Austin had said they'd gotten eight inches of snow already. And she'd seen eight inches of snow plenty of times in her life. But the world had been completely transformed between the time she'd gone into church this morning and now.

The parking lot had been recently plowed, but a thick layer of snow covered the few remaining cars. Snowflakes filled the sky as well, sparkling in the streetlights that had just turned on. One landed on her lashes, and she blinked it away, smiling. Winter had always been her favorite season, and she was fine with it coming early. It made everything feel more Christmassy.

Austin already had the passenger door open for her, and she climbed into the truck. They rode in silence for a while, but finally she couldn't stand it any longer. "So, are you going to tell me where you learned to cook like that? People were raving about how good the turkey was." More than they usually raved about her turkey. She'd have to get him to spill the recipe.

"Picked it up here and there." He turned down the street that led to her house.

"Well, I feel like a sucker, making you dinner all these nights." Leah kept her voice light, so he'd know she was joking. She enjoyed making food for people, whether or not they knew how to cook for themselves. "Why were you always getting takeout if you could cook like that?"

Austin's shrug was easy, but the line of his jaw tightened.

Apparently, cooking was a touchy subject.

She closed her eyes and snuggled into the warmth of the truck. But too soon, she felt the vehicle slow and turn, and then the engine shut down.

"We're home," Austin whispered. A second later, he was opening her door and reaching to help her down. Against her better judgment, she set her palm into his. She was too tired to trust she could step down herself without landing on her face. A zip of recognition flew up her skin at the touch, but she pretended not to notice it.

As soon as she was down, Austin let go of her hand, but instead of moving ahead of her through the snow, he wrapped an arm around her shoulders and tucked her into his side. She should protest. But she was too sleepy. And his warmth felt too nice.

At the door, Austin let go of her, and the night air crawled down her neck. She shivered.

"I know you're tired." Austin opened the door for her. "But could we talk for a minute?"

Everything in Leah told her to say no.

Austin had hurt Jackson with his refusal to participate in the father-son event the other day.

But he'd also gotten Jackson involved in helping out with the community dinner.

And he'd pretty much saved the whole meal from disaster.

The least she could do was take a minute to listen to him.

Chapter 23

Austin sat on Leah's couch, cracking his knuckles as he waited for her to make the tea she'd insisted they needed.

Now that he'd decided to do this, he just wanted to get it over with.

Not that he was sure doing this was the best idea. But he owed her an explanation for what had happened with Jackson the other night. And if he was going to ask her to consider a more-than-friends relationship with him, she needed to know the truth.

But the longer she took, the less certain he was that he should do it. Not the part about telling her about his leg. That he was going to do one way or the other. But what he wanted to do after that—asking her on a date—that he was a lot less sure of.

"Here we go." Leah's voice sounded strained as she carried two mugs into the living room, and he rose to take them from her, setting them on the coffee table and gesturing for her to sit.

She looked tired.

Maybe he should wait until a better time.

No.

No more excuses.

"So what did you want to talk about?" Leah's fingers fidgeted with a strand of her hair. Was she nervous? Did she sense what he wanted to ask her? Did she want him to?

Austin pushed the questions aside. First, he had to get past telling her about his leg.

He exhaled. Here went everything. "I wanted to apologize for the other night. I feel like I owe you—"

Leah waved a hand for him to stop, and he obeyed. "You don't owe me anything. I get that it was probably weird for you to take your neighbor's kid to a father-son thing. I shouldn't have put that on you." She blew on her tea and took a sip, not lifting her eyes to him.

"That's just it." Austin slid closer to her on the couch, so that their knees nearly touched. "It wasn't weird at all. I was looking forward to it. I like spending time with Jackson." He didn't add that he liked spending time with her too. That would come soon enough, assuming this part went well.

Leah let her eyes meet his for a second, and he had to look away before he kissed her right here and now.

"What was it then? Did I give you the impression I expected more?" Her cheeks grew fiery, and he almost reached a hand to cool them. "You know," she mumbled, "between us?"

Austin nearly laughed out loud. She had most definitely not sent that signal.

"It was hockey," he said simply.

Her forehead creased. She was clearly waiting for more, but he couldn't get the rest out.

"And you didn't want to make a fool of yourself because you don't skate?"

Austin shook his head. "I don't mind making a fool of myself now and then." His voice was hoarse, and he bent to grip the cuff of his pants. "I couldn't skate because of *this.*" With a quick inhale, he pulled the hem up to his knee, exposing his entire prosthetic, from the black carbon fiber shell at the top to the titanium rod that disappeared into the semi-lifelike foot shell inside his shoe.

Leah's hands jumped to cover her mouth, but he heard her gasp through them. Her eyes filled with tears, and his stomach sank.

He didn't know what he'd hoped.

That she'd take one look at it, say, "That's nice," and move on with her night?

"I'm sorry." He spoke past the knives at the back of his throat. "I didn't mean to upset you."

But before he could comprehend what was happening, her arms went around his back. They were warm and soft, and he found himself sinking into them, his arms coming up to circle her. He inhaled her cinnamony scent, and his heart eased for the first time in a year.

"I'm sorry." She pulled away after a minute, and Austin had to fight the urge to gather her back to him. "I didn't mean to—"

He tried to convey that he hadn't minded—far from it—with his smile, and she seemed to accept that.

"I had no idea. I mean you run and you climbed my ladder and . . ." She cut herself off. "But I shouldn't have assumed you were blowing Jackson off about the skating. I'm sure when you tell him, he'll understand."

Austin's stomach flipped. Telling Leah was one thing. But telling Jackson, who'd already seen so many awful things in his short life? That he couldn't do, not yet.

Leah must have read it in his expression. "You don't have to tell him yet. But I think you should. Soon."

He nodded. He wasn't making any promises. But he'd try.

"Do you mind if I ask how it happened?" Leah's voice was tentative.

He longed to say that he didn't mind. That he'd be happy to tell her everything. But he couldn't talk about it. Not with her. Not with anyone. His last therapist had called it avoidance. He called it survival.

Still, he owed her something at least. "I was in Afghanistan." Saying it felt like peeling off his own skin.

He looked at the ceiling, trying to come up with something else he could tell her without collapsing the careful walls he'd built up around that day.

Next to him, he could hear the quiet in and out of her breathing. Its softness calmed him.

Without meaning to, he found himself talking.

He tipped his head back to rest on the couch cushion and closed his eyes. "It was last Christmas."

"Oh." Her voice said that she finally understood why he didn't like Christmas.

He could feel the muscles in his jaw working, but it took a minute to get the words out. "We were on a routine patrol, my buddy Tanner and I. I was supposed to be driving, but he wanted to. Said it would remind him of being home for Christmas and driving his wife and kids to visit family." Already he had to stop and clear his throat. "He was driving, and we saw this kid we'd befriended playing along the side of the road."

He opened one eye a crack and tipped his head toward her. She watched him, her expression a mixture of compassion and tension. "He was about Jackson's age. Isaad." He rubbed a hand over the rough scar on his jaw. That kid had been something special. "I told Tanner to pull over and pick Isaad up and we'd give him a ride, kind of as a Christmas present."

His hands fisted and he pressed them into his eyelids. "We weren't supposed to do that, and Tanner was a rule follower. But he was also a good guy." He licked his lips. "He stopped, and Isaad got in. I was joking with him about giving him a lump of coal, and he was laughing." Even now he couldn't help smiling at the memory of the sound. "He had the best laugh, and I was watching him. I wasn't scanning the road in front of us, the way I was supposed to be." His voice cracked, and he sucked in several deep breaths.

A soft hand fell into his, and he squeezed it, unable to look at her. But now that he'd started talking, he couldn't stop. Even though he knew he should. Leah shouldn't have to carry this burden too.

"It all happened so fast. One minute Isaad was laughing, the next everything was chaos. It felt like the world had blown apart." He exhaled. "Which I guess it had."

Leah slid closer, pressing her other hand into his arm.

"It was an IED." He opened his eyes and stared at the ceiling. "I mean, I had seen what they could do. I'd picked up bodies that had—" He cleared his throat again. She didn't need that image in her head. "But I never knew what it was like to go through it. The funny thing is, some guys don't remember it at all afterward. But I can't forget." He gripped the back of his neck.

He remembered what it felt like to fly through the air, his body completely out of his control. He remembered hitting the ground and having no idea where he was or what had happened to Tanner and Isaad. He remembered sitting up and seeing his leg completely mangled and knowing right in that moment that there was no way he'd be able to keep it.

"I prayed," he whispered. "Before I looked for them. I prayed so hard that Isaad and Tanner had survived too." But when he'd opened his eyes, the first thing he'd seen was Isaad, staring up at the sky with empty eyes. He'd clawed his way to the boy's side, even though he knew it was too late. Then he'd crawled across the sand and rocks, pain screaming through his shattered leg, to find Tanner. Only he'd blacked out before he got to him. He didn't find out Tanner was gone until he woke in the helicopter.

He pressed his lips together and closed his eyes again, but moisture rained down on his cheeks, and his breath was ragged. "Neither of them made it."

"I'm so sorry." Leah's whispered words washed over him, and he dared to look at her. Tears glistened on her cheeks too, and he reached to wipe them away.

The feel of her soft skin under his fingertips reminded him of the reason he hadn't wanted to tell her any of this in the first place.

He sat abruptly, pulling his hand away and scrubbing at his own cheeks. "I'm sorry. I didn't mean to burden you with all of that." He shifted to stand—he should go—but she grabbed his arm and held him in place.

"Thank you for telling me." Her voice was a balm, and he leaned closer to her.

Her eyes went to his jaw. "Is this from then too?" Her fingers lifted to touch the jagged scar that ran from his jaw up to his hairline, and he flinched involuntarily.

She lifted her hand. "Sorry, does it hurt?"

He shook his head. "No. It's just kind of hideous."

Her eyes locked onto his. "It's not hideous. It's beautiful. A reminder of what God brought you through."

"Yeah. Right." He wasn't exactly sure it was God who had brought him through. More like sheer dumb luck. Otherwise, why hadn't Tanner and Isaad made it too? They certainly deserved to survive more than he did.

"It is," Leah insisted. "And God knows what it's like to be scarred. Jesus had scars too. For us."

Austin swallowed. It sounded like something Tanner would say. But he wasn't in the mood for a conversation about Jesus.

Even so, he couldn't make himself leave her side.

"I should get home," he whispered. "Let you get some rest."

She nodded, but neither of them moved.

Austin searched her eyes. There was something there that hadn't been there before.

He bent his head a fraction closer. She didn't move. He dared another fraction. And then another.

One more fraction, and their lips would meet. Austin inhaled and closed his eyes. He could already feel—

"Ned needs more food." Jackson's voice sent Leah rocketing to the far end of the couch.

Austin exhaled a long breath, watching the squirrel scurry from one of Jackson's shoulders to the other.

The critter would be a lot cuter if he hadn't just cost Austin the kiss he'd been dreaming of for days.

"I'll put it on my list." Leah's voice was stilted, and Jackson gave each of them a weird look before retreating to his room.

Leah jumped to her feet, and Austin pushed himself off the couch more slowly, heading for the door. Ever since that first time he'd almost kissed her, she'd stopped seeing him out when he left. But this time he could feel her right behind him.

He turned to say goodnight, but before he could say anything, she lifted a hand to his scar again.

He closed his eyes as her fingers traced it.

She was making it nearly impossible to fight the urge to kiss her.

"Austin." Her whisper drew him closer. He only had a second to grasp what was happening before her lips met his.

His gasp was buried in their kiss as his arms went around her back. Her lips were just what he'd imagined—warm and soft, with the slightest hint of cinnamon.

When she pulled away, a smile tickled her lips, but worry lines furrowed her brow.

"I'm—"

He lifted a hand and smoothed a palm over her cheek. "Don't you dare apologize for that."

Her giggle was slightly giddy, and the sound went right through him. He could not make himself stop grinning.

"I was planning to decorate the tree tomorrow." Her smile was just as persistent as his. "If you wanted to come over and join us."

Decorating a Christmas tree was the last thing he wanted to do.

But if it meant spending time with Leah . . .

"I'll be there."

Chapter 24

J oy hummed through Leah, and she did a twirl in her bedroom as she got dressed the next morning.

She should be absolutely freaked out. She should be trying to figure out a way to stuff Austin back into the friend zone he'd so deftly escaped.

But she didn't want to. Not even a little bit.

She brushed a finger over her lips, swiping on a thin layer of gloss.

Hoping to attract Austin to your lips again?

Leah giggled to herself. She couldn't deny that she'd very much enjoyed kissing him. She could still taste the faint peppermint of his lips on hers. Another giggle sneaked out, and she covered her mouth. Jackson was going to think she was crazy, laughing to herself in here.

Her eyes fell on the bouquet of silk flowers she'd caught at Dan and Jade's wedding. Though, to be fair, she hadn't so much caught it as Jade had chucked it right at her head.

Obviously, Leah didn't put any stock in that old superstition. She'd only kept the bouquet as a fun memento of the wedding.

But as she considered the flowers now, she flashed back to all the times she'd prayed for a husband in the past. When God hadn't seen fit to answer that prayer with a yes, she'd switched to praying for contentment with her single status. And God had more than given her that.

She was beyond content on her own.

Or, at least, she had been.

But now? Now everything was a mess. A big, confusing, delicious, kissing mess.

Should she start praying for a husband again?

With a sigh, she sank onto the bed. Look at her. She was being foolish. One kiss and here she was, picturing herself walking down the aisle.

Help me to know your will in this, Lord. She ducked her chin as she sank into the familiar intimacy of prayer. *Guide Austin and I in our relationship, whether that's as friends or as . . . more.*

The thought sent a thrill through her, but she ignored it. She had to wait on God's will.

A knock echoed through the house, and Leah jumped, pressing a hand to her middle as an unexpected case of the flutters hit her. How was she going to greet him? Would he try to kiss her? Did she want him to kiss her?

She couldn't decide if it was fortunate or unfortunate that she'd never find out, since Jackson was already on his way to answer the door, Ned balanced on his outstretched arm.

"Don't let him get outside," Leah called down the hallway. The squirrel had grown a lot, but after it had been hand-raised, Leah didn't want to contemplate what would happen if it got outside.

"Duh," Jackson shot over his shoulder as he pulled the door open, then snatched the squirrel's tail just in time to keep it from jumping.

Leah's eyes went from the squirrel to the doorway. Maybe it was the morning light, or maybe it was his soft smile, but Austin looked different today. Happy.

"Good morning." His voice reached for her, and she stepped closer.

"Morning." She couldn't make herself speak louder than a whisper.

"How did you sleep?" Austin's eyes held a gentle light.

Jackson thrust the squirrel at Austin before she could answer. "Ned wants to say hi."

Austin turned to the boy as the squirrel scampered up his arm. "He's gotten big. You must be taking good care of him."

Leah let out a slow breath. She had to get her feelings in check. She could be in the same room with Austin without needing to kiss him the entire time.

Or even one time.

Anyway, they had a Christmas tree to decorate.

Two hours later, as she placed the last ornament on a branch, Leah had to wonder. Maybe she'd been wrong. Maybe she and Austin were best off as friends.

Jackson had ducked out of decorating almost immediately, leaving her to work side by side with Austin. Alone.

And yet Austin hadn't made a single attempt to kiss her again. Or to hold her hand. Or to touch her in any way.

If anything, he seemed to be doing everything he could to keep his distance.

They'd talked. Laughed. The same way they had dozens of times before.

As friends.

Which was . . . fine.

Like she'd said, she'd wait for God's will on this one. And if his will was for them to remain nothing more than friends, she could live with that.

Scratch that. She could more than live with it. She preferred it.

"There." She stepped back from the tree. "Perfect."

"Mmm hmm." But Austin's eyes were on her, and she felt suddenly self-conscious.

"How about some hot cocoa?"

Austin nodded, but he seemed to be deep in thought. As she retreated to the kitchen and got out the mugs, she worked to convince herself that she was content. That they could pretend last night had never happened and move on with their friendship intact.

By the time the cocoa was ready, she had a plan. She knew exactly what she was going to say.

She wouldn't apologize for the kiss, exactly, since he'd asked her not to. But she'd make it clear it wouldn't happen again.

Confident that it was the right decision, she picked up the mugs and carried them to the living room. But the moment Austin's eyes landed on her, she nearly lost her resolve.

He strode across the room, took the mugs from her, and set them on the table, then caught both of her hands in his.

"Austin, wait." She had to get this out. "I think we need to talk about last night."

He shook his head. "I told you not to apologize for that."

"I'm not." She had to look away, or she wouldn't go through with this. "I'm just saying I didn't mean for it to happen. And it won't happen again."

She tugged her hands out of his and moved toward the Christmas tree, her eyes falling on the heart ornament her dad had given her two years ago—his last Christmas on earth.

He'd reminded her that there were many kinds of love in this world and that they were all wonderful. But the one love she always needed—the one love that would always be there for her—was the love of God. His agape, never-ending love.

"Why not?" Austin's voice was soft, and she appreciated that he didn't move closer.

She shrugged. "It's not a good idea."

"Why not?" he repeated, and Leah blinked back the sting behind her eyelids. She wanted so badly to say, never mind, they should absolutely kiss again.

But what happened when Austin realized that kissing had been a mistake? When he came to his senses and realized he only wanted to be friends with her after all—and maybe not even that?

She didn't have only herself to think about. There was Jackson to consider too. If she and Austin dated and then broke up, what would that do to the boy?

She heard Austin come up behind her, but he didn't touch her. "Peyton and Jade warned me that you've been hurt before." His voice was so gentle.

She swallowed but nodded. There was no point in denying it.

"You know I would never hurt you, right?"

But Leah couldn't answer. It was what Gavin had said too. And she believed he'd meant it. No one ever *wanted* to hurt someone. It was just what happened.

"Look, I'm not asking you to kiss me again."

Leah couldn't help but laugh at that. She glanced over her shoulder at him. He looked completely earnest and slightly vulnerable—and entirely adorable.

"All I'm asking—" He reached for her, and she let him wrap his hand around hers. "Is if we can do something together sometime. Go somewhere."

"I was going to take Jackson—"

"Without Jackson." His voice was firm, and he spun her to face him. "Peyton said I had to be absolutely clear about this, so— I want to go as more than friends, Leah. I want to take you on a date."

Coming from him, the word had a pleasant undertone that made her feel warm and kind of melty inside.

She bit her lip, and his eyes tracked to that spot.

Did he suddenly want another kiss as much as she did?

"Okay." Her whisper came out sounding uncertain, and she cleared her throat and tried again. "Okay."

"Yeah?" The smile that spread across his face was so wide it brought out a dimple she'd never noticed before. "Are you sure?"

She swatted at him with a laugh. "Are you trying to unconvince me now?"

"No, absolutely not. In fact, just in case you need a little more convincing . . ." He bent his head closer, moving slowly, as if giving her time to change her mind.

But she lifted her face to his, closing her eyes. She had no desire to move away.

The instant his lips fell on hers, she knew.

They'd gone way past the line of friendship.

And she couldn't be happier.

Chapter 25

Austin couldn't believe he'd managed to wait an entire week for this day.

Although he'd continued to have dinner with Leah and Jackson every night—and although he and Leah had exchanged more than one goodnight kiss—he'd been half waiting all week for her to cancel their date.

He finished ironing his blue and white dress shirt, then pulled it on. As he buttoned it, his mind hooked on his physical earlier today. He'd already analyzed it from every angle three dozen times. But no matter how he looked at it, the exam felt . . . anticlimactic. And disconcerting.

The doctor had asked a few questions, performed a regular physical exam on him, and then dismissed him. When Austin had asked whether the doctor could tell him if he qualified for reinstatement to active duty, all the bushy-eyebrowed man had said was, "You'll get a letter in the mail in the near future." He hadn't been able to give Austin a date or a time frame.

Which meant Austin was left with more waiting. More worrying about Chad, whom he still hadn't heard from.

He fastened the final button and shook off the thought. There was nothing he could do for Chad right now. All he could do was trust that his brother was safe.

Chad's words from the last time they'd spoken rang in his head yet again. *I wouldn't mind a prayer or two.*

Austin sighed and lifted his chin toward the ceiling. He'd gone to church with Leah and Jackson again on Sunday—and this time he'd managed to stay in his seat for the whole service. He even had to admit that some of the things Dan said—like about how this world was a bleak place full of man's corruption—made sense. No one had to tell Austin that twice. He was living proof. What he wasn't sure of yet was what Dan had said after that: That despite the evil in this world, people could know peace because Jesus promised he had overcome the world. That one day, those who believe in him would be called from this world of pain and sorrow to be with him forever in heaven.

"If there really is a heaven," he muttered now to his ceiling. *Please keep Chad safe.* It was the fullest extent of a prayer he could offer, but if God *was* real, it would have to be enough.

He pulled on his jacket and stocking cap, picking up the flowers he'd bought this afternoon.

A shot of adrenaline coursed through him as he opened the door and the night air hit him. A fresh layer of snow blanketed the grass. That would make tonight even more perfect.

With Peyton's help, he'd found a place so perfectly Leah, she could have created it herself.

At her door, he considered letting himself in, as he'd started doing lately. But this wasn't just dinner with a friend. It was a date with someone he hoped was becoming much more than that.

He rang the doorbell, examining the lights they'd hung together as he waited. But the door remained closed.

She wasn't going to stand him up, was she? Her car was in the driveway, and the lights inside were on. If she was trying to pretend she wasn't home, she was doing a pretty poor job of it.

He was reconsidering letting himself in when the door opened.

Austin gasped as his eyes fell on Jackson. The boy's nose was swollen to twice its normal size, and ugly black and purple bruises extended from the bridge of his nose down the sides and under his eyes.

"What happened?"

"She says she'll be ready in five minutes." Jackson turned and shuffled into the house.

"Seriously, dude. Did you get in another fight? I thought you were done with that." Austin followed the boy to the kitchen and laid a hand on his shoulder.

But Jackson shrugged him off. "What's it to you?"

"It's a lot to me, actually." Austin blocked the boy's exit from the room, and Jackson's eyes darted past him. "I care about you. And your mom."

"Whatever." Jackson grabbed a plate stacked with a PBJ off the counter and shoved around Austin.

Austin watched the boy march toward his room, debating whether to follow. But he decided to let it go for now. Instead, he moved to the cabinets and found a vase for the flowers, placing them in the middle of the counter. Then he went to the sink and started putting away the clean dishes. After so many meals here, this kitchen was more familiar to him than the one in his own rental house.

His back was to the kitchen entryway, but still he knew the moment Leah was there. He set down the plates he'd been stacking and crossed the room to wrap her in his arms.

"The flowers are beautiful. Thank you." She sighed and leaned into him, and he pressed his lips to the top of her head.

"I saw Jackson. I understand if you need to cancel tonight. We can stay here and watch a movie or something."

Leah leaned back far enough that he could see her eyes. She looked tired, but that familiar light still shone in them. "There's nothing else I can do at this point. I've talked and talked and talked. And I'm not sure if I'm getting through to him at all. I think I need a little space from him right now, to be honest."

Austin smiled at her. "In that case, grab your coat. And a hat. And gloves. Maybe a scarf. Oh, and make sure to wear boots."

She gave him a startled look. "Where are we going? Sledding?"

He grinned as he waited for her to bundle up. "Not exactly."

He wouldn't ruin this surprise for anything.

Not even for the adorable pout she was giving him right now.

Chapter 26

She'd tried pouting. She'd tried cajoling. She'd even tried kissing.

But Austin wasn't budging. The man could keep a secret.

A ripple of anticipation winged through Leah as Austin squeezed her hand and looked over with a smile. "Almost there."

After the way her day had gone, this was exactly what she needed.

Just when she'd thought she was making progress with Jackson—or, to be more specific, that she and Austin were making progress with him—he went and punched a kid again. For no apparent reason, according to Mrs. Rice. She'd have to take the principal's word for it, since Jackson hadn't said a thing to her since she'd left work early to bring him home from school.

She didn't understand why every step forward with him brought forty steps back.

"Here we are." Excitement crept into Austin's voice as he pulled into a narrow gravel driveway. Leah worked to force out thoughts of Jackson. Tonight was about her and Austin.

"Where is here?" She peered out the window. There was a small handmade sign near the entrance, but in the dark, it was impossible to read what it said. As far as she could tell, they were in the middle of nowhere.

"You'll see." Austin's grin lit up the inside of the truck, and she couldn't help but return it.

He drove toward a large barn and parked the car behind it.

"Are we milking cows?"

Austin's chuckle warmed her. He jumped out of the truck and jogged around to open her door for her, holding out a hand to help her down.

"Come on." He tugged her toward the far side of the barn. A jingling reached her ears before they got there, followed by the soft nickering of a horse.

"Is this— Are there—" Leah's mouth fell open. He couldn't possibly have known. She swiped a gloved finger under her eyes.

"I'm sorry." Austin's face fell. "I should have asked if you liked— I wanted it to be a surprise, but we can leave if you don't want—"

She tightened her grip on his hand. "It's not that. I love sleigh rides. When I was a little girl, my dad started taking me on one every year, just me and him. Last year was the first year I hadn't been on one in probably twenty-five years. I really missed it, and . . ." She swiveled to take in the trees, the velvet of the night sky, and the man standing next to her. "And it's perfect. Thank you."

He let go of her hand and wrapped his arm around her shoulders instead, hugging her close to his warmth. "I'm glad you like it."

She could only nod, breathing in that warm scent that always said Austin to her.

A sleigh pulled by two beautiful black horses—one with a white patch over its eye—stopped alongside them, and the woman driving it invited them to step up.

Austin's hand moved to the small of her back as he helped her into the sleigh, then followed her up and slid onto the seat next to her. He unzipped his jacket to reveal a red plaid blanket, and she laughed as he tucked it around them.

"What other surprises do you have in store?"

But he only smiled and held her closer as the horses set off, their bells jingling merrily.

She relaxed in Austin's arms as the sleigh slid into a wooded area. With the tree branches glittering above them, the snow shushing beneath them, and a few snowflakes dancing around them, it was like a scene from a painting.

A very romantic painting.

When Austin had asked her on a date, she'd pictured dinner at the Hidden Cafe. Not a moonlit sleigh ride. Thank goodness Austin had a more romantic imagination than she did.

She sighed, completely content, and he leaned over and pressed a kiss onto the top of her head. "You like it?"

She nodded, her head rocking against the firm muscles of his arm.

Too soon, the sleigh slowed, and Austin helped her down. She tried not to show her disappointment that the ride was over already.

But as her feet hit the ground, she realized they weren't in the same place they'd started. "Wait. Where are we? Where's the barn?"

Austin steered her toward a trail lined with small lanterns. "Let's take a hike. There's a surprise at the end."

"Another surprise?" Leah let herself be led along, her gloved hand tucked into his. In spite of the cold, she'd be happy to stay out here all night.

But after a few minutes, they came to a bend in the trail.

Austin pulled her to a stop. "Close your eyes."

"What?" She spun in a circle, but there was nothing to see here aside from more trees. "Why?"

"Trust me."

She nodded and closed her eyes. She did trust him.

He wrapped a hand around her elbow, leading her forward. They walked like that for maybe fifty yards—it was hard to judge with her eyes closed—before Austin told her to open them.

"What was that all— Oh." She pressed her hands to her cheeks.

She'd never seen anything like this.

In front of them was a small village of glass-enclosed gazebos, each lit by strings of Christmas lights, each with smoke puffing out of a chimney on top, each with a single couple inside, seated at a candlelit table.

"We're in that one." Austin pointed to the left, toward an empty gazebo with white fairy lights strung across the ceiling and a flame dancing in the fireplace.

"What is this place?" Leah gazed around in wonder. It was like they'd been transported to some sort of winter wonderland. "How'd you find it?"

"I have my sources." He pulled her toward the gazebo and opened the door for her. A heady mix of wood smoke and savory herbs—thyme and rosemary, if she had to guess—drew her inside. The small space was warmer than she'd expected, and she pulled off her hat and gloves, running a finger through her locks to combat the hat head she was undoubtedly sporting.

As if reading the self-consciousness in the action, Austin stepped closer and caught her hands in his. "You look beautiful." He ducked his head and lowered his lips to hers.

She let herself be drawn into the kiss, but he pulled away much too soon.

"Sorry." He took a step back. "I promised myself I wouldn't do that until the end of the date." His eyes danced in the firelight, and Leah couldn't resist closing the space between them.

"Maybe we should call this the end of the date then."

His eyes widened, and she offered a smile. Where had those words come from? She wasn't the flirty type. Couldn't remember a time in her life she'd ever flirted, actually.

But right now, she was feeling playful, and the room made everything slightly magical, slightly unreal—or better than real.

"I guess we could do that." Austin's throaty response drew her closer, and before she could overthink it, she rose onto her toes and brought her arms around his neck, drawing him in until their lips met in a long, slow kiss.

Before Austin, she'd never known a kiss could make her feel like this. That it could make her feel precious and safe and beautiful and cared for and—

She refused to let herself think the last word that hovered at the edge of her thoughts. It was much too soon for that.

When they at last pulled apart, Austin ran a hand over her cheek. "Looks like you're full of your own surprises."

"I guess I am." She led the way to the table at the center of the gazebo, where candles flickered on either side of a covered platter.

She pulled off the lid.

"Oh my goodness. Seared scallops. My favorite. How did you know?"

He gave her a mysterious grin. "I told you—"

"It was Peyton." Leah laughed. She should have known. "Peyton helped you set this up, didn't she?"

Austin's expression turned sheepish, and he lifted his hands in surrender. "Sorry, I—"

But she shook her head. "Don't apologize. I think it's sweet that you went out of your way to make this special." She stepped around the table to kiss him again.

When she pulled back, she could not stop smiling. Goodness, she liked kissing this man.

Austin smiled too and reached for her plate to serve her a generous helping.

Leah took it from him with a grateful sigh and sat at the cozy table as he filled his own plate.

When he was seated, she folded her hands and bowed her head to offer a silent prayer.

"You can pray out loud if you'd like." Austin's voice was low and guarded, and she looked up to find him watching her.

"Do you want me to?" She wasn't going to force it. If praying with her made him uncomfortable, she wouldn't do it. Though she'd pray for a time when he might want to join her.

But he nodded. "I think so."

She gave him a gentle smile, then took a deep breath, sending up a quick silent prayer before she began. *Guide my words, Lord.* "Heavenly Father, thank you for this beautiful night you have given us together. Thank you for Austin, who is a thoughtful and giving man who has sacrificed so much for people who will never know what he's done for them." She swallowed back the emotion at the thought. If there were a way for her to tell the whole country what Austin had given up for them, she would. But she knew that wasn't what he was looking for. "Thank you for everything he has done for me and for Jackson. We ask, Lord, that you would touch Jackson's heart and help him to know not only how much we care about him, but how much you do. How you love him more than anyone on this earth ever could. Thank you that you love us so much that you sent your son to die for our sins. Even after Jackson has only been with me for such a short time, I can't imagine giving him up to save someone else. And yet you did that, Lord. You gave up your perfect son to save us, though we were anything but deserving. Help the knowledge of that guide everything we think, say, and do every day. Amen."

She kept her eyes closed for a moment after ending the prayer. She was afraid to lift her gaze to Austin's. Had she gone on too long? Had she scared him off?

But when she made herself meet his eyes, the look he was giving her wasn't one of anger or fear.

If she wasn't mistaken, it was one of hope.

Chapter 27

The truck's heater purred, pouring warmth from the vents and thawing their toes and fingers. Despite the frigid temperatures, the sleigh ride back to the truck had been much too short for Austin's liking.

If he could have, he would have stayed in that gazebo with Leah all night. After they'd finished eating, they'd sat and talked for an hour, and he'd even convinced her to dance with him. In spite of his bad leg, he hadn't moved too badly, if he did say so himself.

The gazebo had felt like a separate world. Like none of the cares and concerns that weighed on them out here existed in there. Leah had been carefree and happy and even—dare he say it?—slightly flirtatious. And he hadn't thought once about his physical or Afghanistan or Chad.

But he'd felt it all stealing back over them as they'd ridden in the sleigh, as if it was borne on the cold wind that snaked down their blanket and slipped through to their core.

Leah had grown quieter, and even he had a hard time keeping up the light tone.

He sneaked a glance at her out of the corner of his eye now. She caught his look and dropped the piece of hair she'd been absently twirling around a finger.

"What are you thinking about?" Though it'd only take one guess for him to figure it out.

Her sigh was heavy. "Sorry. I was thinking about Jackson. I'm going to have a talk with him when we get back. Tell him—" She shook her head. "I don't know what I'll tell him."

She angled toward him. "What were you thinking about?"

Somehow, his sigh was even heavier than hers had been. "Chad."

"I've been praying for him." Her hand came to rest on his arm.

How could one tiny touch like that be so reassuring?

"Me too." He could barely get the words out, but Leah's face lit up.

He didn't know how to tell her that his prayers weren't anything like hers. When she'd prayed before dinner, he could hear the conviction in her voice. She really believed God would hear her. That he would answer.

His prayers were more like shots fired wildly into the dark at a target he wasn't sure was there.

"I'd feel better if I heard from him. I can't wait to get back over there. Then I can be the one to watch his back."

Her hand tensed against his arm, and he turned his head to find her staring at him, open mouthed.

"You're going back? I thought— With your leg—"

"I've been on the temporary disability retired list for the past year. But with any luck, I won't be for much longer. I had my physical today, and if they find me fit for duty, I could be redeployed."

"When?" Leah's voice sounded strangled, and he glanced at her again. Her left hand remained on his arm, but her right was balled in her lap.

"Soon. I thought you knew."

She shook her head, blinking rapidly, and he repositioned his arm so he could take her hand. This was not how he'd have chosen to tell her.

"This doesn't change anything, you know. Unless you want it to." His heart nearly crumbled at the thought, but he had to let her decide this. It wouldn't be fair to drag her into a long-distance relationship she hadn't been prepared for. "I'm not saying it wouldn't be hard. But lots of guys have girlfriends or wives back home while they're deployed. And I do get leave and—"

"Austin." Leah squeezed his hand. "It doesn't change anything. I mean, I'd be worried about you, but I know that God is bigger than I am, and he's always watching over you."

He let out a long breath. Whether that was true or not didn't matter. What mattered was that she'd said yes.

"But can I ask you something?" Leah's voice was gentle, and Austin nodded, though he felt like he should protest. But that was ridiculous. There was nothing she could say right now that would tamp down the joy building in his chest.

"You said *if*. What happens if you're not found fit for duty?"

Austin shook his head. "Not going to happen."

It couldn't. He had to get back over there.

"But *if*, Austin," Leah insisted.

He sighed. Fine. He'd tell her the process. But he was going back.

"They could find that my injuries haven't stabilized enough and keep me on the temporary disability list and order another physical in a few months. Or—" He pressed his lips together. He hated to consider the other possibility.

"Or?"

"Or they could move me to the permanent disability list. Retire me."

He could feel Leah's eyes on him as she considered his answer. "And could you be content with that?"

The gentle question ripped through him like shrapnel.

"No." His answer was flat and immediate.

Leah didn't say anything, and he risked a look at her. But she was staring out the window.

"We're home." And just in time too. If this conversation continued, they might end up destroying this relationship before it had gotten off the ground.

He pulled into her driveway and walked her to the door.

"Do you want to come in and have some cocoa?" Her voice was tiny, hesitant, and it sliced him to know he was responsible for that.

He stretched his neck, trying to force himself to relax. She hadn't been trying to crush his hopes.

"I actually have a little bit of a headache. I think I'll go home and go to bed." He touched a hand to hers, then took a step backward.

"Austin, don't—" Tears sprang to Leah's eyes, and he silently cursed himself.

Did he call this not hurting her?

He moved close enough to wrap his arms around her. "I'm not upset. I promise. I just need some sleep. I'll see you tomorrow, okay?"

At her slight nod, he slid his hands to the back of her head and leaned in for a kiss, telling himself it was only his imagination that she barely returned it.

Chapter 28

Leah swiped at a stray tear as she pulled off her coat.

Austin hadn't meant to hurt her. He just had a headache. One she'd probably caused.

She'd only been trying to help, trying to make sure he saw the situation realistically—that he was prepared in case things didn't work out the way he wanted.

She wanted him to know that God was with him no matter what.

But instead of reassuring him, she may have ruined everything.

She dragged herself down the hall, rubbing at her head.

"Jackson, I'm home." She knocked on his as-always closed bedroom door, running a hand over her face one more time. Jackson didn't need to know anything was wrong.

She'd go over to Austin's in the morning and they'd talk, and everything would be fine. Wouldn't it?

She drew in a rough breath and knocked again.

Of course it would be fine.

"Jackson? Please open the door so I can say goodnight." Another, longer sigh slipped out.

A mutiny from Jackson was not what she needed right now.

Not when she just wanted to pull on a pair of fuzzy socks to warm her still tingling toes and curl into bed.

"You have ten seconds." She raised her voice to make sure Jackson could hear. "And then I'm coming in there whether you open the door or not."

She counted backward in her head. When she got to three, she switched to counting out loud. "Three. Two. One."

Weariness tugged at her shoulders. She'd rather go to bed and deal with Jackson in the morning. But she'd said she was coming in, so now she had to follow through.

She lifted her hand to the doorknob slowly, giving him one last chance.

When it didn't open, she turned it.

The lights were off inside, and she opened the door farther to let light from the hallway brighten the space. "Don't tell me you're sleeping . . ."

Her eyes fell on the empty bed, and she flipped on the light. The peanut butter and jelly she'd made him sat untouched on his dresser, and the room was vacant, aside from Ned, who gave an excited squeak and ran back and forth in his cage with his tail lifted over his back.

"Jackson?" She backed out of the room and retraced her steps toward the front door. Had he been in the living room or the kitchen and she'd missed him when she walked past? She *had* been rather distracted.

But the kitchen was empty, as was the living room.

She opened the door to the basement, quashing down the rush of panic that threatened to take over. There was no reason to overreact. He'd probably gotten bored and was exploring downstairs.

She pounded down the wooden steps, calling his name.

No answer.

She stood at the bottom of the staircase, her breaths coming heavier than they should. "Jackson, this isn't funny. If you're down here, come out."

The furnace kicked in, making her jump, and she pressed a hand to her heart.

After a quick search of the mostly empty basement, she sprinted up the stairs and straight out the back door. Maybe he was collecting nuts for Ned.

But the yard was dark and empty, no footprints marring the fresh snow.

She tore through the house to Jackson's room. Clues. She needed clues about where he could be.

Maybe there was something going on at school tonight that he hadn't told her about, and he'd gotten a ride with a friend. It was a long shot, one she already knew couldn't be true, but she clutched at it, searching the floor for his backpack. There might be a note in it.

But the backpack was gone, as was, she noticed now, the sweatshirt from Austin that always hung on the closet doorknob and the watch she'd given him for his birthday, which had remained in its box on top of the bookshelf since then. Nausea rose in her gut as she lunged for his dresser and yanked the top drawer open.

Empty.

So was the next.

And the next.

The room seemed to spin, but she staggered out of it, down the hallway, and to the front door.

She needed Austin's help.

Right now.

Chapter 29

Austin leaned into his crutches as he reached for a bottle of water from the refrigerator. He popped the aspirin into his mouth and took a swig out of the bottle. He hadn't been lying to Leah about the headache, though he'd also needed some space before he said something he'd regret.

He knew she was only doing what she thought was best when she'd asked what he'd do if he weren't redeployed.

But that possibility wasn't something he could think about.

He hooked the water bottle between his fingers and maneuvered his crutches to the couch, propping his good foot on the coffee table. His laptop taunted him, silent as ever.

When are you going to call, Chad?

The wallpaper on the screen—a picture of him and Chad in front of a spectacular sunset in the Afghan mountains—mocked him, and he dropped his face into his hands, the edges of his scar rough against his skin.

A second later, he jumped as footsteps pounded up his porch stairs, followed by someone beating on the door.

"Austin!" Even through the door, Leah's voice set his heart on fire. As much as he'd wanted space, he hadn't wanted to leave things the way he had tonight.

He glanced at his crutches.

She knew about his prosthetic. But she'd never seen him without it on.

"Austin!" The urgency in her voice made him forget the debate. He grabbed his crutches and hopped to the door, wearing his best apologetic smile. "I'm sorry, Leah. I shouldn't have—"

The look on her face stole whatever he'd been planning to say next. "What is it? What's wrong?"

Her eyes were too wide and wild, skipping past him to the living room, and her breath came in short gasps even though she lived fewer than fifty steps away.

"Is he here?" She barreled past him into the house. "Please tell me he's here." Her voice pitched up an octave.

"Is who here?"

But Leah was no longer in the living room. She'd sprinted down the hall and was popping her head into every bedroom.

"Leah." He followed her, his crutches thumping quietly against the wood floor. "Leah, stop." He grabbed her elbow, pulling her to face him. "What's going on?"

She shook her head, gasping harder than before. "I thought maybe he—" She choked on a short breath. "I thought he'd be here. I thought—"

"Jackson?" His own pulse spiked. Was she saying she couldn't find him?

"I was sure he must be here. But if he's not—" Face ashen, she clutched at her arms.

"Shh." He leaned one crutch against the wall so he could pull her close. "It's okay. We'll find him. You looked everywhere at your place? Outside?"

She nodded into his chest. "Everywhere." Her voice was muffled by his sweatshirt. "Austin, his backpack is gone."

"That doesn't mean—"

"So are his clothes."

Austin's heart dropped, but he schooled his face into a calm expression, gripping her shoulder and sliding her back until he could look into her eyes. "We're going to get through this. Together. Okay?"

He waited for her slow nod. "It's so cold out there." Her teeth chattered as if she were the one out in the cold. "It's so cold, and he's just a kid."

Austin shook his head. "No. It's going to be all right. We're going to find him. He's probably nice and warm somewhere. I'm going to call the police and file a report. Why don't you call everyone else and ask them to start driving around to look for him? Maybe someone can call his classmates."

Leah's hand shook as she pulled out her phone, but she started dialing.

Austin took out his own phone and dialed the police. He didn't mean for the prayer to come out as he waited for someone to pick up, but it did.

Please let us find him.

Chapter 30

Two hours. They had been searching for her son for two hours, and no one had seen a sign of him. Austin's breath puffed into the air between them as he leaned on his crutches and studied the map of Hope Springs on his phone.

They'd already searched the entire downtown, and Grace and Emma were calling all of Jackson's classmates. Not that she had much hope he'd gone to one of them, since he'd never referred to any as friends. The rest of her friends were going door to door through the town, asking if anyone had seen the boy, and Jade had offered to sit at Leah's house in case Jackson came home.

Because of the extreme cold, the police were organizing their own search of the fields and forests around the town as well. They'd already sent patrolmen to search the beach, and Leah's breath locked in her chest every time she thought about the cold Lake Michigan water washing up on shore.

Jackson wouldn't have gone into the water.

She was sure of it.

Wasn't she?

A strangled sob fought its way up from her core, and she lifted a hand to her mouth to stifle it, but she couldn't keep it in any longer.

Austin pulled her into his arms without a word, their embrace slightly awkward around the crutches. She leaned into him, letting his strength hold her up.

"It's going to be okay," he murmured into her hair. "We're going to find him."

But she knew he was just as uncertain—just as scared—as she was.

She pulled away, a completely unjustified anger straightening her back. "You don't know that. He's a kid, Austin. He has no food. No shelter. No money. Nothing. He's one hundred percent alone." She crossed her arms over her chest, so he couldn't take her hand and give her empty assurances that everything would be fine.

"He has you." Steam rose from Austin's mouth, floating on the cold night air.

"A lot of good that does." Leah snarled at her own helplessness. "I can't do anything for him now."

"Look, let's go check—"

But Leah shook her head, defeat engulfing her. "Let's split up. We'll cover more ground that way."

"I'm not going to leave you alone, Leah." Austin moved his crutches toward her, but she backed up, ignoring the hurt in his eyes. She knew it was unfair, knew this wasn't his fault. But if she had been home with Jackson instead of on a date with Austin, none of this would have happened.

"I want to be alone right now, okay?" She bit back the fresh sobs that tried to wriggle free of the tight hold she had on them. She could deal with her emotions later. Right now, the only thing she cared about was finding Jackson.

"Okay." Austin's whisper cut at her, but she turned away and started walking toward her storefront. Maybe Jackson had sneaked in there for the night.

"Leah," Austin called behind her. She stopped but couldn't bring herself to turn around. "I'll pray for him."

Leah's nod was stiff. She knew she should be grateful that Austin would consider it. And she should do the same—had been trying to do the same all night.

Up until now, she'd always rejoiced to know God was in control. It was why she'd always been fine when he answered her prayers with no.

But if she prayed for Jackson's safe return and God answered that prayer with a no, she wasn't sure her faith could survive.

So she walked away, keeping her mind carefully blank.

379

The toes of Austin's good foot had gone numb. If only there was a way to numb his heart too.

The punch of Leah's words—"I want to be alone"—hit him right in the solar plexus as he watched her walk away.

When she disappeared around the corner, he forced himself to go in the opposite direction, all his senses on full alert for the slightest sign of movement. It was so cold out here. How warmly was Jackson dressed? How long could he survive out here on his own? Would they find him in time, or would—

It was too much. First his brother.

And now Jackson.

He shook off the thought. He might not be able to do anything for Chad right now. But he could help find Jackson.

Come on, Austin. Think.

A thirteen-year-old who didn't have any money couldn't get farther than he could walk. Unless he had hitchhiked. Austin nearly choked at the thought, and he had to knock it aside so he wouldn't fall into the same despair as Leah.

His eyes fell on the dark bus station. It was the only form of mass transportation in the small tourist town, and it was only open during the day. But if Jackson had left Leah's house right after she and Austin had gone on their date, the boy could have gotten here before it closed.

And if he had . . . A sick feeling rose in the back of Austin's throat. If he had, he could be in another state by now.

Heaviness dragged at his limbs, but he forced himself to make his way to the station. Maybe there was a phone number on the door he could call to find out who'd been working. Ask them if they'd seen a young boy traveling alone.

But the glass door boasted only a closed sign and posted hours—the station wouldn't reopen until nine the next morning. That was nine hours from now. They couldn't wait that long.

He called the police station and filled them in on his hunch, and they promised to investigate who had been working and where the last buses of the day had been headed.

Then he circled the perimeter of the small building, checking in every nook and cranny he could find, even the dumpster. But there was no sign anyone had been there recently.

He didn't understand. This wasn't how it was supposed to be. Leah was a good person. She was only trying to help this kid. To give him the family he'd never had. She shouldn't have to go through something like this.

It just went to show that she was wrong when she said God was in control. When she said to trust him. She'd trusted this so-called God, and look where it'd gotten her.

There was no God.

When he returned to the front of the building, Austin tried to peer inside. In the faint glow of the security lights, he could see the building was empty.

But he didn't care.

He lifted a hand to pound on the door as hard as he could.

The shock of the impact reverberated through his body, and he hit the door again. And then again, putting all his fear and pent-up anger into each blow.

It didn't make sense. It shouldn't make him so angry to realize, once again, that there was no God.

But he'd been starting to hold onto a tiny tendril of hope that maybe Leah was right and there was a God and maybe he did answer prayers.

And now.

Now he knew he'd been wrong about that. Again.

He dropped his forehead to the glass, letting its cold pierce through him. He'd run out of ideas. There was nowhere else to look.

A knifing pain sliced through him at the thought of Leah's loss.

Of his loss.

He hadn't meant to get close to Jackson—he'd warned himself not to—and yet over the past few weeks, Jackson had become more than the neighbor kid to him. The boy felt more like a son.

He almost didn't register the clicking sounds over the harsh in and out of his own breaths. He kept his eyes closed and worked to slow his breathing so he could hear better. It sounded kind of like the bolt of a lock.

His eyes popped open just as the door next to him pushed out.

Jackson stood on the other side, mouth open, staring at the spot where Austin's foot should have been.

Austin swung forward on his crutches, then let them drop to the ground as he pulled the boy into him with one arm. With the other, he reached into his pocket for his phone.

Chapter 31

L eah had never understood happy crying.

Until tonight.

She hadn't been able to slow the tears flowing down her cheeks since the moment Austin had called to tell her he'd found Jackson.

As the three of them sat crammed into the front of Austin's truck now, she swiped at her eyes. If she didn't get herself under control soon, both guys were going to think she was crazy.

She'd insisted that Jackson sit up here with them instead of in the back so that he could warm up after spending half the night in the bus station.

From the little Jackson had told Austin—and Austin had relayed to her—by the time Jackson had gotten to the bus station, the last bus had already left for the day. So he'd hidden in a supply closet until the station was closed and locked up for the night. He'd been planning to use money he'd swiped from Leah's purse to buy a ticket in the morning.

Every time she thought of it, her heart skipped. If they hadn't found him—if Austin hadn't been there—Jackson might have disappeared from her life forever.

But God had put Austin in exactly the right place at exactly the right time.

Even after her faithless refusal to pray.

Leah's heart swelled at the reminder that in spite of her own frailties and sins, God loved her. He was still working in her life even when she failed to acknowledge him.

She turned toward Jackson and Austin. It was impossible not to notice how the boy's gaze kept tracking to Austin's missing limb.

Leah wanted to tell him that it was okay, that it didn't change who Austin was, but she needed to let Austin be the one to address that.

When they pulled into the driveway, Austin shut off the truck's engine, and the three of them sat, their breaths the only sound in the small space.

Finally, Austin opened his door and slid off his seat, then reached into the back to grab his crutches.

The movement unstuck Leah from her seat, and she opened her door as well. The moment she was on the ground, Jackson scooted out past her and trundled to the front door.

Austin came around the truck to stand at her side.

"Thank you." There was so much more she needed to say, but she couldn't. She wound her hands between Austin's crutches and his torso to crush him in the tightest hug she could manage.

His hands rested on her back, and he dropped the lightest touch of a kiss onto the top of her head. "I'll let you get some sleep."

She nodded, though she didn't see how that would be possible. What if Jackson ran away again the moment she closed her eyes?

Austin glanced toward her house. "Unless you want me to stay. I don't sleep much anyway. I could sit up in the living room . . ."

Leah shook her head, but even she could tell the gesture lacked conviction. "You don't have to do that."

But Austin was already working his crutches toward the house. "Whatever makes things easier for you, that's what I have to do."

Leah followed him inside, offering her eightieth prayer of the night to thank God for him.

"I'm going to go talk to Jackson. Or try to at least." She didn't hold out much hope that he'd respond, given the fact that he hadn't said a word to her since he'd been found.

Austin squeezed her arm as she walked past, and she tried to gather what strength she could from the gesture. It was well after one in the morning, and the need for sleep pulled at her eyelids, but she couldn't go to bed without talking to her son first.

She knocked on his door but didn't wait for his response before opening it. The relief of seeing him in here shouldn't slam into her like this—after all, they'd been home for all of three minutes—but still, she sagged against his door.

Her eyes fell on the PBJ on his dresser, and she reached for it, then passed it to him. "You have to be hungry. Why don't you eat this before you go to sleep?"

Jackson shrugged but snatched the plate from her and took a bite that devoured half the sandwich.

"I know things have been a little rocky between us lately." Well, not so much lately as from the moment Jackson had arrived at her house. "But I don't understand why you felt like you needed to run away. Are you that unhappy here?" She managed to hold off the tears that threatened but couldn't prevent the crack to her voice.

When Jackson didn't answer, she lowered herself to the edge of his bed. He watched her but kept eating.

"Look, Jackson. I love you."

The boy's eyes focused on his plate, but Leah wasn't going to let his lack of a reaction keep her from telling him how she felt. "I love you so much that no matter how many times you run away, I'll come find you. I'll search and search and search. Even if it's a hundred times."

"Like Jesus with the sheep," Jackson muttered.

Leah's heart just about burst. She knew Dan had preached about the parable of the lost sheep a couple weeks ago. But she could never be sure if the message was getting through to Jackson.

"Exactly like that." She swallowed. She wasn't sure she could make herself say the next part.

She gathered her hair at the nape of her neck and took a long, shaky breath. "If you really don't want to stay with me—" She sniffed and blinked to clear the moisture from behind her lids but forced herself to keep going. She had to do what was best for Jackson. No matter how much it hurt her. "If you think you'd be happier with someone else or in a group home, then I'll respect that. You're old enough to make that choice."

At last, Jackson looked at her, but she couldn't read his expression. Was he happy? Angry? Hurt?

His eyes were blank.

"I don't want to go to another family." Jackson's hands fisted in his comforter.

"Do you want to go to a group home?" Leah tried not to let the hope lifting her heart leak into her voice.

The boy shook his head, and any prayer she had of not getting her hopes up was shattered.

"Do you want to stay here? Maybe talk about adoption?" She bit her lip, trying to resist the smile that threatened to burst out. If that's what tonight had been about—showing Jackson that he belonged with her—then maybe it had been worth all the worry and fear.

"I don't want any family."

Leah's heart crashed to the floor of Jackson's bedroom. "Why not?" she managed to whisper past the glass shards blocking her windpipe.

Jackson got out of the bed and stomped to the other side of the room, leaning against the wall and crossing his arms in front of him.

"What's the point?" The combination of hurt and anger in his voice tore at her. "Families tell you they'll be there for you forever, but it's all lies. You know what my mom said the morning she—" His gaze collided with hers, and Leah longed to go to him and wrap him in her arms. No kid should have to know this kind of pain. But she forced herself to keep her seat and let him talk.

"She said, 'It's you and me forever, baby.' I'll never forget that, the way she called me 'baby.' And she made me a peanut butter and jelly, my favorite, and said that after lunch we could go to the park if I sat at the table and ate like a big boy."

"And I trusted her." Jackson shook his head as if he couldn't believe how stupid he'd been. "I ate my sandwich, and then I went to find her to ask if we could go to the park. But she—" He dropped his eyes to the floor, kicking at the crack between floorboards with his toe.

"She was dead," Leah filled in for him.

Jackson nodded, not blinking. "So forever lasted less than an hour with her. And then they put me with this family that I thought was nice. But they kept me for less than a year before they got rid of me. And then there was another family. And another one. Some of them promised to adopt me. But none of them did."

Leah stood, daring to take a few steps toward him. "Jackson, I'm so sorry you've had to go through all of that. I wish I could take it away. I really do. But I can't. The only thing I can do is tell you I'm not them. I *do* want to—"

"No." Jackson's yell startled her into stillness. "Don't say it. I don't want you to. You're dumber than me if you think I'll believe it this time. Why don't you save us some time and admit what all those other families found out? I'm a bad kid, and nothing's going to change that."

"You're not a bad kid."

Jackson pushed off the wall, striding past her to get to the other side of the room. "Yes, I am. I didn't know why until yesterday. But now I know there's nothing I can do about it."

"Until yesterday? You mean punching Trent? That doesn't mean you're—"

"It's not about punching Trent. He deserved it. He was making fun of Adam because he has one arm that's shorter than the other. He's a total—"

"Wait." Leah had never considered that Jackson might be standing up for someone weaker than himself when he punched Trent. Not that it made punching acceptable, but it did change her perception of the situation. "You were defending Adam?"

"He can't exactly defend himself."

Leah tried to sort out her thoughts. "We'll talk about why hitting isn't the way to do that later. But first, I want to know why you say you're a bad kid."

Jackson slouched against the wall. "I just am," he mumbled.

Leah waited. Maybe that was all she was going to get. Already, he'd said more in the past twenty minutes than in the entire month they'd been together.

"My mom was an addict." The boy's voice was low, and Leah moved closer so she wouldn't miss anything.

"I'm afraid she was, honey. But that doesn't mean—"

"Mr. Giles said in health class that addiction is hereditary." He lifted his gaze to hers as if challenging her to argue.

She paused, thinking. She didn't want to mislead him. But nor did she want him to go through life thinking he was destined to fall into addiction. "It's not quite as clear-cut as that. It's not like inheriting your blue eyes. Just because your mom was an addict doesn't mean you'll be one. God gives us all a free will, to make those choices about things like what we put into our bodies. And it's my job to help you make good choices. To resist those temptations. And, if you ever fall into them, to always love you and forgive you. And to remind you that Jesus loves and forgives you too."

Jackson didn't say anything, but the tension in his shoulders eased, and his head drooped.

"Why don't you get some sleep now, and we can talk more in the morning?"

Jackson moved to the bed. Leah waited until he was tucked under the covers, then flipped off the light. She stood in his doorway, watching him lying still in bed for a moment.

"Goodnight, Jackson. I love you."

He didn't respond, but that was okay. She hadn't expected him to.

She only hoped that he'd believed her when she said it this time.

Chapter 32

"Pancakes?" Leah's sleepy voice from the entryway to the kitchen lifted Austin's mouth into a smile.

"I thought you could use them after last night."

Leah had been too worn out after talking with Jackson to tell him much about their conversation, but from what he'd gathered it had made her, at least, feel somewhat better.

He, on the other hand, had sat up on the couch the entire night, unable to shut off the images of what could have happened.

It had been too close. Way too close.

Thinking about what he could have lost had almost brought him to his knees more than once during the night. He'd even gone so far as to say a quick prayer of thanks for Jackson's safe return.

"Is Jackson up yet?" Leah shuffled into the kitchen and started setting the table.

"He got up a while ago. We talked for a bit." Austin had used their time alone together to apologize to the boy for not telling him the truth about why he couldn't play hockey. Jackson hadn't had too many questions about Austin's leg—other than how it had happened and if it hurt—and afterward, he'd returned to his room.

Austin wasn't sure yet if that was a good sign or a bad sign.

"Thank you for staying." Leah touched a light hand to his arm as she reached past him for the butter, but her voice was semi-guarded.

Because of the way he'd left her last night after their date? Before everything with Jackson?

"Leah. About last night. I'm sorry."

She set the butter down and slipped her arms around him, crutches and all. "I am too. And I really am praying for you. That things will work out the way you want, and you'll be redeployed."

He nodded and let himself do what he'd been dying to do all morning.

Her lips were soft and yielding against his, and he let himself sink into the moment.

Until Leah pulled back abruptly, snatching at the butter and moving around the table.

Austin blinked. It took him a second to figure out why she'd pulled away.

But then he spotted Jackson, staring between them with a revolted expression.

"Good morning." The forced casualness in Leah's voice almost made Austin laugh, but he managed to hold it in.

"Want some pancakes, dude?" He only asked it out of habit, though he knew what the answer would be.

But Jackson wiped his hands on his shirt and said, "Sure."

Austin could feel his mouth open as he turned to Leah, but she grinned at him and raised her eyebrows. Apparently she had the same thought as he did—don't make a big deal about this, or Jackson might change his mind.

So, as if this was what he did every day, Austin loaded a plate with three pancakes and passed it to Jackson. Then he filled one for Leah and another for himself.

As they sat there eating together, Austin couldn't keep the thought from edging its way in: They made a nice family.

Chapter 33

"So, when will we be planning one of these for you?" Peyton nudged Leah as she dropped her cake decorating supplies onto the counter.

Leah continued garnishing the elegant cups of tomato soup with basil. The bride and groom had chosen the perfect meal for a December wedding, from the tomato soup appetizers to the beef tenderloin and roasted potatoes to the hot chocolate bar.

"You're getting a little ahead of yourself."

Sure, the week since her date with Austin had been perfect. She and Austin and Jackson had eaten dinner together every night, and they'd actually convinced Jackson to play a board game with them last night. And then there'd been the kisses she and Austin had shared, and the quiet conversations they'd enjoyed together.

But that didn't mean she was planning their wedding. It'd taken her this long to be ready to date anyone. She was nowhere near ready to get married.

Even if the flutter in her tummy every time she considered it said otherwise.

"Oh, come on, Leah. Anyone can see that's where this is going." Peyton bent to pipe a flower onto the three-tiered cake.

"*I* can't."

"Of course you can." Peyton added a last flourish to the flower and lifted the piping tip. "I can see it in the way you look at him. You're in love."

"I know, but—" Leah threw the basil to the counter and wiped her hands on her apron. She couldn't deny that she loved him, even if they hadn't said it out loud yet.

"You don't look very happy about it." Peyton laid a hand on Leah's shoulder.

To her chagrin, Leah burst into tears at the gesture. "I'm sorry. I—" She picked up the basil again, but Peyton pulled her into a hug.

"Did something happen?"

Leah shook her head and wiped her eyes, laughing at herself. "That's the thing. I don't want to get my hopes up. In case nothing does. Happen. Because what if I'm expecting it and then—nothing?"

Peyton patted her back, then pulled away to fill another piping bag. "I know this is hard for you because you like to be in control, but—"

"Are you calling me a control freak?" She sniffled through her half smile.

Peyton raised an eyebrow. "You've always had your whole life planned. You like to know how everything is going to go. You thought you were going to stay single. You *planned* for it. So now that things are changing, you're scared."

Leah searched for an argument. But she had nothing.

"But you've never been in control," Peyton continued. "You know that. That's God's job."

Leah nodded. She knew that.

And yet . . . did she?

What if remaining single wasn't God's will for her? What if she'd only told herself that so she wouldn't have to risk getting hurt?

"You need to submit it all to God, Leah." Peyton examined her handiwork on the cake. "Trust he's got this. He's got you."

Leah nodded.

But she had a feeling that was going to be harder than it sounded.

"You good?" Dan didn't break his stride, but Austin caught his glance.

"I'm good." Austin huffed the words out. He knew Dan was probably used to running at a faster pace than this, but he felt good about holding his own this morning.

After how cold November had been, the days this week had warmed into the thirties, and there were only a few patches of brownish snow left at the sides of the road.

Much as Austin hoped Leah would get her white Christmas, he was grateful that the sidewalks were clear and dry enough to run again.

They pushed it hard for the last mile, and by the time they slowed to a walk in the church parking lot, Austin's lungs burned.

But he felt good.

"So, Leah tells me you hope to redeploy." Dan lifted his hands behind his head as they walked it off.

He should have known this was coming when Dan had invited him on a run this morning. But he'd agreed to it because he had something he wanted to ask Dan too.

"Yeah." He tried to gauge Dan's level of overprotectiveness. "It won't affect my relationship with Leah, though, if that's what you're worried about."

Dan stopped at the sidewalk that led from the parking lot to his house and gave Austin a long look. "Of course it will. But she's strong. She can handle that. Can you?" Dan leveled a look at him, but Austin met it full on.

His love for Leah was one thing he had no doubts about. "I can. In fact, I wanted to talk to you about that."

Dan nodded, and Austin took it as an invitation to continue. "I'd like to ask Leah to marry me."

Another nod. Either the guy had the best poker face in the world, or Austin's declaration hadn't surprised him.

"I know your dad passed away last year," Austin continued. "So I was kind of hoping you'd be willing to give me your blessing."

Dan studied him, and Austin forced himself to stay still and not look away.

"You should know that Leah has a strong faith," Dan said finally. "It's important to her."

It was Austin's turn to nod. He did know, and it was one of the things he loved about her.

"She's not going to be content with someone who only goes to church to please her." Dan regarded him. "Who doesn't have a genuine faith."

Austin swallowed. He knew that too. And although he'd once sworn to himself that he'd never believe again, over the past few weeks, as he'd sat at her side in church, as he'd listened to God's Word, he'd almost wondered if he could believe again.

It was taking more and more work not to, especially after the way they'd found Jackson unharmed last week. It was hard to believe that was a coincidence.

Which meant God had answered that prayer.

Now if he'd just answer Austin's prayers for Chad's safety and his own redeployment, he might be convinced.

"So I don't have your blessing?" Somehow the words found their way out.

Dan clapped a hand to his shoulder. "You have my blessing. And my prayers. That you see how much God loves you, no matter how things turn out."

That wasn't exactly the vote of confidence he was looking for.

But at least Dan hadn't said no.

Chapter 34

As Leah gazed around the table at Austin and Jackson, one verse kept running through her head: My cup runs over.

It was the only way to describe how she felt right now.

Surely God had blessed her and made her heart run over with joy.

For the past week, she'd been unable to stop thinking about her conversation with Peyton. The one about giving over control of her life to God.

At first, she'd been annoyed and tried to force her thoughts to something else every time it came to mind. But over the past couple of days, she'd found herself softening to the idea.

And last night, as she'd lain in bed, she'd finally prayed the prayer she'd been putting off maybe her whole life. *Lord, you made me, and you know me better than anyone else in this world. You know I like to be in control. Because I feel like if I'm in control, I can't be hurt. But the truth is, Lord, I need you to be in control. Because you love me and know what's best for me. Help me to trust that. And help me, if it is your will, to be open to a future with Austin.*

Peace had enveloped her as she prayed. Not the peace of knowing she and Austin would marry—that she was still completely unsure of—but the peace of knowing that whatever happened with Austin was in God's control. And that no matter what, she would always have the agape love of her Heavenly Father.

"What's up with you?" Jackson asked around a bite of spaghetti. Leah couldn't help the surge of happiness she felt every time he talked to her voluntarily.

Dan had been counseling the boy for the past couple weeks, and it seemed to be making a huge difference. It was such a blessing that her brother could not only help Jackson deal with some of the trauma of his past but could also share God's Word with him in the process. The other day, Jackson had come home and told her that he thought he might want to be a pastor someday. Or a soldier.

"Nothing. Why?"

"You're smiling really weird."

"Am I?" But Leah already knew she was. And she couldn't stop.

"What about me? Am I smiling weird?" Austin stuck his tongue out the side of his mouth and crossed his eyes.

Jackson pushed away from the table, picking up his empty plate. "And adults think kids are weird."

"But you love us." The words rolled off Leah's tongue. Jackson hadn't yet gone so far as to say it, but Leah could tell his heart was changing—and if he didn't love her yet, he at least didn't seem to hate her anymore.

"Whatever." As Jackson fled the room, Leah could feel Austin's eyes on her.

He reached across the table and laced his fingers through hers. "Before we clean this up, there's something I want to tell you."

A shiver of anticipation went up her spine. They hadn't said "I love you" to each other yet. But Leah didn't need to hear the words to know that was what this was.

Which wasn't to say she'd mind hearing the words—or saying them.

"There's something I want to tell you too."

"Yeah?" His grin was slow and sweet, and she leaned closer to kiss him.

But as their lips met, his phone blared a sharp ringtone. He pulled back with a quick apology, then snatched the phone off the table and lifted it to his ear.

Leah worked not to be disappointed. He'd been jumping at every phone call lately, hoping it would bring news about his brother.

She couldn't imagine how agonizing this must be for him, not knowing if Chad was safe.

It was agonizing for her to watch him go through it.

She squeezed his arm, then got up to clear the dishes. She hummed a hymn under her breath as she worked, and it took her a second to realize that Austin had called her name.

"Hmm?" She looked over her shoulder with an easy smile, but the moment she saw his white face and shaking hands, she dropped her rag and rushed to him. "What is it?"

He pulled the phone away from his ear and hit the speaker icon.

"We're still looking, Austin. And I have no doubt he'll show up any day. But I wanted you to hear it from me first."

Austin stared at the phone, not blinking, not moving.

Leah reached to put her hand in his, and he gripped it as if afraid she'd disappear if he let go.

"I'm sorry." She directed her comment toward the phone, even as her eyes remained on Austin. "Is this about Chad?"

"Sorry, who is this?" The man on the other end of the line sounded confused. "Where's Austin?"

"I'm here." Austin's voice was rough, as if someone had scraped sandpaper over his vocal cords. "This is my—" He broke off, staring at their linked hands.

"I'm a friend." She couldn't worry about labels right now. And no matter what else they were—what else they might become—they were friends first.

"Did I understand you correctly? Are you saying Chad is missing in action?" Even though her voice was barely above a whisper, the words seemed to blare across the kitchen, and Austin's arm convulsed under hers. She gripped his hand tighter.

"No ma'am. Not officially. But he was on an intel assignment, and he's missed a couple of check-ins. I was just calling to prepare Austin. In case . . ."

Thankfully, he left the rest of the sentence off.

Austin asked a few more questions about people and places Leah had never heard of, then hung up the phone. As the room fell silent, Leah turned to wrap her arms around him. He returned the hug briefly, then slid back from the table.

"I have to make some calls."

"Of course." She told herself it was ridiculous to be upset by his abrupt tone. "You can use the living room. I'll stay out of your hair. Unless you want me to—"

"I think I'll go home. I've got some info on my computer." He'd already moved to the front door and was pulling on his sweatshirt and hat.

Leah followed him, a wave of helplessness washing over her. She grabbed his arm as he reached for the door.

He lifted his head but refused to meet her eyes.

Pushing past her own hurt, she offered him the same comfort he'd given her when Jackson ran away. "We're going to get through this. Together."

With a nearly imperceptible nod, Austin pulled his arm away and left.

Chapter 35

Austin slammed his phone to the table.

Twenty-four hours of phone calls had gotten him no closer to answers.

What he really needed was to get his own boots on the ground. If he were there, at least he'd feel like he was actually doing something. Instead of being stuck here, useless.

He scrubbed his palms over his face. His eyes begged for sleep, but there was no way his mind would allow it.

His gaze went to the front window. The mail truck was just pulling up to his house.

Feeling as if he'd aged ten years in the past day, he forced himself to his feet. Maybe his reinstatement letter was in there today. Then he could get where he needed to be to help his brother.

Yeah, because your life always works out that way.

But he pushed the thought aside. God had taken enough from him. It was about time he cut Austin a break.

Outside, he couldn't keep his eyes from going to Leah's house. She'd stopped by three times already today, and each time he'd reassured her that he was fine and there was nothing she could do. He'd had to look away from the hurt in her eyes when he'd declined her offer to stay with him.

He had to be alone right now. He couldn't have any distractions as he tried to figure out how to find his brother from seven thousand miles away.

He reached into the mailbox, pulling out a stack of envelopes. An electric bill, a Christmas card, two credit card offers, and, at the bottom of the stack, an envelope marked *Department of the Army.*

His heart roared, and the world moved in slow motion as he ripped the letter open, slid the single sheet of paper out, and unfolded it. He gulped in a quick breath before letting his eyes skim the letter.

The shaking in his hands intensified as he scanned the page. He couldn't seem to focus. But four words stood out to him: *permanent disability retired list.*

He rubbed at his eyes and tried reading it again.

He had to be seeing it wrong.

But as he read the words more slowly this time, making himself absorb each one, his chest grew tighter and tighter, until he wasn't sure he was breathing anymore.

His eyes caught on more phrases now: *condition has stabilized, not fit for active duty, right to appeal the decision.*

Darn right he was going to appeal the decision.

He tilted his head up, squinting into the brilliant blue of the winter sky. "Guess you don't care after all."

Chapter 36

The scent of garlic and herbs made Leah's mouth water. She may have gone a little overboard, experimenting with four new recipes today. But she hadn't known what else to do, when Austin kept pushing her away.

She understood, she really did, that he wanted to be alone. But that didn't make her any less heartsick.

Heartsick not only for herself but for him and what he was going through and for his brother and whatever might have happened to him.

Please be with him, she prayed, trusting that God understood that by *him* she meant both Austin and his brother.

"Jackson, come help me carry some of this food over to Austin's."

It was too much to expect that Austin would come over for dinner. But the man still had to eat.

Jackson appeared in the kitchen. "Austin's not coming over?" Lines of worry puckered the boy's brow.

"I don't think he's up for it." She'd already explained to Jackson what she knew of the situation, and her heart had nearly burst when he'd volunteered to pray for Austin.

"Here, you take that plate and this container, and I'll take the pie." In truth, she probably could have carried it all herself. But she hoped seeing Jackson might help Austin. And it might make things less awkward between the two of them.

Not bothering to make the boy put on a coat, Leah followed him out the door and across the now snowless yards.

Austin's bloodshot eyes and haggard skin told her what she already knew—he hadn't slept since he'd gotten that call yesterday.

"Hope you don't mind being a guinea pig." She worked to keep her voice cheerful. "I tried a bunch of new recipes today and had way too much food, so here you go."

Austin gestured for them to come in. Jackson headed straight for the kitchen with his load, but Leah stopped to greet Austin with a kiss.

His lips were stiff on hers, and he pulled away after a quick peck. Leah stumbled slightly at his abrupt retreat but regained her footing and followed him to the kitchen.

"Any news?"

"No."

She set the pie she'd been carrying on the counter and reached for him. But he flinched away.

Blinking back the moisture that threatened, she busied herself dishing food onto a plate for him.

"I know what I forgot to tell you." She reached for the thin book she'd brought along with the food. "Dan did some digging, and he found out that your parents *did* go to Hope Church. There's even a picture of them." She paged through the book until she came to it. "This must be before you and your brother were born."

Austin's eyes flitted to the book, then jumped away. He pressed his lips together. "Thanks for dinner."

Leah blinked at the clear dismissal. Maybe he wanted to be alone. But too bad.

They were in this together.

"I know this is hard, Austin." She kept her voice low. "But we're just trying to help. To be here for you. I wish you'd talk to us."

"You want me to talk?" The words exploded out of Austin, and she had to stop herself from taking a step back. "Okay, what should I talk about? The fact that my brother is missing? And that there isn't a single thing I can do about it since the army has found me unfit to serve my country?" His chest heaved.

"What?" Leah dared to take a step closer, but Austin paced out of her grasp.

"Don't act all shocked. It's what you said would happen. What you wanted to happen."

"Austin, I never—" She reached for him again, but again he sidestepped her. "Can we talk?"

"Stop trying to fix me." Austin's voice lashed into her. "All your talk about going along with whatever God's will is. Well, God's will may have cost me my brother."

"Don't talk to her like that."

Leah's head lifted in surprise. Jackson had been so quiet on his perch at the breakfast bar that she'd almost forgotten he was there.

But now he jumped off his stool, facing Austin head-on.

"It's all right, Jackson." Leah moved toward the boy. "Why don't we give Austin some space? Come on."

Jackson stared down the larger man for another few seconds, then walked to the front door.

Leah followed more slowly, not quite sure how her heart was staying in one piece when it wanted to break for him.

And for herself.

"Leah. Jackson. Wait." Austin blinked back the moisture in his eyes as he reached for her. What was he doing? Was this who he'd become now? A man who yelled at the woman he loved? Who set this kind of example for the kid he'd come to think of as a son?

They both stopped. Jackson stared at the floor, but Leah was watching him with a look of mingled hurt and compassion.

He opened his mouth, but he couldn't force the words out past the missile-sized lump that had lodged there.

Finally, he managed to pull out two words. "I'm sorry."

Jackson threw him a disgusted look and marched out the door, but Leah's look was longer, more penetrating.

"I want to help." Her voice broke. "I really do. But you're right—I can't fix you. Only God can do that." She stepped outside but then turned back to him. "I pray you'll let him."

With a sad smile, she made her way down the porch steps and to her own house.

For a long time after she'd gone inside, Austin stood staring at her house, with the twinkling Christmas decorations they'd worked so hard to put up together.

They made the house look cozy and homey—the perfect place for a happy family.

Too bad he had finally realized the truth: He was too broken to have a family.

Chapter 37

C offee.

She needed coffee.

Leah stumbled out of bed, banging her shin on the hope chest at the foot of it, and limped toward the kitchen. The sun was barely up, and only the dimmest light illuminated the hallway, but she didn't bother to flip on any light switches. She had never had such a horrendous night's sleep in her life, and she was pretty sure her eyes would seal themselves shut if she exposed them to light right now. It didn't help that she'd spent half the night on her knees, in tears. At first, she'd prayed that God would fix whatever it was that had broken between her and Austin. But after a while, her prayer had transformed into one for healing for Austin. She whispered it to herself again now as she turned on the stove to boil water.

"Please let Austin find what he needs, Lord. Help him find the one thing that can fix him. Help him find you. And if he has to lose me to find you, please give me peace with that."

When she'd told Austin yesterday that she couldn't fix him, it had been a revelation to her too. She'd been trying so hard to make everything better for him—and for Jackson. But she had to surrender all of that to God. Because he was the only one who could give them what they truly needed—the truth that they were forgiven in Jesus.

Leah blew out a long breath. She'd always thought she was good at surrendering to God. Hadn't she gladly sacrificed her desires for marriage years ago? But now she knew better. Peyton was right—she'd accepted being single because she'd wanted to be in control.

Now, though. Now she wasn't in control. And she was trying to be okay with that.

In spite of the tiredness that clung to her eyelids, a restless energy compelled her to the living room.

It had finally snowed again overnight, and the faintest light hit the tops of the trees across the street, setting their snow-covered limbs aglow. The image soothed her soul. If God could make such beauty with a little snow and light, imagine what he could do in her life. And in Austin's.

She let her eyes track to his house just in time to see him jump into his truck. Exhaust steamed the air behind the vehicle as he started the engine. Leah watched, a vague uneasiness creeping in as she wondered where he'd be going so early in the morning.

A second later, he hopped out of the truck and headed back into the house, emerging after a minute carrying a large duffel bag in one hand and his crutches in the other. He threw them into the back of the truck, then moved toward the house again.

Her stomach dropped. When she'd said she was willing to lose him so he could find God, she hadn't meant right now. Not this way.

Please give me peace with your will, Lord. The prayer had never hurt so much.

But if he *was* leaving, she couldn't let him go without giving him the Christmas gift she'd found for him. If nothing else, maybe it would remind him that there were people in the world who cared about him.

She ran to her room and grabbed the gift, which she'd wrapped in a silver and blue foil paper, then pulled on her coat and tucked the gift into her pocket.

She jogged across the yard, snow seeping into the slippers she'd forgotten to change. Oh well. She wasn't going to go back inside and risk missing him.

Austin looked up when she was halfway across the yard, and she couldn't tell if his expression held relief or regret.

He came around the truck to meet her as she reached the driveway.

"Going somewhere? Without saying goodbye?" She tried to keep the accusation out of her voice.

He didn't come closer but squinted at her through the morning light. "I didn't think you'd want to see me." His eyes slid to the road, and he tucked his hands into his sweatshirt pocket. "But I did want to say that I'm sorry about yesterday. I shouldn't have taken out my frustrations on you."

"I understand." Leah shuffled a few steps closer, and Austin's eyes traveled to her feet. "What are you doing out here in slippers?"

She let herself smile a little. "It's what I do. Remember?" That first night they'd met, when she'd yelled at him for chopping wood at midnight, she never would have guessed that this was where they'd end up.

Although she could see him trying to fight it, a slight smile lifted Austin's lips, softening his face. She closed the rest of the space between them, though she was careful not to touch him.

"Where are you going?"

Austin sighed and leaned against the tailgate. "To see my old commander at Fort Benning. He has worked with other guys who wanted to appeal the decision to put them on the permanent disability list. If anyone can help me get where I need to be, it's him."

Leah pressed her lips tight but nodded. She wanted to argue, to tell him that was the worst thing he could do right now, that he belonged here in Hope Springs, where it was safe and there were people who loved him. But she held her tongue.

"I should make sure I have everything." He stepped away from the truck and started toward the house, but she reached for his arm.

"What will you do if you can't redeploy? Will you come back here?"

But she knew the answer before the dejected head shake. "I can't, Leah. You were right. I'm too broken. And you can't fix me." Red rimmed his eyes, and he sniffed and cleared his throat, opening his arms and pulling her in tight.

She wanted to argue, but there was nothing she could say. She would happily accept him as the broken man he was. But if she needed to let him go so he could find the One who could truly fix him, that was what she'd do.

"I really am sorry," he said into her hair. "For everything."

She inhaled his warmth, wondering how long she'd remember his comforting scent after he left.

Probably forever.

The realization gave her the courage to finally say the words she'd been holding back. "I love you, Austin."

He loosened his hold on her and slid his hands to her shoulders, nudging her back so that she could see his face. The torment in his eyes was clear, but so was how he felt about her. "I love you too." He swept a hand over her cheek, wiping away the moisture that had collected there, and she did the same for him.

"Would you—" Austin looked away, blinking hard. "Would you say goodbye to Jackson for me? Tell him I'm sorry and I'm proud of him."

She sniffled but managed to rasp, "I'll tell him."

Austin pulled away and took a few backward steps toward his house. "I have to check if I missed anything."

He walked backward nearly all the way to the door, his eyes not leaving hers until he disappeared inside. Leah took the gift out of her pocket as she reached numbly into the back of the truck for his duffel bag. She slid the gift into the bag, then zipped it and walked toward her house.

It'd be easier for both of them if she wasn't out here when he drove away.

Chapter 38

A ustin slowed as the GPS told him to take the exit toward Omaha, his shoulders knotting and stomach churning now that he was close. He'd made it to Indianapolis yesterday, with the plan of driving the rest of the way to Georgia today. But last night, he'd felt compelled to open the emails from Tanner's wife—all fifty of them. As he'd read them, the love and forgiveness she'd poured into them had left him gasping for air until he'd had to give in to the sobs he'd been stuffing down for an entire year. He'd buried his face in a pillow to keep from alarming the people in the room next door, giving full vent to his grief for the first time. When he'd finally managed to calm himself, he'd picked up the phone and honored the request she signed each of her emails with. *Please call.*

And now he was on his way there. Omaha was nine hours out of the way, but it didn't matter. Somehow, he *knew* he had to go there. Today. Now.

Two more turns, and the GPS announced he was at his location. He parked on the street, rolling his shoulders and letting out a long, slow breath.

It took a few minutes to work up the courage to step out of the truck and make his way toward the front door.

The house was quaint, its Christmas lights not quite as elaborate as what they'd done to Leah's house but still festive. Two sleds lay in the middle of the yard, and boot prints crisscrossed the snow.

The home looked completely normal. Like a happy family lived here. Austin wasn't sure what he'd expected—curtains drawn, a black veil over the door, an empty yard?—but it wasn't this.

When he got to the door, he just stood there, staring at the doorbell. Could he really do this? Could he really stand here and talk to Tanner's wife? Could he ever justify why he was the one standing here, and not her husband?

Before he could retreat, he lifted his hand to the doorbell.

The action set off chaos in the house. A dog took up wild barking, and children's voices shrieked. Through the sidelight, Austin watched a boy of six or so walk toward the door, followed by his little sister. They were a little older than the last picture he'd seen of them, but Tanner had talked about them so much that Austin felt like he knew them already.

The sight of the kids set up an ache in his chest at the thought of his makeshift family in Hope Springs, but he stuffed it down.

The boy opened the door and sent a grin his way, and the air caught in Austin's lungs. Aside from the gaps where his front teeth should have been, the boy was nearly a mirror image of his father.

"Are you Mr. Austin?" The boy's voice was innocent and filled with admiration.

Austin nodded, but he couldn't speak.

The boy didn't seem to mind. "I'm Matthew. This is my sister Martha." He patted the little girl who had finally managed to catch up with him.

Austin swallowed. The kids were both so young, neither would remember their father. It was a blessing in some ways, he knew. He'd been young enough when his father was killed that he'd never experienced the sharp pain of missing someone who'd once been a regular part of his life. But he also knew they'd grow up with questions about their father—questions maybe he could help answer. Someday.

"Sorry. I was elbow-deep in dishwater." A slender, dark-haired woman hurried up behind the children. "I'm Natalie."

Austin shook the hand she held out. He recognized her from Tanner's photos too.

"I'm so glad you could make it." Natalie gestured for him to come in, then sent the kids to play in the playroom. "I've got some coffee and cookies in the kitchen."

Austin followed her and took the seat she indicated at the table, but he waved off the cookies and coffee. He couldn't have eaten right now if he'd gone weeks without food.

Natalie pulled out the chair next to him and poured herself a cup of coffee, picking up a cookie and dunking it. "I was surprised to get your call last night. I'd actually told myself that if I didn't hear from you by Christmas, I'd stop sending the emails. I figured either I had the address wrong or you didn't want to hear from me."

Austin slid his finger over a crack in the table. "I got them," he said quietly. "But I couldn't bring myself to open them until last night."

"And what changed last night?"

"I have no idea," he answered in all honesty. Maybe it was the anonymity of the hotel room. Maybe it was the emotional conversation with Leah that morning. Maybe it was loneliness. All he knew was that when he'd turned on his phone and noticed a new email from her, he'd clicked right to it and read it—and he hadn't stopped reading until he'd gotten through all of the messages.

"I'm glad you did." Natalie's smile was warm and kind. If he'd expected to find bitterness or anger toward him, he couldn't spot any.

He glanced around the cozy room. One wall was dedicated to pictures. Tanner stared at him out of nearly all of them. One holding each of his kids as newborns. Several family photos. One of him and Natalie on their wedding day.

Austin deliberately turned away from the photos. It was too painful to look at the face he'd only seen in his memory for the past year.

"How do you do it?" The question came out before he could consider whether it was insensitive. "How do you get through the days without him?"

Natalie paused with her coffee cup halfway to her mouth. Her eyes went to the wall of pictures behind him, but Austin didn't follow her gaze.

"Some days I miss him so much, I think there must be a hole clear through the middle of me." She pressed a hand to her stomach, and Austin was sorry he'd asked.

"I'm sorry. I shouldn't have—"

But she gave him a gentle smile. "But I know he's in his true home. In heaven. And I know I'll join him there one day. When it's time."

Austin grimaced. He hadn't come here to debate heaven. But as long as she brought it up. "How could it possibly have been Tanner's time? He was way too young."

Natalie shook her head. "There's no such thing as too young or too old. God calls us home when he knows the time is right. There's nothing that's outside of his control. Not even this."

Austin wanted to be angry at her answer. How could she believe in a God who would "call someone home," as she put it, on a whim?

"I get mad sometimes," she said, as if reading his thoughts. "But then I remind myself of the promise I made to Tanner every time I talked to him."

"What was that?" His throat burned around the question, but he needed to know.

"I promised him 'even if.'" She looked at Austin, as if waiting to see if he understood. He didn't. "Even if?"

Her gentle smile held no judgment. "Have you ever heard the Bible account of Shadrach, Meshach, and Abednego?"

Austin shrugged. He'd probably learned about them in Sunday School. Long ago.

"It was Tanner's favorite Bible story."

A pang shot through Austin. Tanner had tried to talk to him about the Bible on so many occasions, but Austin had shut him down every time.

"Shadrach, Meshach, and Abednego worshiped the true God," Natalie continued. "And when they refused to bow down to a false god, the king of Babylon threatened to throw them into a fiery furnace. But these three men said, basically, 'Go ahead and throw us in there. Our God will save us. But even if he doesn't, we won't worship your false gods. We'll still worship the true God. Even if.'"

She leaned toward him, expression earnest. "That's the kind of faith Tanner wanted for us. Faith that even if something happened to him, we would continue to worship God. To trust in him and his will for our lives. I have to pray every day for that *even if* kind of faith. And God has been faithful in answering that prayer."

Austin blinked and looked away from her sincere eyes. He wasn't sure he could ever pray for that kind of faith.

"There's something Tanner wanted you to have." Natalie pushed her chair back and stepped toward the kitchen counter, grabbing a well-worn book and passing it to him. "This was his personal Bible."

But she didn't have to tell him that. He'd seen Tanner pull the beat-up book out of his pack more times than he could count. He'd offered to let Austin borrow it dozens of times. But Austin had always declined.

He half laughed as he took the book now. Apparently Tanner had gotten his way in the end.

"There's a letter for you in it," Natalie added. "It's from Tanner. Just so you're not freaked out when you open it and see your name in his handwriting."

Austin's throat threatened to close, but he managed to squeeze out a thank you.

"I'm glad you came." Natalie bent down to hug him, and Austin closed his eyes, wishing more than anything that she could be hugging her husband instead. "Tanner would be glad too."

Chapter 39

"How many of these are we going to make?" Jackson set down the candy cane-shaped cutout cookie he'd been frosting and picked up an angel-shaped one, dipping his knife into a bowl of blue frosting.

Leah couldn't help the laugh. They'd been working on the cookies for three hours already, and the boy hadn't shown any sign of tiring. Of course, it helped that for every ten cookies he frosted, he ate one.

But she couldn't bring herself to be upset about that. Not when she was having such a wonderful Christmas Eve with him.

The results of the house decorating contest had been announced earlier this morning. Their house had taken third place, earning them a fruit basket that sat in the middle of the counter now.

For the life of her, Leah couldn't remember why she'd thought it was so important to win the contest. She didn't need Hawaii to bond with Jackson. They were doing that right now, in the simple act of baking cookies.

With a thick layer of frosting covering the angel, Jackson set it down and sprinkled colored sugar over its wings. "Austin's not coming back, is he?"

Leah stopped frosting her own cookie and set it down, the heaviness of heart she'd managed to shake off for a short time returning. When she'd told Jackson two days ago that Austin had to go to Fort Benning, the boy hadn't said much. But Leah hadn't missed how many times he looked out the window toward Austin's driveway.

Wiping her hands on her apron, Leah stepped around the counter to stand next to Jackson. "I don't think so."

She wasn't sure she'd fully come to grips with it herself, but she was trying. Instead of being bitter about the time they wouldn't have together, she was focusing on being grateful for the time they had enjoyed together. And for the fact that he'd changed her outlook on life—on love.

Even though she was in no rush to meet someone and get married, she was no longer so certain that God had written that out of his plan for her life. Maybe someday . . . if the right man came along. Although at the moment, the only face she saw when she pictured the right man was Austin's.

Please be with him, Lord. She'd been repeating the same prayer constantly since Austin had left. She'd never stop praying for him, even if she never saw or heard from him again.

"Can't you call him?" Jackson looked at her as if it were the most obvious thing in the world. "Tell him to come back?"

Leah sighed. It wasn't like she hadn't contemplated doing that very thing. Every. Single. Moment.

But every time she pulled her phone out to dial, she put it away. If this was what Austin felt he had to do, she had no right to make it harder on him.

"It's not that simple." She piled the cooled cookies into a plastic container. She'd bring them to Christmas at Dan's tomorrow.

Jackson bit the head off a snowman. "Seems pretty easy to me. Call and tell him he's being an idiot."

Leah's heart twisted for the boy. Just when he'd thought he finally had a steady father figure in his life. "Austin loves you," she said quietly. "And so do I."

Jackson looked at her expectantly. "So . . ."

"It's complicated," she repeated.

"Mrs. Jenkins always says a problem is never as complicated as it seems if you break it down into its smallest parts."

Leah snapped the lid on one container and pulled out another. "Who's Mrs. Jenkins?"

"My math teacher. I think the smallest part is that you're scared to call him. Because you're afraid maybe he *might* come back."

"That's ridiculous." Leah pushed a piece of hair out of her eyes. "I'll clean this up. You go get ready for church."

Jackson popped the rest of the cookie into his mouth. "It's simple," he said as he trotted down the hallway toward his room.

Leah shook her head. She was so, so grateful for their wonderful day together. But this was not a conversation she wanted to have with him.

He was just a kid. What did he know about being scared to love people?

Probably a whole lot.

Wasn't that the reason he'd tried so hard to push her away? Because he'd been burned by people claiming to love him so many times?

But that was different. Leah wasn't afraid to love. She was just giving Austin the space he needed. She was completely willing to sacrifice herself for his sake.

That was all that was going on here.

Chapter 40

Austin threw his bags on the floor of the hotel room. After another whole day of driving, he'd made it back to Indianapolis. If it hadn't been for the detour to visit Tanner's family, he'd be in Georgia by now. But he couldn't regret making the trip to see them. Knowing that they were okay—that in spite of everything they could smile and laugh and pray—had eased his heart at least a little.

He dropped onto the edge of the bed and rummaged in his bag for Tanner's Bible. He hadn't been able to bring himself to look at it last night, but the promise of a letter from Tanner had been hovering in the back of his mind all day.

He ran his fingers over the Bible's soft leather cover. How many times had he seen Tanner do exactly the same thing, as if the book were an old friend?

Ignoring the tremor in his hands, he lifted the cover and inhaled as his eyes fell on the envelope. Despite Natalie's warning, the sight of Tanner's handwriting jarred him, and he had to look up quickly.

After a second, his heart rate slowing only slightly, he lifted the envelope out of the Bible and slid a sheet of paper out of it.

Hey Texas—

Austin couldn't help the soft laugh at the nickname. He was from nowhere near Texas, and Tanner knew it, but for whatever reason, he enjoyed the play on Austin's name. He let his eyes continue over the scrawled words.

So you're reading this, huh? I guess that means I'm chilling in heaven right now.

Austin blew out a breath. It was Tanner's voice, as sure as if he were sitting right here next to him.

I hope you know it's pretty awesome here, and I'm happy. And I also know that you did everything you could to keep this from happening. You might be wondering how I know this, since I'm dead and all. It's because I know you. And I also know that no matter how many people tell you my death isn't your fault, you'll insist it is.

Austin swiped at the tears blurring the words on the page.

Look, buddy, I'm sorry, but it wasn't your choice when I went home. That was all God. And another thing: I suppose you're using my death as one more excuse to harden your heart to him. Totally boneheaded move, man.

Austin shook his head. Even when he was writing his goodbye letters, Tanner couldn't be serious.

That's why I want you to have my personal Bible. I've been reading it and writing notes in it since I was thirteen. I hope you'll read it and that you'll let God open your heart through it. Because no matter how much you resist him, he loves you. He loves you so much that he sent his son to die for your sins so that you could come hang out with us here one day too. Looking forward to seeing you then.

Your brother,

Tanner

PS Check out Daniel chapter three.

For a long time after he read those last words, Austin sat holding the letter. How could one little sheet of paper covered with squiggles hold so much meaning? How had Tanner managed to capture the essence of himself in this letter? How had he known exactly what Austin needed to hear?

Finally, slowly, he opened the Bible and paged through it until he came to Daniel chapter three. He laughed as he read the heading—apparently Natalie knew her husband well. Tanner had directed him to the story of the fiery furnace.

With a sigh, Austin started to read it. He owed Tanner that much at least.

More than the story itself, Austin's attention hooked on the copious notes Tanner had written in the margin. But it was the final note that stuck with him the most. "Faith isn't faith if it only believes in God when he answers our prayers in the way we want him to. Faith is faith when we believe *even if*."

As Austin closed the Bible, his head spun.

416

He'd had faith once. And he'd thought it was an *even if* kind of faith. But after the things he'd seen, after he'd lost one too many buddies in battle, he'd let go of that faith, pretended it had never existed.

Could he find it again?

Not on his own. That much he was sure of. Bible still clutched in his hands, he closed his eyes.

"Lord, help me." He could only manage a whisper. "I need an *even if* kind of faith. I need faith to believe that you are with me even if things don't go the way I think they should. That you love me even if I can't be redeployed. That you are here even if something happens to Chad." Saying it nearly destroyed him, but somehow he knew this was what he needed to pray right now.

Eyes still closed, he focused on regaining control of his ragged breathing. He needed peace.

His mind slid to the first sermon he'd ever heard Dan preach. About asking God for peace with the things he was angry about. He hadn't wanted to be at peace then. He'd wanted to hold on to his anger.

But now he knew he couldn't live like this, always angry with God. "Please give me peace, Lord." His voice was stronger now. "Peace with Tanner's death and Isaad's. Peace with losing my leg. Peace with not knowing where Chad is. With all of it. Take my anger and give me your peace."

At last, his breathing slowed, and he opened his eyes.

Had the prayer done anything? He didn't feel different. Not really.

He reached for his duffel bag to put the Bible away and grab his sweats. He needed to at least attempt to get some sleep.

But as he reached into the bag, his hand fell on something sleek and thin. Another book?

He grabbed it out of the bag.

It was the church directory Leah had given him. He'd almost left it behind, but at the last minute, he'd thrown it in his bag. Even if he never looked at it, it was part of his family's history.

But something compelled him to open it now. As his eyes fell on his parents, young and obviously in love, smiling at the camera as if they had no fears about the future, he realized they hadn't known that their life wouldn't turn out as planned either. And yet, even after his dad was killed, his mom didn't turn away from God. She continued to bring Austin and his brother to church, continued to pray with them, continued to encourage them in their faith. She had been his living example of an *even if* kind of faith, and he hadn't even realized it.

Setting the book aside, Austin reached for his bag again. Now he really did have to get to bed.

But as he tugged his sweatshirt out of the bag, something hit the floor with a soft thump.

A present, wrapped in blue and silver paper, lay in the middle of the floor. He stared at it, uncomprehending. That hadn't been there when he'd packed.

And then he realized.

Leah.

As he reached for it, the ache he'd carried with him for the past three days of not being with her blazed into a need to hold her.

But that wasn't possible—would never be possible again.

Maybe if he opened the present and got it over with, he'd get some closure.

He snatched the gift up and tore the paper off in one quick movement.

His breath caught. It was a ceramic ornament in the shape of a gingerbread house that looked startlingly like Leah's house after they'd decorated it. But in place of the door was a picture—one they had taken during a walk on the beach last weekend. Austin stood with an arm around Leah, and Jackson stood in front of the two of them. There'd been no one else around, so Austin had extended his arm as far as he could to take the group selfie. The image was slightly out of focus, and he'd cut off the top of his own head—but the picture was perfect. All three of them were smiling as if there was nowhere else they'd rather be.

He ran his hand over the photo, regret slicing at him. If only things had turned out differently. If only he weren't so broken.

Austin flipped the ornament over. On the flat white ceramic of the back, in flowing handwriting, Leah had written, "'Though the mountains be shaken and the hills be removed, yet my unfailing love for you will not be shaken nor my covenant of peace be removed,' says the Lord, who has compassion on you. -Isaiah 54:10."

Austin laid on the bed, resting the ornament on top of his heart. God's covenant of peace, the verse said.

For the first time in a long time, he felt like maybe that covenant was for him too.

He reached for his phone to set the alarm. But as his finger hovered over the clock icon, a notification popped onto his screen—an email from Hope Church that the Christmas Eve service would begin live streaming in five minutes.

Austin hesitated. He was supposed to be leaving Hope Springs behind. But maybe one last night to remember wouldn't hurt.

Chapter 41

In the glow of hundreds of candles, Leah joined the rest of the packed church in singing the final verse of "Silent Night." Listening to Jackson singing next to her, she knew she had gotten more than she ever could have hoped for Christmas.

The final chord of the song rang out, and Leah joined the others in blowing out her candle and sitting as the lights came up just enough to illuminate Dan at the front of the church.

A twinge of pride lifted her lips at the sight of her little brother up there, fulfilling the role their father had once filled. She missed Dad more than ever tonight, but it was a sweet sort of missing him. He was happier in heaven than any of them could ever imagine being here on earth—and someday, when it was her turn to go to her heavenly home, she'd see him again.

"Traditionally, I would preach from the account of Jesus' birth in Luke chapter two on Christmas Eve," Dan began his sermon. "But you all know I'm not a terribly traditional guy." There was a smattering of laughter among the congregation, and Leah couldn't help smiling along.

"Instead, I'd like to look at Isaiah 54:10."

Leah fought to keep from gasping out loud. Her brother couldn't have known that was the same verse she'd written on the gift to Austin. She hadn't shown it to anyone.

Dan read the verse she knew by heart: "'Though the mountains be shaken and the hills be removed, yet my unfailing love for you will not be shaken nor my covenant of peace be removed,' says the Lord, who has compassion on you."

Jackson gave her a strange look, and she realized she'd been mouthing the words along with her brother. She shrugged. This was too wonderful to ignore. She sat forward as her brother paused to take in the congregation.

"Here's a dumb question: Do bad things ever happen to you?" Dan paced from one side of the church to the other as all around people nodded. "Of course they do. It's part of living in this sin-fallen world, right? But you think you have it rough? Look at all those people in the Bible who went through bad things. There was Joseph—his brothers stole his coat, threw him in a pit, and sold him to slave traders. And what about David? He served King Saul loyally, and how did the king repay him? By chasing him down with the intention of killing him. Oh, and let's not forget Job. He probably had it the worst of all, right? God let Satan take everything from him—his land, his home, his health, and, most painfully, his children."

"Makes our problems seem pretty insignificant, doesn't it?" Dan paused.

In front of her, Leah could see a few heads nod, but she knew her brother well enough to know this was where he was going to flip everyone's expectations upside down.

"Actually—" Dan held up a hand. "Actually, I don't think it does. Because God doesn't see any of our problems as insignificant. He knows our hurts. He knows when we're sick. He knows when we worry that we won't be able to pay the bills. He knows when our hearts are broken because a relationship has ended."

Leah blinked back the moisture that pricked her eyes. It did hurt to know that her relationship with Austin had ended. And yet, it was comforting to know that Jesus understood. That he cared.

"And he knows what we're going through when we have to say goodbye to someone we love because they've gone before us to be with him."

Dan spread his arms wide, as if encompassing the whole room. "And how does he know all of this? Why can he relate to it?" After a heartbeat, he answered his own question. "Because he was one of us. He chose to set aside his glory and humble himself and come into this world to be born as a baby and live among us. He hurt the same ways we hurt—worse, because he knew what he had created us to be, the perfect life he had intended for us, and we had thrown it all away."

"But here's the thing to remember." Dan's smile took in the entire congregation. "These verses from Isaiah. God says that no matter what, his love for us will not fail. Even if the mountains are shaken. Even if the hills fall to the ground and are no more. Even if we are filthy, wretched sinners who fail him at every turn. Even then, his covenant with us will always stand. His promise to us. And what promise is that? It's the promise he was born on Christmas and died on Good Friday to fulfill. The promise he made at the beginning of the world, when Adam and Eve fell into the first sin. The promise that he forgives us for all of our sins. That we have the peace of knowing the promise of heaven."

Leah sighed, relaxing into her seat. No matter how many times she heard that promise, she'd never tire of the good news. Next to her, Jackson was leaning forward, taking in Dan's sermon. God's Word was working in his heart. Leah could tell.

But there was one more person's heart she prayed it worked in. *Please let Austin know this good news too, Lord. It's the only thing that will heal him.*

Chapter 42

Austin had sat up in the bed of his hotel room halfway through the sermon, and as Dan said "Amen" and the congregation began to sing a new song, he sprang to his feet.

That sermon. Those words. That *even if*. Again.

"Okay, Lord, you have my attention," he said out loud into the mirror over the room's small dresser. "Now what?"

But he already knew now what.

He shoved his phone in his pocket, grabbed his duffel bag, and cradled the ornament from Leah. With one last look around the room to make sure he hadn't forgotten anything, he jogged toward his truck. It was nearly nine o'clock, but if he drove through the night, he should reach Hope Springs by tomorrow morning—Christmas morning.

He set the ornament on the seat beside him, then started the engine and pointed the truck north. As he drove, he found himself falling into prayers he hadn't known he needed to pray.

Prayers for Tanner's wife and children.

Prayers for Isaad's family.

Prayers for himself, that he would find peace with the life God had given him instead of seeking the one he'd thought he'd have.

Dan had said once that he could be thankful even for his hardships. That God knew what he was doing with his life even when Austin didn't. He hadn't seen it at the time—hadn't wanted to see it. But now he did.

These scars were exactly what had led him to where he was supposed to be—with Leah and Jackson. And more than that, walking with his Savior.

Thank you for your scars too, Lord. The scars that you willingly endured to save us when we were helpless to save ourselves.

Austin drove and prayed through the night, stopping only twice to stretch his legs. By the time the sun was peeking over Lake Michigan, he was pulling into Hope Springs. A fresh layer of snow had fallen overnight, giving the town the perfect Christmas atmosphere.

He wanted nothing more than to go straight to Leah's house and fold her into his arms. But there was something he had to do first.

He pulled into the church parking lot and stopped in one of the spots near Dan's house. Since it was Christmas morning, the preacher was likely already awake and preparing for services. But Austin didn't want to wake his family. So he sent a quick text.

Got any wrapping paper?

The immediate *yes* from Dan set off a grin he couldn't hold back.

Chapter 43

"It's not much, sorry." Christmas morning, Jackson passed her a card and a box it looked like he'd wrapped himself. She'd wanted to wait until after church to open gifts, but he seemed so eager to give her hers that she hadn't been able to say no.

She slid her finger under the flap of the envelope and pulled out a Christmas-tree shaped card. When she opened it, speakers inside started playing "O Christmas Tree," and she had to laugh.

But her laughter died as her eyes fell on the words Jackson had written:

Dear Mom,

Thank you for not giving up on me. I know I haven't made it easy.

Merry Christmas,

Jackson

She tried to blink back the tears but failed. "Thank you, Jackson."

The boy looked at the floor, a slight pink tinging his cheeks, and she couldn't resist pulling him into a hug.

He didn't exactly return the hug, but he didn't squirm away either.

After a few seconds, Leah released him and swiped at her eyes, then carefully unwrapped the box he'd given her.

"Austin helped me pick it out," Jackson mumbled as she opened the lid, and she nodded, trying not to let the name affect her.

A small laugh escaped as she lifted a pair of oven mitts out of the box. They were almost the same as her old ones—red and white checked—but had none of the worn patches.

"We thought you could hang up your dad's. So they wouldn't get more wrecked."

She hugged them to her. "I love them. Thank you."

Jackson's face grew pinker.

"How about you open one of your presents now?" Leah stood and moved to the tree, rummaging through the gifts she'd stacked there to find the perfect one to give him first.

"Uh, Le— Mom?" Jackson stumbled over the word, but it was still the most beautiful sound Leah had ever heard. She buried her head deeper under the tree. If he saw how emotional she got every time he called her that, he'd stop.

"Mom." Jackson's voice was more urgent now, and Leah stopped digging to look at him.

"What's up?"

But he was staring out the window. "Austin's here."

"What are you talking about?" Leah's mouth went dry, even as she knew he had to be mistaken. Austin was in Georgia by now.

She jumped as the doorbell rang, but Jackson was already running to answer it.

Leah's hands shook as she straightened, and she smoothed down her rumpled flannel pajamas.

The door blocked her view at first. All she saw was a hand reaching out to pull Jackson toward him.

But it was enough. She'd recognize that hand anywhere.

She wanted to take a step closer, but her feet refused to obey her brain. From the other side of the door came the sound of Austin's hand clapping Jackson's back.

She should tell him not to get the boy's hopes up. That if he wasn't here to stay, he shouldn't have come at all. Because it wasn't fair to Jackson. Or to her.

But like her legs, her mouth refused to follow her orders.

At last, Jackson took a backward step into the room, a massive grin filling his face. A second later, Austin followed, closing the door behind him.

"Hi." His eyes met hers, and all she could do was nod. He held a large wrapped box in one arm and, not taking his eyes off her, bent to set it on the coffee table. "I got your message."

"You called him?" It was the loudest she'd ever heard Jackson speak—so loud she should probably reprimand him for yelling, but she still couldn't get her voice to work.

"Yes! I knew it." The boy clapped his hands.

Austin laughed, but Leah's heart dove. This was exactly why she hadn't wanted to call Austin. She'd left only a super short message right before she went to bed last night, wishing him a merry Christmas. But he'd obviously heard the sadness in her voice and let his guilt bring him back.

"You didn't have to come back."

"I know I didn't." His voice was too tender, and Leah had to look away as he stepped toward her. Still her legs wouldn't work.

"Leah, look at me. Please." His hands closed around hers, and her eyes were drawn to his.

"I didn't come back because of your call. I was already on my way. I came back because I realized you were right. Dan was right. Chad was right. Tanner was right. Everyone was right except me, apparently." He gave an ironic laugh. "I was so angry about everything that happened, so busy thinking that everything had to work out exactly how I wanted it to, that I missed the whole point. It's not about what I want. It's about what God wants for me. What he knows is best for me." He closed the last little bit of space between them. "And that's you." He lowered his face toward hers.

Leah's heart thrummed a thousand beats a minute as she lifted her chin.

"Eww." Jackson's voice behind them made them both pull back. But both were smiling.

"And that goes for you too," Austin said to Jackson. "You're one of the best things that has ever happened to me, and I'm not going to run away from that."

Jackson blinked and cleared his throat, staring at the floor, and Leah had to brush a tear from her own cheek at seeing his reaction to being so loved.

"I got you something." Austin lifted the present off the table, passing it to her.

Although it appeared easy for him to handle, she braced for the weight of the big box. But when he set it into her arms, she almost dropped it because it was so light.

"You got me air?" she teased.

"Guess you'll have to open it to see."

Leah lowered herself to the couch so she could set the box on her lap, then began carefully peeling the layers of wrapping paper.

"You might want to grab something to drink," Austin said over his shoulder to Jackson. "We might be here a while."

"This is how I open gifts," Leah shot back. "Take it or leave it."

"I'll definitely take it." Austin grinned at her, and she turned her attention to the box.

Once she had the paper all peeled off, she folded it and set it aside, then lifted the lid off the box, groaning at the sight of another wrapped box inside it.

"You're one of *those* present wrappers," she accused. But she started unwrapping the box immediately.

Three boxes later, she came to the smallest box she'd ever seen. This had to be the last one. There was no way another would fit inside it.

When the paper was finally off, she held a small velvet box in her hand—the kind jewelry came in. Her hands shook as she pried it open, and she nearly dropped it as her eyes fell on the ring inside.

She looked up, but Austin was no longer standing next to her. She'd been so busy unwrapping the boxes that she hadn't noticed him drop to one knee at her side. His left leg was propped at a slightly odd angle, but she still knew what the pose meant.

She could only blink at him, her heart leaping. Was this really happening? She hadn't been looking for it. And it was all so fast.

He cradled her hands in his. "Before I came to Hope Springs, I didn't realize anything was missing from my life." He laced his fingers through hers. "When I met you, I thought maybe that was it. Maybe you were what I had been missing." His smile went all the way to his eyes, which shone brighter than she'd ever seen them. "But you helped me see that what I was missing couldn't be found in a person. Or in redeploying. Or in anything else. What I was missing was God. And you helped me find him again."

Leah dropped the box into her lap and threw her arms around him. That was the best thing anyone had ever said to her.

After a second, Austin gently unwrapped her from his neck and slid her back so that he could see her face.

"The thing is, though, God had something to show me too." He lifted his palm to her cheek, caressing it with his thumb. "He showed me that even if my life didn't turn out the way I thought it would, he has been with me every step of the way. And he has led me to you. To both of you." He looked over his shoulder at Jackson, who was watching them with a half-disgusted, half-intrigued expression. "And I'd like to stay with the two of you for a very long time. Forever, in fact, if you'll let me." He dropped his hand from her face and reached for the ring still in her lap, pulling it out of the box and holding it out to her. "Leah, will you marry me?"

Her first instinct was to blurt the yes that had been hovering on her tongue the whole time he'd been speaking. But this was a big decision. It didn't affect only her. It affected Jackson too.

She swallowed. "Can I think about it?"

Chapter 44

"**M**erry Christmas, Austin." Sophie leaned in to hug him, juggling one of her twins on her hip, as Spencer carried the other, along with what looked like a year's worth of baby supplies.

"Merry Christmas." Austin reached to help Spencer with the extra highchair. Friends had been coming in and out of Dan and Jade's house all day, in between visits with their own families. Dan and Leah's mother had arrived just in time to go to church with them, and though Austin had nearly panicked at the prospect of meeting Leah's mother, he'd found her as easy to talk to as Leah was.

He hadn't mentioned this morning's proposal to anyone, though. He'd let Leah do that—after she made her decision.

Every time his eyes met hers, he felt it. This was *right*. This was where he was supposed to be. Who he was supposed to be with.

But he wasn't going to force it. For the past year, he'd been trying so hard to force his will that he'd lost sight of what mattered. But that stopped now. He was going to accept his permanent retirement and wait and see where God led him from here.

And right now, that meant giving Leah the time she needed to make a decision.

In his pocket, his phone vibrated, and he pulled it out, intending to decline the call. It was Christmas, after all.

But the moment his eyes fell on the name, his hands shook so hard, he nearly dropped the phone.

He swiped to answer the video call.

"Hey bro."

At the sight of Chad's pixelated face, Austin lost it.

Covering his mouth with his hand, he rushed down the hallway to the nearest empty room.

"Where have you— I thought—" He couldn't talk around his gasps. *Thank you, Lord.*

"It's okay." His brother's voice sounded so close and so far away at the same time. "I'm okay." He repeated it a few times, until Austin managed to pull himself together.

Finally, he scrubbed a hand over his face and cleared his throat. "Sorry. I—"

A knock on the door cut him off. "Austin?" Leah opened the door. "Is everything all right?"

"Is that your gorgeous neighbor?" Chad's voice was unnecessarily loud, likely intended to embarrass him, but Austin didn't care.

"Yes it is." He hurried to the door and grabbed Leah's hand, pulling her into the room.

"Leah, this is my brother Chad. Chad, Leah."

The tears that sprang to Leah's eyes touched him more than anything else could have, and he had to blink back his own emotion again.

"It's nice to meet you, Leah." Chad's voice was warm, and Austin still couldn't believe it was really him.

"You too." Leah wiped her eyes. "You had us all pretty worried. A lot of prayers were said here for your safe return."

"I appreciate that." Now it was Chad's turn to sound choked up.

"I'll let you two talk." Leah lifted onto her tiptoes to kiss Austin's cheek, and he reached an arm around her in a quick hug.

"Just neighbors, huh?" Chad's voice pulled his attention off Leah as she waved and closed the door.

"A lot has changed since the last time we talked." Austin chuckled, his heart buoyant.

Chad was alive and unharmed, he and Leah were together again, and he was in a home full of people he cared about—and who cared about him.

"So your girlfriend—"

"Possibly fiancée." Austin could not stop grinning.

Chad's eyes widened, and he leaned closer to the screen. "Seriously?"

Austin could only nod, still grinning. The only way this day could get better was if Leah answered his question with a yes.

But even if she didn't, it was shaping up to be a pretty amazing Christmas.

"Okay, then, your fiancée said that there have been a lot of prayers said there. Does that include you?"

Austin studied his brother. Despite the poor video quality, he could see the hope on Chad's face. His brother had been almost as persistent as Tanner in trying to talk to him about God.

Austin had never appreciated it before, but now he realized that each of those seeds Chad and Tanner—and later Leah and Dan—had planted had sprouted in his heart.

"I prayed for you, Chad. And I prayed for me, that I'd be redeployed so I could come watch your back." He blew out a breath. "God only answered one of those prayers with a yes."

On the screen, Chad blinked but didn't say anything, and Austin wasn't sure if it was because his words hadn't gone through or if his brother was waiting.

He gripped the phone tighter. "They moved me to the PRDL."

Still just a blink from his brother.

"Did you hear me?" Austin held the phone closer to his face, raising his voice in case the connection was bad. "They put me on the permanent disability retirement list."

"I heard." Chad's voice was quiet, but his expression didn't change. "How do you feel about that?"

"I'm—" Austin hesitated. Three days ago, he would have said he was furious, outraged, ready to tear down every obstacle to return to active duty.

But God had worked an amazing change in his heart since then.

"I went to see Natalie," he said quietly. "She gave me Tanner's Bible, and I read some of it."

Chad's laugh held admiration. "Gotta hand it to that guy. He never gave up."

"Yeah." Austin shook his head. There'd never be anyone quite like Tanner. "He wrote something in there about trusting in God *even if*." He licked his lips. He could hardly believe the next part. "So I'm at peace with it. I trust God has something else planned for me. And that he's got your back better than I ever could."

"I'm happy for you, Austin." The sincerity in Chad's voice carried through the phone. "Looks like my prayers were answered today too."

Austin nodded, not trusting himself to say anything.

"I have to get to all kinds of debriefings, but I'll talk to you soon."

Austin expected the familiar panic to take over at the thought of not hearing from his brother for a while, but a new sense of peace cloaked him. Another answered prayer.

"Merry Christmas, bro."

After Chad hung up, Austin sat staring at the phone for a few minutes, pouring out his thanks to God for so many blessings, hidden and otherwise.

Then he pushed to his feet and hurried to the living room. He had to thank Leah and their friends for all the prayers they'd offered up for Chad—and for him.

"Today was a good day." Leah leaned into Austin as they walked up the steps to her porch. She couldn't remember ever feeling more content in her life.

"The best." Austin dropped a kiss onto the top of her head, then opened the door for her. When he hesitated on the porch, she grabbed his hand and pulled him inside.

"Can we talk?" She barely found the courage to say the words, and she could tell by the way his breath hitched that he knew what she wanted to talk about.

While Austin had been on the phone with Chad—praise the Lord for answered prayers—she'd had a chance to talk to Jackson about Austin's proposal and what it would mean for both of them, especially if he chose to let her adopt him.

"Austin—"

"Leah, wait." Austin took her hands and led her to the couch. "Before you give me your answer, can I say one more thing?"

She bit her lip but nodded. There was nothing he could say to change her mind, but she'd let him speak first.

"Whatever you answer, I want you to know that I will always be here for you and Jackson. As friends, if that's what you want. But I'm not going anywhere either way. And also, I want you to know that saying yes would mean being with a man who is broken but healing in his Savior, a man who makes mistakes but seeks forgiveness. Above all, a man who will love you and Jackson for the rest of his life." He sucked in a long breath. "I realize that was like four things. But I just wanted you to know. In case it makes a difference."

But Leah shook her head. At the flash of disappointment in his eyes, she rushed to clarify. "None of that makes a difference, Austin, because I already knew all of it." She lifted her hands to his cheeks.

"But before I give you an answer, there are a few things I need you to know. One is that you have totally upended my world. I had everything planned. I thought I knew where my life was going. I was happily single. And then you came along and—" She slid her hands along the light layer of scruff on his cheeks. "And I love you so much it literally steals my breath sometimes. And another is that I'm a mess too. I can't promise I'm not going to ever meddle or try to control things I need to leave to God. But I'm going to trust that you'll call me out when I do. And also, I want you to be a real father to Jackson—to teach him how to be a man of God. And finally—" She paused, and her eyes locked on his. "Finally, yes, I will marry you."

Austin's arms instantly engulfed her, and their lips came together, the long kiss solidifying everything they'd said—and all the things words could never express.

When they pulled apart, they both had tears on their cheeks, and both were laughing.

"Best Christmas ever," Austin whispered into her hair.

Epilogue

One Year Later

"Best Christmas ever." Leah could not stop smiling as she walked down the aisle on her new husband's arm. Technically, it was three days after Christmas because they hadn't wanted to take people away from family on Christmas day, but who was counting?

Austin had not stopped smiling once the entire day either.

The moment they exited the sanctuary into the lobby, he swept her up in his arms and brought his lips to hers.

"Eww. Are you guys going to keep doing that all day?" Jackson followed them, dapper in the tux he wore as Austin's best man and carrying a laptop under his arm. Chad hadn't been able to make it back for the ceremony, so they'd set up a video call with him so he could watch everything live.

"Not all day." Austin rumpled the boy's hair. "*Forever.*"

Jackson groaned but stepped into their outstretched arms for a family hug.

Leah had a fleeting wish that she could freeze time right at this moment and live it forever. But that wasn't how life worked. The three of them had a whole life to live together—so many more memories to create. She prayed that the majority of them would be happy, but even on this happiest day of her life, she knew they wouldn't all be.

But that was okay. Because they would weather them together—with God.

As the rest of the bridal party and then all the well-wishers at church gathered around them, Leah kept a careful watch on Austin. He'd been doing better in crowds lately, but she had promised herself that she'd do everything she could to make this day enjoyable for him. And if that meant escaping the crowds, that's what they'd do. Besides, that'd give them more opportunities to kiss.

As his eye caught hers, she leaned over for a quick kiss, whispering, "You okay?"

"Never better."

The rest of the afternoon and evening passed in a whirl of joy. After a delicious dinner prepared by her staff—she made a mental note to give Sam a raise—and a scrumptious cake made by Peyton, Jackson stepped up to the microphone that had been set up for toasts.

Leah gripped Austin's hand. "What's he doing?"

Austin grinned at her. "Best man toast."

Leah pushed down a flutter of nerves. When Austin had suggested Jackson as best man, she'd been so moved, she hadn't even considered this part of the job duties. He was only a fourteen-year-old kid. What was he supposed to say at a wedding?

But Jackson pulled an index card out of the inside pocket of his tux and cleared his throat, glancing at his wrist, which sported the watch Leah had given him for his birthday last year.

She stilled to listen.

"Uh, hi everyone. My name is Jackson Zelner. I'm Leah's son." His gaze flicked her way, and Leah gave an encouraging smile, telling herself that this was not the time to cry. "And, uh, I guess Austin's son too now—or at least I will be once the adoption paperwork goes through for that."

Well, it may not be the time to cry, but that didn't stop the tears that trickled down her cheeks. She was learning that there was definitely something to be said for happy crying.

"Uh, anyway," Jackson continued. "I just wanted to say that I don't think I ever really knew what love was growing up. I mean, people would tell me they loved me, but then they would leave me. Sometimes on purpose, sometimes not."

The wedding guests had stilled, and Leah didn't think a single person dared to lift a fork.

"Then this woman came along, and for some reason she decided she wanted to be my foster mom. I still have no idea why." A few people laughed gently. "I tried really hard—"

He held out a hand. "I mean, really hard, to push her away. To get her to prove once again that there was no such thing as love. That it was just a word. But she wouldn't give up." He turned to Austin. "Just a warning that she's really stubborn."

The guests laughed harder this time.

"So anyway—"

Leah could tell Jackson was warming up to having everyone's attention. She never would have guessed that this was the same young man who'd barely said two words to her when she'd first brought him home last fall.

"Then there was this guy. Austin. Our neighbor. I thought he was pretty cool. But I don't think my mom liked him very much at first. Especially when he let me keep a squirrel."

Next to her, Austin laughed and wrapped an arm around her shoulders.

"But I could tell he liked her. And pretty soon she liked him too. And then they were in love. And I watched them. I was waiting again. Since Leah wouldn't give up on me, I needed different proof that love wasn't real. But the more I watched them, the more I wondered if maybe it *was* real after all." Jackson turned to face the two of them. "I don't think it was until last Christmas morning, though, that I really believed it. Austin came barging into our house and asked my mom to marry him. And I was sure she was going to say yes—it was pretty obvious she wanted to. And I figured that would leave me on my own again, since she'd found someone else to love. But she didn't say yes. She said she had to think about it. She wanted to talk with me about it. I think that was when I knew love was real, because she put aside what she wanted to make sure things were okay with me." Jackson blinked and looked down at his card, then raised a champagne goblet that had been filled with sparkling grape juice. "So what I guess I'm saying is that love is actually pretty great. And congratulations, Mom and Dad."

"Congratulations," the rest of the guests cried as both Austin and Leah flew out of their seats and trapped Jackson in a long hug.

When they finally pulled apart, Jackson looked from one to the other. "I can't believe I'm going to say this, but you two should kiss now."

He grabbed a spoon off the table and clinked it against his glass. The sound was echoed by people throughout the hall.

"What do you say Mrs. Hart, should we kiss?" Austin's hands were already around her waist, and he pulled her closer, his breath tickling her cheek and sending a warm shiver down her back.

She'd never thought she'd be Mrs. *Anyone*. And now here she was, married to a man God had created to be her perfect match.

She wrapped her arms around his neck. "Yes, Mr. Hart, I think we should."

As Leah's lips met her husband's, her heart welled with joy. She hadn't fixed Austin, and he hadn't fixed her. But God had taken the broken pieces of both of their lives and transformed them into something beautiful.

For Christmas and for always.

Not Until This Day

A HOPE SPRINGS NOVEL

VALERIE M. BODDEN

The Lord is my light and my salvation—
whom shall I fear?
The Lord is the stronghold of my life—
of whom shall I be afraid?

Psalm 27:1

Chapter 1

R*ed.*

Why had she chosen red?

Isabel combed her fingers through her hair and leaned closer to the gas station restroom's grimy mirror as she waited for her daughter to finish up. Of course Gabby hadn't been able to wait the five minutes until they got to their new apartment.

But this was fine. It gave Isabel a chance to steady her nerves before they started their new life.

Again.

"How you doing in there, Bunny? Need any help?"

The sound of a toilet flushing answered, and her daughter emerged, swinging her long blonde locks behind her. Locks that looked exactly like Isabel's own hair had once upon a time.

"I like your hair, Mama." Gabby flashed her signature toothless grin at Isabel as she walked to the sink.

"You don't think it's too red?"

Gabby shook her head as Isabel helped her reach the soap. "It's not red. It's burnt umbrella. That's what the box said, remember?"

Isabel laughed, ripped off a piece of paper towel, and passed it to her little goofball. "Burnt auburn. Not umbrella."

Gabby shrugged and wiped her hands on the paper towel, then threw it in the trash and slipped her still-damp fingers in between Isabel's.

Isabel squeezed. Her daughter couldn't possibly know what a lifeline she was. "Come on. We'd better get back out there before Chancy tears apart the car."

Outside, the sun had started to sink, and the air had cooled enough that Isabel shivered and hurried Gabby toward the car. She hadn't thought to pull their sweatshirts out of their bags this morning, since temperatures to the south had been hot and sticky for weeks already. She should have realized that early June would still be cool this far north.

Gabby giggled as she spotted Chancy in the driver's seat, poking his nose through the slight crack Isabel had left in the window. "I think Chancy wants to drive."

Isabel angled her ear toward her shoulder in a deep stretch. "He's welcome to." After driving for three days straight, she'd had enough. Thankfully, this was it. They'd finally reached their destination.

She settled Gabby into her booster seat in the back, then moved to her own door. Chancy licked her hand as she nudged him out of her seat and slid the temperature control from air conditioning to heat.

"Mama, I'm hungry."

"I know, Bunny. We'll get some supper as soon as we get settled in."

Settled in.

That had a nice ring to it. For half a second, Isabel let herself imagine what it would be like to settle in for good.

But they couldn't. Not here. Not yet.

Maybe not ever.

If they stopped moving, if they settled in for too long, Andrew would find them. And if he found them—

Isabel shivered and cranked the heat up another notch.

That wasn't going to happen. As long as she followed the rules she'd made for herself, they'd be safe: Keep moving. No friends. No men.

She let out a quick exhale and nodded to herself. Easy enough.

"What does that sign say?" Gabby piped up from the back seat.

"Hope Springs." The large wooden sign was painted in bright, welcoming colors, and the tightness in her shoulders eased as she said the words. In three years, this was the farthest they'd moved. She still wasn't sure what had made her choose this place. Not really. Except that when she'd Googled "where to find hope" a few days ago, an ad for this town had come up. The name had caught her eye. As had the fact that it was clear across the country from Andrew, small, out of the way, and picturesque. The last one she knew was frivolous, but if she was going to keep uprooting her daughter like this, she at least wanted her to have beautiful memories of the places they'd lived.

"Are we going to stay here this day?" Gabby asked around a yawn.

"*Today*. Not 'this day.'" Isabel shook her head. She corrected Gabby on that phrase nearly every day, but it was one of those things her daughter seemed to ignore. "And, yes, we're going to stay here for a while. What do you think of it?"

They crested a steep hill, and both of them gasped at the same time.

"Wow, Mama. I thought we were far away from the ocean."

Isabel blinked at the expanse of water, burnished with the red-gold of the sunset, a hint of peace filling her for the first time since she could remember. "That's not the ocean. It's Lake Michigan."

"Look at all those boats down there." Gabby rolled her window down, and Chancy pounced into the back seat to climb over her and stick his head out the window. "I hope we can go on one."

"Close your window." Isabel frowned into the mirror. The last thing they needed was for the dog to jump out of the car. "Those boats are too expensive. And too dangerous." Though she had to admit the bobbing masts made a pretty picture, glowing against the backdrop of the water.

She tore her eyes off the lake and examined the stores that lined either side of the street. A fudge shop, a bakery, an antique store. They probably couldn't afford anything in any of them, but at least they could have some fun window shopping. The tightness in her shoulders eased a little more.

This had been the right place to come, she could feel it.

She followed the directions her phone's GPS announced, taking a right and then two lefts, until she pulled into the parking lot of a small but well-kept apartment building.

"Looks like this is the place." She was careful not to use the word home.

Home implied somewhere you planned to stay, if not forever, for a good, long time.

"I like it." Gabby's voice pitched up with enthusiasm. "It has a playground." She pointed to the single swing and small slide, both of which had probably been old already when Isabel was Gabby's age.

Isabel was grateful it took so little to make her daughter happy. Though she couldn't ignore the twinge of regret—she'd wanted to be able to give her daughter the world.

Too bad you're not fit to be a mother.

She shook her head against the thought. Though she'd left Andrew three years ago, his voice had been a constant refrain in her head every single day. But she wasn't going to let it win today.

She wasn't.

She pushed her door open, reaching to snap Chancy's leash onto his collar before he could take off across the parking lot. Keeping a tight hold on the leash, she opened her daughter's door.

"Can I walk Chancy, Mama?"

Isabel studied her daughter. The dog was strong but well-behaved. And maybe it would help their case if the landlord saw kid and dog together. She'd sort of neglected to mention they had a dog when she'd inquired about the apartment on the phone. She'd figured once they got here and the landlord saw how sweet Chancy was, there was no way he'd turn the dog away.

At the building's door, she pressed the button to buzz the landlord, and a few seconds later, they were standing face-to-face with a grumpy looking older man. "What're you doing with that mutt?"

"Oh, um— Hi." Isabel squeezed Gabby's hand tighter as she held out her other hand to the man. He peered at it as if suspecting she'd just cleaned up after the dog, before finally giving it a half-hearted shake. "I'm Isabel. We spoke on the phone about the apartment you have for rent."

The man eyed her. "I know who you are. You didn't say nothing about a dog."

"I know. I'm sorry. I thought—"

"Gonna have to get rid of it if you wanna live here."

Next to her, Gabby burst into loud tears, and Isabel pulled her closer, torn between a desire to comfort her daughter and an urge to tell her to cry harder to win this man's sympathy.

"Please, sir. This dog has been through a lot with us, and—"

The man jabbed his finger at a sign in the small window next to the door. "No pets. No exceptions. Now do you want the apartment or not?"

Isabel stared at him, her heart faltering. Could he really ignore her daughter's tears?

"I do, sir. I really need it. But we can't get rid of the dog. My daughter—" She gestured helplessly at the sobbing Gabby, blinking back her own tears. "Isn't there any way? I'd be willing to pay extra . . ." Not that she had any idea how she'd manage that. All the money she had in the world would be going into the security deposit and first month's rent.

The lines around the man's mouth softened. "I'm sorry. I'd help you if I could. But my granddaughter lives in the building, and she's allergic to dogs. Breaks out in hives and can't breathe when she's around them."

Isabel clamped her mouth shut. It hadn't occurred to her that he could have a good reason for not giving in.

"I understand." She tugged Gabby down the walkway. "We'll find somewhere else to stay."

"If you decide to get rid of the dog . . ."

But Isabel shook her head. Chancy had saved her life. There was no way she was going to give him up. And after everything else her daughter had left behind, Isabel refused to make her say goodbye to her only friend.

They'd just have to find hope somewhere else.

"Strike three!"

The umpire's call jerked Tyler's attention back to the baseball game. He held out a hand for a high-five as his son Jonah jogged to the bench, head down.

"It's all right. Shake it off." But he knew Jonah wouldn't. That kid took every loss as a personal affront. Kind of like his dad.

But dwelling on the strikes wasn't going to help his performance in the outfield. Tyler clapped a hand on his son's shoulder, forcing himself to talk like a coach and not a dad. "I mean it. Shake it off. Game's not over yet."

Even if they were down three to five in the bottom of the sixth.

Tyler scrubbed his hands over his face as the team of boys from his church took their positions in the outfield. Jonah was having a rough night. So was his twin brother Jeremiah. And since they were the team's two leading scorers, it was having a cascade effect.

It's not them. It's you.

He clapped his hands, working to shake it off. "All right, boys. Watch left field."

But his eyes drifted to the stands for the hundredth time tonight. Usually, he could tune out the crowds. Focus solely on the game. But tonight he couldn't seem to keep his mind on what he was doing.

Julia's voice from their call earlier refused to leave his head. "So, I'll come pick up the boys July 9. And I want to keep them for two weeks this year."

Why had she called today of all days? And then not even acknowledged what day it was. Did she really not know? Did this date really mean nothing to her now?

June 3 was supposed to be a date they'd both remember forever.

As he scanned the stands, Tyler spotted his brother Spencer and sister-in-law Sophie, sitting with their two-year-old twins on their laps. Tyler's parents were seated right behind them. And beyond them, more people. Or, more precisely, more couples. More families.

Just like he and Julia were supposed to be.

He shook his head and forced his eyes back to the game. Just because Julia had left him didn't mean he wasn't part of a family. For the past six years, it'd been just him and his boys. And that was all he needed.

All he wanted.

The smack of a ball hitting the bat's sweet spot made Tyler groan. He squinted against the lights as the ball rose toward center field.

"Jonah." It was half-whisper, half-shout. Now they'd see if his son had shaken off his strikeout.

The ball arced high above the field, then rocketed toward the ground.

Tyler eyed Jonah. He was running, head tipped skyward, glove extended. Tyler held his breath.

He was going to be too late. He was going to . . .

The ball hit Jonah's glove with a satisfying thwack, and Tyler leaped into the air, yelling to his son to throw to second. But Jonah was already on it, and they had the double play.

For the rest of the game, Tyler managed to keep his focus on coaching. When it was over, he brought the team in.

"You guys did awesome." He grinned at each one of them.

"Uh, Coach, we lost." The twins' friend Mason frowned at him.

"Yeah. So you lost. But you didn't give up. You went into the bottom of the sixth down by two and you could have walked away, given up a bunch more runs. But you didn't. You played hard all the way to the end. You didn't let your disappointment with how things had gone so far stop you from trying again. Let's all fold our hands and thank God for this game."

He waited until all the boys had stilled, then prayed. "Dear Heavenly Father. Thank you for this awesome group of boys you've brought together to play baseball, but more importantly to glorify you in all they do, whether they win or lose. Help that be the way we all live our lives every day. In Jesus' name we pray. Amen."

"Amen," the boys repeated.

Tyler waited to make sure all the boys were picked up by their parents, then made his way to where his twins had joined Spencer, Sophie, and his parents in the stands. Jonah and Jeremiah were giggling with their twin cousins, and a few of the unhealed cracks in Tyler's heart filled. If he and Julia were still together, he might still be stubbornly refusing to come home—and then the boys would never have known their aunt and uncle or cousins or even their grandparents.

"Good game." Dad clapped a hand to his shoulder.

Tyler shrugged. He could have done a better job if he'd gotten his head into the game right from the first pitch, but he was proud of how the boys had played.

"How about some ice cream?" Mom winked at the boys.

Tyler wanted to protest. Though he loved time with his family, he wasn't exactly in the mood for company tonight. All he wanted to do was go home, plop into his favorite chair, and try to resist the urge to pull out the wedding album.

"Please, Dad. I read that it takes fifty licks to finish an ice cream cone, and I want to test it." Jeremiah gave him the pleading eyes, and his brother soon joined in.

"No fair double teaming." Tyler ruffled both boys' hair, then yanked his hands away, wiping them onto his shirt. "Nice. You guys need a shower."

"Please, Uncle Tyler." Now Rylan and Aubrey gave him the look. Their two-year-old eyes were much more convincing.

"Fine." He pretended to tickle them. "But I get to choose the place."

"Deal," everyone said at once. There was only one ice cream place in Hope Springs: the Chocolate Chicken.

As they started for the cars, Tyler swung Rylan up into his arms. His nephew giggled and buried his face in Tyler's shirt. Something squeezed against Tyler's heart. It wasn't that long ago that his boys were this small.

Of course, then he and Julia had still been together. And he'd assumed they would be forever.

"Hey." Sophie laid a hand on his arm, slowing her pace until he had to slow too. Rylan reached for his mother, and Tyler passed the boy over, letting himself hope that once Sophie had her son, she'd move on to catch up with the others. He should have known his sister-in-law better than that.

"You doing okay today?" Her voice said she knew what day it was, even if Julia didn't. Which was ironic, since Sophie hadn't been around when they'd gotten married.

Tyler gazed straight ahead to where moms and dads were getting into their cars with their kids. "Yeah. I'm fine. It's just hard not to think about, you know?"

Sophie nodded. "I know. But I think instead of dwelling on the past, you need to start thinking about what God has in store for you next."

Tyler gaped at her. Next? What next?

The way his life was right now—that was how he planned for it to be forever. Or at least until his boys were in college. He'd continue to live on the family land, work the cherry orchard he and Spencer had bought from their father, and do his best to muddle through raising two boys on his own. That was enough.

"I'm just saying." Sophie started walking again, and he made himself walk alongside her. "Don't shut yourself off to possibilities. God might have something—or someone—in store for you yet."

Tyler forced a laugh. "That's what I love about you, Sophie. You're crazy." He threw an arm around her shoulder and squeezed. "But I'm happy with things just the way they are."

Even that ache in his heart wouldn't convince him otherwise.

Chapter 2

"Finish your ice cream, Bunny." Isabel eyed her own half-eaten scoop of plain vanilla as she waited on hold for yet another hotel.

If this one didn't have a room . . .

"Miss?" The woman on the other end of the line sounded apologetic. "I'm sorry. We're completely booked tonight. I could get you a room next Thursday if that would work."

Isabel pinched the bridge of her nose, willing patience into her voice. It wasn't the woman's fault that this was the last hotel in her price range. "No, that won't work. Thank you anyway."

"Look, Mama. I swooshed it up." Across the table Gabby had created a messy swirl of ice cream and fudge, half of which was now dripping down the front of her shirt. "I like having ice cream for supper."

Isabel nodded, forcing herself to swallow a bite of her own. She'd been so full of hope when she'd driven into this town two hours ago. But now she felt like a rag that had been used to scrub floors until it was threadbare.

She clutched her phone, staring at the search bar. Finally, she forced herself to type it in: women's shelter.

It's only for one night, she promised herself. But even so, it felt too much like going backwards. She'd always been so grateful that Gabby had been too young during their brief stay in the women's shelter in Houston to remember it. But if they stayed in one now . . . kids remembered stuff from when they were five, didn't they?

Still, what choice did she have?

She clicked on the map of listings that came up. That couldn't be right. The nearest one was over three hours away.

Her heart slipped down her throat with her ice cream.

It was already after eight, and she was completely exhausted. The thought of driving that far yet tonight, of living that whole part of her life all over again was too much.

Which only left one option.

"Hey—" She injected as much enthusiasm into her voice as possible. "You want to have an adventure tonight?"

Gabby's eyes lit up as if Isabel had announced that they could have ice cream for supper every night. "What adventure?"

"How would you like to camp out in the car?" She'd noticed a huge parking lot down by the marina next door. Surely no one would bother them there.

Really, Isabel? Sleeping in the car? This is how you raise our daughter? At least I always made sure there was a roof over her head.

She forced herself to take a long, slow breath. She was starting to lose the fight against Andrew's voice.

"What about Chancy?" Gabby wiped her mouth with a napkin, missing nearly every drop of ice cream.

"He'll be our guard dog."

Gabby giggled. "He snores too loud for that."

Isabel let herself laugh with her daughter, feeling Andrew's voice slip a little farther to the background.

She was doing all of this for Gabby. If it weren't for this silly girl, she would have gone crazy long before now.

"Come on. We should get back out to him. He'll want to clean you up." She winked at Gabby as she picked up the mess from their table, tucking the newspaper that had been left there under her arm. If it took all night, she'd find an apartment and a job in there.

At the door, she and Gabby paused as a group of adults and kids entered. Isabel tried not to let her eyes linger on the smiling faces. What was it—three generations? All laughing and talking at once. She glanced down at her daughter. She didn't need three generations and loud gatherings.

As long as she had Gabby, she had everything she needed.

"After you," a man's voice said, and she nodded, not looking up as she tugged Gabby forward.

But her foot got caught on the rug in front of the door, and she stumbled.

Before she could catch herself, a hand landed on her elbow. "Are you all right?"

Panic shot up Isabel's back, and her heart rate quadrupled in preparation for flight. She snatched her arm out of his grip and with a muttered thanks pushed through the door, practically dragging Gabby to the car.

Her breath didn't ease until she'd pulled out of the parking lot. Thankfully, by the time she'd driven down the steep hill that led to the marina, her heart rate had returned to normal too.

She pulled into a parking space on the far end of the lot, near what appeared to be a restroom building.

"Come on, we'll go get ready for bed in there, and then I'll tell you a bedtime story."

After getting Gabby washed up and settled in the back seat with her pillow and the few blankets they'd brought, Isabel told the little girl her favorite story, about princess Megan Rose, who lived in a land of cotton candy trees and lollipop forests. She'd first started telling the stories when they were staying in the shelter because she needed Gabby to believe that such a magical place was possible. She only hoped it'd be a long time before her daughter realized it was all a lie.

By the time she'd finished the story, Gabby's breathing had deepened, and her eyelids twitched. Chancy curled up on the girl's legs, sighing as he laid his head across her knees. Isabel kissed her fingertips, then reached into the back seat to press the kiss to her daughter's forehead. Working to find a comfortable position for her stiff limbs, she opened the newspaper as silently as she could. Folding it in half, she scanned the apartment listings. All two of them. Both far, far out of her price range.

She swallowed past the burn in her throat. So there were no listings in the paper. That didn't mean there weren't other places available. She could ask around tomorrow. For now, she'd focus on finding a job. At a daycare, preferably, so she could keep Gabby with her—there was no way she'd be able to bring herself to leave her daughter with strangers. There was too much of a risk that Andrew would find her. She pushed the thought out.

That was not going to happen. She wouldn't let it.

But when she flipped to the help wanted ads, the last morsel of hope she'd managed to hold onto through the course of the day crumbled. There wasn't a single daycare job available. And none of the other jobs would work for their situation.

Letting the newspaper fall to her lap, she pressed her fingers to her eyelids, as if that could lock the tears behind them. But it was no use. After three years of holding them in, she had reached the end of her strength. Pressing her lips together so she wouldn't wake her daughter with the force of the sobs that threatened to escape as well, she buried her face in her hands.

She didn't know how long she cried, but finally she didn't have the energy left to do even that. She wiped her cheeks, turning her eyes toward the sky.

There were so many stars up there. But they were so distant. So far away.

Just like all the dreams she'd once had. Dreams for herself. Dreams for her daughter. Dreams . . .

She was so tired, and dreams sounded so nice.

She closed her eyes and let herself drift. Maybe when she woke up in the morning, she'd find that this nightmare was over and her dreams had at last come true.

Chapter 3

Tyler sighed and pushed the blankets off, cringing as something heavy clunked to the floor. He may have fallen asleep paging through the wedding album he'd promised himself he wouldn't open.

He grabbed his glasses off the nightstand so he could check the time. Four a.m.

With another sigh, he sat. He'd been lying here awake for at least an hour already. Falling back to sleep obviously wasn't going to happen.

He moved to the chair next to his bedroom window and flipped on the small table lamp, picking up his Bible. But instead of reading, he let his eyes wander to the still-dark sky. Millions of stars blinked back at him.

He let out a breath. He didn't know why he was so restless today. But the sight of all those stars up there calmed him. He knew the One who had made them, the One who had made him and his boys and who knew their every need.

It was just—he didn't know *what* he needed right now.

He took in the wide expanse of land behind the house, the open field and beyond it, a deep patch of trees. God had brought him and his boys here and given them a life filled with love.

So why was he so lonely?

Tyler blinked away the thought. He wasn't lonely.

And even if he was, it wasn't like he wanted to do anything about it. After everything with Julia, he was one hundred percent certain that he never wanted to marry again.

Ironic, when he considered how all the guys used to tease him for being the only man alive not afraid of commitment. From the time he and Julia had started dating in high school, he'd made it clear he wanted to spend his life with her. But he'd learned the hard way that just because he was committed didn't guarantee it was a two-way thing.

And there was no way he was going to put his boys through the heartache of finding out it wasn't, again.

Sighing, he flipped his Bible open to the spot he'd left off in Lamentations. The words washed over him as he read: "Yet this I call to mind and therefore I have hope: Because of the LORD's great love we are not consumed, for his compassions never fail. They are new every morning; great is your faithfulness."

He lifted his head to the window again. The sky to the east was just starting to lighten, and with it, Tyler's heart lightened too. God's mercies were new this day. He would never fail them. No matter how lonely he might feel in this world, he had the promise that God was with him in everything. That was all he needed.

He finished reading the chapter, then folded his hands and poured out his heart to God, asking him for peace with his life, contentment with his situation, and joy in knowing God's love.

By the time he finished, night had lifted, and the early morning sun had tipped the grasses in the field behind the house with gold. It was going to be a beautiful day.

A perfect day for fishing.

He and Spencer had plenty of work to do out in the orchard later today, but if he and the boys left now, they could get in a good couple hours on the lake before he had to be back.

He pushed to his feet, a new energy surging through him, and stepped across the hall to the boys' room. It was summer, which meant they would be up already, since the only time they seemed to have trouble getting up early was school days.

Sure enough, both boys were stirring.

"Fishing?"

Both boys sprang out of their beds instantly, and within twenty minutes, they'd all gotten ready and grabbed a quick breakfast. Tyler threw some water bottles and snacks into a cooler, and they were on their way.

As they pulled into the marina parking lot, Tyler sucked in a deep breath of the refreshing early morning lake breeze. "I'm going to go get things ready on the boat. You two go use the bathroom, then meet me down there." In the year he'd owned the boat, he'd learned that if he didn't have the boys use the bathroom before they went out, they'd be making a trip back to the marina within twenty minutes.

Tyler watched the boys as they crossed the nearly empty parking lot, until they reached the restrooms, then he strode toward the docks, squinting against the morning light to check the lake conditions. There was a slight chop on the surface—just enough to keep the bugs away but not enough that he needed to be worried about the boys getting seasick.

He climbed into his modest vessel, ignoring the yachts that flanked it on each side, thankful that he'd chosen a motorboat so he didn't have to mess with sails. After checking that everything was in place and the gas tank was full, he stashed the cooler and started setting up the fishing lines.

As he worked on the last pole, he lifted his head, squinting toward the restrooms. The boys should be on their way down here by now.

Instead, he spotted them up on the hill beyond the marina's parking lot, playing with a dog.

Tyler shook his head, laying the fishing pole aside. If he didn't go get them, they'd likely stay up there all day. His boys were dog crazy. Ever since the old farm dog Buck had died, they'd been begging Tyler to get them a dog of their own.

He jogged down the dock. Hopefully the boys weren't making a nuisance of themselves with the dog's owner, who likely wanted to get on with his or her walk.

Then again, Tyler didn't see anyone with the boys aside from a little girl who looked a bit younger than them. Her mom or dad must be farther up the hill. Or maybe using the restroom.

"Boys," he called when he was close enough, gesturing for them to come his way.

They both looked up and waved but didn't make any move to leave the dog.

Tyler dropped his arms. Apparently he wasn't going to get out of this without greeting the dog as well.

"Hey," he said when he reached them. "Are we going to go fishing or stay here and play with a dog? Don't answer that," he added before they could choose the second option.

"Isn't he cute, Dad?" Jeremiah was sitting on the ground, letting the dog—which looked to be a cross between a border collie and a beagle—lick his face. "Did you know dogs only have one-sixth as many taste buds as humans?"

"I guess he'll have to lick you six times as much then." Tyler bent down to pet the dog.

Fine, he had a soft spot for dogs too.

He just wasn't sure he wanted the extra responsibility of caring for one. Not when there were days he barely survived caring for his two boys.

"His name is Chancy." The little girl, who was missing her two front teeth, said.

"It's nice to meet you, Chancy." Tyler gave the dog another pat. "Come on, boys. If we don't get out there now, we're not going to have a chance to fish." He gazed around, looking for the girl's mom or dad. He didn't feel right leaving her here by herself.

But there wasn't a single other person in the area, as far as he could tell.

He turned to the girl. "Are you here with your parents?"

The girl nodded. "My mama."

He glanced around again. But the hillside was most definitely empty. "Where is she? In the bathroom?"

The girl grinned and pointed to a car parked next to the restrooms. From here, Tyler could make out a vague form slumped against the passenger window. The head was tipped forward, and a mass of red hair blocked his view of the face.

His heart jumped. Was she dead? Or maybe passed out? Drunk? High?

He eyed the little girl. He couldn't leave her here with no one watching her. And obviously her mom wasn't doing a bang-up job of that.

"Could I meet your mom?" He offered the girl a reassuring smile, so she wouldn't see what he thought of her mom right now.

"Sure." She skipped down the hill, and the dog followed at a full-out run. Tyler walked behind them more slowly.

He really wasn't sure he wanted to get involved in whatever was going on here. But he also couldn't just walk away.

"Stay over here," he told the boys as they got to the bottom of the hill.

Then he approached the car and knocked on the window.

Chapter 4

Isabel jumped, her eyes snapping open. What was that knocking? Where was she?

Why was there a strange man peering through the window at her?

And why was her daughter outside next to him?

Her hand shot to the door handle, and she shoved against the door hard, slamming it into the man's hip. He jumped backwards grabbing at his side.

"What are you doing with my daughter?" Her hand darted out and snatched Gabby to her, heart ripping at her chest.

The man adjusted his glasses, eyeing her. "Your daughter was wandering out here alone." He leaned closer, peering at her face as if searching for something. "You're not . . .?" He raised an eyebrow and mimicked taking a swig.

"Of course not." Isabel tucked Gabby behind her, keeping one hand on her daughter and the other on her hip. "We stopped to watch the sunrise, and I must have gotten sleepy." That sounded plausible, didn't it?

"You're sure you're okay?" The man studied her, and she had a sudden urge to smooth her hair, which she was sure was a great rat's nest on top of her head. Not to mention the puffiness she could feel in her eyelids after last night's crying bout.

"I'm sure." But her voice was none too steady. No matter how hard she tried, she couldn't get her heart to settle down. If anything had happened to Gabby . . .

I told you that you were an unfit mother.

Isabel stuffed Andrew's voice aside. Even if in this case it was right, she had more immediate concerns.

"Then I guess we'll be on our way. Got some fishing to do." The man gestured to the two identical boys who'd been hovering in the background, and they each stepped forward and bent to pet the dog.

"What's your names?" Gabby asked them. Isabel fought the urge to close her eyes. They did not need to be making friends right now. They needed to move on and forget this whole encounter.

"Jonah," one of the boys said.

"Jeremiah," the other offered.

"We have to get going . . ." Isabel opened the back door of the car and nudged Gabby inside. Chancy followed at her heels. Isabel winced at the blankets still spread on the back seat. Hopefully the man would assume they were for the dog.

"I'm Tyler, by the way. Tyler Weston." The man held out a hand, and Isabel eyed it, her own palm growing sweaty.

It's only a handshake. He's not going to hurt you.

Her own voice tried to fight through the panic, but she wasn't sure she could trust it. She wiped her hand against her shorts and forced herself to reach for his. She managed to avoid grimacing at the contact but pulled her hand back as soon as he'd pumped it once. "I'm Amb—" She caught herself, nearly gasping at her mistake. "Isabel. Isabel Small."

Tyler pressed his lips together, and his eyebrows lifted toward his cropped hair, but all he said was, "Take care."

And then he ushered his boys toward the docks, giving one last glance over his shoulder that Isabel could have sworn was to take in her license plate number.

She rounded the car and ducked into the driver's seat, her hands shaking as she attempted to fit the key into the ignition.

That sneering laugh Andrew had always turned on her echoed in her head. *You are such an idiot.*

How could she have done that? She hadn't slipped like that in the two years since she'd legally changed both hers and Gabby's names and social security numbers.

At last, the engine turned over, and she pulled out of the parking spot, sparing one last glance at the lone boat motoring away from the marina. She didn't know where she was driving, only that she had to put some distance between them and the marina.

After a minute, she finally felt like her voice would be steady enough to talk to her daughter without losing it. "I told you not to leave the car without me. Ever."

"I'm sorry, Mama. Chancy was crying and I didn't want him to wake you and—"

"And nothing—" Isabel fought against the urge to ease up on the sharpness in her own voice. Her daughter had to know how serious this was. "It won't happen again. Do you understand?"

"Yes, Mama."

She could hear the tears in Gabby's voice, but she steeled herself against them. Her daughter had no idea how dangerous the world was.

Isabel drove into the parking lot of a small restaurant with a sign saying Hidden Cafe. She turned in her seat, so she could see Gabby. "I'm sorry I yelled. But I need you to promise that from now on you won't leave my side. Not even for a minute."

Gabby giggled. "That's silly, Mama."

Isabel frowned at her. "Why is it silly?"

"Well, what about when I go to the bathroom? Or go to sleep in my bed? And when I start school? I can't wait, I can't wait." Her eyes lit up with her chant, but Isabel tried to ignore it. She'd been putting off thinking about Gabby starting school for years.

Maybe she'd homeschool.

Right. Because a high school dropout would make such a good teacher.

She closed her eyes. She hated when Andrew's voice was right.

"Come on." She tapped her daughter's nose, trying to force some lightness into her tone. "Let's go eat breakfast."

She pushed her door open, every muscle in her body protesting that sleeping in the car had been a bad idea. Telling Chancy to stay, she led Gabby toward the restaurant.

"Why did you lie, Mama?" Gabby tilted her head up toward Isabel. "You said we should never lie."

"When did I lie?" Isabel was half-preoccupied with figuring out if she actually had enough money for them to eat here. Spending the money she'd saved for rent felt too much like giving up. But her daughter needed food.

"You told that man we stopped to see the sunrise. But we didn't. It was dark when we stopped."

Isabel sighed, biting her lip as she opened the cafe door and held it for Gabby. "That was different."

"How?" That look Gabby was giving her, like she had all the answers, tore at Isabel. What would happen when her daughter realized someday that she had none?

"It just was." She pushed her hair out of her face, her fingers catching in a massive tangle. At least she'd been right about the rat's nest then. "I said that to keep us safe."

Gabby's eyes widened. "Was he a bad man?"

"I'm sure he wasn't. But you can never be too careful."

Isabel nodded to the hostess, who held up two fingers, and they followed her to a table near the window.

"I'm glad." Gabby slid into a seat. "I liked him. And his boys were okay too."

"Boys?" Isabel lifted an eyebrow at her daughter. "I think you're a little young to be noticing boys."

Gabby rolled her eyes. "Not like that, Mama. Boys can be good friends. And anyway, they liked Chancy, so that makes them good."

Isabel chose to ignore that comment. She only wished it was that easy to figure out which guys were good guys and which were only pretending. "Make sure you eat enough. After breakfast, we'll hit the road again, and I'm not sure how long it will be until we stop." She still didn't know where they were going, though the women's shelter weighed at the back of her mind as an option.

"I thought we were staying here. I like it here." Gabby's pout almost broke Isabel's resolve.

But there was nothing for them here. No home. No jobs.

And a man who was now suspicious of her.

Her eyes went again to the lake that gleamed below.

Something about it called to her.

This is where we're supposed to be, I can feel it. She pushed away the stray thought.

Barring some miracle, there was no way they'd be able to stay in Hope Springs.

And her life had been awfully short on miracles lately.

"Ready to get in the car?" Isabel eyed Gabby's nearly uneaten pancakes, acid swirling in her own gut. How could this be the life she'd made for her little girl? While other girls were taking ballet lessons and going to Disney World, her daughter was stuck with her, moving from town to town, limited to the few toys she could fit in a garbage bag.

Someday things would be different.

Someday they'd settle somewhere. Buy a house. And Gabby could have as many toys as she wanted, take as many dance classes as she could fit into her schedule.

But that someday was too far in the future for Isabel to see yet.

"I'm tired of driving. I want to stay here." Gabby crossed her arms in front of her.

"I know, Bunny. I'm tired of driving too." Which was why she'd been stalling for the past hour. "But it should only take a few hours to get where we're going. And then we can stay for a while." She swallowed hard. She didn't want to stay in the shelter any longer than they had to. But she had no way of guessing how long that would be.

"Where are we going?" Gabby's innocent look was more potent than any tantrum could be.

Isabel stacked their dishes at the edge of the table, then took Gabby's hand and led her to the car. She waited until her daughter was buckled in to speak.

"We're going to a women's shelter. We lived in one once before, but you probably don't remember." She peeked at Gabby in the rearview mirror.

The girl's forehead crinkled as if in concentration. "Nope. I don't remember. What's a women's shelter? Is it fun?"

Isabel pulled in a quick breath. It was no big deal. "It's a place where moms and their kids can live for a little while. Until they can find somewhere else to go."

"Oh." Gabby's expression smoothed. "There are other kids there? That sounds fun."

Isabel nodded, letting it go at that. As she pulled out of the parking lot and aimed the car back the way they'd come yesterday, she let herself imagine how different her life would be if she'd never met Andrew. She certainly wouldn't be a nomad now. But she wouldn't have Gabby either. And she'd gladly relive every horrible moment of her life with Andrew if it meant having Gabby at her side. Her little girl was the best thing that had ever happened to her.

"Look, Mama." Gabby's shout as they turned onto a road beyond the town startled her, and she jerked her gaze to the passenger window.

"It's cotton candy trees." Gabby was nearly shouting in her excitement. "I thought you made those up. But they're real."

Sure enough, the road was lined with rows and rows of trees covered in pink blossoms. Isabel could see how Gabby would mistake them for cotton candy.

Her eyes flicked to the sign up ahead. "It says this is Hidden Blossom Farms. I think those are cherry trees."

"Can we go there?"

"To a cherry orchard?" Isabel gave her daughter a quick look over her shoulder. "What do you want to do there?"

Gabby bounced in her seat. "I want to see the trees. Like Megan Rose."

Isabel eyed the orchard's quickly approaching driveway. If she was going to turn in, she needed to slow down right now. But what were they going to do at a cherry orchard?

"Puh-lease, Mama?"

Isabel sighed. Her daughter didn't ask for a lot. The least she could do before relegating her to life in a shelter was let her check out some trees. She turned on her signal light and tapped the brake.

From the back seat, Gabby let out a cheer, and Isabel couldn't help her own smile. Making this girl happy was one of the few things that brought her joy these days.

She followed the winding driveway until it opened onto a small parking lot in front of a cute country store to the right side. Across the driveway was a large farmhouse, and another hundred yards or so down, she could see two newer looking houses and a decent-size pole shed.

She pulled into a parking spot and unlocked the car door so Gabby could get out.

"You stay." She pointed a finger at Chancy, who lifted his eyes, then closed them and went back to sleep. "Some guard dog," she muttered. A good guard dog would have chased away that guy at the marina this morning.

She blew out a breath. She had to stop worrying about that. It was over. Gabby was safe. And she'd never see that man—Tyler—again.

As they stepped into the store, a mix of baking scents and fresh wood hit her, making her heart ache in a way she couldn't explain. Jars of bright red cherries lined the shelves, and a table in front of them was loaded with boxes of cherry pies. On the other side of the store, wooden furniture and home decor items beckoned. Isabel let them pull her forward. Her hand went out to touch the smooth wood of a rocking chair. Someday, when she and Gabby had a house, they'd get a set of chairs like this for their porch.

"Good morning." The friendly voice from across the store made Isabel jump.

"Sorry." A smiling woman carrying a toddler on each hip emerged from a door at the back of the store. "I didn't hear you come in. How can I help you folks today?" She set down the babies—one a boy, the other a girl, but if Isabel had to guess, twins—passing each a sippy cup.

"I wanna see the cotton candy trees." Gabby shot her toothless grin at the woman.

"Cotton candy trees, huh? I'm not sure we have any of those." She winked at Gabby. "But you sure are welcome to explore and see. Maybe the cherry trees will interest you."

A beeping sounded from behind the door the woman had come out of, and she bustled toward it. "Sorry. I'll be right back." As she disappeared behind the doors, the toddlers waddled out from behind the counter. Gabby was immediately at their side, oohing and ahhing over them.

A pang went through Isabel that her daughter would never have a sibling, never know what it was like to have a family.

But she'd worked hard to make sure Gabby knew she'd always have her mom. Which was more than she could say for her own mother.

She let her gaze move to the wooden carvings on the table in front of her. There were several animals, some people, an angel, and a baby. She picked up the baby. Though its face was featureless, something about the form awed Isabel. Whoever had carved it had obviously poured a lot of love into it.

"Sorry about that." The woman reemerged from the back room, and Isabel set the carving back in place. "I've been swamped trying to keep up with everything in the store lately. Our other employee quit last week, and I haven't had a chance to get an ad in the paper yet."

Isabel stared at the woman. "You're hiring?"

"Yeah." The blonde woman gave her a thoughtful smile. "You know someone who might be interested?"

Isabel hesitated. She needed to work somewhere she could keep Gabby with her.

She glanced again at the two toddlers. Maybe that wouldn't be a problem.

"I'm actually looking." She readjusted the angel carving, just for something to do with her hands.

"You're kidding." The blonde woman's voice was warm and inviting. "Why am I always surprised when God does something like that?"

"Sorry." Isabel had no idea where God had come from in this conversation. "Something like what?"

"Like delivering exactly what we both need at the same time." The woman ducked below the counter and reappeared a few seconds later, holding out a clipboard. "If you want to fill this out, I'll take a look at it right away." The woman's voice bubbled with enthusiasm—and relief.

"Actually—" Isabel bit her lip. They were supposed to be moving on from this town. Hadn't everything lined up to show her this wasn't the place for them?

"I don't know," she hedged. "I have Gabby, and I don't know where she would go while I worked and I don't know how long we'll be in town . . ."

The woman waved off her protest. "You'd bring Gabby here with you, of course. We're a family company. Anyway, my twins are here almost every day, and I sure could use someone to play with them. Would you be up for that?" She squatted so that she and Gabby were eye to eye.

Gabby gave a vigorous nod. "They're cute."

"That settles it then." The woman shook the clipboard. "Come on. It'll only take a minute."

Isabel took it slowly. This all seemed very strange. What were the chances that the cherry orchard they just happened to stop at on Gabby's whim would have not only a job opening but one that would allow her to keep her daughter with her?

Could it be that the woman was right? Had God made this happen?

She dismissed the thought as she started to fill out the application. God hadn't looked after her once in her life. Sure would be odd if he'd decided to start now.

The application was short, a few basic questions about employment history, and when she was done, she passed it back to the woman, who immediately scanned it.

You really think she wants someone like you? You're not qualified to do anything.

She almost gave in to Andrew's voice and told the woman never mind, but before she could speak, the woman looked up. "This is great. Do you think you could start today? Right now?"

Isabel's mouth fell open. "Wait. You want to hire me?"

The woman's smile grew even warmer. "If that's okay with you."

Isabel squinted at her. She couldn't really be that nice, could she?

"I'm Sophie, by the way." The woman held out a hand, which Isabel managed to shake after only a couple seconds of hesitation. "And these two rug rats are my twins, Rylan and Aubrey."

"We saw twins this morning too." Gabby perked her head up from her spot on the floor.

But Isabel was determined to forget about that whole incident. "What do you need me to do?"

"How are you at pie-making?"

Isabel had made a pie as a surprise for Andrew once. He'd taken one bite, then picked up the entire pie pan and tossed it in the garbage can, curling a lip at her and congratulating her on being truly good for nothing.

She swallowed. She could try to pretend she was good at it—but the truth would come out soon enough.

"Not great," she admitted. "Thanks anyway." She gestured for Gabby to come to her side. She should have known this had been too easy. Things in her life were never easy.

"Wait." Sophie stepped toward her. "It's fine. I'm sure you'll pick it up quickly. And in the meantime, I can make the pies while you help customers. Sound good?"

All Isabel could do was nod. She had no idea why this woman was being so nice to her. She knew she should probably examine it, probably walk away and not look back because when something seemed too good to be true, it usually was. But maybe, just this once, things would actually work out.

"Let me call my husband to see if he can come give you a tour. And when you get back, we'll start training." She lifted her head at the sound of a vehicle stopping in the parking lot. "Actually, there's my brother-in-law Tyler and his boys. I'm sure they'd be happy to take you."

Isabel froze. Had Sophie said Tyler?

She fought the urge to flee.

Surely there was more than one Tyler in this town.

Chapter 5

"Hey, it's Chancy." Jonah had his door open before Tyler had shut off the van.

"Who?" Tyler worked to drag his mind back to the present. He hadn't been able to stop thinking about the woman in the car all morning. He shouldn't have been so hard on her. Shouldn't have assumed she'd been drinking—or worse.

He hadn't bought her story about stopping to see the sunrise—for one thing he'd recognized her from the Chocolate Chicken last night, so he knew she and her daughter had been in town long before daybreak. For another, the car was facing the wrong direction for the sunrise. And for a third—as if he needed a third—the car had blankets and pillows spread across the back seat, as if someone had slept there overnight. But that didn't mean he couldn't have been politer.

He'd been half-hoping she'd still be there when they returned from fishing so he could apologize, but the spot where her car had been parked had been taken over by a large SUV.

Oh well. Not seeing her again definitely made things easier.

"The dog from the marina. Chancy." Jonah said it in the tone nine-year-olds used to show what they thought of adults who didn't have a clue.

Tyler glanced at the car parked in front of the shop. The dog running back and forth on the back seat did look an awful lot like the one they'd met this morning. His eyes flicked to the car's Texas license plates, the number he'd memorized this morning—just in case—confirming what he already knew. This was the woman's car. Isabel, she'd said her name was. Although he was almost sure she'd started to say something else first—something that began with an A, maybe.

What was she doing here? It seemed a little too coincidental to be an accident.

Had she looked him up? Was she targeting his family for some sort of scam?

Tyler followed the boys into the shop, shoulders tense. If this woman thought she could play his family, she was very, very wrong.

"Hey boys, how was fishing?" Sophie grinned at her nephews as they went straight for where the little girl from the marina was playing with Rylan and Aubrey. Isabel hovered a few steps behind her daughter but kept her head down.

Was she avoiding his gaze? Hoping he didn't recognize her?

"We didn't catch anything." Jeremiah said it cheerfully. "Dad almost had one, but then it let go of the hook. But he said it was probably this big." Jeremiah spread his hands to twice the width of his thin body.

"He did, did he?" Sophie's laughing eyes took him in. "I think that's twice as big as the last one he said got away."

Tyler shrugged. "Telling stories is half the fun."

"Spencer said he's going to work in the south orchard today, if you want to join him. But could you do me a quick favor first?" Sophie asked.

"You know even if I say no, I'm going to end up doing it." One of the hazards of having a sister-in-law he adored. Even if he may have tried to convince Spencer not to give her a second chance once upon a time. Thankfully, his brother had more sense than to listen to him.

Sophie took a step toward Isabel. "I'd like you to meet our newest employee. Isabel. And this is her daughter, Gabby."

Before Tyler could digest what she was saying, Jeremiah broke in. "We know. And their dog is Chancy."

"You know each other?" Sophie lifted an eyebrow at Tyler, a grin tickling her lips, but he gave a subtle shake of his head.

"We met at the marina this morning." He surveyed Isabel, debating how much to say. Now that her hair was combed and the fog of sleep was gone, she looked pretty normal. Pretty *pretty*, actually. Not that he needed that kind of thought clouding his judgment. "You know the boys and dogs. Once they saw Chancy, there was no keeping them away."

Isabel's eyes met his, and something like gratitude flashed in them.

Whatever.

It didn't mean he trusted her.

In his book, she was still some sort of con artist.

"Well, good. You can get to know each other a little better while you give Isabel and Gabby a tour of the orchard." Sophie winked at him, and Tyler nearly threw his hands in the air. Would his sister-in-law never give up?

But he nodded. There was no point in arguing.

And anyway, this would give him a chance to feel this stranger out, figure out what she was up to.

"Let's go."

Gabby popped to her feet and bounded toward him. Her mom eyed him for a few seconds first, but as Gabby reached the door, she hurried behind her.

Tyler opened the door for Gabby, the little girl firing questions at him the whole time. "Can Chancy come with us? Can we go see the cotton candy trees? Do you have a lollipop forest?"

"Gabby, calm down. Don't ask so many questions." Isabel's voice was low and guarded as she followed her daughter, offering a quick "thank you" to him for holding the door.

"Sorry, Mama." The girl's blue eyes were so full of energy, Tyler had to grin at her.

"Ask away. I have two boys, so that means I get twice as many questions as the average parent. Which also means I'm very good at answering them. Let's see. Yes, Chancy can come with us. Yes, we can go see the cotton candy trees—if you tell me which ones those are. And we might have to explore a little to see if we have a lollipop forest."

"Explore?" Gabby sounded awed. "Like an adventure?"

Tyler laughed. He may not be sure what to make of Isabel yet, but this little girl had won his heart over already. "Do you like adventures?"

Gabby nodded, eyes wide. "We had an adventure last night. We—"

"Gabby." Isabel's voice from behind them was sharp, and Gabby spun toward her mom.

It was a moment before Isabel spoke, and when she did, she seemed shaken. "Could you get Chancy out of the car, please?"

"Yes, Mama." Gabby skipped ahead of them to the car, and then a whir of fur and legs exploded out of the back seat.

"Wait!" Jeremiah and Jonah burst out of the store. "We want to come too."

"Why don't you two run ahead and get the trailer hooked up? We'll be right behind you." That was one of the best parts of working on the orchard. He could spend his days with his boys and still get his work done.

"Wait for us." Gabby and Chancy started to run after the boys.

"Gabby Mae." Isabel's voice was sharp. "You stay with me."

Gabby stopped to look at her mom, then back to where his boys were running ahead.

"It's fine if she wants to go with them." Tyler kept his voice low enough that Gabby wouldn't hear. He hated when other parents said his kids could do something he'd told them not to do. But still, Gabby should be able to run ahead with the boys. There was nothing to hurt her between here and the shed.

"She can stay with me." Isabel's words were clipped, and she didn't look at him.

Fine. If she wanted to be uptight about it, that was her problem.

When they reached the shed, the boys had already attached the trailer to the ATV and were sitting inside it.

"There's room for you and Chancy," Jeremiah said to Gabby, pointing to the open spot they'd left.

"We are not riding in that." Isabel grabbed her daughter's hand to keep her from getting in.

"Well, no. The kids can ride in the trailer. You can ride on the ATV with me. It's perfectly safe. We even have helmets." He lifted a helmet his boys had worn when they were smaller off a shelf and held it out to Gabby.

But Isabel intercepted it, shoving it back into his arms. "I said we're not riding on that. We'll walk. Or we'll skip the tour."

Tyler stifled his retort that they were welcome to skip the tour. He had plenty of work to get to anyway.

But he'd promised Sophie.

"Fine. We'll walk. But you'll only get to see a fraction of the orchard."

Isabel gave a curt nod. "That's fine."

"Fine," he repeated, gesturing for his boys to get out of the trailer. "We'll have to go to the north orchard if we're going to walk."

The twins led the way out of the shed. Gabby glanced at her mother, then took a few tentative steps ahead of her. Next to him, Isabel's hands were clenched, her jaw tight, but she didn't say anything.

Apparently, Gabby took that as permission because she was soon running ahead with his boys as they raced toward the nearest section of orchard, which was a good quarter mile walk.

"So where did you live in Texas?" If they were going to walk together, he might as well attempt to make small talk. And maybe it would help him figure out what exactly she was hiding.

Her head snapped toward him. "How did you know we lived in Texas?"

Wow. Jumpy much? "I noticed your license plates."

Her expression eased an iota. "Oh. We lived all over."

Okay. That was plenty evasive. "And what brings you to Hope Springs?"

The sound of their feet crunching on the gravel trail was the only answer.

When a full minute had gone by, he grabbed her elbow, pulling her to a stop. She jerked away from him and took a step backward, fear hovering in her eyes as she wrapped her hand over the spot he'd touched.

"Sorry." He hadn't meant to scare her. But he had to say this. "I don't know what you're doing here. But if you're trying to con my family in some way, you might as well leave now."

Her eyes widened, and to his surprise, a slight chuckle escaped her mouth, though she didn't smile. "I'm not conning your family. I had no idea this place was here until we were driving past and Gabby asked me to stop. And then your sister-in-law mentioned she was hiring, and next thing I know, I had the job. If it makes you uncomfortable, I'll leave. I just— Gabby likes it here, and—" She shook her head. "But it doesn't matter. It was obviously a mistake to come to Hope Springs."

She looked away but not before Tyler caught the hopelessness in her eyes.

Great.

He sure could be a class A idiot sometimes. The poor woman was new to town, he didn't even know her, and here he was trying to run her out of town.

"No. I'm sorry. You shouldn't leave. Hope Springs is a great place. I'm just a little . . ." Burned? Overly suspicious? Paranoid? "Anyway—" He started walking again, and after a moment she followed, keeping a step or two behind him. "We do really need the help. Sophie's been swamped in the store, and it's only the beginning of tourist season."

He kept his face pointed straight ahead. He didn't need to see that vulnerable look in her eyes again. The one that made him feel like he should be protecting her instead of protecting himself and his family from her.

As they reached the edge of the trees, he slowed, pulling in a deep breath of the sweet blossom-scented air as he let her catch up to him. "This is our oldest section of orchard. It's on its second generation of trees. And even then, some are getting close to fifty years old."

"Wow." Isabel appeared genuinely enchanted as she wandered under the blossoming trees.

He paused, watching her. Something in his heart unfurled just a crack, and he worked to roll it back up.

He didn't need to be feeling anything like that about anyone. Especially not this newcomer he didn't trust.

"So what are these cotton candy trees your daughter wants to see?" He kept his voice gruff, indifferent.

Because that was how he felt.

A hint of pink colored Isabel's cheeks, nearly matching the shade of the blossoms. "They're from a story I tell her. I guess from the road the blossoms on the cherry trees looked like cotton candy to her."

"Ah." He turned toward where his boys and Gabby were chasing each other around the trees, Chancy leaping after them. He cupped his hands around his mouth and yelled, "Gabby."

The little girl came running over without hesitation.

How had someone as obviously uptight as Isabel raised such a carefree little girl?

He held out a hand for a fist bump. "Do you want to pick some cotton candy?"

"Can I?" Gabby's grin went straight to his heart. Maybe it wasn't her Mama he had to watch out for.

"Sure." He bent to put his hands around her waist and popped her onto his shoulders. Next to him, Isabel inhaled sharply, and he waited for her to demand he put the girl down, but she simply hovered at his side, arms outstretched as if she expected him to drop her daughter.

He moved closer to the tree, maneuvering Gabby under a branch heavy with blossoms. "Go ahead and pick some of those flowers."

Gabby wiggled on his shoulders, and he tightened his grip on her legs. "Make sure you pick some for your mom too." He angled his head toward Isabel, whose face didn't loosen in the slightest.

"I don't need any." She crossed her arms in front of her but immediately spread them out again.

Wow. She really didn't trust him not to drop her daughter.

"I got them." Gabby giggled as he lifted her back over his head, setting her smoothly on the ground.

At last Isabel lowered her arms, and Gabby held out the biggest sprig of blossoms to her. "Put it behind your ear, Mama."

Isabel opened her mouth, and Tyler was sure she was going to come up with some excuse about how putting flowers behind your ear wasn't safe. But instead of saying anything, she ran a finger over the petals, then tucked the flowers into her hair.

Gabby grinned at her. "It's pretty."

Tyler had to look away.

Otherwise, he might be tempted to think the same thing.

Somehow, after spending an hour with Isabel, Tyler knew less about her than he had to begin with.

He had never been a terribly talkative person himself, but compared to her, he was downright loquacious.

As they walked in silence back toward the store, he examined her out of his peripheral vision. He couldn't help noticing the way she let her eyes rove all over the scenery, as if drinking it in. Or the way she smiled whenever her daughter did. Or the way her reddish hair flowed over her narrow shoulders.

What are you doing? So she was attractive. It wasn't like that mattered. He was surrounded by attractive women every day, and he never felt a need to dwell on their caramel eyes.

Oh, for heaven's sake.

That was not the kind of watching her he was supposed to be doing.

He put on a burst of speed to reach the store ahead of her, then made a show of checking his phone as he held the door open for her.

"Thank you." Her words were quiet, and he had to force himself to ignore whatever it was that made him want to look into her eyes again.

He'd done enough foolish things for one day.

"How was it?" Sophie greeted them as he let the door close behind himself.

"I didn't know there could be places this beautiful." The awe in Isabel's voice tugged at Tyler.

Anyone who loved Hidden Blossom that much could be trusted. Couldn't they?

Still, that nagging suspicion that she was hiding something hung over him.

"Be careful." Sophie smiled at their guest. "Once this place gets in your blood, you might just want to stay forever." Her eyes darted to Tyler, and her smile turned mischievous.

That was enough of that.

"Can I talk to you for a minute?" He shot Sophie a pointed look.

She frowned at him but nodded. "Isabel, could you hang out by the counter here and welcome anyone who comes in? I'll be right back."

Isabel's eyes bounced between him and Sophie, but she moved toward the register.

Tyler sized up the cash drawer. This was the kind of community where they didn't worry too much about theft, so the drawer was rarely locked. What if she decided to clean them out while they were in the back?

"You should probably lock that." He gestured to the register.

Sophie glared at him but did it, then stormed past him into the small kitchen at the back of the store, where she prepared the pies and jams they sold.

He nearly bowled her over as she spun on him, a hand on her hip. "Tell me you weren't that rude to her the whole time."

"What?" Tyler gaped at her. He wasn't being rude. He was being cautious.

"Well, that wasn't exactly friendly." Sophie pinned her eyes to his. "Here God drops the perfect person for the store right into our laps, and you're going to scare her away."

Tyler rubbed at his jaw. "Maybe that wouldn't be such a bad thing."

He didn't want to question God's work in this. But what if it was some darker force that had brought Isabel here?

Sophie's frown deepened. "You don't like her?"

He lifted his hands at his sides. "I don't know her, Sophie, and neither do you. How do you know we can trust her?"

"Why wouldn't we trust her?"

He shrugged. How did he explain it? "It's just a feeling I get. Like she's hiding something."

Sophie shook her head, her eyes laced with pity. "Not every woman is hiding something." Her voice was soft, but the words hit their mark.

"This has nothing to do with Julia," he snapped. "This is about Isabel. We met because she was sleeping in her car at the marina. Gabby was out frolicking around with the dog, and Isabel had no idea. I thought maybe she was drunk or . . ."

Sophie tilted her head at him.

"And I don't even think Isabel is her name," he continued, needing Sophie to understand just how untrustworthy this woman was.

But Sophie snorted. "Come on, Tyler. You've watched too many cop shows. Why would she be using a fake name?"

He threw his hands in the air. "How should I know? Why's she sleeping in her car with her kid?"

Sophie regarded him, disapproval hovering in her gaze. "It's not like you to be so suspicious and judgmental."

Tyler's hands fisted. He knew she was right. And yet . . .

"Please tell me you're at least going to do a background check."

Sophie studied him. "I wasn't planning on it. But I can if it'd make you feel better."

"It would."

"Okay." Sophie grabbed a couple of water bottles from the fridge and passed them to him. "I'll do a background check if you promise you'll be nice to her in the meantime."

"Fine." Tyler opened one of the bottles and took a long drink. He could pretend to be nice—it'd give him more of an opportunity to keep an eye on Isabel.

"And then," Sophie added, "when the background check comes back clean—"

"*If* it comes back clean," he interrupted.

Sophie ignored him. "You can ask her on a date."

Tyler nearly choked on his water.

"I can what?" he gasped as he finally managed to swallow.

"You heard me."

Tyler shook his head.

He'd heard her all right. And it just confirmed what he'd already begun to suspect: she'd lost all common sense.

Chapter 6

T he breath Isabel had been holding for the past ten minutes slipped out of her as Tyler banged out of the back room and through the store's front door without so much as a glance at her.

She had a feeling the conversation between him and Sophie had been about her and that she was about to get fired.

What kind of loser can't even hold a job for an hour?

She pushed the voice aside as Sophie re-entered the room. If she quit now, technically she couldn't be fired.

"Should we get started?" Sophie smiled at her, and Isabel blinked, swallowing the words that had almost tripped off her tongue and giving a mute nod.

Either she'd been wrong about what Tyler had been talking to his sister-in-law about, or this woman next to her was kind-hearted enough to overlook it. Maybe Sophie pitied her.

At this point, it didn't matter. If pity got her the job she needed to take care of her daughter, she'd take it.

For the next couple hours, Isabel was absorbed in learning the ins and outs of the cash register and of their inventory system.

It turned out that the store's beautiful wooden furniture and carvings were made by none other than Sophie's husband and her brother-in-law. Isabel tried to picture Tyler standing over a piece of wood, shaping it into a work of art. She supposed she could see it. He seemed sort of quiet and artistic. Somewhat sensitive too, maybe not toward her, but in the way he treated his boys. And her daughter.

Goodness, Gabby had taken right to that man. Isabel wanted to be worried about that, but the truth of it was, it had been nice seeing someone take an interest in her daughter and watching Gabby thrive under his attention.

Was that what it would be like if the girl had a father who loved her?

Isabel gave herself an internal shake as the door to the store opened. There was no reason to let her thoughts dwell on what could never be.

"Why don't you take this customer?" Sophie nudged her forward.

"You're sure?" Isabel wasn't at all confident that she knew what she was doing.

But Sophie nodded and stepped aside.

Isabel greeted the customer—a sweet older woman—and helped her find the perfect gift for her granddaughter, then rang up her purchase.

By the time the woman left, a sense of accomplishment completely out of proportion to the task had washed over her.

Between talking to Sophie, entertaining the kids, and helping customers, the rest of the afternoon slipped by so quickly she barely noticed.

Before she knew it, Sophie was flipping the store's sign to closed.

"I'd say that was a successful first day." Sophie's generous smile met her. "We're closed on Sundays, but I hope you'll be back on Monday."

"I'll be here. Thank you again for the opportunity."

Sophie waved off the gratitude. "Can I ask you something?"

Isabel's stomach clenched, and she felt her smile waver. If there was one thing she tried to avoid, it was being asked questions. But she nodded.

"Do you have a place to live?" Sophie's voice was gentle, not a trace of judgment in it, but still it fell heavy on Isabel's shoulders.

"Of course. We're staying at—"

"We slept at the big boat park," Gabby sang from across the room where she'd been putting together a puzzle, Chancy curled up on the floor by her feet, Sophie's twins watching from a set of portable cribs. "It was an adventure."

Isabel closed her eyes. She hadn't thought to tell Gabby that sleeping in the car was a secret.

"It was late when we got here," she rushed to explain. "But we're going to go check some apartment listings now."

Sophie's gaze didn't carry even a trace of the suspicion Tyler had regarded her with earlier. "Because I have a friend who is looking to rent out an apartment. I mean, it's being renovated right now because her last renters kind of trashed the place, but I think it might be close enough that you could move in, if you don't mind a little construction. Do you want me to call her?"

Isabel felt like a fish, her mouth opening and closing but no sound coming out. This had to be a dream. That was the only possible explanation. People in real life weren't this nice. Especially not to complete strangers.

"I'm not sure I could afford it," she finally managed to croak. "My budget is pretty small."

Sophie waved off her concern. "I'm sure she wouldn't ask for much. Vi is such a sweetheart. And if you don't have enough right now, we can always give you an advance on your pay."

An advance on her pay? Isabel grasped for the counter, expecting it to fade as she woke up. But it was solid under her hands.

"What about Chancy?" She prepared for the dream to come to an end. There was no way Sophie's friend would happen to have a pet-friendly apartment.

"Oh, Chancy will be just fine there." Sophie pulled out her phone. "Violet's husband had a dog in the building when he lived there. And now that they have their own house, they have three."

"Three dogs?" Gabby's eyes grew wide with hope. "Mama, can we—"

"Absolutely not." Isabel cut her off before she could ask the question.

Sophie fell silent as her thumbs flew across her phone screen. After a minute, she looked up and tucked the phone into her pocket. "There. I texted Vi a heads-up that you're interested. She'll be here for dinner in half an hour, so you can talk to her about it then."

"Oh, we couldn't intrude on your party."

"Of course you could. We're just having a couple people over. No big deal. They're practically family."

What would that be like, Isabel wondered. Having friends over for no particular reason? Thinking of them as family?

It sounded kind of . . . nice.

No friends. She'd made that rule for a reason.

But she wasn't going to dinner to make friends.

She was going to secure a place for her and Gabby to live.

It was a necessity. "Sure. I guess we could do that."

"Perfect." Sophie picked up Aubrey and held her out toward Isabel. "Would you mind? I thought Spencer would be back by now to help me cart these two home, but he must have gotten caught up."

"Oh, um— Okay." Isabel reached for the little girl, who promptly wrapped her arms around her neck. She let Aubrey's warmth soak into her as Sophie scooped up Rylan and they left the store, Gabby skipping behind them.

Sophie led them toward the end of the driveway they'd come in on—had that only been this morning? How had her life changed so drastically since then?

"That's Tyler's house." Sophie pointed to a cute ranch at the very end of the driveway, and Isabel tried to picture him living there with his boys.

And his wife.

How had she not considered the fact that he must have a wife?

Probably because it didn't matter to her one way or the other.

But still the question came out. "What does his wife do?"

Sophie cut her a sideways glance before answering. "He's divorced."

"And he has custody of the kids?" She didn't mean to sound so surprised.

"He's a good father." Sophie's answer held a defensive edge.

"Yeah. No. I noticed that. I just mean . . ." She trailed off. She had no idea what she meant.

"And this is us." Sophie turned toward a house nearly identical to Tyler's, only painted a deeper shade of brown. "Come on in." She opened the door, and Isabel stepped into the homey space.

"If you want to make yourself comfortable out back, I'm going to get a few things ready." Sophie gestured to a patio door that led out to a spacious yard.

"Is there anything I can help with?" Not that Isabel had ever been much good in the kitchen, but it was the least she could do after Sophie had been so kind to her.

"Sure." Sophie set Rylan down in the living room, and Isabel followed suit with Aubrey, instructing Gabby to stay with the twins. Then Sophie led Isabel to the kitchen and passed her a cutting board and knife. "Do you mind cutting veggies?"

Isabel shook her head. That, at least, she shouldn't be able to mess up.

I wouldn't be so sure. You always find a way to mess up.

But Andrew's voice was weak this time. Pathetic.

Things were going too well to listen to it now.

As Sophie bustled in and out of the kitchen, setting food out on the large patio table, Isabel fell into the rhythm of cutting and chopping. It was soothing somehow, and one by one, her muscles relaxed. She hadn't felt this comfortable, this at ease, in three years—longer than that really. Probably since she'd married Andrew.

Sophie pulled out her phone as she made another trip into the house. "I'd better text Spencer and let him know it's time to come in. Those two tend to lose track of time out there."

"Two?" Isabel's stomach looped.

"Spencer and Tyler." Sophie's answer only confirmed what she already feared.

How had she not considered the fact that Tyler would likely be coming to dinner at his sister-in-law's house?

She wracked her brain for an excuse to back out of this.

But it was too late now.

"Sophie says everyone will be there in a few minutes." Spencer jabbed his shovel into the ground near Tyler's feet. "Are you ready to call it a day yet?"

Tyler dug his own shovel into the mulch pile on the trailer behind him and dropped the wood shavings at the base of a tree before straightening and stretching his back. He lifted his head to the sky. The sun was hovering just above the treetops to the west. Which meant it was likely after six by now.

And that meant the store would be closed—and Isabel should be gone. Much as he felt a need to keep an eye on the newcomer, he feared that being around her more today would only confuse him. Because no matter how hard he tried to hold onto his suspicions about her, the only thing he'd been able to think about all afternoon was the way she'd looked at him when he'd helped Gabby pick those cherry blossoms.

"Yeah. Let's head back." He turned to call to the twins, who'd been climbing trees in the narrow strip of land that divided their property from the neighboring farm.

"You really went at it today. I think you got twice as many trees mulched as I did." Spencer took Tyler's shovel from him and threw it in the back of the trailer. "Not too bad for a numbers guy."

Tyler snorted. Sure, he did all the books for the orchard, but this time of year, he was out here almost as much as his brother. "Maybe you were slacking today." Though his stiff arms told him he'd definitely worked harder than usual.

Spencer gave his shoulder a light punch. "Or maybe you were trying to outrun your demons. You have to stop dwelling on what happened with Julia. Move on."

Tyler pulled up short. Aside from when he'd woken up this morning, he hadn't actually thought about Julia once today. A certain other woman seemed to have crowded thoughts of her out.

But there was no need for his brother to know that. "Yeah."

"Do you want to talk about it?" Spencer sat on his ATV but didn't start it up.

Tyler shook his head, jumping onto his own ATV and bringing it roaring to life as the boys climbed into the trailer. He waved for Spencer to go ahead of him.

His brother studied him for a minute, then started his vehicle and throttled in front of Tyler.

As they reached the orchard's long driveway, he followed Spencer into the pole shed to park his ATV.

"We should have come back earlier so we'd have time to wash up." Spencer brushed at his dusty t-shirt. "Guess they'll have to deal with us like this."

That was fine by Tyler. His friends had been with him through his worst. And he didn't have anyone to impress.

As they started toward the house, Tyler let his eyes drift over the land that surrounded them. How had he ever convinced himself he didn't belong here? Thankfully, now that he was back, there was no question in his mind—this was home.

Jeremiah and Jonah raced ahead, and Spencer reached an elbow out to nudge him, then started to jog, raising an eyebrow. "Last one there does the dishes?"

Tyler didn't bother to answer. Just lengthened his stride and let his lanky legs pull him in front of his brother.

"Hey, wait," Spencer called from behind him, but Tyler was too smart for that. His little brother was easily faster than him. He'd let Tyler get almost to the house, then put on his own burst of speed and pass him at the last second. It was how Spencer won every time.

But Tyler wasn't going to let that stop him from trying.

This time, when Spencer drew even with him, Tyler shot out a hand to grip his wrist. The move apparently caught Spencer by surprise, and Tyler used it to his advantage, lowering his head and wrapping his arms around his brother in a tackle. They both went down, and Tyler scrabbled to get his feet under him, but he was laughing too hard.

"Come on. We'd better get inside before you get in trouble with your wife." He finally managed to get to his feet and held out a hand to help Spencer up.

His brother took the hand, but the moment he was on his feet, he yanked it away, leaving Tyler off balance as Spencer sprinted the last few steps to the house.

"Cheater," Tyler called at his back.

But Spencer flashed him a grin and disappeared through the front door, calling over his shoulder, "Looks like you're on dishes duty."

Tyler followed his brother into the house, still chuckling. Dishes duty wasn't so bad, especially when some friend or another was sure to step up and help.

But that didn't mean he wasn't going to give his brother a hard time.

"Sophie, you should know that your husband is a—" He stopped short at the kitchen, no idea what he'd been planning to say. There was no sign of Spencer or Sophie.

Instead, Isabel looked up from the carrot she was chopping. Her eyes locked on his for a second before she jumped back, dropping the knife and pulling her hand to her mouth.

"Are you okay?" He hadn't meant to cross to her side, and yet here he was. He reached for her hand, but she hissed and dodged away as if she'd been cut again.

He backed off, reaching for a paper towel and passing it to her.

She grabbed it, pressing it to the spot where blood swam down her finger. A bright red drop fell onto the white countertop, and she gasped, pulling the paper towel off her finger to wipe at it. But without the makeshift bandage to soak them up, three more drops fell to the counter.

"Sorry. I'm such a klutz." She kept her face turned away from his as she muttered about her own stupidity.

Silently, Tyler ripped off two more paper towels, passing one to her and using the other to wipe the blood off the counter.

"How bad is it?" His voice came out gruffer than he meant it to, but it was clear she didn't want his help. "You might need stitches."

"It's fine." But the way she winced as she clutched her hand close to her chest told a different story.

The patio door opened, and Sophie and Spencer came in from the backyard.

"Oh my goodness, what happened?" Sophie rushed to Isabel's side.

"I just slipped with the knife. I'm fine."

"I think she might need stitches. It's bleeding pretty good." Tyler pointed to the paper towel, which was already nearly soaked through with blood.

"I'm fine," Isabel repeated, more than a hint of irritation in her voice.

Tyler shrugged and moved out of the room.

If she didn't want help, he didn't want to give it. And getting away from her was safer, anyway. Because that protective urge that had come over him when he'd seen her hurt—he didn't need that messing with his head.

Thankfully, the house and yard were soon filled with people, and he tried to lose track of Isabel as he greeted friends.

Except that he couldn't seem to keep his eyes from constantly searching her out.

Sophie appeared to be making the rounds with her, introducing her to everyone. Isabel kept Gabby close to her side, and though she smiled with every introduction, she also looked ready to bolt at any moment.

A pinprick of compassion went through him. This had to be awkward for her.

But that didn't stop him from searching for an escape route as Sophie steered Isabel toward where he'd been talking to Dan and Jade. Unfortunately, Sophie's eyes were locked on him, and if he bailed now, he'd never hear the end of it.

"Isabel, this is Dan and Jade and their daughter Hope. And of course you already know Tyler," Sophie said.

Isabel's smile looked glued in place as she came to a stop next to Tyler and shook the hands Dan and Jade offered, followed by the one their two-year-old stuck out. That one, at least, seemed to earn a genuine smile.

A subtle scent of cherry blossoms drifted toward him from the flowers she still wore in her hair.

Tyler rubbed a hand down his shirt. How bad did he smell right now?

"Dan is the pastor at our church," Sophie added, and Tyler noticed Isabel do a double-take, though Sophie seemed oblivious to it. "And actually," his sister-in-law continued, "I think we're ready to eat, if you'd say the blessing, Dan."

"Of course." Dan brought his fingers to his mouth and let out a piercing whistle that elicited a giggle from Gabby. "I've been informed that we're ready to eat. Let's thank God for another delicious meal together."

Next to him, Isabel's jaw clenched, but she turned to Gabby, whispering to fold her hands and close her eyes.

"Why, Mama?" Gabby's whisper was just below shouting volume.

"We're going to pray," Unlike her daughter's, Isabel's whisper was nearly undetectable. "Now, shh. Just listen."

"Heavenly Father," Dan began. "You are the source of all good things. Thank you for the meal you have prepared for us and for the friends—new and old—we get to share it with. Help us to be a blessing to one another every day. In Jesus' name we ask it. Amen."

As everyone's Amens rang out, Gabby's voice rose above them. "Mama, who's Jesus?"

Tyler turned in time to see Isabel's cheeks light up nearly as red as her hair.

He wanted to tell her that it was all right, that plenty of the people standing here right now had had questions about Jesus at one point or another, that they'd all be happy to tell Gabby about him.

But before he could say anything, Isabel had taken her daughter by the hand, muttered something about using the restroom, and then disappeared into the house.

Chapter 7

The wooden swing creaked softly as Isabel pushed at the ground with her toe. Behind her, the sound of the party—there was no other way to describe a gathering of this many people, even if Sophie insisted on calling it a few friends for dinner—continued in full swing. Gabby was playing a game of tag with the other kids, and every once in a while Isabel peeked over her shoulder and around the lilac bush that half-shielded the swing to check on her daughter. Though there was little need, since she couldn't miss Gabby's joyful shrieks.

The sound filled her even as a warning bell dinged in her head. She shouldn't be letting Gabby make friends here. It would only make it harder on her when they moved on in a few months. But how could she make Gabby leave right now, when she was having real fun for the first time in possibly her entire life? And anyway, Violet and Nate didn't seem to be ready to leave yet, and Isabel had to wait for them to take her and Gabby to their new apartment.

Isabel still couldn't believe how generous Sophie's friends had been. They'd insisted on giving her the first month rent-free, since the apartment wasn't fully ready yet. And the rate they'd given her had been so low that she'd had to ask them to repeat it three times before she was sure she'd heard right.

She tipped her head toward the sky, watching the pink and orange of the setting sun flirt with the clouds.

Today had been some day. She'd woken in her car, ready to take her daughter back to a shelter, and now she had a job, an apartment, and even some friends.

Not friends, she reminded herself.

Just people she knew. Who happened to be nice.

She felt bad that she didn't remember most of the names Sophie had told her earlier. Not that it mattered, since this party or gathering or dinner or whatever you wanted to call it was a one-time thing.

After this, she'd have to make sure she and Gabby kept to themselves.

The sound of footsteps in the grass behind her had her whirling around—just in time to see Tyler, frozen, his body halfway between turning toward her and turning away.

"Looks like you found my secret getaway spot." His eyes landed on hers. They were rich and cocoa-y and warm, the suspicion he'd regarded her with all day seemed to have somewhat faded.

"Oh sorry. I can go." Isabel worked to slip the foot she'd been sitting on out from under her.

"No, that's okay." Tyler gestured for her to remain seated, but instead of walking away, he moved closer, then took a seat on the far end of the swing.

Every muscle in her body tensed. She sensed an interrogation coming on.

But Tyler sat in silence, and after a few minutes, her muscles loosened in spite of herself.

"I see you got your cut taken care of." He gestured to the gauze wrapped around her index finger.

"Oh." She lifted her hand. "Sophie asked someone . . . Jared, I think it was, to look at it. He said it didn't need stitches."

"That's good."

She nodded, not quite sure what else to say. The swing squeaked as he nudged it into motion, and he tilted his head up, frowning. "Going to have to oil that."

"Did you make this?" The question came out so naturally it was almost like she was used to making conversation.

Tyler's face seemed to redden slightly, although that could have been the sunset shining on it. "Spencer did, mostly, but I helped a bit."

"The furniture you two make for the store is really beautiful." Okay, now that was going beyond what was necessary, conversation-wise. She could stop anytime now.

"Thank you. I mostly do the carving and just help Spencer out with the furniture when he needs someone to hold something." For some reason, his smile made her want to keep talking.

"Sophie said you all get together like this often?" The idea was so foreign to her.

"Couple times a month, yeah." Tyler shrugged like it was no big deal. Like everyone in the world had a group of friends like this.

Then again, maybe everyone did. Except her.

Because no one would want you, Andrew's voice slithered through her head.

She swallowed, fighting off the ugly words, reminding herself that she didn't want friends anyway.

"Did you get a chance to meet everyone?" It took her a minute to register Tyler's question.

"What?" She shook herself. "Oh. Yeah. I think so. Though I'm not sure I remember everyone's name."

Tyler turned toward her, lifting one arm to the back of the swing as he pointed toward the house. "Over there, you've got Grace, Emma, Jared, and Peyton. And the couple with the little girl is Ethan and Ariana."

Isabel had no choice but to slide closer to him to see around the lilac bush. A faint scent of sandalwood and hard work drifted from him, but it wasn't unpleasant. More like . . . comforting.

She brushed aside the thought as Tyler pointed to a group gathered around the small firepit. "That's Leah and her husband Austin and their son Jackson."

"She looks too young to have a teenager." Isabel bit her lip. Maybe that wasn't an appropriate thing to say.

"She adopted him last year. Just before she and Austin got married. And Austin's adoption paperwork just went through too."

"That's great."

Tyler smiled at her, and she used all her willpower to ignore the tiny flurry it sent up from her stomach. There was no reason to react like that.

"And that's the pastor and his family with them?" She had no idea why people would invite their pastor to a party. All she knew was she couldn't have made a good impression with him, what with her daughter not knowing who Jesus was and all.

"Yeah. Dan is Leah's brother, and his wife is Jade. Their little girl is Hope. And you know Sophie and Spencer." This time when he shifted, his arm brushed against hers. Before she could pull away, it was gone, but she couldn't get the sensation out of her head.

"And the other couple with them is Nate and Violet." Tyler kept talking as if he hadn't noticed the contact. Probably because he hadn't.

"Yeah. I definitely remember Nate and Violet." She worked to reel her attention back to the conversation. "They offered to let me stay in their apartment."

"That's good." Tyler seemed sincere. "It's a nice place. You'll like it."

They lapsed into silence, but the question balancing on the tip of her tongue refused to stay put. "Can I ask you something?"

Tyler gave her a wary look. "Okay."

"Are all of you for real?"

A rich, full, warm, kind of endearing laugh burst out of him.

No, not kind of endearing.

Annoying.

It was a serious question, and she wanted a real answer.

"Yeah," he finally said, but that stubborn smile wouldn't leave his lips. "We're for real. Why do you ask?"

She shook her head. "This all just seems so Mayberry or Leave It to Beaver or something. I don't know."

He was still smiling, and she faltered. That smile was throwing her off.

And anyway, didn't she know more than anyone that looks could be deceiving? They were all likely putting on a good show for her benefit.

After all, how many times had she done that—stood holding Andrew's arm, smiling and laughing and pretending she had the perfect life, so no one would know the truth?

"No reason," she mumbled as Nate and Violet approached them.

"Ready to go home?" Violet asked.

Isabel started. That word—home—she'd promised she wouldn't use it. But it sure did have a nice ring to it.

"Yeah." She pushed off the swing. "I'm ready."

Chapter 8

This was the fifth day in a row Isabel had woken with a smile on her face. Living in this apartment, with its hardwood floors, soft blue walls, and best of all, view of the lake, was still surreal to her. Apparently Violet had lived here once upon a time, and though the people who'd rented the apartment after her had done some damage to the place, Violet and Nate had done a beautiful job of fixing it up.

Chancy popped into her bedroom, toenails clacking, followed by Gabby.

"You two are up early." Isabel slid out of the bed that the apartment had been furnished with. Its high mattress and four posts made her feel like a princess, as ridiculous as that might be for a thirty-two-year-old woman to feel.

"Can we have eggs for breakfast?" Gabby bounced onto the bed, and Isabel considered reprimanding her but decided against it. Let the girl have fun for once.

"Sure." Isabel stretched, checking the time. She didn't have to be at Hidden Blossom for an hour yet, although a small part of her wanted to get there early.

Only because she was a diligent worker. Not because if she got there before the store opened, there'd be a better chance of seeing Tyler before he and Spencer headed out to the orchard. Though, hard as she tried, she couldn't convince herself that she hadn't enjoyed the few conversations she'd had with him over the past week. And each day, he seemed to regard her with a little less suspicion, a little more . . . what?

She wasn't sure exactly, and she probably shouldn't like it.

Which didn't change the fact that she did.

"Oh no." Isabel frowned at the second egg she'd burned and scraped it into Chancy's bowl.

Can't even make an egg. Because your thoughts are on some guy who would never want you. Didn't I tell you I was the only one who ever would?

Cracking another egg, Isabel hummed to drown out Andrew's voice. This time, she turned a perfect sunny-side-up egg onto Gabby's plate.

But her clumsiness in the kitchen meant they arrived at Hidden Blossom just in time to see Tyler and Spencer roaring down the trail on their ATVs.

That was *not* disappointment Isabel felt.

It was anticipation for the day ahead.

To her own surprise, she was really enjoying this job. Though the store could go from empty to swamped in the space of two minutes, she enjoyed the challenge, and the days flew by. Plus, Sophie was easygoing and fun to spend the days with.

She opened the door and waited for Gabby to walk through. "I can't believe what a beautiful day—"

One look at Sophie, and her words evaporated. The woman she was coming to think of as a friend in spite of her own rules was clutching a piece of paper in her fist, her face grim.

But she looked up and gave Isabel a gentle smile. Too gentle. "Gabby, why don't you take the twins into the office and watch a movie."

Isabel's heartbeat stumbled. If Sophie had something to say to her that she couldn't say in front of the kids, it couldn't be anything good.

After Gabby had led the twins to the office, Sophie turned to Isabel and held out the paper.

Isabel's hand shook as she took it and her eyes fell on the words: "Background Check." She swallowed, scanning it but not really seeing. Not that she had to see it to know what it said.

"According to this, Isabel Small has only existed for three years." Confusion and hurt mingled in Sophie's statement.

Isabel made herself meet her employer's eyes, trying not to flinch at the compassion she saw there.

"I know," Isabel rasped.

"Could you tell me why?" There was no judgment in Sophie's question.

Isabel's mind swirled with potential answers. Hadn't she rehearsed exactly this scenario a thousand times?

But no matter how desperately she wanted to clutch onto a lie, she found she couldn't.

"I changed my name and Gabby's a couple years ago."

Sophie nodded, waiting for more.

"It was for safety reasons, after I left my ex."

"He was abusive?" Sophie reached for her arm, offering a gentle squeeze.

Isabel gave a silent nod. She couldn't handle talking about it.

"Did he hurt Gabby? Did he—" Sophie's eyes darted to the closed office door.

Isabel shook her head. But he could have. That's the part that haunted her. She hated herself for not leaving sooner. Hated that her fear could have cost her daughter everything.

"Thank the Lord for that," Sophie breathed. "Is there anything I can do? Are you in danger now?"

"I don't think so. We've changed our name, stayed on the move, that sort of thing. There shouldn't be much of a chance he'll find us." Which didn't stop the fact that she lived with the dread of that possibility pressing heavy in her stomach every day.

"That's a relief." Sophie wrapped an arm around her shoulder, and Isabel found herself leaning into her.

"I can give you our former names if you need them." She didn't say *real* names, because she didn't think of them as their real names anymore. Isabel and Gabby were their real names now—and always would be.

"I don't think that's necessary," Sophie said. "This background check came back clean, and I trust you."

Isabel let herself relax a little. As much as she trusted Sophie wouldn't do anything with the knowledge, she felt better if she was the only one who knew their former names.

"Listen," Sophie continued, "the twins have a doctor appointment later this afternoon. Would you be comfortable holding down the fort and closing up for me?"

Isabel's mother had taught her it was rude to stare. But she couldn't help it. "You're not firing me?"

"For having a past?" Sophie laughed lightly. "Of course not. But you have to promise me that if you ever feel like you're in danger, you'll come to me."

Isabel hesitated. She couldn't see what good Sophie would be if Andrew did find her. But she nodded.

"Can I ask for a favor too?" Isabel swallowed past the anxiety that said this woman had already done her way too many favors.

"Of course."

"I'd prefer if no one else knew about the name change. Just in case . . ."

Sophie nodded. "Your secret's safe with me."

Tyler could not stop whistling as he worked.

He'd tried. But every time he managed to be silent for a few minutes, the melody found its way back to his lips.

"You're awfully chipper these days." Spencer's eyes gleamed as he jumped off the backhoe he'd been using to dig holes for the new trees they'd plant come fall.

Tyler shrugged. "It's a beautiful day."

And it was. Hot but not too hot. Sunny with just enough cloud cover to provide shade every now and again. Even the grass seemed greener than usual today after the light rain they'd gotten last night.

"Or you're thinking about a beautiful girl." Spencer stopped in front of him, arms crossed over his chest, as if waiting for confirmation.

Tyler looked down, kicking a small mound of dirt back into the hole. "You know I have no interest in dating."

"Yeah. And I've also noticed how you find little excuses to talk to her every day."

Tyler crammed his hands in his pockets. "You're delusional. I don't talk to her any more than you do."

Spencer held up his hands. "Hey, I'm not saying it's a bad thing. It's about time you moved on."

"I've already moved on." Tyler gritted his teeth. When would his brother see that? "But that doesn't mean I want to date. You know my only priority is the boys. Speaking of which—" He checked the time on his phone. "I'd better go get them from the tree house. We've got a baseball game tonight."

"Long as you're going that way . . ." Spencer's careful drawl had Tyler on guard. What did his brother want him to do now? "Why don't you drop this week's deposit off at the bank? It'll give you an excuse to stop in the store and—"

Tyler held up a warning finger. "Don't."

Spencer's only response was an oversized grin.

Tyler jumped on his ATV and sped off without waiting for his brother.

It wasn't like he'd been going out of his way to see Isabel. It was just that when he *did* happen to see her, he didn't mind talking to her.

Fine. He enjoyed it.

But that didn't mean he had any interest in dating her. A man could enjoy talking to a woman without necessarily being attracted to the way her hair made a perfect frame for her face or the way her smile was slow to start but finished larger than life.

Good grief.

Time to think about something else.

Like the fact that he still wasn't one hundred percent sure he trusted her. Although he'd accepted that she probably wasn't conning them, he remained all but certain she was hiding something.

He stopped at the tree house to tell the boys to get home and change, then drove the ATV into the shed, briefly contemplating a quick stop home to at least put on a clean shirt—and maybe a little cologne. But he dismissed the idea because, for one, it was ridiculous, and for two, he didn't have time to get home and change before the store closed, which meant he'd be too late to see Isabel. He'd change after he got the deposit.

He pulled open the door to the store, pausing as the cool of the air conditioning refreshed him.

"Oh hey." Isabel looked up from the display of homemade jams she was arranging. She wasn't quite wearing a smile, but she didn't look unwelcoming either.

"Hi, Tyler." Gabby came bounding from behind the counter. "Sophie had to take the twins to the doctor, so Mama said I could sit at the register while she cleaned up. But no one came in." She turned hopeful eyes on him. "Do you want to buy something?"

Tyler literally had five dollars in his pocket, but he couldn't let the little girl down. "All right. I'll take one jar of that strawberry jam your Mama is putting out."

Isabel's mouth eased into that slow smile as she passed it to him, and he got caught up in admiring it.

"You have to bring it over here, so I can beep it, silly." Gabby called from the perch she'd resumed behind the register.

"What? Right." Tyler tore his gaze off Isabel. That had been . . . weird. When their eyes had met, something had gone through him. Something he couldn't place. Something he hadn't felt in a very long time. Something he wasn't sure he wanted to feel again.

"So Sophie left you to close up on your own?" he asked as Isabel followed him across the store. He set his jam on the counter, and Isabel helped Gabby ring it up. She nodded in answer to his question.

"Do you need any help with anything or . . .?" Or what? Or did she want him to stay and keep her company?

"No. I think we'll be fine, thanks."

And you have a baseball game to get to.

Tyler paid Gabby and thanked her as she passed him his change. "I'll just grab this week's deposit and be out of your hair then."

Gabby giggled. "You're not in our hair. You're too big to fit." She held her hair straight above her head as if to prove it.

"It's an expression." Isabel rumpled Gabby's hair.

"What's a ex-special-son?" Gabby shifted her gaze to her mother, and Isabel gave a half-suppressed sigh.

Tyler was still chuckling as he headed for the office. He remembered those days of endless questions. He hadn't even noticed when the boys had grown out of that phase. He should warn Isabel that kids grew up fast.

Twisting the combination lock on the small safe that sat in the corner of the office, Tyler started whistling again.

He couldn't help it. God was good.

It looked like they were going to have an abundant harvest this year. His family was all healthy. And they had enough help at the orchard.

And it didn't hurt that the help was so sweet.

He shook his head at himself. Nothing was going to dampen his mood right now. Not even his own foolishness.

The lock on the safe clicked, and he opened it and grabbed the bank deposit bag.

The bag was lighter than usual, and Tyler glanced down at it. At least counting it should go quickly.

But his whistle died on his lips as he unzipped the bag and pulled it open.

Empty.

There wasn't even a penny in the bag, though he'd watched Sophie put a stack of bills in here the other day.

"Isabel." The whisper came to his lips unbidden, but who else could it have been?

There were only three people who knew the combination to the safe—himself, Spencer, and Sophie.

And apparently Isabel.

Tyler kicked the safe shut as he stood, but the bolt was turned, and the heavy door jolted back toward him, hitting his shin. Ignoring the bruising pain, he marched toward the front of the store, bag still clutched in his hands.

But there was no sign of Isabel or Gabby.

Had they already made their getaway?

A low growl grew in his throat.

He'd known Isabel was hiding something from the moment he met her. How could he have been stupid enough to let her beautiful face and treacherous smile lull him into a sense of security?

"Did you say something?" Isabel emerged from the kitchen. "Sorry, I was washing—"

The moment her eyes landed on him, all the color slid off her cheeks, and the dish towel she'd been using fell to the floor.

A worm of self-loathing crawled through Tyler. He'd been hoping he was wrong, though he knew he couldn't be. But didn't her expression say it all?

She was guilty.

"What is it?" She took a step toward him but then backed off two steps, fear dancing in her eyes as she scanned the room.

Looking for an escape route, no doubt.

He held up the empty bank bag, shaking it to emphasize the nothingness of its interior. "Where's the deposit?"

"In the safe?" The way she raised her voice at the end made it more of a question than a statement.

He shook the empty bag again. "It's gone." He held out his hand, as if she was just going to put the money right back into it.

Isabel's eyes widened, the fear in them growing along with her pupils. "You think I took it?" The words sliced like glass across his ears. She sounded genuinely upset.

But he supposed he would be too if he'd just been caught stealing from his employer.

The shine of tears gleamed in her eyes, and Tyler glared at her feet so he wouldn't lose his resolve, his hand still extended. "Look, just give it to me now and be on your way, and we won't press charges." He should discuss that with Spencer and Sophie first, but he knew them well enough to know they'd agree.

"But I didn't—" Isabel's swallow was audible. "I don't even know the combination to the safe."

"You expect me to believe that Sophie left you here alone to close without giving you the combination? How were you supposed to put today's cash in there?"

"I guess she forgot. Anyway, we didn't have much cash today, so I probably would have just left it in the drawer."

Tyler sneered. The woman was a good actor, he'd give her that. Almost as good as Julia, insisting that she hadn't been having an affair when he'd found another man's socks in his drawer. He may have bought Julia's story—that obviously the socks were his and he'd just forgotten he had them—but that had only earned him six more months of heartache.

He wasn't going to make the same mistake this time.

"Get out." His voice was low and void of emotion. "Just get out and don't come back."

Her tears spilled over then, a great torrent of them down her cheeks, but she nodded and called for Gabby, her voice wobbly.

Tyler clenched his jaw and slammed the door of his heart. Julia had cried too. He'd thought that had meant she was innocent.

It hadn't.

"Mama?" Gabby's eyes went from her mother's teary face to Tyler, and he dropped his head, grinding his teeth tighter.

He might be smart enough not to give in to Isabel's tears, but he couldn't guarantee the little girl wouldn't move him.

"It's okay, Bunny. Just time for us to go. Come on." She took Gabby's hand and led her toward the door, not meeting Tyler's eyes as she passed.

"What's wrong, Mama?" Gabby asked again as the door opened.

But if Isabel answered, Tyler didn't hear. The door closed with a soft click, but it might as well have been a gong for the way it hammered his ears.

He'd done the right thing.

He'd had no choice.

So why had it left him so shaken?

It was just that it all cut a little too close to Julia's lies, Julia's betrayal.

That was the only reason.

With a heavy sigh, he moved to the cash register, emptied what little money it held into the bank bag, and redeposited it in the safe. Then he pulled out his phone and dialed first Sophie, then Spencer. But neither answered, and this wasn't the kind of thing he wanted to tell them in a message.

He'd talk to them after the boys' baseball game.

His movements were slow and lethargic as he locked up the store. But the moment he got outside, he forced himself to pick up his head. His boys didn't need to know anything was wrong.

He was only glad this had happened now—before he'd gone and done something foolish, like deciding he liked her.

Yep.

Looked like his heart had been spared that pain.

Chapter 9

Isabel picked at her piece of the pizza she'd bought on the way home from the orchard. They really couldn't afford it, especially now that she didn't have a job, but she was in no condition to cook.

She'd finally managed to stop crying by sheer force of will so she wouldn't freak Gabby out. But inside, her soul still wept.

How could Tyler think that? How could he accuse her of stealing from the first people she'd put her trust in, in so long?

Underneath the sorrow, anger built.

Tyler hadn't liked her since the moment he'd met her, when he'd asked if she'd been drinking. She'd seen the contempt and suspicion in his eyes that day, and even though it had faded over the past week, it'd been back on full display today.

That was fine.

She'd been making it on her own since she was seventeen. She didn't need him or anyone else.

A stab of regret needled her over the thought of letting Sophie down, but that was why she wasn't supposed to make friends in the first place.

"Mama, Jonah and Jeremiah said they want to show me the creek tomorrow. Is that okay?" Gabby's question was more subdued than usual, her eyes holding a trace of worry.

Isabel worked to smooth her own forehead. "Actually, I was thinking we could do something fun tomorrow, just you and me."

"Going to the orchard is fun." Gabby looked at her as if she was crazy if she thought otherwise.

"I know. But I think I'm going to find another fun job. Maybe at a daycare. Then there will be lots of kids for you to play with."

Gabby popped her lower lip out. "But Jonah and Jeremiah are my friends. They'll be sad if I don't come back."

Isabel bit her own lip. She liked the orchard too. More than she ever would have guessed she would. But she didn't have a choice. It was either a daycare or move again.

Although maybe leaving would be better. By now, everyone here probably thought she was a criminal anyway.

It was just, now that she'd let herself think the word *home*, she was having a hard time letting go of it.

Call Sophie and explain what happened. It was the tenth time she'd had the thought since she'd left the orchard.

But every time, Andrew's voice drowned out her own: *She's not going to believe you. Not over her own brother-in-law.*

She rubbed at her temples, too exhausted to unwind her mixed up feelings.

"Eat your pizza." She set another piece on Gabby's plate as she handed her own half-eaten slice to Chancy. "It's almost time for bed."

Thankfully, Gabby hadn't learned to tell time yet, so she couldn't protest that it wasn't even seven o'clock.

But Isabel had a long night of worrying ahead of her. And she didn't want Gabby to be part of it.

Seven-zero.

Tyler shook his head at the scoreboard.

That had not been a pretty game.

As the team huddled around him, he searched for some encouragement to offer them. But the day had left him fresh out.

Guilt still pulled at him over making Isabel cry, mingled with anger that he felt that way. She was the one who had played him—played them all. She should be the one who felt guilty.

Anyway, he was sure the tears had only been for show. All part of the act.

"Dad?" Jonah tugged at his arm, and Tyler made himself focus on the dejected faces staring up at him.

"Good game, boys."

From the way every last one of them blinked at him, it was obvious they could tell his heart wasn't in it. He had to shake himself out of it. These boys deserved better than that.

He tried again. "I know it's disappointing to lose, but I want each one of you to remember that whether we win or lose, you are precious in God's sight." He made an internal face at himself. Precious in God's sight? That was the best he could come up with right now?

The verse he'd been studying this morning came to him, and he blurted it, without considering whether it fit the situation: "Forgetting what is behind and straining toward what is ahead, I press on toward the goal to win the prize for which God has called me heavenward in Christ Jesus." He took a breath as the relief of the verse washed over him. "Do you guys know what prize this is talking about?"

Jonah raised a hand, and Tyler nodded to him.

"Heaven." His son said it with confidence, and Tyler's heart surged. This was what it was all about. Not whether they won or lost a game but whether these boys knew their Savior.

"That's right. And knowing that heaven is our prize, we can keep going, keep serving God in the way we play baseball and the way we live our lives. Sound good?"

The boys all mumbled something that seemed like an assent.

"I said, 'Does that sound good?'" Tyler lifted his voice and put force behind his words.

This time the boys shouted a loud, "Yes, sir," and Tyler gave them each a high-five as he sent them off to their parents.

And speaking of forgetting the past, that was exactly what he was going to do.

He'd forget he'd ever met Isabel, had ever enjoyed her conversation, had ever admired her smile. Just as soon as he told Sophie and Spencer what had happened.

"Why don't you boys go load up the van?" He passed the keys to Jeremiah and the equipment bag to Jonah. "I need to talk to your aunt and uncle, but I'll be there in a minute."

As the boys took off, he made his way toward Spencer and Sophie, each of whom held a sleeping twin on a shoulder.

"Rough game." Trust his brother to cut right to the chase.

"Yeah. Listen. We need to talk."

"We saw you called." Sophie shifted Rylan on her shoulder. "Man, these two are getting heavy. Why didn't you leave a message?"

"I had to fire Isabel." He'd planned to preface the words with an explanation of what had happened, but they splattered out of him with about as little forewarning as an earthquake.

Both Sophie and Spencer blinked at him, Spencer's lips slightly parted, Sophie's jaw hard.

"Without talking to us first?" Sophie was the first to recover, but her tone was none too friendly.

Tyler held up his hands. "I didn't have a choice. I caught her stealing."

"Stealing what?" Sophie was on the defensive, and Tyler didn't blame her.

He hadn't wanted to believe it either, and he'd seen it with his own eyes. "The bank deposit. I went into the safe to get it, and—"

"Tyler Michael Weston, you are quite possibly the biggest idiot on the face of the planet." Sophie's words may have been quiet, but they carried the full heat of her anger. "*I* took the bank deposit. I texted Spencer to let him know."

She turned toward her husband, who nodded. "Right after you took off. I texted you not to worry about it, since Sophie was doing it."

A sick feeling started low in Tyler's stomach and crept toward his esophagus as he pulled out his phone and opened his texts.

Sure enough, there was an unopened message from Spencer.

He opened it now. *Never mind about bank deposit. Soph has it.*

"She didn't steal the money?" His voice was dull.

"No she didn't." Sophie said sharply.

Tyler dropped his head and scrubbed his hands over his cheeks, shoving his fingers under his glasses to rub his eyes.

501

Isabel hadn't stolen the money.

That was a relief.

But also—

The way he'd accused her. Had refused to even listen to her. Had ignored her tears.

"You need to stop letting your issues with Julia cloud your judgment of other women," Sophie shot at him.

"Soph." Ever the peacemaker, Spencer jumped in.

"No. She's right." Tyler deserved Sophie's anger.

And Isabel's.

"You're right, I'm right." Sophie pulled out her phone and waved it in his face. "I'm going to call her and try to straighten everything out. Apologize and beg her to come back to work tomorrow."

"Yeah, of course." Tyler swallowed. "I'll call her too."

But Sophie shook her head. "Don't think you're going to get off that easily. Call her, yes. But tomorrow, assuming she comes back, you owe her an apology in person."

Tyler's mouth went dry. How could he ever make up for something like this?

And worse, what if she didn't give him a chance?

Chapter 10

Isabel juggled her phone from hand to hand, staring at the congealed yolk of her uneaten egg.

She hadn't had the courage to answer Sophie's half-dozen calls last night. But she'd listened to her messages.

Listened to Sophie's explanation that everything had been a misunderstanding. Listened to her begging for Isabel to come back. By the last message, Sophie had sounded near tears.

And Isabel did feel bad about that. None of this was Sophie's fault.

You might as well cut your losses and leave.

Even if it had been a misunderstanding, she wasn't sure how she could face Tyler now, knowing what he'd thought about her.

Tyler had left a message too—a single one—but she'd deleted it without listening to it. The decision may have been hasty, she saw now, but there was no way to undo it. She'd never know what he'd said, though she could guess. Probably something along the lines of "Go away and never come back."

Absently, she shoved a forkful of cold egg into her mouth, nearly gagging as she choked it down, then emptied the rest into Chancy's bowl. If she didn't pull herself together soon, the dog was going to get used to eating like a king.

"Mama, look what happened." Gabby emerged from her room holding something crumpled and brown in her palm. It took Isabel a moment to recognize it as petals from the cherry blossoms they'd picked the first day at the orchard.

"Sorry, Bunny. That's what happens after you pick them. They stay nice for a little while, but then they die."

Kind of like hope.

"Can we get some more?"

Isabel brushed the crumpled blossoms from her daughter's hand and deposited them in the trash. "The trees are done blossoming now. They won't have flowers again until next year. Remember how Tyler told you about the life cycle of a cherry tree?"

She hit her phone against her palm. Tyler had been so patient, explaining everything to Gabby and answering her twenty bazillion questions.

"Oh yeah, I forgot for a second." Gabby's eyes brightened. "He said he'd take me to see what happens to the tree when the flowers fall off. He said it was a big surprise. So we have to go there today."

Isabel gave the phone in her hand a hard stare. Maybe they *should* go to the orchard, if only to say goodbye to Sophie in person. After all Sophie had done for her, she owed her that much at least.

Besides, she needed to get her first—and last—paycheck, or she and Gabby would be eating ramen indefinitely.

"Just for a little while," she warned. "And I don't think we'll have time for Tyler to show you the cherries." If she had her way, they wouldn't run into Tyler at all. Thankfully, it was late enough that he should already be in the orchard.

"But Tyler might be sad if he doesn't get to show me. I promised he could." Gabby's expression was so earnest that Isabel nearly laughed in spite of the dread angling its way through her stomach.

What if she did see him?

She tried to push the worry aside. If she did see him, she'd ignore him. Simple as that.

"I'm sure he'll be fine," she assured Gabby. "Now go get your shoes on."

Gabby was back in a jiffy, with her shoes on and tied.

"Okay then, Speedy Gonzalez, let's go." Isabel tucked Chancy into his crate and followed her daughter out the door.

By the time they got to the store, Isabel had nearly convinced herself this was a bad idea. She could have Sophie mail her paycheck.

But Gabby was out of the car before Isabel could change her mind.

All right. They'd stay for five minutes and be on their way.

The moment she opened the store door, she stopped in her tracks. She'd never seen such a long line of customers before. And a faint scent of something burning wafted toward her.

Sophie looked up from behind the counter, her eyes instantly registering relief. "Isabel, I'm so happy to see you."

The eyes of everyone in the long line swung to Isabel, and she ducked her head, trying to ignore their curious looks as she hurried to Sophie's side. The sound of the twins' cries carried from the kitchen, where Isabel knew they were likely in their portable cribs.

"I'm so sorry about yesterday," Sophie said between counting out a customer's change, sounding more than a hair frazzled. "I should have made sure Tyler knew—"

"We'll talk about it later." Isabel reached for the next customer's items. "Go check your pies. I think they're burning. Gabby, go help with Rylan and Aubrey."

Sophie's arm came around Isabel in a sideways hug. "You're a lifesaver."

Isabel tolerated the squeeze for three seconds. "Go. Your pies."

As she helped the next few customers, Isabel tried not to think about the fact that she was supposed to be on her way out of here by now.

How could she not stay to help Sophie, when Sophie had done so much for her?

"Hey, Sugar."

Isabel froze with her hand on the next customer's jar of jam.

Sugar was what Andrew had always called her—at least before his pet names had turned into curses. And the man's drawl had a hint of the south in it.

"How are you today?" She made herself make small talk, though she was careful not to angle her eyes up.

"Better now." The voice was smooth and charming, but it sent little sparks of panic all up and down her spine. Andrew's voice. Andrew's charm.

She looked up quickly. It only took half a second to realize the man bore no similarity to Andrew. And yet that look on his face. The way his eyes were traveling down her body. He leaned closer, and the sharp scent of his cologne hit her—spicy with a hint of black licorice. The same cologne that had cloaked her that last night, strangled her almost as completely as Andrew's hands around her neck.

The room started to spin around her, and she reached for the counter. She needed something to lean on. Something to hold her up. But all she could find was air.

Tyler was not looking forward to this.

He still hadn't figured out how he was going to apologize to Isabel. Hopefully the message he'd left last night had at least broken the ice.

He opened the door to the store, still rehearsing potential apologies in his head.

As if by reflex, his eyes went immediately to her.

But something didn't look right.

The usual pink in her cheeks had faded to a chalky white, and she seemed to be swaying, her hands grasping in front of her but not touching anything.

Tyler's feet pulled him across the store before he could make up his mind about what to do.

The moment his hands grasped her elbows, she sagged into him. He readjusted to get a better grip.

"I'm just going to rest here." Her mumbled words were indistinct.

"I got you." He spoke softly into her ear.

"Is she all right?" The customer at the counter—a tall dude with a southern twang—leaned closer.

Isabel swayed again, and Tyler carefully steered her toward the kitchen. "Let's get you some air."

He tightened his arms around her, but she pulled out of his grasp. "I'm fine."

She reached for the counter again, closing her eyes, her torso starting to lean backward.

"You're not fine." Tyler couldn't keep the irritation from bleeding through. "You need a break."

She started to take a step toward the kitchen but stumbled. This time when Tyler wrapped an arm around her, she didn't protest but leaned into him.

"Someone will be with you in a moment," he said to the man at the counter as he half-led, half-dragged her from the store.

"Oh my goodness." Sophie rushed to their side the minute they entered the kitchen. "What's wrong? Are you all right? Should I call an ambulance?"

"Mama." Gabby rushed to Isabel's side and threw her arms around her mother's waist. "I'm fine."

Somehow, even though Tyler could feel the effort she was making to remain on her feet, she managed to pull an arm out of his grasp and wrap it around Gabby. "Just got a little dizzy."

"Come on. You need to sit." Tyler led her to one of the wooden stools perched at the countertop workspace, not letting go until she was settled onto it, with her elbows propped against the countertop and her head braced in her hands. When he did finally let go, his arms felt oddly empty.

He told himself to give her some space, but he couldn't help hovering over her. What if she got dizzy again and fell off the stool? He should have put her on a lower chair.

After a moment she raised her head. "Much better now. I'd better get back out there."

Tyler pressed a hand to her shoulder. "You need to rest some more."

Her eyes came to his, traces of the fear she'd worn yesterday when he'd accused her of stealing still lingering there, and a stab of regret went through him again. How could he have jumped to such terrible conclusions about her?

"Tyler's right. You need to rest." Sophie reached for Isabel's arm, and Tyler made himself remove his hand from her shoulder. "You get some lunch and don't come back out there until you feel better." Sophie wore her concern for Isabel all over her face, and Tyler wondered if he looked the same.

"I'll stay with her," he offered. "We need to talk anyway."

Sophie nodded and patted his arm, then bustled into the store. "Thanks for your patience, everyone," Tyler heard her chirp before the door between the two rooms closed, leaving him alone with Isabel, Gabby, and Sophie's twins.

"I have an idea." He clapped his hands, looking at Gabby instead of Isabel. If he was going to sell this, he'd need the girl's help. "How about a picnic?"

The light that filled Gabby's eyes could have given the sun a good run for its money. "Yay! Please, Mama, can we?"

Isabel massaged her temples.

"If you feel up to a short walk," Tyler was quick to add.

Isabel gave him a grim look, but as her gaze shifted to her daughter, her face softened. "Just a short picnic. Then I need to get back in here and help Sophie."

"Deal." He held out a hand, and she eyed it, not taking it.

He supposed he deserved that. He may have kept her from landing head-first on the floor, but that didn't make up for the way he'd treated her yesterday. He pulled his hand back. He'd apologize once they were outside and the kids were busy playing.

"I'll go make some sandwiches. Gabby, why don't you let Sophie know we're taking the twins, and I'll come get you all when everything's ready."

Isabel looked for a moment like she was going to protest, but she nodded.

It may have been a nod of sheer exhaustion, but Tyler would take it.

Chapter 11

"Wow, Mama, what's that? It looks like there's a house in that tree." Gabby pointed with one hand, tugging Isabel forward with the other as they reached a small tree line on the other side of the field behind Tyler's house.

Fortunately, the fresh air had cleared the spots from Isabel's vision. Unfortunately, that meant she could see perfectly clearly that what Gabby was pointing to was exactly what it sounded like.

From the other side of Gabby, Tyler—impossibly carrying Rylan on his back and Aubrey in front—gave an incredulous chuckle. "You've never seen a tree house?"

"Nope." Gabby sounded cheerful and also a little awe-struck.

"Well, the boys are already up there, if you want to go join them."

Isabel shook her head, catching Gabby's arm just as she was about to skip off. "No tree houses."

Tyler eyed her with disbelief. "What do you mean no tree houses? Every kid loves a tree house."

"That may be." Isabel massaged her temple. Shaking her head had caused the spots to start blinking again. "But every mom does not. No tree houses."

"Please, Mama." Gabby's eyes welled with tears, but she blinked them back. Which only made saying no harder. But it was Isabel's job to consider not only her daughter's happiness but her safety. She just wished the two could line up more often.

"It's perfectly safe. I built it with the boys." Was that an edge of hurt in his voice?

Too bad.

Even if the Dalai Lama of Construction himself had built it, Gabby wasn't going up there.

It was too dangerous.

"Here, I'll show you. Watch these two."

Before Isabel could process what he was doing, he'd set Rylan and Aubrey down and was jogging to the base of the tree. "Boys, I'm coming up."

Two seconds later, Jonah and Jeremiah emerged from the enclosed part of the tree house onto the balcony that surrounded it.

They grinned down at Gabby. "Come up."

Gabby's pleading eyes fell on Isabel again, but Isabel shook her head. No tree house.

As Tyler reached the top of the makeshift ladder bolted to the tree, his head poked through a trap door in the floor of the tree house, and Gabby giggled. "It looks fun, Mama."

Tyler stood, huddled with his boys, and whispered something.

"Be careful," Isabel couldn't resist calling.

All three of them turned and grinned, then started jumping and stomping and pulling on railings, like a bunch of gorillas.

Isabel gave a little shriek and covered her ears. She wasn't in the mood to watch someone fall to their death. But Gabby giggled and clapped, chanting, "More!" Rylan and Aubrey soon joined her.

After what felt like two years, Tyler finally raised an arm, and they stopped.

"See?" He gave one last stomp on the tree house floor. "It's safe. We can't break it if we try." Between his boyish grin, his twins' earnest expressions, Gabby's hopeful pout, and Rylan's and Aubrey's ongoing giggles, Isabel felt herself nearly caving.

But she stiffened her spine. She had one job to do: protect Gabby.

"I'm sorry. No. Should we eat?" She moved to spread the picnic blanket Tyler had hooked onto his pack, pretending not to notice Gabby's crocodile tears or Tyler's muttered words to his boys as they climbed down from the tree house.

Silently, Tyler pulled out sandwiches and apples and passed them to everyone.

"Should we pray?" He gave her a questioning look, as if not quite sure how she'd react, but folded his own hands. His boys and Rylan and Aubrey did too. Gabby looked around at all of them, then did the same. Isabel stifled her sigh and folded her hands as well. It wasn't like it would hurt to go through the motions.

"Heavenly Father," Tyler began, and Isabel closed her eyes in spite of herself. His voice was warm and filled with a kind of trust she'd never known. Much as she hated to admit it, something about that intrigued her.

"Thank you for the food you have given us and the beautiful day to enjoy it. Help us always to put our trust in you alone and to remember that you have not given us a spirit of fear but of love. In Jesus' name. Amen."

"Mama, you still didn't tell me about Jesus." Gabby stuffed a giant bite of sandwich into her mouth and looked at Isabel expectantly.

But Isabel was still stuck on Tyler's prayer. Was that a dig at her? At her refusal to let her daughter climb the tree house?

"I can tell you about Jesus," Tyler said to Gabby. "If that's okay with you?" He turned to Isabel, his eyes holding a gentle question.

She wanted to say no. She didn't need her daughter's head filled with all the things Christians claimed to stand for but then did the opposite of.

But they were all looking at her, waiting. And she'd already let them down once, with the whole tree house thing.

Anyway, if she had to choose between the tree house and Jesus, she supposed Jesus was the less dangerous option.

***

Tyler leaned back on his elbows, searching for a relaxed posture. But the tightness in his shoulders told him he was never going to find it.

He'd sent the kids off to play—though Isabel had been careful to stress that Gabby was not to go in the tree house. He couldn't suppress a twinge of pride that his boys had elected to stay on the ground with her.

Currently, Gabby appeared to be instructing Jeremiah and Jonah in a game she'd invented, while Rylan and Aubrey toddled around them.

Isabel sat about as far away from him as she could without venturing off the picnic blanket, her entire body rigid.

They were as alone as they were going to get. Which made this the perfect time to apologize. So why did his tongue seem suddenly incapable of speech?

Maybe he could ease into it. "I hope you didn't mind me telling Gabby about Jesus." He'd only been able to scratch the surface of who Jesus was, telling Gabby that he was the Son of God who had been born as a baby and grown up to die for the sins of the world. By then, Gabby had finished eating and was ready to play, but Tyler had seen that hunger in her eyes for more of God's Word.

"You know," he said to Isabel now, "if you ever want to bring her to church, we have a great service. Dan's a fantastic preacher. And there's Sunday school . . ." He trailed off as her posture grew even stiffer.

Right.

That wasn't the place to start.

The place to start was with an apology for the way he'd acted yesterday. Right now, he was probably coming across as nothing more than a hypocrite.

"Look, I know your words before were aimed at me." Isabel's statement shot at him out of nowhere.

"I . . . What words?" Quite honestly, he had no idea what she was talking about, but it seemed better not to come out and say that.

"About a spirit of fear and all that." Her eyes landed on his, and they were fierce, their caramel color sparking into fiery embers. "I know you think it's ridiculous that I won't let Gabby in the tree house, and maybe if I had a little Jesus in my life, I wouldn't be so scared about everything, but—"

"Whoa, Isabel." He leaned forward, sitting crisscross applesauce style and leaning his elbows on his knees. "If you must know, it was a prayer for myself."

Isabel's mouth opened, but it was a few seconds before any sound came out. A few seconds during which he found himself admiring the curve of her lips.

"For yourself?" She finally said, and he worked to put her lips out of mind and pick up the thread of their conversation.

"Yeah." He scratched at a non-itchy spot on his cheek. "So I'd have the courage to apologize to you. Did you happen to get my message last night?"

She blinked at him, and he blew out a breath.

Okay, he didn't deserve for her to make this easy.

"I deleted it," she finally said.

He scooted a fraction closer to her on the blanket but then scooted right back. "I don't blame you. I'm so sorry I accused you of taking that money. I was way out of line jumping to that conclusion. Sophie says I have trust issues." He ducked his head, running a hand over his hair.

"Do you? Have trust issues?"

He looked up to find her watching him with a strange expression—almost a sort of kinship.

His laugh came out short and sharp. "Yeah. I guess you could say that. My ex-wife . . ." But she didn't want to hear all of that. And he didn't want to tell it. "Anyway. It's no excuse for the way I treated you, and I'm sorry. I hope you'll forgive me and that you'll stay on at the store."

Isabel bit her lip, drawing his attention back to her mouth.

"Please." He folded his hands and shifted so he was a tad closer to her. "If you don't, Sophie will never forgive me. I'll throw in a free bucket of cherries at harvest if you'll stay."

He could see Isabel trying to fight the grin. The moment it peeked out, he knew she had relented.

"Thank you." He only hoped his sincerity came through in the simple words.

"I didn't do it for you. I did it for the cherries." But her posture had eased, and a true smile had found its way to her lips.

Whatever the reason, he could only thank God that she'd decided to stay.

Because he was starting to believe that Isabel Small was a woman worth getting to know.

Chapter 12

"Come on, Mama. We're going to be late." Gabby popped through the door of Isabel's bedroom, dressed in her princess nightgown. Isabel had braided her daughter's hair earlier this morning too, to create more of a bedtime effect.

Gabby skidded to a stop in front of Isabel, hitting her with a disapproving look. "That's not pajamas. It's shorts and a shirt."

"It's what I sleep in, so it's pajamas." Besides, Gabby should be happy she'd agree to do this at all.

One moment, Sophie had been telling them about Hope Church's entry in the Hope Fest parade, the next Isabel had been accepting Sophie's invitation to join them in it.

She tried to deny the sneaking suspicion that she'd said yes because Tyler would be there too.

Sure, they'd had a couple more picnics together over the past week. And sure, she'd enjoyed talking to him. And sure, he made her laugh until she snorted—an unattractive sound she'd worked hard since grade school to suppress. And sure, he'd even convinced her to let Gabby go in the tree house and then proceeded to gently tease her when she called out "be careful" every three seconds.

But none of that had anything to do with the reason she'd said yes to the parade. That was simply because Gabby had never been in a parade, and she'd been so enamored with the idea that Isabel couldn't say no.

"Maybe if you put your hair in piggies." Gabby was still watching her with a critical eye.

"Pigtails?" Isabel frowned. She'd probably been Gabby's age the last time she'd worn her hair in that particular style. But she supposed it wouldn't hurt. Pulling her hair into a quick, uneven part, she snapped a rubber band around each side, wondering for the hundredth time why they'd been instructed to wear pajamas for the parade. When she'd asked, Sophie's only response had been a mysterious smile.

"Good now?"

Gabby nodded and pointed to her feet. "And wear slippers."

Isabel shook her head. She wasn't sure how long the parade route was, but she was pretty sure she didn't want to walk the whole thing in slippers. "How about I carry Bugsy instead?" Bugsy being the ratty stuffed rabbit she'd had since she was a kid—the one and only thing she'd held onto from that life. It had been her rock whenever things between her parents had gotten too heated.

"Okay," Gabby relented. "But only because we're going to be late, and I don't have time to argue with you."

Hearing her own words parroted back at her from a five-year-old made Isabel chuckle, but she quickly stifled the laugh. "I think that's my line. Now let's go before you make us late."

"Can we bring Chancy?" At the sound of his name, the dog came padding over, and both canine and girl turned puppy dog eyes on her.

"He doesn't have pajamas."

Gabby giggled. "He's a dog. Wait. I know." She dashed into her room, emerging a few seconds later with her baby blanket draped over her arm. She tossed it over Chancy's back, and the dog turned to sniff it but left it in place.

"He looks more like a superhero now, but sure. Let's bring him." She snapped the leash on the dog, who instantly pulled her to the door.

Passing the leash to Gabby, she turned to lock the door, smiling at the patter of feet as Chancy and Gabby tromped down the stairs.

As she returned her keys to her pocket, a loud crash sounded from the apartment across the hall.

Isabel jumped, her gaze landing on her neighbor's door. She'd met the young couple who lived there—Kendra and Kyle—only once, though she'd heard loud fights through the door on a few occasions.

I'm sure someone just dropped something. She struggled to push away the uneasiness, the little nudge that told her she should knock and make sure everything was all right.

"What was that, Mama?" Gabby called from the bottom of the stairs.

Isabel swallowed. What if no one had asked "what was that" when they'd heard Chancy barking that last night with Andrew? What if they'd walked on past?

"Stay down there," she called to her daughter.

In three strides, she was across the hall and knocking on the neighbors' door.

She didn't hear anything for a moment, then heavy footsteps approached the door.

Kyle stood in front of her, broad and bare chested, and Isabel averted her eyes, searching beyond him for any signs of trouble.

"Can I help you?" Kyle's voice was low and lazy.

Isabel made herself bring her eyes to his face. "Sorry. I thought I heard a crash, and I wanted to make sure everyone was okay." She hated that her voice trembled over the words.

"Everything's fine. Thanks for checking." Kyle started to close the door, but Isabel jammed her hand against it.

He gave her an appraising look that made her want to run, but she forced herself to hold her ground. "Actually, I was wondering if Kendra is home."

He lifted a slow eyebrow until it came to a neat peak. "Kendra." The bellow made Isabel jump, and he chuckled.

A petite brunette hurried into the room, dabbing at her forehead with a kitchen towel. When she noticed Isabel, she pulled the towel away and tucked it behind her back, but not before Isabel noticed the circle of blood on it.

"Are you okay?" The words were out before Isabel could consider their wisdom.

"She's fine." Kyle was still sporting that half-lazy, half-amused voice. "Just clumsy. First she drops a glass, then she hits her head on the cupboard trying to clean it up."

That was almost as good as the time Isabel had claimed she bruised her cheek walking into the bathroom door.

Isabel's gaze went to Kendra, and she hoped the other woman could read her unspoken words: *I've been there. I can help.*

But Kendra's eyes jumped to the floor.

"If you're sure you're all right . . ." *Look at me, Kendra.*

But Kendra simply nodded, eyes focused on her feet.

"Thanks again for checking." This time when Kyle closed the door, Isabel didn't try to stop him.

But she vowed that the next time she saw Kendra alone, she'd talk to her, let her know there were places she could go for help.

Isabel tried to put the incident out of her head as they stepped outside and made their way toward the parade lineup. Although the parade didn't start for over an hour yet, throngs of people already crowded the sidewalks, lined up on blankets and chairs from the curb all the way back to the shop entrances on both sides of the street. Isabel and Gabby had to walk on the road—which had been closed to motorized traffic—to get through.

Isabel's anxiety spiked, and her heart ramped itself up. The familiar fear that Andrew was hidden in the crowd, disguised among all the friendly faces, crept over her. Keeping her stuffed bunny tucked under her arm, she tightened her hold on Chancy's leash and reached for Gabby's hand, gripping it until the girl cried out.

"Sorry." Isabel forced herself to loosen her hold.

"Look, there they are." Gabby wiggled out of her grip and took off toward a large group of people.

"Gabby, wait!" Isabel's heart shot through her chest as she lunged after her daughter, but Gabby was too fast.

Thankfully, the girl came to a stop as a man in flannel pajamas peeled off from the rest of the group. Isabel's heartbeat shifted rhythms, becoming less panicky, more jittery, as she recognized Tyler.

Only because she knew it meant Gabby was safe.

Tyler greeted Gabby, and Isabel could tell he was complimenting her princess pajamas, then they both turned to wait for her. Her silly heart jittered harder, but she ignored it.

"Hey. I'm glad you made it." Tyler's smile was easy and relaxed—the smile of someone who didn't have any jittery symptoms to worry about at all.

"Thanks." She didn't know why the word came out all breathless, except the lingering anxiety over the way Gabby had taken off.

"I was talking to Chancy." Tyler hit her with a wicked grin, and she almost gave his shoulder a playful slug but pulled back at the last second.

Physical contact was a big no.

"Nice pajamas." She smirked at the red and black checkered pattern. "They make you look like a cowboy." She meant for it to be a lighthearted insult, but it came out more like a compliment.

Tyler's grin grew. "Thank you kindly, ma'am." He pretended to tip a hat. "The boys and I picked these up special for the parade."

Isabel glanced in the direction he pointed. Sure enough, Jonah and Jeremiah wore matching flannel pajamas, the only difference being that Jeremiah's were blue and Jonah's were green.

Something about the sight of the three of them dressed alike stirred Isabel.

Did those boys know how lucky they were to have a dad like that? One who took the time to build a tree house with them and wore matching pajamas in public. One who looked at them with love every single day.

"Aren't you warm?" It had to be at least eighty degrees out here. She was hot in her t-shirt and shorts.

"Sweltering." But Tyler's smile never faltered. "Come on. I'll show you the float."

He led them toward a pickup truck hitched to a large flatbed trailer. Along the way, several people greeted them—Sophie and Spencer, their twins in matching strollers, Grace, Jared and Peyton, and even a bunch of people she'd never met.

"Ta-da." Tyler held his hands out toward the trailer as if revealing a prize.

A band stood tuning their instruments at the end of the trailer closest to the truck, and Isabel recognized Nate among them.

The rest of the trailer had been decorated to look like a child's bedroom. Kids who looked to be about Gabby's age sat on a low mattress on the floor of the trailer, all talking and laughing with one another.

"I thought maybe Gabby would like to ride up there." Tyler's words were barely out before Gabby was jumping up and down, asking if she could.

But Isabel couldn't answer right away. Her eyes had caught on the sign hanging on the side of the trailer.

Yes, my soul, find rest in God; my hope comes from him. –Psalm 62:5

Those two words: *rest* and *hope*. Weren't they exactly what she'd been searching for when she moved here?

She didn't feel like she'd quite found them yet, but maybe this was a sign—a literal sign—that she would.

"Can I, Mama?" The tug on Isabel's arm brought her back to the conversation at hand.

She studied the float, gnawing her lip. There were no railings on the side, so if Gabby wasn't careful or if the truck stopped too quickly or if—

"It's safe. I promise." Tyler's gentle smile said he'd read her thoughts. "Austin is driving the truck, and I'd trust him with my life. Plus, you can walk right alongside."

Isabel nodded, relenting. "As long as you promise to—"

"Be careful," Gabby and Tyler chanted with her.

Chapter 13

Dusk dusted the lake in shades of rose as Tyler and his boys picked their way through the crowds gathered on the hill above the marina. The Hope Fest fireworks was the event of the year in their small community, and it felt like the whole town packed the broad hillside. But as Tyler's eyes roved over the crowd, he couldn't deny that he was looking for one person in particular. Or two really. He couldn't imagine Isabel without Gabby.

He was wading into dangerous territory here, Tyler knew that. He had sworn to himself that he'd never open his heart to another woman. But as he'd gotten to know Isabel a bit better over the past week, he couldn't help wanting to get closer to her. And considering how opposed to the idea he'd been before, it had to be a God-thing, didn't it?

As he spotted his parents, along with Sophie and Spencer, sitting with a large group of their friends near the gazebo, a current of disappointment swept through his middle. When he'd invited Isabel after the parade, she'd seemed less than certain about coming, but he'd hoped she might change her mind, especially if she knew he'd be here.

He frowned at himself. How presumptuous had that been? Especially considering that most of the time, far from showing interest in him, she seemed to begrudgingly tolerate him.

But then there were those other times—like when he'd made her laugh so hard she snorted and when he caught her unaware with a compliment—that he thought she might just do more than tolerate him. He'd almost let himself think she might even like him.

As he and the boys wound their way through the people covering the hillside, he resolved to put Isabel out of his mind for tonight.

Fortunately, his friends and family had spread out several large blankets, so there was plenty of room for Tyler and his twins. He greeted everyone and plopped down next to his dad, behind Sophie.

His sister-in-law glanced at him over her shoulder, and instead of saying "hi" as he'd intended, what came out was, "Isabel decided not to come?"

Sophie smirked. "Hello to you too. And yes, she's here. She just went to get some cotton candy for Gabby. Here they come." She nodded past Tyler's shoulder, and he managed to resist turning around for a full two seconds.

Maybe it was the pigtails, or maybe it was the smile that sat easy on her lips, or maybe it was the reflection of the lowering sun off her cheeks, but she looked different tonight. Happier. Less on guard. More at peace.

She wore the look well.

"Ah, is this the famous Isabel who would be perfect for Tyler?" Dad elbowed him, and Tyler ignored Sophie's peal of laughter. Apparently his sister-in-law had been talking.

"I'm not looking for someone who would be perfect for me." His protest wasn't nearly as convincing as he'd hoped.

"The very one." Sophie waved to Isabel to make sure she saw them, and apparently Chancy recognized her because he pulled Isabel forward, forcing her to half-jog, half-leap over the people between them and the blanket.

"She's a dog person. Gotta love that." Dad's voice boomed, and Tyler shushed him as Isabel reached them, out of breath but laughing.

"Hey." Tyler was careful to direct his greeting at Gabby, who settled onto the blanket next to him, Isabel sinking down on her daughter's other side.

Gabby grinned at him, her face half-buried in her cotton candy. Chancy leaped over Gabby and greeted Tyler with a lick on the chin.

"Looks like the dog likes you, anyway." Dad nudged him, and Tyler barely held back his groan.

Dad leaned past him, holding out a hand to Isabel. "Nice to meet you, Isabel. I've heard a lot about you."

Isabel shook Dad's hand, shooting Tyler a quick questioning look.

"This is my dad, Marcus Weston." Tyler made the introduction begrudgingly, praying Dad would be content to leave it at that. "And my mom, Mary."

Mom offered Isabel a friendly wave, though Tyler was amazed she resisted climbing over everyone to engulf her in a hug. Thank goodness for large crowds and sticky bodies.

"Two things you need to know about my son," Dad started, ignoring the groan Tyler didn't hold back this time. "One: he doesn't believe in peanut butter."

"Dad—" Tyler could only imagine what number two would be. The fact that he'd played with G.I. Joes until he was fifteen maybe. Or that he hadn't learned to ride a bike until he was ten. Or that he had a lifelong fear of thunderstorms.

"And two—" Dad ignored the warning finger Tyler lifted to stop him. "He's one of the two best men you'll ever meet."

"Dad—" But that one caught him completely off guard, and all he could do was stare at Gabby's cotton candy as Dad clapped a hand to his shoulder.

After a second, he found the courage to raise his eyes to Isabel. She scrutinized him, a slightly perplexed smile working its way across her lips. "You don't believe in peanut butter?"

"It's not so much that I don't believe in it." Tyler leaned back on his hands. "More that I don't think it's right. Too sticky."

"Hey, Isabel." Sophie turned to interrupt their conversation, handing Isabel her phone. "Look at this great picture of you and Gabby at the parade."

Tyler glanced across Gabby to look at the screen. It was a shot of Isabel walking next to the float, wearing the most relaxed expression he'd seen on her yet, her eyes trained on her daughter. For her part, Gabby's mouth was open, clearly singing, her eyes bright.

"Is this—" Isabel lifted a finger to scroll. "Did you find this on social media?"

"Yep. Our church's account. I can forward it to you if you want."

"Oh. I don't need—"

But her answer was interrupted by a loud boom, followed by ribbons of light crackling above them.

Gabby let out a loud cheer, but Chancy sprang to his feet and shot off the blanket.

Tyler grabbed for the dog's collar but was too slow. Chancy raced through the crowd, leaping over reclined bodies and knocking into camp chairs.

"Chancy, come back." Isabel's cry was sharp and scared as she pushed to her feet and took off after the dog, telling a crying Gabby to stay put.

Tyler was already on his feet too. "We'll catch him," he promised Gabby, praying it was a promise he'd be able to keep.

Doing his best to apologize as he tripped over people and trampled on their blankets, he attempted to keep one eye on the dog and the other on Isabel.

But by the time he'd reached the edge of the crowd, Isabel had drawn up short, and Chancy was nowhere in sight.

"Which way did he go?" Tyler puffed.

"I don't know." Isabel's voice skirted the edge of panic.

"It's okay. We'll find him." Tyler scanned the parking lot below them, the darkened store fronts above them, and the small area of woods that lined the beach.

"I was so stupid to bring him." Isabel sounded near tears. "We can't lose him."

Tyler gave her forearm a quick squeeze, not allowing himself to linger over the sensation of her smooth skin under his fingertips. "My money is on those trees over there. Let's spread out a little so we can cover more ground."

Isabel nodded and moved about twenty yards away from him. They both called the dog's name again and again, sometimes unintentionally calling at the same time, their voices mixing in a pleasant harmony.

By the time they came to the end of the trees, there was still no sign of the dog.

"Maybe he went another way." Tyler tried to sound upbeat and sure. "Let's double back."

Isabel nodded, her lips pressed tight. This time, Tyler was the only one calling for the dog.

As they returned to where they'd started searching, Tyler examined every possible direction the dog could have gone.

"I need to go check on Gabby," Isabel murmured.

"I'll keep looking." He moved down the street toward the closed stores. Maybe the dog was hunkering down in one of the alleys that had been converted into a flower garden. Fireworks continued to burst above him, washing the ground in color, then returning it to shadows, but Tyler didn't look up. He couldn't risk missing Chancy.

For half a second, he imagined himself finding Chancy, imagined the gratitude in Isabel's eyes. The hug she'd give him.

But fifteen minutes later, he had to let go of that fantasy. Either Chancy was very good at hide-and-seek, or he wasn't here either.

Tyler wasn't sure if he dreaded Isabel's or Gabby's disappointment more as he made his way back to the marina. The sky burst into sound, and Tyler lifted his head to watch the finale. It had always been his favorite part of the show, but within seconds, it was over. Aside from muted applause and a few whistles that drifted from the marina, silence reigned.

When he finally reached the hillside again, it had largely cleared. There was still a crowd around the gazebo, though, and Tyler made his way in that direction, not noticing until he was a few feet away that among the two-legged people standing there was a four-legged dog.

"Chancy!"

The dog wagged its tail and sprang for him, but Isabel gripped his leash tightly, and Chancy came up short.

Still, he went nuts licking Tyler's hand the moment Tyler stepped close enough.

"I tried to text you." Isabel sounded apologetic.

"Where'd you find him?"

"Funny story." Isabel grimaced. "Apparently he came right back here after we left to search for him. Your dad snagged his collar and managed to calm him down. I guess the loud noise scared him, the big chicken. He sat with his tail between his legs for the whole show."

"Troublemaker." But Tyler bent to pet the dog's head. Truth was, he'd grown fairly fond of the creature. "I'm glad you made it back."

"I feel terrible." Isabel slid her hand up and down on the leash. "You missed the entire fireworks show."

Tyler shrugged. "No biggie."

"It is a biggie." Isabel smirked around the word. "I want to make it up to you somehow."

"Come biking with us tomorrow." The invitation was out before he could think it through. He'd been planning for it to be just him and the boys. But he was sure the twins wouldn't mind having Isabel and Gabby along.

"Biking?" Isabel wrinkled her nose as if she'd never heard the word.

"Yeah. You know, mechanical device. Powered by pedals."

She swatted at the air in front of him with a laugh that made him want to keep teasing. "I know what a bike is. But I don't have one. Haven't ridden in years."

"You could ride Sophie's. She won't mind. And riding a bike is riding a bike. You don't forget how."

"What about Gabby? She doesn't have a bike either. And she can't ride a two-wheeler yet."

"I have a pull-behind trailer she can sit in." Before she could protest, he added, "It's one hundred percent safe. I even have a helmet she can use."

He waited for her next excuse, ready to lob it back at her.

But the corners of her mouth lifted. "Biking might be fun."

Chapter 14

B^{*lue.*}

Of course the sky would be a blinding blue today.

Isabel readjusted her sunglasses as she turned into Hidden Blossom's driveway.

She'd half-hoped to wake up and find it raining, so she would have an excuse to get out of biking with Tyler and his boys.

She'd spent half the night pondering what had led her to agree in the first place. She was almost convinced it was because she'd promised herself she'd give Gabby as normal a life as possible—and nothing seemed more normal than a bike ride.

And then there was the fact that Tyler had spent his entire night running around chasing after her dog, so she did kind of owe him.

Not to mention that it gives you the chance to spend the day with him.

She knocked the thought aside, but her tummy swirled as she parked in his driveway.

"I can't wait! I can't wait! I can't wait!" Gabby was out of the car and dancing in place before Isabel had her seat belt off.

With only a little less outward enthusiasm than her daughter, Isabel stepped out of the car. She was tempted to join Gabby in skipping toward the front door but forced her feet to walk instead.

Gabby pressed the doorbell, and they waited, Isabel working to get her conflicted feelings under control. It was just a bike ride. With three kids along—definitely nothing anyone could misconstrue.

Least of all her heart.

Gabby pressed the doorbell again while Isabel studied the silent house and pulled out her phone to check if Tyler had sent a message.

But the only notification was for the social media post Sophie had promised to forward her. Isabel still hadn't figured out what to do about that. It hadn't occurred to her when she'd agreed to be in the parade that she could be putting herself or her daughter at risk. What if Andrew saw the post? What if it led him straight to them?

The likelihood of that was minuscule, she knew. What were the chances that Andrew would see a post from this tiny church in this tiny town so far from him? But still, she'd have to be more careful from now on.

She clicked off her phone, turning back to the obviously empty house.

Tyler had said to meet them here, hadn't he? Maybe she'd gotten the time wrong. Or the day.

Or maybe you're an idiot to think that anyone besides me would bother with you. The subtle hiss of Andrew's voice slinked through her head and roped around her heart, cinching tight. *How many times did I tell you that you were lucky to have me? That no one else could love you?*

But she didn't want Tyler to love her. She didn't need anyone to love her. All she wanted was to take her daughter on her first-ever bike ride.

"There they are!" Gabby's yell drew Isabel's eyes down the driveway, where a minivan was barreling toward them, a fine fog of dust billowing behind it.

Isabel let out a breath, the swirling in her belly resuming. Only because she was relieved she wouldn't have to let Gabby down.

The sun glinting off Tyler's glasses hid his eyes from her, but the way he and the boys were smiling and waving eased her heart a tad more. They hadn't been trying to ditch her and Gabby.

The moment the van was parked, all three of them jumped out.

"I'm so sorry. Church ran late this morning, and then we . . ." Tyler stopped in front of her, peering at her face. "What's wrong?"

Isabel shook her head. *Stop staring.*

With effort, she pulled her eyes off his dress shirt and tie. She'd rarely seen him in anything aside from shorts and a t-shirt or polo. The dress clothes made him look . . . a little too much like Andrew, who never left the house without a tie.

"Sorry. Nothing's wrong," she managed to croak.

"Good. Give us ten minutes to change, and we'll be ready to go."

Isabel nodded mutely, but Gabby eyed the boys. "Why are you dressed so fancy? Were you playing tea party?"

Isabel couldn't help the snorting laugh that escaped. Trust her daughter to lighten the mood.

"We were at church." Jonah wrinkled his nose as if the very idea of a tea party was repulsive. Which Isabel supposed it was for a nine-year-old boy.

"Oh. Can I come next time? I like to get fancy."

It seemed to Isabel that Tyler was avoiding her eyes, as if he could sense how she'd feel about that. Instead, he smiled at Gabby. "We'd love to have you come along next time. And you could even go to Sunday school." He lowered his voice to a conspiratorial whisper. "Sometimes they have snacks there."

"I love school. And snacks. Please can we go, Mama?" Gabby wrapped her arms around Isabel's waist as a laughing Tyler disappeared into the house.

She aimed a glare at his back. It was totally not fair to use Gabby against her like that.

"We'll see" was all she felt comfortable answering Gabby.

True to their word, ten minutes later Tyler and the twins emerged from the house, Tyler looking much more like himself in a pair of cargo shorts and a gray t-shirt that looked soft enough to touch.

Not that she wanted to touch it.

Isabel's face heated, and she turned away before anyone could notice, pretending to scan the orchard. "So where are we going?"

"There's a great trail about a mile down the road." Tyler led them toward the pole shed. He pointed out Sophie's bike and helmet, then started attaching a covered bike trailer to his own bike.

"I can pull that." The thought of entrusting Gabby's safety to someone else—even Tyler—was a little unnerving.

But Tyler fastened the last pin on the trailer and stood. "Considering you haven't ridden a bike in years, she's probably safer with me. Besides, my bike has the attachment."

He passed Gabby a helmet, then helped her fasten it.

Unable to argue, Isabel worked the straps of her own helmet, then stepped closer to examine Gabby's.

"Don't trust me?" Tyler's voice held only a note of serious under the teasing.

Isabel gave her daughter's helmet a good tug. When she was certain it wouldn't fall off, she turned to Tyler. "Just double-checking."

Tyler nodded at her helmet. "Your straps need to be tightened."

Isabel reached up, feeling for the end of the strap, but when she tried to adjust it, it didn't budge.

"Here, let me." Tyler lifted his hands to the straps. His fingers accidentally brushed Isabel's chin, and she held her breath even as her heart decided to be a wild clodhopper all over her chest. Again the heat rose to her face.

Thankfully, Tyler didn't seem to notice either the touch or her reaction.

"There." He rocked the helmet gently. "All set."

Isabel swallowed and nodded, not trusting her voice to sound normal if she attempted to talk.

It was only the close contact, she told herself. She would have reacted that way to anyone who had touched her.

Except it hadn't been a reaction of fear.

It had felt more like . . . longing.

Need, even.

She dismissed the thought. She neither longed for nor needed anyone.

Jonah and Jeremiah were already on their bikes, and after buckling Gabby into the trailer under Isabel's watchful eye, Tyler slung his leg over his bike.

They all watched Isabel, waiting.

She eyed Sophie's bike, her mouth reaching Sahara levels of dryness.

It had been at least fifteen years since she'd been on one of these.

"It's okay." Tyler's voice was light, but Isabel could hear the reassurance in it. "It's just like riding a bike."

"Ha ha." Isabel gave him her best eye roll but threw a leg over the seat and perched one foot on the pedals.

She eyed Tyler, with Gabby behind him. "You're sure you'll be—"

"Careful, yes." The smile lines around Tyler's eyes stood out as he lifted his feet to the pedals and took off, leaving Isabel no choice but to follow.

She wobbled a time or two, but once she found her balance, the movement felt familiar and reassuring.

"Good job, Mama," Gabby called, peering out the back of the trailer.

Isabel pushed the pedals faster, pulling up even with Tyler. By the time they reached the end of Hidden Blossom's driveway, she felt like she'd never stopped riding.

But the feeling she got in her stomach when he looked at her? That feeling was nothing like the familiarity of riding a bike. It was new and uncertain and scary.

And maybe just a little bit exciting.

His smile landed on her again, lifting from his mouth all the way to his eyes.

Make that more than a little bit exciting.

Things that seem too good to be true usually are, she reminded herself, looking away from that smile. *Even men.*

Especially men.

He really had to stop looking over at Isabel. For one thing, she'd never forgive him if his inattentiveness to the trail caused him to crash while pulling her daughter. And for another, every time he looked over at her, that *feeling* swept over him. The one that said his interest in her was growing beyond friendship.

And it sure didn't help, the way she was smiling today. Somehow, it made it impossible for him to keep a straight face.

"How far do you want to go?" He didn't have to raise his voice much, since she was easily keeping pace with him—or, fine, maybe he had slowed his typical pace so they could ride next to each other.

The boys were a decent distance ahead, but Tyler could still see them.

"How far does the trail go?"

"About twelve hundred miles." Tyler just managed to keep the smirk off his lips as she gasped.

"You're kidding right?"

He shook his head. "Nope. It starts here, goes southwest to the Illinois border, turns straight north, and then jogs to the Mississippi River. I've always thought it would be kind of fun to bike the whole thing someday." He'd gone so far as to investigate camp sites along the route, before he'd decided it'd have to wait until the boys were older.

"That's— Wow. That would be an adventure." Isabel glanced back at Gabby. "Do me a favor and don't mention that to Gabby quite yet. I'm not sure my legs would make it that far today."

"Fair enough." Tyler's heart bounced. Did that mean she'd consider it someday? He made himself rein in his hope—he was reading way too much into that simple answer. "There's a clearing ahead. How about we stop there to have some lunch, then head back?"

Isabel nodded her agreement, and half an hour later, after a peaceful lunch, the kids were running around the clearing, playing yet another game of Gabby's invention. Tyler reclined on the picnic blanket he'd packed, closing his eyes against the sun and patting his stomach. "I do make a mean ham sandwich, if I do say so myself."

"Yeah." Isabel's voice came from slightly above him. "Though I sure could have gone for some peanut butter."

Tyler snorted. "You pack the picnic next time then." His grin straightened as he realized what he'd said. He hadn't meant there would necessarily be a next time. Though as the moments went by, he was hoping more and more that there would be.

"Maybe I will." Isabel's easy answer shouldn't have sent his heart scampering all over the place like that.

"So I don't think I ever asked—" He rolled over onto his stomach and propped himself on his elbows. "What brought you to Hope Springs?"

Though he wasn't looking at her, he could feel the shift—like a cloud had covered the sun, though the landscape was as bright as ever.

"It sounded like a nice place."

It was a canned answer, and he considered calling her out on it.

But one glance over at her said that would be a bad idea. She'd gone absolutely rigid, her fingers shredding the stem of the flower Gabby had picked for her earlier.

"And is it?" he risked asking. "Nice?"

"It's growing on me."

Not exactly a glowing endorsement, but it would have to do.

"You grew up in Texas though?"

She shook her head. "Montana. I moved to Texas after I left home."

"Are your parents still in Montana then?"

Uh-oh. Wrong question.

If he could rewind and take it back, he would.

Her lips had drawn tight, causing little lines to stand out around them, and her hands crushed what remained of the poor flower.

"My dad died a few years ago."

"Oh, I'm sorry." *Smart move, Tyler.*

"Don't be." Her voice was hard, and she pushed to her feet. "My family wasn't exactly like yours."

"And what is my family like?" He worked to keep the defensive note out of his voice. Heaven knew he'd had his share of issues with his family over the years, but when it came down to it, they were his family, and he wouldn't trade them for anything.

"You're all so . . ." Isabel waved her hand as if searching for the right word, and Tyler tensed. "Brady Bunch."

His tension unspooled on a laugh. If that was the worst anyone could say of his family, he'd take it. "Fair enough. What about your mom? Still around?"

Isabel shrugged, bending to pick up the remnants of the kids' lunches still scattered on the blanket. Tyler pushed to his knees to help her.

"I think so," she said. "We don't stay in touch."

"Why not?" He didn't want to pry, but she seemed to be carrying such a burden, and he just wanted to help.

She studied him for a long heartbeat, as if trying to decide if she could trust him.

But he apparently came up lacking, because she shook her head and said, "We just don't."

"You should contact her." He didn't mean to tell her what to do, but he'd found out the hard way what life without family was like.

Her eyes hardened, and she reached to pick up the blanket, sending him scrambling off it. "Spoken like a true member of the Brady Bunch."

"I cut myself off from my family for ten years." Tyler's confession brought her head up, shock scribbled across the furrows in her brow.

"Not as Brady Bunch as you thought, huh?" Regret hung on his words. How many times had he wished he could go back and redo that time in his life? Set different priorities?

"Why?"

He pondered the question. He'd never really taken the time to examine why he'd done what he'd done. He supposed he was afraid to find out the answer would reveal some ugliness in his own character.

"My dad had always taken it for granted that I would run the orchard one day," he said finally. "I grew up spending my weekends helping him, my entire summers devoted to working with him."

"And you didn't like it?"

Tyler considered. "Actually, I never minded the work. But it was the sense of responsibility, you know? The feeling that I didn't have a choice and this was going to be the rest of my life."

Isabel nodded, her eyes trained on him.

He didn't know why he was telling her this, but he did know he didn't want to stop. "My senior year of high school, Dad and I got in a big fight, and I basically told him what he could do with his orchard." The familiar heaviness of shame washed over him, though Dad had long since given Tyler his forgiveness. "Anyway, the moment I graduated, I took off for college, and then Julia and I were married, and then my dad had a heart attack . . ."

"That's why you came back." Understanding and sympathy and maybe even a little admiration bloomed on Isabel's face.

Shame pressed hard on his chest. "Not the first time. I didn't even come back to visit. I called. Once, I think." Yes, there was definitely ugliness to this story. To who he'd been then. "It wasn't until his second heart attack, right after Julia left me, that I came back. So it was more selfish than anything else." He'd spent too many nights lying awake, wondering what would have happened if he hadn't come back, if his dad hadn't made it.

All he could do was thank God he'd gotten a second chance.

And try to get Isabel to see the importance of a second chance too. "Promise me you'll at least think about calling your mom."

Isabel folded the blanket and passed it to him. "No promises." But her voice had lost just enough of its hard edge to give him hope.

He couldn't press the subject any further now, though, as the kids ran up to them, all three loading Isabel down with flowers.

"What about me? What's a guy gotta do to get some flowers around here?" Tyler mock protested, although he'd give up all the flowers in the world to see that easiness that had returned to her face.

"Boys don't like flowers," Gabby protested with a giggle.

But Tyler gave an emphatic nod. "Common misconception. Those purple ones are my favorite."

"Just a minute." Gabby slipped a few feet away and bent to pluck another flower, then returned and handed it to him. "For you."

Oh boy. If Tyler's heart hadn't already been completely melted by Isabel, it didn't stand a chance against Gabby.

He broke off the stem of the flower, then lifted it to his ear, tucking it behind the bow of his glasses. "How do I look?"

Jonah and Jeremiah groaned, but Tyler ignored them, his heart flipping at Isabel's and Gabby's matching smiles. If he could see those smiles every day for the rest of his life, he'd be a happy man.

Whoa, there, mister. Every day for the rest of your life is a little extreme. Let's take it one day at a time, okay?

As they packed up and got back on their bikes, he deliberately kept his eyes off their smiles.

On the trail, he and Isabel rode side by side in silence, though he could hear Isabel breathing as she worked to keep up. Halfway back, he turned toward her and lifted an eyebrow. "Race?"

Before she could answer, he put on a burst of speed, easily pulling ahead.

"Hey." Her half-laughing shout carried to him. "No fair."

But he didn't slow. He had to put some distance between them before he lost his mind and did something crazy like let himself fall in love again.

After a quarter mile, he chanced a peek over his shoulder. Isabel had fallen a few bike lengths behind, but she was pedaling fast, her mouth set. Tyler faced forward to watch the trail again, grunting as they came to a steep uphill. Pulling Gabby would slow him down pretty sharply. He'd be lucky if Isabel didn't pass him. He stood on the pedals to get more leverage, but by the time they reached the top of the hill, he could hear Isabel only a few feet behind him.

The trail descended on a wicked curve. Tyler had slid out here once before and had ended up with a nasty scrape down his shin.

He gently applied his brakes, calling over his shoulder, "Be careful on this downhill."

But Isabel surged in front of him. There was a nasty screech as she applied her brakes, and he saw the moment her wheels locked up. There was nothing he could do as her back wheel skidded out from under her, tipping the bike onto its side and spilling Isabel to the ground.

"Mama!" Gabby's frightened cry spurred Isabel to push at the bike, even though every nerve in her body was zinging.

"I'm okay," she managed to grit out, though she was definitely on the losing end of this wrestling match with the bike.

Footsteps skidded through the gravel, and then the bike was off her. She should thank Tyler, but right now, her only goal was to get to Gabby, whose worry had risen to a wail. Ignoring the protest from her hip, she sprang to her feet and rushed to the bike trailer to unbuckle Gabby. But she winced at the sting of the seat belt against her shredded palms.

Somehow, Tyler was at her side, and catching her hands in his, he gently tugged her out of the way. "I'll get it."

In two seconds, he had the buckle undone, and Gabby's arms were glued around Isabel's waist. She stroked her daughter's hair with the back of her hand so she wouldn't dirty it with the blood that oozed from her palms.

Tyler grabbed Isabel's hands to examine them. "You got scraped up pretty good." He stepped back, his eyes traveling to her leg. "Your knee is bleeding too. We need to get you cleaned up."

He moved to the back of the bike trailer and rummaged around behind the seat, digging out a small bag and holding it up in triumph.

Isabel raised an eyebrow. She wouldn't have expected him to be so prepared. "A first aid kit?"

Tyler grinned. "I'm more safety conscious than you give me credit for."

"Hey, I told you to pack that." The boys had ridden back to check on them, and Jonah aimed an accusing finger at his father.

"Busted," Tyler muttered, and somehow, even through the smarting pain and the worry over Gabby, Isabel managed to laugh.

She held out a hand for the kit, but Tyler moved it away from her. "Step into my office, and I'll get you patched up." He gestured to a fallen log at the side of the trail.

Isabel watched him for a minute. Surely she could take care of her own injuries. Had been doing it for years.

But she had to concede that it'd be difficult to bandage her own hands. She settled onto the log, sitting with her knee outstretched and her palms up.

Tyler grabbed his water bottle off his bike and uncapped it, then squatted in front of her and poured a slow stream over her palms. Then he bunched up the corner of his shirt and lifted it to her hand. It took her a moment to realize what he was doing.

"Oh, don't, you're going to wreck—"

But he'd already used his shirt to brush away the first pebble. A light stain of her blood darkened the corner of the fabric.

"Your shirt," she finished.

"I'm sorry. I shouldn't have goaded you into racing." Tyler's words were outlined in regret, and her heart bobbled, not because of the words, but because of the sincerity in his eyes. How many times had Andrew said he was sorry for hurting her? But never once had he looked at her like this.

"I'm the one who let myself be goaded." She took a lighthearted tone, so he wouldn't see how much his apology meant to her.

Tyler finished cleaning the scrapes, then pulled out an antibiotic spray. "This is probably going to sting."

She drew in a sharp breath as the cool medicine hit her skin.

"Sorry." Tyler winced too. "There. Now we just have to bandage it up." He pulled out a roll of gauze and started to wrap it around her hand.

Isabel sniffed and blinked hard. No one in her life had ever taken care of her like this.

"I'm sorry." Tyler's voice was low, and he lifted his eyes to meet hers. "I'm being as careful as I can. Does it hurt a lot?"

She could only nod. Because there was no way she could tell him it wasn't the sting that had caused her reaction. It was him. The way he'd winced, like it hurt him to see her in pain—that was the same way she felt whenever Gabby got hurt.

Only she couldn't remember anyone ever feeling that way for her sake.

Tyler finished the bandages, then helped her up. "Do you think you can ride? Otherwise, I can walk both bikes."

"I can ride." Isabel moved to the bike, keeping her eyes off Tyler.

Because he was being too nice to her. Too tender.

And if he didn't stop, she was going to be tempted to break all her rules.

Chapter 15

"**S**trike three!"

Isabel stood with the rest of the crowd to cheer as Tyler's team surged from the outfield to surround him.

He lifted Gabby, whom he'd dubbed honorary assistant coach and allowed to sit on the bench with him, to his shoulders.

Isabel waved to her daughter, suppressing the instinct to call out to Tyler to be careful. She knew he'd never let her daughter get hurt. And that look of sheer elation on Gabby's face right now—she'd do nearly anything to keep that expression there permanently.

Even risk your own heart?

She dodged the question. That wasn't an issue. She'd spent plenty of time with Tyler in the two weeks since their bike ride, and he hadn't once come anywhere close to asking her out—or even indicating he was interested in her that way.

Thankfully.

In fact, they hadn't been alone together once since then that she could recall. At the orchard, Sophie was always around, a whole slew of friends always showed up for the twins' baseball games, and they'd gone to the county fair with Tyler's whole family, including Spencer and Sophie and their twins, as well as Tyler's parents. She couldn't deny that she enjoyed watching Tyler interact with his friends and family. It was clear that every last one of them respected him and looked up to him. And he, in turn, never hid the fact that he cared about each of them.

"Hey." The smile Tyler wore as he walked up to their group threatened to ignite a smile on her own face as well. "Who's up for some ice cream?"

"Sure." The answer slipped off her tongue before Isabel had time to make a conscious decision. Only because she was craving some ice cream, clearly.

"We have to get the twins to bed," Sophie jumped in.

"Yeah, we should get Hope to bed too." Jade scooped up her daughter.

"It's only—" Dan started, but Jade grabbed her husband's elbow and steered him toward the parking lot. Isabel smiled as Dan repositioned his arm around his wife's shoulders. Much as she'd tried not to, she really did like the pastor and his wife, even if she had to work to dodge their—and everyone else's—invitations to church from time to time.

"Well, I could go for some ice cream." Tyler's dad rubbed his stomach. "Been too long since I've been to the Chocolate Chicken."

"Sorry, dear." Tyler's mom gave a quick head shake. "Sophie and Spencer wanted to show us that thing."

"What thing?" Tyler's dad wrinkled his brow at his wife.

"That *thing*." Tyler's mom tilted her head to the side, and after staring at her blankly for a moment, his dad shrugged and let his wife lead him away.

Isabel glanced from Tyler to the dissipating crowd. Had he arranged that little disappearing act?

Don't flatter yourself. Andrew's voice, which had fallen nearly silent for the past couple weeks, flared as a nervous wave went through her belly.

She was sure she wasn't imagining the slight sheepishness to Tyler's grin. "Looks like it's just the five of us. You still want to go?"

Isabel pretended to debate, but now that Gabby had heard the words ice cream, there was really no way out of it. Oddly, Isabel was more than a little happy about that.

The baseball diamond was only a few blocks from the Chocolate Chicken, so they decided to walk, Gabby and the boys running ahead. The evening had cooled a little, though it was still plenty sticky. Isabel grabbed the ponytail holder she always kept on her wrist and pulled her hair into a quick bun. It was likely a ridiculous mess, but at least it kept her neck cooler.

When she lowered her arms, Tyler was watching her.

"What?" She fluttered her fingers over her hair. Was it that bad?

"Nothing. You just look really pretty like that. I mean, not that you don't usually—I mean, you always—" He fumbled to a stop with a self-deprecating laugh. "Clearly I'm not very good at this."

"No, you're great. I mean, I think you're— Well, you have—" Oh brother. Clearly neither was she.

Thankfully, they reached the Chocolate Chicken before either of them could stumble over more awkward comments. Jonah held the door for everyone, and Isabel couldn't help but think as she thanked him that these two boys were a wonderful reflection of their father.

She moved to the counter to study the ice cream flavors as Tyler ordered for himself, the boys, and Gabby.

"Take your time," he encouraged. "It's an important decision."

Isabel smirked at him, then stepped to the register. "I'll have a single scoop of vanilla in a dish."

"Wait, wait, wait." Tyler held up a hand to stop the high school kid dishing out the ice cream. "You did not just spend twenty minutes studying that list to choose vanilla. Live a little."

"It was five minutes." Isabel stuck her tongue out at him. But he wasn't wrong that there was a flavor calling to her. "But fine. I'll have a scoop of strawberry river."

"That's better. And make it a double in a waffle cone," Tyler directed the kid behind the counter.

Isabel rolled her eyes. She supposed she could go along with that, especially since it did sound rather heavenly.

With her first lick, her eyes closed of their own accord, the sweet tang of the strawberries mixing perfectly with the cool smoothness of the ice cream.

"See?" Tyler nudged her, and she opened her eyes to find him smiling. "Sometimes you have to be open to something new."

She studied him, searching for a double meaning. But there didn't appear to be one.

"Can we go eat these in the park?" Jeremiah licked at a drip about to escape the side of his cone.

Tyler gave her a questioning look, and she nodded. The park sounded like a perfect way to end the night.

They stepped outside, Jonah and Jeremiah each moving to one edge of the sidewalk to make room for Gabby between them. That, even more than walking next to Tyler, made her heart flip upside down and forget how to right itself.

Because it felt like Gabby *belonged* here. Like they both did. But that was only going to make it harder when they left.

Unless you don't leave.

The thought had been creeping its way into her head more and more lately. She had no choice but to ignore it.

They couldn't stay.

"What are you thinking?" Tyler's question caught her out, and she shook her head.

"I was just thinking that you were right about the ice cream. It was so worth it."

Tyler cast his eyes over her, as if trying to decide if that was what she'd really been thinking.

Fortunately, whatever conclusion he came to, he seemed content to let it go.

"Did you call your mom yet?"

Too bad letting it go meant he'd decided to focus on his new favorite topic.

She couldn't remember the last time she'd seen him that he hadn't asked.

She gave a quick head shake. He knew by now that she didn't want to talk about it.

"You have to trust me on this." It was about the thirtieth time he'd told her that. "You'll feel better if you do it."

But Isabel highly doubted that. Because every time she'd pulled her phone out of her pocket with the intention of following his advice, a sick feeling had churned her stomach. A feeling that said all the hurt of the past she'd worked so hard to bury would only come surging to the surface the moment she heard her mom's voice. It would be just one more reminder that her mom hadn't loved her enough to leave her dad. One more reminder that she'd almost doomed Gabby to the same life.

"We'll see," she muttered to appease Tyler.

Apparently content to let it go at that—for now—Tyler led her along a flower-lined path toward the gazebo perched at the top of the hill. Gabby and the boys, who had all apparently inhaled their ice cream, aimed for the park at the bottom of the hill.

Isabel watched them, trying to hold back the words perched on her tongue. But it was no use. "Be careful, Gabby!"

Gabby turned and gave her a quick wave, then set off at lightning speed for the jungle gym.

Next to her, Tyler was chuckling softly.

"What?" She lifted the hand without an ice cream cone to her hip. But she already knew what.

"Those are your favorite words, aren't they?"

Isabel shrugged. She didn't see anything wrong with wanting to keep her daughter safe. And it was a bigger job than she ever could have known she was signing up for. "Don't you ever worry?"

Tyler popped the last bite of his cone into his mouth and stepped into the gazebo, leaning his forearms on the edge of the wall that rose halfway up its height, his gaze traveling to his boys.

Isabel leaned her hip against the wall, still licking her ice cream.

"When Julia first left, I was terrified all the time. I was sure I was going to feed the boys wrong, or I'd forget to put them in their car seat, or they'd roll off the changing table." He laughed, but Isabel nodded. She'd had all those same fears, and they'd only grown as Gabby had gotten older. What if she ran into traffic? Or took candy from a stranger? What if Andrew found her?

"But you don't worry anymore?" Maybe he could tell her the secret. Show her how to let go of all this fear.

"Sometimes, yeah. But I've learned that worry only gives us the illusion of control. But it's a lie. Because the only one in control is God. And somehow, he loves my boys even more than I do. So if he's watching over them and he holds their lives in his hands, what good is my worrying going to do?" He paused, giving her an uncertain look. "Would you mind if I shared a verse from the Bible with you? I've always found it comforting when I'm tempted to worry."

She wanted to say no. But something in her heart cried out to hear reassurance—even if it was from the Bible.

"Okay," she whispered.

"Yeah?" Tyler's smile glowed. "It's from Matthew chapter six. Jesus is talking to a group of his followers, and he tells them, 'Look at the birds of the air.' He says the birds don't spend all their time working and worrying, and yet he takes care of them and feeds them. And then he goes on to say—" Tyler turned to her, his eyes warm, inviting. "'Are you not

541

much more valuable than they? Can any one of you by worrying add a single hour to your life?'" He paused, watching her. "Does that make you feel any better?"

Isabel wanted to say yes, for his sake. But saying "do not worry" and actually not worrying were two very different things. And just because Tyler said God cared about her and Gabby didn't mean it was true. Because God sure hadn't done anything to show them that care so far.

He brought you here.

The voice was a soothing whisper in her head. A voice she wanted to give in to.

"I'll try to let it" was the best she could offer Tyler.

"Fair enough." He didn't seem deterred by her less-than-enthusiastic response. If anything, he seemed more optimistic than ever.

Which probably made it a bad time to ask him this question. But she couldn't stop herself. "What happened with you and your ex? You said she walked out on you. Why?"

She cringed, not believing she'd dared to ask something so personal.

But a worry had been scraping at the back of her mind since they'd met—if Tyler was really the good guy he seemed to be, why would his wife have left? From where she stood, any woman would be lucky to have a man like this.

But that was only based on what she'd seen. And it was what she may not have seen that scared her.

Tyler rubbed a hand over his jaw, his gaze focused on the lake.

"Never mind. You don't—" She'd had no right to ask.

"You have no idea how many times I've asked myself that question." He studied his hands as if they might have the answer. "All I know is one day I came home, and she had a suitcase packed. Said the boys were napping and she was leaving. I thought she meant on a trip." He gave an ironic laugh that made Isabel want to reach for him.

But she didn't.

"Turned out, she'd met someone else. Had been seeing him for almost a year already." His jaw hardened. "I think that was the hardest part. Knowing she'd lied to me all that time. I felt so . . . betrayed."

"But you got custody of the boys."

"I did." The hardness in his jaw eased. "She didn't want custody. And I thank God for that every day." He gazed toward the playground, where the boys and Gabby appeared to be playing tag. "Actually, I feel kind of sorry for her, for what she's missed out on. These two guys are pretty awesome." He cleared his throat and looked away, but not before Isabel detected a sheen of emotion in his eyes.

"You've done a good job with them." She stepped closer to him, though she was careful not to brush his arm with hers.

"Thanks." Tyler bumped her shoulder with his, and waves of warmth went through her at the contact.

"What about Gabby's father?" He said it quietly, but the question pulled her upright, away from him.

"What about him?"

"Was he ever in the picture? Were you married? Does he see Gabby?"

She chomped her lip hard enough to taste blood. Part of her wanted to trust Tyler with the truth, but the other part of her—the practical part, the part that worried day after day that Andrew would find them—said it wasn't safe.

"We were married." Maybe that would be enough.

But Tyler looked at her, clearly waiting for more.

"He died before Gabby was born." The lie slipped out even as Isabel tried to convince herself it wasn't really a lie. The Andrew she'd thought she'd married—the one who had called her beautiful and charmed her with his expensive cars and fancy meals and exotic trips—had died almost the moment they'd married.

"I'm so sorry."

She had to look away from the compassion in Tyler's eyes. "It was a long time ago."

"Still, it must have been difficult." That blasted sincerity in his voice.

"I don't like to talk about it." That much, at least, was one hundred percent true.

"Of course."

They both fell into silence, and Isabel watched the kids play in the deepening twilight. They should leave before full dark, but she was reluctant to move. Somehow, just standing here with Tyler, the last remnants of day glinting on the water, was comforting.

Here she could pretend her life was what could have been instead of what was.

Chapter 16

Tyler would be content to stay here all night. But he supposed he had to get his boys to bed at some point.

And Isabel looked ready to drop.

Reluctantly, he pushed off the gazebo. "It's getting late."

Isabel nodded, and he tried to imagine that was disappointment on her face.

"I'll walk you home." He gestured for her to step out of the gazebo ahead of him.

"You don't have to. We'll be fine."

"It's getting dark. I'm not going to let you walk home alone."

"I thought you weren't afraid of anything." Isabel smirked at him.

"I didn't say that." He escorted her toward the playground. "What I said was that God says we don't have to worry. But unfortunately, I forget that too often. And if you must know, I'm scared of thunderstorms."

Isabel snorted. Which didn't do much for his ego.

But now that he'd confessed it, he might as well tell her the whole story. "When I was a kid, I got lost in the neighbor's cornfield when the tornado siren went off. I was terrified." Still jumped every time the weekly test of the siren caught him by surprise.

"You did not." She shoved him lightly.

"I did. My dad found me and got me to the basement. But I've been scared of storms ever since. Just don't tell the boys. I don't want to pass my fear on to them." Which was why he was thankful Hope Springs didn't get many tornado warnings each year.

"You're serious?"

"One hundred percent."

"And was there a tornado?"

"Couple towns to the south. Didn't do any damage here."

They fell silent as they reached the kids and then headed together toward Isabel and Gabby's apartment. There was no room for either Tyler or Isabel to say a word the whole way back, as Gabby talked nonstop about the fun they'd had at the park, aided by an occasional comment from Jeremiah and Jonah.

Which was fine. Because Tyler's mind had been seized by a crazy idea that he was struggling to fight.

When they reached the apartment building, Gabby gave an excited squeak and pointed to the hill that led down to the lake. "Fireflies. Can we catch some, Mama?"

Isabel watched the blinking yellow lights, and he saw the wistfulness in her eyes. "You can try. Five minutes."

With the twinkling flickers of light, the kids' laughter, and the moonlight reflecting off the lake as a backdrop, the night felt almost magical.

Maybe his idea wasn't so crazy after all.

He cleared his throat and took a step closer to Isabel, letting himself breathe in the strawberry scent that he was coming to recognize as hers. He stuck his hands in his pockets.

"So—"

"You ever caught fireflies?" The question burst out of her mouth, strangely loud in the quiet night.

"Of course. Who hasn't?" His eyes went to her. "Right. You haven't."

She shrugged. "Like I said, not exactly a Brady Bunch family. But I'm glad Gabby gets the chance."

Tyler was starting to wonder what that meant, not a Brady Bunch family. But he had a feeling she wouldn't tell him if he asked.

Still, he may not be able to change whatever her family life had been like, but he could change the fact that she'd never caught fireflies. "Let's catch some now."

"Oh no. I don't—"

But he grabbed her wrist and led her toward the hill. "Hold out your hands like this." He held a cupped hand in front of him. "They're actually pretty slow fliers, so you don't need to be aggressive. Just watch for a light and slip your hand under it, and then . . ." He scooped a firefly out of the air and closed his other hand over it.

He turned to show it to her, lifting his hand a crack so she could see it glow. "You try."

She gave him a playful grin. "Looks easy enough."

But after a few attempts, she still hadn't managed to grab one. After another close miss, he stepped to her side.

"Here." He slid his hand under hers, guiding it to a spot directly under a firefly.

His heart rate notched up at the feel of her hand in his, but he ignored it, keeping her hand steady and lifting it slowly, until the firefly stopped moving its wings and came to a landing on her finger.

Her laugh sounded almost like Gabby's, youthful and full of wonder.

"Now bring your other hand over it."

Isabel nodded and slowly cupped her other hand over the top of the insect. But after a moment, she lifted the hand.

He gave her a curious look, and she smiled. "I'd rather see it fly away and glow than keep it trapped in my hands where I can't see it."

The firefly lit up on her finger, then, with a slow whir of its wings, lifted straight into the air.

And Tyler suddenly realized her hand was still resting in his. Instead of pulling his hand back, he turned it over, onto the top of her palm, and wrapped his fingers around hers.

Her eyes came to his. In the moonlight, their caramel color had lightened to gold.

"Isabel, would you ever—"

"Oh wow." She pulled her hand out of his and took a giant step backwards. "It's getting late. I'd better get Gabby to bed."

She lunged toward the other side of the hill, where Gabby and the boys were giggling as they continued to chase fireflies.

"Gabby Mae." Her voice was sharp. "It's been way more than five minutes. Bedtime now."

Gabby looked up and skipped to her mother, who marched her toward the apartment building.

Tyler remained rooted in his spot, trying to wrestle his confusion down. Had she known what he was going to ask? Or was it only a coincidence that she'd decided they needed to go in at that exact moment?

As they passed him, she offered a quiet goodnight but didn't quite look at him. And that answered his question.

The moment the building's door closed behind her, Isabel had to fight the temptation to crumple onto the bottom step.

Tyler had been about to ask her out, she was certain of it.

What she was less certain of was why she had literally run away from him.

She could have at least declined graciously. He deserved that much.

But she wasn't entirely convinced she would have had the strength to say no.

And that was what she had to do.

For Gabby's sake.

And her own.

She followed Gabby up the stairs, her feet itching to turn around and carry her back out the door to tell Tyler to wait. To say she wanted to hear the rest of his question.

As they reached the landing, she passed the apartment keys to Gabby, who liked to unlock the door herself. Isabel leaned against the wall as she waited, and when the door clicked open, she didn't move.

"Coming, Mama?"

"Be right there. Just thinking. You go get ready for bed."

As Gabby skipped into the apartment, Isabel tipped her head back.

What was she so scared of?

Maybe Tyler was right. Maybe she needed to stop worrying and trust that God was in control. But then, trust had never been her strong point. With God or with people.

Tyler is one of the good ones.

Or at least she was pretty sure he was. But it was that little sliver of uncertainty that held her back. Because Andrew had seemed like one of the good ones too—until he wasn't.

It had crept up on her so slowly. First the half-mocking comments when she'd had an innocent conversation with a waiter on their honeymoon. Then the insistence that he know where she was at all times. Later the insults, the manipulation, the fists.

Tyler isn't Andrew.

She knew that. And yet . . .

Why did this all have to be so hard? If she'd just followed her own rules in the first place, if she had avoided getting to know anyone, she wouldn't be in this position right now.

No, you'd be lonely.

And that would be fine.

Lonely she could deal with. Because if she was lonely, it meant she was safe. Gabby was safe.

"Ready, Mama."

Isabel sighed and pushed herself off the wall. She was too tired to think about this anymore tonight.

The door across the hall opened, and Kendra emerged, her eyes darting to Isabel before she ducked her head. But it was long enough for Isabel to spot the blue-black bruise under her eye.

"Kendra." Isabel rushed forward. "Are you okay?"

Kendra's eyes skipped from her closed apartment door to Isabel and back. "I'm fine. Just ran into a—"

"Cupboard door?" Isabel crossed her arms in front of her. "Your cover stories need some work. If Kyle is hurting you—"

"He's not." The response was quick, automatic.

"Kendra—" Isabel tamped the frustration down, pulling out compassion instead. She'd been in this exact spot—unwilling to tell anyone what was happening. Unwilling to ask for help. "Let me at least get you the number for the nearest women's shelter." Though considering it was three hours away, the chances that Kendra would actually go were slim.

"I said I'm fine." Kendra looked to the door of her apartment again. "I have to go pick up dinner."

"Of course." Isabel stepped aside, though she kept her eyes pinned on Kendra. She so desperately wanted the girl to know she had an ally.

But Kendra pushed past her and ran down the steps, her feet barely making a sound on the treads. She'd learned to step lightly, just as Isabel had.

Isabel let out a rough breath as the door at the bottom of the stairs clicked shut.

And *that* was why she couldn't get involved with a man.

Not even Tyler.

Because until men went around wearing name tags that identified the good ones, there was always a risk.

Chapter 17

"Hey, I don't know if anyone told you, but it's the Fourth of July. You're supposed to be having fun." Spencer clapped a hand on Tyler's shoulder before settling next to him on the outdoor sofa that took up the corner of their parents' patio.

Tyler offered a muttered response that he wasn't even sure was words.

How could he have been so stupid? What had possessed him to attempt to ask Isabel out last night?

He'd told himself he'd never get involved with a woman again.

And a date was the very definition of getting involved.

He should be thanking Isabel for running away from the question, really.

She'd spared him from any further stupidity.

But the worst part was, he didn't want to be spared from that particular stupidity when it came to her.

"Wow." Spencer gave him an appraising look as he tucked into the food on his plate.

Tyler shouldn't take the bait, but he couldn't help it. "Wow what?"

"Nothing. I just would have thought you could go one day without seeing Isabel. Why don't you bring her some soup or something? I'm sure it will make her feel better."

Tyler snorted. "Soup's not going to help. She's not sick."

"She told Soph—"

"I know." Tyler pushed to his feet, then sat back down. He didn't know what to do with himself right now. "But she's not sick. She didn't come because she didn't want to see me."

"Don't be so dense." Spencer took a big bite of hamburger. "Anyone can see you two are crazy about each other."

Yeah. He was the only crazy one. "Is that why she practically ran away when I tried to ask her out last night?"

Spencer lifted an eyebrow. "Define practically ran away."

"Didn't let me finish the sentence, grabbed Gabby, and escaped into the house."

Spencer looked thoughtful as he chewed. "So you didn't actually ask her out?"

Tyler shook his head. Why was this so difficult for his brother to grasp? "She didn't let me."

"So she may not have known that was what you were going to say?"

"She knew. It's for the best anyway. I have no desire to—"

But Spencer leaned forward, cutting him off. "You're my brother, Tyler, and I love you. I don't want to see you get hurt any more than you want to get hurt. But don't you think it's time to drop the whole 'I'll never date again' thing? Especially seeing as how you're in love with her."

"I'm not—"

But he was. He so was.

How had he not realized it before? He was ridiculously in love with Isabel.

The question was, what was he going to do about it?

But what Tyler wanted to do about his new realization—ask Isabel out for real this time—was impossible, since she had become a ninja at avoiding him. All week, she'd scurried out of the store whenever she saw him coming. Yesterday, he'd almost caught her by surprise, but she'd disappeared into the restroom. He'd contemplated hanging around to see just how long she'd stay in there but had decided against it. If she was really that set against him asking her out, he would honor her wishes.

He could be patient and wait for her to come around.

And if she never did, that was fine too.

Easier really.

Anyway, he couldn't dwell on Isabel today. Not when Julia would be here to pick up the boys any minute. Seeing his ex-wife took enough of an emotional toll the way it was.

"Do you have your toothbrushes?" He stood in the door to the boys' bedroom, trying to quash the ache that rose in his chest every year when he had to say goodbye to them. He kept wondering when it was going to be the year they decided they wanted to stay with their mother—permanently.

"Yeah, Dad."

Tyler stepped into the room, grabbing each boy's favorite stuffed bear off the pile that had been unceremoniously stuffed into their closet. He stuck the toys in the boys' suitcases, but both Jonah and Jeremiah pulled them right back out.

"We don't need these, Dad. We're nine, you know." Jonah's voice had an edge of sassiness, and Tyler bit back his reprimand. An argument was not how he wanted to leave things with his boys. He knew only too well how much damage that could do.

He set the bears on the boys' dressers, remembering the days when they couldn't sleep without them. He'd spent two hours one night searching for Jonah's bear, his son crying the entire time, until Tyler had finally found the stuffed animal tangled in the blankets at the bottom of the bed.

The doorbell rang as the boys were zipping their suitcases, and Tyler moved with heavy limbs to answer it.

"Tyler." Julia greeted him with a forced smile, her hair shorter than the last time he'd seen her, makeup all in place.

"Julia." He waited for the familiar gut punch of loss at seeing his ex, but it didn't come. Instead, his eyes traveled past her, down the driveway, to the store, where Isabel was probably considering going to lunch right about now.

"Are the boys almost ready? We have reservations at LeMarque tonight. You did pack nice clothes for them, right?"

Tyler gave a weary nod. "They should have everything they need."

Jeremiah and Jonah entered the room, wheeling their suitcases behind them.

"Darlings." But Julia didn't move to hug them. She'd never been demonstrative, not even with Tyler.

"Can we go to Six Flags?"

"Jonah, at least say hi to your mother first." This time Tyler couldn't avoid the reprimand.

Jonah gave a sheepish grin. "Hi, Mom. Six Flags?"

Julia smoothed a hand down her designer jeans. "Of course. Tom already bought the tickets."

Tyler told himself the lurch in his stomach wasn't jealousy that the boys would be spending time with the man Julia had left him for. He followed Julia and the boys out the door, then helped them load their things into Julia's car.

"Let's hit the road, then." Julia opened her car door.

"Wait. I promised Aunt Sophie we'd say goodbye before we left." Jeremiah headed for the store, Jonah right behind him.

Julia heaved an exaggerated sigh but followed as well. Tyler dragged his feet alongside her, not bothering with the effort of small talk.

The boys clamored into the store, letting the door close behind them. Julia stood to the side, waiting for Tyler to open it.

He did, offering a small, unnecessary gesture to wave her through ahead of him.

Sophie already had her arms around the boys. "I'm going to miss you two so much. Don't grow too much while you're gone." She dropped a kiss onto each one's head. Both boys pretended to dislike it, but Tyler knew better.

As Sophie let the boys go, a little voice from the other side of the store called out, "Wait."

Everyone's eyes went to Gabby, who was perched on a stool behind the counter, Isabel's arm wrapped protectively around her shoulders.

"Are you leaving?" Gabby's eyes were wide and sad.

The twins nodded. "Just for a couple weeks."

Gabby scampered down from her stool and scurried toward the boys, Isabel taking a few hesitant steps behind her.

"Here!" Gabby reached into her pocket and fished out a package of gummy bears, distributing them equally between the boys. "Sophie gave these to me for helping with the pies, but I want you to have them. So you won't forget me."

"Thanks, Gabby. You can play in the tree house whenever you want while we're gone." Jeremiah tucked the gummy bears into his pocket. Tyler considered warning Julia to check for them before she did the laundry but decided against it.

"Bye, Gabby. Bye, Isabel."

Isabel lifted her head, looking surprised—and maybe a little touched—that the boys had thought of her. Tyler wanted to tell her that of course the boys had thought of her. They adored her almost as much as he did. But he held his tongue.

"Bye, boys. Take care." She shot an uncertain look toward Julia before retreating behind the counter.

"All right. Enough goodbyes. Let's go." Julia pushed the door open, and Tyler waited for the boys to exit, daring a quick glance over his shoulder.

Isabel's eyes slipped to his, and she offered him a sad smile that was somehow comforting. Like she understood how hard this was for him.

He pulled his gaze away and followed the boys and Julia out the door. Before they got in the car, he gave each boy a long hug. Thankfully, even if they'd outgrown their stuffed animals, this they still tolerated.

Then they were getting in the car and driving away, and he was lifting a hand and waving until he couldn't see them anymore.

A tiny fracture opened in his heart that he knew wouldn't close until they returned home.

Chapter 18

Isabel tossed her dust rag down, turning away from the window display she'd been arranging.

She needed a walk. Not for the exercise. But for the clarity.

To help her sort some things out.

Because ever since she'd escaped Tyler's question last week, she'd been a mess, oscillating between certainty she'd done the right thing and a crushing sense that she'd let what could have been one of the best things in her life slip away.

And watching him say goodbye to the boys the other day—it had nearly broken her not to go to him and offer comfort. She'd only seen him once in the three days since then, and he'd looked miserable. Aside from a nearly inaudible "hi," he hadn't said a word to her.

Not that she blamed him.

In fact, it had been her goal—avoiding him until he gave up.

But now that he had, she couldn't suppress the feeling that she'd made a terrible mistake.

"Hey, Sophie?" She moved to the kitchen, where Gabby was helping Sophie roll out a pie crust. "Do you mind if I take an early lunch?"

Sophie glanced up, studying her, and Isabel tried to keep her expression flat.

"Of course." Sophie waved her off. "It's slow today anyway. Take your time. We've got things covered here, right Gabby?" The sympathetic look said Sophie knew she needed some time to herself.

"Thank you." Once again she wondered how she'd gone all her life without a friend like this. "I'll get Gabby her lunch first."

But Sophie winked at Gabby. "My little helper isn't ready for lunch yet. I'll get it for her when we're done here. But make sure to watch the sky. Looks pretty nice out there now, but they're calling for storms."

Isabel nodded, her mind slipping to Tyler's confession that he was afraid of thunderstorms. He'd seemed a little embarrassed, but she'd found it kind of cute. Something that made him more real.

Outside, the still, humid air wrapped around Isabel's face like a wet rag, making it nearly impossible to pull in a deep breath. She briefly considered retreating back into the air conditioned shop.

And then she imagined Tyler coming in for lunch. Pictured him ignoring her again.

Surveying the landscape, she set off toward the end of Hidden Blossom's long driveway, veering right toward the orchard Tyler had taken her to her first day here. Within seconds, sweat plastered her hair to the back of her neck, but she kept going, flicking off a large winged grasshopper that landed on her arm.

She strode purposefully through the trees, laden now with reddening fruit, and continued into the wide, grassy field beyond them. She had her eyes set on a distant tree line. Tyler had pointed it out to her one day, said the orchard's namesake tree was located within it. He'd also promised to take her there sometime. But since that promise was likely to go unfulfilled, she'd just go see it for herself.

What she had thought was a single large field turned out to be two fields—separated by a dry creek bed. There was no bridge, but there was also no water in the creek.

With a quick inhale, she plunged down the bank, her feet scrabbling against the loose rocks.

At the bottom, she peered both upstream and downstream. In both directions, the creek disappeared from her line of vision quickly. Her thoughts swirled like eddies in the nonexistent current. Thoughts about Tyler. And Hope Springs. And the friends she was making here.

She'd come here with three rules.

But she was so close to breaking all of them.

She tried to convince herself that was a bad thing, but she couldn't quite do it.

Standing there, in the middle of the creek bed, Isabel felt stuck, unable to go forward or backward. Going back to the way things were before would be stifling, now that she'd gotten a taste of what life could be like without the rules. But going forward, letting herself forget the rules—that was terrifying and unknown and possibly dangerous.

She let out a long breath. If this walk was supposed to help her figure these things out, it wasn't working.

The climb up the far bank was harder, and she got a fresh gash on her recently healed hand, but when she made it to the top, she set out for the trees at a faster pace. She had no idea why she thought she'd find peace and clarity there, but at this point, she was ready to try just about anything.

Fifteen minutes later, as she finally stepped into the trees, a bird trilled. Isabel stilled as something moved in her heart at the sound.

What did it remind her of?

Look at the birds of the air. Wasn't that the Bible verse Tyler had told her about? About how God took care of the birds. And how he cared for his people even more.

She hadn't told anyone, not even Sophie, but ever since that night, she'd been paging through the Bible she'd found on the bookshelf in the apartment. It must have been Violet's at one time, because certain verses were highlighted, and there were notes in the margins. Those were the verses that drew her attention, since she figured there must have been a reason Violet marked them. The verse she'd read last night popped into her head. She didn't remember it word-for-word, but basically, it said don't be anxious about anything but bring your requests to God in prayer.

That idea, "do not be anxious about anything," was so appealing. But also so unrealistic.

She had so many things to be anxious about. She recited the list in her head as she pushed through the trees: She had to keep Gabby safe and figure out how long to stay in Hope Springs and decide where they were going to live next and keep Andrew from finding them and dye her hair again before the color faded completely and pick up groceries and figure out what to do about Tyler . . .

The list kept going, and Isabel nearly bowed under it. It was too much.

All this worry was going to crush her under its weight.

Her feet slowed as she emerged from the trees into a large clearing. Awe drew her to a stop as she spotted the giant cherry tree at the center of the clearing. Heavy with fruit, it stood all gnarled and twisted but still exuding a sort of strength that called to her.

This must be the hidden blossom tree Tyler had told her about. The one that had started this whole orchard generations ago.

She moved toward it, her steps still heavy, as thunder rolled in the distance.

As she reached the tree, the words of the verse looped through her head. *Present your requests to God. Present your requests to God.*

All right then.

Isabel ducked under the tree, letting its earthy scent surround her, and sat with her back against its trunk. Though she'd never really prayed on her own, she'd listened to Tyler and Dan and the others pray plenty of times. Didn't seem that hard.

She closed her eyes and leaned her head back. *Well God, I hope you have some free time. This might take a while.*

Chapter 19

The weather alert on Tyler's phone buzzed, and he pulled it out of his pocket, swiping at the sweat that never seemed to evaporate in this humidity. Thunder had been rumbling in the distance for half an hour already, but they'd been trying to get as much done as they could before the storm hit.

He clicked on the notification and read the alert, then tipped his head up to study the sky. Although the towering cumulonimbus clouds that had built up directly above the orchard were still interspersed with patches of blue, to the west, he could see the dark line of the approaching thunderstorm.

"All right." He strode to show the alert to his brother. "That's a thunderstorm warning. And it says this storm has a history of hail and the potential for a tornado to develop."

Spencer abandoned the fencing they'd been working all day to fix. "Let's head in. We'll want to make sure we can get everyone to safety if need be."

Thankfully, it was a couple weeks from harvest yet, or there would be people scattered all across the orchard picking their own cherries. As it was, they only had to worry about any customers in the store.

And the employees.

Tyler tried not to think about spending half an hour or more enclosed with Isabel in his parents' basement—the storm shelter they'd designated in the disaster plan Sophie had insisted they write a few years ago.

Fortunately, there'd be plenty of other people down there, so it would be easy enough to avoid her.

And at least he didn't have to worry about the boys, since they were safe with Julia. Although the heaviness of their absence still hung over him, at least he'd gotten to chat with them online last night.

By the time he and Spencer had parked their ATVs in the shed, the roll of thunder was almost constant, and the dark wall of clouds was nearly overhead. The unnaturally still air muted all other sounds. Even the birds had stopped singing.

"This could be a bad one," Spencer muttered.

Tension raked through Tyler's system as they jogged toward the store, the sky darkening enough that the dusk to dawn lights sprang to life.

A cold, hard rain started, spurring the brothers to a sprint. By the time they reached the store, their clothes and shoes were waterlogged.

The moment they were inside, Tyler wiped his glasses, then scanned the room, taking a quick inventory of the people gathered there. As he'd hoped, they had only a handful of customers right now. His phone blared with another alert, and he pulled it out.

Tornado warning. Brown County.

That was the next county to the west.

"If everyone will follow us—" He worked to infuse his voice with a confidence he was far from feeling. "We're going to lead you to the storm shelter. Just as a precaution."

Tyler held the door open as customers filed out of the building, followed by Spencer, holding one of his twins in each arm, and Sophie, gripping Gabby's hand.

Wait.

"Where's Isabel?" Tyler started toward the kitchen.

"She went for a walk a while ago." Sophie's forehead creased. "I told her to take as long as she wanted, but I'm sure she's on her way in. Hopefully, she's not getting too soaked."

Too soaked? If she wasn't careful, she was about to get blown away by a tornado.

He tried to tell himself that was highly unlikely. Aside from the tornado that had hit Delison when he was a boy, Tyler was pretty sure the peninsula hadn't seen a tornado in at least a hundred years.

Still.

What if it did happen?

And what if Isabel was in the middle of it?

Gabby's frightened eyes landed on him, and he tried to give her a reassuring smile as Sophie bent to tell the girl to run through the rain.

As he turned to close and lock the store door, the low wail of the tornado siren stationed a mile down the road knifed through the throbbing rain, rising to a piercing note that pulsed through his jaw.

Everything inside him went colder than the rain that was pelting him full force.

Run, his instincts screamed. *Run to shelter.*

He'd been caught outside during a tornado warning once in real life—and hundreds of times in his nightmares. He had no desire to repeat that experience.

Isabel was a big girl. She was smart enough to start back when the storm began. She'd be here any second.

But what if she was hurt? Or lost?

He squinted through the rain to see Sophie and Gabby reach the door to Mom and Dad's farmhouse.

Decision made his footsteps firm as he sprinted into the rain.

Away from safety.

✑

Isabel tore through the forest, gasping as she pushed her legs to their limit.

Around her, the trees whipped at odd angles as the eerie sound of the tornado siren seemed to rise straight up out of the ground.

She had to get to Gabby. Had to get her to safety. What had she been thinking, leaving her? What had she been doing, spending her time praying, trying to convince herself God was real and was listening to her and there was nothing to worry about?

She didn't care what the Bible said. *This* was something to worry about.

As she emerged from the forest onto the path through the open field, cold rain pelted her head and bounced off her arms. She nearly rolled an ankle as her foot slipped, and she spared a quick glance at the ground.

Hail the size of marbles was collecting in the field.

She'd lived in Texas long enough to know that hail during a thunderstorm wasn't a good sign.

Please keep Gabby safe. It was her only thought. The only thing that mattered. She'd spent the past twenty minutes praying for God to help her and Gabby make a real home here, to give them a future that was brighter than their past. But she'd trade all that for just the promise that God would keep her daughter safe through this storm.

She skidded again, catching herself just before she hit the ground, and sharp pain shot from her foot up through her ankle. But she kept running. *Please God. If you're ever going to hear me, hear me now. Help me get to Gabby.*

A strange roar filled her ears, and she looked wildly around for the source. She'd never heard a tornado up close. But she'd heard they sounded like a freight train.

This sounded more like . . .

An ATV.

A wild half-cheer, half-sob ripped out of her as the bright yellow of Tyler's ATV barreled down on her.

He stopped the machine inches from her. "Get on."

She could barely hear him, but she was close enough to read his lips.

"Where's Gabby?" She reached to the bottom of her lungs for the strength to yell loud enough as she threw her leg over the seat and her arms around his chest.

"With Sophie." Tyler revved the engine into gear and took off.

She pressed her face into his back to protect herself from the lashing hail.

No matter how hard she tried, she couldn't catch her breath.

Tyler was here. Even though he was afraid of storms, he'd come for her. He was bringing her to Gabby.

Thank you. Thank you. Thank you. She hoped he could read her thoughts through the spot where her cheek pressed against his soaked t-shirt.

In an instant, what little light was left seemed to be sucked from the sky and a rushing sound, like a waterfall, filled her ears.

She lifted her head enough to peer over her shoulder.

She'd never seen a tornado in real life before, and she stared at it for a moment, fascination warring with her fear.

It was wider than she'd imagined and black against the dark gray of the sky. It undulated in a hypnotic pattern, a funnel of clouds swirling down from the sky and up from the ground, working its way toward them.

Toward them!

"Tyler!" The scream tore out of her as she whipped her head forward. "It's coming this way!"

Tyler's head bobbed up and down, and she felt the ATV accelerate.

But the sound behind them grew louder, becoming closer to that freight train comparison she'd always heard. If you crossed the freight train with the howl of a wounded animal.

Isabel tightened her grip on Tyler.

If I die, who will take care of Gabby?

The question socked Isabel in the gut. She didn't even have a will. What if she died and the courts gave Andrew custody?

"Go faster!" But there was no way he heard her scream now. The sound of the tornado seemed to come from every direction, erasing all other sound.

It took her a second to realize he'd shut down the ATV and was trying to pull her off it.

"What are you doing?" She tried to push him away, but he hauled her off the machine and stood her on the ground.

"We're not going to make it." He grabbed her arm, dragging her away from the ATV. From their only way to get to safety. "It's too close. We have to shelter here."

She reared back, looking around wildly. "Where?" Unless he saw some magical structure that was invisible to her, there was nothing here.

Tyler pointed to her left. "The creek bed. It's the lowest point." He pulled on her arm again, and she swiveled her head from him to the tornado.

It writhed, looming closer, snaking just behind the forest she'd been in ten minutes ago.

Everything in her screamed that she couldn't do what Tyler was asking her to do. She had to get to Gabby. Had to keep her daughter safe.

Who of you by worrying can add a single hour to your life?

But it wasn't her life she wanted to add to, it was her daughter's. She needed to know her daughter was safe.

"Where's Gabby?" she asked again.

"She's in my parents' basement. With Spencer and Sophie. I promise she's safe."

Behind them, the tornado's roar shifted to a high-pitched, unearthly whistle that made her want to cover her ears. Rain and hail still lashed at her skin.

Tyler moved closer, placed one hand on each of her arms. Somehow, his palms were warm in spite of the cold rain. "Isabel, if you're ever going to trust me, it has to be now."

He was right. She had no choice but to trust him.

She nodded, and he slid his hand into hers, tugging her along with him to the creek bed.

Together they slid down the bank, Tyler never letting go of her hand.

"Lie down flat on your stomach," he yelled when they got to the bottom. "And cover your head with your arms."

Isabel eyed the creek bed, where a trickle of water had begun to flow. With a quick breath, she dropped to the ground, shivering as the cold water seeped into her already soaked clothes. She lifted her arms to cover her head.

This was crazy. How were her little arms supposed to protect her from that beast bearing down on them?

Tyler settled on the ground next to her, the solidness of his side warm against her ribs, giving her a grounding. He pulled her in close, tucking her head against his chest and wrapping his arms over her. Something solid settled across her legs, and Isabel realized it was his leg.

In the absence of shelter, he was becoming a shelter for her.

But why?

Why would he do that? Why would he protect her instead of himself?

"God is our refuge and strength, an ever present help in trouble." Somehow Tyler had bent his head close to hers and was speaking right into her ear. She didn't know how she heard him, with the tornado still whistling, the siren still blaring, her heart still roaring, but she took in the words, letting them settle over her.

"He says, 'Be still, and know that I am God,'" Tyler's voice continued, rumbling through his chest. "'I will be exalted among the nations, I will be exalted in the earth.' The Lord Almighty is with us; the God of Jacob is our fortress."

Be still. The words whispered against her mind. *Be still.*

The trembling in her legs stopped, and her breathing slowed.

Whatever happened, in this moment there was nothing she could do but be still.

Chapter 20

I t had to be close.

Tyler closed his eyes and pressed his head down on top of Isabel's, shifting so that both of his arms shielded as much of her skull as possible.

The ragged edges of his breaths tore at his lungs as the tornado filled his ears, trying to drown out the Psalm he'd recited to Isabel.

He scrunched his eyes tighter, listening for the sound of his own voice in his head.

Be still, he commanded his roaring heart. *Be still and trust.*

The whistling of the tornado intensified, and Tyler tightened his arms around Isabel as his ears popped. If it got any louder, his ear drums were going to blow.

How long had they been in the creek already? How much longer would this last?

He started to count in his head.

One. Be still. Two. Be still. Three. Be still.

When he got to thirty, the sound lifted, its pitch shifting slightly, and his breath loosened as the pain in his ears lessened. Still, he kept his head down, his arms around Isabel.

By the time he'd reached ninety, the roar had faded significantly, and the rain eased to a steady drum.

Slowly he raised his head, sliding his arms from Isabel's head to her shoulders.

She lifted her face, her eyes landing on his for a second before she shoved to her feet, her gaze jumping across the landscape. "Did it hit the houses?"

Tyler pushed to his feet, the water pooling around his ankles now, and pulled off his rain- and mud-splotched glasses, squinting until he spotted the dark form of the tornado in the distance. He lifted a hand to point it out. "It passed to the south. It didn't hit the houses." Relief socked him in the gut. His family was safe.

Isabel grabbed his arm, her fingers surprisingly strong as they locked around his wrist. "You're sure?"

Tyler nodded, eyes still fixed on the tornado. If it kept going at that trajectory, it would sweep right through Hope Springs.

A punch against his shoulder made him jerk his head toward Isabel. She had her fist drawn back, as if she were about to do it again.

Tyler caught her wrist, holding it lightly. "What was that for?"

"Why did you do that?" Isabel's eyes were wild.

"Do what?" It wasn't like he had control over the tornado.

"Why did you come out here? You should have stayed with Gabby. What if something happened—" She broke off, bending in half and pulling her hand from his grasp.

He gaped at her. Why did he do it? "Gabby was safe with Sophie and Spencer. I came to find you . . ." He scrubbed his hands over his face. He couldn't bring himself to think what could have happened to her if he hadn't. She never would have made it to the creek.

She straightened, nailing him with a stern frown. "I'm not worth that kind of risk, Tyler. Next time, you just see that my daughter is safe and don't worry about me."

He stared at her, blinking away the rain that continued to fall in his eyes. Did she really believe that? That she wasn't worth it?

"You know that day we talked about what I'm scared of?"

Her brow wrinkled. "Yeah. Storms. Which is why you should have—"

He took a step closer to her, letting himself raise a hand to her cheek. "I was more scared to think that something might happen to you."

The shift in her expression, from anger to something much, much softer, much, much nicer, much, much more open, made him lean in. "Isabel." Her name was so beautiful.

"Tyler, I—" She fell silent, and it was like they were suspended like that. Stuck in this in-between place where he didn't know if she was going to hit him or kiss him.

She had forgotten everything she was going to say.

Some sort of argument. Something to put some distance between them again. To make him stop looking at her like that, stop talking to her like he cared about her.

Instead, she felt herself leaning forward, felt her lips moving closer to his, felt herself letting go of every rule she had ever made.

As their lips met, her hands came to his arms, and his circled her waist.

This was right. This was good. This was—

No.

What was she doing?

She pulled away, taking a step back.

"Sorry." This time she remembered what she'd been about to say. "I think we should get back."

"Yeah." His eyes were still on hers, slightly confused, but still with that look that was almost sweeter than a kiss. "We probably should."

She turned to take a step up the bank, but the pain in her ankle had sharpened, and she gasped, trying to catch her footing with her other leg.

"You're hurt." Tyler was instantly at her side, one arm wrapped around her back, the other supporting her arm.

She shook her head. "Just twisted my ankle. I'm fine."

Still, he kept his arm around her and helped her up the bank.

She should shrug out of his grasp, insist she could do this herself. But the truth was, she wasn't sure she could.

All the adrenaline that had driven her down the path toward Gabby was seeping out of her, like a slow leak from a tire, and she was pretty sure she'd collapse soon if Tyler wasn't there to hold her up.

He nudged her forward, arm still firmly wrapped around her, and helped her onto the ATV.

"I'm glad to see this still here." Isabel had never thought she'd say that about an ATV.

"We're fortunate the tornado angled the way it did." Tyler's face was grim. "It must have been a few hundred yards from us." He held up a hand and pointed to a section of decimated trees to the south.

Isabel's head swiveled to the forest where she'd been when the siren first went off. A path of sawed-off and mangled trees had been cut right through the middle of it.

If Tyler hadn't come for her, she'd be like one of those trees right now.

Her stomach rolled as she collapsed onto the ATV, sliding back so Tyler could climb on in front of her.

She leaned into him and wrapped her arms around his waist as he throttled forward.

Within minutes, they were approaching the farmhouse. From here, she could see that a few shingles had been ripped off the roof, and the outdoor furniture that had been so carefully arranged was now scattered across the driveway. But all in all, the damage appeared minimal, and the tightness in her chest eased an inch.

Tyler pulled the ATV right up to the house, and before he had shut off the engine, Isabel launched herself off it.

She had to see Gabby.

Before she could get to the front door, people were pouring out of it.

"Mama." Gabby threw herself at Isabel, then pulled back, wrinkling her nose. "Why are you all wet and dirty?"

Isabel laughed—the sound may have been slightly hysterical, but she didn't care, she was so relieved they were all in one piece—and pulled her daughter back to her, despite Gabby's attempts to wriggle away.

When she finally let Gabby go, Sophie engulfed her in a hug. "We were so worried about you. I'm glad you were safe."

Isabel nodded into Sophie's shoulder, brushing away the prickle of tears. "Thank you for keeping Gabby safe."

"Of course." Sophie squeezed her tighter. "Come on. Let's go find you some dry clothes before you end up with pneumonia next. You too, Tyler." Sophie released her and peered over her shoulder. "Tyler? You okay?"

Isabel turned to see Tyler still on the ATV, still grasping the handlebars, head bowed.

"Yeah. I'm okay." But his voice was all raspy. "It was headed straight for Hope Springs."

Isabel couldn't tell if the gasp came from her alone or if they'd all gasped at once.

Sophie already had her phone out and was typing furiously. "Dan and Jade," she muttered. "Vi and Nate. Peyton and Jared. Ethan and Ariana. Emma. Grace. Leah and Austin." She looked up, her face drawn, and Isabel realized she'd been messaging all their friends who lived in and around Hope Springs.

They all stared at the phone as if it held some sort of psychic power to tell them what was happening ten miles down the road.

A minute went by.

Then another.

Just when Isabel didn't think she could take it anymore, Spencer blew out a loud breath. "Service is probably down. Why don't you two get dried off, and then we'll take a drive into town. See how bad things are. Help where we can."

They all nodded.

"Come on, I've got some stuff over at my house you can wear." Sophie gestured to Isabel, and she nodded, grabbing Gabby's hand and following her friend.

But she couldn't resist looking back at Tyler, who was finally climbing off the ATV. His eyes met hers, and a tiny smile lifted his lips.

Lips that had been kissing her a few moments ago.

Chapter 21

Tyler's grip on the van's steering wheel tightened, and tension pulled across his shoulders. The closer they got to Hope Springs, the worse the damage got. Out in the country, near the orchard, they'd seen some downed trees, but now that they were closer to town, they'd seen a handful of houses with smashed out windows and missing roofs. Thankfully, it didn't appear that anyone had been hurt.

In the seat next to him, Isabel was silent, her hands clutching at the fabric of the shorts she'd borrowed from Sophie. In the back seat, Sophie and Spencer were equally mute. They'd left Rylan and Aubrey with Grandma and Grandpa, but Isabel hadn't wanted to leave Gabby, and the little girl exclaimed every time she spotted another sign of damage.

Tyler muttered as he turned down the main road into town, only to find it blocked by a police cordon. Liam Cline, an old classmate of Tyler's and the town's newly appointed police chief, lifted a hand and made his way toward them. Tyler rolled down his window, letting in a refreshing breeze that had to be at least twenty degrees cooler than before the storm.

"Sorry, Tyler, you're going to have to turn around. We've got some downed power lines this way."

"Yeah." Tyler ran a hand over his face. "We're trying to check on some friends. Just wanted to lend a hand wherever we can."

The chief nodded. "People seem to be gathering at the church. If you go around on the county roads, you can get there. Just be careful."

Tyler shifted the van into reverse, but Liam's hand landed on his door. "The church took the worst of it, Tyler. Just so you know."

Tyler's gut clenched. "What about the parsonage?" Dan and Jade and their little girl lived right next door to the church. If it had been hit, then . . .

"Pretty badly damaged, but everyone's okay."

Tyler let his head fall back against the seat, closing his eyes, and offering a silent prayer of thanks. When he opened them, Liam was gone, and Isabel was watching him.

"Do you want to go check your apartment first?" He'd almost forgotten that she may very well have lost everything in the storm.

But she shook her head. "Let's go to the church. Hopefully we can find out if everyone is safe there."

With a terse nod, Tyler turned the van around and took the winding county roads to the far side of town.

As he drove, he let himself breathe easier. The damage didn't appear so bad in this direction. Maybe Liam had been wrong—

"Where'd the church go?" Gabby's question from the back seat made Tyler jerk his head forward.

He blinked. Then blinked again.

It couldn't be.

"Oh my goodness." Isabel covered her mouth and rolled down her window, leaning her head into the opening. "It's gone."

She was right. Only a pile of rubble stood where the church had once been.

Debris covered areas of the parking lot as well as the cemetery where Tyler's grandparents were buried.

His gaze shifted to the parsonage as he parked the van along the curb and shut off the engine. Half of the top floor appeared to be missing.

"Maybe you should stay in the car with Gabby." Tyler turned to Isabel.

But she was already out of the van, opening the back door and reaching for Gabby's hand to help her out.

"It might be dangerous," he added, surprised she hadn't already thought of that.

"I want to help." Her voice held a fierce note he didn't recognize, and he nodded, eyeing her. Was this the same woman who'd refused to let Gabby go in the tree house at the beginning of summer?

Spencer and Sophie got out behind Gabby. Before any of them could take a step toward the church, Jade was barreling at them, followed by a whole group of people.

"We were so worried." Jade wrapped one of them after another in a hug. "You're the last ones we've heard from."

"Worried about us?" Sophie laughed as she wiped at her cheeks. "Look at your house."

Jade waved a dismissive hand. "That can all be fixed. I'm just so grateful God protected everyone. So far, it sounds like there wasn't a single injury, praise the Lord."

As the others launched into a hug exchange, Tyler turned, his feet pulling him toward the church. He didn't want to see it.

But he had to.

He stopped fifteen feet away, his path blocked by the large oak that had once stood proudly in front of the church. The tree was now half-crashed on top of the building.

A sharp grief started deep in his chest and expanded toward his limbs.

He knew it was only a building. Knew it could be rebuilt. Knew God had a plan even in this.

But still.

It hurt to see the place where he worshiped every week, where he had long conversations about God, where he spent time with so many of the people he loved, completely decimated.

He swallowed and pinched the bridge of his nose, willing the emotion away. After a few seconds of deep breathing, he lowered his hand.

A soft hand slipped into his. "Are you okay?"

The concern in Isabel's voice wrapped around his heart.

"Yeah." But he didn't suppose his croak sounded too convincing. "Where's Gabby?"

He couldn't believe she'd let the girl out of her sight after everything they'd been through today.

"Someone brought some cookies for the kids. Jade's watching her."

He nodded. "Did you hear anything about your apartment?"

"Violet said Hope Street was largely missed. I guess there's some debris there, and a few broken windows on cars that were parked on the street, but overall, it's fine. Our apartment wasn't damaged at all."

"Good." His eyes went back to the demolished church in front of him. Already a few people were venturing into the ruins, apparently searching for anything that could be salvaged. "I'm glad to hear that."

"Thanks." He could feel her watching him. "I'm so sorry about the church. I can't even imagine what it's like for all of you who grew up here. How long have you been going to church here?"

He counted in his head. "Only six years or so. Growing up, my family went to church on the other side of the peninsula. But when I moved back, Spencer was going here, and I started coming with him, and—" His eye snagged on the large cross that had stood on the wall at the front of the sanctuary. Somehow, it was still half-standing. "And this is where I really started to get it, you know?"

Isabel's forehead wrinkled. "To get what?"

He shrugged. "All of it, I guess. That God's love isn't like people's love. That it's unconditional and eternal and that he won't ever, ever betray us. That no matter how many times I screw up, he's always right there, loving me and forgiving me. That I can put my full trust in him."

"And does this change any of that?"

It wasn't a rhetorical question, like one believer might have asked another, knowing the answer would be "of course not." She genuinely wanted to know if the destruction of the church building had shaken his faith.

He contemplated the ruins as he prayed for wisdom in answering. "It doesn't change God's love for me. It doesn't change my faith in him. The only thing it changes is it reminds me that each day is precious. *This* day is precious." He squeezed her hand, and she nodded, letting her eyes search his.

He willed her to see what was there. To see that he cared about her.

She couldn't breathe.

That look in Tyler's eyes was too pure. Too open. Too full of everything she'd never dared to hope she could have.

"Excuse me, everyone."

She jumped as the sound of an amplified voice boomed across the parking lot.

Tyler's eyes held hers a moment longer, before he turned toward the voice. Isabel let out a long exhale, following his gaze to find Dan in the middle of the parking lot, standing on a kitchen chair that had come from who knew where. He held a large megaphone like the ones cheerleaders used in movies.

Next to her, Tyler laughed, and she flipped a glance at him out of the corner of her eye. Had he lost it?

"I knew that white elephant gift was going to be useful someday. Come on." He tugged her toward the crowd that was starting to circle Dan.

As they slipped into a spot next to Sophie and Spencer, Sophie's eyes landed on their still interlocked hands, and her lips lifted in a knowing smile.

Isabel would have to tell her later that it wasn't like that. She was just being a friend. Providing moral support.

Jade brought Gabby and the other children over to the group, and Isabel took her daughter's sticky hand in her own free hand, trying to ignore the fact that having Tyler on one side of her and Gabby on the other made her feel . . . complete. For the first time maybe ever.

"It means so much to me," Dan said into the megaphone once the crowd had stilled, "that you all made your way here after the storm. I have to be honest with you. After the storm had ended and it was safe, I came out here, and my heart about crashed to my feet. Because I remember my dad preaching in this church." His voice cracked, and he cleared his throat. "And I remember going to youth group at this church. I remember marrying my wife in this church." On the other side of Gabby, Jade swiped a quick finger under her eye, bouncing her daughter on her hip. "And I know all of you have similar memories. And maybe you're asking, like I confess I did, 'Why would God take my church from me?'" Dan's eyes went over the crowd, and several people nodded.

Isabel shifted on her feet. Well, why *would* God do that? It seemed rather counterproductive and even kind of mean-spirited.

"But here's the thing God reminded me of," Dan continued. "I don't need this church. You don't need this church. It's just a building. What we need is the faith God has worked in our hearts. What we need is his love for us that is so great that he sent his Son into the world to die for us."

A pulse of energy rippled through the crowd as Dan shifted the megaphone to his other hand.

"No storm can take that away." Dan gestured at the destruction surrounding them. "Not even a tornado. Because our refuge isn't in a building. *God* is our refuge. *He* is our strength and our fortress."

"Amen," someone called, and several others repeated it.

Isabel startled as a voice rose in song.

"Jesus, refuge of the weary," the voice sang, and soon nearly the entire crowd joined in.

How? How could they be singing when they'd just lost everything? She felt like the Grinch, staring down at the Whos on Christmas morning, trying to figure out why they were so happy when he'd stolen their Christmas.

But despite her confusion, despite her wonder, something tickled at her heart.

What would it be like to have a faith like that? To believe that even in the storms God had her back?

The thought was a little too scary for now, so Isabel tucked it away and just listened to the song.

Chapter 22

The whining buzz of the chainsaw, the vibration of the tool in his hands, the constant rain of pungent sawdust had all become constants in Tyler's life over the last week.

As had the woman who was approaching him now, her hair half-escaping a wild ponytail, streaks of dirt across her cheeks, the glisten of hard work on her forehead.

Good heavens, she was beautiful.

He shut down the chainsaw as she stopped in front of him.

She held a dripping water bottle out to him. "Thought you might need this."

"Thank you." Tyler took a long drink, using the opportunity to study her over the bottle.

She seemed different since the tornado. That old aloofness she'd worn like a shield had been lowered. These days, she was much quicker to smile, much more playful, much . . . happier, it seemed to him.

It wasn't the first time he'd wondered if he should ask her out again. They hadn't talked about the kiss or the hand-holding, and they certainly hadn't done either again. But that didn't mean he didn't want to.

"Hey, Tyler." A hand clapped his shoulder, accompanying Jared's voice.

Tyler barely suppressed his sigh. Despite the hundred or so other people who'd turned out to work at the church, he'd almost managed to convince himself that he and Isabel were going to get a moment alone.

"Think you could give us a hand with some demo?" Jared asked.

"Yeah. Of course." He could talk to Isabel later. He raised the water bottle toward her. "Thanks again."

Though he kept an eye out for her the rest of the day, she seemed to have disappeared. It wasn't until the crowds began dispersing as the sun lowered that he spotted her again in the front yard of the parsonage.

"Hey." He stopped a few inches farther away than necessary. "I thought you left hours ago."

She shook her head, pushing a rogue strand of hair out of her eyes. "I was helping Jade clean up and sort through some things. Figure out what could be saved."

"How are they holding up?"

"A little too well." Isabel's laugh seemed forced. "I'm still wondering if they're for real. If any of you are."

Tyler touched a light hand to her arm. "We're all for real. We just know that the troubles of this world are temporary. Our true home is in heaven."

Something flickered in her eyes, and he held his breath. Was this it? Was this the breakthrough he'd been praying for? Was her heart finally going to be opened to the truth?

But the moment passed, and she looked over her shoulder, calling for Gabby.

The little girl skipped up to them. "Sorry, Mama. I was saying goodbye to Hope. She's so cute. I wish I had a little sister. Or brother."

Even in the twilight, Tyler could pick out the faint pink coloring Isabel's cheeks.

Gabby turned to Tyler. "I miss Jonah and Jeremiah. When are they coming home?"

The fresh ache of his earlier conversation with Julia flared. "I'm not sure. Their mom wants to keep them a little longer, because of the tornado." Tyler did not see how that was necessary. If anything, he wanted his boys to come home sooner, so they could take part in helping to rebuild their community.

Gabby's hand landed in his. Though small, it was surprisingly comforting. "Are you sad?"

Tyler blew out a breath and nodded. "Yeah. I guess I am. I like having them with me."

"Then you should come have supper with us. Mama is making macaroni and cheese 'cuz it's my favorite and she said I worked hard today."

The pink stain on Isabel's cheeks deepened to crimson. "Gabby, I'm sure Tyler has something yummier to eat at his house."

"Yup." Tyler nodded. "I have some bread and some moldy cheese and some mustard."

"Eww." Gabby wrinkled her nose. "You can't eat that. You're coming with us."

Isabel studied him as if trying to decide if he was being serious about the food available at his house. "You're more than welcome to come, if you don't mind mac and cheese."

"It's my favorite." Tyler winked at Gabby.

He supposed he could have bowed out of the invitation graciously—considering it hadn't been Isabel who'd invited him in the first place.

But he couldn't get over the need to spend more time with her.

And if that meant snagging a dinner invitation from a five-year-old, so be it.

Why was she so flustered about making a box of macaroni and cheese?

Isabel blew a stray hair out of her face as she poured the noodles into the boiling pot of water. She'd nearly dumped the powdered cheese in when she'd added the water, only catching herself at the last second.

With the noodles on the stove, she turned to the refrigerator, trying to figure out what else she could serve. If it were only her and Gabby, she wouldn't bother. But since they had a guest—and since that guest was Tyler . . .

What had Gabby been thinking, inviting him? And what had he been thinking, accepting?

He had to have noticed that she wasn't exactly throwing a parade to encourage him to come.

Thankfully, the moment they arrived, Gabby had tugged Tyler to her room, promising to introduce him to all her stuffed animals.

"And this one's Bo. He's my best friend. Besides Jonah and Jeremiah."

"Of course." The smile in Tyler's voice was obvious, even from here, and Isabel suddenly couldn't regret that Gabby had invited him.

The poor guy had to be missing his boys so much. And she couldn't deny that he was good with Gabby.

She pulled out a questionable bag of spinach, studied it, then tossed it in the trash.

Maybe some corn?

She grabbed a bag out of the freezer and popped it into the microwave.

By the time she had everything on the small kitchen table, Tyler and Gabby had wandered into the room.

"Smells great," Tyler said.

Isabel's eyes cut to him. Was he patronizing her?

But his smile was completely sincere as he took the spot next to Gabby. She'd deliberately put him there, across the table from herself, instead of next to her.

As they sat, Tyler folded his hands in front of him, as he did at every meal.

Gabby followed suit. "Can I say the prayer tonight?"

Isabel's eyes shot to her and then to Tyler. Had he put her up to this? But he raised an eyebrow and shrugged.

"Do you really want to?" Isabel asked her daughter.

"Yes, Mama."

Isabel nodded and folded her hands, one hundred percent unsure of what to expect from Gabby's prayer.

"Dear God." Gabby's voice had the ring of confidence that said she thought she knew what she was doing. "Thank you for my favorite food. And Tyler's. Thank you that he's our friend, and help him not to be sad that his boys are gone right now. Help him be happy with me and my mama. Amen."

That wave of heat steamrolling its way to her face had nothing to do with what it had sounded like Gabby was saying in her prayer. It was only because she'd shut down the air conditioning while they were gone, and it was taking an inordinate amount of time to cool the place off again.

Tyler cleared his throat, and though she didn't dare lift her eyes to his, she could hear the laughter in his voice when he said, "Thank you for that prayer, Gabby. As a matter of fact, I am very happy with you and your mama. And I feel less sad about missing my boys already."

Isabel kept her head down as she dished some macaroni onto Gabby's plate, then passed the pan to Tyler. But a smooth kind of warmth filled her middle at the knowledge that he was happy with them.

Gabby kept up a constant flow of chatter through the meal, and Isabel was grateful. After a week of steady manual labor, she was too exhausted to think. It was a good kind of exhaustion, though. The kind that came from feeling like she had a purpose, like she was part of something bigger than herself. Like she was part of a community—or even a family.

Danger.

But she didn't have the energy to heed the warning.

Maybe it was okay if the people here felt like a family. Maybe it was even okay if she'd picked up the papers to register Gabby for school here in the fall. She hadn't filled them out yet—she wasn't quite ready to go that far—but she had been thinking about it pretty seriously.

She hadn't come to Hope Springs planning to find a real home. But it almost felt like she had found one anyway.

"May I be excused, Mama?" Gabby pushed her empty plate away from her.

Isabel forced her attention off the future and back to the present. "Of course."

But the moment Gabby disappeared, Isabel regretted her quick dismissal. Because now that she and Tyler had a moment alone, only one thought consumed her: What if Tyler wanted to talk about what had happened the other day? After the tornado? Worse—or maybe better—what if he wanted to do it again?

A fresh flush of heat seeped from her neck up through her face, and she pushed back from the table, scooping up a stack of dirty dishes.

She couldn't deny that the kiss had been . . . Well, the kiss had been wonderful, if she was being honest.

But that didn't mean she wanted to do it again. Or, well, it did mean she wanted to do it again. But it didn't mean she *should* do it again.

Tyler got up too, grabbing the rest of the dishes and following her into the kitchen, which suddenly felt much too small.

She considered trying to skirt around him to escape, but there was too great a risk that would involve one of those awkward dances where both people moved in the same direction, trying to get out of each other's way.

Instead, she filled the sink with dishwater. If Tyler wanted to take that as his cue to leave, that was fine with her.

But he stepped next to her and picked up a dish towel.

She concentrated on wiping the first glass clean, careful not to bump his hand as she passed it to him.

"Thanks for dinner. I'm sorry if I made you uncomfortable by accepting."

She let her eyes flick to him for a second, ignoring the way her heart did a little kick-flip as the warm cocoa of his gaze fell on her.

"It didn't make me uncomfortable." She sought a breezy tone. "I'm just sorry it wasn't much of a meal. I'm not much of a cook."

"Why do you do that?" He set the towel down and turned so that he was facing her head-on—or he would be if she hadn't remained facing the sink.

"Do what?"

"Why do you put yourself down like that all the time? It was a very nice meal, and I'm thankful that you made it for me. Why can't you accept that?"

Huh. *Did* she put herself down a lot? "I guess it's because it's true."

"Isabel." His voice hardened—not in a threatening way but more in a this-is-important way.

She scrubbed furiously at the spotless plate in her hand, until he took it gently from her and dropped it back into the water.

He wrapped his fingers around hers. "You're an amazing woman. I hope you know that."

Isabel stared at the floor with a big, wet blink. Yeah, she was really amazing. "So amazing I didn't even graduate high school."

Yipe! She hadn't meant for that to come out.

"You didn't?" The surprise in Tyler's voice told her exactly what he thought of her now. That she was the loser she'd always known herself to be.

"Pretty amazing, huh?" She could only hope the layer of sarcasm would provide a convincing disguise for the shame swimming in her belly.

"It *is* amazing." Tyler squeezed her hand and led her back to the kitchen table, pulling out a chair and gesturing for her to sit. "Look at all the things you've accomplished without the benefit of a diploma."

She stared at a broken nail on her thumb. "I haven't accomplished anything." Unless you counted making a complete mess of her life. That she'd managed pretty handily.

"You've raised a wonderful, bright daughter. You've helped Sophie in the store. You've helped this community recover from a terrible disaster. You listen to people. You care about them."

Isabel shook her head. None of those things were really accomplishments, were they?

"Trust me," Tyler continued, "I know people with all kinds of education and fancy degrees who haven't accomplished half what you have. They wouldn't know what was important in life if you hit them over the head with it. You do."

She swallowed, the task made more difficult by the tightness in her throat. "Thank you."

Tyler smiled and gave her hand another squeeze before letting go. It took all her willpower not to reach for his again.

"If you don't mind my asking," Tyler said as he strode back to the kitchen and resumed his position drying dishes. "Why did you drop out of school?" He fished the extra-clean plate out of the sink and rubbed it with his towel.

Isabel moved to his side, dunking another plate in the water, studying a sudsy bubble that burst with a sudden plop. "My dad was . . ." She chewed her lip. Very few people knew this part about her past. "He wasn't a good guy. He beat my mom."

Tyler set the plate down with a thud, turning toward her. "Did he—"

"He never hurt me," she rushed in. "But I knew it was coming. And my mom didn't love me enough to leave him. As soon as I saved up enough money to buy a car, I left them. Just got in my car and drove south."

"That's how you ended up in Texas?"

She nodded. "Slept in my car sometimes, but mostly I made friends, and they'd invite me to stay with them."

"And is that how you met your husband?" Tyler's question was hesitant, like he wasn't sure he wanted to know the answer.

"I got a job working at this trendy coffee shop. He came in every day, and after a while, he asked me out." She didn't add that he'd told her he didn't like coffee but had been coming in every day to see her. Goodness, had she been naive. A few smooth words, and she'd practically sold her soul to the man.

"You must miss him a lot."

"Mmm." She made a noncommittal sound at the back of her throat, telling herself it wasn't the same as lying. He could interpret that any way he chose.

She passed him the last dish to dry. "I'd better get Gabby to bed."

"Right." Lines of fatigue surrounded his eyes, but they crinkled in a smile. "I should get going. Will I see you tomorrow for more cleanup at the church?"

"I'll be there."

"Good." He stepped toward the door but stopped without opening it. "I don't know if you heard, but we're having a service first. At the community center just down the road. If you'd like to come . . ." He clasped and unclasped his hands, then clasped them again.

Church sounded— Truth be told, she wasn't exactly sure how church sounded right now.

Church with Andrew had always been a trying experience as she'd worked so hard not to do a single thing he would disapprove of, not do anything he'd have reason to berate her about when they got home. As a result, she'd never really been able to concentrate on the message. And anyway, she didn't see the point, when that message fell so far from matching up with what she experienced in her own life, with her own supposedly Christian husband.

But maybe church here—with people like Tyler and Sophie and Spencer and the rest of their friends—would be different.

"We'll see," she conceded.

His face lit into a smile large enough that you'd think she'd just said she'd go out with him. Not that he was asking. Or even thinking about anything in the vicinity of asking.

And neither was she.

Chapter 23

The warm buzz of conversation in the community center petered out as Dan stepped to the front of the room and met the gathered congregation with a smile.

Isabel found herself returning it easily.

Why did she feel so comfortable here? Was it because they were in the community center, instead of a church, so it felt more informal? Or because she already knew so many people, both her friends and the people she'd met helping with the cleanup? Or because Tyler was seated at her side, his shoulder mere inches from hers?

Probably a little bit of all of those, she decided.

"Good morning." Dan was a natural in front of the crowd, somehow making Isabel feel like he was talking directly to her. She joined the rest of the congregation in returning his greeting.

"So that was some storm the other day, huh?"

A few people chuckled, while others nodded.

"I don't know about you, but I felt pretty helpless. Pretty powerless," Dan continued. "Just like I feel helpless and powerless whenever other storms come up in my life. This morning, we're going to talk about how we can defeat this feeling of helplessness, of powerlessness, where we can get the strength to overcome these storms."

Isabel sat forward. Powerless. Helpless. Those two words described how she'd felt most of her life. She'd always figured she'd feel that way forever. But if Dan had the cure, she was listening.

"Here's a hint," Dan continued. "We have no strength, no power in ourselves. Let's begin with the first song."

Isabel sat back as the first strains of music lilted over the church. If Dan's introduction was supposed to be a pep talk, it had failed. What good would having no strength or power in herself do?

"Look, Mama, it's Nate." Gabby pointed, and Isabel pushed down her daughter's arm, letting her eyes travel to where Nate was seated at the piano, his mouth poised in front of a microphone. "When peace like a river, attendeth my way, when sorrows like sea billows roll; whatever my lot, Thou hast taught me to say, it is well, it is well with my soul."

The words floated on his clear voice, and Isabel closed her eyes, feeling herself swaying to the melody. That peace he was singing about, she suddenly realized—she longed to know that peace.

But how could she, when her life had been anything but peaceful? When she felt like she'd been running since the day she left home and couldn't stop now?

As the song ended and Dan turned to the day's readings, a taste of that peace seeped into Isabel. For right now, for this moment, she could let down her guard, stop worrying and being afraid, and just listen.

She let the words of the next song wash over her, and after a couple of times, found herself singing along with the refrain. As the song came to a close, Gabby leaned over and wrapped her arms around Isabel's waist.

That butterfly feeling of overwhelming love fluttered through Isabel's stomach. She leaned to whisper in her daughter's ear, "What was that for?"

Gabby shrugged. "I like church." Her whisper was more like a soft shout, and it came just as the last chord faded.

Isabel shushed her daughter as her own face heated.

But around them, a few people giggled, and others said *aww* and turned to smile at her daughter. Tyler reached over to squeeze Isabel's arm, shifting so that their shoulders remained pressed together even as he resettled his hand in his own lap.

The band members took their seats, and Dan again stepped to the small podium that had been set up at the front of the room. But instead of tucking himself behind it, he grabbed what appeared to be a Bible off it, slid the podium to the side, and took a few steps closer to the chairs.

"So storms," he said. "Like all of you, I've been through a few of them in my life. But last week's was probably the worst."

He flipped open his Bible, paging through it as he talked. "Makes me wonder how it compared to this storm Jesus went through. Well, when I say went through, I guess I really mean slept through." He directed his eyes to the page he'd settled on. "We read in Matthew chapter eight about how Jesus and his disciples were in a boat on the Sea of Galilee, a body of water that was pretty renowned for its fierce storms. And Jesus was tired. He'd been working hard. So he lay down to take a little nap. But while he was sleeping, one of those famous Sea of Galilee storms blew up. It was so bad that waves were washing over the boat, and the disciples were sure they were going to capsize. They woke Jesus up, saying basically, 'Jesus, don't you care that we're going to drown?'"

Isabel shifted in her seat. Didn't Jesus care? Wasn't he supposed to care about everyone?

"But Jesus didn't panic," Dan went on. "He wasn't like, 'Oh no. I didn't see this storm coming. Now what do we do?' Instead, he said to them, 'You of little faith, why are you so afraid?'"

Dan looked up, his eyes roving the congregation. "Let's pause there for a second. Because I have to confess something to you. Jesus could have very easily said this to me the other day. 'You of little faith, why are you so afraid?'" He peered toward the window that looked out on a perfectly clear sky today, but she could tell he was reliving the storm, just like all of them probably were.

"When I heard that tornado and I thought about what it could do to my wife and my daughter, when I came outside and I saw what it had done to our house and our church, I cried out, 'Lord, don't you care?'"

Next to her, Tyler's arm jumped, and she glanced at him. His face wore the same conviction that pulsed through her blood.

But it was a natural reaction, fear in the face of a storm, wasn't it?

Dan turned his eyes back to his Bible. "Then he got up and rebuked the wind and the waves, and it was completely calm. The men were amazed and asked, 'What kind of man is this? Even the winds and the waves obey him!'"

Looking up again, Dan set the Bible on the podium behind him. "So. God stopped that storm. He didn't stop ours. Does that mean he doesn't care about us?"

All around Isabel, people shook their heads. But how could they be so sure?

"How do you know?" Dan echoed her question. "I mean, this isn't the first storm God has let us go through without stopping it, is it? What about the storms of job loss and illness and broken relationships? What about the storm of abuse and addiction and death?" He paused, and Isabel was certain she couldn't be the only one holding her breath.

Dan reached behind him and picked up the Bible he'd just set down. "The apostle Paul had a storm in his life too. He called it a 'thorn in my flesh.' We don't know what it was. There's been all kinds of speculation, but it doesn't really matter. What matters is that Paul asked God three times to take it away, and each time God said no. He told Paul, 'My grace is sufficient for you, for my power is made perfect in weakness.'"

Dan paced in front of the chairs, hand on his chin. "His power is made perfect in weakness." He held up a hand. "I don't know about you, but I felt pretty weak in the face of that tornado. But that's because I took my eyes off the source of my strength. My strength isn't in me, it's in God. Listen to what David says in Psalm twenty-seven: 'The Lord is my light and my salvation—whom shall I fear? The Lord is the stronghold of my life—of whom shall I be afraid?'"

Dan looked up, his serious expression transforming into a smile. "Hear that? *This* is why Jesus called the disciples 'you of little faith.' Because he'd *told* them they had *nothing* to fear. Not a storm in a boat. Not a storm in their lives. Because he had promised he was their strength. Their salvation. And he's our strength, our salvation. That means *you* don't have to be scared of anything—" He pointed to a random spot in the room. "And *you* don't have to be scared of anything." This time his finger came awfully close to pointing at Isabel, and she nearly jumped.

The idea of not being scared of anything sounded nearly preposterous.

And yet.

Dan held up his Bible. "You don't have to be afraid because *this* is where your strength is. In God. In his Word. In the promise he has made to you that no matter how many times you are afraid, no matter how many times he could say to you, 'You of little faith,' he is right here, waiting for you, ready for you, forgiving you. He is right here to guide you and to give you strength no matter how weak you are. Which is why you can say, along with Paul, 'When I am weak, then I am strong.' Because your strength isn't from you. It's from the Lord who 'gives strength to the weary and increases the power of the weak,' who promises that 'those who hope in the Lord will renew their strength. They will soar on wings like eagles; they will run and not grow weary, they will walk and not be faint.'"

It took Isabel a second to realize that the sermon had ended and everyone around her was now standing.

"Mama," Gabby whispered out of the side of her mouth, tugging on Isabel's hand.

Isabel shook herself and pushed to her feet. She was vaguely aware that the rest of the congregation was now singing another song, but all she could think about was Dan's words and the way they had stirred her heart despite her best efforts not to let them.

She had tried her whole life to be strong.

But what if she'd been looking in the wrong place for that strength?

Chapter 24

After another week of nearly nonstop work, demolition at the church was pretty much done, and they'd even managed to start making repairs to the exterior of the parsonage. Between that and cleaning up the section of orchard that had been damaged, Tyler didn't feel like he'd sat down for days.

And neither had Isabel. As he'd watched her throw herself into every task she was asked to do, Tyler had grown more and more convinced that she was the kind of woman he wanted to spend his life with.

Or no—not the *kind* of woman, *the* woman.

Although it might be a good idea to ask her on a date or two before he jumped right to the proposal.

He watched her from across the church parking lot as she bent to say something to Gabby, then straightened, the same joyful smile that had been on her lips all week brightening her whole face.

Yes, he was definitely going to ask her out.

But not right now.

Maybe later tonight, if everything went well.

"You do have a plan, right?" Sophie tapped his shoulder as if she'd been trying to get his attention for a while.

"Um. Yes?"

"Tyler." Sophie crossed her arms. "You have to get her there at seven on the dot."

"I know." Tyler raised his hands in surrender. "I've got a lot of ideas." Most of them unlikely to succeed, but Sophie didn't need to know that.

"All right. I'm heading out to get things set up. But I'm trusting you to get her there. Seven o'clock sharp."

Tyler considered asking her what time to be there again but decided against it. He'd learned not to mess with his sister-in-law when she was in planning mode.

And especially not when she was in stealth planning mode as she had been since she'd learned this morning that today was Isabel's birthday.

"See you at seven," he said dutifully as Sophie marched away with a satisfied nod.

Tyler checked the time on his phone. Five o'clock. What was he going to do to keep Isabel and Gabby with him for the next two hours and then somehow get them to Sophie's without tipping them off about what was going on?

He took his time strolling across the parking lot, wracking his brain a little but mostly just enjoying watching mother and daughter paint the set of shutters that was braced between sawhorses. By the time he reached them, he still hadn't come up with anything convincing.

He stuck his hands in his pockets, trying for a casual pose. "Whatcha doin'?"

Isabel looked up from the shutter, laughing at him. "Painting a shutter."

"Yeah. Uh—" *Smooth.* "What I mean is, are you almost . . . I mean, would you like to . . ."

Gabby set down her paintbrush, her young eyes examining him. "You're being weird."

"Am I?" He pulled his hands out of his pockets and leaned on one of the shutters.

It took a moment for his brain to register that the warm feeling on his hands was wet paint.

He yanked his hands back, examining his now-blue palms as Gabby's giggles rolled across the parking lot.

Isabel eyed the handprints in her otherwise flawless work, then took her brush to them.

"Sorry." Tyler nearly rubbed his hands over his face but caught himself just in time.

"That's okay." Isabel lifted her brush with a flourish. "Done."

"Great. Now what?"

She laughed at him again. "Now I clean up."

"I'll help."

The job took only a few minutes, and when it was done, Isabel pulled her car keys out of her pocket.

"You're not going home, are you?"

She gave him an odd look. "I have to get Gabby some dinner."

He couldn't let them do that. Sophie would kill him if they ate before the party. "How about a walk on the beach first? It's a beautiful day."

"I don't know. I'm really tired and—"

"Please, Mama. You keep promising we can go to the beach and we keep not going."

Isabel's sigh was weary, and he felt a little bad about keeping her from resting, but it would all be worth it.

They made their way down to the beach below the church, kicking off their shoes as they stepped onto the sand.

Gabby ran ahead of them, puffs of sand billowing behind her little feet.

Tyler couldn't resist stepping closer to Isabel as they walked, although he did manage to resist taking her hand in his. For now.

"She really loves it here." Isabel's sigh was surprisingly weighted.

"That's a good thing, isn't it?"

Her nod was slow in coming. "It is. I just . . ."

His feet dragged to a stop, and he turned to her. "Do you not like it here?"

"Actually, I love it here." But her smile seemed perplexed.

"And that surprises you?"

She watched as Gabby chased a seagull. "A little, I guess. It reminds me of my hometown, which doesn't hold many good memories for me."

Tension pulled at Tyler's shoulders, and his hands clenched. Every time he thought of Isabel growing up in a family like that, he felt helpless. Like he should have been there for her.

"I guess I never thought I was the kind of person who would feel at home anywhere." Her caramel eyes grabbed his.

"And does Hope Springs feel like home?" Somehow, as he said it, he must have reached for her hand, because his fingers were now intertwined with hers.

She nodded, the hint of unshed tears in her eyes.

He took a step closer, lifting a hesitant hand to her cheek. If this wasn't the perfect opening to ask her, he didn't know what would be. Her lids flickered closed, and when she opened them again, they held a layer of trust he'd never seen before.

He swallowed, praying he'd prove worthy of it.

"There's something I've been wanting to ask you."

"Look, Mama." Gabby trundled right between them, and Tyler had no choice but to step back.

The little girl blinked up at them with curious eyes. "Why are you touching Mama's face?"

Tyler lowered his hand, relieved to hear Isabel's laugh mix with his. Judging by the sudden temperature increase he was experiencing, his face was likely as red as hers. Though she wore her blush graciously, and if anything, it only made her look more radiant.

"What did you find, Bunny?" Isabel's eyes lingered on Tyler's as she asked, with a look that said she was as disappointed by the interruption as he was.

Or at least that was how he chose to read her expression.

Gabby showed them the shells she'd collected, and then they all began to hunt for shells together. Tyler became so absorbed in the adventure—and in watching the joy that seemed to have become a fixture on Isabel's face—that he completely lost track of the time until Gabby said she was hungry.

"Me too." Isabel pulled out her phone. "No wonder. It's almost seven o'clock."

"It is?"

Yikes! He still hadn't figured out how he was going to convince Isabel to come to Sophie and Spencer's house with him without giving away the surprise.

Isabel used the back of her arm to brush at a hair that had blown into her face but missed. Tyler reached forward to tuck it behind her ear.

"Thanks." The word was soft and inviting, and he so wanted to ask her that question that Gabby had interrupted. But the little girl had taken up her customary position between them. And anyway, he had a job to do.

"What are we eating tonight, Mama?"

Isabel bit her lip, clearly without a plan, and Tyler suddenly had the most brilliant idea. "Why don't you two come to my house for supper? I made a big chicken last night, and it was too much for me without the boys, so I have lots of leftovers." Lord, forgive the white lie. Fortunately, he trusted Sophie would have much better food than invisible chicken to offer them if he got them there in the next—he pulled out his phone and gulped—fifteen minutes.

"Yay!" Gabby grabbed his hand and tugged, and he let her pull him into a jog, reaching behind him to tug Isabel along as well.

"Please." He gave her his best I'll-be-lonely look, mostly to convince her but also because he'd been finding lately that he *was* lonely whenever she wasn't around.

"Okay." She laughed as he raised his arm in triumph, lifting hers with it. "But why are we running?"

He shrugged. "Because I can't wait."

Chapter 25

I sabel cast a quick look at herself in the rearview mirror as she steered her car to follow Tyler out of town. Her hair was a mess of flyaways, and her face was sunburned, with a smudge of sand on her cheekbone. She brushed away the sand, at least. The rest she couldn't do anything about.

Tyler thinks you're beautiful anyway. She didn't know where this new voice had come from. It had just showed up gradually over the past few weeks as Andrew's had faded. The thing was, she was almost certain she recognized it from long ago. She was almost sure it was her own voice.

Wherever the voice had come from, she knew it was right. She didn't know how she knew, exactly, since Tyler had never come out and said those words. But she could tell just the same. In the way he looked at her with that softness in his eyes. In the way he spoke to her. In the way he'd been about to ask her—

What had he been about to ask her?

And would he try again while they were having dinner at his house? Maybe if they occupied Gabby with some toys or a movie?

The bigger question was, did she want him to ask what she suspected he'd been about to ask?

Yes.

That voice again. Her voice.

Very emphatic.

Yes, she did want Tyler Weston to ask her on a date.

A soft giggle worked its way up from the tickle in her belly and escaped into the car.

"What's so funny, Mama?"

Isabel clamped down on her smile as she turned into Hidden Blossom's driveway. "Nothing, Bunny. Just thinking."

"Why are there so many cars at Sophie's house?"

Isabel had been focusing on Tyler's car in front of her, but she directed her eyes down the driveway toward Sophie and Spencer's house as Gabby counted. "One. Two. Three. Four. Five. Six. Seven. Seven cars."

Isabel's smile slowly dried up. "Maybe they're having a party." One they hadn't invited Isabel and Gabby to.

Because you don't really belong here. Andrew's voice found its way to the front of her mind. *You didn't really think you had friends, did you?*

Isabel swallowed. *Tyler isn't there, either. He chose to spend time with me. With us.* Thankful that her own voice hadn't pulled a disappearing act, Isabel opened her car door just as Tyler reached them.

He seemed oblivious to the fact that he hadn't been included in whatever was going on over at Sophie and Spencer's. A wave of unexpected gratitude went through her at his loyalty.

"There are seven cars at Sophie's," Gabby informed Tyler.

"There are?" He put on a surprised expression and turned to count them. "You're right. I wonder what's going on over there."

Tyler stepped back from the car, but instead of leading them to his own house, he headed the short distance down the driveway toward Spencer and Sophie's place.

"What are you doing?" Isabel called, even as Gabby skipped to catch up with Tyler.

"Going to see what they're doing. Come on."

"What? No." She crossed her arms in front of her. The only thing worse than being excluded was barging into the very place she'd been excluded from.

But Tyler marched back to her, grabbed her arm, and tried to tug her forward.

She yanked her arm out of his grasp. "I'm not going in there, Tyler. Let's just go get some chicken."

His brow crinkled, and he stared at the ground. "There is no chicken."

She felt her own forehead folding into creases. Why would he have lied about chicken?

"Oh man." Tyler looked in her eyes now, his completely open and vulnerable. "I'm totally messing this up, but you're just going to have to trust me."

"Messing what up?" Was this guy talking in riddles? Because he wasn't making any sense.

This time, instead of grabbing her arm, Tyler held out a hand, waiting for her to take it. Slowly, she did, then let him lead her.

Because somehow, inexplicably, in spite of all her rules and all her attempts not to, she did trust him. Completely.

His hand around hers was solid and warm and just right as he walked next to her toward Sophie and Spencer's house.

At the door, he turned to her. "Ready?"

She gave an exasperated laugh. "Yes. No. For what?"

But he nudged her in front of him, Gabby at her side, then reached past her and pushed open the door.

"Aren't you going to—"

"Surprise!"

Isabel shrieked, jumping backwards into Tyler's solid form as people popped out from everywhere.

She pressed a hand to her chest, Tyler's hands warm on her shoulders, as she waited for her heart to catch up with her brain in realizing she wasn't in danger.

Next to her, Gabby had fallen to the ground, giggling.

"Happy birthday." Tyler's breath whispered over her ear.

"Is this— I don't understand."

Sophie strode to the door and pulled her into a hug. "It *is* your birthday, right?"

She nodded dumbly. "But you didn't— How did you . . .?"

"I happened to see the calendar notification on your phone this morning." Sophie winked at her and tugged her farther into the house. "Come on, get some food. Leah brought all kinds of goodies, and Peyton made the most heavenly looking cake."

Isabel swallowed hard, looking around at all the people who had gathered to celebrate her birthday. And just this morning, she'd been moping to think that her phone was the only one who would wish her a happy birthday this year—again. She'd done her best all day to forget it even was her birthday.

"So you were surprised?" Sophie peered at Isabel over her shoulder as she pulled her into the kitchen.

"Uh, yeah. I think it's safe to say that."

"Good. I was afraid Tyler would mess it up."

"Hey," Tyler's voice rose indignantly behind Isabel. "I'm right here."

"I know." Sophie shot him a smirk, then angled off to help with setting out the food.

"Sorry I lied about the chicken." Tyler dipped his shoulder to bump hers. "Hope you're not too disappointed."

"About the chicken? No." She watched him from under her lashes. Would he catch that she was a little disappointed they wouldn't get to have dinner alone together—that he wouldn't get to finish asking that question he'd started?

"All right, everyone." Sophie's voice rose over the din. "The food is ready. Let's bow our heads in prayer, then we'll let Isabel kick off this feast. Dan, will you lead us?"

Next to her, Tyler cleared his throat. "Actually, would you mind if I said the prayer?"

Warmth and sweetness and a trickle of anticipation worked their way through Isabel.

"Heavenly Father," Tyler began, his hand closing around hers.

She drew in a breath and listened.

"We come together this evening to celebrate a wonderful new friend. Thank you for the years you've given Isabel, and thank you that you've brought her right where you want her to be, right when you want her to be here."

Isabel lifted her free hand quickly to her eyes. Could that be? Had God brought her here? It sure was starting to feel like it.

"We ask, Lord, that you would bless her in the year ahead. Help her to know that every one of us is here for her and cares about her. Most of all, help her to know that you love her. In Jesus' name. Amen."

Isabel's quick, one-handed swipe at her eyes wasn't enough now, and she reluctantly tugged her fingers out of Tyler's grasp so she could stem the tears that had blanketed her cheeks.

"What's wrong, Mama?" Gabby wrapped herself around Isabel's waist.

"Nothing's wrong." She sniffed and swallowed back the rest of the tears. "I'm just thankful to have so many good friends."

"Me too. Can we eat?"

Everyone laughed, and Sophie ushered Isabel and Gabby to the front of the line.

The meal was delicious—even if she ate way too much of it—and the cake was heavenly, as promised. But the best part by far was the company.

Isabel couldn't remember when she'd ever smiled so much or laughed so hard.

Once the food had all been cleared away, Sophie presented Isabel with a large canvas tote bag in her favorite shades of peach and sea foam. Across the front, a fancy script scrawled the words "Hope Springs."

"You didn't give us much time," Sophie said, "but we did manage to pull together a little something. I hope you enjoy it."

Isabel opened her mouth. Gifts too? This was too much.

But they were all staring at her in anticipation, so she reached into the bag, letting Gabby help her pull out a jar of her favorite cherry preserves, a scented candle, bubble bath, a framed portrait of a little girl reading that she'd been admiring at the antique shop, and a box of fudge.

"These are all really nice presents, Mama." Gabby had already sampled the fudge, and she had a streak of it across her lip.

Isabel nodded, blinking back the emotion.

"Thank you all." Her voice came out kind of rough and jagged, but it was the best she could do if she didn't want to break down again. "I didn't actually know there were people like you in the world. And now I don't know what I would do without you all." She tucked the gifts back into the bag, then, as the chatter resumed around her, made a quick escape out the patio door.

Air. She needed some air.

Because as the night had gone on, an ache sharper than anything she'd ever felt at Andrew's hands had built within her.

The worst part was, it was an ache for something more. An ache for what these people had.

"Hey. You okay?"

Isabel glanced over her shoulder as Sophie stepped onto the deck.

She waited for her friend to reach her side. "Yeah. Sorry. Just needed some air. Thank you for doing all of this."

Sophie shrugged. "It was nothing."

But Isabel knew that wasn't true. It must have taken a heroic effort to put this all together in one day, in the midst of cleaning up from a tornado, no less.

And from the looks of it, they'd all worked hard to make it happen.

For her.

A strand, long and thin as a stretched rubber band, twanged in her heart.

She didn't deserve any of this.

And yet they did it for you anyway. Because they're your friends.

She'd worked for years to keep that word out of her vocabulary. But it kept popping up lately—and she couldn't deny that she liked the sound of it.

"So—" Sophie nudged her side. "How did Tyler get you here?"

"He promised me chicken at his house."

Sophie laughed. "And you believed him? I love the man, but he couldn't cook a chicken to save his life."

Isabel joined Sophie's laughter but then turned to her friend. "We went for a walk on the beach before that." She chewed her lip. She wasn't very good at this girl talk stuff.

Sophie waited, her mouth still upturned in a smile, her eyes patient.

"He said he wanted to ask me something." She poured the words out quickly, before she could change her mind. "But Gabby interrupted him."

"Do you have any idea what he was going to ask?" If anything, Sophie's smile had grown wider.

Isabel wrapped her fingers around the deck railing. "I mean, I think I know, but . . ."

"He cares about you. A lot." Sophie laid a hand on Isabel's arm. "Until you came to town, he insisted he would never date again. I hope you'll give him a chance."

Isabel nodded.

She hoped she would too.

Tyler reached into his pocket to make sure his gift for Isabel was still there.

He'd felt weird about giving it to her in front of everyone, so he'd saved it for now.

With a quick inhale to shore up his courage, he slid open the patio door.

Sophie and Isabel were leaning against the deck railing, whispering together as they watched the last trails of the sun's light slip under the world. Sophie glanced over her shoulder at him, turned to say something to Isabel, then pushed off the railing and headed toward the house.

She squeezed his arm and offered an encouraging smile as she passed him.

"Hey." Tyler took over Sophie's spot near Isabel. "I hope you had a good birthday."

Even in the low light, he could see the joy sparkle in her eyes. "This might be the best birthday I've ever had."

"Good." He reached into his pocket, grasping the small, oddly shaped package and passing it to her.

"What is it?"

"Open it." Instead of watching the gift, he watched her face. He could tell the moment she got the paper off because she gasped and lifted a hand to her mouth.

"Is this me and Gabby?" She ran a finger over the spot where he'd carved a little girl's arms wrapped around her mother's waist, the mother's arms circling the girl's shoulders.

He toed the patio, suddenly embarrassed, though there was no reason to be. "I noticed that you two stand like that a lot, so . . ."

Her smile was tender, as she brought her eyes to his. "Yeah, I guess we do. But you couldn't have made this in one day."

He pushed his hands into his pockets. "No, I've been working on it for a while. Honestly, I had no idea when I'd give it to you. *If* I'd give it to you."

"Well, I'm glad you did." She wrapped her fingers around the figure, holding it close to her. "Though I feel bad that everyone went to so much trouble for me."

"Do you really not know why we did this?"

She tilted her head at him, as if she didn't understand the question. "I just mean, I'm not really worth all this fuss."

He dared to reach a hand out to touch hers. "You are worth it, Isabel. Everyone here cares about you very much. You know that, right?"

He saw her throat bob as she swallowed. "I'm starting to," she whispered.

"Good." As long as their hands were still linked, maybe now would be a good time to ask her the question Gabby had interrupted earlier. "So, you remember before, at the beach?"

"Vaguely, yes." Isabel hit him with a teasing look that only made his desire to kiss those laughing lips grow. "There was water and sand, right?"

"Okay, okay." He slid closer. "What I meant was, do you remember that I said I wanted to ask you something?"

Isabel licked her lips, swallowed, and nodded. "I remember."

Tyler turned toward her, watching her profile, telling himself that if she showed even the slightest sign that she didn't want him to continue, he'd walk away.

But she tilted her head toward him, expectation clear in her eyes.

His mouth went dry. He was really going to say this.

"What I wanted to ask was—" He hesitated, fully expecting that they'd be interrupted again. But the only sound was the symphony the crickets had begun to strum. "Would you like to go out with me sometime?"

Her eyes didn't widen in surprise, and she didn't shriek or jump backward. But her smile did grow, and her eyes did brighten, and her lips did whisper a single word. "Yes."

Chapter 26

Isabel snapped the back on her earring, then stepped to the mirror to survey the completed look.

Tyler had told her to dress casually. She hoped her blue and pink plaid shorts and sleeveless white shirt qualified.

"How do I look?" She turned to Gabby, holding out her arms.

"Happy."

Isabel pressed a kiss to her daughter's head. She'd tried so hard over the years to hide her misery from Gabby, but she had a feeling the girl had picked up on it. But now—now she didn't have to hide how she was feeling anymore.

Because Gabby had gotten right to the heart of the matter.

"You're sure you'll be okay with Violet?" Isabel was so grateful her friend had been available on short notice. Of course, it helped that the moment she'd said yes to their date, Tyler had wrapped her in a wonderful hug, then marched her into the house and demanded to know who would babysit Gabby the next night. Nearly everyone had volunteered, touching Isabel once again with their generous spirits, but in the end, Violet had won out.

"Of course I'll be okay, Mama. We're going to play dolls and school and hairdresser and then we're going to eat ice cream."

Isabel held up a finger. "After you eat a decent dinner."

Gabby nodded and rolled her eyes. "Yes, Mama. Don't be so silly."

"You want silly?" Isabel leaned over to tickle her daughter. "*This* is silly."

Gabby squealed, but before Isabel's fingers could find their way to Gabby's ticklish armpits, there was a knock on the door.

Isabel's heart gave a cheerleader-sized leap.

Tyler was early.

But she opened the door to find Kendra, sobbing, blood dripping from a wicked gash on her puffy lip.

"What happened?" Isabel darted a glance at the door across the hall, then reached to pull Kendra into the room.

But Kendra could only cry, and Isabel led her to a chair, then crossed to the kitchen to wrap an ice cube in a wash rag. She returned to the living room and passed it to Kendra, who pressed it to her mouth. Gabby was already patting Kendra's arm, and Chancy had rested his head in her lap, so Isabel settled on the coffee table, waiting for her neighbor to talk.

Finally, the younger woman drew in a long, shaky breath. "You were right. I have to get away. But I don't have anywhere to go."

"Where is Kyle now?" Isabel was already pulling out her phone.

Kendra shrugged. "Probably at the liquor store." She closed her eyes, her whisper smaller than the smallest rustle of a leaf. "I'm scared."

"I know. Do you think he'll come home after the liquor store?"

Kendra nodded silently.

"Okay. I want you to go over there and grab only what you need. A change of clothes. Toothbrush. Anything you can't bear to part with. Can you do that?"

Another mute nod.

"Good. I'll be right here. I just have to make a couple of calls, and then I'm going to get you somewhere safe."

"Mama?" Gabby watched Isabel uncertainly.

"It's all right, Bunny. You're still going to hang out with Violet. I'm just going to see if she'd mind having you visit her at her house instead." She swiped at her phone as she talked to Gabby, grateful when Violet answered on the first ring and easily agreed to babysit Gabby at her house.

Isabel only hoped the next call would go as well.

But Tyler's phone rang and rang, finally going to voice mail. She listened as his warm greeting played in her ear. This was not the kind of thing she wanted to leave in a message. But she didn't see what choice she had.

At the beep, she drew in a quick breath. "Hey, Tyler. It's Isabel. I am so sorry to do this, but I'm going to have to cancel for tonight. Something has come up, and I—" She fumbled, unsure how much to tell him. "Anyway, I hope you'll understand . . ." She trailed off. How did she close? Just saying "bye" seemed too abrupt. But anything else seemed too . . . presumptuous. Finally, she hung up without saying anything else.

"Okay, Gabby, let's go." She locked Chancy in his kennel and grabbed her daughter's hand, working to beat back the fear that threatened to lock her in its stranglehold. What if Kyle came back before they got Kendra out? What if this time he hurt Isabel? Or Gabby?

She tightened her grip on her daughter's hand. She wasn't going to let that happen. And she wasn't going to let fear keep her from helping her neighbor. Not the way she'd let fear keep her tied to Andrew for too long.

Kendra emerged into the hallway, and with a grim nod, they started down the stairs.

"Sit in the back with Gabby and keep your head down," Isabel ordered her passenger.

Kendra's fear-bright eyes landed on Isabel's for a second before she obeyed.

Lord, help us. The prayer flitted through her head, along with the verse Dan had quoted the other day: "My power is made perfect in weakness."

Well, she felt pretty weak right now.

I sure hope you're planning to show off some of your power right now, God.

Tyler did his best to ignore the flowers sitting cheerfully in a vase in the center of his kitchen table.

He must have been in the middle of buying them last night when Isabel had decided she didn't want to go out with him after all.

He hadn't gotten her message until he'd showed up at her apartment and knocked, only to find it empty.

All because "something had come up."

Had he made a mistake to put his heart out there?

Again.

He'd warned himself not to get involved with anyone, not to let his heart feel the things it had felt, but then he'd gone ahead and done it anyway.

"Arrgh." He growled at his tie as he cinched it too tight around his neck.

He'd go to church.

He'd come home.

He'd go about his ordinary life.

And he'd forget all about Isabel.

Resolve firmly in place, he set off for the community center. By the time he arrived, the parking lot was already full, so he parked a couple blocks down the street, across from the antique shop. He resisted looking toward Isabel's apartment as he pushed out of the car, but her voice was the first thing he heard.

"Tyler!"

As if they were incapable of following the instructions his brain sent, his ears tuned right in to her. He lifted a hand in the same wave he'd give any acquaintance and almost turned to start walking again, but the decorum his mother had drilled into him wouldn't let him.

Isabel ran across the street, stopping as she came to his side. "I'm so sorry about last night. I can explain."

Her hair was pulled into a loose ponytail, and he noticed the blue-gray circles that hugged the bottom of her eyes. Apparently she'd been out late.

He shrugged, turning to walk toward the community center. Her shoes clicked on the sidewalk as she worked to keep up.

"No need to explain. It's fine." He sought an indifferent tone. "You actually saved me from having to cancel on you. So no worries."

Her feet slowed, but he kept going.

"You were going to cancel?" she asked from behind him.

"Yeah. I realized I had something else already planned. So—"

"Oh." Her exhale rang with hurt, and Tyler's conscience stabbed at him for the lie.

You're being childish. Yeah. He knew that. But sometimes being childish was the only way to keep from being hurt.

He pushed open the door of the community center, almost letting it close behind him. But the gentleman in him wouldn't let him. Instead, he contented himself with looking at his feet as he waited for her to pass.

Inside, she turned to him. "Do you think we could reschedule?"

He shrugged. "Maybe."

"Maybe?"

He was spared from answering by the sound of the band beginning the first song.

He held a hand in front of him, gesturing for her to make her way to a seat.

With one more confused look at him, she walked down the aisle that had been formed between the rows of folding chairs, and he followed.

As Isabel slid into the row where most of their friends had taken seats, Gabby leaped from the chair next to Violet to tackle her mother in a hug.

Wait.

Gabby?

Why hadn't she been with Isabel? How had she gotten here?

Tyler shook his head, taking the last seat in the row, and picked up his worship folder.

It didn't matter. From now on, nothing Isabel did mattered to him.

But he couldn't concentrate on the service, not with Isabel sitting so close to him, the light strawberry scent of her drifting toward him every time she moved her hair, though she was careful to hug the far edge of her seat, practically sitting on Gabby's lap.

In the middle of Dan's sermon message, Tyler realized his mind had drifted, and he worked to call it back.

"I know this is a big topic," his friend was saying. "And we could spend a lifetime talking about it. But if you only take one thing away from this message, I hope it's this: You are a redeemed child of God. Period. You did not have to do anything to earn that. That is God's free gift of grace to you. He has forgiven all of your sins." The familiar truth wrapped around Tyler—it was one he would never tire of hearing.

"Now, as forgiven children of God, what are we called on to do?" Dan turned to the Bible Tyler had seen him read from countless times. "Get rid of all bitterness, rage and anger, brawling and slander, along with every form of malice," his friend read. "Be kind and compassionate to one another, forgiving each other, just as in Christ God forgave you."

"Forgiving each other . . ." Dan trailed over the words, and Tyler shifted uncomfortably in his chair. Why did he have a feeling he was about to experience the sharp sting of the law?

"You probably don't need me to tell you this," Dan continued, "but sometimes people screw up. They hurt us. They disappoint us. They let us down. The worst is when it's someone we trust. Someone we love."

Tyler held back his ironic snort just in the nick of time.

"And what's our reaction when that happens? Do we say, 'It's okay,' forgive them, and move on? Or do we hold onto our hurt and anger, pack it tight inside and bring it out the next time they do something wrong? Do we let it color the whole future of our relationship with them? Maybe even affect our relationships with others?"

And there it was. Tyler winced.

He hadn't exactly been forgiving to Isabel this morning. And, as long as he was being honest with himself, she hadn't really done anything wrong.

"Is there someone in your life you haven't forgiven?" Dan asked. "Someone you've maybe been angry with for a long time?"

An image of Julia popped into Tyler's mind, though he didn't understand why.

He'd forgiven her years ago. Hadn't he?

But if that were true, would he really keep dwelling on how she'd betrayed him? Would he really still be jealous when she wanted to spend time with their boys?

A rock worked its way down Tyler's throat, settling in his stomach with a solid thud.

No, he may have told himself he'd forgiven Julia because that was what he knew he was supposed to do. But in his heart, he'd let his anger at Julia harden into a barrier. And that barrier had blocked his relationship with Isabel. Had made it impossible for him to trust her.

Had made him assume the worst of her without even giving her a chance to explain.

Dan was still talking, but this couldn't wait. He leaned his head closer to Isabel. "I'm sorry." His whisper was nearly silent, but he knew she heard it by the way her shoulders stiffened.

She pressed her lips together but then gave him a quick nod.

He supposed it was the best he could hope for, for now. He'd make a full apology the minute the service was done.

Isabel had planned to make a quick getaway.

But then Tyler had leaned over, had whispered that he was sorry, and now she didn't know *what* to do.

As she joined in singing the last song, Isabel debated. She'd almost made her mind up to leave, but then, as Dan dismissed the congregation, Tyler turned his warm eyes on her. "Can we talk?"

Isabel glanced at Gabby, then sent her off to get a cookie. She crossed her arms in front of her. It didn't offer much protection, but it made her feel a little better just the same. "About what?"

"About the way I treated you before church. I don't know what came over me, and all I can say is I'm sorry."

She blinked. Nodded. Kept her arms crossed.

"Please." His hands reached for her, fell to his sides. "I was hurt that you canceled last night. I thought you just didn't want to go out with me. But I should have listened to you. Given you a chance to explain. Clearly I'm still working on those trust issues." This time his hand did land on hers, just briefly. "Can we start today over? Pretend I just pulled up across the street and you just came out of your apartment, and I waved and said, 'Good morning, Isabel. I'm so happy to see you'?" His eyes wore a look of tentative hope, and even though every instinct told her to resist, she felt herself nodding.

"What would happen next?"

Relief welling in his voice, he said, "Next I would say I'm sorry we didn't get to go out last night but I completely understand. And I'd let you explain."

"Mmm hmm." She knew she shouldn't be softening, but she was. "And then what?"

"And then I'd ask if you and Gabby would like to go on a picnic with me after church."

"Yes!" Gabby's voice answered, and Isabel looked down in surprise. She hadn't noticed her daughter return to her side.

She tried to frown at Gabby's acceptance of Tyler's invitation, but her lips kept twitching upward. Even though her entire body ached with exhaustion, she nodded.

Half an hour later, stocked with carryout from the Hidden Cafe, they strolled to the park at the marina to eat. By the time they were done, Isabel's eyelids were heavy, and a pleasant sleepiness rolled over her.

She failed at stifling a yawn.

"You seem tired." Tyler shot her a concerned look. "Do you want to go home?"

"I'm okay. Just had a late night."

"Oh."

She cracked one tired eye open to look at him, but there was no trace of suspicion on his features.

She rolled onto her elbow. "I still owe you an explanation."

He shook his head. "I trust you. If something came up, something came up."

Isabel watched Gabby picking a blade of grass with her toes. "Hey, Bunny, you can go on the playground if you want."

"By myself?" Gabby's eyes widened.

A little flurry of worry pushed through Isabel's stomach, but she ignored it. They were twenty yards from the playground. Nothing was going to happen to her daughter.

She waited until Gabby was climbing the playset, then turned to Tyler. "I've suspected for a while that my neighbor's husband was abusing her, but she kept denying it. Last night, she came to me with a split lip and admitted she needed help getting away from him. I took her to the shelter in Adams."

The line of Tyler's jaw had hardened as she spoke, and she thought for a second that he didn't believe her.

"Where is he?" His voice was low, protective.

She shrugged. "I don't know if he ever came home last night. I had Gabby sleep at Violet's, and when I got back at two this morning, the place was quiet."

Tyler pinned her with a penetrating look. "You yelled at me for coming after you in a tornado. But this was just as risky. Maybe riskier. What if this guy comes after you? Or Gabby?"

She pushed herself upright, meeting his gaze head-on. She'd thought of that, and she'd been praying nonstop that God would keep her and Gabby safe. But this was something she had to do.

"I was as careful as I could be. There's no way he'll know we helped her."

"You don't know that." Tyler sounded almost angry. "What if Gabby says something to him?"

"Gabby knows how to keep a secret." It wasn't the first time she'd been grateful for that.

"Still, you could have called someone else to help. Your neighbor must have family, or there are groups that handle these kinds of things."

Indignation rose in her even though her heart knew his reaction was out of concern for her.

"There aren't any places to help around here." Or at least not yet. Although maybe that would change if she could make the idea that had sprouted in her head last night a reality.

"I just don't understand why you'd risk your own life. Promise me you won't do that again."

Anger drove her to her feet. "I can't promise that." She'd never be able to watch someone else go through what she'd gone through without trying to help. "You would have done the same thing."

Tyler stood too, his eyes on hers. After a moment, his face softened. "I'm sorry." He moved closer to her. Close enough that she should move away, though she couldn't seem to get her body to understand that. "You're right. You did the right thing. I just worry about you."

"Worry only gives you the illusion of control," she murmured.

"True." His hands lifted to cup her face, and she watched them as if she were watching a movie. It didn't seem real until his warm skin made contact with her cheeks.

Her hands came to his wrists, though she couldn't have said how, and his eyes locked on hers.

"Do you think—" Her voice came out as a whisper, but it was a whisper filled with certainty. "Maybe we could reschedule our date?"

Hands still on her cheeks, Tyler drew her closer, until their foreheads were touching. "I think we could."

He tilted his head slightly to the side, angling his lips toward hers.

Her breath caught at the promise of finally kissing him again.

"Mama, why is Tyler touching your face again?"

Their breath mingled on a laugh, and Tyler pulled back, murmuring, "Friday night."

Isabel nodded. "I'll find a sitter."

Chapter 27

T hank goodness the lake was nearly empty this evening. Because Tyler could not stop glancing away from the water to watch the woman next to him on his boat.

He'd been half-afraid to tell Isabel his plan for their date, sure she would shoot that down with a comment about boats being unsafe. He'd even had a backup plan—dinner at the Hidden Cafe—just in case.

But by some miracle, she hadn't resisted. Hadn't even hesitated. As he looked at her again, her hair swirling wildly around her head in the wind, he couldn't help it. He reached over and took her hand.

He only meant to hold it for a second, sure she'd feel more comfortable if he had both hands on the wheel, but she met his gaze with a smile and cinched her fingers tighter around his.

At the same time, something cinched tighter in his chest.

Tyler had prayed about this evening at least a dozen times already. But the words rose to his mind again as he aimed the boat for their destination. *I care about this woman, Lord. So much. But help me not to get so caught up in that, that I fail to seek your will. Most of all, help me to be an example of your love to her. Amen.*

After a few minutes more, he pulled back on the throttle. As the boat slowed and the noise of the engine faded, Isabel leaned closer. "Why are we stopping?"

Tyler grinned, pointing to the small island a few hundred yards in front of the boat. "We're here."

Isabel stood, grabbing at his shoulders as a wave slipped under the boat.

He got to his feet too, maneuvering the boat toward shore with one hand and sliding the other around her waist.

"Don't tell me you own an island." Her voice held a slight trace of awe.

But Tyler laughed. "Nah. It's public land. But not many people know about it." Which was why he'd been able to come out here earlier today to set everything up.

He cut the engine and let the boat drift until the hull slid against the sandy lake bottom.

"Hope you don't mind getting your feet wet." He grabbed a coil of rope from the front of the boat, then vaulted over the side.

Isabel gave a quiet yelp, then peeked over the side at him.

"Come on." He held out a hand to help her down.

But she was already splashing into the water next to him.

Maybe this woman was more adventurous than he'd given her credit for.

Isabel sighed as she lay back on the picnic blanket. She had no idea how Tyler had prepared all of this—the blanket, the flowers, the cooler full of food—but she was grateful he had.

The sky deepened into shades of mauve and navy, and she supposed she should be worried about how they'd get back in the dark. But she was too content to worry. And she trusted Tyler to keep her safe.

As she searched the sky for the first star, hundreds of twinkling lights suddenly blinked on above her.

She gasped, pushing to her feet and squinting into the trees.

Fairy lights. Somehow, Tyler had strung fairy lights in the trees.

He came up behind her, resting his hands on her shoulders.

"You're cold." His hands fell away, and she wanted to ask him to put them back. The warmth of his hands on her skin was all she needed.

But he had moved to the side of the blanket and was rummaging in a backpack.

"Here." He held out a gray hoodie.

"Don't you need it?"

He shook his head. "I'm never cold."

"Then why did you pack it?" She stuck her arms into the sleeves, bunching them to find her hands.

"Because I thought you might need it."

As her head emerged from the sweatshirt, an inexplicable prickle started behind her eyes. She sniffed, then sniffed again. She was not going to cry on their date.

But it was no use.

A tear swam down her cheek. Followed by another. Then another.

She turned away, mortified.

But Tyler's arms spun her gently, pulled her against his chest, cradled her head. "I understand if this is hard for you. We can take things as slowly as you want."

Although she'd started to relax into him, she pulled away at his words.

She walked slowly to the water's edge.

What was she doing? Was she delusional to think she could ever have a normal relationship? That anyone would ever actually want her, with all her baggage and brokenness?

He doesn't even know your name.

She pulled the hood of the sweatshirt over her head, sinking into the scent of Tyler that enveloped her, willing her mind to go blank.

After a few seconds, Tyler's bare feet stopped next to hers in the sand. "Do you want to leave?" The words were quiet, but they didn't carry hurt or anger.

Only understanding.

She rubbed at her forehead. The truth was, she didn't know what she wanted.

Or she did.

But she was too afraid to admit it.

"Would you just hold me?" She didn't know where the request came from, but suddenly she knew that was what she wanted more than anything—to be held.

A whoosh of air sounded from Tyler, as if he'd been waiting for her to ask. "Of course."

He pivoted so that he was facing her, then wrapped his arms tight around her, one hand resting on the small of her back, the other in her hair.

His heart beat strong and steady under her ear, and the sound mixed with the shushing waves to soothe her.

The peace she'd been feeling from time to time lately stirred in her heart.

"Tyler," she murmured, making the effort to get the words out past her relaxation.

"Yes?" His fingers slid up and down through her hair.

"Do you really believe God is here with us, right now?" God had always seemed so distant to her, so impersonal.

But right now, she could almost believe God cared about her. Cared about her life.

"I do." He nodded against her head.

"And do you think he wants us to be together?"

Tyler's hand stilled in her hair, and under her ear, his heart seemed to pick up speed.

It had been a bold question, and she wasn't sure she wanted to know his answer. Maybe he would say God didn't care what they did or who they ended up with.

"I've been praying for a long time now that he does." His voice was hoarse, and his arm snugged her to him.

Slowly, she lifted her head off his chest, pulling back enough to find his eyes. They were clear and bright and filled with something no one had ever looked at her with before.

"You prayed about that?" Her gaze went to his lips as they lifted into a tender smile.

"I'm praying about it right now."

She rose onto her toes, all the fear she'd clung to for so long suddenly falling away. If this man cared about her enough to pray for her, there was nothing to be afraid of.

As their lips met, she knew—this was what a kiss was supposed to feel like.

In her head, her voice whispered a quiet assent.

Chapter 28

Was it possible to float?

Because that's what Isabel felt like she'd been doing for the past two weeks.

Every once in a while, a little niggle of worry would work its way in, warning that soon the other shoe would drop, like it always did. But so far, she'd managed to push that worry away.

Because Tyler had been right. Worry had never gotten her anywhere.

And she was truly starting to believe that God had good plans for her future.

Last weekend, Dan had preached on a verse that had worked its way into her heart so far she was pretty sure it had made a home there. She didn't remember the reference, but the words that had stuck with her were, "to grasp how wide and long and high and deep is the love of Christ."

All her life, she'd been aching for a love like that. She'd wanted so desperately to find it in her parents, in Andrew, even in Tyler. And though what she and Tyler had together had only grown stronger day by day, she was starting to understand that there was no one on earth who could provide that kind of love that God freely gave—his *agape* love, Dan had called it.

Now she understood—or at least she thought she did—what made her friends here so different. It wasn't that they weren't for real—it was that they knew the very real love of God.

"Don't need a penny for your thoughts," Sophie sang from across the store as she flipped the sign to closed after another busy day. "They're written all over your face."

"Oh hush." Isabel started counting out the cash drawer, her eyes cutting to Gabby, who was listening from her perch in front of the candy display. "I was thinking about Dan's sermon from last weekend."

"Of course." Sophie winked. "What else did you think I meant? Or should I say *who* else?"

"Mama and Tyler kissed last night." Gabby covered her mouth, but the giggles escaped around her hand.

"Oh they did, did they?" Sophie's grin was as wide as the little girl's.

"You can pick out one piece of candy, Bunny." Hopefully that would distract Gabby from saying any more.

Although, truth be told, Isabel was relieved by her daughter's reaction. She'd thought Gabby was safely in her room when she'd kissed Tyler at the door last night, so when cheering had erupted from behind them, it'd taken her a moment to figure out what was going on.

But when she and Tyler had pulled apart, he'd already been laughing. Gabby had run to them, demanding that they both kiss her at the same time—one on each cheek.

Isabel's eyes had jumped to Tyler, but he'd looked completely smitten by her little girl. Together, they'd each kissed a cheek with a loud lip-smacking sound, and Gabby had giggled, wrapped an arm around each of their necks, said "I love you" to her and then to Tyler, and then dashed to her room.

Isabel had stared after her daughter, afraid to meet Tyler's eyes. What did it mean that Gabby had said she loved him before they'd said it to each other? Would it freak him out?

But Tyler's voice had been full of emotion when he'd said, "That's one special little girl you've got there."

Isabel could only nod, her own heart too full to say anything but "Goodnight."

"Isabel?" Sophie's voice called her back. "What did you get?"

"What? Oh." She glanced down at the money in her hand, having no idea what number she'd been on. "One second." She counted it again, her cheeks flaming as she felt Sophie's eyes on her.

"He really cares about you." Sophie's voice was gentle, and Isabel lifted her head.

"I know. And I—" Oh. She cared about him too. So much. But putting it into words . . .

"I know." Sophie patted her hand, then took the cash from her and counted it herself. Isabel moved to the kitchen to find a less thought-intensive task, but Sophie followed her.

"Can I ask you something?" Sophie sounded hesitant, and Isabel turned to her.

"Of course." She was careful not to promise to answer.

"When you took the job at Hidden Blossom, you told me you didn't plan to stay in Hope Springs long. Is that still true?" Concern hovered in Sophie's eyes, and Isabel saw where this was going.

"Yesterday I went to the school and registered Gabby." The funny thing was, she'd walked into that building with such certainty, such a conviction that this was the right thing to do. That they belonged here. In this town. With these people.

It was like nothing she'd ever felt before.

"Really?" Sophie squealed and engulfed her in a hug. Isabel's arms wrapped tight around her friend.

"I know you probably won't have work for me after fall," Isabel said as they disentangled. "But that's okay. Because there's something else I've been thinking of doing."

"What's that?" Sophie leaned forward, as if nothing could interest her more than what Isabel was planning. It was still a new feeling, this having friends who cared what she did with her life, but Isabel was slowly coming to realize she liked it.

She liked it a lot, actually.

"Well, I was thinking I'd like to open a women's shelter." It was the first time she'd said it out loud, and it felt a little audacious to think that she—without any education or training—would even consider it. But it felt amazing too. "I know it will be hard, and I'm not sure if I can do it, but I'd like to try."

"Count me in." Sophie squeezed her arm. "Whatever you need, you just let me know."

Isabel tipped her head in thanks. She shouldn't have been surprised that her new friend would support her in this.

The back door opened, and Tyler stepped through, a light sheen of sweat on his forehead.

"Hey, there's two of my favorite ladies." But his eyes went straight to Isabel, and she felt the warmth all the way through her.

"Don't forget about me." Gabby stepped over to him.

"Oh, don't worry. I meant you and your mama." He smirked at Sophie, who chucked a dish towel at him.

"And what have you done with my husband?"

"He was right behind me." Tyler glanced over his shoulder and laughed. "Trying to show me up as usual."

Spencer stepped into the store, holding out a bouquet of day lilies to his wife.

Sophie let out a little exclamation and crossed the room to take them, brushing a quick kiss across her husband's lips.

A little twinge of jealousy moved in Isabel. If only she could express her feelings for Tyler as openly.

Well, why couldn't she?

Gabby had already seen them kiss, and Sophie knew it, as did Spencer, undoubtedly.

Overtaken by a sudden boldness, she strode toward Tyler, planted her hands on his arms, and boosted herself onto her toes to press her lips to his.

She could feel his surprise in the way his lips lifted under hers, and then she was flat on her feet again, smiling up at him, completely ignoring the rush of heat to her face. It had been so worth it.

"And he didn't even have to bring flowers," Spencer complained.

"Neither did you." Sophie gave Spencer a kiss on the cheek, then grinned at Isabel. "Now, I believe you two have a date to get ready for."

"I just need to grab a quick shower, then I'll swing by your place to pick you up." Tyler pressed a kiss onto her forehead and then ducked out the door, leaving her with a grin so large Sophie and Spencer both made fun of her.

Which somehow only made her grin wider.

Chapter 29

Tonight was the night.

Tyler rearranged the much bigger bouquet of day lilies in his arms as he climbed the stairs to Isabel's apartment.

He'd been wanting to do this for days—weeks really—but something had been holding him back.

Fear of spooking her, mostly.

But after the way she'd kissed him in the store this afternoon, in front of Sophie and Spencer and Gabby, he knew—it was time.

He knocked on her apartment door, holding the flowers in front of his face.

There was a clatter of dog paws on the floor, accompanied by Isabel's gentle voice telling Chancy to settle down, and then the door was opening, and her laugh washed over him. "Now who's trying to show who up?"

He lowered the flowers, about to make a smart comeback, only to find himself suddenly speechless. She was wearing an ordinary pair of cutoff shorts and a shirt that set off her red hair, but it was the look on her face that had him captivated.

He held the flowers to the side and reached for her cheek with one hand, lowering his lips to hers. She inhaled and settled into him, her hands coming up to grasp the front of his shirt.

When she at last pulled away, he had to make an effort to open his eyes.

"Um, hi." It came out scratchy, and he cleared his throat. "These are for you."

Her laugh filled him. "I surmised. Come in. I just have to grab some shoes and put Chancy in his kennel. Violet picked Gabby up a couple minutes ago. They're going to go to a movie and then get ice cream, so we have a couple hours."

Tyler wanted to say that he wished he had longer—he wished he had forever—but for now, this would do.

Ten minutes later, after Isabel had put on her shoes and they'd stolen a kiss and put Chancy in his kennel—and then stolen another kiss—Tyler finally held the door open for her.

She smiled as she stepped past him, then turned to give him another kiss.

He wasn't sure what had sparked her new open affection, but he certainly wasn't going to complain.

The sound of a door opening carried up the stairs, and he pulled away reluctantly.

Isabel took his hand and turned to lead him down the steps. But she froze as she spotted the person coming up.

"Kendra?" Isabel's grip on his hand tightened, and even though the woman peering up the steps at them didn't look like a threat, he felt a sudden urge to protect her. He stepped forward.

"Hi, Isabel." The woman moved to the door across the hall without glancing up.

Isabel lurched toward her, and Tyler followed, trying to catch up with what was going on.

"What are you doing back here? Where's Kyle?"

The woman stared at the floor. "I called him. Just to see how he was doing."

"Oh Kendra." Isabel reached for the other woman, but Kendra pulled back.

"He said he missed me. He promised he'd never do it again."

"Kendra, you can't—"

But Kendra opened the door to the apartment and slipped inside. "I'm fine." The door closed with a sharp click.

Isabel's shoulders dropped as she stared at the door.

Tyler touched a hand to her elbow, and she jumped, as if she'd completely forgotten he was there. "Are you okay?"

She nodded, but it was clearly a lie.

"I take it that was the neighbor you helped."

Another nod.

"Why would she come back?" After Isabel had gone to all that trouble—risked her own safety to get her out—why would this woman come back to a man who had hurt her?

"I really don't know," Isabel whispered. She gave him a wobbly smile. "Come on, let's go to dinner."

He took her arm. "We don't have to go. If you want to stay here, help her leave again . . . If you want me to beat the pulp out of the guy . . ." That drew a laugh.

"No. But thank you. She has to be willing to leave. I can't make her, much as I'd love to. About all we can do for her right now is pray."

Those were words he'd never thought he'd hear Isabel say, and he savored them.

They were just one more sign that tonight was the night.

By the time dinner was over—he'd taken her to a new place called Toivoa, which the owner had informed them was Finnish for *hope*—he felt like he had Isabel fully back.

"Want to go for a walk on the beach?" He tried to sound casual, even as nerves kicked up in his gut.

She nodded and took his hand, and they walked together silently.

"Wow." Isabel halted as they stepped onto the beach, gazing at the bands of pink and orange that swiped across both the sky and the water. "Kind of takes your breath away, doesn't it?"

"Yeah." He couldn't take his eyes off her, and she looked up with a shy smile.

"You are so beautiful." It wasn't just outward beauty, either. It was everything about her. He bent and touched his lips to hers.

"I'm not. I'm—"

He bent to kiss her again.

"That doesn't change anything," she said around a laugh. "I'm not—"

This time, his kiss was deeper, longer, fuller. His hands slid from her shoulders into her hair, and his lips searched hers.

When he finally pulled away, her laugh was breathless. "Okay. You win. Only because I'm not sure my heart will survive another kiss like that."

"We could always try and find out." But he took her hand and led her along the edge of the water.

The beach was full tonight, and they dodged around couples and families and dogs.

Tyler glanced around. He'd envisioned somewhere a little more private for this.

His eyes landed on the water. It was nearly flat, gentle lapping waves creating little splooches on the sand in place of the big rollers they usually got out here.

"Hey, can I show you something?"

Isabel nodded.

"You'll have to get a little wet though."

Looking slightly less sure, she nodded again.

He took her hand and led her another hundred yards down the beach, looking over his shoulder to check the shoreline and make sure it was the right spot, straight down from the Hidden Cafe.

He stepped into the water, pulling her with him, pausing to give them both a second to acclimate to the chill.

"Ready?"

"I think so."

He clutched her hand tight, then started running through the water. After a couple dozen yards, it rose to his knees and a little farther on, it reached his thighs.

"Tyler," Isabel laugh-shrieked.

He kept pulling. "Almost there."

About a hundred yards out, the bottom abruptly rose, and the water was at their knees again, then their ankles.

"How on earth?" Isabel looked around in wonder.

"It's a sandbar."

"It feels like we're walking on water." She shielded her eyes and peered at the shore. "This is amazing."

The sandbar continued about twenty yards in each direction parallel to shore, though its width was only ten feet or so. Tyler followed Isabel as she explored its length and breadth.

She finally stopped and took his hands. "Thank you for showing me this."

All he could do was nod, all the words he'd prepared as he'd worked in the orchard today floating away on the water that surrounded them.

He didn't need fancy words or rehearsed speeches.

All he needed was for her to know the truth.

"Isabel," he whispered, brushing the hair away from her face.

"Yes?"

The trust in her eyes almost undid him.

What if she didn't want to hear this? What if she wasn't ready?

A flicker of fear crossed her face when he didn't say anything. "Tyler, what is it?"

"It's nothing." He choked on a small laugh. "Well no, actually, it's something. I wanted to tell you . . ."

She tilted her head, waiting.

The waves lapped at his ankles, but his heart drowned out the sound. He'd sworn he'd never say these words to a woman again. But how could he not, when he knew they were true with all his being? He let out a quick exhale, then belted the words at her. "I think I love you."

Her eyes widened. "You think you love me?" The whisper was incredulous and scared and oh-so-beautiful.

Tyler shook his head, and her expression fell.

"What I meant to say—" He tried again, savoring each word. "Is, I *know* I love you."

He reached into his pocket and pulled out a small box.

Isabel took a step backward, nearly falling off the sandbar.

He darted out a hand to catch her. "I promise it's not a ring."

She gave him a guarded look but took the box and opened it, her gasp mingling with the soft splash of the waves.

"They're beautiful." She fingered the tiny teardrop diamond earrings.

"I don't want to pressure you or rush you or anything like that. But I do want you to know that I'm all in. My heart is yours. Forever. And I hope that someday, maybe, you'll consider being my wife."

Chapter 30

Be his . . .?

She was still trying to process the fact that he'd said he loved her, and now he was saying that he wanted her to be his wife one day?

No pressure.

No rush.

Just someday.

His *wife*.

Isabel tried to swallow, but her mouth was ironically dry considering the water all around them.

How long had she been silent?

A minute?

Two?

Twenty?

She kept running her fingers over the diamonds. She could feel that Tyler's eyes were still on her, but she couldn't bring herself to look up and face the disappointment that was undoubtedly in his eyes.

He'd told her he loved her, that he eventually wanted to marry her, and all she could do was stand here.

Just say it.

But it wasn't as easy as that. She'd thought she loved Andrew and that he had loved her, and that had been a disaster. Plus, to Tyler, she was Isabel Small, widow, not Amber Perkins, domestic violence survivor.

And there was still that part of her—the part Andrew had put there—that said she wasn't good enough for him. That Tyler might be deluded enough to think he loved her now, but eventually he'd realize the truth.

"Isabel?" Tyler's fingers came to her chin, lifted it gently until she was looking at him. There was no disappointment in his eyes. Only understanding. Somehow, that made it worse.

"It's okay." He rubbed a thumb across her cheek. "You don't have to say anything. I just wanted you to know."

She nodded. Opened her mouth. Closed it again.

Three words.

Just say it.

Her phone dinged, and she grabbed for it as if it were a life raft.

"Violet texted that she and Gabby are back."

Tyler nodded and held out a hand to her. "Ready to get wet again?"

This time, they didn't run, and she didn't let out any wild, laughing shrieks.

By the time they reached the shore, she was shivering.

"Here." Tyler pulled her close, wrapping his arm around her shoulders as he walked her home.

Her phone dinged again just before they reached the apartment, and Tyler lowered his arm so she could grab it out of her pocket.

"Gabby wants you to come up and say goodnight." She tucked the phone away without clicking on the message. That way she could always claim she hadn't seen it if Tyler said no. "You don't have to if you don't want to."

"Of course I want to." He followed her to the door.

Do you see how this man loves your little girl? How could you not have told him you love him? Say it right now.

She tromped silently up the steps.

"Mama!" Gabby met her at the door with a giant hug, and Isabel squatted down to pick her up and squeeze her tighter.

"How was the movie?"

"It was the bestest movie I ever saw. And we got ice cream. And went for a walk."

"Sounds like you had a busy night." Isabel put Gabby down, and her daughter went straight to Tyler, wrapping him in a hug too.

Oh, Isabel, you are such an idiot to let a man like that get away.

Because surely that was what would happen, now that she'd failed the *I love you* test.

She turned to Violet to thank her for taking Gabby for the evening.

"Okay, Bunny, time to get you to bed. What do you say to Violet?"

"Thank you, Violet." The little girl gave Violet a hug.

"Anytime your Mama is willing to give you up for a few hours, you know who to call." Violet winked at Gabby, waved to Isabel and Tyler, and disappeared.

Gabby bounced in front of her. "Can Tyler stay to tuck me in? Please, Mama."

Isabel sent Tyler a questioning look, but the way his face had lit up, she didn't have to wait for him to answer.

"Go put on your pajamas and brush your teeth, and then we'll come tuck you in."

We'll tuck you in.

Goodness, those words had a nice ring to them.

If she *did* become Tyler's wife, they could say that every night.

She blew out a long breath.

That was a very big *if.*

Chances were, by morning Tyler would come to his senses and realize what a mistake he'd made even suggesting it.

Gabby galloped toward the bathroom, leaving them way too alone. She'd been alone with Tyler before of course, but that had been before he'd said he loved her. Before she'd been a fool and refused to say it back.

She turned to the kitchen. Surely there had to be something to clean up in here. She grabbed a rag and held it under the running water.

"Isabel." Tyler took the rag from her hand and reached past her to turn off the water. "I'm sorry if I made you uncomfortable. I didn't mean to scare you." He started to reach for her but then pulled back as if he wasn't sure she'd want him to. "I guess I just couldn't hold it in anymore. But I won't say it again if you don't want me to. I'll wait until you're ready. Just—" This time he did take her hand. "Just please don't shut me out. Or run away— Or— Or— Whatever else you're thinking."

The relief that coursed through Isabel made her laugh wobbly. "What if what I'm thinking is that I'd like to kiss you?"

She wasn't quite sure where she'd managed to summon up the teasing tone, but she was thankful when Tyler stepped closer, lowering his face toward hers. "Then I take back everything I just said. Please, do whatever you were thinking."

She lifted a hand to his cheek, the soft prickle of his stubble warm and real against her fingers, then boosted herself onto her toes to bring her lips to his. His hands slid around her waist and then up her back and into her hair.

Isabel sighed around the kiss. So this was what it was like to be loved.

How had she thought that anything she'd ever felt with Andrew had come close?

And in that moment she realized—this wasn't only what it felt like to *be* loved. It was what it felt like to *love*.

It wasn't passive.

It was active and full and amazing.

She pulled back from their kiss, gasping. "Tyler, I—"

"Ready, Mama."

Isabel closed her eyes. How was it that her daughter always managed to have the worst timing?

But Tyler laughed and slid his hands out of Isabel's hair, squeezing her arm as he slipped past her. "So how do we do this?"

Gabby giggled. "You're a daddy. You must know how to put kids to bed."

"Ah, yes, well." Tyler scooped her up. "At my house, we always start with a tickle, then another tickle, followed by the before-bed tickle, the in-bed tickle, and the turn-out-the-light tickle. Is that how you do it too?"

Gabby's giggle was wilder as Tyler reached for her foot. "No. Mama tells me a bedtime story and then sometimes we say our prayers. And then Mama gives me five kisses. And then I go to sleep."

"Five kisses?" Tyler opened his eyes wide in pretend amazement. "Why five?"

"One for yesterday. One for today. One for tomorrow." Gabby counted them off on her fingers. "One for good dreams. And one just because."

"I like that." Tyler looked over his shoulder at Isabel as he set Gabby on her bed, careful not to tangle her in the pink canopy Violet had made for her. "I might need to keep that in mind when I say goodnight to your mama."

Isabel's face heated, but she couldn't deny that she looked forward to those five kisses very much.

"All right." Tyler pulled the covers up around Gabby. "You're in bed. Now what? You said we read a bedtime story, right?"

Gabby shook her head. "Not *read* it. Mama tells it."

"We can read a story for tonight." Isabel picked a book off Gabby's bookshelf. "That way Tyler can help us."

"I want a Megan Rose story." Gabby's pout stuck out past her chin.

"Who's Megan Rose?" Tyler settled onto the edge of Gabby's bed.

"She's five just like me. And she goes on adventures. Like to the cotton candy trees and the lollipop forest." Gabby sat up in bed, and Isabel gestured for her to lie back down. She may have had a little too much sugar tonight. "Mama named her after me."

Isabel froze, her mouth suddenly the texture of sandpaper. She'd assumed—hoped—Gabby had forgotten.

Tyler quirked an eyebrow. "How is Megan Rose named after Gabby? The names don't sound alike."

"Not me, Gabby, silly." Gabby rolled her eyes as if she couldn't believe adults could be so slow. "Me, Megan Rose. That I used to be."

"Used to be?" Confusion was scribbled in the lines around Tyler's eyes, and Gabby's eyes opened wide. "Oops."

"Before she was born." Isabel rushed to cover her daughter's slip. "It was one of the names we were considering for her."

"Ah." Tyler nodded. "We almost named Jonah and Jeremiah Macaroni and Cheese, so I get it."

Gabby burst into wild giggles, and Isabel let her shoulders relax a little as she launched into the story of Megan Rose and the bubble gum pond. As she talked, Tyler reclined against the foot of Gabby's bed, his gaze alternating between Isabel and Gabby but never losing that expression of complete contentment she'd seen him wear so often.

She had a feeling the same expression was written on her own face.

When the story was done, Gabby asked if Tyler could say the bedtime prayer, and Isabel nodded, gesturing for him to go ahead.

"Dear Father in heaven," Tyler began. "Thank you for the families you put in our lives. The ones we are born in. The ones we make. And the ones we come to love." Isabel felt his eyes land on her, and she couldn't help lifting her head to him. He smiled as he continued. "You bless us in so many ways, Father. Sometimes in ways we're looking for. Sometimes in ways we never knew we needed. For that and for all good gifts, we thank you. Amen."

Isabel just barely managed to blink back the tears. What more proof did she need that this man was for real?

After they'd each given Gabby her five kisses and turned out the light, Tyler swept a light kiss onto Isabel's forehead. "I'd better head out. I have to take off early tomorrow morning to pick up the boys."

"Okay," she whispered, walking him to the door. *Say it. Say it now.*

"Tyler?" His name warbled out, and she cleared her throat and tried again. "Tyler?"

He turned to her, his eyes filled with questions she longed to answer.

"I—" She licked her lips. "I'll see you tomorrow night, right? At Leah and Austin's?"

"Of course." He bent to kiss her one, two, three, four, five times. And then he was gone.

Chapter 31

Tyler rolled his shoulders as he finally pulled into the driveway of Julia's house.

He'd had way too much time to himself to think during the drive here.

Had it been a mistake to tell Isabel he loved her? That he wanted her to be his wife someday?

He hadn't meant to pressure her, but he supposed he could understand how it might have felt that way to her. Especially since she was likely still mourning the death of her husband. Not that he could be sure, since she rarely talked about him.

Then again, he wasn't sure how much he wanted to know about the man she'd been in love with before him.

Assuming she even was in love with him.

She hadn't said as much—which was fine. He hadn't expected her to, though if he was being honest, he'd held onto a sliver of hope that she would.

Which wasn't fair to her.

He shouldn't be trying to force a confession of love.

Eesh. He had to stop thinking about Isabel for five minutes, so he could face his ex.

Rubbing at the kink in his shoulders, he got out of the van. It sure would be nice if love could ever be simple.

Before he'd made it two steps up the walk, the front door of Julia's stately three-story brick house banged open, and both boys zoomed at him, crushing him in a bear hug.

His arms went around them.

This love, at least, was easy.

"They haven't stopped asking when you'd be here since they got up." Julia walked down the flagstone path more slowly, and he was surprised to see her in bare feet, with no makeup. She actually looked relaxed.

"Boys, why don't you go grab your stuff." She stopped in front of him as the twins raced each other back inside. "Thanks for letting me keep them longer. We had a really good time."

"I'm glad." To his surprise, Tyler meant it. It was a good thing for his boys to know more than just his love. "Where'd you all go?"

"We mostly hung out here, actually. They're surprisingly good at making their own entertainment."

Tyler chuckled. "Yeah, that they are." After a moment of hesitation, he plunged forward with the question he'd avoided asking for six years. For some reason, today he couldn't wait any longer. "What happened to us, Jules?"

She gave him a sad smile. "Do you know how long I've been waiting for you to ask that? And now that you have, I really don't know the answer."

Tyler's shoulders dropped. That was less than helpful.

"Was it something I did or didn't do or . . .?" If Isabel *did* give him a chance, he didn't want to make the same mistake twice.

"All I can tell you is that I felt neglected and alone after the twins were born. You were out there, still living your life, and I wanted to be living mine too, but I was struggling. I felt like you didn't see me."

A retort was sharp on Tyler's tongue, but he bit it back, considering her words. He'd always looked at Julia as the bad guy, the one who had abandoned their marriage. But was it possible that he'd been just as much to blame?

"I'm not saying I handled it well." Julia looked at her bare feet. "And I know it's probably hard to believe, but I *am* sorry for that."

"I believe you," Tyler said quietly. "And I forgive you." A burden the size of Julia's house lifted off his shoulders. "I hope you can forgive me too."

"I do." Julia tilted her head to the side. "There's something different about you."

Tyler shrugged.

Julia tapped his shin with her bare toe. "It wouldn't have anything to do with this Isabel the boys keep telling me about, would it?"

Again he shrugged. It wasn't really the kind of thing he wanted to talk to his ex-wife about.

"I'm happy for you, Tyler." She squeezed his arm as the boys came out carrying their bags.

He nodded. He was pretty happy for himself too.

Chapter 32

"Ready to go, Gabby?" Little zaps of anticipation shot through Isabel's entire body.

In a few minutes, she'd see Tyler. And she knew exactly what she was going to do the moment she saw him.

First, she was going to kiss him. Then she was going to take him aside, tell him she loved him, and share the truth of her whole life with him—every single ugly part of it. Because she knew now that he could handle it, that he would love her no matter what he learned about her. She didn't want any part of what they had together to be based on a lie.

She wanted it all to be beautifully, messily, imperfectly real.

"Coming, Mama." Gabby emerged from her room, holding up two pictures. "I made these for Jonah and Jeremiah. I can't wait to see them."

"Me neither. Let's go." She was about to put Chancy in his kennel when there was a knock on the door.

"Oh." She pressed a hand to her stomach. They were supposed to meet Tyler and the boys at Leah and Austin's house, but maybe he'd decided to surprise them by picking them up. "You want to get that, Bunny?"

She held Chancy's kennel open as Gabby skipped to the door, but the dog refused to move.

"Chancy, get in," Isabel commanded.

A low growl rose from the dog's throat, and Isabel jumped. He'd never done that before.

"Chancy, what—"

"Hello, Amber."

She froze as Chancy's growl turned to a bark, and he sprang for the door.

It couldn't be. He couldn't have found them. He couldn't be here.

She spun, reaching for Gabby and pushing her daughter behind her as Chancy kept up his wild barking.

"Good to see you again too, dog." Andrew aimed a sharp kick at Chancy's side, and the dog whimpered and stopped barking but didn't leave the post he'd taken up between Isabel and her ex-husband.

The scent of black licorice threatened to overtake her as she shook her head frantically from side to side, wildly searching for a way out, though she knew there was none.

"Mama?" Gabby sounded confused but not frightened. Of course. She'd been too young when they left to remember. Isabel had always figured it was better if she didn't know her father was a monster.

"It's okay, Gabby. Can you go in your room for now? I need to talk with this man."

"*This man* is her father." Andrew took a step closer, and Chancy's growl deepened.

"Gabby. Room. Now," Isabel commanded.

Thankfully, the girl obeyed.

Andrew smirked at her. "It's been too long. I wouldn't have thought red would be your color, but you look good." He reached for her hair, and she flinched out of his way. Instead, his hand landed on her upper arm, locking around it.

"How did you . . .?" Not that it mattered how he'd found them. Only that they got away.

"Good thing you never were very smart." He fished a phone out of his pocket, casually scrolling through it. He flicked the screen toward her, zoomed in on a picture of her and Gabby in the Hope Fest Parade.

"You need to leave, Andrew." She tried for forceful, but her voice came out as more of a whimper. "We've been divorced for three years. You have no claim on me anymore."

Please give me courage, Lord. Show me a way out of this. Keep my daughter safe.

The knot of fear that had cinched around her lungs eased a fraction.

Whatever happened next, God was with them.

"Maybe not on you, sugar, but Megan Rose is still my daughter. I got a right to see her."

Just like that, the knot was back, squeezing tighter, threatening to cut off her air.

"The courts gave me full custody. You know that."

"Only because I didn't contest it at the time. But now I'm thinking I just might. Might try for full custody myself. Judge owes me a favor after I got him out of a tight spot."

No. No. No. No. No.

This could not be happening.

She turned her head to the side, seeking an escape from the sharp cologne that blocked her ability to think straight. All she wanted to do was drop to the floor in a sobbing puddle, but she couldn't give in.

For Gabby's sake, she had to stand up to him.

"No judge is going to give you custody after the things you did. Not even if they owe you a favor." Her voice didn't exactly ring with confidence, but at least it wasn't shaking.

Andrew grabbed her face, turned it toward his. "Do you have any proof of that?"

She forced herself to hold eye contact. "It's all in the divorce proceedings."

That horrible smirk twisted, morphing into a grotesque smile. "I wouldn't be so sure about that. I told you, the judge owes me a favor."

Nausea rolled from Isabel's stomach up her esophagus, and she had to swallow down the bile. It wasn't true. It couldn't be. That wouldn't be legal.

This was just what he did, what he'd always done. Using her fears and doubts and insecurities to manipulate her. Make her think she had to do what he said.

"It doesn't have to be like this." Andrew stepped closer, so that his body was nearly pressed against hers.

She fought off the need to gag as his cologne nearly overwhelmed her.

His voice turned sugary. "Just come back with me. I'll be better this time. Treat you real sweet."

She wanted to ask if bruising her arm the way he was right now was part of real sweet but held her tongue. Angering him more was not the way out of this.

"Come on." He gave her a loose semblance of that smile she had found so charming all those years ago. "I miss being a family."

That word.

Family.

That was all Isabel had ever wanted her entire life. It was what had drawn her to Andrew in the first place. What had made her stay with him long after she'd discovered what he was really like.

But now she knew. What Andrew was offering her wasn't family.

Family was people who loved you no matter what. People who watched out for you and cared for you and laughed with you and cried with you. Family was what she had here. In Hope Springs.

"We're not going with you," she said as firmly as she could. "You're going to let me go right now and get in your car and leave and never come near us again."

Andrew let out a hearty chuckle. "And who's going to make me?"

He pushed her farther into the room. Closed the door. "I'll help you pack."

"I told you, we're not going."

Andrew lifted his free hand to her neck. Flashes of panic went off in her head. She'd been in this position before.

Almost hadn't survived it.

The same helplessness that had rolled over her three years ago threatened to suffocate her.

But now she knew she wasn't alone.

Call on me in the day of trouble. She'd read those words just last night.

Please help me, Lord. Please help.

Spots flickered in front of her eyes.

What if God didn't help her?

Chapter 33

"God is good boys," Tyler said as he drove into Hope Springs, past the church. Construction was in full swing now, and they were already planning the dedication service for this fall. Their great Father had brought good out of the storm.

Both out of the tornado and in his life.

Six years ago, he never would have thought it was possible. He still wouldn't have chosen to go through a divorce, but God had turned even that to good, bringing him to Isabel.

"We're back earlier than I thought we'd be. Why don't we swing by and surprise Isabel and Gabby. We can all drive over to Leah and Austin's together."

The three of them sang along to the Christian song on the radio as he steered down Hope Street. None of them had the best voices, but it didn't matter—their praises filled the car with their exuberance.

Tyler imagined God smiling from heaven.

A twist of nerves pinched his gut as he pulled into the parking lot behind the antique store. She'd had all day to think about what he'd said last night, and he wasn't sure if that was a good thing or a bad thing.

God's got this, he reminded himself as he and the boys spilled out of the van.

They thundered up the steps, Jonah and Jeremiah arguing about who got to knock on the door.

"Boys." At the top of the stairs, Tyler stepped past them, about to knock himself. But as the boys fell silent, the sound of wild barking and someone screaming bled through the door.

"Stay here." Adrenaline spiked through Tyler as he pushed the boys to the side of the hall. He couldn't even imagine what was going on inside. But if Isabel and Gabby were in danger—

He grabbed the doorknob and shoved hard. It slammed open with a bang.

Isabel was pinned on the couch, a large man hunkering over her, hands wrapped around her neck. A screaming Gabby was trying to get to them, but Chancy blocked her path, alternately growling at the man and barking at Gabby.

Tyler didn't think.

Just reacted.

Five long strides, and he had the man's collar in his hands, was yanking him off Isabel. His fist met the guy's face. Once. Twice.

Rage made him draw back for a third punch, but the guy had crumpled to the floor.

He lunged for the couch, arms engulfing Isabel. She clutched at his shirt, gasping for air.

"You're okay. You're okay." He didn't know if his words were a question or a statement, but she nodded into his chest. "Oh, thank you, Lord."

Still holding her to him, he pulled out his phone, dialing 911 with shaking hands.

That had been too close. He could have lost her. She could have . . .

He couldn't even think the words.

"Mama?" Gabby ran across the room and launched herself at them.

"Dad?"

He looked up to see Jonah and Jeremiah in the doorway, and he gestured them into the room too.

"911. What's your emergency?"

Tyler quickly relayed what had happened, and the dispatcher promised an officer would be there in a few minutes. "Do you feel you are safe now?"

"We're safe." Tyler eyed the man's form as he started to stir. He let go of Isabel and moved to jerk the man's arm behind him in an armbar, thankful that he and the boys had taken a martial arts class together last year. This would hold him until the police arrived at least.

"Mama, why did that man say he's my daddy?"

Tyler's head jerked up in time to see Isabel's face lose all the color it had started to regain.

Beneath him, the man stirred again, and Tyler tightened his grip.

"Because I *am* your daddy, Megan Rose."

Tyler's heart jolted to a stop. That name. He recognized it. Wasn't that the girl Gabby liked to hear stories about? The name Isabel had said she'd almost given Gabby.

His eyes went to Isabel, but she refused to look at him.

That said it all, didn't it?

But still, he had to ask. "Isabel, who is this man?"

She shook her head, tears slipping down her cheeks. And still she refused to look at him.

"Isabel, huh?" The man on the floor grunted. "Doesn't suit you, Amber."

Amber?

Tyler's head spun. He needed a minute to figure out what was going on here.

Because either this guy was delusional or—

Or Isabel had lied to him.

The force of the realization hit him like a falling tree.

She'd lied to him.

"Isabel," he asked again, voice oddly calm. "Who is this man?"

Chapter 34

There was no way to explain.

The hurt in Tyler's voice. The betrayal.

Telling him who Andrew was wouldn't make that go away.

From underneath Tyler, Andrew gave a sharp laugh. "Go ahead, *Isabel*. Tell him who I am."

She pressed her lips together. If only she could get these stupid tears to stop. She hated that Andrew still had this power over her.

"Fine. I'll tell him. I'm her husband." Andrew grunted as Tyler jerked harder on his arm. "Watch it man, or I'll have you arrested for assault. I'm a lawyer."

Tyler ignored him, and she could feel his eyes on her. "You said your husband was dead."

Andrew's chuckle rumbled through the room. "Gave you that whole I'm a helpless widow act, right? Don't worry, man, she got me with it too."

No. But Isabel's voice stuck in her throat.

Tyler wouldn't believe that would he?

"Act?" His voice was dull.

"And now she has the single mom vibe going for her too, right? But that's *my* daughter. You can keep Amber. Or Isabel. Or whatever you want to call her. I'm just here to get my daughter back."

No. The voice was a scream in her head, but still she couldn't get it to come out.

640

The doubt in Tyler's eyes was clear.

With one little twist, Andrew had turned him against her.

You turned him against yourself. With your lies.

"Tyler, I didn't—"

"Is he your husband?" Tyler's voice was too quiet.

"Ex-husband," she whispered. "We're divorced, Tyler. I didn't— I shouldn't have—"

The sound of police sirens in front of the store brought their conversation to a stop. Within seconds, Liam Cline and two other officers were bursting into the room. They handcuffed Andrew, then the two officers led him to the door, while Liam said he'd stay to take their statements.

"She's my daughter too." Andrew called over his shoulder, doing a convincing representation of a broken father who just wanted to see his child. Isabel prayed she wasn't the only one who could see through it.

Liam asked Jonah and Jeremiah to take Gabby in her room to play, then asked her and Tyler to take a seat so he could get their statements. She remained where she was on the couch, trying not to flinch when Tyler chose the chair on the opposite side of the room.

But his voice shook as he told the chief how he'd found Andrew with his hands around her neck, how he'd thought she was dead, how he'd pulled the man off of her and punched him. Isabel swiped at a fresh round of tears. This man had risked his life for her more than once. And she hadn't even been able to tell him she loved him.

She doubted very much that she'd ever get that chance now.

"Thank you, Tyler," Liam said after he'd asked a few follow-up questions. "You're free to go if you'd like. I'll be in touch if I need anything else."

She felt Tyler's eyes slide to her, and she dared for a second to meet his gaze. The warmth that she'd come to expect there was gone, but his voice was gentle as he asked if she wanted him to stay.

She nodded, offering him what she hoped came across as a grateful smile. She was pretty sure she couldn't do this without him.

She kept her eyes on him the entire time she made her statement. She told the chief about how Andrew had abused her for years before she'd left him, how she'd had to change her name and Gabby's to keep them safe, how she'd prayed he wouldn't find them in Hope Springs. Through it all, Tyler sat rigid, his jaw clenched, not meeting her eyes, though she saw a muscle in his neck jump every time she said anything about Andrew hurting her.

She wanted so badly to go to him, to tell him she was sorry she'd lied, to feel him wrap his arms around her and tell her it was okay, that he was here, and he was never going to let anything bad happen to her again.

But that kind of ending only happened in fairy tales.

As the chief got up to leave, she told him again of Andrew's connections, of his threat to blackmail a judge into giving him custody of Gabby.

"I wouldn't worry about that." Liam patted her shoulder. "From what I've heard here, I think we can make a case for attempted murder. He's not going to be in any position to do any blackmailing."

Isabel swallowed, blinking back the gratitude. "Thank you."

After Liam left, Tyler sat staring at his hands.

She approached his chair but stopped several feet in front of it. He didn't look up at her.

"Tyler, I'm sorry." Her voice was stronger than she'd expected. "I should have told you the truth. I guess it was just easier to pretend that none of it had ever happened. To pretend that this was my real life." She gestured around her. "I was embarrassed and ashamed of my past, and I didn't want you to know . . ."

When his eyes met hers, the certainty she'd seen there yesterday had been replaced by doubt. He pushed to his feet but didn't step closer.

"I am so glad that you're okay. That he didn't . . ." Tyler looked out the window, clearing his throat. "And I am so sorry that you had to go through all of that. In the past. I wouldn't wish that on anyone, least of all you."

She held her breath. Next he would take a step forward and wrap those powerful, comforting arms around her and tell her everything was all right.

"I just . . ." He blinked, bringing his eyes to her. The sheen in them made her blink back her own tears. "I don't understand why you lied to me. Why you couldn't trust me."

She wanted to tell him that she did trust him. That she trusted him with her life.

But she could see that it was too late. She'd known the one thing he couldn't handle was being lied to. And she'd lied to him anyway.

"I think I just need some time." His voice was hoarse, and he rubbed his fingers over his eyelids as he passed her.

Please. But the voice was only a whisper in her head.

She stepped out of his way, and he collected the boys.

And then they were gone.

⸎

"I don't want to go, Mama." Gabby's eyes were red-rimmed, and Isabel's heart, which she'd thought had already been shattered into as many pieces as possible, broke a little farther as she pulled the covers up to Gabby's chin.

It was late, and today had been too much to handle. For both of them.

"I know, Bunny. But we have to."

"Why?" Gabby's brow wrinkled, as if her five-year-old brain were being asked to comprehend far more than it should ever have to. "The police took that bad man away. My daddy."

"I know." Isabel swallowed against hearing her daughter call Andrew her father. If only she could have gone her entire life without finding out. "It's complicated."

But even that answer was a lie. Because it was actually very simple. They had to leave because it was too hard to be here, knowing what she'd almost had, what she'd lost.

"But I'm supposed to start school next week." A fresh batch of tears slipped down Gabby's cheeks.

"I know, Bunny. And you will. Just not here."

"But this is our home, Mama."

Home.

Gabby couldn't have known how that word stabbed into Isabel's heart.

She'd promised herself she'd never call anywhere home.

But hard as she'd tried to keep it from happening, Hope Springs had become home. And she doubted very much that she'd find anything like it anywhere else she went.

"I know." She dusted a kiss onto Gabby's forehead. "Try to get some sleep now."

A snuffle was Gabby's only response, and Isabel had to fight against her own tears as she closed her daughter's bedroom door.

Weariness pulled at her limbs, but she still had packing to do if they were going to leave first thing in the morning.

Fortunately, she knew Vi kept a stack of empty boxes in the furnace room under the stairs. She trundled down to collect some, thinking about how Sophie had showed up at her door not fifteen minutes after Tyler had left.

It shouldn't soothe her to know that Tyler had asked his sister-in-law to check on her, but it did.

Even if she'd sent Sophie away, telling her she just needed to be alone for a bit.

She should have at least thanked Sophie—for everything.

Maybe once she got settled somewhere else she'd work up the courage to call and do that.

Settled.

The word didn't have the same appeal it once had. But even if she didn't fall in love with another place, even if she never found somewhere else to call home, she could at least learn to live in a new town—she was pretty sure.

It took less than an hour to pack up the living room and kitchen, and then she moved on to her bedroom. She grabbed the framed picture of her and Gabby off the nightstand, then reached for the Bible.

But instead of packing it, she sat down on the bed and pulled it into her lap.

"Lord, what am I doing?" she whispered into the dim room.

There was no answer, not that she'd expected one. Though she'd continued to go to church, though she was starting to believe that God was in control, somehow he still felt distant. Like he was managing things from far away, not sitting right here next to her, as she'd heard her friends talk about.

Last week, she'd asked Dan about that, asked how she could know God was with her. He'd suggested that she read First John chapter four. She'd been putting it off all week, not sure if she was really ready to hear it, but tonight, she didn't know where else to turn.

She flipped her Bible open, paging through it until she came to the chapter. At first, her eyes skimmed the words, unable to take them in.

But when she came to verse eighteen, she froze: "There is no fear in love. But perfect love drives out fear."

Her finger went back and forth over the words as she mouthed them to herself.

Sometimes it seemed like every decision she'd ever made in her life was driven by fear. She'd tried to convince herself she was driven by love—love for Gabby, a desire to keep her safe. But the truth was, she'd been driven by fear of losing Gabby. Fear of opening her heart again. And now, fear of staying here and facing the consequences of what she'd done.

Perfect love.

What would that be like?

But she already knew.

It wouldn't be like Tyler's love. Because as much as she knew he loved her—or at least he had loved her until she'd ruined everything—she also knew he made mistakes.

Perfect love was the love she kept reading about in the Bible, kept hearing about in church. She went back to the beginning of the chapter and read it again, more slowly this time, letting the words seep through every barrier she'd ever erected. Phrases emblazoned themselves on her heart: "Love comes from God," and "This is love: not that we loved God, but that he loved us and sent his Son as an atoning sacrifice for our sins," and "God lives in us."

A stir moved in her heart, and she knew God had been knocking there for weeks, but she'd kept telling him to go away. What if this time she let him open the door? She closed the Bible and folded her hands on top of it. At first she just sat like that, still and quiet. But after a while, the words came, and she poured them out to God.

"Lord, I have been so afraid of everything. Of Andrew. Of losing Gabby. Of love. Of Tyler. Even of you." She swiped at a stray tear. How could she ever have been afraid of the One who loved her more than anything? "Please help me to know the perfect love that drives out fear. Take my fear and weakness and turn it into strength—not strength in myself, but strength in you. I don't know what to do next. I don't know where to go. But I know that I need you. None of the rest matters without you."

She closed her eyes as something settled over her. If she had to put words to it, she'd call it peace—that elusive peace she'd been chasing all her life. She didn't really understand it. She still didn't know where they would go or what would happen next. She didn't know if she could fix things with Tyler or if they were broken forever. She didn't even know if she could stay in Hope Springs.

But she knew peace—God's peace. A peace that was beyond her understanding.

Chapter 35

Tyler rubbed at his bleary eyes, whispering a soft "Amen." He lifted his head, surprised to see dawn breaking on the horizon. He'd spent all night in this chair. Thinking. Praying.

But now that morning was here, he was at peace. He knew what he had to do.

He sent Sophie a quick text. *You up?*

The reply was immediate. *Never went to bed.*

Same here. His fingers flew across the keypad. *Can you stay with the boys for a bit?*

He didn't want to wake them, after it had taken so long to get them to sleep last night. They'd been pretty shaken by everything they'd seen.

Then again, so had Tyler.

His fists clenched in his lap as he saw that vulgar man's hands around Isabel's neck again. As he imagined for the seven thousandth time what could have happened to her. Realized that he could have lost her.

And that was how he knew. As much as he'd been confused yesterday and hurt that she'd lied to him, he knew without a doubt now that he didn't ever want to lose her. Which was why he had to see her right now.

There was a soft tap on the front door, and then Sophie was letting herself in.

She was a mess, her hair in disarray and her eyes heavy with shadows, and he knew this was as hard on her as it was on him. She crossed the room and wrapped him in a hug.

"He hurt her, Sophie." The whisper scraped at Tyler's throat as he tried to hold back the emotion. He wasn't too macho to admit he'd cried for Isabel last night. For what she'd been through when she was married to that monster. For the fact that there was nothing he could do to change that.

"I know." She rubbed his back. "But you won't. You'll be there for her."

He nodded, swallowing hard.

"Give her my love." Sophie gave him one last pat on the back, then sent him out the door.

The sun was just lifting over the lake when Tyler drove into town, and he slowed to watch it sparkle off the water. He hated the fact that Isabel had had to experience so much of the ugliness of this world.

And he prayed that he could show her some of its beauty.

Its hope.

He pulled into the parking lot behind the antique store, closing his car door quietly.

But when he got to her apartment, he hesitated. He didn't want to wake her and Gabby if they were sleeping.

Pulling out his phone, he deliberated, finally texting, *Can we talk? I'm here.*

He stared at the door, listening hard for sounds of movement. After a minute had gone by, he started to pace. After another minute, he laced his hands behind his head, still pacing.

Finally his phone dinged. *Still here?*

Before he could reply, the door opened.

"Hey." It was all he could get out, since all the air had escaped him. The urge to hold her nearly overpowered him, but the way she was looking at him, sort of wary and guarded, warned him off.

"Hey." She crossed her arms over her middle.

He tried to figure out what to do with his hands, finally stuffing them into his pockets. "I just wanted to say that I'm sorry. I shouldn't have left like that yesterday. I was confused and hurt, I guess. I didn't understand why you didn't trust me with the truth." He shook his head. He hadn't come here to blame her.

"I do trust you, Tyler. I should have told you," she whispered, eyes aimed at the floor. "I'm so sorry I lied. I don't even know why— I just thought . . ."

He took a step closer, then tentatively placed a hand on her cheek, letting his thumb sweep over the soft skin. "I'm not going to pretend to understand everything. But I want you to know that I understand *you*. I understand why you didn't tell me. You wanted to keep Gabby safe." He thought again of everything she'd been through. "You're so brave, Isabel."

But she shook her head, lifting her eyes to his. "I'm not brave."

He started to argue, but her eyes flashed, and he fell silent.

Whatever she had to say, he'd let her say it. "I didn't tell you because I was afraid. Fear has driven every single thing I've done since Gabby was born, maybe longer." A new light seemed to shine in her eyes. "But I don't want to live in fear anymore. I want to trust in God's perfect love. The love that drives out fear."

"That's—" Tyler swallowed, his heart fuller than it had ever been. "That's the best news I've ever heard." He wrapped his arms around her, pulling her tight to him.

From somewhere in the apartment, Chancy whined, and Isabel laughed. "Someone wants a hug too."

"Well, he deserves one, after the way he protected you and Gabby yesterday." Tyler glanced toward the dog's kennel.

But something about the room was different.

He straightened, stepped past Isabel.

Boxes.

Everything was in boxes.

"I don't understand. Are you—" But she wouldn't. Would she?

"Are you leaving?"

"Tyler," her whisper was weighted.

"No." He turned and grabbed her hands. This was too perfect. He wasn't going to let go of it this time. "Don't say it. Don't say you're leaving."

"Tyler—"

"No. Please let me say this. I never meant to fall in love again. I thought I'd hardened my heart. Thought nothing and no one could ever move it."

"Tyler—"

But he rushed on, desperate not to let her speak. "But you moved it, Isabel. You filled it. Please stay here. With me."

He'd never felt so vulnerable in his life.

And yet he wouldn't take back a single one of those words, even if she said she didn't feel the same way.

She raised an eyebrow. "Are you done?"

"Actually, there's one more thing."

Slowly, he brushed the hair off her face. Slowly tilted his head. Slowly lowered his lips to hers, letting them linger in a tender kiss.

Her hands came to his shoulders, and he sighed, contentment welling in his soul. Couldn't she feel it too? How right this was?

When they finally parted, she slipped her hands into his. "Now, if you would let me talk, what I was going to tell you is that I'd already decided to stay in Hope Springs."

"You had?" Tyler tilted his head to the side, studying her. "Why?"

She looked around the room, out the window, toward Gabby's bedroom, then back at him. "Because it's the only real home Gabby has ever known. Because she has friends here. And so do I. Because I know we're loved here. Because I love people here. Because—" She broke off, swallowed, and he held his breath.

"Because I love you."

Tyler's eyes locked onto hers. "You do?"

She nodded, her hands coming to his shoulders and pulling him toward her. "I do. Now if you don't mind, I'd like you to kiss me again."

He did not mind at all.

Epilogue

"**R**eady to get the kids?"

Isabel looked up from the small alcove she'd converted into an office in the new women's center. It had taken nearly the entire school year to get the place up and running, and she still couldn't believe it had really happened.

Thanks largely to this man's unwavering support.

She pushed back from her desk and stood to greet him with a kiss. "Yep. Let me just tell Kendra I'm leaving."

She'd already told her assistant that she'd only be in until noon today, since it was the last day of school, and she and Tyler had planned to spend the afternoon with the kids.

She popped her head into the kitchen, where Kendra was preparing lunch with the other two women who were currently staying in the shelter. Thankfully, Kendra had finally left Kyle for good, and Isabel had been able to help her file a restraining order against him.

After a quick goodbye and a reminder to call her if they needed anything, Isabel slipped her hand into Tyler's and let him lead her to the front door of the Old Victorian he'd helped her transform into the women's center.

Outside, she paused. There was something she had to tell him. "I called my mom today."

Tyler turned to face her, waiting silently. She loved that he knew when she needed a moment to collect her thoughts.

"It was totally awkward," she confessed, and he gave a gentle laugh, pulling her closer.

"We both said we were sorry, both cried. I asked her if maybe she'd like to meet Gabby sometime." She directed a shy smile at him. "And you, if you'd like. And the boys."

Tyler beamed, lifting her hand to his lips and dusting a kiss onto her knuckles. How was it that such a simple gesture could hold so much love? "There's nothing I'd love more."

"Good." And it *was* good. So good.

"So what's the plan for this afternoon?" she asked as he held open the van door for her. She'd been so busy with the shelter that Tyler had offered to plan their afternoon off.

"I thought we could go over to the island this afternoon. I packed a picnic."

"It's like you read my mind." He was getting pretty good at that. And she was getting better at learning that if she needed something, it was okay to ask. Better than okay. He *wanted* her to ask. He *wanted* to know how he could best serve her.

It was a totally different feeling from any she had ever known in her life, not having to fend for herself.

It made her feel . . . precious.

So different from how she'd felt a year ago today, when she'd pulled into Hope Springs, alone, afraid, and unsure what the future held.

And even though she couldn't predict the future any better today than she could a year ago, she was no longer alone or afraid. She knew that whatever came next, the One who had walked beside her every step of the way would continue to be with her.

They pulled into the school parking lot just as the school bell rang. Kids spilled from the building, their cheers and laughter testifying to the promise of the carefree summer that stretched before them. She spotted Gabby hugging her teacher and waving to her friends, and a shot of joy went through her. Somehow, even after everything she'd been through in her young life, her daughter remained a little ball of sunshine.

Jonah and Jeremiah approached Gabby, and she smiled and walked between them, chatting the whole while. Isabel couldn't help the thought that the boys treated her like a sister.

She glanced at Tyler out of the corner of her eye to see if he'd noticed. But he was leaning into the back seat, digging frantically in the picnic bag.

"What are you doing?" Isabel leaned to peer over his shoulder, but he tugged the bag's zipper closed.

"Nothing. Just thought I forgot something."

651

"What?"

He shook his head. "Nothing. It's all there."

Before she could question him further, the back doors of the van opened, and the kids poured in, all three talking at once. Isabel soaked up their energy as Tyler pulled out of the parking lot and drove to the marina.

When they got to the boat, she didn't hesitate but stepped aboard and handed out the life vests. Tyler stowed their picnic and pulled slowly out of the marina.

As soon as they hit the open water, Isabel gave him the thumbs-up, and they shot off across the waves.

She leaned back in her seat, savoring the moment. She was happy, yes. But it was more than that. As she looked from her daughter to the boys she'd come to love as sons to Tyler, she realized what it was—she was content.

Tyler slowed the boat as they approached the island, and they all jumped easily into the water. When they reached the shore, Tyler tugged her toward their usual picnic spot, telling the kids they could play in the sand for a few minutes before lunch.

Isabel wanted to protest that it would make more sense to eat first, then play in the sand, but she resisted. It wasn't like she minded the extra time alone with Tyler.

As they spread out the picnic blanket and set out the food, he grew quiet, his gaze flitting to the kids and back every few seconds.

She turned to look over her shoulder. What was going on over there that had him so interested?

"Hey, Isabel—"

She swiveled toward him, waiting.

But he cleared his throat and continued to take items out of the bag.

"Tyler, what on earth is going on?" She reached to take the container he'd just pulled out of the bag, setting it aside.

"Nothing." But his eyes darted beyond her again.

"I swear, Tyler, if you put them up to dumping a bucket of water over my head again—" They'd all gotten a good laugh out of that—even her, once she'd gotten over the shock of the cold water.

"No, I promise—"

"Dad, we're ready," Jonah called from behind her.

"Thank goodness," Tyler murmured, jumping to his feet and holding out a hand to help her up.

She studied him. What kind of a trap had they set for her this time? But she set her hand in his and let him tug her to her feet.

As they walked down the beach toward the kids, she eyed the three of them, standing in a neat row, fighting off grins.

Yep, they were definitely up to something.

"What's going on?" she asked again, but Tyler simply gave her a mysterious smile and steered her forward.

By the time they reached the kids, Gabby was bouncing up and down. "Mama, we made something for you."

She and the boys stepped aside, and Isabel's eyes fell on a series of lines that had been drawn in the sand.

Words, she realized.

But she couldn't read them from this angle.

Letting go of Tyler's hand, she moved to stand at the edge of the water, her back to the lake, and let her eyes scan the words.

We want to be a family. Will you marry us?

Isabel's eyes filled, but she blinked back the moisture and threw her arms around all three kids at once.

They all laughed and cheered, and when she finally pulled away, there was Tyler, standing with his hands at his sides, studying her, his eyes searching.

"If it's too soon, I understand. We all understand."

But she shook her head, and with a smile that rivaled the sun shining down on them, he stepped forward and took both of her hands in one of his. "In that case—" He opened his other hand to reveal a ring lying flat on his palm, then slowly lowered to one knee. "Isabel, will you marry me? Marry us—" He nodded toward the kids, who stood in a cluster, watching them and giggling. "So that we can be a family from this day until forever?"

The word *family* filled Isabel until she couldn't contain the joy inside of her. The "yes" burst from her, loud and sure and laughing, and suddenly Tyler's arms were around her, and then Gabby's and the boys', until she felt like she was in the middle of a sandwich. A family sandwich.

And she never wanted to be anywhere else.

Tyler managed to untangle his arms enough to slip the ring onto her finger and drop a soft, lingering kiss on her lips.

"Eww, gross." The boys ran away, but Gabby tugged on Tyler and Isabel until they bent and kissed her too.

When they straightened, Gabby grinned. "I like this day."

Then she ran after the boys, who were already halfway to the picnic blanket.

Tyler wrapped an arm around Isabel's shoulders as they followed. "I like this day too."

Isabel laughed, leaning her head on his shoulder and savoring the warmth that pooled inside her as he pressed a kiss into her hair. A year ago, she never would have believed a day like this was possible.

She'd thought that the only way to stay safe, to keep from being afraid, was to guard her heart against everyone.

But now she knew. The only way to truly be safe, to truly be fearless, was to know perfect love.

That love, the love of her Heavenly Father, made it possible to know this love with Tyler.

"Hey." She tugged him to a stop.

"What is it?" His eyes locked on hers. "Is it too soon? Are you having second thoughts?"

"I just wanted to say—" But words weren't adequate to express this. She reached her arms around his neck and drew him closer, bringing her lips to his.

When she finally pulled back, she grinned at him. "I just wanted to say that I like this day too."

Thank you for reading books 4-6 in the Hope Springs series! I hope you loved becoming friends with Dan and Jade, Leah and Austin, and Tyler and Isabel as each found their happily ever after! Catch up with them and the rest of the Hope Springs friends in the Hope Springs Books 7-9 Box Set!

And be sure to sign up for my newsletter to get Ethan and Ariana's story, Not Until Christmas, as a free gift.

Visit www.valeriembodden.com or use the QR code below to join.

A preview of **Not Until Someday (Hope Springs book 7)**

Chapter 1

"Hey, aren't you Levi Donovan?"

Levi grabbed the bottled water out of the rest stop vending machine and turned toward the kid standing behind him.

"Sure am." His eyes tracked from the freckle-faced boy—maybe twelve years old, if Levi had to guess—to the attractive woman standing with her hand on the kid's shoulder. A hand that didn't sport a wedding ring. "I see you're a Titans fan." He gestured to the boy's cap. "You want me to autograph that?" He directed the question to the kid but kept his eyes on the mom.

The kid shrugged and passed his cap to Levi.

Levi patted the pocket of his leather riding jacket. Time was, he'd never left home without a pen for just such an occasion.

"You used to be pretty good," the kid said. "You ever going to play again?"

Pretty good? Levi resisted the urge to correct the kid. His rookie season, he'd set a new passing yards record. A record he'd then beaten three years in a row, until he'd been sidelined by an ACL injury.

"Nah. I'm retired now." At twenty-nine. Not that he'd had much of a choice. His comeback attempt had been less than stellar, with a broken thumb and a stress fracture in his foot.

Anyway, he'd been released, no teams had picked him up, and now here he was, getting a rush from signing some kid's cap in a rest stop.

Or not signing it. He gave his pocket another pat. "Sorry, Sport. I don't have a pen. Maybe your mom does?" He returned his gaze to the woman.

"I'm sure I do." She rummaged in her purse, retrieving a pen with a smile and passing it to Levi. He let his fingertips subtly brush hers as he took it, then signed his name across the cap with a flourish.

"Where you folks headed?" He passed the cap back to the kid.

"Disney World." The kid bounced on his toes. "Where are you going?"

"Nowhere as exciting as that." Actually, every time Levi thought about where he was going, he considered turning his Harley right back around.

"Thank you." The mom smiled at him. "This was sweet of you."

He tipped his chin and headed for the parking lot. "Have a good trip."

When he reached the Harley he'd purchased the moment he was no longer under a contract that prohibited riding, he tucked his water into the saddlebag and pulled on his helmet. He had hundreds of miles of open road ahead of him before he arrived in Hope Springs.

And he was going to enjoy them.

Because goodness knew he wasn't planning to enjoy his time there.

Grace dipped her head to pull in a deep breath of the mixed bouquet—asters, roses, tulips, some sort of lilies, and tiny white flowers she couldn't identify but that gave the whole arrangement a heavenly scent.

This was it. The perfect bouquet.

She meandered toward the flower shop's counter, smiling at the high school student working the register.

"These are pretty." The girl wrapped the flowers in paper. "Who are they for?"

"Myself. A birthday indulgence."

"You're buying yourself birthday flowers? That's so sad." The girl gave her a pitying look, eyeing her as if she were an old maid, and Grace bit her tongue against the urge to say she was only twenty-nine. She supposed that would seem like an old maid to a sixteen-year-old.

"Don't feel bad for me." Grace was careful not to let her smile slip. "I happen to love buying myself flowers. I always get the ones I want that way."

Actually, the last few years, a guy *had* bought her birthday flowers—but not the way the employee meant it. It had been her grandfather. This was her first birthday without him, and she'd found herself missing him so much that she'd decided to come out and buy herself a bouquet.

She took her credit card back, tucked it into her purse, and scooped up the flowers, keeping her chin up as she made her way to the door.

In the car, she nestled the flowers into the passenger seat, then leaned back against the headrest and blew out a long breath. It wasn't that she minded buying flowers for herself—or even that she minded being alone. It was just that she was so tired of everyone assuming that because she didn't have a boyfriend, her life was empty.

She wouldn't mind having someone someday—but only if it was the right someone. She'd learned the hard way that it was better to have no one than the wrong one.

It was why she kept a checklist in her head: loves and serves the Lord, good with kids, sensitive enough to show emotion, kind to others, and drives a sensible car.

If she could find a man who checked all those boxes, she'd be happy to settle down. But until then, she was perfectly content on her own.

She slid the key into the ignition, but before she could start the car, her phone rang. She dug it out of her purse, suppressing a groan as Mama's picture flashed on the screen. Speaking of people who assumed she needed a man—not to mention, a passel of kids.

Maybe she should let it go to voicemail. But Mama would know Grace was ignoring her call. And she was probably only calling to wish Grace a happy birthday—maybe as a gift, she'd avoid mentioning Grace's lack of a boyfriend.

Here was hoping. "Hi, Mama."

"Happy birthday, Grace." Mama's Southern accent was soft but slightly more pronounced than Grace's. "How's your special day going?"

"Great." Grace made sure to fill her voice with cheer. "I just came from working on a fundraiser at church." She left out the part about buying flowers for herself. Mama would certainly take the flower shop cashier's view of things. "Now I'm headed home to make sure everything is ready to start the renovation on Grandfather's place next week."

A flutter of excitement went through her as she backed out of her parking space. She still couldn't believe Grandfather had left her the house that had been in the family for four generations. She'd spoken to him so many times about what a beautiful bed-and-breakfast it would make, but never had she imagined he would leave her the home—and the money to make her dream possible.

"I still don't understand why you feel the need to do this." Mama put on the voice she always assumed for guilt trips.

"I know you don't, Mama." Even though Grace had tried to explain it to her about a million times. "It's just something I need to do." She didn't add that it felt like a calling—like she'd at last found her purpose in life.

As far as Mama was concerned, she should only have one purpose. Babies.

"You're not getting any younger, you know."

"Yes, Mama, I know that." Mama had only reminded her every birthday for the past five years.

"By the time I was twenty-nine," Mama kept going, "I'd been married eight years and had five children."

"Four children, Mama. I'm number four."

"Whatever." Impatience shortened the word. "The point is, that's a lot more children than you currently have."

"Yes, Mama." That was a tension headache starting behind her eyes.

"Isn't it time to sell that old house and come home? Get married. Settle down. Give me some grandbabies."

"Mama, I told you, I don't—" Grace glanced down as the car's gas light dinged on.

"Before you tell me you're not interested in coming home, I've got some news that will change your mind," Mama chirped.

Grace shifted her phone to her other hand as she turned onto Hope Street and followed it past the fudge shop and the bakery and the antique store toward the edge of town.

"What are you talking about, Mama?"

"Remember Aaron Cooper? He just moved back to Heart's Bend. He's our new youth pastor."

Grace could almost picture Mama waving pom-poms on the other end of the line.

"Of course I remember Aaron Cooper." His daddy and hers had served together at the Bible camp her daddy had run when Grace was younger. Aaron had practically been a part of her family, until the camp had closed when she was in middle school. Last she'd heard, his family had been in the mission field.

"Well, he's all grown up now. Very good-looking too. And single."

"That's nice, Mama."

"You know, I always thought he'd be a good match for you."

Grace snorted. "Mama, we were eleven when he moved away."

"I know, but if he had stayed, maybe everything with Hunter wouldn't have happened."

"But it did happen." She didn't exactly want to spend her birthday dwelling on the biggest mistake of her life.

She slowed and pulled into the gas station.

"Well, he's back now," Mama repeated. "And I still think you two would be perfect together."

"We haven't seen each other in nearly twenty years."

"Yes, but when I showed him your picture and told him you were single, he—"

"Mama!" Grace yanked the steering wheel toward a gas pump.

"What?" Mama's voice was all calm innocence. "He happens to be looking for a wife. It's perfect."

Grace shook her head violently enough that she'd be surprised if Mama didn't get dizzy through the phone. "Mama, it's not perfect." Heavens to Betsy, she couldn't believe they were having this conversation. "I don't even know Aaron Cooper anymore. And he's in Heart's Bend, and I'm in Hope Springs."

"That's easy enough to fix."

"And I'm seeing someone." The words popped out of Grace's mouth before the thought had fully formed in her mind.

"You are?" Mama's voice rang with surprise. "Why didn't you say so?"

Grace rubbed at her temple. She couldn't very well say it was because she'd just thought of it.

"It's new, Mama." She opened her car door and stood waiting at the pump. There had to be a way to wrap up this conversation before she said anything even stupider.

"Well, who is he? What's his name? You're sure he's a good one? You know your judgment can be . . ."

A motorcycle roared up to the other side of Grace's gas pump.

Thank you, Lord.

"Sorry, Mama," she shouted to be heard over the motorcycle's engine. "I can't hear you. We'll talk more later." She hung up and tossed the phone into the car just as the motorcycle's engine cut off.

She lifted the gas pump, trying to figure out what she'd been thinking, telling Mama she was seeing someone when she hadn't been on a date in years.

She'd just have to pray that Mama would forget she'd said anything.

Sure. Mama was about as likely to forget as the right guy was to materialize right here at the gas station.

"Long day?"

The deep voice made her jump, and Grace spun around. "Excuse me?"

The motorcyclist on the other side of the pump had pulled his helmet off to reveal mussed dark hair and a charming smile, complete with dimple.

"Sorry, you looked like you were having one of those days. Can I get you a coffee? Cheer you up?"

"Ah, no. I'm fine, thanks." Grace gave him a tight smile. Though she usually enjoyed meeting new people, she was very much not in the mood for small talk right now.

"Do you have a piece of paper and a pen I could borrow?" the stranger asked.

"Uh. Sure." Ducking her head back into the car, Grace rummaged in her purse until she'd found the requested items, then passed them to the guy and busied herself washing the car windows.

When she was done, he was leaning against the gas pump, waiting. He passed her the pen, then the paper. "For you."

"What's this?" She glanced at the handwriting scrawled on the paper. A name and a phone number.

"My number. In case you decide you want that coffee after all. I'd love to take you out."

Grace stared at him. How could he know he'd love to take her out? Until two minutes ago, he'd never seen her before in his life.

"Thanks." She forced a smile as she passed the paper back to him. As certain as she was of what she wanted in a man, she was equally sure of what she *didn't* want. And a motorcycle-riding bad boy topped that list. She'd been down that road once before, and it had almost cost her everything.

"I'm actually seeing someone." Well, why not? If her imaginary boyfriend could get her out of a conversation with Mama, why not use him to make this guy back off too?

"Oh." He looked mildly surprised, as if no one had ever turned him down before. "Sorry. I should have realized." He gestured toward her car. "He must be a good one if he got you flowers."

"Yeah." Grace flipped the gas pump off though her tank wasn't full yet. "It was nice to meet you."

She jumped into her car and sped away before she had to tell any more lies about Mr. Invisible.

Chapter 2

Oh well.

There'd be others.

Levi shrugged as he watched the woman drive off, then got on his bike and pulled away from the gas station.

It was her mocha eyes. That was what had made him ask her out in the first place. He'd always been a sucker for dark eyes.

That and the way she'd stood at the gas pump, looking so forlorn.

He'd been so sure she would be an easy yes that he hadn't even taken a moment to consider that she might turn him down.

It didn't matter. It wasn't like he'd been interested in anything more serious than a single date, maybe two.

Never more than that.

Levi leaned into a turn, the town feeling strangely familiar and yet new at the same time. He hadn't been home in over two years, and he suddenly couldn't remember if the awning over the antique store had always been blue and white or whether the sign at the marina had always been so big.

Too soon, he was slowing for the turn into his parents' driveway. As he parked and took off his helmet, the house too felt strangely new and old all at once. He would have sworn on his Super Bowl ring that the home he'd grown up in was yellow, but the siding was now taupe, with blue shutters. And the plum tree that he'd climbed as a kid was missing from the front yard. He double-checked the address.

Yep. This was the right place.

Modest. That was the word to describe this house.

Not bad. But nothing compared to what he could have bought his parents if they'd let him.

But every time he'd offered, he'd received the same answer—they were comfortable here.

So he'd stopped offering.

Hanging his helmet from the bike's handlebars, Levi grabbed his pack from the luggage rack, then made his way up the porch steps to the front door. It all felt a little surreal, as if maybe this was one of those dreams where everything was the same as in real life but different.

Until the front door sprang open and Mom was launching herself at him, pulling him into a ferocious hug. "I wasn't sure you'd come."

Levi squeezed her tight, her comforting citrus scent making him aware of how much he'd missed her. "I wasn't either."

He still wasn't sure why he was here. Only that Mom's message that Dad needed his help had touched something in him. After two years of refusing to speak to Levi, the fact that Dad would ask for his help felt like a big step.

When Mom finally let go, Levi took a step back, examining her. She had maybe one or two extra lines around her eyes now, but other than that, she looked as young and strong as ever.

"Hey, is that my brother?" The voice from behind Mom was deeper than Levi remembered but as cheerful as ever.

"Come see," Mom said over her shoulder, moving aside and gesturing for Levi to enter the house.

But he froze in the doorway, his chest tightening as his eyes fell on the cane in Luke's hand. Since the day his brother had been diagnosed with Becker muscular dystrophy eleven years ago, they'd all known there might come a time when Luke would need help getting around—when he might even need a wheelchair. But Levi had assumed that day would be far in the future.

Luke was only twenty-five. He should be out running and throwing footballs. Not limping around with a cane.

"Hey, brother." Luke's grin swept from his mouth all the way to his eyes as he made his way to the door. "Long time no see."

"Yeah." Levi swallowed, painfully aware of his own smooth steps as he walked toward his brother and held out a hand, realizing too late that Luke held the cane in his right hand. Instead of taking his hand, Luke shifted his cane to the side and wrapped his other arm around Levi's back.

Levi gingerly put an arm around his brother.

"Dude, I'm not going to break." Luke tightened his grip on Levi until Levi lifted his other arm and pulled Luke in closer, still not one hundred percent sure he wouldn't hurt him.

When Luke finally let go, Levi looked around.

Though the outside of the house had changed, everything in here was identical to what he remembered. Pictures of Luke and Levi still decorated the walls. The big beige couch they'd piled on for family movie nights still took up one side of the living room. And Dad's old recliner was still tucked into the corner, his worn Bible perched on the table next to it.

"Where's Dad?" Might as well acknowledge the elephant in the room—or not in the room.

"At work." Mom gestured him toward the couch. "Come on, let's sit down."

"Maybe I should go over to the shop. Find out what he needs help with."

Mom and Luke exchanged a look.

"What?" Levi's head swiveled between them. Luke stared at the floor, and Mom busied herself rearranging throw pillows. "He didn't want me to come, did he?"

"It's not that." Mom gave up on the pillows.

"This is more of an intervention," Luke cut in. "Before he works himself to death."

"I'm sure there are plenty of people he could hire." Actually, this was good. It meant Levi didn't have to stay.

"Probably." But Mom's eyes filled, and Levi had to look away. He'd only seen his mom cry twice in his life—the day Luke was diagnosed, and the day Levi left for college—and he'd been shaken both times.

"But we wanted to see you." Luke had always been good at coming out and saying what he meant, whether or not it came across as sappy. "We've missed you."

Levi softened. "I've missed you guys too. But we all know Dad isn't going to be happy to see me here. I think it's best if I go now, before he gets home." He stood.

But the sound of the door from the garage to the kitchen pulled their attention toward the next room.

"Sandra, whose Harley is that blocking the garage?" Dad's voice boomed as loud as Levi remembered.

"Come and see." Mom pushed to her feet and moved toward the kitchen, throwing a pleading look at Levi over her shoulder.

He shook his head but dropped back onto the couch. It wasn't like he had much of a choice. He wasn't going to go sneaking out of here like some coward. He'd stay and face Dad.

Then he'd leave.

The murmur of Mom's low voice carried from the kitchen, followed by Dad's more explosive one.

"So how've you been?" Luke leaned forward, clearly trying to distract Levi.

"Bored." The word came out before Levi could think it through.

Funny. He hadn't been able to put his finger on the feeling before today. But that was it. He was bored.

He'd kept up with his training for the first year or so after he'd retired, until he'd realized there was no point. Mostly, he spent his days playing video games and his nights going out with friends.

It wasn't such a bad life, he supposed. But it lacked the thrill of getting onto the field, the satisfaction of a game well-played, the purpose of striving to be the best he could be.

"What about you?" Levi asked, but Dad burst into the room, followed by Mom.

"What are you doing here, Levi?" Dad's voice was flat. "You need money or something? Blow through your riches already?"

Seriously?

"No, Dad, I don't need money." He knew plenty of guys who blew through their salaries in record time, but he was smarter than that. He'd made enough on his investments that he'd probably never have to work another day in his life if he didn't want to.

"Well, I didn't know." Dad unbuttoned the Donovan Construction shirt he always wore over a white t-shirt. "All those pictures of you with all those women. Figured it must get expensive."

"Whatever, Dad." Judgment was the one thing Dad had always been good at. "I didn't come here so you could stand over me and judge me."

"What *did* you come for? To make a mockery of your family again?"

"A mockery?" Levi turned helplessly from Dad to Mom and Luke, who offered him a sympathetic look that was no help at all. "When did I ever—"

"That interview, Levi. Your whole lifestyle. Different woman every night."

"Hold on. I'm not with a different woman every night. And I didn't say anything against my family in that interview. All I said was—"

Mom stood, holding out a hand toward each of them. "Stop. Please."

Levi fell silent.

"I asked Levi to come." Mom's voice was firm as she turned to Dad. "You need help on your crews. You've had three guys quit in the last two weeks, and you're working yourself to death. And," she continued as Dad opened his mouth, "I need to see my son."

"She's right, Dad," Luke piped from his spot next to Levi. "We've got half a dozen jobs lined up for the next month alone. There's no way we're going to get them all done without help. And Levi knows what he's doing already. He doesn't need any training. He can step in and lead a crew."

That was true enough. From the time he could swing a hammer, Levi had been helping Dad on the various renovation projects he took on. During college, he'd spent summers managing the company's top crew. Before he'd been drafted into the NFL, he and Dad had talked about the possibility of partnering and expanding the company.

But none of that changed the fact that Dad no longer wanted anything to do with Levi.

The feeling was mutual.

"And you want to work for me?" Dad's cloudy blue eyes met Levi's.

The answer to that was an unequivocal no. But his gaze flicked to Mom, then to Luke. Both looked so hopeful.

He nodded once, painfully.

"Fine." Dad marched toward the kitchen. "Luke, get him up to speed on the Calvano project."

"Thank you." Mom squeezed his shoulder as she followed Dad out of the room.

Levi tried to muster a smile. It was only for the summer, he reminded himself. And if nothing else, at least he shouldn't be bored anymore.

KEEP READING NOT UNTIL SOMEDAY in the HOPE SPRINGS BOOKS 7-9 BOX SET

More Books by Valerie M. Bodden

Hope Springs

While the books in the Hope Springs series are linked, each is a complete romance featuring a different couple.

Not Until Forever (Sophie & Spencer)

Not Until This Moment (Jared & Peyton)

Not Until You (Nate & Violet)

Not Until Us (Dan & Jade)

Not Until Christmas Morning (Leah & Austin)

Not Until This Day (Tyler & Isabel)

Not Until Someday (Grace & Levi)

Not Until Now (Cam & Kayla)

Not Until Then (Bethany & James)

Not Until The End (Emma & Owen)

River Falls

While the books in the River Falls series are linked, each is a complete romance featuring a different couple.

Pieces of Forever (Joseph & Ava)

Songs of Home (Lydia & Liam)

Memories of the Heart (Simeon & Abigail)

Whispers of Truth (Benjamin & Summer)

Promises of Mercy (Judah & Faith)

River Falls Christmas Romances

Wondering about some of the side characters in River Falls who aren't members of the Calvano family? Join them as they get their own happily-ever-afters in the River Falls Christmas Romances.

Christmas of Joy (Madison & Luke)

Want to know when my next book releases?

You can follow me on Amazon to be the first to know when my next book releases! Just visit amazon.com/author/valeriembodden and click the follow button.

Acknowledgements

First and above all, I thank my Heavenly Father, who gave me this gift of writing and has led me to this point in my life where I can use that gift to serve him daily. I certainly haven't done anything to earn or deserve this privilege—and I stand in awe every day of what he is doing with my books. I thank him for leading me to these stories of hope, love, and redemption. And most of all, I thank him for forgiving every last one of my sins through the blood of his Son, Jesus Christ. I pray that through my books, readers will be reminded that all their sins are forgiven in Jesus as well.

I thank God every day for the blessing of my family. For my husband, who not only sets an example of Christ's love for me every day but who is also my number one fan and strongest supporter—not to mention an incredible book cover designer. For our four children, who have taught me more about love and grace and trust and forgiveness than I'll ever be able to teach them. For my parents, who raised me in a Christian home, where I knew God's love from before I can even remember. For my sister, my in-laws, and my extended family, who have supported and encouraged me as I have worked to get this series into the world.

A heartfelt thank you also goes out to my amazing Advance Reader Team. If I named all the people who have contributed their thoughts and feedback on the three books in this volume, the list would go on for another two pages! So let me just say that I'm so grateful for all of you. It's been wonderful to get to know you and to consider you friends.

Thank you for sharing your honest thoughts on my books, brainstorming with me when needed, and giving so generously of yourselves to encourage me.

One of the amazing and unexpected benefits of writing books in the digital age is that I have had an opportunity to connect with readers from around the world. Thank you for being one of them! I know this world is a busy place—and I thank you for choosing to spend some of your time with me and the characters of Hope Springs. I hope you've enjoyed their journey.

About the Author

Valerie M. Bodden has three great loves: Jesus, her family, and books. And chocolate (okay, four great loves). She is living out her happily ever after with her high-school-sweet-heart-turned-husband and their four children. Her life wouldn't make a terribly exciting book, as it has a happy beginning and middle, and someday when she goes to her heavenly home, it will have a happy end.

She was born and raised in Wisconsin but recently moved with her family to Texas, where they're all getting used to the warm weather (she doesn't miss the snow even a little bit, though the rest of the family does) and saying y'all instead of you guys.

Valerie writes emotion-filled Christian fiction that weaves real-life problems, real-life people, and real-life faith. Her characters may (okay, will) experience some heartache along the way, but she will always give them a happy ending.

Feel free to stop by www.valeriembodden.com to say hi. She loves visitors! And while you're there, you can sign up for your free story.

Printed in Great Britain
by Amazon

51975884R00380